THE LEW AR

Vol

ROSS MACDONALD was born near San Francisco in 1915. He was educated in Canadian schools, and then travelled widely in Europe. In 1938 he married a Canadian, the now well-known crime novelist Margaret Millar. For over twenty years he lived in Santa Barbara and wrote mystery novels about the fascinating and changing society of his native state. He was a past president of the Mystery Writers of America. In 1964 his novel *The Chill* was given a Silver Dagger award by the Crime Writers' Association of Great Britain, which also named *The Far Side of the Dollar* as the best crime novel of 1965. In 1966, *The Moving Target* was made into the highly successful film, *Harper*, starring Paul Newman. Ross Macdonald died in 1983.

THE LEW ARCHER OMNIBUS

Volume 1

ROSS MACDONALD

This edition first published in Great Britain in 1993 by
Allison & Busby
an imprint of Wilson & Day Ltd
5 The Lodge
Richmond Way
London W12 8LW

A catalogue record for this book is available from the British Library

ISBN 0 74900 109 7

Printed and bound in Great Britain by
Cox & Wyman Ltd, Reading, Berkshire

THE DROWNING POOL
1

THE CHILL
219

THE GOODBYE LOOK
457

THE DROWNING POOL

To Toni

CHAPTER 1

If you didn't look at her face she was less than thirty, quick-bodied and slim as a girl. Her clothing drew attention to the fact: a tailored sharkskin suit and high heels that tensed her nylon-shadowed calves. But there was a pull of worry around her eyes and drawing at her mouth. The eyes were deep blue, with a sort of double vision. They saw you clearly, took you in completely, and at the same time looked beyond you. They had years to look back on, and more things to see in the years than a girl's eyes had. About thirty-five, I thought, and still in the running.

She stood in the doorway without speaking long enough for me to think those things. Her teeth were nibbling the inside of her upper lip, and both of her hands were clutching her black suede bag at the level of her waist. I let the silence stretch out. She had knocked and I had opened the door. Undecided or not, she couldn't expect me to lift her over the threshold. She was a big girl now, and she had come for a reason. Her stance was awkward with urgency.

"Mr. Archer?" she said at last.

"Yes. Will you come in."

"Thank you. Forgive me for hanging back. It must make you feel like a dentist."

"Everybody hates detectives and dentists. We hate them back."

"Not really? Actually, I've never been to a dentist." She smiled as if to illustrate the point, and gave me her hand in a free gesture. It was hard and brown. "*Or* a detective."

I placed her in the soft chair by the window. She didn't mind the light. Her hair was its natural brown, without a fleck of gray that I could see. Her face was clear and brown. I wondered if she was clear and brown all over.

"What tooth is bothering you, Mrs. —?"

"Excuse me. My name is Maude Slocum. I always forget my manners when I'm upset."

She was much too apologetic for a woman with that figure, in those clothes. "Look," I said. "I am rhinoceros-skinned and iron-hearted. I've been doing divorce work in L.A. for ten years. If you can tell me anything I haven't heard, I'll donate a week's winnings at Santa Anita to any worthy charity."

"And can you whip your weight in wildcats, Mr. Archer?"

"Wildcats terrify me, but people are worse."

"I know what you mean." The fine white teeth were tugging again at the warm mouth. "I used to think, when I was younger, that people were willing to live and let live—you know? Now I'm not so sure."

"You didn't come here this morning, though, to discuss morals in the abstract. Did you have a specific example in mind?"

She answered after a pause: "Yes. I had a shock yesterday." She looked close into my face, and then beyond. Her eyes were as deep as the sea beyond Catalina. "Someone is trying to destroy me."

"Kill you, you mean?"

"Destroy the things I care about. My husband, my family, my home." The rhythm of her voice faltered and ceased. "It's dreadfully hard to tell you, the thing is so underhanded."

Here we go again, I said to myself. True confession morning, featuring Archer the unfrocked priest. "I should have gone to City College and been a dentist and gone in for something easy and painless like pulling teeth. If you really need my help, you'll have to tell me what with. Did someone send you here?"

"You were recommended. I know a—man who does police work. He said you were honest, and discreet."

"Unusual thing for a cop to say about me. Would you care to mention his name?"

"No, I wouldn't." The very suggestion seemed to alarm her. Her fingers tightened on the black suede bag. "He doesn't know about this."

"Neither do I. I don't expect I ever will." I let a smile go with it, and offered her a cigarette. She puffed on it without relish, but it seemed to relax her a little.

"Damn it." She coughed once over the smoke. "Here I've been up all night, trying to make up my mind, and I still haven't made it up. No one knows, you see. It's hard to bring myself to tell anyone else. One acquires the habit of silence, after sixteen years."

"Sixteen years? I thought it happened yesterday."

She colored. "Oh, it did. I was simply thinking of how long I'd been married. This has a good deal to do with my marriage."

"So I gather. I'm good at guessing-games."

"I'm sorry. I don't mean to offend you or insult you." Her contriteness was unexpected in a woman of her class. It didn't go with hundred-dollar suits. "It isn't that I think you'll spread it around, or try to blackmail me—"

"Is somebody else trying to blackmail you?"

The question startled her so that she jumped. She recrossed her legs and leaned forward in the chair. "I don't know. I haven't any idea."

"Then we're even." I took an envelope out of the top drawer of my desk, opened it, and began to read the mimeographed enclosure. It informed me that the chances were one in three that I'd enter a hospital within the year, that I couldn't afford to be unprotected by health insurance, and that he who hesitates is lost. "He who hesitates is lost," I said aloud.

"You're making fun of me, Mr. Archer. But just what is the arrangement? If you take the case, you'll naturally be governed by my interests. But if you don't, and I've told you about this thing, can I trust you to forget it?"

I let my irritation show in my voice, and this time I didn't smile, or even grimace. "Let's both forget it. You're wasting my time, Mrs. Slocum."

"I know I am." There was self-disgust in her tone, more than there should have been. "This thing has been a physical blow to me, a blow from behind." Then she spoke with sudden decision, and opened her bag with taut white fingers: "I suppose I must let you see it. I can't just go home now and sit and wait for another one."

I looked at the letter she handed me. It was short and to the point, without heading or signature:

> Dear Mr. Slocum:
>
> Lilies that fester smell far worse than weeds. Can you possibly enjoy playing the role of a complaisant cuckold? Or are you strangely unaware of your wife's amorous activities?

The message was typed on a sheet of cheap white typing paper that had been folded to the size of a small envelope. "Is there an envelope to go with this?"

"Yes." She rummaged in her purse, and handed me a crumpled white envelope, which was addressed to James Slocum, Esq., Trail Road, Nopal Valley, California. The postmark was clear: Quinto, Calif., July 18.

"This is Wednesday," I said. "It was mailed Monday. Do you know people in Quinto?"

"Everybody." She managed a strained smile. "It's only a few miles from Nopal Valley, where we live. But I haven't the faintest notion who could have sent it."

"Or why?"

"I have enemies, I suppose. Most people have."

"I take it your husband hasn't seen it. James Slocum *is* your husband?"

"Yes. He hasn't seen it. He was busy in Quinto when it came. I usually bicycle down to the mailbox, anyway."

"Is he in business in Quinto?"

"Not in business. He's very active in the Quinto Players—it's a semi-professional theatrical group. They're rehearsing every afternoon this week—"

I cut her short: "Do you usually read your husband's mail?"

"Yes, I do. We read each other's—I hardly expected to be cross-questioned, Mr. Archer."

"One more question. Is the allegation true?"

The blood coursed under the clear skin of her face, and her eyes brightened. "I can't be expected to answer that."

"All right. You wouldn't be here if it weren't true."

"On the contrary," she said.

"And you want me to find out who sent the letter, and prosecute him or her?"

"Oh, no." She wasn't clever. "I simply want it stopped. I can't stand guard over the mailbox to intercept his mail, and I can't stand the strain of waiting and wondering—"

"Besides, the next note might be handed to him personally. Would it matter so much if he read it?"

"It would matter terribly."

"Why? Is he violently jealous?"

"Not at all, he's a very quiet man."

"And you're in love with him?"

"I married him," she said. "I haven't regretted it."

"If your marriage is a good one, you don't have to worry about a poison-pen or two." I tossed the letter on the desk-top between us, and looked into her face.

Her mouth and eyes were tormented. "It would be the last straw. I have a daughter who is still in school. I simply won't permit this thing to happen."

"What thing?"

"A breakup and divorce," she answered harshly.

"Is that what it means if your husband gets one of

those?" I pointed my cigarette at the scrap of white paper.

"I'm afraid it does, Mr. Archer. I could cope with James, perhaps, but he'd take it to his mother, and *she'd* hire detectives."

"Could they find grounds for divorce? Is there evidence against you?"

"There must be," she said bitterly. "Someone knows." Her entire body moved slightly, twitched like a worm on a hook. For the moment she loathed her sex. "This is very painful for me."

"I know," I said. "My wife divorced me last year. Extreme mental cruelty."

"I think you might be capable of it." There was gentle malice in her voice; then her mood changed again: "Please don't imagine I take divorce lightly. It's the last thing I want."

"On account of your daughter, you say?"

She considered that. "Ultimately, yes. I was the child of a divorced couple myself, and I suffered for it. There are other reasons, too. My mother-in-law would like it much too well."

"What sort of a woman is she? Could she have sent the letter?"

The question caught her off guard, and she had to think again. "No. I'm sure she didn't. She'd act much more directly. She's a very strong-minded woman. As I told you, I haven't the slightest idea who sent it."

"Anybody in Quinto then. Population about twenty-five thousand, isn't it? Or anybody who passed through Quinto on Monday. It's a pretty tough setup."

"But you will try to help me?" She wasn't too much of a lady to arrange herself appealingly in the chair, and dramatize the plea. There was a chance that she wasn't a lady at all.

"It will take time, and I can't promise any results. Are you fairly well-heeled, Mrs. Slocum?"

"Surely you don't reserve your services exclusively for the wealthy." She looked around at the plain, small, square office.

"I don't spend money on front, but I charge fifty dollars a day, and expenses. It will cost you four or five hundred a week, and with what I've got to go on it may take all summer."

She swallowed her dismay. "Frankly, I'm not well off. There's money in the family, but James and I don't have it. All we have is the income from a hundred thousand."

"Thirty-five hundred."

"Less. James's mother controls the money. We live with her, you see. I do have a little money that I've saved, though, for Cathy's education. I can pay you five hundred dollars."

"I can't guarantee anything in a week, or a month for that matter."

"I have to do something."

"I have an idea why. The person who wrote that letter probably knows something more definite, and you're afraid of the next letter."

She didn't answer.

"It would help if you'd let me know what there is to be known."

Her eyes met mine levelly and coldly. "I don't see the necessity for me to confess adultery, or for you to assume that there is anything to confess."

"Oh hell," I said. "If I have to work in a vacuum, I'll waste my time."

"You'll be paid for it."

"You'll waste your money, then."

"I don't care." She opened her purse again and counted ten twenties onto the desk-top. "There. I want you to do what you can. Do you know Nopal Valley?"

"I've been through it, and I know Quinto slightly. What does your husband do with the Quinto Players?"

"He's an actor, or thinks he is. You mustn't try to talk to him."

"You'll have to let me do it my own way, or I might as well sit in my office and read a book. How can I get in touch with you?"

"You can phone me at home. Nopal Valley is in the Quinto book. Under Mrs. Olivia Slocum."

She stood up and I followed her to the door. I noticed for the first time that the back of the handsome suit was sun-faded. There was a faint line around the bottom of the skirt where the hem had been changed. I felt sorry for the woman, and I liked her pretty well.

"I'll drive up this morning," I said. "Better watch the mailbox."

When she had gone, I sat down behind the desk and looked at the unpolished top. The letter and the twenties were side by side upon it. Sex and money: the forked root of evil. Mrs. Slocum's neglected cigarette was smouldering in the ash-tray, marked with lipstick like a faint rim of blood. It stank, and I crushed it out. The letter went into my breastpocket, the twenties into my billfold.

In the street when I went down the heat was mounting toward ninety. In the sky the sun was mounting toward noon.

CHAPTER 2

An hour north of Santa Monica a sign informed me: YOU ARE ENTERING QUINTO, JEWEL OF THE SEA. SPEED 25 MILES. I slowed down and began to look for a motor court. The white cottages of the Motel del Mar looked clean and well-shaded, and I turned into the gravel apron in front of the U-shaped enclosure. A thin woman in a linen smock came out of the door marked OFFICE before I could stop the car. She danced towards me smiling a dazed and arty smile.

"Did you wish accommodation, sir?"

"I did. I still do."

She tittered and touched her fading hair, which was drawn tightly back from her sharp face in a bun. "You're travelling alone?"

"Yes. I may stay for a few days."

She blinked her eyes roguishly, wagging her head. "Don't stay too long, or the charm of Quinto will capture you. It's the Jewel of the Sea, you know. You'll want to stay forever and ever. We've a very nice single at seven."

"May I look at it?"

"Of course. I believe that you'll find it delightful."

She showed me a knotty pine room with a bed, a table, and two chairs. The floor and furniture shone with polishing wax. There was a Rivera reproduction on one wall, its saffrons repeated by a vase of fresh marigolds on the mantel over the fireplace. Below the western window the sea glimmered.

She turned to me like a musician from his piano. "Well?"

"I find it delightful," I said.

"If you'll just come up and register, I'll have Henry fill the carafe with ice water. We *do* try to make you comfortable, you see."

I followed her back to the office, feeling a little uncomfortable at her willingness to tie herself in knots, and signed my full name in the register, Lew A. Archer, with my Los Angeles address.

"I see you're from Los Angeles," she said, taking my money.

"Temporarily. As a matter of fact, I'd like to settle here."

"Would you really?" she gushed. "Do you hear that, Henry? The gentleman here would like to settle in Quinto."

A tired-looking man half-turned from his desk at the back of the room, and grunted.

"Oh, but you'd love it," she said. "The sea. The mountains. The clear, cool air. The nights. Henry and I are awfully glad we decided to buy this place. And it's full every night in the summer, no-vacancy sign up long before it's dark. Henry and I make quite a game out of it, don't we, Henry?"

Henry grunted again.

"Are there many ways to make a living here?"

"Why, there are the stores, and real estate, all sorts of things. No industry, of course, the Council won't permit it. After all, look what happened to Nopal Valley when they let the oil wells in."

"What happened to Nopal Valley?"

"It was ruined, absolutely ruined. Great hordes of low-class people, Mexicans and dirty oil crews, came in from gosh knows where, and simply blighted the town. We can't let it happen here."

"Absolutely not," I said with a phoniness she had no ear to catch. "Quinto must remain a natural beauty spot and cultural centre. I've heard quite a lot about the Quinto Players, by the way."

"Now have you really, Mr. Archer?" Her voice sank to a simpering whisper: "You're not a Hollywood personage, are you?"

"Not exactly." I left the question open. "I've done a good deal of work in and about Hollywood." Peeping on fleabag hotel rooms, untying marital knots, blackmailing blackmailers out of business. Dirty, heavy, hot work on occasion.

She narrowed her eyes and pressed her lips together as if she understood me. "I sensed you were from Hollywood. Of course you'll be wanting to see the new play this weekend. Mr. Marvell wrote it himself—he's a very brilliant man—and he's directing it, too. Rita Treadwith, a very dear friend of mine, is helping with the costumes, and she says it has great possibilities: movies, Broadway, anything."

"Yes," I said. "I've had reports of it. Where's the theater they're rehearsing in?"

"Right off the highway in the center of town. Just turn right at the courthouse, and you'll see the sign: Quinto Theatre."

"Thank you," I said, and went out. The screen door slammed a second time before I reached my car, and Henry came plodding toward me across the gravel. He was leathery and lean, beaten and parched by long summers. He came up so close to me that I could smell him.

"Listen, friend, you mean it what you said about settling down here?" He looked behind him to make sure that his wife was out of earshot, and spat in the gravel. "I got an income proposition if you're interested. Ten thousand down and the rest out of earnings. Fifty thousand for the works, that's twelve good cottages and the good will."

"You want to sell this place? To me?"

"You'll never get a better at the price."

"I thought you were mad about Quinto."

He shot a contemptuous yellow glance at the door of the office. "That's what *she* thinks. Thinks, hell.

She lets the Chamber of Commerce do her thinking for her. I got a chance for a liquor license in Nopal."

"Money in Nopal, I hear."

"You can say it again. The Valley's lousy with money since they struck oil, and there's no spenders like oilmen. Easy come, easy go."

"I'm sorry," I said. "I'm not interested."

"That's O.K., I just thought I'd raise the question. *She* won't let me put up a sign, or list the god-damn place." He plodded back to the office.

The men and women in the streets had the rumpled, sun-worshipping look of people on holiday. Many of them were very young or very old, and most of the former wore bathing-suits. The white Spanish buildings seemed unreal, a stage-setting painted upon the solid blue sky. To the left at the bottom of the cross-streets the placid sea rose up like a flat blue wall.

I parked in front of a restaurant near the courthouse and went in for a cold lunch. The waitress had a red-checked apron that matched the tablecloth, and a complexion that matched the coffee. I tipped her very lightly, and walked around the block to the Quinto Theatre. It was two o'clock by my watch, time for the rehearsal to be under way. If the play was scheduled for the week end, they'd be running the whole thing through by Wednesday.

The theatre stood back from the street in a plot of yellowing grass: a massive windowless box of a building with its stucco scabbing off in patches to show the aged plaster. Two weather-pocked plaster pillars supported the roof of the portico. On each of the pillars a playbill announced the World Premiere of *The Ironist*, a New Play by Francis Marvell. On the wall beside the box office there was a layout of photographs mounted on a large sheet of blue cardboard. Miss Jeanette Dermott as Clara: a young blonde with luminous dreaming eyes. Mrs. Leigh Galloway as The Wife: a hard-faced woman smiling professionally, her bright teeth ready to eat an imaginary audience.

The third of the glossy trio interested me. It was a man in his late thirties, with light hair waving over a pale and noble brow. The eyes were large and sorrowful, the mouth small and sensitive. The picture had been taken in three-quarters face to show the profile, which was very fine. Mr. James Slocum, the caption said, as "The Ironist." If the picture could be believed, Mr. James Slocum's pan was a maiden's dream. Not mine.

A prewar Packard sedan drew up to the curb in front of the theatre, and a young man got out. His long legs were tightly encased in a pair of faded levis, his heavy shoulders bulged in a flowered Hawaiian shirt. The levis and the shirt didn't go with the black chauffeur's cap on his head. He must have been conscious of the cap, because he tossed it on the front seat of the Packard before he came up the walk. The glistening dark hair frothed on his head in tight curls. He looked at me from eyes that were paled by the deep tan of his face. Another maiden's dream. They pastured in herds in the California resorts.

Dream Two opened the heavy door to my left, and it swung shut behind him. I waited a minute and followed him into the lobby. It was small and close and dimly lit by the red glow of the Exit lamps. The young man had disappeared, but there was a murmur of voices beyond a further door. I crossed the lobby and entered the main auditorium. It was blacked out except for the stage, where there were lights and people. I sat down in an aisle seat in the back row, and wondered what the hell I was doing there.

The set had been erected, an English drawing-room with period furniture, but the players were not yet in costume. James Slocum, looking as pretty as his picture, in a yellow turtleneck sweater, shared the stage with the blonde girl, in slacks. They were talking at each other in center stage.

"Roderick," the girl was saying, "have you honestly

been aware of my love for you, and never breathed a word of it to me?"

"Why should I have?" Slocum shrugged his shoulders in weary amusement. "You were content to love, and I was content to be loved. Naturally, I did my best to encourage you."

"You encouraged me?" She overdid the surprise, and her voice screeched slightly. "But I never knew."

"I took care that you should not, until you had passed the narrow line that lies between admiration and passion. But I was always ready with a match for your cigarette, a compliment for your gown, a touch of the hand at parting." He moved his hand in the air, and unconsciously underlined the corn.

"But your wife! What of her? It seems incredible that you should deliberately lead me on to the dark edge of adultery."

"Dark, my dear? On the contrary, passion is radiant with the radiance of a thousand suns, luminous as the dayspring, shot through with rainbow splendors!" He spoke the words as if he meant them, in a ringing voice which held only a trace of reediness. "Beside the love that we may have—shall have—the legal mating of the married is the coupling of frightened rabbits in a hutch."

"Roderick, I hate and fear and adore you," the girl announced. She cast herself at his feet like a ballerina.

He gave her both his hands and lifted her to her feet. "I adore to be adored," he answered lightly. Clinch.

A thin figure had been pacing nervously in the orchestra pit, silhouetted against the reflection of the footlights. Now he vaulted onto the stage in a single antelope bound, and circled the mugging pair like a referee.

"Very fine," he said. "Very fine, indeed. You've caught my intention beautifully, both of you. But would it be possible, Miss Dermott, to bring out just a shade more emphatically the contrast between *hate and fear* on the one hand, and *adore* on the other?

After all, that's the very keynote of the first act: the ambivalence of Clara's response to the Ironist, externalizing the ambivalence of his attitude to love and life. Would you take it again from 'rabbits in a hutch'?"

"Of course, Mr. Marvell."

Which made him the author of the play, as I'd suspected. It was the kind of play that only a mother or an actor could love, the kind of stuff that parodied itself. Phony sophistication with a high gloss, and no insides at all.

I turned my attention to the darkened auditorium, which seemed larger than it was because it was almost empty. A few people were clustered in the first rows, silently watching the actors rehash their tripe. The rest of the plywood seats were unoccupied, except for a couple a few rows ahead of me. As my eyes became used to the dim light, I could make out a boy and a girl, their heads leaning close together. At least the boy was leaning toward her; the girl sat straight in the seat. When he raised his arm and placed it along the back, she moved to the next seat.

I saw his face as he leaned sideways to speak to her: Dream Two. "God damn you," he said. "You treat me as if I was dirt. I think I'm getting someplace with you, and then you crawl into your little igloo and slam the door in my face."

"Igloos don't have doors, you crawl in through a tunnel." Her voice was soft and prim.

"That's another thing." He was trying to whisper, but anger jerked at his vocal cords and made the words uneven. "You think you're so damn superior, the big brain. I could tell you things you never even heard of."

"I don't care to hear of them. I'm very interested in the play, Mr. Reavis, and I wish you'd leave me alone."

"*Mr.* Reavis! What makes you so bloody formal all of a sudden. You were hot enough last night when I took you home, but now it's '*Mr.* Reavis'."

"I was not! And I won't be talked to like that."

"That's what you think. You can't play around with me, do you understand? I'm big stuff, and I got ideas, and there's plenty of women I can have if I want them, see?"

"I know you're irresistible, Mr. Reavis. My failure to respond is unquestionably pathological."

"Two-bit words don't mean nothing," he cried in frustration and fury. "I'll show you something that does mean something."

Before she could move again, he was crouching in front of her, holding her down in her seat. She let out a stifled squawk and beat his face with closed hands. But he found her mouth and held on, with one of his large hands on either side of her head. I could hear their breath whistling, the seat creaking under the weight of their struggling bodies. I stayed where I was. They knew each other better than I knew them, and nothing could happen to her where they were.

He released her finally, but stayed bending over her, with something hopeful in the arch of his shoulders.

"Dirt!" she said. "You dirt."

The words hit him hard, a spatter of mud in the face. "You can't call me that!" He had forgotten about whispering. His hands were groping for her shoulders, or her neck.

I was halfway out of my seat when the overhead lights came on. The dialogue on the stage had ceased, and everyone in the theatre was running up the aisle, with Marvell at their head. He was a flaxen-haired man in Harris tweeds and a dither. The trace of an English accent fogged his voice:

"Really! What on earth is happening here?" He sounded like a spinster schoolteacher who has caught a pupil in the act.

The boy had scrambled to his feet and half-turned, leaning over the back of the seat. There was shamed awkwardness in his movements, but danger, too. His muscles were strained taut, and his eyes were black ice.

Slocum stepped forward and laid his hand on Marvell's shoulder. "Let me handle this, Francis." He turned to the girl, who was sitting tense in her seat. "Now, Cathy, what's been going on?"

"Nothing, father." Her voice was demure again. "We were sitting here talking, and Pat got mad, that's all."

"He was kissing you," Slocum said. "I saw you from the stage. You'd better wipe your face, and I'll talk to you later."

Her hand flew up to her mouth. "Yes, father," she said between her fingers. She was a pretty girl, much younger than I'd thought from the words she used. The auburn hair blossomed at the back of her neck into curls that were alive with copper glints.

The boy looked down at her head, and back to her father. "No," he said. "She had nothing to do with it. I tried to kiss her, and she wouldn't let me."

"You admit that, do you, Reavis?"

The boy walked up to Slocum, and dwarfed him. With his thin shoulder-blades projecting under the yellow sweater, it was Slocum who looked like the youngster. He stood where he was, unbending and outraged.

"Why shouldn't I admit it?" Reavis said. "There's no law against kissing a girl—"

Slocum spoke in deliberate cold fury: "Where my young daughter is concerned, certain things are impossible and inconceivable and"—he groped for a word and found it—"foul. No lout of a chauffeur—"

"I won't always be a chauffeur—"

"You're quite right. You're not one now."

"I suppose you mean I'm fired." His tone was flat and scornful.

"Absolutely."

"Why, you poor damn ninny, you can't fire me. You never paid my wages, anyway. Not that I want your friggin' job. You can stick it."

The two men were facing each other, so close they were almost touching. The rest of the people in the aisle surged forward around them. Marvell insinuated himself between them, and laid a graceful hand on Reavis's chest. "That will be about enough of that." He omitted the "my man" tag, but it was implied. "I advise you to get out of here before I summon the police."

"For calling a phony's bluff?" Reavis tried to laugh, and almost succeeded. "I'd of walked out months ago if it wasn't for Cathy. The little buzzard's doing me a favor."

The girl Cathy got out of her seat, her eyes bright with tears about to spill. "Go away, Pat. You mustn't say these dreadful things to father."

"You heard her, Reavis." Slocum was flushed in the neck and white around the mouth. "Get out of here, and don't come back. We'll send your things to you."

The tension was leaking out of the situation as Reavis, its center, gradually relaxed. He knew that he was beaten, and his shoulders showed it. He turned to look at Cathy, and she wouldn't meet his eyes. Before the focus of attention could shift to me, I slid out of my $7.70 seat and into the lobby.

The photograph of the Ironist on the portico was staring unblinkingly into the afternoon sun. The offstage drama in Quinto, I told it silently, was better than the kind they rehearsed. It didn't answer; it was lost in a dream of its own loveliness.

CHAPTER 3

I found a phone booth in a drugstore down the block. There was no James Slocum in the Nopal Valley section of the directory, but there was a Mrs. Olivia Slocum, presumably his mother. I made the ten-cent toll call and got a cracked dry voice which could have belonged to man or woman:

"The Slocum residence."

"Mrs. James Slocum, please."

There was a click on the line: "All right, Mrs. Strang. I'll take it on my extension."

Mrs. Strang grunted and went off the line.

"Archer speaking," I said. "I'm in Quinto."

"I hoped you would call. Yes?"

"Look here, Mrs. Slocum, I'm practically handcuffed. I can't ask questions, or I'll start talk where there isn't any. I have no lead and no contacts. Isn't there some way I can meet your family—your husband, at least?"

"But he has nothing to do with it. You'll only rouse suspicion."

"Not necessarily. If I float around without an explanation, I'll rouse suspicion for sure. And I won't find anything out if I can't talk to anybody."

"You sound discouraged," she said.

"I was never encouraged, I told you that. Operating

in a vacuum, I don't stand much chance of helping you. Even a list of suspects—"

"But there are none. I can't name a single person. Is the case really so hopeless?"

"Unless I get a lucky break, like somebody running up to me in the street and confessing. This is a very intimate business, there's nothing overt in it like the ordinary divorce setup, and I need to get closer to your life."

Very softly, she said: "Are you proposing to spy on me, Mr. Archer?"

"Hardly. I'm working for you. But I need a center to work from, and you and your family are it. I got a look at your husband and daughter just now, but a look is not enough."

"I specifically instructed you not to approach my husband."

Her moods were hard to follow and match. I changed mine: "If you don't let me handle the thing my own way, I'll have to drop it. I'll mail you your money."

In the silence that followed, I could hear her tapping with a pencil on the base of the telephone. "No," she said finally. "I want you to do what you can. If you have any reasonable suggestion—"

"It's not very reasonable, but it should do. Do you have any friends in Hollywood? Picture people?"

Another silence. "There's Mildred Fleming, she's a secretary in one of the studios. I had lunch with her today."

"Which studio?"

"Warner's, I think."

"All right. You told her how good the play is. She has a boy-friend who works for an agent who deals in literary properties. Me."

"I see," she answered slowly. "Yes, that's reasonable enough. Actually, it will fit in very well. A few of James's friends are coming in for cocktails. If you could be here at five?"

"I'll come early."

"Very well, Mr. Archer." She gave me directions, and hung up.

My shirt was dank from sitting in the steaming booth. I drove back to my motel, changed to shorts and went down to the beach for a swim. The blue-green swells were heaving slowly beyond the surf. Further out, a few white sails leaned across the horizon, curved sharp like wings in the wind, but motionless in the distance. I met a wave head-on as it broke and took the cold shock running. My feet kicked out behind me and I swam straight out for a quarter of a mile. There the kelp-beds stopped me, a tangled barrier of brown and yellow tubes and bulbs floating low in the water. I hated the touch of underwater life.

I turned on my back and floated, looking up at the sky, nothing around me but cool clear Pacific, nothing in my eyes but long blue space. It was as close as I ever got to cleanliness and freedom, as far as I ever got from all the people. They had jerrybuilt the beaches from San Diego to the Golden Gate, bulldozed super-highways through the mountains, cut down a thousand years of redwood growth, and built an urban wilderness in the desert. They couldn't touch the ocean. They poured their sewage into it, but it couldn't be tainted.

There was nothing wrong with Southern California that a rise in the ocean level wouldn't cure. Except that there were too many Ararats, and I was no Noah. The sky was flat and empty, and the water was chilling me. I swam to the kelp-bed and plunged down through it. It was cold and clammy like the bowels of fear. I came up gasping and sprinted to shore with a barracuda terror nipping at my heels.

A wave thrust me up on the beach, where a cold late afternoon wind took over, armed with small needles of sand. I wasn't a noble savage after all.

I was still chilly a half-hour later, crossing the pass to Nopal Valley. Even at its summit the highway was wide and new, rebuilt with somebody's money. I could smell the source of the money when I slid down into the valley on the other side. It stank like rotten eggs.

The oil wells from which the sulphur gas rose crowded the slopes on both sides of the town. I could see them from the highway as I drove in: the latticed triangles of the derricks where trees had grown, the oil-pumps nodding and clanking where cattle had grazed. Since 'thirty-nine or 'forty, when I had seen it last, the town had grown enormously, like a tumor. It had thrust out shoots in all directions: blocks of match-box houses in raw new housing developments and the real estate shacks to go with them, a half-mile gauntlet of one-story buildings along the highway: veterinarians, chiropractors, beauty shops, marketerias, restaurants, bars, liquor stores. There was a new four-story hotel, a white frame gospel tabernacle, a bowling alley wide enough to house a B-36. The main street had been transformed by glass brick, plastic, neon. A quiet town in a sunny valley had hit the jackpot hard, and didn't know what to do with itself at all.

More had changed than the face of the buildings, or the number and make of the cars. The people were different and there were too many of them. Crowds of men whose faces were marked by sun and work and boredom walked in the streets and in and out of the bars, looking for fun or trouble. Very few women showed on the main street. The blue-shirted cop on the main corner wore his holster on the front of his hip, with the flap unbuttoned and the gun-butt showing.

Trail Road turned off to the right on the far side of the town, and climbed through the oil fields to a gently sloping mesa which overlooked the valley. As it climbed it dwindled down to a narrow blacktop looping up the side of the sunbaked hill. The mountains rose sheer in front of the nose of my car, starkly shadowed by the declining light. A long, low house half-hidden by giant oaks sat in the middle of the mesa, as indigenous as a boulder. Before I reached it I had to stop and open a gate which barred the road.

On either side of it a six-foot cyclone fence topped by strands of barbed wire stretched out of sight.

The road inside the gate was freshly gravelled, and sentineled by twin rows of young palms. There were a couple of cars parked in the circular drive that curved around in front of the house. One was the old Packard sedan I had seen in front of the Quinto Theatre. I left my car beside it and crossed the terraced lawn, dodging the rainbowed spray from a sprinkling system.

The house was built of adobe brick the color of the earth, pressed down to the earth by a heavy red tile roof, and massive as a fortress. A deep veranda ran along its front. I climbed the low concrete steps. A woman in a red sweater and slacks was curled like a scarlet snake in one corner of a green canvas porch swing. Her head was bent over a book, and red harlequin spectacles gave her shadowed face a look of queer concentration. The concentration was real; she gave no sign of hearing me or seeing me until I spoke:

"Excuse me. I'm looking for Mrs. Slocum."

"Excuse *me*." She looked up in real surprise, her eyes refocusing like a sleeper's, and flicked the spectacles off. It was Cathy Slocum; I hadn't recognized her until then. The glasses and the look they gave her had added ten years to her age, and the shape of her body was misleading. It was one of those female bodies that bloomed very young. Her eyes were large and deep like her mother's, and she had better lines. I could understand the chauffeur's passion for her. But she was very young.

"My name is Archer," I said.

She gave me a long, cool look, but didn't know me. "I'm Cathy Slocum. Is it mother or grandmother you want to see?"

"Mother. She asked me to the party."

"It's not her party," she said under her breath to herself. A spoiled-little-girl look made two black vertical lines between her eyebrows. Then she remembered me, and smoothed them out, and asked me very sweetly: "Are you a friend of mother's, Mr. Archer?"

"A friend of a friend's. Would you like my Bertillon measurements?"

She was clever enough to get it, and young enough to blush. "I'm sorry, I didn't mean to be rude—we see so few strangers." Which might account for her interest in a rough-talking chauffeur named Reavis. "Mother's just come up from the pool, and she's dressing, and father hasn't come home. Would you care to sit down?"

"Thank you." I followed the tall fine body to the swing, amused by the fact that it contained an adolescent who had to be reminded of her manners. Not a usual adolescent, though. The book in her hand, when she laid it down on the cushion between us, turned out to be a book on psychoanalysis by Karen Horney.

She began to make conversation, swinging the spectacles back and forth by one end: "Father's rehearsing a play in Quinto, that's what the party's about. He's really a very fine actor, you know." She said it a little defensively.

"I know. Much better than the play."

"Have you seen the play?"

"I caught a scene of it this afternoon."

"And what did you think of it? Isn't it well written?"

"Well enough," I said, without enthusiasm.

"But what do you really think of it?"

Her look was so candid and girlish that I told her. "They should jack up the title and build a new play under it and change the title. If what I saw was a fair sample."

"But everyone who's seen it thinks it's a masterpiece. Are you interested in the theatre, Mr. Archer?"

"Do you mean do I know what I'm talking about? Probably not. I work for a man in Hollywood who deals in literary properties. He sent me up to look at it."

"Oh," she said. "Hollywood. Father says it's much too literary for Hollywood, and it's not written to a formula. Mr. Marvell plans to take it to Broadway. Their standards are much subtler, don't you think?"

"Much. Who is Mr. Marvell? I know he's author-director of the play . . ."

"He's an English poet. He went to Oxford, and his uncle's a lord. He's a good friend of father's, and father likes his poetry and I tried to read some of it but I couldn't understand it. It's awfully difficult and symbolic, like Dylan Thomas."

The name rang no bell. "Is your father going along, when Marvell takes the play to New York?"

"Oh, no." The swinging spectacles described a full circle and struck against her knee with an audible tap. She put them on again. They lengthened and aged her face, and gave it piquancy. "Father's just helping Francis out. He's putting it on to try and get some backing. Father has no histrionic ambitions, though he is a really fine actor, don't you think?"

A mediocre amateur, I thought. I said: "No question about it." When the girl mentioned her father, as she frequently did, her mouth went flower-soft and her hands were still.

But when he mounted the veranda a few minutes later, with Marvell skipping beside him up the steps, she looked at James Slocum as if she were afraid of him. Her fingers interlaced and strained against each other. I noticed that the nails were bitten stubby.

"Hello, father." The words left her mouth ajar, and the tip of her tongue moved along her upper lip.

He walked toward us purposefully, a middle-sized, thin-chested man who should have had a Greek torso to support his startling head. "I've been wanting to talk to you, Cathy." The sensitive mouth was stern. "I expected you to wait for me at the theatre."

"Yes, father." She turned to me. "Do you know my father, Mr. Archer?"

I stood up and said hello. He looked me over with his sad brown eyes, and gave me a limp hand as an afterthought. "Francis," he said to the blond man at his shoulder: "See if you and Archer can find a drink for yourselves. I'd like to have a moment with Cathy here."

"Right." Marvell touched me in the small of the back, ushering me to the front door. Cathy watched us go. Her father stood looking down at her with one hand on his hip, the other at his chin, in an actorish pose.

We entered a living-room as dim and cool as a cave. The windows were few and small, masked by venetian blinds which laid horizontal bars across the light. The barred light fell on a floor of black oak, partly covered with faded Persian rugs. The furniture was heavy and old: a rosewood concert grand at the far end of the room, carved elaborately to nineteenth-century taste, stiff-backed chairs of mahogany, a tapestried divan in front of the deep fireplace. The beams that supported the time-stained plaster ceiling were black oak like the floor. A chandelier of yellowing crystal hung down from the central beam like a misshaped stalactite.

"Queer old place, what?" Marvell said to me. "Well, what shall it be, old boy? A Scotch and soda?"

"Fine."

"I expect I'll have to look you up some ice."

"Don't bother."

"No bother at all. I know where everything is." He trotted away, his light hair flying in the wind of his own motion. For the nephew of a lord, he was very obliging. I myself was the nephew of my late Uncle Jake, who once went fifteen rounds with Gunboat Smith, to no decision.

I tried to remember what my Uncle Jake looked like. I could remember the smell of him, compounded of bay rum, hair oil, strong clean masculine sweat and good tobacco, and the taste of the dark chocolate cigarettes he brought me the day my father took me to San Francisco for the first time; but I couldn't remember his face. My mother never kept his pictures, because she was ashamed to have a professional fighter in the family.

The murmur of voices drew me to a window which

opened outward onto the veranda. I sat down in a straight chair against the wall, hidden from outside by the heavy drapes and the half-closed blind. Cathy and her father were talking on the swing.

"I didn't see him afterwards," she said tensely. "I walked out and got in the car and drove myself home. He wasn't even in sight."

"But I know he drove you home. I saw his cap on the front seat of the car just now."

"He must have left it before. I swear I didn't see him after."

"How can I believe you, Cathy?" The man's voice held genuine torment. "You've lied to me before, about him, too. You promised me you'd have nothing to do with him, or any other man, until you were older."

"But I didn't! I didn't do anything wrong."

"You let him kiss you."

"He made me. I tried to get away." A trace of hysteria came into her voice like a thin entering wedge.

"You must have encouraged him in some way. A man doesn't act like that without a reason, surely. Think about it, Cathy, didn't you do or say something which might have led him on?" He was trying to be cool and fair, the impersonal cross-examiner, but hurt and rage buzzed like blundering insects in his tone.

"Led him on, father. That's a hideous thing to say." The onset of sobbing rocked her words.

"Darling," he said. "Poor darling." The swing creaked as he leaned toward her, and the sobs were smothered. "I didn't mean to hurt you, Cathy, you know that. It's simply because I love you that I'm so concerned about this—this ugly thing."

"I love you too, father." The words were muffled, probably by his shoulder.

"I wish I could believe that," he said gently.

"But I do, father, I do. I think you're the best man in the world."

There was something queer about the conversation,

made stranger still by the girl's extreme urgency. They could have been two lovers, of the same age.

"Oh, Cathy," he said brokenly. "What am I going to do about you?"

A third voice entered the colloquy: "What are you trying to do to her, James?" It was Maude Slocum's voice, and it was cold with anger.

"This is no affair of yours," he answered.

"I should think it is. She is my daughter, you know."

"I'm well aware of that, my dear. It doesn't necessarily follow that she can't have a good, decent life."

"She won't have if you go on like this, stirring her up and torturing her nerves."

"For heaven's sake, mother." Cathy spoke as if the older woman were the child. "The way you talk about me, you'd think I was a bone for two dogs to fight over. Why can't you treat me like a human being?"

"I try to, Cathy. You'll never listen to me. I know something about these things—" She faltered.

"If you know so much, why don't you put them into practice? There've been nothing but scenes in this family since I was old enough to talk, and I'm sick of it."

The girl's footsteps crossed the veranda, and the elder Slocums were silent. A full minute passed before the woman said, in a voice I barely recognized: "Leave her alone, James. I'm warning you."

The throaty whisper made the short hairs prickle at the back of my neck.

CHAPTER 4

I moved to the center of the room and leafed through a *Theatre Arts* magazine that was lying on a table. In a little while Marvell came back with a bowl of ice, glasses, Scotch, and soda, clinking together on a myrtlewood tray. "Excuse the delay, old man. The housekeeper's busy making canapes, and gave me absolutely no help at all. Do you like it strong?"

"I'll pour my own, thanks." I made a tall highball with plenty of soda. It was still early, a few minutes after five by my watch.

Marvell made himself a short one and took it in two gulps, his Adam's apple bobbing like a soft egg caught in his throat. "The Slocums aren't inhospitable," he said, "but they're nearly always late. One has to fend for oneself. Cathy informs me you're a literary agent?"

"Of a kind. I work for a man who buys fiction if he thinks it has movie possibilities. Then he tries to interest a producer, or make a package deal with a star."

"I see. Would I know the gentleman's name?"

"Probably not. I'm not allowed to use his name, anyway, because it's worth money. It bids up prices." I was improvising, but I knew twenty men in the game, and some of them operated like that.

He leaned back in his chair and hitched one thin knee over the other. His legs were pale and hairless above the drooping socks. His pale blond gaze seemed lashless. "You don't seriously think my play is cinematic material? I've sought a rather difficult beauty, you know."

I dipped my embarrassment in whiskey and soda, and waited for it to dissolve. It stayed where it was, a smiling mask on my face. "I never make snap decisions. I'm paid to keep tabs on the summer theaters, and that's what I do. There's a lot of young acting-talent floating around. In any case, I'll have to see all of your play before I can make a report."

"I noticed you there this afternoon," he said. "What *did* happen before that frightful scene between Cathy and her father?"

"I wouldn't know. I was watching the play."

He got up for another drink, moving sideways across the room like a shying horse. "The girl's quite a problem," he said over his shoulder. "Poor dear James is positively hag-ridden by his womenfolk. A less responsible man would simply decamp."

"Why?"

"They bleed him emotionally." He smiled palely over his second drink. "His mother began it when he was a very small boy, and it's gone on for so many years that he actually doesn't know he's being imposed upon. Now his wife and daughter are carrying on the good work. They're wasting the dear man's emotional substance."

He realized then that he was talking too much, and changed the subject abruptly: "I've often wondered why his mother chooses to live on a barren slope like this. She could live anywhere, you know, absolutely anywhere. But she *chooses* to wither away in this dreadful sun."

"Some people like it," I said. "I'm a native Californian myself."

"But don't you ever weary of the soul-destroying monotony of the weather?"

Only of phonies, I thought. Of the soul-destroying

monotony of phonies I wearied something awful. But I explained, for the hundredth time, that Southern California had two seasons, like any Mediterranean climate, and that people who couldn't tell the difference lacked one or more of the five senses.

"Oh, quite, quite," he told me, and poured himself another stiff drink, while I was still sipping the dregs of my first. The whisky didn't seem to affect him at all. He was an aging Peter Pan, glib, bland and eccentric, and all I had really found out was that he was fond of James Slocum. Everything he said and did was so stylized that I couldn't get at his center, or even guess where it was.

I was glad when Maude Slocum came into the room, her straight white smile gleaming in the amber light from the windows. She had left her emotions on the veranda, and seemed in control of herself. But her eyes looked past me, and far beyond the room.

"Hello, Francis." He half rose from his chair, and slumped back into it. "You really must forgive me, Mr. Archer, I'm a most unsatisfactory hostess—"

"On the contrary." She was dressed to attract attention in a black-and-white striped linen dress with a plunging neckline and a very close waist. I gave her attention.

"Francis," she said sweetly, "would you see if you can find James for me? He's somewhere out front."

"Right, darling." Marvell seemed pleased with the excuse to get away, and trotted out of the room. Nearly every family of a certain class had at least one hanger-on like him, dutiful and useless and untied. But unless Maude Slocum and he were very smooth actors, Marvell wasn't the apex of her triangle.

I offered to make her a drink but she poured her own, straight. She wrinkled her nose over the glass. "I hate Scotch, but James so loves to make the cocktails himself. Well, Mr. Archer, have you been probing the household secrets, rattling the family skeletons and so on?" The question was humorously put, but she wanted an answer.

I glanced at the open window and answered in a lower tone: "Hardly. I've had some talk with Marvell, and some with Cathy. No light. No skeletons." But there was electric tension in the house.

"I hope you don't think Francis—?"

"I don't think about him, I don't understand him."

"He's simple enough, I should think—a perfectly nice boy. His income's been cut off by the British government, and he's trying desperately to stay in the United States. His family's the fox-hunting sort, he can't abide them." The chattering stopped abruptly, and her voice went shy: "What do you think of Cathy?"

"She's a bright kid. How old?"

"Nearly sixteen. Isn't she lovely, though?"

"Lovely," I said, wondering what ailed the woman. Almost a total stranger, I was being asked to approve of herself and her daughter. Her insecurity went further back than the letter she had given me. Some guilt or fear was drawing her backward steadily, so that she had to enthuse and emote and be admired in order to stay in the same place.

"Loveliness runs in the family, doesn't it?" I said. "Which reminds me, I'd like to meet your mother-in-law."

"I don't understand why—"

"I'm trying to get a picture, and she's a central figure in it, isn't she? Put it this way. You're not so worried about who sent the first letter—that's safe in my pocket—as you are about the possible effects of a second letter. If I can't stop the letters at their source, I might be able to circumvent their effects."

"How?"

"I don't know. The main thing is that your husband, and your daughter, and your mother-in-law, shouldn't take the letters seriously. Your husband might divorce you, your daughter might despise you—"

"Don't say that." She set down her glass peremptorily on the coffee-table between us.

I went on evenly: "Your mother-in-law might cut off your income. I've been thinking, if I launched a poison-pen campaign against the whole family, and made a lot of different accusations, the one that hurts could get lost in the shuffle, couldn't it?"

"God no! I couldn't stand it, none of us could." The violence of her reaction was surprising. Her whole body heaved in the zebra-striped dress, and her breasts pressed together like round clenched fists in the V of her neckline.

"I was only playing with the idea. It needs refining, but there's something there."

"No, it's horrible. It would cover us all with filth to hide one thing."

"All right," I said, "all right. To get back to your mother-in-law, she's the one that would break you, isn't she? I mean it's her money that runs the house?"

"It's really James's, too. She handles the income in her lifetime, but his father's will requires her to provide for him. Her idea of providing is three hundred a month, a little more than she pays the cook."

"Could she afford to pay more?"

"If she wanted to. She has income from half a million, and this property is worth a couple of million. But she refuses to sell an acre of it."

"A couple of million? I didn't realize it was that big."

"There's oil under it," she said bitterly. "As far as Olivia is concerned, the oil can stay in the ground until we all dry up and blow away."

"I take it there's no love lost between you and your mother-in-law."

She shrugged her shoulders. "I gave up trying long ago. She's never forgiven me for marrying James. He was her pampered darling, and I married him young."

"Three hundred a month isn't exactly pampering, not if she has a couple of million in capital assets."

"It's the same as he got in college." The details of her grievances poured out, as if she'd been waiting for a long time to borrow somebody's ear. "She never increased it even when Cathy was born. For a while before the war we managed to live on it in a house of our own. Then prices went up, and we came home to mama."

I put the important question as tactfully as I could: "And what does James do?"

"Nothing. He was never encouraged to think of making a living. He was her only son, and she wanted him around. That's the idea of the allowance, of course. She's got him."

Her eyes were looking past me at a flat desert of time that stretched backward and forward as far as she could see. It occurred to me for an instant that I'd be doing her a favor if I showed her mother-in-law the letter in my pocket, and broke up the family for good. It was even possible that that was her own unconscious wish, the motive behind her original indiscretion. But I wasn't even certain that there had been an indiscretion, and she would never talk. After sixteen years of waiting for her share, and planning for her daughter, she was going to wait for the end.

She rose suddenly. "I'll take you to meet Olivia, if you must. She's always in the garden in the late afternoon."

The garden had fieldstone walls higher than my head. Inside, the flowers broke the light into almost every shade of the spectrum, and held it glowing. The sun was nearly down behind the western mountains and the light was fading, but Mrs. Slocum's flowers burned brightly on as if with fires of their own. There were fuchsias, pansies, tuberous begonias, great shaggy dahlias like separate pink suns. Olivia Slocum was working among them with a pair of shears, when we came up to the gate. Of indeterminate shape and size in a faded linen dress and a wide straw hat, she was bent far over among the blooms.

Her daughter-in-law called to her, with a slight nagging tone in her voice: "Mother! You shouldn't be straining yourself like that. You know what the doctor said."

"What did the doctor say?" I asked her under my breath.

"She has a heart condition—when it's convenient."

Olivia Slocum straightened up and came toward us, removing her earth-stained gloves. Her face was handsome in a soft, vague, sun-flecked way, and she was much younger than I'd expected. I'd imagined her as a thin and sour old lady pushing seventy, with gnarled hands grasping the reins she held on other people's lives. But she wasn't over fifty-five at most, and she carried her age easily. The three generations of Slocum women were a little too close for comfort.

"Don't be ridiculous, my dear," she said to Maude. "The doctor says mild exercise is beneficial to me. Anyway, I love to garden in the cool of the day."

"Well, as long as you don't overtire yourself." The younger woman's voice was grudging, and I suspected that the two never agreed on anything. "This is Mr. Archer, mother. He came up from Hollywood to see Francis's play."

"How nice. And have you seen it, Mr. Archer? I've heard James is quite distinguished in the leading role."

"He's very accomplished." The lie came easier as I repeated it, but it still left a bad taste on my tongue.

With a queer look at me, Maude excused herself and went back to the house. Mrs. Slocum raised both arms to take off her woven straw hat. She held the pose a moment too long, and turned her head so that I could see her profile. Vanity was her trouble; she was fixed on her own lost beauty, and couldn't grow old or let her son grow up. The hat came off after the long moment. Her hair was dyed bright red, and combed over her forehead in straight bangs.

"James is one of the most versatile people in the world," she said. "I brought him up to take a creative interest in everything, and I must say he's justified my faith. Of course you know him only as an actor, but he paints quite passably, and he has a beautiful tenor voice as well. He's even taken to writing verse lately. Francis has been a great stimulus to him."

"A brilliant man," I said. I had to say something to stem her flow of words.

"Francis? Oh, yes. But he doesn't have a tithe of James's energy. It would be a boon to him if he could rouse some Hollywood interest in his play. He's been urging me to back it, but naturally I can't afford to speculate in that sort of thing. I presume that you're connected with the studios, Mr. Archer?"

"Indirectly." I didn't want to get involved in explanations. She chattered like a parrot, but her eyes were shrewd. To change the subject, I said: "As a matter of fact, I'd like to get out of Hollywood. It's ulcer territory. A quiet life in the country would suit me fine, if I could get a piece of property in a place like this."

"A place like this, Mr. Archer?" She spoke guardedly, and her green eyes veiled themselves like a parrot's eyes.

Her reaction surprised me, but I blundered on: "I've never seen a place I'd rather live in."

"I see, Maude sicked you on me." Her voice was unfriendly and harsh. "If you represent the Pareco people, I must ask you to leave my property at once."

"Pareco?" It was the name of a gasoline. My only connection with it was that I used it in my car occasionally. I told her that.

She looked closely into my face, and apparently decided I wasn't lying. "The Pacific Refinery Company has been trying to get control of my property. For years they've been laying siege to me, and it's made me a little suspicious of strangers, especially when they express an interest in real estate."

"My interest is entirely personal," I said.

"I'm sorry if I've maligned you, Mr. Archer. The events of the last few years have embittered me, I'm afraid. I love this valley. When my husband and I first saw it, more than thirty years ago, it seemed our earthly paradise, our valley of the sun. When we could afford to, we bought this lovely old house and the hills around it, and when he retired we came here to live. My husband is buried here—he was older than I—and I intend to die here myself. Do I sound sentimental?"

"No." Her feeling for the place was stronger than sentimentality, and a little frightening. Her heavy body leaning on the gate was monumental in the evening light. "I can understand your attachment to a place like this."

"I am a part of it," she continued throatily. "They've ruined the town and desecrated the rest of the valley, but they shan't touch my mesa. I told them that, though they'll never take no for an answer. I told them that the mountains would be here long after they were gone. They didn't know what I was talking about." She rolled a cold green eye in my direction: "I believe you understand me, Mr. Archer. You're very sympathetic."

I muttered some kind of an affirmative. I understood a part of her feeling all right. A friend of mine who lectured in economics at UCLA would call it the *mystique* of property. What I failed to understand was the power of her obsession. Perhaps it was explained by the fact that she felt besieged, with her daughter-in-law a fifth column in the house.

"I sometimes feel that the mountains are my sisters—" She cut herself off short, as if she'd suddenly realized that she was going off the deep end. I was thinking that she had enough ego to equip a dictator and leave enough over for a couple of gauleiters. Perhaps she noticed the change in my expression.

"I know you're wanting to go to the party," she said, and gave me her hand briefly. "It was nice of you to come and talk to an old woman like me."

I started back to the house through an aisle of tall Italian cypress. It opened on a lawn in which a small swimming-pool was sunk, its filter system masked by a cypress hedge. At the far end a burlap-covered springboard stuck out over the water. The water in the pool was so still it seemed solid, a polished surface reflecting the trees, the distant mountains, and the sky. I looked up at the sky to the west, where the sun had dipped behind the mountains. The clouds were writhing with red fire, as if the sun had plunged in the invisible sea and set it flaming. Only the mountains stood out dark and firm against the conflagration of the sky.

CHAPTER 5

The sound of an approaching motor stopped me at the corner of the veranda. There were several more cars on the apron of the drive: a Jaguar roadster, a fishtail Cadillac, an ancient Rolls with wire wheels and a long, square British nose. Another car came into sight between the lines of palms, a quiet black machine with a red searchlight mounted on the front. I watched it being parked. A police car in that company seemed as out of place as a Sherman tank at a horse show.

A man got out of the black car and came up the flagstone walk which ascended the terraces in front of the house. He was tall and thick, a bifurcated chunk of muscle that moved with unexpected speed and silence. Even in slacks and a sports jacket, with a silk shirt open at the neck, he had the authority of a uniform, the bearing of a cop or a veteran soldier. Shadowed eyes, cragged nose, wide mouth, long jaw; his face was a relief map of all the male passions. Short hair the color of faded straw bristled on his head and sprouted from the shirt-opening at the base of his heavy red neck.

I moved a step to show myself and said: "Good evening."

"Good evening." He bit the words off with clean

white teeth, smiling automatically, then mounted the steps to the veranda.

He glanced around as though he were ill at ease, before knocking on the door. I watched him over the veranda railing, and our eyes met for a meaningless instant. I was about to speak again—something about the weather—when I noticed Cathy curled in the porch swing as she'd been an hour before. She was leaning forward, watching the man intently.

His eyes shifted to her, and he took a step toward her. "Cathy? How are you, Cathy?" Hesitant and uncertain, the tone of a man talking to a child he didn't know.

Her only answer was a clucking deep in her throat. With a slow boldness she rose from the swing and walked toward him in silence. Past him and down the steps and around the far corner of the veranda, without once turning her head. He pivoted on his heels and half-raised one hand, which stayed forgotten in the air until she was out of sight. The large hand, open and futile, curled into a fist. He turned to the door and struck it twice as if it had a human face.

I climbed the steps behind him while he was waiting. "Fine weather we're having," I said.

He looked at me without hearing what I said or seeing my face. "Yeah."

Maude Slocum opened the door and took us in in a single swift glance. "Ralph?" she said to the other man. "I wasn't expecting you."

"I met James downtown today, and he asked me to come over for a drink." His heavy voice was apologetic.

"Come in then," she said, without graciousness. "Since James invited you."

"Not if I'm not wanted," he answered sullenly.

"Oh, come in, Ralph. It would look rather strange if you came to the door and went away again. And what would James say to me?"

"What does he usually say?"

"Nothing, nothing at all." If they had a joke between them, it didn't fit my wave length. "Come in and *have* your drink, Ralph."

"You twisted my arm," he said wryly, and passed her in the doorway. Almost imperceptibly, her body arched away from his. Hatred or some other feeling had drawn her as tight as a bowstring.

She remained in the doorway and moved her hips so that she blocked my way. "Please go away, Mr. Archer. Pretty please?" She tried to make it pleasant and light but failed.

"You *are* kind of inhospitable, aren't you? Apart from the curious fact that you hired me to come up here."

"I'm sorry. I'm afraid a situation is developing, and I simply couldn't stand the extra strain of having you around."

"And here was I, thinking I was a welcome addition to any group gathering. You lacerate my ego, Mrs. Slocum."

"It's no laughing matter," she told me sharply. "I don't lie very well. So I avoid situations in which lying is necessary."

"Then who's the large character with the thirst?"

"One of James's friends. I don't see the point of these questions."

"Does James have many policeman friends? I didn't think he was the type."

"Do you know Ralph Knudson?" Surprise made her face look longer.

"I've seen the pattern they're made from." Five years on the Long Beach force were in my record. "What's a tough cop doing at an arty party in the hills?"

"You'll have to ask James—but not now. He takes peculiar fancies to people." She wasn't a competent liar. "Of course, Mr. Knudson isn't an ordinary policeman. He's the Chief of Police in town, and I understand he has a rather distinguished record."

"But you don't really want him at your parties, is that it? I used to be a cop, and I'm still one in a way. I've felt that kind of snobbery myself."

"I'm not a snob!" she said fiercely. Apparently I'd touched something she valued. "My parents were ordinary people, and I've always hated snobs. But why I should be defending myself to you!"

"Then let me come in for a drink. I promise to be very suave and smooth."

"You're so terribly persistent—as if I didn't have enough to contend with. What makes you so persistent?"

"Curiosity, I guess. I'm getting interested in the case. It's quite an interesting setup you've got here; I've never seen a fishline with more tangles."

"I suppose you realize I can dismiss you, if you continue to make yourself completely obnoxious."

"You won't."

"And why won't I?"

"I think you're expecting trouble. You said yourself that something was building up. I can feel it in the air. And it's possible your policeman friend didn't come up here for fun."

"Don't be melodramatic. And he isn't my friend. Frankly, Mr. Archer, I've never had to deal with a more difficult—employee, than you."

I didn't like the word. "It might help you," I said, "if you thought of me as an independent contractor. In this case I'm expected to build a house without going near the lot." Or perhaps demolish a house, but I didn't add that.

She looked at me steadily for twenty or thirty seconds. Finally a smile touched her generous mouth and parted it. "You know, I think I rather like you, damn it. Very well, come in and meet the wonderful people, and I'll buy you a drink."

"You talked me into it."

I got my drink and lost my hostess in the same motion, as soon as we entered the big living-room. Ralph Knudson, the big man who was no friend of hers, caught her eye as she handed me my glass. She went to him. Her husband and Francis Marvell were sitting on the piano bench with their heads together, leafing through a thick volume of music. I looked around at the rest of the wonderful people. Mrs. Galway, the amateur actress, with the professional smile clicking off and on like a white electric sign. A bald-headed man in white flannels setting off his mahogany tan, who daintily smoked a small brown cigarillo in a long green-gold holder. A fat man with a cropped gray head, in a tweed suit with padded shoulders, who turned out to be a woman when she moved her nyloned legs. A woman leaning awkwardly on the arm of the chair beside her, with a dark long tragic face and an ugly body. A youth who moved gracefully about the room, pouring drinks for everybody and smoothing the receding hair at his temples. A round little woman who tinkled on and on, whose bracelets and earrings tinkled when her voice paused.

I listened to them talk. Existentialism, they said. Henry Miller and Truman Capote and Henry Moore. André Gide and Anais Nin and Djuna Barnes. And sex—hard-boiled, poached, coddled, shirred, and fried easy over in sweet, fresh creamery butter. Sex solo, in duet, trio, quartet; for all-male chorus; for choir and symphony; and played on the harpsichord in three-fourths time. And Albert Schweitzer and the dignity of everything that lives.

The fat man who had been listening to the tinkling woman closed his face against her and became absorbed in his drink. She looked around brightly and gaily like a bird, saw me, and picked up her drink. It was short and green. She sat down on a hassock by my chair, crossed her plump ankles, so that I could see the tininess of her feet, and tinkled:

"I *so* love creme de menthe; it's *such* a pretty drink, and I always drink it when I wear my emeralds." She bobbed her birdlike head, and the earrings swung. They were the right color, but almost too big to be real.

"I always eat oyster stew when I wear my pearls," I said.

Her laughter had the same quality as her voice, and

was an octave higher. I decided not to make her laugh, if possible.

"You're Mr. Archer, aren't you? I've heard such interesting things about you. My daughter's on the stage in New York, you know. Her father's constantly urging her to come home, because of course it costs him a great deal of money, but I tell him, after all, a girl is only young once. Don't you agree?"

"Some people manage it twice. If they live long enough."

I meant it as an insult, but she thought it was funny, and made me the curious gift of her laughter again. "You must have heard of Felice. She dances under the name of Felicia France. Leonard Lyons has mentioned her several times. Mr. Marvell thinks she has dramatic talent, too; he'd love to have her play the ingénue in his play. But Felice has given her heart and soul to the dance. She has a very, very beautiful body, dear child. I had a lovely body myself at one time, really utterly lovely." Meditatively, she fingered herself, like a butcher testing meat which had hung too long.

I looked away, anywhere, and saw James Slocum standing up by the piano. Marvell struck a few opening chords, and Slocum began to sing, in a thin sweet tenor, the *Ballad of Barbara Allen.* The trickle of melody gradually filled the room like clear water, and the bubbling chatter subsided. Slocum's face was untroubled and radiant, a boy tenor's. Everyone in the room was watching it before the song ended, and he knew it, and wanted it that way. He was Peter Pan, caught out of time. His song had killed the crocodile with the ticking clock in its belly.

"Quite utterly lovely," the emerald earrings tinkled. "It always reminds me of Scotland for some reason. Edinburgh is really one of my favorite places in the world. What is your favorite place in the whole wide world, Mr. Archer?"

"Ten feet underwater at La Jolla, watching the fish through a face-glass."

"Are fish so terribly fascinating?"

"They have some pleasant qualities. You don't have to look at them unless you want to. And they can't talk."

Below her bird-brained laughter, and drowning it out, a heavy male voice said clearly: "That was very nice, James. Now why don't you and Marvell sing a duet?"

It was Ralph Knudson. Most of the eyes in the room shifted to him, and wavered away again. His thick face was bulging with blood and malice. Maude Slocum was standing beside him, facing her husband. Slocum stood where he was, his face as white as snow. Marvell was motionless, his eyes fixed on the keyboard and his back to the room. Short of homicidal violence, the atmosphere around the piano was as ugly as I had ever seen.

Maude Slocum walked through it, moving easily from Knudson to her husband, and touched him on the arm. He drew away from her, and she persisted.

"That would be nice, James," she said simply and quietly, "if only Francis had a voice like yours. But why don't you sing by yourself? I'll accompany you."

She took Marvell's place at the bench, and played while her husband sang. Knudson watched them, smiling like a tiger. I felt like going for a long drive by myself.

CHAPTER 6

The fire in the sky had died, leaving long wisps of cloud like streaks of ashes livid against the night. All I could see of the mountains was their giant shadowed forms shouldering the faintly lighted sky. A few lights sprinkled their flanks, and a car's headlights inched down into the other side of the valley and were lost in darkness. Then the night was so still that motion seemed impossible, all of us insects caught in the final amber. I moved and broke the spell, feeling my way down the dew-slick terraces beside the flagstone walk.

I closed a contact when I took hold of the left doorhandle of my convertible. The headlights and dashlights came on with a click. My right hand moved by reflex under my coat for a gun that wasn't there. Then I saw the girl's hand on the switch, the girl's face like a ghost's leaning towards me.

"It's only me, Mr. Archer. Cathy." There was night in her voice, in her eyes, night caught like mist in her hair. In a soft wool coat buttoned up to her soft chin, she was one of the girls I had watched from a distance in high school and never been able to touch; the girls with oil or gold or free-flowing real-estate money dissolved in their blood like blueing. She was also young enough to be my daughter.

"What do you think you're doing?"

"Nothing." She settled back in the seat and I slid under the wheel. "I just turned on the lights for you. I'm sorry if I startled you, I didn't mean to."

"Why pick on my car? You've got one of your own."

"Two. But father took the keys. Besides, I like your car. The seat is very comfortable. May I ride along with you?" She gave her voice a wheedling little-girl inflection.

"Where to?"

"Anywhere you're going. Quinto? Please, Mr. Archer?"

"I don't think so. You're a little young to be running around nights by yourself."

"It's not late, and I'd be with you."

"Even with me," I said. "You'd better go back to the house, Cathy."

"I won't. I hate those people. I'll stay out here all night."

"Not with me you won't. I'm leaving now."

"You won't take me along?" Her clenched hand vibrated on my forearm. There was a note in her voice that hurt my ears like the screech of chalk on a wet blackboard. The smell of her hair was as clean and strange as the redheaded girl's who sat ahead of me in senior year.

"I'm not a nursemaid," I said harshly. "And your parents wouldn't like it. If something's bothering you, take it up with your mother."

"*Her!*" She pulled away from me and sat stonily, her eyes on the lighted house.

I got out and opened the door on her side. "Good night."

She didn't move, even to look at me.

"Do you get out under your own power, or do I lift you out by the nape of the neck?"

She turned on me like a cat, her eyes distended: "You wouldn't dare touch me."

She was right. I took a few steps toward the house, my heels grinding angrily in the gravel, and she was out of the car and after me. "Please don't call them.

I'm afraid of them. That Knudson man—" She was standing on the margin of the car's light, her face bleached white by it and her eyes stained inky black.

"What about him?"

"Mother always wants me to make up to him. I don't know if she wants me to marry him, or what. I can't tell father, or father would kill him. I don't know what to do."

"I'm sorry, Cathy, you're not my baby." I moved to touch her shoulder, but she drew back as if I carried disease. "Why don't you get the cook to make you some hot milk and put you to bed? Things usually look better in the morning."

"Better in the morning," she repeated, with toneless, empty irony.

She was still standing tense and straight, with her hands clenched at her sides, when I started to back the car. The white beam swerved as I turned, and left her in darkness.

I stopped at the gate, but it was open, and I went on through. A few hundred yards beyond it a tall man appeared in the road, lifting his thumb for a ride. I was passing him up when I caught a glimpse of his face: Pat Reavis. I barked to a quick stop and he came running.

"Thanks very much, sir." He smelled strongly of whisky, but he didn't look drunk. "Your dashboard clock working?"

I compared the lighted dial with my watch. Both indicated twenty-three minutes after eight. "Seems to be."

"It's later than I thought, then. God, I sure hate walking. I walked enough in the Marines to last me the rest of my life. My own car's in the garage, front end smashed."

"Where did you do all the walking?"

"One place and another. I landed on Guadal with Carlson's Raiders, for one. But we won't go into that. You know the Slocums?"

To get him talking, I said: "Anybody who is anybody knows the Slocums."

"Yeah, sure," he answered in the same tone. "All that class. What the Slocums need is an equalizer." But he said it in a good-humored way. "You trying to sell them something?"

"Life insurance." I was tired of the farce of pretending to be interested in Marvell's play.

"No kidding? That's a laugh." He laughed to prove it.

"People die," I said. "Is it so funny?"

"I bet you ten to one you didn't sell any, and you never will. The old lady's worth more dead than she is alive already, and the rest of them don't have one nickel to clink against another."

"I don't get it. I heard they were good prospects, well-heeled."

"Sure, the old lady's sitting on a couple of million bucks in oil, but she won't sell or lease. Slocum and his wife can't wait for her to bump. The day she bumps, they'll be down at the travel bureau buying tickets for a de luxe round-the-world cruise. The oil under the ground's their life insurance, so you can stop wasting your time."

"I appreciate the tip. My name is Archer."

"Reavis," he said. "Pat Reavis."

"You seem to know the Slocums pretty well."

"Too damn well. I been their chauffeur for the last six months. No more, though. The bastards fired me."

"Why?"

"How the hell do I know. I guess they just got sick of looking at my pan. I got sick enough looking at theirs."

"That's a nice-looking kid they got, though. What was her name?"

"Cathy."

But he gave me a quick look, and I dropped the subject. "The wife has her points, too," I offered.

"She had it once, I guess. No more. She's turning into another bitch like the old lady. A bunch of women go sour like milk when they got no man around to tell them where to get off."

"There's Slocum, isn't there?"

"I said a man." He snorted. "Hell, I'm talking too much."

The car went over the little ridge that marked the edge of the mesa. The headlights swept empty blackness and dipped down into the valley. There were a few islands of brightness on either side of the road where night crews were working to bring in new wells. Further down the slope, aluminum-painted oil tanks lay under searchlights like a row of thick huge silver dollars in a kitty. At the foot of the hill the lights of the town began, white and scattered on the outskirts, crowded and crawling with color in the business section, where they cast a fiery glow above the buildings.

The traffic in the main street was heavy and unpredictable. Fenderless jalopies threatened my fenders. Hot rods built low to the ground and stacked with gin-mill cowboys roamed the neon trails with their mufflers off. A man in a custom-made Buick stopped in my path abruptly to kiss a woman in the seat beside him, and drove on with her mouth attached to the side of his neck. Eats, Drinks, Beer, Liquor, the signs announced: Antonio's, Bill's, Helen's, The Boots and Saddle. Little knots of men formed on the sidewalk, jabbered and laughed and gesticulated, and broke apart under the pull of the bars.

Reavis was feeling that pull, his eyes were glistening with it. "Anywhere along here," he said impatiently. "And thanks a million."

I angled into the first empty parking space and turned off the lights and ignition. He looked at me with one long leg out the door. "You staying in town tonight?"

"I've got a room in Quinto. Right now I could use a drink."

"You and me both, friend. Come on, I'll show you the best place in town. Better lock your car."

We walked back a block and turned into Antonio's. It was a single large room, high-ceilinged and deep, with restaurant booths along one wall and a fifty-foot bar to the left. At the far end a fry cook worked in a cloud of steam. We found two empty stools near him. Everything in the place looked as if it had been there for a long time, but it was well-kept. The cigarette butts on the floor were new, the scarred mahogany surface of the bar was clean and polished. Reavis rested his arms on it as if it belonged to him. The sleeves of his gaudy shirt were rolled up, and his forearms looked as heavy and hard as the wood under them.

"Nice place," I said. "What are you drinking?"

His answer surprised me: "Uh-uh. This is on me. You treat me like a gentleman, I treat you like a gentleman, see?"

He turned and smiled wide, full in my face, and I had my first chance to study him. The teeth were white, the black eyes frank and boyish, the lines of the features firm and clean. Reavis had quantities of raw charm. But underneath it there was something lacking. I could talk to him all night and never find his core, because he had never found it.

He offered the smile too long; something for sale. I put a cigarette in my mouth. "Hell, you just lost your job. I'll buy the drinks."

"There are plenty of jobs," he said. "But buy 'em if you want. I drink Bushmill's Irish whisky myself."

I was reaching for a match when a lighter flicked under my nose and lit my cigarette. The bartender had approached us noiselessly, a middle-sized man with a smooth hairless head and a lean ascetic face. "Good evening, Pat," he said without expression, replacing the lighter in the pocket of his white jacket. "What are you gentlemen drinking?"

"Bushmill's for him. A whisky sour for me."

He nodded and moved away, narrow-hipped and poised as a ballet-dancer.

"Tony's a cold-blooded bastard," Reavis said. "He'll take your money for six months and then cut you off with a cup of coffee if he thinks you're eighty-six. Now I'm not Jesus Christ—"

"Excuse my mistake."

"You're a right gee, Lew." He smiled the big raw

smile again, but he got to first names too quickly. "What do you say we pull the rag and have ourselves a time? I got me a neat blonde stashed over at Helen's. Gretchen can find you a playmate. The night's still young."

"Younger than I am."

"What's the trouble, you married or something?"

"Not at present. I have to hit the road early tomorrow."

"Aw, come on, man. Have a couple of drinks and you'll feel better. This is a wide-open town."

When our drinks arrived he took his quickly and went out through a swinging door marked Gents. The bartender watched me sip my whisky sour.

"Good?"

"Very good. You didn't spend your apprenticeship in Nopal."

He smiled bleakly, as a monk might smile over the memory of an ecstasy. "No. I began at fourteen in the great hotels of Milan. I graduated before twenty-one to the Italian Line." His accent was French, softened by a trace of native Italian.

"All that training so you can mix 'em for a gang of oilfield winos."

"Nopal Valley is a fine place to make money. I bought this place for thirty-five thousand and in one year paid off the mortgage. Five years and I can retire."

"In Italy?"

"Where else? You are a friend of Pat Reavis?"

"Never saw him before."

"Be careful then," dryly and quietly. "He is a very pleasant boy most of the time, but he can be very unpleasant." He tapped the side of his lean skull. "There is something wrong with Pat: he has no limit. He will do anything, if he is drunk or angry. And he is a liar."

"Have you had trouble with him?"

"Not me, no. I don't have trouble with anybody." I could see why in his face. He had the authority of a man who had seen everything and not been changed by it.

"I don't have much trouble myself," I said, "but thanks."

"You are welcome."

Reavis came back and draped a ponderous arm over my shoulder. "How you doing, Lew boy? Feeling younger now?"

"Not young enough to carry extra weight." I moved, and his arm dropped away.

"What's the matter, Lew?" He looked at the bartender, who was watching us. "Tony been running me down as usual? Never believe a dago, Lew. You wouldn't let a dago spoil the beginning of a beautiful friendship."

"I like Italians very much," I said.

The bartender said slowly and clearly. "I was telling the gentleman that you are a liar, Pat."

Reavis sat and took it. The lips drew back from his fine white teeth, but he didn't say a word. I put a cigarette in my mouth. The lighter flicked under my nose before I could reach for a match.

Normally I objected to being waited on. But when a man was perfect in his role it was a pleasure to see him walk through it.

"Two more of the same," I said to his slim impassive back as he walked away.

Reavis looked at me like a grateful dog. Which I was observing for rabies.

CHAPTER 7

Two more drinks, which I paid for, restored Reavis's opinion of himself and the use of his tongue. He told me how he was promoted in the field on Guadalcanal, to become the youngest captain in the whole Pacific. How the OSS heard of his prowess and gave him a hush-hush assignment tracking down spies and saboteurs. How the *Saturday Evening Post* offered him several thousand dollars for an article about his personal experiences, but he was sworn to secrecy and besides he had other sources of income. He told me he could walk a city block on his hands, and frequently did. He was going through an interminable list of the female friends he had served and sent on their way rejoicing, when someone came up behind me and tapped my shoulder.

A dirty gray fedora, dirty-gray eyes, a long probing nose with a slightly bulbous tip, a lipless mouth like the wrinkle formed by a scar. His face was lopsided in the bar mirror and still looked lopsided when I turned. The corners of his mouth had tobacco-juice stains.

"Lewis Archer?"

"Right."

"I found your car down the street and I figured

you were in one of the places along here. I'm Franks, Detective-Sergeant."

"Parking trouble? I didn't see any signs."

The scar tore open and showed some yellow teeth. It seemed that Detective-Sergeant Franks registered amusement in this way. "Death trouble, Mr. Archer. The Chief phoned down and said to pick you up."

"Mrs. Slocum," I said, and I realized I'd liked her pretty well. Too often the human ones were the ones that got in the way.

"Now how would you know it was the old lady—"

"It's not the young Mrs. Slocum then—James Slocum's wife?"

"Naw, the old lady," he said, as if that could be taken for granted.

"What happened to her?"

"Don't you know? I thought maybe you'd know. The Chief says you're the last one that seen her alive." He averted his face coyly and spat on the floor.

I got up suddenly. His hand went to his right hip and stayed there. "What happened to her?" I said.

"The old girl got drowned. They found her in the swimming-pool a little while ago. Maybe she jumped in for fun, or maybe somebody pushed her. You don't go swimming at night with all your clothes on. Not if you can't swim a stroke and got a weak heart in the bargain. The Chief says it looks like murder."

I glanced at Reavis, and saw that his stool was unoccupied. The door marked Gents was oscillating slightly on its hinges. I moved for it and pushed it wide. At the far end of the passage the shadow of a big man moved in an open doorway and disappeared. Simultaneously a gun went off behind me and something jarred the door under my hand. A spent slug dropped to the floor at my feet among a shower of slivers. I picked it up and turned to face Franks, tossing the slug from hand to hand because it was hot. He advanced crabwise, with a service .45 steady in his hand.

"You coming peaceable, or do I shoot to maim this time?" The people in the room had formed a group behind him, a heaving body with twenty staring heads. Antonio, still and scornful, watched from behind the bar.

"Trigger-happy, Sergeant? Who gave you a gun with real live shells in it?"

"Hands up, you, and watch your lip."

I tossed him the piece of lead and put my hands on my head. My hair was thinner than it used to be. He caught the slug in his left hand and dropped it in the coat-pocket of his shiny blue umpire suit. "Now march, you."

He circled me cautiously, and the crowd made way for us. When I opened the door a small shiny object whizzed past my head and rang on the sidewalk. It took me a minute to realize what it was: the fifty-cent piece I had left on the bar as a tip for Antonio. Then I began to get angry.

When Franks unsnapped the handcuffs from his belt, I was ready to fight him for them. He saw that, and didn't insist. Instead, he put me in the front seat of the police car, beside the uniformed driver, and sat in the back where he could watch me.

"The siren, Kenny," he said. "The Chief wants him there in a hurry."

A fool in an official job, with guns and gadgets to play with, could cause a lot of disturbance. The siren purred, growled, whooped, screeched and ululated like a mountain lion as we went up the hill. I didn't say a word. Detective-Sergeant Franks wouldn't know an explanation if it bit him in the leg and called him brother.

His Chief was another story. He had set up a temporary office in the kitchen and was questioning the witnesses one by one, while a uniformed policeman took notes in shorthand. When the sergeant took me in to him, Knudson was talking to Francis Marvell. The authority I had noticed in his bearing had flared up in the emergency, like a slow fire doused with gasoline. The opaque eyes and the thick face were full of life and power. Homicide was his dish.

"Archer?" The heavy voice was crisp.

"This is him, Chief." Sergeant Franks was staying close to me, still with his hand on his gun.

"I'd like to congratulate the sergeant," I said. "He only needed one shot to bring me in. And I'm a witness in a murder, and you know how serious that is."

"Murder?" Marvell spread his hands on the red plastic-topped table and pushed himself to his feet. His jaw moved down and up silently before more words came out. "I understood it was an accident."

"That's what we're trying to find out," Knudson snapped. "Sit down." He used the same tone on Franks: "What's this about shooting?"

"He tried to escape, so I fired a warning shot."

"Yeah," I said. "I made a wild break for freedom."

He whirled on me: "If you didn't try to escape, why did you go for the door?"

"I needed a breath of fresh air, Sergeant. Now I need another one."

"Break it up," Knudson cut in. "Franks, you go out and help Winowsky with his photographic equipment. You, Archer, sit down and I'll be with you shortly."

I sat down in a straightbacked kitchen chair on the other side of the room and lit a cigarette. It tasted bitter. A large wooden tray of what had been hors d'oeuvres stood on the tiled sink beside me: the remains of anchovies, a little earthenware crock half full of caviar. I helped myself to some caviar on a cracker. Mrs. Slocum had lived well.

Marvell said: "You didn't tell me she was murdered. You permitted me to think it was an accident." He sounded badly shaken. His yellow hair was wet, but the water that glistened on his forehead came from his own pores.

"They're no deader when they're murdered. In any case, we don't know if she was."

"Murder is such a perfectly dreadful thought." His blurred gaze wandered around the room and skipped past me. "It was bad enough when I found the poor woman's body. Now I simply know I shan't sleep a wink tonight."

"Take it easy, Mr. Marvell. You did exactly the right thing and you should be feeling more than satisfied with yourself." Knudson's rippling bass was gentle and bland. "One thing I don't quite understand, though, and that is why you decided to take a swim all by yourself after dark."

"I don't entirely understand it myself," Marvell answered slowly. "It was one of those half-conscious motivations, I believe. I'd just stepped outside for a bit to smell the jasmine, and I was strolling in the loggia, when I thought I heard a splash from the swimming-pool. It had no sinister connotations, you know, nothing like that; I must have thought that someone else was taking a dip, and I decided to join them. I'm always one for fun and games, you see—"

"I see."

"Well, first I went down to the pool to see who it was—"

"Right after you heard the splash?"

"No, not immediately. It took a little while for the idea to grow on me—"

"And meanwhile the splashing continued?"

"I believe it did. Yes, I think it must have. By the time I got down there, however—it's quite a piece from the house—"

"Nearly a hundred yards. By the time you got down there?"

"It was perfectly silent again, and perfectly dark. Naturally I was a little surprised to find that the lights weren't on. I stood by the pool for a moment, wondering what had happened, and then I made out this round dark object. It was a large straw hat floating upside down in the water, and when I realized that I became alarmed. I switched on the underwater lights, and saw her. She was lying face down at the bottom of the pool, her hair swirling round her head, her skirt billowing, her arms spread out. It was ghastly." The water from his pores had made bright marks along his cheeks and formed a single clear droplet at the point of his chin. He brushed it away with the back of a nervous hand.

"Then you went in after her," Knudson stated.

"Yes. I took off my clothes, all but my underthings, and brought her to the surface. I found I couldn't raise her onto the side, so I pulled her to the shallow end and got her out there. She was terribly hard to handle. I'd thought that dead people were stiff, but she seemed loose all over. Like soft rubber." A second droplet formed.

"It was then that you raised the alarm?"

"Yes. I should have done before, but all I could think of was to get that poor dear woman out of the cold water."

"You did just fine, Mr. Marvell. A minute or two didn't make any difference, anyway. Now I want you to think carefully before you answer this: how much time elapsed between the initial splash and the alarm? It was twenty to nine when you called for help. You see, I'm trying to fix the time of death."

"I understand that. It's very hard to say how long it was, impossible in fact. I was lost in the beauty of the night, you know, and I wasn't consciously taking note of time, or of what I heard. It might have been ten minutes, or it might have been twenty, I really couldn't say."

"Well, think about it some more, and let me know if you can set it more definitely. You're perfectly certain, by the way, that you didn't see anybody else at all at the pool, or while you were back of the house?"

"As certain as I can be, yes. Now if you'll excuse me—"

"Of course. And thank you."

Marvell left the room in a nervous sidewise movement, stroking his hair with his hand.

"Jesus," Knudson said as he stood up. "He never saw a stiff before, let alone touched one, and it hit him in the middle. It takes guts to dive for a cadaver at night, though. You get all of that, Eddie?"

"All but the gestures." The man in uniform stroked himself elaborately from hairline to nape.

"Okay, take a little walk while I talk to Archer here." He crossed the room and stood above me with fists on hips until the door had closed. I put some caviar on a cracker and ate it daintily, in two bites.

"Have some?"

He didn't answer that. "Just who the hell are you, anyway?"

I took out my wallet and showed him the photostat of my license. "Now ask me what the hell I'm doing here. Unfortunately my chronic aphasia has taken a bad turn for the worse. It always goes like that when a dumb cop takes a shot at me."

He wagged his stubbled head good-humoredly. "Forget Franks, eh? I can't help it if he's a ward-heeler in the Mayor's party, and the Mayor is *ex officio* on the Police Commission. Can I?"

"You could put him on a desk, or issue him blanks."

"Yeah. You're a fast talker, Archer, but you needn't get your back up. Maude Slocum told me about you."

"How much?"

"Enough. The less said about that the better. Right?" His mind was quick and cold, out of place in his big, full-blooded body. I could almost see it turning a leaf and writing a new heading at the top of a clean page. "So far as she knew, you were the last one to talk to the old lady before she died. Exactly when did you see her?"

"Just before sunset. That would be a few minutes after seven."

"A couple of minutes before. It's earlier here on account of the mountains. You talked to her in the garden, I believe? If you'll tell me now exactly what was said—" He went to the door and called his shorthand writer, who took his position at the kitchen table. I told him what was said.

"Nothing much there, eh?" He sounded disappointed. "No sign of suicidal impulse? Or illness? She had a pretty bad heart, the doctor says."

"Nothing that I could put my finger on. She

seemed a little screwy to me, but nearly everyone does. What's the physical evidence?"

"Everything external points to drowning. That's the presumption, anyway, when you find a corpse in water—though how the hell she got there I can't say. About the body, we'll know more tomorrow. The Coroner's ordering an autopsy and an inquest."

"What's the assumption in the meantime? Fell, or got pushed?"

"Fell, but I'm handling it as homicide until I know for sure. Old ladies do fall into swimming-pools, I guess."

"She wasn't so old."

"I know. And there's no good reason why she should go near the pool, let alone into it. She never used it. It was built for her husband's arthritis years ago. She was forbidden the water, on account of her heart, and she was afraid of it, anyway."

"Not without reason."

"No." His thick, square-nailed fingers drummed on the hard tabletop. "I tried a reconstruction from the condition of the lawn around the pool. The trouble was, when Marvell yelled for help, everybody came running. They trampled out any traces there might have been."

"One thing, if it's murder, you'll have most of your suspects accounted for. The people at the party."

"It's not that simple." To the man with the notebook he said, "Don't bother with this," and turned back to me: "They had a buffet lunch in the dining-room, and at the time it happened the guests were moving in and out. Even Marvell could have pushed her in, then fished her out himself."

"Why pick on Marvell?"

"Figure it out. He wants money to take his play east. He's very close to Slocum. Now Slocum has money."

"You're skipping Slocum, aren't you?"

His face twisted sourly. "James is a mother's boy. He wouldn't touch a hair of his mother's head."

"And Maude Slocum?"

"I'm skipping her, too." His mind flicked another page, and started a new heading: "Assuming she was murdered, there's a possibility it was an outside job. A woman like that makes lots of enemies."

"Like Pareco," I said.

He grunted: "Huh?"

"The Pacific Refining Company."

"Oh. Yeah. Only the oil companies don't go in for murder any more. Not for a little matter like an oil lease. I meant to ask you, you didn't see any strangers around the place?"

This was the question I'd been waiting for, and wondering how to answer. Reavis was the logical suspect: on the spot, drunk, and with a grievance. The only trouble was that when I picked him up, he hadn't looked or talked or acted like a man who had just committed a crime. And the timing was wrong. But if the police were looking for a quick and easy out, they could probably send him to the gas chamber on circumstantial evidence. I'd seen it happen before, in the L.A. jungle, and I had to be sure about the Nopal Valley police. I decided that Knudson could be trusted, but I kept one card face down. I didn't tell him that when I picked Reavis up a mile or more from the house, it was exactly 8:23 by my dashboard clock and my wristwatch. It was Reavis who had called attention to the time, and that could mean that Reavis was trying to use me for a phony alibi. I hated to be used.

Knudson didn't like the delay, but he kept his temper. "All right. So you gave this boy a lift from outside the gate sometime after eight. You realize we don't know when she was killed, and probably never will know. Marvell's evidence is inconclusive. In his first account he didn't even mention the splash he heard, or thinks he heard. Did Reavis have murder on his mind?"

"Not unless he enjoys it. He was in a good mood."

"What sort of a boy is he? I've seen him around, but never talked to him."

"There's nothing wrong with him a pre-frontal

lobotomy wouldn't fix. He'd steal his widowed mother's rent-money to play the ponies, but I don't see him pushing her into the water. Psychopath, maybe, but not extreme. He takes it out in talking."

He leaned toward me, as wide as the tabletop. "You like the boy? Is that why you let him slip away from Franks?"

"I lose my well-oiled precision when a slug just misses my kidneys. I don't like Reavis at all, but some people do." I pitched him a curve, low, on the outside: "Cathy Slocum likes him pretty well."

His face swelled up with blood, and he leaned closer. "You're a liar. Cathy doesn't mess with trash like that."

"Take it easy, Knudson." I stood up. "Ask her father about it, if you like."

The life went out of his face and left it stupid. "What goes on here?" he said to himself. Then he remembered me, and the shorthand man.

He took the notebook out of the man's hands, and ripped out the last page of pencilled shorthand. "All right, Eddie, take a rest." And to me: "What are you going to do? Help us find Reavis?"

"I'll talk to Mrs. Slocum."

"Do that. She's in the front sitting-room with her husband. It's across the hall from the living-room."

I said: "I'm not a liar."

"What?" He stood up slowly. He was no taller than I was, but he was wide and powerful. His thick body dominated the room even though the mind behind his pale blue eyes was turned elsewhere.

"I'm not a liar," I said.

The eyes focused on me, cold with hostility. "All right," he said after a time. "You're not a liar." He sat down at the table again, with his shoulders slumped like a padded coat on an inadequate hanger.

CHAPTER 8

Passing the open door of the living-room, I caught a glimpse of the people waiting inside. Voices were subdued, faces white and strained. Nobody seemed to be drinking, and all the gay conversation had run out. The party was a group hangover, the dim old room the ancestral cave of death. A policeman in a blue shirt sat hunched in a chair by the door, studying the visored cap on his knee as if it were the face of a dear friend.

The door of the sitting-room across the hall was locked. I was about to knock on it, when a man on the other side uttered a four-letter word. It sounded incongruous in his high tenor. He was answered by a woman's voice, rapid and low, too low to penetrate the heavy door and let me hear her words. The only sounds I could make out plainly were the sobbing gasps that punctuated the sentences.

I moved to the next door on that side and entered the dark room beyond it. The light from the hall made crouched shadows of the chairs along the wall and gleamed among the silver and dishes that cluttered the buffet. There was still a little light in the room when I closed the door behind me: a thin shining under the old-fashioned sliding doors that separated the dining-room from the sitting-room. I crossed the room quietly and lay down by the sliding doors. Maude Slocum's voice slid under them:

"I've stopped trying. For years I did my best for you. It didn't take. Now I'm giving up."

"You never tried," her husband answered, flatly and bitterly. "You've lived in my house, and eaten my bread, and never made the slightest attempt to help me. If I'm a personal failure, as you say, the failure is certainly yours as well as mine."

"Your mother's house," she taunted him. "Your mother's bread—a very unleavened loaf."

"Leave Mother out of it!"

"How can I leave her out?" Now her voice was purring smoothly, in control of itself and of the situation. "She's been the central figure in my married life. You had your chance to make a clean break with her when we were married, but you hadn't the courage to take it."

"I had no real chance, Maude." The actorish voice wobbled under the burden of self-pity. "I was too young to get married. I was dependent on her—I hadn't even finished school. There weren't many jobs in those days, either, and you were in a hurry to be married—"

"*I* was in a hurry? You begged me with tears in your voice to marry you. You said your immortal soul depended on it."

"I know, I thought it did." The simple words held echoes of despair. "You wanted to marry me, too. You had your reasons."

"You're damned right I had my reasons, with a child in my belly and nobody else to turn to. I suppose I should have been the true-hearted little woman and swallowed my pride and gone away somewhere." Her voice sank to an acid whisper: "That's what your mother wanted, wasn't it?"

"You were never little, Maude."

She laughed unpleasantly. "Neither was Mother, was she? Her lap was always big enough for you."

"I know how you feel about me, Maude."

"You can't. I have no feeling at all. You're a perfect blank as far as I'm concerned."

"Very well." He struggled to keep his voice steady. "But now that Mother's dead, I'd think you'd be a little kinder to—her memory. She was always good to Cathy. She had to go without things herself to send Cathy to school and dress her properly—"

"I admit that. What you don't understand is the fact that I'm thinking about myself. I put Cathy first, of course. I love her, and I want the best of everything for her. But that doesn't mean I'm ready for the shelf. I'm a woman as well as a mother. I'm only thirty-five."

"That's rather late to start all over again."

"Right now I feel as if I haven't started—that I've been saving myself for fifteen years. I won't keep much longer. I'm going rotten inside."

"Your version at the moment. This is the chance you've been waiting for. If Mother hadn't died, you'd have been perfectly willing to go on as before."

"I'm afraid you don't know what you're talking about."

"Approximately as before, then. I know that something's been happening to you since you made that trip to Chicago."

"What about that trip to Chicago?" A threat tightened her voice like an unused muscle.

"I haven't asked you any questions about it. I don't intend to. I do know that you'd changed when you came back that spring. You had more life—"

She cut him short contemptuously: "You're well advised not to ask questions, James. I could ask questions, too, about Francis, for instance. Only, I know the answers."

He was silent for a time. I could hear one of them breathing. Finally, he sighed. "Well, we're getting nowhere. What do you want?"

"I'll tell you what I want. Half of everything you have, and that includes half of this property now."

"*Now!* Mother's death has been exceedingly convenient for you, hasn't it? If I didn't know you, Maude, I'd believe that you killed Mother yourself."

"I won't pretend I'm sorry that it happened. As soon as this unpleasantness is over with, and you've agreed to a settlement, I'm going to court."

"I'll make a settlement," he said thinly. "You've waited long enough for your share of the property. Now you can have it."

"And Cathy," she insisted. "Don't forget Cathy."

"I have not forgotten her. Cathy is staying with me."

"So she can live *à trois* with you and Francis? I think not."

He spoke with great effort: "Francis doesn't enter into the picture."

"Francis or someone like him. I know your penchant, James."

"No." The word exploded from his lips. "Cathy is all I want."

"I know what you want. You want a healthy life so you can twine around it like a vine. You tried it with me, but I tore you loose, and you shan't twist yourself around Cathy. I'm moving out of here, and taking her with me."

"No. No." The second word trailed off in a painful whimper. "You mustn't leave me alone."

"You have your friends," she said with irony.

"Don't leave me, Maude. I'm afraid to be left alone. I need you both, much more than you believe." His voice was quite unmanned, a hysterical boy's.

"You've neglected me for fifteen years," she said. "When I've finally got my chance to go, you insist I have to stay."

"You must stay. It's your duty to stay with me. I can't be left alone."

"Be a man," she said. "I can't have any feeling for a whining jellyfish."

"You used to love me—"

"Did I?"

"You wanted to be my wife and look after me."

"That was a long time ago. I can't remember."

I heard breath drawn in, feet moving quickly on the floor. "Whore!" he cried in a harsh choking voice. "You're a horrible cold woman, and I hate you."

"It chills a woman off," she said clearly and firmly, "being married to a fairy."

"Horrible. Woman." The caesura between the words was marked by a blow on flesh. Then something bony, his knees perhaps, bumped unevenly on the floor. "Forgive me," he said, "forgive me."

"You struck me." Her voice was blank with shock. "You hurt me."

"I didn't mean it. Forgive me. I love you, Maude. Please stay with me." A retching sob tore through his babbling and lengthened rhythmically. For a long time there was nothing but the sound of the man's crying.

Then she began to comfort him, in a gentle lulling voice. "Be quiet, Jimmie. Dear Jimmie. I'll stay with you. We'll have a good life yet, won't we, my dear?"

I staggered slightly when I got to my feet. I felt as if I'd been listening in on a microphone built into the walls of hell. I passed the closed door of the sitting-room without breaking my stride, and went out onto the lawn. The sky was black and moving. Long gray clouds streamed across the mountains to the sea, flowing like a river over the jagged edge of the world.

I was halfway across the lawn to the drive when I remembered that my car was parked on the street in Nopal Valley. I went around to the back of the house and found the kitchen empty except for the housekeeper. Mrs. Strang was an elderly woman with a long, soft face and fading hair. She was cooking something in a saucepan on the stove.

She jumped sideways at the sound of my footsteps. "Heavens! You frightened me."

"I'm sorry. I'm Archer, a friend of Mrs. Slocum's."

"Oh yes, you phoned, I remember." Her lips were trembling and blue.

I said: "Is Cathy all right?"

"Yes, she's all right. I'm making her some hot milk

to put her to sleep. The poor child needs her rest after all these terrible things happening."

In a way I felt responsible for Cathy, if only because there was nobody else to feel responsible. Her parents were completely involved in their private war, negotiating their little armistice. Probably it had always been like that.

"You'll take good care of Cathy?" I said to Mrs. Strang.

She answered me with pride: "I always have, Mr. Archer. She's very well worth it, you know. Some of her teachers think she is a genius."

"This place is lousy with geniuses, isn't it?"

I left before I got into an argument. From the kitchen door, I saw a white flash splatter the darkness below the garages like a brushful of whitewash. They were still taking pictures around the pool.

Knudson was there with three members of his department, directing a series of measurements. Near them the body lay under a blanket, waiting patiently to be taken away. The underwater lights of the pool were on, so that the water was a pale emerald depth with a luminous and restless surface filming it.

When he saw me Knudson moved away from his group and lifted his chin at an angle. When I was near enough to hear his low voice: "What did she say? Co-operate with us?"

"I didn't see her. She was locked in the room with her husband."

His nostrils flared in a private nasal sneer, not intended for me. "I've got our radio cars out looking for Reavis. You could be a help, since you know him to see."

"It's a little off my beat, isn't it?"

"You be the judge of that." His shoulders rose and fell in a muscular slow-motion shrug. "It seems to me there's a certain responsibility—?"

"Maybe so. Can you get me a lift into town? *Not* with Franks."

"Sure." He turned to the photographer, who was

kneeling by the body. "Just about finished, Winowsky?"

"Yeah." He threw back the blanket. "A couple more shots of the stiff. I want to do her justice, my professional honor demands it."

"You take Mr. Archer into town with you."

"Yeah."

He stood over the body in a crouching position and flashed the bulb attached to the top of his camera. The white magnesium light drew the dead face from the shadows and projected it against the night. The freckles grew like acne on the lime-white skin. Bulbous and white, like deepsea life, the foam bulged from the nostrils and gaping mouth. The open green eyes gazed up in blank amazement at the dark sky moving between the darker mountains.

"Once more," the photographer said, and stepped across the body. "Now watch the birdie."

The white light flashed again on the unmoving face.

CHAPTER 9

The building was pink stucco, big and new and ugly. It had a side entrance with "Romp Room" lettered above it in red neon. The wall was blind except for the door and a couple of round screened ventilators. I could hear the noise of the romping from the outside: the double-time beat of a band, the shuffling of many feet. When I pulled the heavy door open, the noise blasted my ears.

Most of it came from the platform at the rear end of the room, where a group of young men in white flannels were maltreating a piano, a guitar, a trombone, a trumpet, drums. The piano tinkled and boomed, the trombone brayed, the trumpet squawked and screeched. The guitar bit chunks from the chromatic scale and spat them out in rapid fire without chewing them. The drummer hit everything he had, drums, traps, cymbals, stamped on the floor, beat the rungs of his chair, banged the chrome rod that supported the microphone. The Furious Five, it said on his biggest drum.

The rest of the noise came from the booths that lined three walls of the room, and from the dance-floor in the middle where twenty or thirty couples whirled in the smoke. The hight titter of drunk and flattered women, the animal sounds of drunk and eager men. Babel with a wild jazz obbligato.

A big henna redhead in a shotsilk blouse was making drinks at a service bar near the door. Her torso jiggled in the blouse like a giant soft-boiled egg with the shell removed. The waitresses came and went in an antlike stream, and all the whiskies came from the same bottle. In an interval between waitresses, I went up to the bar. The big woman smashed an empty bottle under it and straightened up, breathing hard.

"I'm Helen," she said with a rubber-lipped public smile. "You want a drink, you find a seat and I send a waitress to you."

"Thanks, I'm looking for Pat."

"Pat who? Does she work here?"

"He's a man. Young, big, with curly dark hair."

"Friend, I got troubles of my own. Don't you go away mad, though. Try the waitresses if you want." She took a deep breath when she finished, and the egg swelled up almost to her chin.

"Two bombs, beer chasers," a waitress said behind me.

I asked her: "Is Gretchen here?"

"Gretchen Keck, you mean?" The waitress jerked a flat thumb at a tall girl on the dance floor. "That's her, the blonde in the blue dress."

I waited till the music stopped, and crossed to an empty booth. Some of the couples stayed where they were in the center of the room, arms locked, face to face. A Mexican boy in blue jeans and a white shirt stood with the tall blonde. Gretchen was as light as the boy was dark, with a fair skin and a pull-taffy pompadour that made her taller than he was. They couldn't stand still. Their hips, pressed flat together, moved in a slow weaving round and round until the music started and quickened their beat.

While she danced on a dime by herself, he moved in a circle about her, turkey strutting, flapping his arms like a rooster, leaping and stamping. He moved his head and neck in the horizontal plane, Balinese fashion, danced squatting on his heels like a Cossack, invented new gyrations of the hips, body and feet jerked by separate rhythms. She stood where she was, her movements slightly mimicking his, and his circle tightened about her. They came together again, their bodies shaken and snaked through their length by an impossible shimmy. Then she was still on his arched breast, and her arms fell loose. He held her, and the music went on without them.

In the booth behind me, a woman called in *bracero* Spanish upon the Mother of God to witness her justifiable act of violence. She thrust herself out of her seat, a gaunt Mexican girl with hair like fresh-poured tar. From her clenched right fist, a four-inch knife-blade projected upward. I moved, bracing one hand on the seat and pivoting. My left toe caught her instep and she fell hard, face down. The spring-knife struck the floor and clattered out of her reach. At its signal the dark boy and the blonde girl sprang apart, so suddenly that the girl staggered on her high heels. The boy looked at the knife on the floor and the woman struggling to her knees. His eyes watered and his bronze face took on a greenish patina.

Slouching and woebegone, without a backward look, he went to the woman and tried awkwardly to help her rise. She spat out words in Spanish that sounded like a string of cheap firecrackers. Her worn black satin dress was coated with dust. Half of her sallow pitted face was grimy. She began to weep. He put his arms around her and said, "Please, I am sorry." They went out together. The music stopped.

A heavy middle-aged man in a fake policeman's uniform appeared from nowhere. He picked up the knife, broke it across his knee, and dropped the blade and handle in the pocket of his blue coat. He came to my booth, stepping lightly as if he was walking on eggs. His shoes were slit and mis-shapen across the base of the toes.

"Nice work, son," he said. "They flare up so fast sometimes I can't keep track of 'em."

"Knife-play disturbs my drinking."

His red-rimmed eyes peered from a face that was gullied by time. "New in these parts, ain't you?"

"Yeah," I answered, though I felt as if I'd been in Nopal Valley for days. "Speaking of my drinking, I haven't been doing any."

He signalled to a waitress. "We'll fix that." She set down a trayful of empty glasses grained with the leavings of foam. "What'll it be?"

"A bottle of beer." I distrusted the bar whisky. "Ask Gretchen what she's drinking, and if she'll have one with me."

The drink and Gretchen arrived simultaneously. "Helen says no charge," the waitress said. "Your drinks are on the house. Or anything."

"Food?"

"Not this late. The kitchen's closed."

"What, then?"

The waitress set my beer down hard so that it foamed, and went away without answering.

Gretchen giggled, not unpleasantly, as she slid into the seat across from me. "Helen's got rooms upstairs. She says there's too many men in this burg, and somebody has to do something to take the pressure off." She sipped her drink, rum coke, and winked grotesquely over the rim of the glass. Her eyes were naïve and clear, the color of cornflowers. Not even the lascivious red mouth constructed with lipstick over her own could spoil her freshness.

"I'm a very low-pressure type myself."

She looked me over carefully, did everything but feel the texture of the material my coat was made of. "Maybe. You don't have the upstairs look, I admit. You can move, though, brother."

"Forget it."

"I wish I could. I never get scared when something happens, it always come over me later. I wake up in the middle of the night and get the screaming meemies. God damn that babe to hell."

"She's there already."

"Yeah, I know what you mean. These Spanish babes

take things so hard, it's getting so a girl can't have any fun any more."

"You do all right," I said. "If Pat can be believed."

She blushed, and her eyes brightened. "You know Pat?"

"He was my buddy," I said, almost gagging on the word. "In the Marines."

"He really *was* in the Marines, then?" She seemed surprised and pleased, and was sharper than I thought.

"Sure. We were on Guadal together." I felt just a little like a pander.

"Maybe you can tell me." She bit her lower lip and got lipstick on her teeth. Even her front teeth were bad. "Is it true what he says, that he's a secret agent or something?"

"In the war?"

"Now. He says him being a chauffeur is only a blind, that he's some kind of an undercover man."

"I wouldn't know."

"He tells so many stories, half the time I don't know what to believe. Pat's a swell joe, though," she added defensively. "He's got a good brain, and he'll go far."

I agreed, as heartily as I could. "Yeah, a good guy. I was hoping to see him tonight. There's a business opportunity in our organization, and he could get in on the ground floor."

"A business opportunity?" The words had a magical four-color advertisement quality, and she repeated them with respect. The cornflower eyes saw Gretchen in an apron freshly laundered in the new Bendix, cooking for Reavis in the tiled kitchen of a new one-bedroom G.I. house in the suburbs of what city? "In L.A.?"

"Yeah."

"He might be at my place. He waits for me in the trailer sometimes."

"Can you leave now?"

"Why not? I'm a freelance." The patter went on like a record she'd forgotten to turn off, but her thoughts were far ahead, on Gretchen in a new phase: attractive young wife of rising young executive Reavis.

She stroked the fender of my car as if it was an animal she could win by affection. I wanted to say, forget him. He'll never stay long with any woman or pay his debts to any man. I said: "We're doing good business these days. We can use a boy like Pat."

"If I could help to get him a real good job—" she said. The rest of it was silent but unmistakable: he'd marry me. Maybe.

A few blocks off the main street I turned, as she directed, down a road lined with large old houses. The eroded asphalt rattled the tools in the trunk of the car. It was one of those streets that had once been the best in town. The houses were Victorian mansions, their gables and carved cornices grotesque against the sky. Now they were light-housekeeping apartments and boarding houses, wearing remnants of sleazy grandeur.

We went up an alley between two of them, to a yard oppressed by the black shadows of oaks. There was a trailer under the trees, on the far side of the yard. In the light of the headlights I could see that its metal side was peeling and rusting like an abandoned billboard. The littered yard gave off an odor of garbage.

"That's our trailer there." The girl was trying to be brisk, but there was a strain of anxiety rising in her voice. "No lights, though," she added, when I switched off the headlights and the engine.

"He wouldn't be waiting in the dark?"

"He might have gone to sleep. Sometimes he goes to sleep here." She was on the defensive again, describing the habits of a large and troublesome pet whom she happened to love.

"You said 'our trailer,' by the way. Yours and Pat's?"

"No sir, he just visits me. I got a bunkmate name of Jane, but she's never home nights. She works in an all-night hamburger up the line."

Her face was a pale blur, swallowed completely then by the shadow of the oaks. Their sharp dry leaves crackled under our feet. The door of the trailer was unlocked. She went in and turned on a light in the ceiling.

"He isn't here." She sounded disappointed. "Do you want to come in?"

"Thanks." I stepped up from the concrete block that served as a doorstep. The top of the door was so low I had to duck my head.

The little room contained a sink and butane stove at the end nearest the door, two narrow built-in bunks covered with identical cheap red cotton spreads, a built-in plywood dresser at the far end cluttered with cosmetics and bobbypins and true-romance comic-books, and above it a warped, dirty mirror reflecting a blurred distorted version of the girl's room, the girl, and me.

The man in the mirror was big and flat-bodied, and lean-faced. One of his gray eyes was larger than the other, and it swelled and wavered like the eye of conscience: the other eye was little, hard and shrewd. I stood still for an instant, caught by my own distorted face, and the room reversed itself like a trick drawing in a psychological test. For an instant I was the man in the mirror, the shadow-figure without a life of his own who peered with one large eye and one small eye through dirty glass at the dirty lives of people in a very dirty world.

"It's kind of cramped," she said, trying to be cheerful, "but we call it home sweet home."

She reached past me and closed the door. In the close air, the smell of spilled rancid grease from the stove and the sick-sweet odor of dime-store perfume from the dresser were carrying on an old feud. I wasn't rooting for either. "Cozy," I said.

"Sit down, sir," she said with forced gaiety. "I'm out of rum and cokes, but I got some muscatel."

"Thanks, not on top of beer."

I sat on the edge of one of the red-covered bunks. The movements of the man in the mirror had the quickness and precision of youth, but none of youth's enthusiasm. Now his forehead was bulbous like a cartooned intellectual's, his mouth little and prim and cruel. To hell with him.

"We could have a little party if you want," she said uncertainly. Standing in the full glare of the light, she looked like a painted rubber doll, made with real human hair, that wasn't quite new any more.

"I don't want."

"Okay, only you don't have to be insulting about it, do you?" She meant to say it in a kidding way, but it came out wrong. She was embarrassed, and worried.

She tried again: "I guess you're pretty anxious to see Pat, eh? He might be down in his place in L.A., you know. He don't usually go down in the middle of the week, but a couple of times he did."

"I didn't know he had a place in L.A."

"A little place, a one-room apartment. He took me down one week end to see it. Gee, wouldn't that be funny if you came all the way up here to find him and he was down in L.A. all the time."

"That would be a scream. You know where it is, so I can look him up tomorrow?"

"He won't be there tomorrow. He's got to be back on the job, at Slocum's."

I let her think that. "Too bad. I have to get back to L.A. tonight. Maybe you can give me his address."

"I don't have the number, but I could find it again." Her eyes flickered dully, as if she hoped to promote something. She sat down on the bunk opposite me, so close that our knees touched. A pair of nylons hanging from a towel-rack above the bed tickled the back of my neck. "I'd do anything I could to help," she said.

"Yeah, I appreciate that. Does the place have a name?"

"Graham Court, something like that. It's on one of the little side streets off North Madison, between Hollywood and L.A."

"And no phone?"

"Not that I know of."

"Thanks again." I stood up. She rose like my shadow, and we were jammed in the narrow aisle between the beds. I tried to move past her to the door, and felt the touch of her round thighs.

"I kind of like you, Mister. If there was anything I could do?"

Her breasts were pointed like a dilemma. I pushed on past. The man in the mirror was watching me with one eye as cold as death. "How old are you, Gretchen?" I asked her from the doorway.

She didn't follow me to the door. "None of your business. A hundred years, about. By the calendar, seventeen."

Seventeen, a year or two older than Cathy. And they had Reavis in common. "Why don't you go home to your mother?"

She laughed: paper tearing in an echo chamber. "Back to Hamtramck? She left me at Stanislaus Welfare when she got her first divorce. I been on my own since 1946."

"How are you doing, Gretchen?"

"Like you said, I'm doing all right."

"Do you want a lift back to Helen's?"

"No thank you, sir. I got enough money to live on for a week. Now that you know where I live, come and see me sometime."

The old words started an echo that lasted fifty miles. The night was murmurous with the voices of girls who threw their youth away and got the screaming meemies at three or four a.m.

CHAPTER 10

I stopped at a lunch-bar east of the cemetery on Santa Monica Boulevard, for a sandwich and coffee and a look at the telephone book. It hung by a chain from the pay telephone on the wall beside the front window. A Graham Court on Laredo Lane was listed. I dialed the number and watched the sidewalk roamers. The young hepcats high on music or weed, the middle-aged men on the town, the tourists waiting for something to fulfill their fantasies, the hopeful floozies and the despairing ones, the quick, light, ageless grifters walked the long Hollywood beat on the other side of the plate glass. The sign above the window was red on one side, green on the other, so that they passed from ruddy youth to sickly age as they crossed my segment of sidewalk, from green youth to apoplexy.

A dim voice answered on the twelfth ring. Pat Reavis didn't live at Graham Court, he never had, goodnight.

The counterman slid a thin white sandwich and a cup of thick brown coffee across the black lucite bar. He had pink butterfly ears. The rest of him was still in the larval stage.

"I couldn't help hearing," he said moistly. "You're looking for a contact, I know a good number to call."

"Write it in blood on a piece of rag-content paper and eat it with your breakfast."

"Huh?" he said. "Blood?"

"What makes you think that sex is the important thing in life?"

He laughed through his nose. "'Name another."

"Money."

"Sure, but what does a guy want money for, answer me that."

"So he can retire to a lamasery in Tibet." I showed him a Special Deputy badge which I'd saved from a wartime case on the Pedro docks. "Pimping will get you a couple of years up north."

"Jesus." His face underwent a sudden and shocking change. Old age ran crooked fingers over it, and held it crooked. "I was only kidding, I didn't mean nothing, I don't know any number. Honest to God."

His whine followed me onto the sidewalk. The closing door shut it off. I was in an unpleasant mood.

Laredo Lane was one of the little lost stucco-and-frame streets between the two big boulevards. Its street lights, one to a block, spaced long patches of gloom. There were occasional houselights where after-midnight parties were going on. I caught fragments of music and laughter, glimpses of dancing couples in the windows as I drove past. Some of the dancers were black, some white; some had brown Indian faces. Most of the small marginal houses were dark behind closed blinds. One entire block was empty, its broken row of concrete foundations bared by an old fire.

I felt like a lonely cat, an aging tom ridden by obscure rage, looking for torn-ear trouble. I clipped that pitch off short and threw it away. Night streets were my territory, and would be till I rolled in the last gutter.

The letters GRAHAM COURT were cut in the front of a rectangular metal box lit from inside by an electric bulb. Nailed to the post which supported the sign was a piece of white-painted board on which an unsteady hand had lettered VACANCY. The NO was hidden by a weathered cardboard flap. I parked two hundred feet past the sign and left my engine running. The exhaust made little blue puffs like pipe-smoke in the chilling air.

The Court was a row of decaying shacks bent around a strip of withering grass. A worn gravel drive brought the world to their broken-down doorsteps, if the world was interested. A few of the shacks leaked light through chinks in their warped frame sides. The building marked Office, which was nearest the street, was closed and dark. It looked abandoned, as if the proprietor had given up for good. Over my head a red-flowering eucalyptus moved in a wind as soft as night-time breathing, and dropped its thin small petals to the ground. I picked one off the sidewalk for no good reason and ground it to red powder between my fingers.

I was deciding between the direct approach and a long dull wait in the car, when the door of one of the cottages opened, halfway down the row. It dropped a yellow plank of light across the grass. A man's shadow moved in it, and then the light went out. I walked on up the street, away from my car. After an interval, quick footsteps followed me.

I turned up the walk of an unlighted house, casually and with a sort of reluctance, to give the impression that I belonged there. My long vague shadow merged with the shadows of bushes, and I knew that no more than my outline would be visible to the man behind me. A car was parked in the driveway beside the house, and I moved out of sight behind it. The footsteps on the sidewalk went by without a pause.

At the corner, the man crossed under the streetlight. It was Reavis, walking with an eager swagger, chin up and shoulders held back consciously as if he was pied-piping a bevy of girls at broad noon. When he had turned the corner, I ran back to my car and drove it around the block in time to shut off the lights and see the one-man parade cross the next intersection.

I took no chances. Because he knew my car, I

locked it and left it parked where it was. I let him stay nearly a block ahead and used whatever cover was convenient: trees, hedges, parked cars. He never looked back; he moved like a man whose conscience was clear, or lacking. When he got to Sunset, he turned left. I crossed the boulevard and closed the distance between us. He had on a hounds-tooth suit in clashing black and tan. I could practically hear the suit across the wide traffic-humming thoroughfare.

Reavis headed for a taxi stand, where several cabs stood in line along the curb. I expected him to take one, and was set to follow him in another. Instead, he sat down on the bench at the bus-stop, crossed his legs, and lit a cigarette. I went a few yards up the cross-street and watched him from the shadow of the building on the corner. Off to my left, the tall apartment hotels stood against a sky whose moving reddish color was like the inside of closed eyelids. The late night traffic flowed between me and Reavis at a steady thirty-five to forty.

A long black car nosed out of the stream and into the red curb where Reavis was sitting. He stood up and flipped his cigarette away. A man in a dark gray livery got out of the chauffeur's seat and opened the back door for him. I was halfway across the street, in the thin aisle of safety between the moving lanes, when the limousine got under way again. I opened the door of the first cab in the line and told the driver to follow it.

"Double fare?" he said above the starting roar of his motor.

"Sure thing. And an extra buck for the license number."

The cab left the curb in a jet-propelled takeoff that threw me back in the seat, and went up to fifty in second. Cutting in and out of traffic, it gained on the black limousine.

"Don't pull up on him too fast. Drop back when you get the number."

He slowed a bit, but gradually narrowed the space

between the two cars. "The number is 23P708," he said after a while. "You tailing the guy or what?"

"This is a game I play."

"Okay, I was only asking a natural question."

"I don't know the answer." That ended our conversation. I wrote the number inside a match-folder and slipped it into my watch-pocket.

The black car drew into the curb unexpectedly, dropped Reavis, and pulled away again. He swaggered across the sidewalk under a sign which spelled out Hunt Club. The leather-padded door swung to behind him.

"Let me out here," I said to the driver. "Park as near as you can and wait for me."

He raised his right hand and brushed the ball of his thumb back and forth across the first two fingers. "Show me a little green first, eh?"

I handed him a five.

He looked at the bill and turned to look at me over the back of the seat. His face was Sicilian, black-eyed, sharp-nosed. "This wouldn't be a heist or nothing like that?"

I told him: "I'm a private cop. There won't be any trouble." I hoped there wouldn't.

Dennis's Hunt Club was dim and chilly and crowded. Indirect lights shone with discretion on polished brass and wood, on polished pates and highly polished faces. The photographs that lined the panelled walls were signed by all the big names and the names that had once been big. Dennis himself was near the door, a gray-haired man wearing undertaker's clothes, clown's nose, financier's mouth. He was talking with an air of elegant condescension to one of the names that had once been big. The fading name glanced at me from under his fine plucked eyebrows. No competition. He registered relief and condescension.

The place was built on two levels, so that the bar commanded a view of the dining-room. It was nearly two o'clock. The bar was doing a rush-hour business before the curfew knelled. I found an empty stool, ordered a Guinness stout for energy, and looked around me.

The hounds-tooth suit was raising its visual din in the middle of the dining-room. Reavis, his back to me, was at a table with a woman and a man. The man leaned across his four-inch steak in Reavis's direction, a blue dinner-jacket constricting his heavy shoulders. The wide neck that grew through his soft white collar supported an enormous head, covered with skin as pink and smooth as a baby's. Pinkish hair lay in thin ringlets on the massive scalp. The eyes were half-closed, listening: bright slits of intelligence in the great soft, chewing face.

The third at the table was a young ash blonde, wearing a gown of white pleated chiffon and the beauty to outshine it. When she inclined her head, her short bright hair swung forward, framing her features chastely like a wimple. Her features were fine.

She was trying to hear what the men were talking about. The big face looked at her and opened its eyes a little wider and didn't like what it saw. A babyish petulance drove a wedge between the invisible eyebrows and plucked at the munching mouth, which spoke to her. The woman rose and moved in the direction of the bar. People noticed her. She slid onto the empty stool beside me, and was served before I was. The bartender called her by name, "Mrs. Kilbourne," and would have tugged at his forelock if he'd had one. Her drink was straight bourbon.

Finally the bartender brought me my stout, foaming in a chilled copper mug. "Last call, sir."

"This will do."

I stole a look at the woman, to confirm my first impression. Her atmosphere was like pure oxygen; if you breathed it deep it could make you dizzy and gay, or poison you. Her eyes were melancholy under heavy lashes, her cheeks faintly hollowed as if she had been feeding on her own beauty. Her flesh had that quality of excess drawn fine, which men would turn and follow in the street.

Her hands fumbled with the diamond clasp of a

gold lamé bag, and groped inside. "God damn and blast it," she said. Her voice was level and low.

"Trouble?" I said it not too hopefully.

She didn't turn, or even move her eyes. I thought it was a brush-off, and didn't especially mind, since I'd asked for it. But she answered after a while, in the same flat level tone: "Night after night after night, the run-around. If I had taxi fare I'd walk out on him."

"Be glad to help."

She turned and looked at me—the kind of look that made me wish I was younger and handsomer and worth a million, and assured me that I wasn't. "Who are you?"

"Unknown admirer. For the last five minutes, that is."

"Thank you, Unknown Admirer." She smiled and raised her eyebrows. Her smile was like an arrow. "Are you sure it isn't father of five?"

"Vox populi," I said, "vox dei. I also have a fleet of taxis at my disposal."

"It's funny, but I really have. My husband has, anyway. And I don't have taxi fare."

"I have a taxi waiting. You can have it."

"Such sweetness, and self-denial to boot. So many unknown admirers want to be known."

"Kidding aside."

"Forget it, I was talking. I haven't the guts to do anything else *but* talk."

She glanced at her table, and the large head jerked peremptorily, beckoning her. Downing her drink, she left the bar and went back to the table. The large head called for its check in a rich, carrying voice.

The bartender spread his arms and addressed the people at the bar: "Sorry now, good people, it's time to close now, you know."

"Who's the Palomino?" I asked him quietly.

"Mrs. Kilbourne, you mean?"

"Yeah, who's she?"

"Mrs. *Walter* Kilbourne," he stated with finality. "That's Walter Kilbourne with her." The name had connotations of money for me, but I couldn't place it definitely.

I was waiting in the taxi across the street when they appeared on the sidewalk. Simultaneously, the limousine drew up to the curb. Kilbourne's legs were small for his giant torso. As they crossed the sidewalk, his great head moved level with his wife's. This time Reavis sat up front with the chauffeur.

My driver said: "You want to play tag some more?"

"Might as well, it's barely two o'clock."

"Some guys," he grumbled, "got a very peculiar sense of humor."

He made a U-turn at the corner and came back fast. The traffic had thinned, and it was easy to keep the widely spaced red tail-lights in sight. In the center of the Strip, the black car pulled into the curb again. The blonde woman and her husband got out and entered The Flamenco. Reavis stayed where he was, beside the chauffeur. The black car U-turned suddenly, and passed us going in the opposite direction.

My driver had doubled-parked a hundred yards short of The Flamenco. He slammed the gear-shift savagely into low and wrestled with the steering wheel. "How long does this go on?"

"We'll have to wait and see."

"I usually get myself a bite and java round about two o'clock."

"Yeah, it's sure hell. Murder certainly breaks up a man's schedule."

The speedometer needle jumped ten miles, as if it was attached directly to his heartbeat. "Did you say murder?"

"Right."

"Somebody get it, or somebody going to get it?"

"Somebody got it."

"I don't like messing with killings."

"Nobody does. Just keep that car in sight, and vary your distance."

The black car stopped with a blaze of brake-lights at the Cahuenga stoplight, and my driver made a mistake. Before it turned left, he pulled up close to it. Reavis looked back, his eyes wide and black in our headlights, and spoke to the chauffeur. I cursed under my breath, and hoped that he was discussing the beauty of the night.

He wasn't. Once the limousine got onto the Freeway, it began to move at the speed it was built for. Our speedometer needle moved up to eighty and stayed there like the hand of a stopped clock. The tail-lights disappeared around a curve and were gone when we rounded the next curve on whining tires.

"Sorry," the driver said, his head and body rigid over the wheel. "That Caddie can hold a hundred from here to San Francisco. Anyway, it probably turned off on Lankershim."

CHAPTER 11

Graham Court had changed in the hour or so since I had seen it last. The place had the same abandoned ugliness, the same foul-breathed atmosphere of people living desperately on their uppers, but these things had lost a part of their reality. By stepping out of it into a limousine which took him into the company of Mrs. Kilbourne, Reavis had given the place a new dimension: the possibility that there was more behind the thin warped walls than drinking and poverty, copulation and despair. For Reavis, at least, Graham Court was a place where anything could happen: the low-life set where actors played at being poor for a thousand dollars a day; the slum where the handsome prince lived incognito.

In the first cottage, a woman sighed mournfully in her sleep, and a man's blurred growl instructed her to shut her big loud yap. A radio chirped like a frenzied cricket in the shack at the front of the row, where someone was listening to an all-night disc-jockey or had forgotten to turn it off. Reavis's was the third from the street on the left. The door opened at the first try with an ordinary passkey. I closed it behind me and found the light-switch beside it.

The room precipitated out of darkness and enclosed me in a dingy wallboard cube. The light was a paper-shaded bulb in a hanging double socket, drawn sideways by a cord which ran to a nail in the wall and down the wall to a two-burner electric plate. There were dark crumbs on the oilcloth-covered table beside the burner, and some of them were moving. A chest of drawers sagged against the opposite wall, its veneer flaked like crackleware. Its top, indented with charred cigarette burns, held a bottle of barbershop hair-oil and a pair of military brushes in a pigskin case initialed P.M.R.

I went through the drawers and found two laundered shirts, two pairs of cotton socks in brilliant patterns, a change of underclothes, a cardboard box bearing a Sheik label and a colored picture of the Sheik himself, a blue silk ribbon signifying second place in Junior Field and Track at Camp Mackenzie, wherever that was, in 1931; and a carton of cardboard matchfolders. The carton was nearly full, and each of the folders bore the legend, printed in gold on black: Compliments of Patrick "Pat" Reavis. The bottom drawer contained dirty clothes, including the Hawaiian shirt.

An iron bed in the left-hand corner of the room opposite the door took up about a quarter of the floor space. It was covered with a U.S. Navy blanket. The pictures on the wall above the bed seemed to go with the blanket. They were photographs of nude women, both glossy prints and cutouts, perhaps a dozen of each. Gretchen Keck was among them, the face above the soft young body set in a smiling tetany of embarrassment. The pictures in the drawer of the table by the bed were more unusual. They included a set of the Herculaneum murals, which did not mean that Reavis was an amateur archaeologist. There was nobody there that I knew. Opposite the bed a faded green curtain, hung from a curved iron pipe, enclosed a sink and toilet and a portable shower stall sheathed with rusting metal. A pool of dirty water spread across the rotting linoleum and darkened the hem of the curtain.

Without getting down on my knees, I reached far

under the bed and brought out a cardboard suitcase with scuffed leather corners. It was locked, but the cheap clasp loosened when I gave the lid a sharp upward kick with my heel. I dragged it under the light and wrenched it open. Beneath a mouldy smelling tangle of dirty shirts and socks, the bottom of the suitcase was lined with disordered papers. Most of them were personal letters written in unformed hands and signed with girls' names or nicknames; exceedingly personal letters. I sampled one which began: "My Dearest Darling: You drove me just wild the other night," and ended: "Now that I know what love is all about, my Dearest Darling, you won't go away and leave me—write and say you won't." Another, in a different hand, began: "Dear Mister Reavis," and ended: "I love you pashunitly with all my haert."

There were official discharge papers which stated that one Patrick Murphy Ryan, born in Bear Lake County, Kentucky, on February 12, 1921, had enlisted in the U.S. Marine Corps on June 23, 1942, in San Antonio, Texas, and been discharged in San Diego in December of the same year, dishonorably. Ryan's civilian experience was listed as agriculturalist, garage mechanic, and oil well maintenance apprentice, and his preferred occupation as commercial airplane pilot. There was a copy of an application for National Service Life Insurance in the amount of two thousand dollars, made out by the same Patrick Ryan, and dated July 2, 1942. It requested that the policy be mailed to Elaine Ryan Cassidy, R.R. 2, Bear Lake, Kentucky. She could be his mother, his sister, or his ex-wife.

The name Elaine appeared again, this time with a different surname, on a torn and empty envelope crumpled in a corner of the suitcase. The envelope was addressed to Mr. Patrick Ryan, Graham Court, Los Angeles, and postmarked Las Vegas, July 10, that year. The return address was scribbled across the ripped flap: Mrs. Elaine Schneider, Rush apts., Las Vegas, Nev. If this was the same Elaine who had been sent Pat's insurance policy, she was one woman he trusted. And Las Vegas wasn't far, as the buzzard flies. I memorized the address.

I was going through the bundle of letters, looking for the one that matched the empty envelope, when a breeze blew light and cold on the back of my neck. I picked up one of the letters and straightened slowly without turning, as if to have light to read by; then slowly turned with the letter in my hands. The door was ajar a few inches, pure darkness beyond.

I reached for the light-switch. The step I took threw me a little off balance. A hand came through the aperture, pushing it wider, and closed on my wrist: fingers like curled white sausages, speckled with short black bristles. It pulled me further off balance and my head slammed against the wall. The wallboard crunched. A second hand closed on my arm and began to bend it around the edge of the door. I set one foot against the door-jamb and brought the hands into the room. The hands, then the arms, then the shoulders. When the whole man came, he brought the door along with him. It fell against the green curtain with very little noise.

His nose and brows were brown fungus growing on a thick stump of face. Small eyes like shiny black beetles lived in it. They burrowed out of sight when I struck at them with my free hand, and reappeared again. I hurt my hand on the thick chin. The head rolled away with the punch and came back grinning at me.

He turned suddenly, raised his arms and swung me off balance. His fingers ground on my wristbones. His heavy shoulders labored. I would not turn in to his hold. His coat split up the back with a sharp report. I twisted my hand free, joined both hands under his chin, and set my knee in the small of his back. Gradually he straightened, came over backwards and down. The floor cracked against the back of his head, then the ceiling fell on the back of mine.

I came to, lying face down in darkness. The surface under my face seemed to be vibrating, and the same vibration beat savagely at the base of my skull. When

I opened my mouth I tasted dusty cloth. Something heavy and hard pressed down on the small of my back. I tried to move and found that my shoulders and hips were tightly enclosed on both sides. My hands were tied together, pressed hard into my stomach. Coffin fear took me by the back of the neck and shook me. When the shaking subsided my head was clearer and more painful. I was on the floor of a moving car, wedged face down between the front and back seats.

The wheels bumped and slid across two sets of car tracks. I raised my head from the floor.

"Take it easy, buster," a man's voice said. One heavy object was removed from the small of my back and placed on the nape of my neck.

I said: "Take your feet off me."

The foot on my neck shifted, pressing my face into the floor. "Or what will you do, buster? Nothing? That's what I thought."

I lay still, trying to memorize pitch, tone, inflection, so that I would not mistake them if I ever heard them again. The voice was soft and liquid in the way that molasses is liquid, with a fruity tremor of vanity running through it. A voice like the stuff cheap barbers put on your hair before you can stop them.

It said: "That's right, buster, you can do your talking later. And you will."

More car tracks. A left turn. Pitted city pavement. Another turn. The blood was roaring angrily in my ears. Then there was no sound but the roaring of my blood The feet were lifted, a car door opened. I struggled upright to my knees and tore at my bound wrists with my teeth. They were bound with wire.

"Now take it *easy*. This is a gun I have at your back. Don't you feel it?"

I felt it. I took it easy.

"Backwards out of the car, buster. Don't raise a hullabaloo or you'll take another ride and never know it. Now you can stand up and let me look at you. Frankly, you look like hell."

I looked at him, first at the steady black gun. He

was slender and tall, pinched at the waist by over-elaborate tailoring, heavily padded at the shoulders. The hair on top of his head was thick and black and glossy, but it didn't match the gray hair over his ears. I said: "You're showing a little middle-aged sag yourself."

He nicked me under the chin with the front sight of his gun. My head snapped back and I fell against the open door of the car, slamming it shut. The sound rang out along the deserted street. I didn't know where I was, but I had the Glendale feeling: end of the line. No lights went on in any of the dark houses. Nothing happened at all, except that the man pressed his gun to my sternum and made threats like cello music into my face.

The other man leaned out of the front window. A little blood flowed from a cut over his right beetle. "You're sure you can handle this screw?"

"It will be a pleasure," the tall man said to both of us.

"Don't mark him up unless he asks for it. We just want to get his story and put him on ice for a while."

"How long?"

"You'll hear in the morning."

"I'm not a baby-sitter," the tall man grumbled. "What about your place, Mell?"

"I'm going on a trip. Goodnight sweetheart." The car went away.

"Quick march," the tall man said.

"Goosestep, or plain?"

He put one heel on my instep and his weight on the heel. His eyes were dark and small. They picked up the light of a distant streetlamp and reflected it like a cat's.

I said: "You're very active for an elderly man."

"Cut the comical chatter," he said throatily. "I never killed a man, but by Jesus—"

"I have, Amy. He kicked me in the head when I was down."

"Stop calling me Amy." He backed away and held

the gun higher. Without it he was nothing. But he had it.

I quick-marched up the cracked and slanting concrete to the porch. It was cavernous and sunken, a place of shadows. He kept his eyes and gun on me while he fumbled for his key-ring and snapped back the lock. A woman's voice spoke from the shadows then:

"Is it you, Rico? I've been waiting for you."

He turned catlike from the door, shifting his gun from me to the darkness behind me. "Who is it?" His voice was jangled.

I leaned on the balls of my feet, ready to move. The gun came back to me. The key-ring forgotten in the lock.

"It's me, Rico," the voice from the shadows said. "Mavis."

"Mrs. Kilbourne!" Amazement raked his face, and his voice choked. "What are you doing here?"

"Mavis to you, tall and handsome. I haven't been out by myself for a long time. But I haven't forgotten how you looked at me."

She moved out of the shadows past me as if I wasn't there, immaculate in a high-shouldered ermine jacket. Her left hand was behind her with the forefinger extended. It curled and straightened, pointed at the floor.

"Be careful, Mrs. Kilbourne." The man's voice was wretched, straining to repress an impossible hope. "Please go home, Mrs. Kilbourne."

"Won't you call me Mavis?" She brushed the side of his face with a white-gloved hand. "I call you Rico. I think of you when I'm lying in bed at night. Aren't you ever going to give me a break?"

"Sure I will, baby, only be careful. I'm holding a gun—"

"Well, put it away," she said with coy petulance. She pushed the gun to one side and leaned heavily on him, her arms around his shoulders, mouth on mouth.

For an instant the gun wavered. He was still, enclosed by her in a white and perfumed dream. I raised my doubled fists and brought them down. Something snapped in his hand. The gun rattled on the floor. The woman went down after it, scurrying on her knees, and Rico went after her. My arms looped over his head, hugged him and lifted him. I held him suspended by the neck until his hands stopped scratching at me and dragged on the floor. Then I let him fall on his face.

CHAPTER 12

The woman stood up with the gun. She held it in a gingerly way, as if it were a reptile. "You catch on quickly, Archer. That is your name, isn't it?"

"Unknown admirer," I said. "I didn't realize I had this fantastic power over women."

"Didn't you? I knew when I saw you you were for me. Then I heard my husband telling them to bring you here. I came. What else could I do?" Her hands made a pretty gesture, spoilt by the gun.

"Unlike Rico," I said, "I'm allergic to ham." I looked down at the man at my feet. His toupee was twisted sideways, so that the straight white line of the part ran from ear to ear. It was funny, and I laughed.

She thought I was laughing at her. "Don't you dare to laugh at me," she said in a blind white rage. "I'll kill you if you do."

"Not if you hold the gun that way. You'll sprain your wrist and shoot a hole in the roof. Now put it away and kiss your boyfriend goodnight and I'll take you home. I suppose I should thank you, too? Mavis."

"You'll do as I say," but her heart wasn't in what she said.

"I'll do as I think best. You hadn't the guts to tackle Rico alone, and I'm a tougher proposition than Rico."

She dropped the gun in her coat pocket and

clasped her white silk hands below her bosom. "You're right. I need your help. How did you know?"

"You didn't go to all this trouble for fun. Unwire my hands."

She slipped off the gloves. Her fingers unwound the thin steel wire. The man on the floor rolled onto his side, the breath whistling tinnily in his throat. "What can we do with him?" she said.

"What do you want to do with him? Keep him out of mischief, or get him into mischief?"

A smile brushed her lips. "Keep him out, of course."

"Give me the wire." My fingers were nearly numb, pierced by shooting pains from returning circulation, but they worked. I turned the tall man onto his back, doubled up his knees, and wired his wrists together behind his thighs.

The girl opened the door, and I dragged him over the threshold by the shoulders. "Now what?"

"There's a closet here." She closed the front door and switched on the light.

"Is that safe?"

"He lives here by himself."

"You seem to have cased the joint."

She touched a finger to her mouth and glanced at the man on the floor. His eyes were open, glaring up at her. Their whites were suffused with blood. His hair had fallen off entirely, so that his skull looked naked. The toupee lay on the floor like a small black animal, an infant skunk. Its master's voice came thin between purplish lips:

"I'm going to make bad trouble for you, lady."

"You're in it now." To me: "Put Tall and Handsome in the closet, will you?"

I put him in under a dirty raincoat, with a muddy pair of rubbers under his head. "Make a noise and I'll plug the cracks around the door." He was still.

I shut the closet door and looked around me. The lofty hallway belonged to an old house which had been converted into an office. The parquetry floor was covered with rubber matting, except at the edges where the pattern showed. The walls had been painted grey over the wallpaper. A carved staircase loomed at the rear of the hall like the spine of an extinct saurian. To my left, the frosted glass pane of a door bore a sign in neat black lettering: HENRY MURAT, ELECTRONICS AND PLASTICS LABORATORY.

The woman was bent over the lock of this door, trying one key after another from the keyring. It opened with a click. She stepped through and pressed a wall-switch. Fluorescent lights blinked on. I followed her into a small office furnished in green metal and chrome. A bare desk, some chairs, a filing cabinet, a small safe with a phony dial that opened with a key. A framed diploma on the wall above the desk announced that Henry Murat had been awarded the degree of Master of Electronic Science. I had never heard of the school.

She knelt in front of the safe, fumbling with the keys. After a few attempts she looked around at me. Her face was bloodless in the cruel light, almost as white as her coat. "I can't, my hands are shaky. Will you open it?"

"This is burglary. I hate to commit two burglaries in one night."

She rose and came towards me, holding out the keys. "Please. You must. There's something of mine in there. I'll do anything."

"That shouldn't be necessary: I told you I'm not Rico. But I like to know what I'm doing. What's in there?"

"My life," she said.

"More histrionics, Mavis?"

"Please. It's true. I'll never have another chance."

"At what?"

"Pictures of me." She forced the words out. "I never authorized them. They were taken without my knowledge."

"Blackmail."

"Call it that, but it's worse. I can't even kill myself, Archer."

She looked half dead at the moment. I took the keys with one hand and patted her arm with the other. "Why should you think of it, kid? You have everything."

"Nothing," she said.

The key to the safe was easy to pick out. It was made of brass, cut long and flat. I turned it in the keyhole under the dial, pressed the chrome handle, and pulled the heavy door open. I opened a couple of drawers filled with bills, old letters, invoices. "What am I looking for?"

"A roll of film. I think it's in a can."

There was a flat aluminum can on the upper shelf, the kind that was sometimes used for 16 mm. movies. I peeled off the tape that sealed the edges, and pulled off the lid. It contained a few hundred feet of film rolled in a flat cylinder. I held the end frame up to the light: it was Mavis flat on her back in a brilliant sun, with a towel over her hips.

"No. You wouldn't dare." She snatched the film from my hands and hugged it to her.

"Don't get excited," I said. "I've seen a human body before."

She didn't hear me. She threw the film on the linoleum floor and huddled over it. For a moment I didn't know what she was doing. Then I saw the gold lighter in her hand. It flicked open and made sparks, but didn't light.

I kicked the film out of her reach, picked it up, replaced it in the can. She cried out and flung herself at me. Her gloved hands beat on my chest.

I dropped the can in my pocket and took her wrists. "That stuff explodes sometimes. You'll burn the house down and you with it."

"What do I care? Let me go."

"If you make velvet paws. Besides, you need these pictures. So long as we have them, Rico will keep his mouth shut."

"We?" she said.

"I'm keeping them."

"No!"

"You asked for my help. This is it. I can keep Rico quiet, and you can't."

"Who will keep you quiet?"

"You will. By being a good girl and doing what I say."

"I don't trust you. I don't trust any man."

"Women, on the other hand, are extremely trustworthy."

"All right," she said after a while. "You win."

"Good girl." I released her hands. "Who is this Rico?"

"I don't know much about him. His real name is Enrico Murratti, I think he's from Chicago. He did some work for my husband, when they put two-way radios in the cabs."

"And your husband?"

"Let's just talk about human beings for now."

"There are things I want to know about him."

"Not from me." Her mouth set firmly.

"Reavis, then."

"Who's he?"

"You were with him in the Hunt Club."

"Oh," she said. "Pat Ryan." And bit her lip.

"Do you know where he's gone?"

"No. I know where he'll go eventually, and I'll dance at his funeral."

"You're close-mouthed for a woman."

"I have things to be close-mouthed about."

"One more question. Where are we? It feels like Glendale to me."

"It's Glendale." She managed a smile. "You know, I like you. You're kind of sharp."

"Yeah," I said. "I always use my brains to save my brawn. That's how I got this bump on the cerebellum."

His long minutes in the dark had aged and mellowed Rico. The knuckle-taut youthfulness had sagged out of his face. He looked like what he was: an insecure middle-aged man sweating with fear and discomfort.

I pulled him under the hall light and talked down at him: "You said something a while ago about making trouble for my client." I nodded at the woman by the door. "Any trouble you make will be for yourself. You're going to forget you saw her tonight. You're not going to tell her husband or anybody else that she was here. Nobody. And she's not going to set eyes on your pan for the rest of her natural life."

"You can cut the spiel," he said tiredly. "I know where I stand."

I took the can of film out of my pocket, tossed it in the air and caught it a couple of times. His eye followed it up and down. He licked his lips and sighed.

"Flat on your back," I said. "But I'm going to give you a break. I'm not going to beat you, though that would give me pleasure. I'm not going to turn you and the film over to the D.A., though that is what you deserve."

"It wouldn't do Mrs. Kilbourne a lot of good."

"Worry about yourself, Rico. This film is solid evidence of blackmail. Mrs. Kilbourne would never have to take the stand."

"Blackmail, crap! I never took no money from Mrs. Kilbourne." He rolled his eyes, seeking the woman's glance, but she was fixedly watching the film in my hand. I put it back in my pocket.

"No judge or jury would ever believe it," I said. "You're in a box. You want me to nail down the lid?"

He lay still for fifteen or twenty seconds, his lean brown forehead corrugated by thought. "A box is right," he admitted finally. "What do you want me to do?"

"Nothing. Nothing at all. Just keep your nose clean and stay away from my client. A young boy like you deserves a second chance, after all."

He showed vari-colored teeth in a shamed grin: so far gone that he was smiling at my jokes. I unwound the wire from his wrists and let him stand up. All his joints were stiff.

"You're letting him off easy," the woman said.

"What do you want to do to him?"

She turned her eyes on him, gray and lethal under the heavy curtains of her lashes. Instinctively he moved away from her, keeping his back to the wall. He looked willing to be put back into the closet.

"Nothing," she said at last. It was one of her favorite words. But on the way to the door she stepped on the black hairpiece and ground it under her gold heel. The last I saw of Rico, he had his right hand flat on top of his scalp, utter humiliation on his face.

We walked in silence to the nearest boulevard and caught a cruising cab. She told the driver to take her to The Flamenco.

"Why there?" I said, when the cab was under way. "It's closed by now."

"Not for me. I have to go back there anyway. I borrowed taxi-fare from the powder-room girl, and left her my bag for security."

"That's quite a situation you have there. A diamond-studded bag, and nothing in it."

"Tell it to my husband."

"I'd be glad to."

"Oh no!" She moved against me. "You wouldn't really?"

"He's got you frightened out of your wits. Why?"

"You won't ask me any questions, will you? I'm so tired. This business has taken more out of me than you think."

Her head touched my shoulder tentatively, and rested there. I leaned sideways, looking down into her face. Her gray eyes were crepuscular. The lashes came down over them like sudden night. Her mouth was dark and glistening. I kissed her, felt her toe press on my instep, her hand move on my body. I drew back from the whirling vortex that had opened, the drowning pool. She wriggled and sighed, and went to sleep in my arms.

I dropped her half a block from The Flamenco, and asked the driver to take me to Graham Court. He needed directions. It was all I could do to give them to him. My brain and body had gone into a champagne hangover. Through the long ride back, the wearing business of retrieving my car, driving it home, opening and shutting the garage, unlocking the door of my house and locking it behind me, I stayed awake with difficulty. I told my brain to tell my body to do what had to be done, and watched my body do it.

It was twenty after four by the electric alarm on the table beside my bed. Taking off my jacket, I felt for the can of film in the pocket. It was gone. I sat on the edge of the bed and shivered for two minutes by the clock. That made it four-twenty-two.

I said: "Goodnight to you, Mavis." Rolled over in my clothes, and went to sleep.

CHAPTER 13

The alarm made a noise which reminded me of dentists, which reminded me of optometrists, which reminded me of thick-lensed spectacles, which reminded me of Morris Cramm: the man I had been trying to think about when I woke up.

Hilda met me on the third-floor landing with her finger to her lips. "Be quiet now, Morris is sleeping, and he had a hard night." She was blonde and fat and doe-eyed, radiating through her housecoat the warmth and gentleness of Jewish women who are happily married.

"Wake him up for me, will you? Just a minute?"

"No, I couldn't do that." She looked at me more closely. The only light came from a burlap-curtained french door that opened on a fire escape at the end of the hall. "What happened to you, Lew? You look God-awful."

"You look swell. It's wonderful to see nice people again."

"Where have you been?"

"To hell and back. Glendale, that is. But I'll never leave you again." I kissed her on the cheek, which smelt of Palmolive soap.

She gave me a friendly little push that almost sent me backwards over the rail. "Don't do that. Morris might hear you, and he's awful jealous. Anyway, I'm not nice people. I'm a sloppy housekeeper, and I haven't done my nails for two whole weeks. Why? Because I'm lazy."

"I'm crazy about your nails. They never scratch."

"They will if you don't quiet down. And don't think you're going to flatter me into waking him up. Morris needs his sleep."

Morris Cramm was night legman for a columnist, and worked the graveyard shift. He knew everybody worth knowing in the metropolitan area, and enough about them to set up a blackmailing syndicate bigger than Sears Roebuck. To Morris, that idea would never have occurred.

"Look at it this way, Hilda. I am searching for the long-lost son of a wealthy English nobleman. The bereaved father is offering a fantastic reward for the prodigal's Los Angeles address. With Morris, I go halves. If he can give me the address, it will entitle him to this valuable gift certificate, bearing an engraved portrait of Alexander Hamilton and personally autographed by the Secretary of the Treasury." I took a ten-dollar bill out of my wallet.

"You sound like a radio program. A *couple* of radio programs, all mixed up."

"For five minutes of his personal sleeping time, I offer ten dollars in cash. Two dollars a minute, a hundred and twenty dollars an hour. Show me the movie star that gets nine hundred and sixty dollars for an eight-hour day."

"Well," she said dubiously, "if there's money involved. They're selling Beethoven quartets fifty per cent off down at the record shop— Only what if Morris doesn't know the answer?"

"He knows all the answers, doesn't he?"

She turned with her hand on the doorknob and said quite seriously: "Sometimes I think he does. He knows so much it saps the energy right out of him."

Hilda adjusted the blind and let a little light into the bedroom-sittingroom. The floor was covered with newspapers, the walls with shelves of books and record albums. A large Capehart dominated the room and the lives of the two people who lived in it. Morris was sleeping on an uncovered studio bed opposite the window, a small dark man in candy-striped pyjamas. He rolled over and sat up blinking. His eyes looked huge and emotional without his glasses.

He stared at me blindly. "What time is it? Who is it?"

"Nearly nine o'clock, dear. Lew came to ask you a question." She handed him his glasses from a shelf above the bed.

"My God, so early?" He refused to look at me. He put his hands on opposite shoulders and rocked himself and groaned.

"I'm sorry, Morris. It will only take a minute. Can you give me Walter Kilbourne's address? He isn't in the phone book. I have his car license, but this is a personal matter."

"Never heard of him."

"For ten dollars, darling," Hilda said very gently.

"If you don't know where Kilbourne lives, admit it. He looks like money to me, and he's married to the most beautiful woman in town."

"Ten million dollars, more or less," he said resentfully. "As for Mrs. Kilbourne, I don't go for ash blondes myself. My aesthetic taste demands a ruddier coloration." He smiled with frank admiration at his wife.

"Fool." She sat down beside him and ruffled his black wire hair.

"If Mavis Kilbourne was as beautiful as all that, she'd have got on in pictures, wouldn't she? But no, she married Kilbourne."

"Kilbourne or the ten million?"

"More than ten million, come to think of it. Fifty-one per cent of Pacific Refining Company, current quotation 26-⅜, figure it out for yourself."

"Pacific Refining Company," I said slowly and distinctly, thinking of the woman who was drowned. "I thought he was in the taxi business."

"He has some over in Glendale. His finger's in several pies, but Pareco's his plum. They got in early on the Nopal Valley strike." He yawned, and leaned his head against his wife's plump shoulder. "This bores me, Lew."

"Go on. You are cooking electronically. Where does he live?"

"In the Valley." His eyes were closed, and Hilda stroked with maternal awe the forehead that enclosed the filing-cabinet brain. "Staffordshire Estates, one of those private communities you need a special visa to get in. I was out there for a Fourth of July party. They had a Senator for guest of honor."

"U.S. or State?"

"U.S. Senator, what do you think? State Senators are a dime a dozen."

"Democratic or Republican?"

"What's the difference? Haven't I earned my ten dollars, brain-picker? Sweat-shopper?"

"One more question, asphalt intellectual. Where did the money come from in the first place?"

"Am I the Bureau of Internal Revenue?" He started to shrug, but found it required too much effort. "I am not."

"You know things they don't know."

"I know nothing. All I hear is rumors. You are inciting me to commit a libel."

"Spill it," I said.

"Storm-trooper."

"Now that isn't nice to call anybody," Hilda said soothingly.

I reminded him of the question: "The money. Where did it come from?"

"It didn't grow on trees," he said, and smothered a yawn. "I heard that Kilbourne made a fine thing out of black-market cars in Detroit during the war. Then he rushed down here to invest his money legitimately before somebody took it away from him. Now he's grand old California stock and politicians go to his parties. Don't quote me, it's only a rumor. He might have spread it himself to cover up something worse, now that I come to think of it."

Morris looked around the room with a dreaming smile and went to sleep sitting up. Removing his glasses, Hilda laid the limp boyish body out on the bed. I handed her the ten and moved to the door.

She followed me. "Come round in the daytime, Lew, we got the new Strauss from Paris."

"I will when I have some time. I'm on my way to Nevada at the moment."

"Seriously?"

"It looks like it."

"That's where Sue's living, isn't she?" Her round fat face lit up. "You're going to have a reconciliation!"

"Not a chance. This is business."

"I know you'll come back together. Wait and see."

"The bottom dropped out. All the king's horses couldn't put it back in for us."

"Oh, Lew." She looked ready to cry. "You made such a nice couple together."

I patted her arm. "You are lovely and good, Hilda." Morris groaned in his sleep. I went.

CHAPTER 14

From the highway the Staffordshire Estates were a discreet brass marker bolted to a stone arch, through which a new blacktop turned off the public road. A metal sign on one side of the arch informed me further that they were PROTECTED BY PRIVATE PATROL. The rustic redwood gates stood open, and I drove through them. Morning haze was drifting slowly up the canyon ahead, a translucent curtain between the outside world and the privately patrolled world I was entering. There were trees along the road, tall cypresses and elms, and small birds singing in them. Behind adobe walls and thick square-cut hedges, sprinklers were whirling lariats of spray. The houses, massive and low and bright among banks of flowers set in billiard-table lawns, were spaced out of sight of each other, so that no one but the owners could enjoy them. In this corner of the San Fernando Valley, property had become a fine art that was an end in itself. There were no people in sight, and I had a queer feeling that the beautiful squatting houses had taken over the canyon for their own purposes.

Valmy, Arbuthnot, Romanovsky, the mailboxes announced as I drove by them: Lewisohn, Tappingham, Wood, Farrington, Von Esch. WALTER J. KILBOURNE was neatly stenciled on the ninth mailbox and I turned up the drive beside it. The house was built of pink brick and glass, with a flat jutting redwood roof. The drive was lined with twenty shades of begonia. I parked in the gravelled loop that went past the front door, and pressed the button beside it. Chimes echoed through the house. The place was as noisy as a funeral parlor at midnight, and I liked it almost as well.

The door was opened silently by a small Japanese whose footsteps made no sound. "You wish something, sir?" His lips were very careful with the sibilants. Over his white linen shoulder I could see an entrance loggia containing a white grand piano and a white-upholstered Hepplewhite sofa. A pool beyond the white-columned windows threw rippling sapphire shadows on the white walls.

"Mr. Kilbourne," I said. "He told me he'd be home."

"But he is not. I am sorry, sir."

"It has to do with an oil lease. I need his signature."

"He is not at home, sir. Do you wish to leave a message?"

There was no way to tell if he was lying. His black eyes were unblinking and opaque. "If you can tell me where he is—?"

"I do not know, sir. He has gone for a cruise. Perhaps if you were to try his office, sir. They have direct telephone communication with the yacht."

"Thanks. May I call the office from here?"

"I am sorry, sir. Mr. Kilbourne has not authorized me to admit unknown persons to his home." He ducked his bootbrush hair at me in a token bow, and shut the door in my face.

I climbed into my car, closing the door very gently so as not to start an avalanche of money. The loop in the drive took me past the garages. They contained an Austin, a jeep, and a white roadster, but no black limousine.

The limousine met me halfway back to the highway. I held the middle of the road and showed three fingers of my left hand. The black car braked to a stop a few feet short of my bumpers, and the chauffeur got out. His scarred eyes blinked in the brightening sun.

"What's the trouble, mac? You give me the sign."

I hitched the gun from my shoulder-holster as I stepped out of the car, and showed it to him. He raised his hands to shoulder level and smiled. "You're screwy to try it, punk. I got nothing worth taking. I'm an old con myself but I got wise. Get wise like me and put away the iron." The smile sat strangely, like a crooked Santa Claus mask, on his battered face.

"Save it for Wednesday night meeting." I moved up to him, not too close. He was old, but strong and fast, and I didn't want to shoot him.

He recognized me then. His face was expressive, like a concrete block. "I thought you was in the refrigerator." The large hands closed and opened.

"Keep them up. What did you do with Reavis? Refrigerate him, too?"

"Reavis?" he said with laborious foxiness. "Who's Reavis? I don't know any Reavis."

"You will, when they take you down to the morgue to look at him." I improvised: "The Highway Patrol found him by the road outside of Quinto this morning. His throat was cut."

"Uh?" The air issued from his mouth and nostrils as if I'd body-punched him.

"Let me see your knife," I said, to keep his fifty points of I.Q. occupied.

"I got no knife. I had nothing to do with it. I dropped him over the Nevada line. He couldn't come back that fast."

"You came back that fast."

His face worked with the terrible effort of thought. "You're feeding me a sucker's line," he said. "He never went back to Quinto, they never found him."

"Where is he now, then?"

"I ain't talking," the concrete block announced. "You might as well put your iron away and lam."

We were in a dark-green valley walled with close-set laurel on both sides. The only sound was the hum of our idling cars. "You have a deceptive face," I said. "If I didn't know better, I'd think it was alive. You want it gun-whipped."

"Try it on," he said stolidly. "See where it gets you."

I wanted to hurt him, but the memory of the night was ugly in my mind. There had to be a difference between me and the opposition, or I'd have to take the mirror out of my bathroom. It was the only mirror in the house, and I needed it for shaving.

"Run along, quiz kid." I slanted the gun at the road. He went back to his car.

"Punk," he shouted in his thick, expressionless voice as he swerved in the ditch to pass me. His wrap-around bumper nicked the left rear fender of my car, and he blasted my ears with his horn to show it was deliberate. The roar of his accelerating motor rose like a sound of triumph.

I put mine in gear. All the way across the desert I scanned the side of the road for blind cripples and old ladies that I could help across and minister to with potions of camomile tea.

CHAPTER 15

It was late afternoon when I crossed the great level pass. The shadow of my car was running ahead in fleet silence, and slowly increasing its lead. The sun was yellow on the arid slopes, the air so clear that the mountains lacked perspective. They looked like surrealist symbols painted on the shallow desert sky. The heat, which had touched 110 at one, was slackening off, but my hood was still hot enough to fry the insects that splattered it.

The Rush Apartments occupied a two-story frame building on the east side of Las Vegas. Jaundiced with yellow paint, it stood tiredly between a parking lot and a chain grocery store. An outside wooden staircase with a single sagging rail led up to a narrow veranda on which the second-floor apartments opened. An old man was sitting in a kitchen chair tipped back against the wall under the stairs. He had a faded bandana handkerchief around his scrawny neck, and was sucking on a corncob pipe. A week's beard grew on his folded cheeks like the dusty gray plush in old-fashioned railway coaches.

I asked him where Mrs. Schneider lived.

"She lives right here," he mumbled.

"Is she in now?"

He removed his empty pipe from his mouth and

spat on the cement floor. "How do you expect me to know? I don't keep track of women's comings and goings."

I laid a fifty-cent piece on the bony knee. "Buy yourself a bag of tobacco."

He picked it up sulkily, and slipped it into a pocket of his food-crusted vest. "I s'pose her husband sent you? At least she *says* he's her husband, looks more like her bully to me. Anyway, you're out of luck now, slicker. She went out a while ago."

"You wouldn't know where?"

"To the den of iniquity, what do you think? Where she spends all her time." He tipped his chair forward and pointed far down the street. "You see that green sign? You can't make it out from here, but it says 'Green Dragon' on it. That's the den of iniquity. And you want me to tell you the name of this town? Sodom and Gonorrhea." He laughed an old man's laugh, high-pitched and unamused.

"Is that Elaine Schneider?"

"I dont know any other Mrs. Schneiders."

"What does she look like?" I said. "I never saw her."

"She looks like Jezebel." His watery eyes glittered like melting ice. "She looks like what she is, the whore of Babylon rolling her eyes and shaking her privates at Christian young men. Are you a Christian, son?"

I backed away thanking him and crossed the street, leaving my car at the curb. I walked the two blocks to the Green Dragon and worked some of the stiffness out of my legs. It was another seedy-looking bar. Signs in the dirty half-curtained windows advertised LIQUOR, BEER, HOT and COLD SANDWICHES and SHORT ORDERS. I pulled the screen door open and went in. A semi-circular bar with a door to the kitchen behind it took up the rear of the shallow room. The other three walls were lined with slot machines. Kitchen smells, the smell of stale spilled beer, the sick-sour smell of small-time gamblers' sweat, were slowly mixed by a four-bladed fan suspended from the fly-specked ceiling.

There was only one customer at the bar, a thin boy with uncombed red hair hunched desolately over a short beer. The bartender sat on a stool in a corner, as far away from the desolate youth as possible. His greased black head leaned against a table radio. "Three nothing," he announced to anyone who cared. "Top of the seventh." No sign of Jezebel.

I took a seat beside the redheaded boy, ordered a ham and cheese sandwich and a bottle of beer. The bartender went out reluctantly through the swinging door to the kitchen.

"Look at me, eh," the man beside me said. The words twisted his mouth as if they hurt. "How do you like me?"

His thin unshaven face looked dirty. His eyes had blue hollows under them and red rims around them. One of his ears was caked with dry blood.

"I like you very much," I said. "You have that beaten look that everybody admires."

It took the raw edge off his mood of self-pity. He even managed a smile which made him look five years younger, hardly more than a kid. "Well, I asked for it."

"Any time," I said, "any time."

"I asked for it in more ways than one, I guess. I should know better than to go on a bat in Las Vegas, but I guess I'll never learn."

"You have a few more years before you die. What happened to your ear?"

He looked sheepish. "I don't even know. I met a guy in a bar last night and he roped me into a game in a poker-parlor on the other side of town. All I remember, I lost my money and my car. I had three aces when I lost my car, and somebody started an argument: I guess it was me. I woke up in a parking lot."

"Hungry?"

"Naw. Thanks, though. I had a little change. The hell of it is I got to get back to L.A., and I got no car."

The bartender brought my food and drink. "Stick around," I told the young Dostoevsky. "I'll give you a lift if I can."

While I was eating, a woman came through a door at the end of the bar. She was tall and big-boned, with more than flesh enough to cover her bones. The skirt of her cheap black suit was wrinkled where her hips and thighs bulged out. Her feet and ankles spilled over the tops of very tight black pumps. Her north end was decorated with a single gray fox, a double strand of imitation pearls approximately the same color, and enough paint to preserve a battleship. Her chest was like a battleship's prow, massive and sharp and uninviting. She gave me a long hard searchlight look, her heavy mouth held loose, all ready to smile. I took a bite of my sandwich and munched at her. The searchlights clicked off, almost audibly.

She turned to the bar and snapped open a shiny black plastic bag. The yellow hair which she wore in a braided coronet was dark at the roots, obviously dyed. Turn it back to brown, take off a few years and a few more pounds, chip the paint off her face, and she could be Reavis's twin. They had the same eyes, the same thick handsome features.

The bartender clinched it: "Something for you, Elaine?"

She tossed a bill on the pitted woodstone surface. "Twenty quarters," she growled in a whisky voice that wasn't unpleasant. "For a change."

"Your luck is bound to change." He smiled insincerely. "The one you been playing is loaded to pay anytime."

"What the hell," she said, deadpan. "Easy come, easy go."

"Especially easy go," the boy beside me said to the beer-foam in the bottom of his glass.

Mechanically, without excitement or any sign of interest, she fed the quarters one by one into a machine near the door. Somebody phoning long-distance to somebody else who had been dead for years. Some twos and fours, a single twelve, stretched her money out. They went back in as a matter of course. She played the machine as if it was a toneless instrument made to express despair. When the jackpot came in a jangling rush of metal, I thought the machine had simply broken down. Then the slugs and quarters overflowed the bowl and rolled on the floor.

"I told you," the bartender said. "I said she was set to pay."

Paying no attention to her winnings, she crossed to the bar and took the seat beside me. He gave her a double whisky in a shot-glass without being asked.

"*You* pick it up, Simmie." Her voice had a trace of weary coquetry. "I'm wearing a girdle."

"Sure, but I don't need to count them. I'll give you the twenty-five."

"I put thirty-five in." The double shot went down like water down a drain.

"That's the percentage, kid. You got to pay something for all the fun you get."

"Yeah, fun." She folded the twenty and the five he gave her, and tucked them away in her bag.

A newsboy came in with an armful of *Evening Review-Journal's* and I bought one. The third page carried the story I was looking for, under the heading: EX-MARINE SOUGHT IN NOPAL VALLEY DEATH. It gave no information I didn't have, except that the police were maintaining an open mind as to the cause of death. Accompanying the story was a picture of Reavis, smiling incongruously over the caption: WANTED FOR QUESTIONING.

I folded the paper open at the third page and laid it on the bar between me and the big synthetic blonde. She didn't notice it for a minute or two; she was watching the bartender gather up her jackpot. Then her gaze strayed back to the bar and saw the picture, took hold of it. The breath wheezed asthmatically in her nostrils, and stopped entirely for a period of seconds. She took a pair of spectacles from her bag. With them on her face, she looked oddly like a schoolteacher gone astray.

"You mind if I look at your paper?" she asked me huskily. There was more south in her voice than there had been before.

"Go ahead."

The bartender looked up from sorting the slugs and quarters on the bar. "Say, I didn't know you wore glasses, Elaine. Very becoming."

She didn't hear him. With the aid of a scarlet-tipped finger moving slowly from word to word, she was spelling out the newspaper story to herself. When the slow finger reached the final period, she was silent and still for an instant. Then she said aloud: "Well I'll be —!"

She flung the paper down, its edges crumpled by the moist pressure of her hands, and went to the street door. Her hips rolled angrily, her high heels spiked the floor. The screen door slammed behind her.

I waited thirty seconds and went after her. Rotating on his stool, the desolate youth followed me with his eyes, like a stray dog I had befriended and betrayed.

"Stick around," I told him over my shoulder.

The woman was already halfway up the block. Though they were hobbled by her skirt, her legs were moving like pistons. The gray foxtail hung down her back, fluttering nervously. I followed her more slowly when I saw where she was going. She went up the outside stairs of the Rush Apartments, unlocked the second door, and went in, leaving it open. I crossed the street and slid behind the wheel of my car.

She came out immediately. Something metallic in her hand caught a ray of sunlight. She pushed it into her bag as she came down the stairs. The forgotten glasses on her face gave it a purposeful air. I hid my face behind a road map.

She crossed the parking lot to an old Chevrolet sedan. Its original blue paint had faded to brownish green. The fenders were crumpled and dirty like paper napkins on a restaurant table. The starter jammed, the exhaust came out in spasms of dark blue smoke. I followed the pillar of smoke to the main highway junction in the middle of town, where it turned south towards Boulder City. I let it get well ahead as we passed out of town onto the open highway.

Between Boulder City and the dam an asphalt road turned off to the left toward Lake Mead, skirting the public beaches along the shore. Children were playing on the gravel below the road, splashing in the shallow waveless water. Further out a fast red hydroplane was skittering back and forth like a waterbug, describing esses on the paper-flat, paper-gray surface.

The Chevrolet turned off the blacktop, to the left again, up a gravel road which wound through low scrub oak. The brush and the innumerable branching lanes made an accidental maze. I had to move up on the woman to keep her in sight. She was too busy holding her car on the road to notice me. Her smooth old tires skidded and ground among the loose stones as she came out of one curve only to enter another.

We passed a public camping-ground where families were eating in the open among parked cars, tents, tear-drop trailers. A few hundred yards further on, the Chevrolet left the gravel road, turning up a brush-crowded lane which was no more than two ruts in the earth. Seconds later, I heard its motor stop.

I left my car where it was and went up the lane on foot. The Chevrolet was parked in front of a small cabin faced with peeled saplings. The woman tried the screen door, found it locked, pounded it with her fist.

"What gives?" It was Reavis's voice, coming from inside the cabin.

I crouched behind a scrub-oak, feeling as if I should be wearing a coonskin cap.

Reavis unhooked the door and stepped outside. His hounds-tooth suit was dusty, and creased in all the wrong places. His hair curled down in his eyes. He pushed it back with an irritable hand. "What's the trouble, sis?"

"You tell me, you lying little crumb." He overshadowed her by half a head, but her passionate energy made him look helpless. "You told me you were having woman trouble, so I said I'd hide you out. You didn't tell me that the woman was dead."

He stalled for time to think: "I don't know what you're talking about, Elaine. Who's dead? This dame I was talking about isn't dead. She's perfectly okay only she says she's missed two months in a row and I don't want any part of it. She was cherry."

"Yeah, a grandmother and cherry." Her voice rasped with ugly irony. "This is one thing you can't lie out of, sprout. You're in too deep for me to try and help you. I wouldn't help you even if I could. You can go to the gas chamber and I wouldn't lift a finger to save your neck. Your neck ain't worth the trouble to me or to anybody else."

Reavis whined and whimpered: "What the hell are you talking about, Elaine. I didn't do nothing wrong. Are the police after me?"

"You know damn well they are. This time you're going to get it, sonny boy. And I want no part of it unnerstan'? I want no part of you from now on."

"Come on now, Elaine, settle down. That's no kind of talk to use on your little brother." He forced his voice into an ingratiating rhythm and put one hand on her shoulder. She shook it off and held her purse in both hands.

"You can save it. You've talked me into too much trouble in my life. Ever since you stole that dollar bill from maw's purse and tried to shift it onto me, I knew you were heading for a bad end."

"*You've* done real good for yourself, Elaine. Selling it for two-bits in town on Saturday night before you was out of pigtails. You still charging for it, or do you pay them?"

The concussion of her palm against his cheek cracked like a twenty-two among the trees. His fist answered the blow, thudding into her neck. She staggered, and her sharp heels gouged holes in the sandy earth. When she recovered her balance, the gun was in her hand.

Reavis looked at it uncomprehendingly, and took a step toward her. "You don't have to go off your rocker. I'm sorry I hit you, Elaine. Hell, you hit me first."

Her whole body was leaning and focused on the gun: the handle of a door that had always resisted her efforts, and still resisted. "Stay away from me." Her low whisper buzzed like a rattler's tail. "I'll put you on the Salt Lake highway and I never want to see you again in my life. You're a big boy now, Pat, big enough to kill people. Well, I'm a big enough girl."

"You got me all wrong, sis." But he stayed where he was, his hands loose and futile at his sides. "I didn't do nothing wrong."

"You lie. You'd kill *me* for the gold in my teeth. I seen you going through my purse this afternoon."

He laughed shortly. "You're crazy. I'm loaded, sis, I could put you on easy street." He reached for his left hip pocket.

"Keep your hands where I can see them," she said.

"Don't be crazy, I want to show you—"

The safety clicked. The door that had resisted her was about to open. Her whole body bent tensely over the gun. Reavis's hands rose from his side of their own accord, like huge brown butterflies. He looked sullen and stupid in the face of death.

"Are you coming?" she said. "Or do you want to die? You're wanted by the cops, they wouldn't even touch me if I killed you. What loss would it be to anybody? You never gave nothing but misery to a single soul since you got out of the cradle."

"I'll go along, Elaine." His nerve had broken, suddenly and easily. "But you'll be sorry, I warn you. You don't know what you're doing. Anyway, you can put away that gun."

I wasn't likely to get a better cue. I stepped from behind my tree with my gun ready. "A good idea. Drop the gun, Mrs. Schneider. You, Reavis, keep up your hands."

Her whole body jerked. "Augh!" she said viciously. The small bright automatic fell from her hand, rustled and gleamed in the leaves in front of her feet.

Reavis glanced at me, the color mounting floridly in his face. "Archer?"

I said: "The name is Leatherstocking."

He turned on his sister: "So you had to bring a cop along, you had to wreck everything?"

"What if I did?" she growled.

"Hold it, Reavis." I picked up the woman's gun. "And you, Mrs. Schneider, go away."

"Are you a cop?"

"This isn't question period. I could haul you in for accessory. Now go away, before I change my mind."

I kept my gun on Reavis, dropped hers into the pocket of my jacket. She turned awkwardly on her heels and went to the Chevrolet, her hard face kneaded by the first indications of regret at what she had done.

CHAPTER 16

When she was gone, I told Reavis to turn his back. Terror yanked at his mouth and pulled it open. "You ain't going to shoot me?"

"Not if you stand still."

He turned slowly, reluctantly, trying to watch me over his shoulder. He carried no gun. A rectangular package bulged in his right hip pocket. He started when I unbuttoned the pocket, then held himself tense and still as I drew out the package. It was wrapped in brown paper. A melancholy sigh of pain and loss came out of him, as if I had removed a vital organ. I tore one end of the paper with my teeth, and saw the corner of a thousand-dollar bill.

"You don't have to bother to count it," Reavis said thickly. "It's ten grand. Can I turn around now?"

I stepped back, slipping the torn package into the inside breast pocket of my jacket. "Turn around slowly, hands on the head. And tell me who'd pay you ten thousand dollars for bumping off an old lady with a weak heart."

He turned, his blank face twisting, trying to get the feel of a story to tell. His fingers scratched unconsciously in his hair. "You got me wrong, I wouldn't hurt a fly."

"If it was big enough to bite back, you wouldn't."

"I never had nothing to do with that death. It must of been an accident."

"And it was pure coincidence you were on the spot when it happened."

"Yeah, pure coincidence." He seemed grateful for the phrase. "I just went out to say goodbye to Cathy, I thought she might come along with me, even."

"Be glad she didn't. You'd be facing a Mann Act charge as well as a murder rap."

"Murder rap, hell. They can't pin murder on an innocent man. She'll give me a alibi. I was with her before you picked me up."

"Where were you with her?"

"Out in front of the house, in one of the cars." It sounded to me as if he was telling the truth: Cathy had been sitting in my car when I went out. "We used to sit out there and talk," he added.

"About your adventures on Guadalcanal?"

"Go to hell."

"All right, so that's your story. She wouldn't go along with you, but she gave you ten grand as a souvenir of your friendship."

"I didn't say she gave it to me. It's my own money."

"Chauffeurs make big money nowadays. Or is Gretchen just one of a string that pays you a percentage?"

He studied me with narrowed eyes, obviously shaken by my knowledge of him. "It's my own money," he repeated stubbornly. "It's clean money, nothing illegal about it."

"Maybe it was clean before you touched it. It's dirty money now."

"Money is money, isn't it? I'll tell you what I'll do. I'll give you two grand. Twenty per cent, that's a good percentage."

"You're very generous. But I happen to have it all, a hundred per cent."

"All right, five grand then. It's my money, don't forget, I promoted it myself."

"You tell me how you did it, then maybe I'll cut you in. But the story has to be a good one."

He thought that over for a while, and finally made up his mind. "I'm not talking."

"We're wasting time, then. Let's get moving."

"Where you think you're taking me?"

"Back to Nopal Valley. The Chief of Police wants some of your conversation."

"We're in Nevada," he said. "You got to extradite me and you got no evidence."

"You're coming to California for your health. Voluntarily." I raised the barrel of my gun and let him look into the muzzle.

It frightened him, but he wasn't too frightened to talk. "You think you're riding high, and you think you're going to keep my money. All you're gonna do is get caught in a big machine, man."

His face was moist and pallid with malevolence. For less than a day he had been rich and free. I'd tumbled him back into the small time, perhaps into the shadow of the gas chamber.

"You're going to take a ride in a little one. And don't try for a break, Reavis, or you'll limp the rest of your life."

He told me to do an impossible thing, but he came along quietly to my car. "You drive," I said. "I haven't had a chance to look at the scenery."

He drove angrily but well. We passed his sister just out of Boulder City. Nobody waved at anybody. We lost her in no time at all.

Back in Las Vegas, I directed him to the Green Dragon. He looked at me questioningly as he pulled up to the curb.

"We're picking up a friend of mine. You come in, too."

I slid out under the wheel, on his side, and crowded him with the gun in my pocket as we crossed the sidewalk to the screen door. I couldn't trust Reavis to drive across the desert without an accident. I couldn't risk driving myself.

The place looked more cheerful with the lights on,

more people at the bar. The redheaded boy was sitting on the same stool, probably with the same empty beer glass in front of him, as desolate as ever.

I called him to the door. He said hello with a surprised inflection, and heaved up a feeble smile from the bottom of his stomach.

"Can you drive fast?"

"The fastest crate I ever drove would only go ninety, downhill."

"That's fast enough. I'll give you ten dollars to drive me back to the coast. Me and my friend. I'm Archer."

"To L.A.?" He said it as if there were really angels there.

"Nopal Valley. We go back over the mountains. From there you can take a bus."

"Swell. My name is Bud Musselman, by the way." He turned to Reavis with his hand outstretched. Reavis suggested what he should do with it.

"Pay no attention to him," I told the boy. "He suffered a very heavy financial loss."

Musselman took the wheel, with Reavis beside him. I sat in the back of the convertible, my gun on my knees. The downtown streets were brightening into tunnels of colored light under the darkening sky. Its quick nightly tumescence was turning Las Vegas into a city again. Far behind to the east a slice of moon floated low in the twilit sky.

I caught glimpses of it over my shoulder, over the shoulders of mountains, as it slowly rose in the sky, dissolving smaller. The boy drove fast and hard, and no car passed us. I stopped him at a gas station in the middle of the desert. A battered sign advertised Free Zoo: Real live rattlesnakes.

"You still got a third of a tank," he told me eagerly. "We're making good mileage, considering the speed."

"I have a phone call to make."

Reavis had wedged himself in the corner by the door and gone to sleep. One arm was over his face, the fist clenched tight. I reached across him and pushed the hand away from his wet forehead. He sobbed in his sleep, then opened his eyes, blinking in the light of the dash.

"We there already?" he asked me sullenly.

"Not yet. I'm going to phone Knudson. Come along."

Getting out of the car, he walked on loose knees around the gas pumps toward the open glaring door of the office. He looked round at the desert, chiaroscuroed with moon shadows; stole a glance at me, and tensed for movement halfway between the gas pumps and the door. A hunted man in a bad movie, about to risk his two-dimensional life.

I said: "I'm right behind you. My gun is pointed at your hambone."

His knees went loose again. I got change from the attendant and put in a call to the Nopal Valley police station. Reavis leaned beside the wall telephone, yawning wih frustration, so close to me I could smell him. His odor was a foolish hope gone sour.

A metallic voice rasped in my left ear: "Nopal Valley police."

"Chief Knudson, please."

"He ain't here."

"Can you tell me where to reach him?"

"Can't do that. Who's speaking?"

"Lewis Archer. Knudson asked me to report to him."

"Archer. Oh, yeah." A pause. "You got anything to report?"

"Yes. To Knudson."

"He ain't here, I tell you. This is the desk. You can report to me, and we'll take care of it."

"All right," I said reluctantly. "Get in touch with Knudson, tell him I'm coming into town tonight with a prisoner. What time is it now?"

"Five to nine. You on the Slocum case?"

"Yes. We should be there by midnight. We're in the desert now. Tell the Chief, he'll want to know."

"Okay, Mr. Archer." The rasping mechanical voice took on a personal note of curiosity. "You take this Reavis?"

"Keep it to yourself."

"Sure thing. You want a car to meet you?"

"Not necessary. He couldn't fight his way out of a wet paper bag."

I hung up, to meet Reavis's sullen glare. Back in the car, he went to sleep again.

"Your friend seems very unhappy," the boy Musselman said. "Is that a gun you're carrying?"

"It's a gun."

"You wouldn't be a mobster or something, Mr. Archer? I wouldn't want—" He thought better of the sentence.

"Something," I said. "You wouldn't want—?"

"Augh, nothing." He didn't speak to me again for three hours. But he did his job, driving as if he loved it, pushing the long white headlights across the dry-sea floor. The road unrolled like ticker-tape under the wheels.

It was just after midnight when we crossed the second mountain ridge and saw the distant lights of Nopal Valley. Our headlamps flashed on a black and yellow road-sign: Dangerous Grade: Trucks Use Lower Gear. We coasted down.

"Feels like I'm landing a plane," the boy said over his shoulder. Then he was silent, remembering his distrust of me and my gun.

I leaned forward in my seat. Reavis had slipped far down, his arms and shoulders sprawled on the seat, his legs cramped under the dash against the floor-boards. His body had given up, and he looked dead. For an instant I was afraid that he was dead, that all his life had run out through the wound in his ego. I couldn't bear the thought, after the trouble I'd gone to.

"Reavis," I said. "Wake up. We're almost there."

He moaned and grumbled, raised his heavy head, painfully uncoiled his long sluggish body. Suddenly the boy applied the brakes, throwing him against the windshield.

I braced myself on the seat. "Watch it."

Then I saw the truck parked across the road near

the foot of the slope. We traveled a couple of hundred feet with brakes screeching, and came to a jarring halt. The truck was lightless, driverless.

"What do they think they're doing?" the boy said.

On one side the bank rose sharply, studded with boulders, and fell away on the other. No room to pass. A spotlight beam shot out from the side of the truck, wavered and found my windshield.

"Back up," I told the boy.

"I can't. I stalled her." His entire body labored with the starter. The motor roared.

"Douse the glim," somebody yelled. "It's him." The spotlight winked out.

The car shuddered backward a few feet and stalled again. "Christ, the brake!" the boy said to himself.

A knot of men waded into our headlight beam: six or seven gunmen carrying their tools. I pushed Reavis aside and got out to meet them. They had handkerchiefs tied over their mouths. "What is this, the great stage robbery?"

One of the handkerchiefs waggled: "Put your gun down, Jack. We want your prisoner is all."

"You'll have to take him."

"Don't be foolish, Jack."

I shot his gun arm, aiming for the elbow. Things were silent. The echo of the shot repeated itself in the narrow valley like a long low titter of despair.

I said to Reavis, without looking at him: "Better run for it, Pat."

His feet scraped on the road behind me. The man I had shot sat down in the road with his gun between his legs. He watched the blood drip off his hand in the moonlight. The other men looked from him to me and back in a quick tense rhythm.

"There are six of us, Archer," one of them said uncertainly.

"My gun holds seven rounds," I said. "Go home."

Reavis was still behind me, uncomfortably still. "Beat it, Pat, I can hold them."

"The hell," he said.

His arm came around my neck and jerked me backwards. The faceless men came forward in a wave. I turned to grapple with Reavis. His face was a blur in the moonlight, but it seemed to me that the eyes and mouth were wet with satisfaction. I struck at them. His fist came into my face. "I warned you, man," he said aloud.

A blow on the back of the neck chilled me down to the toes. I broke away from Reavis and swung my gun at the front man. Its muzzle raked his cheek and tore the handkerchief loose from his face. He doubled over. The others moved into his place.

"Hold your fire," the man on the ground called out. "We only want the one."

Another blow fell from behind, where Reavis was, and I was out before I hit the road.

I came back to consciousness unwillingly, as if I knew already what I would see. The boy was on his knees, a praying figure between me and the stars. The stars were in the same place in the sky, but they looked old and stale. I felt coeval with them.

Musselman jumped like a rabbit when I sat up. He rose to his feet and leaned over me. "They killed him, Mr. Archer." His voice was broken.

I got up painfully, feeling dwarfed and despised by the mountains. "What did they do to him?"

"They shot him, a dozen times or more. Then they poured gasoline on him and threw him down the bank and a match down after him. Was he really a murderer, like they said?"

"I don't know," I said. "Where is he?"

"Down there."

I followed him around the car and switched my spotlight on. The charred leavings of a man lay ten feet below the road in a circle of blackened sagebrush. I went to the other side of the road to be sick. The thin scrap of moon hung in a gap of the mountains, like lemon rind in a tall dark drink of Lethe. I brought up nothing but a bitter taste.

CHAPTER 17

The man behind the wire partition was speaking into a hand mike in a cheerless monotone: "Car sixteen investigate reported assault corner Padilla and Flower. Car sixteen corner Padilla and Flower."

He switched off the microphone and drew on a wet cigarette. "Yes sir?" He leaned forward to look at me through his wicket. "You have an accident?"

"It was no accident. Where's the Chief?"

"He's out on a case. What's the trouble?"

"I called you around nine. Did Knudson get my message?"

"Not me you didn't call. I just come on at midnight." He took another puff and scanned me impassively through the smoke. "What was this here message about?"

"It should be logged. I called at five to nine."

He turned back the top sheet on his board and glanced at the one underneath. "You must of made a mistake. There's nothing here between 8:45, a drunk on State, and 9:25, prowler over on Vista. Unless it was that prowler trouble?"

I shook my head.

"It wasn't the sheriff's branch office you called?"

"I called here. Who was on the desk?"

"Franks."

"He's a detective. He wouldn't be doing desk duty."

"He was filling in for Carmody. Carmody's wife is going to have a baby. Now what about this call? Name?"

"Archer. I'll talk to Knudson."

"You the private dick in the Slocum case?"

I nodded.

"He's out there now. I can call him."

"Don't bother. I'll drive out. Is Franks around?"

"Naw, he went home." He leaned forward confidentially, crushing out his cigarette. "You want my honest opinion, Franks ain't fit to handle this man's job. He dropped the ball before now. Was the call important?"

I didn't say. An ugly shape was taking form in the dreary, austere room, hanging almost tangibly over my head. It dragged on me, slowing my footsteps as I went out to the car. Anger and fear took over when I got my hands on the wheel. I ran through two red lights on the way out of town.

"We're not going back there?" the boy said shakily.

"Not yet. I have to see the Chief of Police."

"I don't understand what's happening. It's terrible. You tried to save him and he turned on you."

"He was stupid. He thought they were his friends. He didn't have any friends."

"It's terrible," he said again, to himself.

The veranda lights of the Slocum house were on, illuminating the massive walls, the clipped funereal lawn. It was a mausoleum banked with flowers and lit for company. The black police car at the foot of the terraces was fit for death to ride in, quietly and fast. I left the boy in the car and started up the walk. Knudson and Maude Slocum came to the front door together. They moved apart perceptibly when they recognized me. Mrs. Slocum stepped through the door alone, with her hand outstretched.

"Mr. Archer! Police headquarters phoned that you were coming. Where in the world have you been?"

"Too far. I could use a drink."

"Of course, come in." She opened the door and held

it for me. "You'll make him a drink, won't you, Ralph?"

He glanced at her warningly—the hard and practiced glance of an old enemy, an old lover. "Glad to, Mrs. Slocum. What's the good word, Archer?" His manner was cumbersome with a false friendliness.

"The word is all bad."

I gave it to them over my drink, in the sitting-room where the Slocums had quarreled the night before and then made up. Mrs. Slocum had a bruise on her cheekbone, barely visible under a heavy coating of suntan powder. She wore a green wool dress which emphasized the luxury of her figure. Her eyes and mouth and temples were haggard, as if the rich hungry body had been draining them of blood. Knudson sat beside her on a chintz-covered settee. Unconsciously, as I talked, her crossed knees tilted toward him.

"I caught up with Reavis in Las Vegas—"

"Who told you he was there?" Knudson asked softly.

"Legwork. I started back with him between six and seven, with a kid I hired to drive. At nine I called your headquarters from a gas stop in the desert, and told the desk to tell you I was coming."

"I didn't get it. Let's see, who was on the desk?"

"Franks. He didn't even bother to log the call. But he leaked the information to somebody else. Seven men stopped me on the Notch Trail, less than an hour ago. They used a truck for a roadblock. I shot one. Reavis thought the men were there to spring him, and he took me from behind. They knocked me out. Then they ventilated Reavis with a dozen slugs and gave him a gasoline barbecue."

"Please," Maude Slocum said, her face closed like a death mask. "How horrible."

Knudson's teeth tore at his thick lower lip. "A dirty lynching, eh? In twenty years in police work I never had a lynching to cope with."

"Save it for your memoirs, Knudson. This is murder. The boy in my car is a witness. I want to know what you're going to do about it."

He stood up. Beneath his surface show of excitement, he seemed to be taking the thing much too easily. "I'll do what I can. Notch Trail is out of my territory. I'll call the sheriff's office."

"Franks is your boy."

"Don't worry, I'll get to the bottom of that. Can you give me a description of these men?"

"They were masked with handkerchiefs. They looked to me like local products, ranchhands or oilfield hoods. One of them has a bullet hole in the inside right elbow. I'd know two voices if I heard them again. The boy might tell you more."

"I'll let the sheriff talk to him."

I stood up facing him. "You don't sound very eager."

He saw my intention of forcing a showdown, decided to stall it off. "These outbreaks of mob violence are hard to deal with, you know that. Even if the sheriff does get hold of the men, which isn't very likely, we'll never get a jury to convict them. Mrs. Slocum was one of the town's most respected citizens: you've got to expect some pretty raw feeling over her murder."

"I see. Mrs. Slocum's death is murder now. And Reavis's death is vigilante stuff, popular justice. You're not that stupid, Knudson, and neither am I. I know a mob when I see one. Those killers were hired. Amateurs maybe, but they didn't do it for fun."

"We won't get personal," he said in a heavy tone of warning. "After all, Reavis got what was coming to him. Amateur or not, the men that lynched him saved the state some money."

"You think he killed Mrs. Slocum."

"There isn't any doubt of it in my mind. The medical examiner found marks on her back, subcutaneous hemorrhages where somebody pushed her. And the somebody seems to be Reavis. We found his cap about fifty feet from the pool, behind the trees that mask the filter system. That proves that he was there.

He'd just lost his job: motive enough for a psycho. And immediately after the crime he skipped out."

"He skipped out, yes, but publicly and slowly. He thumbed a ride from me outside the gate, and stopped off at a bar for a couple of drinks."

"Maybe he needed a couple of drinks. Killers often do."

Knudson had the red and stubborn look of a man who had closed his mind. It was time to play the card I had been saving: "The timing is wrong. The earliest possible time that Marvell heard the splashing was twenty after eight. It was 8:23 exactly when I picked Reavis up, and it's a mile or more from the pool to the gate."

Knudson showed his teeth. A faint reflection of the grimace passed over Maude Slocum's face, which was intent on his. "Marvell is a very imaginative type," he said. "I took another statement from him today, after he calmed down a bit. He couldn't be certain when he heard the splash, or even if he heard a splash at all. It's possible that Mrs. Slocum was murdered a full hour before he found her. There's no way of establishing how long she was in the water."

"Still, I don't think Reavis did it."

"What you don't think isn't evidence. I've given you the evidence, and it's firm. Incidentally, it's a little late for you to be telling me when you picked Reavis up, and going to bat for him. What happened, Archer, did he sell himself to you? I understand he was a very convincing guy."

I held my anger. "There are other things. They can wait till you've done your phoning."

With arrogant slowness, he took a cigar from his side pocket, asked the woman's permission, bit off the end and dropped it in an ashtray, lit the cigar, blew out the match, puffed smoke in my direction. "When I need a door-knocker to tell me how to conduct my official work, I'll send you a special-delivery letter." He left the room, trailing cigar smoke; and came back from the hall immediately, holding Cathy Slocum by the arm. She twisted in his grasp. "Let me go, Mr. Knudson."

He dropped her arm as if she had struck him. "I'm sorry, Cathy. I didn't mean to be rough."

She turned her back on him and moved toward the door, her low-heeled white fur slippers scuffing the rug. Wrapped in a pink quilted robe, with her gleaming hair brushed down her back, she looked like a child. Knudson watched her with a curious, helpless expression.

"Wait a minute, darling," her mother said. "What are you doing up so late?"

Cathy stopped inside the door, but refused to turn. Her satin-covered shoulders were stiff and obstinate. "I was talking to father."

"Is he still awake?"

"He couldn't sleep, and I couldn't either. We heard voices, and he sent me down to see who it was. Now may I go back to bed, please?"

"Of course you may, dear."

"I'd like to ask Cathy a question," I said. "Do you object, Mrs. Slocum?"

She raised her hand in a maternal gesture. "The poor girl's had to answer so many questions. Can't it wait until morning?"

"All it needs is a yes-or-no answer, and it's a crucial question. Pat Reavis claimed her as an alibi."

The girl turned in the doorway. "I'm not a child, mother. Of course I can answer a question." She stood with her feet apart, her fists thrust deep into the pockets of her robe.

"All right, dear. As you wish." I got the impression that the mother was the one who usually gave in.

I said to her: "Reavis claimed he came out here to see you last night. Was he with you before I found you in my car?"

"No. I haven't seen him since that trouble in Quinto."

"Is that all?" Knudson said.

"That's all."

"Come and kiss your mother goodnight," Maude Slocum said.

The girl crossed the room with an unwilling awkwardness and kissed her mother on the cheek. The older woman's arms moved up around her. The girl stepped out of them quickly, and away.

Knudson watched them as if he was unaware of the tension between them. He seemed to take a simple delight in the forced, loveless transaction of the kiss. He followed Cathy out of the room with a set smile on his face, the glowing cigar held cockily in the middle of the smile.

I sat down on the settee beside Maude Slocum: "Reavis is sewed up tight. I see what Knudson meant."

"Are you still unsatisfied?" she asked me earnestly. "Understand me, Reavis means nothing to me. It's the total picture that bothers me: there are big gaps in it. For example. Do you know a man by the name of Walter Kilbourne?"

"More questions, Mr. Archer?" She reached for a silver cigarette box on the table beside her. Her hand, badly controlled, knocked the box to the floor. The cigarettes spilled out, and I started to pick them up.

"Don't bother," she said, "please don't bother. It doesn't matter. Things in general seem to be going to pieces. A few cigarettes on the floor are the least of my worries."

I went on picking up the cigarettes. "What is the greatest of your worries? Is it still that letter you gave me?"

"You ask so many questions. I wonder what it is that keeps you asking them. A passion for justice, a passion for truth? You see, I've turned the tables on you."

"I don't know why you should bother to." I set the full box on the table, lit her cigarette and one for myself.

She drew on it gratefully. Her answer was visible, written in smoke on the air: "Because I don't understand you. You have mind and presence enough for a better job, certainly one with more standing."

"Like your friend Knudson's? I worked in a municipal police department for five years, and then I quit. There were too many cases where the official version clashed with the facts I knew."

"Ralph is honest. He's been a policeman all his life, but he still has a decent conscience."

"Two of them, probably. Most good policemen have a public conscience and a private conscience. I just have the private conscience; a poor thing, but my own."

"I was right about you. You do have a passion for justice." The deep eyes focused on mine and probed them, as if a passion for justice was something she could see and remember the shape of. Or a strange growth in a man that could be X-rayed out.

"I don't know what justice is," I said. "Truth interests me, though. Not general truth if there is any, but the truth of particular things. Who did what when why. Especially why. I wonder, for example, why you care whether I'm interested in justice. It could be an indirect way of asking me to drop out of this case."

She was silent for a time. "No. It isn't that. I have some regard for truth myself. I suppose it's a woman's regard: I want the truth if it doesn't hurt too much. And I suppose I'm a little afraid of a man who cares strongly about something. You really care, don't you, whether Reavis is innocent or guilty?"

"Doesn't Knudson and his decent conscience?"

"He did, but I don't know if he still does. There are a lot of things going on that I don't understand." That made two of us. "My esteemed husband, for instance, has retired to his room and refuses to emerge. He claims that he'll spend the rest of his life in his room, like Marcel Proust." Hatred flashed in the ocean-colored eyes and disappeared, like a shark-fin.

I crushed out my cigarette, which tasted acrid on an empty stomach. "This Marcel something-or-other, is he a friend of yours?"

"So now you're going to play dumb again?"

"I might as well. It seems to be all the rage in this *ménage*. You're perfectly willing to talk about abstractions like truth and justice. But you haven't told me a single damned fact that might help to find the person that wrote the letter, or the person that killed your mother-in-law."

"Ah, the letter. We're back at the letter again."

"Mrs. Slocum," I said, "the letter wasn't written about me. It was written about you. You hired me to find out who wrote it, remember?"

"So much has happened since, hasn't it? It seems unimportant now."

"Now that she's dead?"

"Yes," she answered calmly. "Now that she's dead."

"Has it occurred to you that the letter-writer and the murderer may be the same person?"

"It hadn't. I can't see any connection."

"Neither can I. With co-operation, I might; if you'd tell me what you know about the relations between the people in this house."

She raised her shoulders and let them fall in a gesture of weary resignation. "I can't claim immunity to questioning on the grounds of extreme youth, like Cathy. I *am* most frightfully tired. What do you want to know?"

"How long you've known Knudson, and how well."

She gave me a second slow and probing look. "Just the last year or so, not at all intimately."

"Yesterday you mentioned a friend of yours, by the name of Mildred Fleming. She might be able to tell me a different story. Or don't you confide in your friends, either?"

She answered coldly: "I think you're being insolent, Mr. Archer."

"Very good, ma'am. We'll play the game according to the formal rules. Unless you want to call it on account of insolence."

"I haven't decided about that. I'll tell you one thing, though, I do know Walter Kilbourne. In fact, I saw him tonight."

Knudson's heavy feet came down the hall, his

sloping shoulders filled the doorway. "I finally routed the sheriff out of bed. He'll meet us at the Notch."

"You," I said, "not me. Mrs. Slocum has just been kind enough to offer me another drink, and I need it. I'll give the sheriff a statement in the morning. Take the kid along. His name is Musselman and he's in my car, probably sleeping by now.—You should get some good tread-marks where the truck pulled onto the shoulder to turn around."

"Thank you very much for the masterly suggestion." His tone was ironic, but he seemed to be relieved that I wasn't going along. He and the sheriff could putter around the scene of the crime, gather up the remains and drive them back to town. Nothing was going to be done.

"See that the kid has a decent place to sleep, will you? And give him this for me, I owe it to him." I handed him a ten-dollar bill.

"Whatever you say. Goodnight, Mrs. Slocum. I appreciate your co-operation."

"It was a pleasure."

Old lovers, I thought again, playing with double entendres. Knudson went out. My initial liking for him had changed to something quite different. Still, he was a man, and a policeman. He wouldn't push his way to what he wanted over an old lady's dead body. He'd choose a harder way.

Maude Slocum rose and took my empty glass. "Do you really want a drink?"

"A short one, please, with water."

"I think I'll join you."

She poured me two fingers of whisky from the decanter, four fingers for herself. She took it at a gulp.

I sipped at mine. "What I really want is the dope on Kilbourne. I'll take that straight."

"God-damned truthoholic," she said surprisingly. The idea of the whisky had hit her before it had time to work. She sat down beside me heavily and loosely. "I don't know anything about Walter Kilbourne, nothing against him I mean."

"That makes you unique, I guess. Where did you see him tonight?"

"At the Boardwalk restaurant in Quinto. I thought Cathy deserved a change after the dreary day she'd had with the police and—her father. Anyway, I drove her over to Quinto to have dinner, and I saw Walter Kilbourne in the restaurant. He was with a blonde young creature, a really lovely girl."

"His wife. Did you have any conversation with him?"

"No. He didn't recognize me, and I'd never particularly liked him. I did ask the headwaiter what he was doing here. Apparently his yacht is in the harbor."

It was what I needed. Tiredness had drained my body of energy and begun to attack my will. I'd been chinning myself on the present moment, too exhausted to see beyond it. Now I could see myself crossing the pass to Quinto.

But there were more questions to ask. "How did you happen to know him in the first place?"

"He was here a couple of years ago. He made a business arrangement with my mother-in-law, to test for oil on her ranch. This was when they'd made a big strike on the other side of the valley, before they'd touched this side. A crew of men came out with Kilbourne and spent several weeks on our property, drilling holes and setting off explosive charges—I forget the technical name for it."

"Seismographing?"

"Seismographing. They found the oil all right, but nothing came of it. Mother"—her lips moved round the word as if it tasted strange—"Mother decided that oil derricks would obstruct her precious view, and broke off relations with Kilbourne. There was more to it than that, of course: she didn't like the man, and I don't think she trusted him. So we've continued to live in genteel poverty."

"Weren't other companies interested? Oil's getting pretty scarce in this part of the world."

"She didn't really want to lease to anyone. Besides, there was something in the original contract for the exploration; it gave Kilbourne's company first refusal."

"Naturally, it would."

Her erratic hand reached blindly for a cigarette. I took one out of the box, put it between her fingers, lit it for her. She sucked on it uncontrolledly like a child. The whisky had combined with her fatigue and given her nervous system a hard one-two. Her face, her muscles, her voice, were rapidly going to pieces.

So I asked her the question that would hurt, and carefully watched her face for its effect: "You won't be living in genteel poverty much longer, will you? I suppose that you and your husband will be getting in touch with Kilbourne. Or is that why he's up here now?"

"It hadn't occurred to me," she said. "I imagine, though, that that's just what we'll do. I must talk to James about it."

She closed her eyes. From the places where it was pinned to the durable bone, the flesh of her face fell in thin slack folds. The folds made dark lines slanting downward from the corners of her closed eyes, the wings of her nose, the edges of her jaw, deep charcoal shadows cartooning dissolution.

I said goodnight and left her.

CHAPTER 18

There was only one light in the lower part of the house, a shaded wall-lamp in the hall midway between the front door and the kitchen. It cast a brownish glow into the alcove under the stairs where the telephone was. A copy of the Quinto-Nopal Valley telephone directory lay on the low table beside the telephone. I flipped through it to the F's. Only one Franks was listed, a Simeon J. residing at 467 Tanner Terrace. I called his number and listened to half-a-dozen rings at the other end. Then a voice answered, harsh and surly:

"Franks speaking. That the station?"

I had opinions to express, but I kept them to myself.

"Hello," he said, "this is Franks."

I hung up. And heard the soft susurrus of feet descending the stairs above my head, a whispering amplified by the sounding-board of the stairs and my keyed-up senses. A face like a pale moon against a cloud of hair leaned over the banister.

"Who is it?" the girl said.

"Archer." I moved out into the hall where she could see me plainly. "Aren't you in bed yet, Cathy?"

"I daren't close my eyes. I keep seeing Grandma's face." Both of her hands clung to the oaken rail, as if she needed a grip on solid reality. "What are *you* doing?"

"Telephoning. I'm finished now."

"I heard Mr. Knudson telephoning before. Is it true that Pat is dead?"

"Yes. You liked him?"

"Sometimes, when he was nice. He was a lot of fun. He taught me how to dance, but don't tell father. He didn't really kill Grandma, did he?"

"I don't know. I don't think so."

"Neither do I." She glanced furtively down the hall, which was choked with shadows. "Where are the others?"

"Knudson has gone. Your mother's in the sitting-room. I think she's asleep."

She drew her hand back further into the soft folds of her robe. "I'm glad that *he's* gone anyway."

"I have to go now, too. Will you be all right?"

"Yes, I'll be all right." She came down the rest of the way, her forearm sliding on the banister. "I'd better wake mother up and send her to bed."

"Maybe you'd better."

She followed me to the door. "Goodnight, Mr. Archer. I'm sorry I was rude to you last night. I must have felt that something was going to happen. I'm very sensitive, you know, at least that's what people tell me. I'm like a dog that howls at the moon when there's trouble in the air."

"But you didn't see Reavis last night."

"No. I was kind of afraid that he might come—I hate emotional scenes—but he didn't." Her finger described a cross on her silken breast. "Cross my heart and hope to die." She giggled in sudden strained mirth: "What a ghastly thing to say: 'hope to die'."

I said: "Goodnight, Cathy."

Number 467 Tanner Terrace was a white frame bungalow in one of the cheaper suburbs, standing among a dozen houses like it. They all had slanting roofs, useless green shutters on the two front windows, and the rootless temporary air of a row of trailers in a vacant lot. You told them apart by the numbers stenciled on the curb. Also, Sergeant Franks's house contained light. It leaked around the edges of the closed venetian blinds in the front windows and sprinkled the struggling lawn.

I drove on past, U-turned at the first intersection and parked a hundred feet short of the house. Franks was a policeman. In his own territory he could make trouble for me. I wasn't the one I wanted trouble to be made for. I turned off engine and lights, slid down in the seat, dozed off with my consciousness slightly ajar. The sound of a nearing motor woke me a moment before bright headlights swept the street.

They straightened out and came to rest in front of Franks's bungalow. There were three blue taxi-lights above the windshield. A man climbed awkwardly out of the back seat and started up the walk. His gait was a little lopsided; in the dim light I thought he was a cripple. The front door opened before he reached the low concrete stoop. He moved forward into the light, a short thick man in a brown horsehide windbreaker. Its right side bulged, and its right sleeve dangled empty. The front door closed on him.

The taxi turned in a driveway and rolled back to the curb in front of the house. Its lights winked out. I waited for a minute or two and left my car without slamming the door. The taxi-driver was stretched out in his seat, waiting for sleep.

I asked him: "Are you busy?"

He answered me with his eyes half-closed: "Sorry. I'm on a return trip."

"To where?"

"Quinto."

"That's where I'm going."

"Sorry, mister. This is a Quinto cab. I can't take Nopal fares."

"You can if you don't charge me."

"Then what's the percentage?" He sat up straight, and his eyes snapped all the way open. They were blue and bulging in a hollow face. "Listen, what goes on?"

I showed him a ten-dollar bill. "Your percentage," I said.

The bill crackled in my fingers, as if it was taking fire under the intensity of his gaze. "Okay, I guess it's okay, if the other guy don't object." He leaned back to open the door for me.

I got in. "He shouldn't object. Where is he going in Quinto?"

"I don't know, where I picked him up, I guess. Down by the boardwalk."

"Ever see him before?"

It was one question too many. He turned in his seat and looked me over. "You're a cop?"

"It didn't used to show."

"Look'it here, I didn't take your money. I didn't say for sure I would take your money. Matter of fact, I wouldn't touch your money. So how about just getting out and leaving me be. I'm trying to make an honest living, for gosh sakes."

"All right. I'll get out, and you beat it back to Quinto."

"For gosh sakes, have a heart. This is a seven-dollar run."

"Take it out of this." I held out the ten-dollar bill.

He shied from it wall-eyed. "Uh-uh. No thanks."

"Then beat it fast. There's going to be trouble here, and you don't want to wait for it."

Before I got out, I tucked the bill between the cushions and the back of the seat, where taxi-drivers had a habit of looking. The forward motion of the cab closed the door. I went back to my car and waited. The man with the bulky right side and the empty sleeve came out almost immediately. He said good-night to someone and turned toward the street. He was on the sidewalk before he noticed that the cab was gone.

He looked up and down the road, and I slid lower in my seat. His left hand pantomimed disgust in an outward-pushing gesture. His voice announced clearly that he would be fornicated with. I recognized his voice. When he turned to look at the house, the lights were gone. Shrugging lopsidedly, he started to walk in the direction of the highway. I let him walk a block before I started my motor, and pulled even with him as he reached the second corner. My gun was on the seat beside me.

"You want a lift?" I blurred my voice.

"I sure could use one, Jack." He stepped off the curb into the road, within the circle of light from the streetlamp overhead. An oil-stained fedora cast a shadow over his dark broad face, from which the eye-whites gleamed.

"Quinto?"

"This is my lucky—" He recognized me or my car, and the sentence was never finished. His left hand dropped to the leather-flapped pocket of his windbreaker.

I swung the door wide open and waved my gun. His fingers were twisting at the leather button that held the flap over the pocket.

"Get in," I said. "You don't want it to happen to the other arm? I have a passion for symmetry."

He got in. I drove left-handed in low to a dark lacuna between streetlights, and parked at the curb. I shifted the gun to my left hand and held it low to his body. The gun I took from his pocket was a heavy revolver which smelt of fresh oil. I added it to the arsenal in my glove compartment and said: "Well."

The man beside me was breathing like a bull. "You won't get far with this, Archer. Better get back to your hunting-grounds before it happens to you."

I told him I liked it where I was. My right hand found the wallet in his left hip-pocket, flipped it open under the dashlights. His driver's license bore the name Oscar Ferdinand Schmidt.

I said: "Oscar Ferdinand Schmidt is a very euphonious name. It will go well in a murder indictment."

He advised me to commit sodomy. I held my impulse to hurt him. Next to the driver's license, an envelope of transparent celluloid held a small blue card which identified Oscar F. Schmidt as a Special Officer of the Company Police of the Pacific Refining

Company. There were bills in the folding-money compartment, but nothing bigger than a twenty. I tucked the bills in his pocket, and the wallet in mine.

"I want my wallet back," he said, "or I slap a charge on you."

"You're going to be busy fighting one of your own. The sheriff is going to find your wallet in the brush by the Notch Trail."

He was silent for a minute, except that the horsehide jacket creaked like a bellows with his breathing. "The sheriff will give it back to me, without no questions asked. How do you think the sheriff gets elected?"

"I know now, Oscar. But it happens the FBI is interested in lynchings. Do you have an in with the Justice Department, too?"

His husky voice had changed when he answered. It had sick and frightened overtones. "You're crazy if you try to buck us, Archer."

I prodded him hard with the gun, so that he grunted. "You'll sit in the cyanide room before I reserve a bed at Camarillo. Meanwhile I want you to talk. How much did you give Franks for the information, and who gave you the money?"

His brain worked cumbrously. I could almost hear it turn over and stall, turn over slowly again. "You let me go if I tell you?"

"For the present. I couldn't be bothered with you."

"And give me back the wallet?"

"I keep the wallet, and the gun."

"I never fired the gun."

"You never will."

His brain turned over again. He was sweating, and starting to smell. I wanted him out of the car.

"Kilbourne gave me the money," he said finally. "Five C's, I think it was. You're crazy if you buck him."

I said: "Get out of my car."

Where Tanner Terrace met the highway, I turned left back into Nopal Valley, instead of right to Quinto. The case was breaking faster than I had expected, faster than I could handle by myself. From where I sat, it looked as if Kilbourne had sparked a double play that would never be recorded on the sports pages: paid Reavis to dispose of Mrs. Slocum, then paid to have Reavis disposed of before he could talk. I didn't like this theory: it explained the more obvious things, the deaths and the money, and gave no clue to the rest, but it was the best I had to go on. In any case, I couldn't act on it without consulting my client. James Slocum's wife was not above suspicion, but she hadn't called me in to tie a noose around her handsome neck.

It was after closing-time, and the main street was almost deserted. A few late drunks were cruising the sidewalks, unwilling to end the night and face the morning. Some had female companions to assure them that fun was still to be had, that there were still doors in the dark walls that would open on romance for a nominal payment. The women were the kind that seldom appear in daylight and look dead when they do. Two plain-clothes men were trying doors on opposite sides of the street.

Passing Antonio's place, I saw a small light behind the bar, half eclipsed by a man's head. I braked the car and nosed in to the curb. I had ten thousand dollars in my breast pocket, which would be hard to explain if I was shaken down by the cops, harder to survive if anyone else found it on me. I wrapped the torn brown package in a piece of newspaper and tied it with friction tape. I'd talked to Antonio once, and didn't know his last name, but he was the man I trusted in Nopal Valley.

He came to the blinded door when I rapped on the plate glass, opened it four inches on a chain. "Who is it, please?" His face was in the shadow.

I showed him mine.

"I am very sorry, I cannot sell after hours."

"I don't want a drink, I want you to do me a favor."

"What kind of a favor?"

"Keep this in your safe until tomorrow." I pushed one end of the package through the narrow opening.

He looked at it without touching it. "What is in the parcel?"

"Money. A lot of money."

"Who is the owner of the money?"

"I'm trying to find out. Will you keep it?"

"You should take it to the police."

"I don't trust the police."

"Yet you trust me?"

"Apparently."

He took the package from my hands and said: "I will keep it for you. Also, I must apologize for what happened in my bar last night."

I told him to forget it.

CHAPTER 19

The house on the mesa was dark and silent. Nothing stirred, inside or out, but the shrill sighing of the cicadas rising and falling in the empty fields. I knocked on the front door and waited, shivering in my clothes. There was no wind, but the night was cold. The insect cry sounded like wind in autumn trees.

I tried the door. It was locked. I knocked on it again. After a long time a light appeared in the hall, footsteps dragged themselves toward the door. The porch light over my head was switched on, and the door opened, inch by inch. It was Mrs. Strang, the housekeeper, her time-bleached hair in double braids, her eyes puffed and reddened from sleep.

The old eyes peered at me: "Is it Mr. Archer?"

"Yes. I have to see Mrs. Slocum."

Her hands plucked at the collar of her blue rayon wrapper. A pink-flowered flannel nightgown showed beneath it. "Mrs. Slocum is dead," she said with a frown of grief.

"Not Maude Slocum. I saw her less than two hours ago."

"Oh, you mean *young* Mrs. Slocum. She's in bed, I guess. Which is where you should be. This is no hour of the night—"

"I know. I have to see her. Will you wake her for me?"

"I don't know whether I ought to. She'll be displeased."

"I'll wake her myself if you don't."

"Gracious, no." She moved as if to bar the door against me, then changed her mind. "Is it as important as all that?"

"A matter of life and death." I didn't know whose life, or whose death.

"Very well, come in. I'll ask her to come down."

She left me in the sitting-room and shuffled out. The twin braids down her back looked stiff and dry, like flowers pressed in an old forgotten book.

When she returned her face and body were sagging with anxiety. "Her door is locked. She doesn't answer."

I moved toward her, hurried her with me into the hall and along it to the stairs. "Do you have a key?"

"There is no key for that door." She was panting. "It's bolted on the inside."

"Show me."

She toiled up the stairs ahead of me and led me down the upstairs hall to the last door. It was made of heavy oak panels. I set my shoulder against it and failed to move it.

The housekeeper took my place at the door and cried out, "Mrs. Slocum!" on a cracked note of despair.

"You're sure she's in there," I said.

"She must be in there. The door is bolted."

"I'll have to break it down. Do you have a crowbar or a pinchbar? Anything."

"I'll go and see. There are tools in the back kitchen."

I switched off the light in the hall and saw that there was light behind the door. I leaned against it again and listened. No snore, no sound of drunken breathing, no sound of any kind. Maude Slocum was sleeping very soundly.

Mrs. Strang came back, her body moving like a lumpy bundle of terror and compunction. Her veined hands held a short steel bar with one flat end, the kind that is used to open packing cases. I took it from her and inserted the flat end between the door and the frame. Something cracked and gave when I pulled on it. I shifted the bar and pulled hard once again. Wood tore, and the door sprang open.

There was a triple-mirrored dressing-table against the wall to my right, an oversize Hollywood bed, its chenille surface uncrumpled, to my left beside the windows. Maude Slocum lay between them. Her face was dark gray shaded with blue, like a Van Gogh portrait at its maddest. The fine white teeth glaring in rictus between the purple lips gave it a grotesque blackface touch. I kneeled beside her, felt for pulse and heartbeat. She was dead.

I stood up and turned to the housekeeper. She was advancing into the room slowly against great pressure. "Has something happened?" she whimpered, knowing the answer.

"The lady is dead. Call the police, and try to contact Knudson."

"Augh!" She turned away, and the pressure of death drove her scuttling to the door.

Cathy Slocum passed her coming in. I moved to shield the corpse with my body. Something in my face stopped the girl in her tracks. She stood facing me, slim and soft in a white silk nightgown. Her eyes were dark and accusing.

"What is it?" she demanded.

"Your mother is dead. Go back to your room."

All her muscles tightened, drawing her body erect. Her face was a white tragic mask. "I have a right to stay."

"You're getting out of here." I took a step toward her.

She caught a glimpse of the thing that lay behind me. The white mask crumbled like plaster suddenly. She spread one hand across her blind face. "How can she be dead? I—" Grief took her by the throat and choked her into silence.

I laid an arm across her shuddering back, turned

her toward the door, propelled her out. "Look, Cathy, I can't do anything for you. Go and get your father, why don't you?"

She blubbered between sobs: "He won't get out of bed—he says he can't."

"Well, get into bed with him then."

It wasn't the right thing to say, but her reaction shocked me. Both of her small fists exploded against my face and sent me off balance. "How dare you say a dirty thing like that?" She followed it up with every Anglo-Saxon word that every schoolgirl knows.

I retreated into the room where the silent woman lay, and shut the door on Cathy. The heavy iron bolt hung loose and useless in its socket; the screws that held it had been torn out of the moulding, but the latch still worked. It clicked, and I heard the girl's bare feet go down the hall. I went to the windows, which stood in a row of three above the bed. They were steel-framed casements, opening outward above the tiled roof of the veranda, and all of them were open. But there were copper screens inside the glass set in metal frames and fastened firmly with screws. No one could have entered the room or left it after the door was bolted.

I returned to the woman on the floor. A lambswool rug was wadded under one shoulder, as if she had crumpled it up in a convulsion. She had on the same dress I had seen her in, pulled high up on her dingy-colored thighs. I had an impulse to pull it down, to cover the sprawling legs I had admired. My training wouldn't let me. Maude Slocum belonged to strychnine and policemen and black death.

The light in the room came from a double-barreled fluorescent desk-lamp on a writing-table opposite the door. A portable typewriter stood uncovered directly under the lamp, a sheet of plain white paper curling from the roller. There were a few lines of typing on the paper. I stepped around the body to read them.

Dear Heart: I know I am being a coward. There are some things I cannot face, I cannot live with them.

Believe me love it is for the best for all. I have had my share of living anyway.

It is strychnine sulphate I think it is from Olivia Slocum's prescription. I won't be pretty I know but maybe now you know they won't have to cut me up I can feel it I can't write anymore my hands zre

That was all.

A small green medicine bottle stood open by the typewriter, its black metal cap beside it. The label bore a red skull-and-crossbones. It stated that the prescription, ordered by Dr. Sanders for Mrs. Olivia Slocum, had been made up by the Nopal Valley Pharmacy on May 4 of that year, and was to be taken as directed. I looked into the bottle without touching it and saw that it was empty.

There was nothing else on the top of the table, but there was a wide drawer in its front. I pushed a chair out of the way, and using a handkerchief to cover my fingers, pulled the drawer halfway out. It contained some sharpened pencils, a used lipstick, hairpins and paperclips, a scrambled mass of papers. Most of these were receipted bills from shops and doctors. A book from a Nopal Valley bank showed a balance of three hundred and thirty-six dollars and some cents, after a withdrawal of two hundred dollars two days before. Flipping through the papers with the point of a broken pencil, I found one personal letter, typed on a single sheet with a Warner Brothers letterhead.

It started out with a bang:

Hi there Maudie-girl:

It seems like a coon's age (as old massuh used to say before they put him in the cold cold ground and a darned good thing it was too I never liked the old bastid) since I've heard from you. Break out the word-making machine and let down the back hair, girl-friend. How goes the latest campaign against the Slocum clan, and also what about Him? The news from this end is all good. Mr. Big has raised me to one-twenty and last week he told Don Farjeon who told his secretary who told me that I never make a mistake (except in matters of the heart, that is, ha ha, but what am I laughing at?) But the biggest news is guess what and keep it under your hat if you ever wear one. England, my sweet. Mr. Big is making a picture in England starting next month, and he's going to take me along!!! So you better duck out from under the trials and tribs of the vie domestique one of these fine days soon, and we'll have a big lunch at Musso's to celebrate. You know where to get me.

Meantime, my love to Cathy and you know what I think of the rest of the Slocum caboodle. See you soon.

The letter was undated, and was signed "Millie." I looked at the woman on the floor, and wondered if she had ever had that lunch. I also wondered if Mildred Fleming had left for England yet, and how much she knew about "Him." "Him" sounded more like Knudson than the deity. And Knudson would soon be here.

I pulled the drawer out further. A folded newspaper clipping, stuck in the crack between the bottom of the drawer and the back, had slipped down almost out of sight. I pulled it out, unfolded it under the light. It was a long newspaper column headed by a two-column picture of two men. One was Knudson, the other a dark young man in a torn white shirt. "Captor and Escapee," the caption said. "Lieutenant of Detectives Ralph Knudson, of the Chicago police, holds Charles "Cappie" Mariano, convicted slayer of three, who escaped from Joliet Penitentiary last Monday. Lieutenant Knudson tracked him down in Chicago's Skid Row, and took him into custody the following day." The news story gave details of the exploit, and I read it slowly and carefully. The dateline was April 12, but there was no indication of the year. I folded the clipping again, put it back where I found it, and closed the drawer.

The message in the typewriter drew me back. There was something funny about it I couldn't name, something that needed explaining. Without a clear idea of what I was doing, I took the letter Maude

Slocum had given me out of my inside pocket, and spread it out on the table beside the typewriter. "Dear Mr. Slocum." It was like a memory of something I had heard a long time ago, way back before the war. "Lilies that fester smell far worse than weeds." The woman on the floor would fester soon; the letter didn't matter now.

My attention fastened on the first word of the salutation, "Dear;" shifted to the note in the typewriter, "Dear Heart;" came back to the letter on the table. The two "Dears" were identical: the initial D of each was slightly out of line, and the 'a' had a barely perceptible break in the middle of the curve. Though I was no typewriter expert, it looked to me as if Maude Slocum's suicide note and the letter to her husband had been typed on the same machine.

I was trying to make sense of it when heavy footsteps sounded in the hall. The door opened and Knudson came into the room. I stood and watched him like a vivisectionist studying an animal under the knife. But his reaction was a man's. When he saw the darkened face on the floor, his entire body buckled. He almost went down, but caught himself and leaned upright against the door-frame. A uniformed policeman looked over his shoulder into the room. Knudson shut the door on the questioning face.

He turned to me. His bloodless skin was a dirty yellow and his eyes glared. "Maude is dead?" The big voice came out small and furred with pain.

"She's dead. Strychnine takes them fast."

"How do you know it's strychnine?"

"It shows on her. And there's a note in the typewriter. I think it was meant for you."

He looked at the woman on the floor between us, and flinched. "Give me the note." His shoulder stayed against the door-frame. He would not walk over or past her.

I pulled the sheet from the roller and brought it to him.

He read it over and over to himself, his heavy lips

forming the syllables. Sweat came out on his face and gathered in its crevices like tears.

"Why did she want to kill herself?" The effort of speaking wrenched his mouth sideways and left it that way.

"You tell me. You knew her better than I did."

"I loved her. I guess she didn't love me. Not enough."

Grief worked on him like truth serum. He had forgotten that I was there, or who I was. Perhaps he had forgotten who he was.

Slowly he remembered. His forces regrouped themselves around a stony core of ego. I could see hard masculine pride come into his face, straightening the mouth and jaw, masking the hurt eyes. He folded the suicide note with large and gentle fingers, thrust it away in a pocket.

"I just got here," he said. "Nothing was said. You didn't find this paper." He patted the pocket.

"And you are George the Sixth, the King of England. Not ex-Lieutenant Knudson of the Chicago police."

His right hand reached for me, took hold of the front of my coat and tried to shake me. "You'll do as I say."

I struck the hand down. The letter I had been holding tore from my fingers and slid to the floor. He stooped and had it in a single movement. "What's this?"

"The letter I was hired to investigate. It was written on the same typewriter as the suicide note. Think about that. When you've finished thinking about that, think about this. Your boy Franks got paid five hundred for the information that I was on my way here with Reavis. Walter Kilbourne paid him. I can identify the leader of the lynching party as one of Kilbourne's men."

"You talk too much." He read the letter, grunting impatiently, then crushed it into a ball and put it away with the other.

"You're destroying evidence, Knudson."

"I said you talk too much. I'm the judge of what's evidence around here."

"You won't be for long. You can take that as a threat if you want to."

He leaned toward me with his teeth bared. "Who's threatening who? I've had enough from you. Now you can get out of town."

"I'm staying."

He leaned closer. His breath was fetid and hot like a carnivore's. "You're getting out of town tonight, now, and you're not coming back. I can send you up for a long time, Archer. You brought Reavis across a state line under duress. You know what that is in the law."

He had me. I'd tied myself up and handed myself to him. Bitter water squeezed from my eyes and burned on my face.

His right hand moved under his coat, loosening the gun in his shoulder holster. "Are you going, or are you staying to take the rap?"

I didn't answer.

He opened the door and I went out past the policeman in the hall. Times and places went through my head in a red rush. There had to be another time and place for me and Knudson.

CHAPTER 20

Mrs. Strang met me at the foot of the stairs. "Mr. Archer, somebody wants to speak to you on the telephone. A woman. She's been on the line for some time but I didn't like to interrupt when you were talking to the Chief of Police."

"No," I said. "That would be *lèse majesté.*"

She looked at me strangely. "At least I *hope* she's still on the line. She said she'd wait. Are you all right, Mr. Archer?"

"I feel fine." There was a roaring hollowness in my head, a tight sour ball at the bottom of my stomach. My case had been taken away from me just as it started to break. I felt fine.

I said, "This is Archer," into the telephone.

"Well, you needn't bite my head off. Were you sleeping?" The voice was sweet and lingering, like a fragrance: Mavis Kilbourne in a melting mood.

"Yeah, I was having nightmares. About a fancy broad who turned out to be a pickpocket whose surname was Trouble."

She laughed: a mountain stream just below the snowline. "I'm not really a pickpocket, or even a broad. After all, I took what was mine. You're not in a very pleasant mood, are you?"

"Improve it for me if you can. Tell me how you knew I was here."

"I didn't. I called your house and office in Los Angeles. Your answering service gave me the number. I don't even know where you are, except that it's Nopal Valley. I'm in Quinto."

The operator cut in and asked for another ten cents please. The bell on the pay telephone sounded clearly over the line.

"I'm running out of dimes," Mavis said. "Will you come to Quinto and talk to me?"

"Why the sudden interest at three in the morning? There's nothing in my pocket but a gun."

"It's three-thirty." Her yawn rustled in the mouthpiece. "I'm dead."

"You're not the only one."

"Anyway, I'm glad you have a gun. You may need it."

"For what?"

"I can't tell you over the phone. I need you to do something for me. Will you accept me as a client?" The siren note again, like distant violins at a fine feast.

"I already have a client," I lied.

"Couldn't you work for both of us? I'm not proud."

"I am."

She lowered her voice. "I know it was a dirty trick to play on you. I had to do it, though. I burned the film, and it didn't explode like you said."

"Forget that. The trouble is that this could be another dirty trick."

"It isn't. I really need you. I may not sound afraid, but I actually am."

"Of what?"

"I said I can't tell you. Come to Quinto and I will. *Please* come." We were talking in circles.

"Where are you in Quinto?"

"In a lunchroom by the beach, but I better not meet you here. You know the big pier by the yacht basin?"

"Yeah," I said. "A perfect setup for an ambush."

"Don't be like that. I'll be out at the end of the pier. There's nobody there at this time of night. Will you come?"

"Give me half an hour."

Quinto was any small seaport at four o'clock in the morning. Dark and empty streets slanted down to the dark and empty ocean. The air was fairly clear but droplets of water formed on my windshield and a sea smell, bitter and fresh, invaded the unpeopled town. At night it was an outpost of the sea, filled by cold tidal winds and shifting submarine blackness.

The reflection of a stop-light made a long red smudge on the asphalt where 101 Alternate crossed the foot of the town. Four or five heavy trucks had gathered at the truckstop on the corner like buffalo at a waterhole. As I turned right onto the freeway, I could see the drivers bent over early breakfast, and a thin-browed, pug-faced waitress smoking a cigarette by the kitchen door. It would have been very pleasant to stop and eat three eggs and talk a while and then go back to bed in the motel. I cut my wheels sharp left at the next crossing, and the tires whined in self-pity: so late, so weary. I said aloud, to myself and the whining tires: "Get it over with."

The Quinto pier was a continuation of the street, carrying the blacktop road two hundred yards beyond the concrete sea wall. Below the pier the long white surges mumbled the sand, lapped at the ancient pilings that supported it, in a work of slow sure destruction. My brights lit up the white railings along the sides. They were bare from end to end, and the road was naked between them. Toward the outer end a group of small buildings huddled against the night: a bait-and-tackle booth, a hot-dog stand, a seashell-souvenir store, a ship's carpenter shop, all closed and lightless. I parked on their landward side, by a ten-cent public telescope, and walked on. The polished wooden butt of my automatic was wet-cold in my palm.

The smell of the sea, of kelp and fish and bitter moving water, rose stronger in my nostrils. It flooded my consciousness like an ancestral memory. The swells rose sluggishly and fell away, casting up dismal gleams between the boards of the pier. And the whole pier rose and fell in stiff and creaking mimicry, dancing its long slow dance of dissolution. I reached the end and saw no one, heard nothing but my footsteps and the creak of the beams, the slap of waves on the pilings. It was a fifteen-foot drop to the dim water. The nearest land ahead of me was Hawaii.

I turned my back on Hawaii and started for shore. Mavis had changed her mind and stood me up. A final goodbye to Mavis, my cold brain chattered; she was unaccountable no-account not-to-be-counted-on. Or had her mind been changed for her. My feet dragged on the planking. Too late, too old, too tired, the deep surge at the back of my mind was sighing.

False dawn was spreading like spilt milk in the sky above the mountains. At their foot the streets of Quinto lay like an unseen cobweb beaded with lights. The highballing trucks from San Francisco and Portland and Seattle went south on 101 like shooting stars. To my right the long arc of the breakwater curved toward the pier. A light on a tower at its end flashed on and off, stroking the narrow channel with intermittent stripes of grayish green. Forty or fifty vessels, of high and low degree, lay in the sheltered basin behind the breakwater. There were swans and ugly ducklings, arrowy racing sloops and broad-beamed Monterey fishing-boats, cabin cruisers and flatties, Star-boats and dinghies. One or two of the fishing-boats showed early-morning lights.

Another light went on as I watched, bringing a triple window into sharp yellow contrast with a low dark cabin. The long hull below it had lines of movement even though it was anchored and dead in the water. It was painted so white that it seemed to shine with its own luminescence. From a quarter mile away it looked like a small neat cruiser. But comparing it with the other boats I guessed it was seventy feet long: except for the purse-seiners, the biggest boat in the harbor. Kilbourne would choose that kind of coracle to ride in.

The light went out, as if by telepathy. I strained my eyes, trying to guess what went on behind the three oblong windows that I could no longer see. A hand from nowhere plucked at my trousers leg. I stepped out of reach, jerked my gun out, snapped a cartridge into the chamber. The wind whistled in my throat.

A head appeared above the planking at the edge of the pier. Light hair frothed out from under a beret. A light voice whispered: "It's me."

"Don't play hiding-games." I snarled, because she'd unnerved me. "A forty-five slug would play hell with your constitution."

She stood up and showed herself, a dark slim shape in sweater and slacks against the dark gray water. With racing lines for a long fast voyage by night, and a sweet full spinnaker bosom. "I like my constitution the way it is." She half-turned into another pose, held it like a model. "Don't you, Archer?"

"You'll get by," I said, and lied in my teeth: "You fascinate me as a source of income solely."

"Very well, sir. We'd better go below. We'll be seen up here." She held out her hand for mine. It was as cold as a fish.

She was standing on a railed gangway which slanted down to the water below the pier. We descended to a floating platform at the edge of the forest of pilings. A little plywood boat was tied to a rusty iron ring at the edge of the platform. Boat and platform rose and fell together with the waves.

"Whose boat?"

"It's a tender from the yacht. I came ashore in it."

"Why?"

"The water-taxis make so much commotion, and besides they'd know where I went."

"I see. Now I know everything."

"Please don't be nasty, Archer. What's your first name, anyway?"

"Lew. You can call me Archer."

"I'm sorry if I frightened you, Lew," in that small, contrite, aphrodisiac voice. "I didn't really mean to. I had to be sure it was you."

"Who else were you expecting?"

"Well. It might have been Melliotes."

"Who in hell," I said, "is Melliotes? Or did you invent the name?"

"If you think Melliotes is a figment, come out to the boat and meet him."

"Is that the family boat?" I pointed to the long white hull on the other side of the basin.

"It is." She thumbed her nose at it. "Some family. Take my husband's dear good friend Melliotes, for example. Last night my dear good husband held me down in my bunk while dear good Dr. Melliotes gave me a shot of morphine to put me to sleep."

I offered her a cigarette, which she took automatically. Lighting it for her, I looked into her eyes. The dark gray pupils were as tiny as a bird's.

"You see," she said, "I'm no liar. Feel my heart." Her hand pressed mine against her ribs below the left breast. There was a pounding in the tips of my fingers, but it was my own heart I felt. "You see?"

"Why aren't you still asleep?"

"I didn't go to sleep. Morphine just stimulates me, I'm like a cat. I feel the hangover now, though. I think I'd better sit down." Still with her hand on my wrist, she sat on the foot of the gangway and drew me down beside her. "I could show you the mark of the needle but that wouldn't be ladylike, would it?"

"Always the lady," I said. "Who are you, Mavis?"

She yawned and stretched herself. I didn't look at her, and she subsided. "A working girl. Used to be, anyway. I wish I still was. Only I was going to tell you about Dr. Melliotes. He was driving the car when Rico brought you home."

I remembered the man I had fought with in Reavis's shack. "He didn't look like a medical man to me."

"He calls himself a doctor, but Folsom's his alma mater if he has one. He's some kind of hydrotherapist, and he runs a sanitarium in Venice. Walter has a spastic colon and he's been going to Melliotes for years. He even brings him along on cruises, which is very convenient when he wants me put to sleep. I fooled them tonight, though. I didn't go to sleep, and I heard what went on.

"I heard my husband conspiring to murder a man. Pat Ryan, the man you asked me about. Walter gave orders to a man called Schmidt to have Pat Ryan killed. A couple of hours later Schmidt came aboard again and said that it was done." She peered into my face. "Doesn't that mean anything to you at all?"

"Plenty. Did anybody say why Reavis had to be shot?"

"Nobody said why, but I know why." She tilted her head toward me, her soft lower lip protruding. "You haven't promised me you'd go to work for me."

"You haven't told me what you want done. I'm not a hired gun like Schmidt."

"I only want justice done. I want you to pin Pat's murder on Schmidt, and on my husband."

"You'll have to tell me why."

"I'll tell you everything if it will help. I want my husband dead or put away, and I haven't nerve enough to do it myself."

"I'm afraid he's too big for me to take alone, but we might get at him through Schmidt. One thing I don't understand, how Kilbourne got you buffaloed. You're frightened to death of him."

"I was. Not any more. I wouldn't be here if I was frightened, would I?" But her voice was light and tinny, and she glanced towards the yacht across the water. A Monterey seiner moved in a semi-circle and nosed towards the channel. Thin shreds of light like metal foil were falling on the water and dissolving.

"Give me the straight story, Mavis. We don't have time to argue."

"Yes. The straight story." Her mouth closed over the words. Her face and body were tense, fighting off sleep. "I feel like a junkie, Archer. The morphine's getting me."

"Let's walk."

"No. We'll stay here. I have to get back to the boat soon. They don't know I'm gone."

I remembered the light that had gone on and off, and wondered.

But she had begun to talk in a steady flow of words, like a pentothal subject:

"I'm partly to blame for what happened. I did a sluttish thing, I suppose, and anyway I wasn't naïve when I married him. I'd been living on the fringes for too long, taking what I could get, waiting on tables, doing extra work and trying for a bit part. I met him at a party in Bel-Air last year. I was doing some modeling at the time, and I was paid to be at the party, but Kilbourne didn't know that, at least I don't think he did. Anyway, he took to me, and he was loaded with money, and I had lost my nerve, and I took to him. He wanted a hostess and a clothes-horse and a bed-companion and he bought me the way he'd buy a filly for his stable. We did the town for ten nights running and married in Palm Springs. We found out over the weekend that we didn't like each other at all. I asked him why he married me and he said that it was cheaper in the end. So I tortured his vanity: Kilbourne's colossally vain. I'd have let him alone if I'd known how nasty he could get.

"I found out later. In the meantime I had new toys to play with and no real kick coming. Then Patrick Ryan turned up last winter. He'd dated me during the war a couple of times, and I liked the guy. I met him at Ciro's one night. We ditched Kilbourne and I went home with Ryan. His place was horribly crummy, but he was good. He reminded me that even sex could be good, and I guess I fell in love with him in an unguarded moment." Her voice was breathless and dry. Her shoulder moved against me restlessly. "You asked for the straight story. It doesn't make me look nice."

"Nobody's straight story ever does. Go on."

"Yes." She leaned against me lightly, and I held her across the shoulders. Her bones were small and sharp in the rounded flesh. "We needed a chauffeur at the time; our old one had been picked up for violating parole. Kilbourne has a weakness for ex-convicts: he says they make faithful servants. I talked him into hiring Pat Ryan so I could have him around. I needed someone, and Pat said he loved me. We were going to run away together and start a new life somewhere. I guess where men are concerned I'm a lousy picker. I haven't told you about the pre-Kilbourne ones, and I don't intend to. Anyway, Kilbourne found out about us. Pat may have told him himself, to curry a little favor. So Kilbourne got me drunk one day and left me alone with Pat and hired a man to take pictures of us together. They were very pretty pictures. He ran them for me the next night, with running commentary, and I haven't got over it yet. I never will."

"But the pictures are gone now?"

"Yes. I destroyed them last night."

"He doesn't need the film to get a divorce."

"You don't understand," she said. "Divorce is not what he wants. I've begged him for a divorce every day for the last six months. He wanted to keep me under his fat thumb for the rest of his life, and that was his way of doing it. If I stepped out of line just once, he was going to let Rico sell the film for distribution. They'd be showing it for years at stag parties and conventions and after-hours nightclubs. My face is known. What could I do?"

"What you did. Does he know the film is gone?"

"I haven't told him. I don't know how he'll react. He could do anything."

"Then leave him. He can't touch you any more, if you're sure there was only one copy."

"There was only one copy. I made up to Rico one night and got that much out of him. But I'm afraid of Kilbourne." She didn't notice the contradiction: her feeling was too real.

"It's a bad habit you have."

"You don't know Kilbourne," she flared. "There's nothing he won't do, and he has the money and men to do it. He killed Pat last night—"

"Not over you, Mavis, though that might have helped. Maybe Kilbourne couldn't forget the pictures, either, but he had more reasons than that. Pat was working for Kilbourne, did you know that? Taking his money up to the day he died."

"No!"

"You still cared for Pat?"

"Not after he ran out on me. But he didn't deserve to die."

"Neither do you. You married one wrong one, and went to bed with another. Why don't you take yourself out of circulation for a while?"

"Stay with you?" She half-turned toward me and her right breast trembled against my arm.

"That's not what I mean. You wouldn't be safe with me. I have some friends in Mexico who are safe, and I'll put you on a plane."

"I don't know. I don't know what to do." Her voice wandered in the scale. Her skin in the growing light was blanched by fatigue. Her eyes moved uncertainly, huge and heavy and dark, with morphine dragging down hard on the lids.

She couldn't make a decision. I made it for her, hoisting her to her feet with my hands in her armpits. "You're going to Mexico. I'll stay at the airport with you till you can get a plane."

"You're nice, you're good to me." She lolled against me, clutching at my arms and sliding down my chest.

The first explosions of a choked motor barked and spluttered on the other side of the basin. The spluttering settled into a steady roar, and a speedboat rounded the stern of the yacht and headed for the pier. Its dark sharp prow cut like shears through the metal water. A man in the cockpit was watching me through binoculars. They made him look like a large goggle-eyed toad.

Mavis hung limp across my arm. I jerked her upright and shook her. "Mavis! We have to run for it." Her eyes came partly open, but showed only white.

I lifted her in both arms and took her up the gangway. A man in a striped linen suit and a washable linen hat was squatting on the pier near the top of the gangway. It was Melliotes. He straightened up, moved quickly to bar my way. He was built like a grand piano, low and wide, but his movements were light as a dancer's. Black eyes peered brightly from the gargoyle face.

I said: "Get out of my way."

"I don't think so. You turn around and go back down."

The girl in my arms sighed and stirred at the sound of his voice. I hated her as a man sometimes hates his wife, or a con his handcuffs. It was too late to run. The man in the linen suit had his right fist in his pocket, with something more than a fist pointed at me.

"Back down," he said.

The motor of the speedboat died behind me. I looked down and saw it coasting in to the landing platform. A blank-faced sailor turned from the wheel and jumped ashore with the painter. Kilbourne sat in the cockpit, looking complacent. A pair of binoculars hung on a strap around his thick neck, and a double-barreled shotgun lay across his knees.

I carried Mavis Kilbourne down to her waiting husband.

CHAPTER 21

The yacht's main cabin was dim and chilly. The early-morning light oozed weakly through the curtained ports and lay in glimmering pools on the built-in mahogany furniture. One bulkhead was almost covered by a photomural of the Acapulco cliffs, the Kilbourne yacht riding below them. Our feet were soundless as undertakers' on the thickly carpeted floor. Kilbourne went to the head of the table that occupied the center of the cabin, and sat down facing me.

"Sit down, Mr. Archer, sit down. Let me offer you some breakfast." He tried a genial smile, but the mouth and eyes were too small to carry it. The voice that issued from the great pink face was little and peevish and worried.

"I'd have to be hungrier than I am," I said.

"Well, if you'll excuse me, I'll have a bite myself." He glanced at the man in the linen suit, who was leaning against the hatch with a gun in his hand. "Melliotes, tell the steward I'll have breakfast. And let's have some light on the subject. I haven't had a good chance to look at our friend's face."

Melliotes switched on an overhead light, then leaned out through the hatch to talk to someone at the head of the ladder. I thought of making a break, and my knees tensed with the thought. But without a gun it was hopeless. And Mavis was lying unconscious in a berth just forward of the cabin. I couldn't run out on her: I hadn't been able to when I had a better chance. Anyway, this was where I wanted to be. Kilbourne was the man I had to talk to. I said it over to myself: this was where I wanted to be. If I said it often enough, maybe I could believe it.

There was a sharp thud at the other end of the table. Kilbourne had drawn my gun and placed it on the polished mahogany surface within reach of his hand. Tiny fingernails glistened like slivers of mica in the tips of his thick white fingers.

"You'll pardon this show of weapons, I hope. I'm very much a pacifist myself, but I understand you're quite the man of violence. I do hope you won't force us to use these ridiculous guns. Physical violence has always unsettled my stomach."

"You're lucky," I said. "Not everybody can afford to have his killings done for him."

Melliotes turned sharply and looked at me three-eyed. His own two eyes were dark and glowing. I preferred the gun's single eye. I couldn't stare it down, but it bore no malice.

"Please, Mr. Archer." Kilbourne raised his hand, dead white as a policeman's in a policeman's gesture. "You mustn't leap to rash conclusions before you know the truth of things. The truth is simpler than you suppose and really not at all sinister. I've had to take one or two extra-legal shortcuts, I admit, in order to protect my interests. If a man won't act to protect his own interests, he can't expect anyone else to. That's one of the home truths I learned when I was a two-for-a-quarter car salesman in Ypsilanti. I came up from small beginnings, you see. I don't propose to return to them."

"Your reminiscences fascinate me. May I take notes?"

"Please," he said again. "We share a mutual distrust, of course, but there's nothing more than distrust standing between us. If we could be perfectly frank with each other—"

"I'll be frank with you. It looks to me as if you hired Reavis to kill the elder Mrs. Slocum, then hired somebody else to kill off Reavis. If that's so, I'm not going to let you get by with it."

"The decision is out of your hands, isn't it?"

I noticed that the table, which was fastened to the deck, was trembling slightly under my forearms. Somewhere aft, the diesels were turning over. Forward, a rattling winch was reeling in the anchor. The screw turned in the water, and the whole craft shuddered.

"After murder," I said, "kidnapping comes easy." But I remembered what I had done to Reavis, and felt a twinge of hypocrisy. Remorse and fear mixed in my veins, and made a bitter blend.

"The correct term is 'shanghaied,'" Kilbourne said, with his first real smile. It was a close-mouthed smile of complacence. Like other self-educated men, he was vain of his vocabulary. "But let's get back to your allegations. You are less than half right. I had nothing whatever to do with the old lady's death. Ryan conceived the plan by himself, and executed it unaided."

"He was in your pay, and you stood to profit by her death."

"Precisely." His fingers clasped each other like mating worms. "You do understand the situation after all. Innocent as I was, I couldn't afford to have Ryan caught and questioned. I gave him money to escape. To that extent I confess I was an accessory to the crime. If Ryan had been brought to trial, I'd have been dragged in willy-nilly."

"So you had to have him silenced."

"Before the District Attorney could take a statement from him. Precisely. You see, in an atmosphere of candor, we *can* have a meeting of minds."

"There's one place we haven't met at all. You haven't explained the important thing: why Reavis wanted to kill her. What was he doing in Nopal Valley in the first place?"

"Let me sketch in the background." He leaned across the table with his hands still clasped in each other. I couldn't understand his eagerness to explain, but while it lasted I could use the explanations. "Ryan had been in my employ less than a year. He was my chauffeur, as a matter of fact, and did one or two other small tasks for me." The shrewd little eyes went blank and imbecile for a moment, as they surveyed the past and Ryan's part in it. In the alcove out of sight, his wife was snoring gently and rhythmically.

A fine American marriage, I said to myself. There wasn't much doubt that Kilbourne himself had hired Pat to make love to his wife.

"Early this year," he continued, "it became inconvenient, for various reasons, to have Ryan as a member of my household. Still, I didn't want to lose touch with him entirely. I have enemies, of course, and Ryan might have become their willing tool. I put him on the company payroll and cast about for a place to use him. As you probably know, I'd had business dealings with the late Mrs. Slocum. You may not know, however, that before the deal broke down I spent nearly a hundred thousand dollars in the exploration of her property. It occurred to me that it might be desirable to have a representative in her home as a partial protection for my investment. If other groups that are interested in the valley made overtures to her, I'd be in a position to know. So I arranged for Ryan's employment by the Slocums as their chauffeur. I had no idea he'd take his responsibilities so very seriously." He raised both hands and smacked them flat on the table. Beneath the sleeves of his blue flannel jacket, the flesh on his forearms quivered for some time.

"Are you sure you had no idea?" I said. "You must have known he was a psychopath, capable of anything."

"No, I did not. I believed him to be harmless." His voice was earnest. "Now don't misunderstand me. I'm not pretending to be free from blame. In a moral sense I know I'm responsible for her death. There may even have been an occasion when, thinking out loud in Ryan's presence, I voiced a wish for her death. I believe there was an occasion of that sort a few weeks ago. In any case, Ryan knew that her continued presence on the scene was costing me hundreds of dollars a day."

"Why split hairs? He was working for you. You wanted her killed. He killed her."

"But I did not incite him to murder. Never, at any time. If I were planning a murder, Ryan is the last man I'd choose as my agent. He was a talker, and I didn't trust him."

That made sense to me. His whole story made sense, in a crazy way. Against my will and my better judgment, I caught myself half believing it.

"If you didn't tell him to kill her, why did he do it?"

"I'll tell you why." He leaned toward me again and narrowed his eyes. The upper eyelids hung in thick overlapping folds. The eyes themselves were of indeterminate color, dull and opaque as unpolished stones. "Ryan saw an opportunity to tap me for a very great deal of money. What seemed to him, at least, a very great deal. By killing Mrs. Slocum he placed me in jeopardy along with himself. His jeopardy was also mine. I had to help him out of it, and he knew it. Now he didn't admit as much when he came to me the night before last, but that certainly was in his mind. He asked for ten thousand dollars, and I had to give it to him. When he was careless enough to allow himself to be captured, I had to take other measures. I'd have been wiser to have him shot in the first place, but my humane impulses deterred me. In the end my hand was forced. So while I can't claim that my motives in this sorry business were wholly pure, neither have they been entirely black."

"Sometimes," I said, "I like a good solid black better than mottled gray."

"You don't have my responsibilities, Mr. Archer. A great company depends on me. A single misstep on my part can destroy the livelihood of thousands of people."

"I wonder if you're that important," I said. "I think life would go on without you."

"That isn't the point at issue." He smiled as if he'd uttered a witticism. "The point is whether life can go on without *you*. I've gone to a good deal of trouble to explain my position. I've hoped that if you understood it, you'd take a somewhat different attitude toward me. You're an intelligent man, Mr. Archer, and, to be frank, I like you. Also, I abhor killing, as I've told you. There's the further fact that my wife seems to admire you, and if I were to have you put away she'd certainly be aware of it and perhaps even try to make trouble. I can deal with her, of course. I can even endure the thought of another death, if you prove its necessity to me. But I'd so much rather handle this thing in a rational, urbane way. Wouldn't you?"

"I'll listen. How much?"

"Good. Fine." The little mouth curled upwards like a cherub's. "I believe you have ten thousand dollars of mine. I don't know for sure, but it stands to reason, doesn't it? If you were to admit that you have it, it would be very valuable proof of your good faith."

"I have it," I said, "out of your reach."

"Keep it. It's yours." He waved his hand in a fat and royal gesture.

"What do I do for it?"

"Nothing. Nothing whatever. I'll put you ashore at San Pedro and you can simply forget that I ever existed at all. Take up your own affairs again, or go for a long vacation and enjoy yourself."

"I have the money now."

"But not the means to enjoy it. That is still in my gift."

The yacht was beginning to pitch and roll in the open sea. I glanced at the man in the linen suit, still stationed by the door with his three eyes on me. His legs were wide and braced against the vessel's movement. The gun was steady. While my glance was on it, he shifted it from one hand to the other.

"You can relax, Melliotes," Kilbourne said. "We're well away from shore." He turned back to me: "Well, Mr. Archer, will you accept the gift of freedom on those terms?"

"I'll think about it."

"I have no wish to hurry you. Your decision is an important one, to both of us." Then his face lit up like a man's who has heard his sweetheart's footsteps: "My breakfast, I do believe."

It came on a silver tray that was almost too wide for the hatchway. The white-jacketed mulatto steward was sweating under its weight. Kilbourne greeted each dish separately as the metal covers were lifted. Next to Walter Kilbourne, food was his one true love.

He ate with a gobbling passion. A piece of ham and four eggs, six pieces of toast; a kidney and a pair of mountain trout; eight pancakes with eight small sausages; a quart of raspberries, a pint of cream, a quart of coffee. I watched him the way you watch the animals at the zoo, hoping he'd choke to death and settle things for both of us.

He leaned back in his chair at last and told the steward to take the empty dishes away.

"Well, Mr. Archer?" The white fingers crawled through his thin pink curls. "What is your decision?"

"I haven't thought it through yet. One thing, how do you know you can trust me?"

"I don't know that I can. Rather than have your blood on my hands, I'm willing to take a certain amount of risk. But I do think I can recognize an honest man when I see one. That ability is the foundation of my success, to be perfectly frank." His voice was still thick with the passion of eating.

"There's a contradiction in your thinking," I said. "If I took your dirty money, you wouldn't be able to trust my honesty."

"But you have my dirty money now, Mr. Archer. You secured it through your own alert efforts. No further effort on your part is required, except that I presume you'll scour it thoroughly before you spend it. Of course I realize how foolish I would be to place my whole dependence on your honesty, or any man's. I'd naturally expect you to sign a receipt for it, indicating the nature of the services rendered."

"Which were?"

"Exactly what you did. A simple notation, 'For capture and delivery of Pat Ryan,' will suffice. That will kill two birds with one stone. It will cancel out my payment to Ryan, which is the only real evidence against me in Mrs. Slocum's death. And more important, it will protect me in case your honesty should ever falter, and the murder of Pat Ryan come to trial."

"I'll be an accessory before the fact."

"A very active one. Precisely. You and I will be in the position of having to co-operate with each other."

I caught the implication. I watched it grow in my mind into a picture of myself five years, ten years later, doing dirty errands for Walter Kilbourne and not being able to say no. My gorge rose.

But I answered him very reasonably: "I can't stick my neck out that far. There were half a dozen men involved in Ryan's death. If any of them talks, that tears it open."

"Not at all. Only one of them had any connection with me."

"Schmidt."

The eyebrows ascended his forehead like surprised pink caterpillars. "You know Schmidt? You are active indeed."

"I know him well enough to stay clear of his company. If the police put a finger on him, and they will, he'll break down and spill everything."

"I am aware of that." The cherub mouth smiled soothingly. "Fortunately, you can set your mind at rest. Oscar Schmidt went out with the tide this morning. Melliotes took care of him for all of us."

The man in the linen suit was sitting on the leather bench that lined the after bulkhead. He showed his teeth in a white and happy smile and stroked the fluted barrel of his gun.

"Remarkable," I said. "Ryan takes care of Mrs. Slocum. Schmidt takes care of Ryan. Melliotes takes care of Schmidt. That's quite a system you have."

"I'm very pleased that you like it."

"But who takes care of Melliotes?"

Kilbourne looked from me to the gunman, whose mouth was expressionless again, and back to me. For the first time our interests formed a triangle, which relieved me of some pressure.

"You ask very searching questions," he replied. "I owe it to your intelligence to inform you that Melliotes took care of himself several years ago. A young girl of my acquaintance, one of my employees to be exact, disappeared in Detroit. Her body turned up in the Detroit River a few days later. A certain unlicensed medical practitioner who shall be nameless was wanted for questioning. I was on my way to California at the time, and I offered him a lift in my private plane. Does that answer your question?"

"It does. I wanted to know exactly what I was being offered a piece of. Now that I know, I don't want it."

He looked at me incredulously. "You don't seriously mean that you want to die?"

"I expect to outlive you," I said. "You're a little too smart to have me bumped before you recover your thousand-dollar bills. That money really worries you, doesn't it?"

"The money means nothing to me. Look, Mr. Archer, I am prepared to double the amount." He brought a gold-cornered wallet out of an inside pocket and dealt ten bills onto the table. "But twenty thousand is my absolute limit."

"Put your money away. I don't want it."

"I warn you," he said more sharply, "your bargaining position is weak. One reaches a point of diminishing returns, where it would be cheaper and more convenient to have you killed."

I looked at Melliotes. His glowing eyes were on

Kilbourne. He hefted the gun in his hand, and asked a question with his knitted black eyebrows.

"No," Kilbourne said to him. "What is it that you want, if not money, Mr. Archer? Women perhaps, or power, or security? I could find a place in my organization for a man that I can trust. I wouldn't waste my words on you, frankly, if I didn't happen to like you."

"You can't trust me," I said, though the fear of death had dried my lips and tightened the muscles of my throat.

"That's precisely what I like about you. You have a certain stubborn honesty—"

"I don't like you," I said. Or maybe I croaked it.

Kilbourne's face was expressionless, but his white fingers plucked petulantly at each other. "Melliotes. We'll give Mr. Archer a little longer to make up his mind. Do you have your pacifier?"

The man in the linen suit stood up in eager haste. His brown hand flicked into a pocket and came out dangling a polished leather thing like an elongated pear. It moved in the air too fast for me to avoid it.

CHAPTER 22

I was walking in the gravel bed of a dry river. Gravel-voiced parrots cawed and flew in the stiff painted air. A girl went by me on silent feet, her golden hair blown out behind by her movement. I stumbled after her on my knees and she looked back and laughed. She had Mavis's face, but her laugh cawed like the parrots. She entered a dark cave in the bank of the dry river. I followed her gleaming hair into the darkness.

When she turned for a second laughing look, her face was Gretchen Keck's, and her mouth was stained with blood. We were in a hotel corridor as interminable as time. Little puffs of dust rose from her feet as she moved. The dust stank of death in my nostrils.

I picked my way after her through the debris that littered the threadbare carpet. Old photographs and newspaper clippings and black-edged funeral announcements, used condoms and love letters tied with pink ribbon, ashes and cigarette butts brown and white, empty whisky bottles, dried sickness and dried blood, cold half-eaten meals on greasy plates. Behind the numbered doors there were shrieks and groans and giggles, and howls of ecstasy and howls of pain. I looked straight ahead, hoping none of the doors would open.

The girl paused at the final door and turned again: it was Cathy Slocum, beckoning me. I followed her into the jasmine-scented room. The woman lay on the bed under a black police tarp. I drew it back from her face and saw the foam.

Someone fumbled at the door behind me. I crossed the room to the casement window and flung it open. The doorlatch clicked. I looked back over my shoulder at the charred featureless face. I said I didn't do it. The calcined man walked towards me, his footsteps soft as ashes. I leaned far out of the window and looked down: far down in the street, the cars marched in antlike procession. I let myself go, fell into wakefulness.

The blood was pounding in my brain like heavy surf on a deserted beach. I was lying on my back on something neither hard nor soft. I raised my head, and a lightning flash of pain blazed in my eyeballs. I tried to move my hands; they wouldn't move. My fingers were in contact with something coarse and damp and insentient. I lay still for a while, hoping the coarse numb surface wasn't my own skin. Cold sweat tickled the sides of my face.

There was yellow light in the room, which came from a high wire-netted window in the canvas-covered wall. I looked down at my immobilized arms and saw that they were bound in a brown canvas straitjacket. My legs were free; not even trousers covered them, but I still had my shoes on. I drew them up and rocked myself to a sitting position on the edge of the cot. A bolt snapped back, and I stood up facing the leather-padded door as it swung open.

Melliotes came into the room. A tiny gray-haired woman loitered behind him. He was wearing white duck trousers and a white Mediterranean smile. Black curling hair like persian lamb covered his naked torso from collarbone to navel. The insteps of his bare feet had a growth of thick black fur.

"Well, well. Good morning again. I hope you enjoyed your rest." His grimace parodied the genial host.

"Your accommodations are lousy. Take this off." I

was ashamed of my voice, which came out thin and dry.

"It wouldn't be very modest to take it off." He looked down at the little woman. "He should have *something* on in the presence of ladies. Isn't that right, Miss Macon?"

She wore a white nurse's uniform. The top of her gray cropped head came just above his waist. Her owlish eyes smiled up into his glowing black ones, and she giggled.

I aimed my head at the hairy abdomen, and rushed him. His feet skipped lightly aside like a matador's. His knee caught the side of my head and caromed me against the padded wall. I sat down on the floor and got up again. The little woman giggled:

"He's violent, doctor. Acts like a mental all right, don't he?"

"We know how to deal with him, Miss Macon." To me he said: "We know how to deal with you."

I said: "Take this off." When I closed my mouth, my back teeth ground together of their own accord.

"I don't see how I can. You're in a disturbed condition. It's my responsibility to keep you out of mischief for a while, until you grow calmer."

She leaned against his thigh, twisting her miniature hand in his canvas belt and looking up admiringly at the source of such fine talk.

"I've killed one man," I said. "I think you'll be the second."

"Listen to him," she simpered. "He's homicidal all right."

"I'll tell you what I think," Melliotes said. "I think a hydro treatment would do him a world of good. Shall we give him one, Miss Macon?"

"Let's."

"We'll give you a hydro treatment," he said between the smile.

I stood where I was, my back against the wall.

He took a bunch of keys from the keyhole and struck me with them sharply across the face.

"You'll be the second," I said.

He swung the keys again. I lost the beat of time in their harsh jangling. The lightning blazed ferociously in my head. A drop of blood crawled down my face, leaving a wet snail track.

"Come along," he said, "while you can see to come along."

I went along. To a room like a burial vault, white-tiled, windowless and cold. The morning light fell through a skylight in the twelve-foot ceiling and gleamed on a row of chromium faucets and nozzles along one wall. He held me by the shoulders while the woman unbuckled the straps across my back. I tried to bite his hands. He jangled the keys.

He pulled the jacket off me and tossed it to the woman. She caught it, rolled it up and stood against the door with the bundle clasped in her arms. There was a gleeful little waiting smile on her face, the smile of a baby that had not been born.

I looked down at my arms. White and shrunken, they were unbending slowly like snakes in the early spring. A ram of water hit me, flung me onto the tiled floor and rolled me against the wall. I sat up gasping. Above the roar of the water, the woman let out a laugh of childish pleasure.

Melliotes was leaning easily against the opposite wall. Waterdrops glistened like dew in his personal thicket. One of his hands held a nozzle attached to a white rubber hose. The other rested on a chromium wheel in the wall. Cold water gushed in my face.

I moved toward him on hands and knees, sideways, with my face averted. Water rushed under me and laid me on my back. I twisted onto my feet and jumped for him, was stopped in midair and dropped, forced back to the wall. I stood up again.

He took another nozzle from its hook, sighted along it like a sharpshooter. "Look at this one," he said. "My prettiest fountain."

A tiny stream of water sprang across the room and stung my chest. When I looked down, a six-inch letter M was printed in red on my skin, oozing droplets of blood.

"Speaking of killing, as you were," he said, "this little fountain will kill."

I moved across the room and got one hand on his throat. He shook me off and I staggered, almost too weak to stand. The heavier stream of water pounded me back to the wall.

"It will kill," he said. "It will blind."

"Do it to him," Macon said, with girlish whinnyings.

"I'd like to. But remember we have to stay on the right side of the law." He said it seriously.

The water took my legs from under me, rapped my head on the wall. I lay where I fell until the door slammed shut and the key turned in the lock. Then I sat up. My chest and stomach were covered with red welts turning blue. And I was wearing his monogram.

The door was made of white enameled steel tightly fitted into the frame. It opened outwards but was knobless on my side. I hit it twice with my shoulder and gave up.

The skylight was frosted glass reinforced with wire netting. But it was a good twelve feet off the floor, beyond the reach of any human leap. I tried climbing the wall by way of the taps and nozzles. All that got me was a shower-bath I didn't need. I closed the tap I had accidentally opened and watched the water with loathing. It ran into a central depression in the floor, where it was caught by a drain. The drain was covered by a circular metal screen. The screen lifted out when I got my fingernails under it. I squatted over the four-inch pipe which was the only way out, and wished I was a sewer rat. A soggy idea moved in my head like a half-drowned animal.

There was another way out of the white room. It was hermetically sealed, built to hold water. If I could fill it with water, I might be able to float myself up to the skylight. A dangerous experiment, but not so dangerous as staying where I was, waiting for Melliotes to think of other games. The first thing I had to do was plug the drain.

I took off my shoes and socks and crammed the toe

of one shoe into the opening, wadding the socks around it. Then I turned all the taps on full. Water hissed and gushed and splattered from the wall. I dodged it as well as I could; Melliotes had given me a bad case of hydrophobia. Standing in the furthest corner, I watched the water creep up over my ankles, up to my knees, all the way up to my waist. In fifteen or twenty minutes I was afloat.

It was pleasantly warm, and I gradually lost my fear of it. I lay on my back and waited for the ceiling to come closer. When I raised my head, I could hear the trapped air hissing out through the cracks around the skylight. After a long time, during which I rose surely and imperceptibly with the water, I was close enough to the ceiling to reach it with my hand.

I trod water and swung a fist at the skylight. Without intending to I pulled the punch; if my fist went through I knew I'd mangle my hand. The blow cracked the reinforced glass but rebounded ineffectually.

I took some deep breaths and dove for one of my shoes. The water was clear and still except where the incoming streams bubbled and tumbled from the nozzles in the wall. A shaft of sun angled down from the skylight and turned the liquid mass to a cube of pale green light. I stroked along the floor and got my hands on the extra shoe. My ears were aching from the pressure of tons of water above me.

There was a sudden movement in the water, a tremor and vibration that turned my stomach over. Something I hadn't counted on was happening to my plan; it looked as if I'd cleverly arranged to die like a rat in a well. I started for the taps to turn them off. But first my lungs needed air and there wasn't much left at the top. With the shoe in my hand I gathered my legs for the upward push.

Another tremor shook the water and me. A metallic crackling sounded from the direction of the door. It had been built to hold water, but not an entire roomful of the stuff. As I turned in swimmer's slow-motion the white door bellied out like a sail and disappeared in a churning rush and welter. The released weight of the water pushed me after it. My free hand reached for something to hold on to, and closed on liquid nothing.

I was swept through the empty doorway, banged against the opposite wall of the corridor, somersaulted along it. I caught a door-frame with one hand and held on while the water tore at me. The current slowed almost as suddenly as it had begun, and the level of the water subsided. I found the floor and braced myself in the doorway.

Melliotes was in the room with the woman. She was struggling in the water, splashing with arms and legs. He bent over her and lifted her in his arms. She clambered on him, a hairless pink monkey gibbering piteously. My shoe was still in my hand; it was a Scotch walking shoe with an iron-shod heel, and I used it on the back of Melliotes' head. He fell in the shallow water with the woman clinging to him. Father chimpanzee and child.

I looked around the room. The woman's white uniform, an up-ended wastebasket, a scattered bunch of flowers, papers and oddments of clothing, floated in the ebbing tide. There was a white oak desk, a leather armchair and couch, all marked by the water. A piece of office stationery on the desk bore the letterhead: ANGEL OF MERCY NURSING HOME. HYDROTHERAPY AND COLONIC IRRIGATION. PRIVATE ROOMS FOR PATIENTS. DR. G. M. MELLIOTES, PROPRIETOR. A Venice address and phone number.

The heavy red drapes at the window dragged soddenly. Through the slats of the Venetian blind I could see a sunlit lawn bright with flowerbeds and deckchairs. A thin old man in tropical cotton was walking from one chair to another, if you could call it walking. He moved erratically, in several directions at once, as if the terminals of his nervous system had been cut. Fortunately he was in good hands. The Angel of Mercy Nursing Home could give him a permanent cure.

Something small and clammy and furious scratched

at my legs. I moved away from her. I didn't like to touch her.

"He's drowning," she cried. "I can't turn him over."

Melliotes was spreadeagled on the wet-dark carpet, his face in a puddle of water. I looked at the bloody back of his head and felt no pain. I took him by an arm and leg and flipped him over. The whites of his eyes were showing, threaded with red. His chest was heaving like a tired dog's.

The woman minced around the desk and opened a drawer. She came back toward me holding Melliotes' gun in both her hands. I didn't intend to die in that company, and I slapped it down. She growled in the back of her throat and hugged her meager breast with pipestem arms.

"I want my clothes," I said. "And put something on yourself. I can't stand the sight of you."

Her mouth opened and closed, opened and closed like a fish's. I picked up the gun and she did as she was told. She opened a closet door and pulled a cotton dress on over her head. My clothes were scrambled on the floor of the closet.

I waved the gun at the woman. "Now go away."

She went, with a backward look at the man on the floor. The pathos of their parting plucked at my heartstrings. I put on my clothes.

CHAPTER 23

The gun was a .38 calibre S. and W. revolver with a six-inch blue steel barrel, serial number 58237. I shoved it into the pocket of my jacket. Melliotes' striped linen coat was draped over a hanger in the closet. In its inside pocket, I found both my automatic and my wallet. I put them where they belonged and made for the door. Melliotes' breathing had slowed down, but he was still sleeping the sleep of the sapped.

My shoes squished on the floor of the corridor. There were heavy doors on either side, all of them closed and locked. The hallway was as dim and ugly as the one in my dream. The only light came from a curtained door at the far end. I had it open and one foot on the porch when someone cried out behind me. It was a woman's cry, muffled by thick sound-proofed walls. I went back into the building.

"Let me out." The consonants were blurred and only the vowels came through: "Lemmeow," like a hurt cat's yowling. "Pleaslemmeow."

The cry was louder at one door than at the others. When I shook that door, the woman said: "Who is it? Let me out." Mavis again. My heart sank into my boots and bounced back into my throat. The burnt child can't stay away from the fire.

I said under my breath, "To hell with you, Mavis," but these were only words.

What I did was go back to Melliotes and take his keys and try them on the door till I found the one that opened it. Mavis stood back and looked at me, then moved into my arms with a little tearing sigh. "Archer. You came."

"I've been here for some time. I seem to be fairy-godfather-in-residence."

"Anyway, you're here."

She walked backward into the room and sat down weakly on the cot. It was a cell much the same as the one that I had occupied, complete with wire-screened window and padded walls. The angels of mercy took good care of their patients.

"What kind of a clientele does Melliotes have? The wet-sheet set?"

Pale and distraught, she looked a little mental herself. She moved her head back and forth, and her eyes swung back and forth as if by their own great weight. "I've never been here before." And in the same tone, quiet and forlorn: "I'm going to kill him." There were flakes of dried blood on her lower lip where she had bitten it.

"There's been too much killing already. Buck up, Mavis. This time you're going to Mexico for sure."

She leaned forward blindly, her small head against my thigh. Her hair parted at the nape and fell forward around her face like two bright wings. From that hiding place she whispered: "If you'll go with me."

We were back where we had left off. The yacht and the water-chamber, Kilbourne and Melliotes, were characters and scenes in a morphine dream. I remembered the fire-blunted features of Pat Reavis, and backed away from her. "I'll go as far as the airport with you. I'll even buy you a ticket, one-way."

"I'm afraid to go by myself." Her voice was a wisp, but her eyes were bright behind the web of hair.

I said that I was afraid to go along. She stood up suddenly and stamped one high-arched foot on the hard composition floor. "What's the matter, Archer, have you got a girl somewhere?"

She was a very bad actress, and I was embarrassed. "I wish I had."

She stood in front of me with her arms akimbo and accused me of *impotentia coeundi.* Those weren't the words she used.

I said: "Men have been spoiling you since grade school, haven't they? But there's no percentage in standing here calling names. In just two minutes I'm walking out of here. You can come along if you like. As far as the airport."

"As far as the airport," she mimicked me. "I thought you liked me."

"I like you. But I have two good reasons for staying clear. One, what happened to Reavis. Two, the case on my hands."

"I thought you were working for me?"

"I work for myself."

"Anyway, aren't I the best part of the case?"

I said: "The whole is always greater than the parts."

But I didn't hear the sound of my own voice. A car door slammed somewhere, and footsteps scraped on concrete, growing louder. Somebody heavy and fast was coming up the walk. She heard the sounds and froze: a nymph on an urn.

I drew my gun and sighted down the corridor. The curtained front door was standing slightly ajar the way I had left it. A shadow rose on the curtain, the screen door creaked. I stepped back into the room and examined the clip of my automatic. It was full, and the cartridge was still in the chamber. The footsteps approached the open doorway of the room we were in, lagging slower each time.

Mavis's fingers bit into my shoulder. "Who is it?"

"Be quiet."

But the heavy feet had stopped. They moved indecisively, and retreated. I stepped out into the corridor. Kilbourne was waddling rapidly toward the open front door.

I said, "Stand," and shot at the wall beside him. The bullet tore a six-inch gash in the plaster, and halted him in his tracks.

He turned slowly, his hands ascending under hydraulic pressure. He was wearing a Homburg and a fresh dark suit with a mottled pink carnation in the lapel. His face was the same mottled pink. "Melliotes was right," he said. "I shouldn't have let you live."

"You've made a lot of mistakes. There are hundreds of people still living—"

The car door closed again, almost inaudibly. I handed the blue revolver to the woman behind me. "Can you use it?"

"Yes."

"Take him into the room and keep him there."

"Yes."

I elbowed Kilbourne out of my way, ran for the front door and slid behind it. A man ran up to the porch, the breath in his ruined nose like a fanfare of trumpets. When Kilbourne's chauffeur came through the door I hooked his shins with my toe. He went down heavily on hands and knees, and I poleaxed him with the butt of my forty-five. The screen door slammed.

Its echo came back to me from the far end of the corridor, amplified to a heavy gun's explosion.

She met me in the doorway, empty-handed. "I had to do it," she chattered. "He tried to take it away from me. He would have shot us both."

"Leave me out of it."

"It's true, he was going to kill me." The parrot screech of hysteria drowned out Mavis. She looked at her hands as if they were evil white birds. A wicked magician named Kilbourne had attached them to her by witchcraft.

Kilbourne was reclining on the floor, one heavy shoulder propped against the cot. A mound of flesh expensively dressed for death, with a single flower which he had bought for himself. A darker carnation blossomed in one eye-socket. Melliotes' gun lay across his lap.

"Will you take me to the airport?" she said. "Now?"

"Not now." I was feeling the flaccid puffed wrist. "You always do the wrong thing, beautiful."

"Is he dead?"

"Everybody is dying."

"I'm glad. But take me away from here. He's horrible."

"You should have thought of that a minute ago."

"Don't uncle me, for God's sake. Take me away."

I looked at her and thought of Acapulco. The fine warm fishing waters and the high sea-cliffs and the long slow tequila nights. Ten million dollars and Mavis, and all I had to do was a little fixing.

It went past the secret eye of my mind like a movie that had been made a long time ago. All I had to do was take it out of the can and dub in dialogue. Not even dialogue was necessary. The chauffeur had been knocked out before the shot. Melliotes was unconscious. And the slug in Kilbourne's brain was from his gun. Mavis and I could walk out of there and wait for the will to be probated.

I took a long hard look at her full body and her empty face. I left it in the can.

She saw my intention before I spoke. "You're not going to help me, are you?"

"You're pretty good at helping yourself," I said. "Not good enough, though. I could cover up for you, but you'd let something slip when the men from the District Attorney's office came around. It would be first degree then, and I'd be in it."

"You're worried about your own damned scrawny neck."

"I only have the one."

She changed the approach. "My husband didn't make a will. Do you know how much money he has? Had."

"Better than you do, probably. You can't spend it when you're dead or in the pen."

"No, you can't. But you're willing to send me there." Her mouth drooped in self-pity.

"Not for long, probably not at all. You can cop a

manslaughter plea, or stick to self-defense. With the kind of lawyers you can buy, you won't spend a night in jail."

"You're lying to me."

"No." I stood up facing her. "I wish you well."

"If you really wished me well, you'd take me out of here. We could go away together. Anywhere."

"I've thought of that, too. No go."

"Don't you want me?" She was distressed and puzzled. "You said I was beautiful. I could make you happy, Lew."

"Not for the rest of my life."

"You don't know," she said, "you haven't tried me."

I felt ashamed for her. Ashamed for myself. The Acapulco movie stirred like a brilliant snake at the back of my mind.

"There's a phone in Melliotes' office," I said. "You call the police. It's better, if you're going to plead self-defense."

She burst into tears, stood sobbing violently with her mouth open and her eyes tight closed. Her wild urchin grief was more touching than any of her poses. When she groped for something to cry on, I gave her my shoulder. And eased her down the corridor to the telephone.

CHAPTER 24

The studio guard was a big ex-cop wrapped in crisp cellophane refinement. He leaned toward the hole in his plate-glass window. "Who was that you wanted to see?"

"Mildred Fleming. She's secretary to one of the producers or directors."

"Oh yes. Miss Fleming. One moment if you please." He talked into the phone at his elbow, looked up with question-mark eyebrows: "Miss Fleming wants to know who it is."

"Lewis Archer. Tell her Maude Slocum sent me."

"Who sent you?"

"Maude Slocum." The name had unexpected reverberations in my interior.

He talked into the telephone again and came up smiling. "Miss Fleming will be with you shortly. Have a seat, Mr. Armature."

I took a chromium chair in a far corner of the big, airy lobby. I was the only living person on the secular side of the plate glass, but the walls were populated by giant photographs. The studio's stars and featured players looked down on me from a lofty unreal world where everyone was young and hugely gay. One of the bright-haired fillies reminded me of Mavis; one of the dark young stallions could have been Pat Ryan thoroughly groomed and equipped with porcelain teeth. But Pat was huddled somewhere on a slab. Mavis was at the Hall of Justice talking to her lawyers about bail bond. The happy endings and the biggest oranges were the ones that California saved for export.

A short woman in a flame-colored blouse came through a plate-glass door that shut and locked itself behind her. Her short bobbed hair was blue-black and fitted her small head like a coat of Chinese lacquer. Her eyes, dark brown and experienced, carried a little luggage underneath.

I stood up and met her as she came toward me, her girdle-sheathed body moving with quick nervous energy. "Miss Fleming? I'm Archer."

"Hello." She gave me a firm cold hand. "I thought Al said your name was Armature."

"He did."

"I'm glad it isn't. We had an assistant director called Mr. Organic once, but nobody could take him seriously. He changed his name to Goldfarb and did right well for himself." Her rate of speech was a hundred words a minute, timed to the typewriter in her head. "Al also said Maude sent you, or is that another of his famous blunders?"

"He said that, but it isn't exactly true."

The smiling crinkle left her eyes, and they raked me up and down in a hard once-over. I was glad I'd changed to a fresh suit on the way from the Hall of Justice. In five or ten years she'd still remember the pattern of my tie, be able to pick my picture from a rogues' gallery.

"Well," she said with hostility, "you tell me what you're selling and I'll tell you how much I don't want whatever it is. I'm busy, brother, you shouldn't *do* these things."

"I sell my services."

"Oh, no, not that!" She was a natural clown.

"I'm a private detective. I worked for Mrs. Slocum until last night."

"Doing what?"

"Investigating. A certain matter."

"It's funny she didn't tell me." She was interested again. "I saw her at lunch the day before yesterday. What happened last night, she fire you?"

"No. She resigned."

"I don't get you." But she understood the finality of my tone. Emotion flowed into her eyes as dark as ink.

"She committed suicide last night," I said.

Mildred Fleming sat down suddenly, perched stiffly on the edge of a green plastic settee. "You're kidding."

"She's dead all right."

"Why in God's name?" Some tears spilled out of her eyes and coursed down her cheeks, eroding the heavy makeup. She wiped them with a ball of crumpled kleenex. "Excuse me. I happened to be pretty fond of the girl. Ever since high school."

"I liked her too. It's why I want to talk to you."

She moved like a hummingbird, toward the outside door. "Come on across the street. I'll buy you a coffee."

The drugstore on the opposite corner contained everything a drugstore should except a pharmacy. Newspapers and magazines, motion picture projectors and pogo sticks, sunglasses and cosmetics and bathing suits, and twenty assorted specimens of human flotsam watching the door for a familiar face. There was a lunch bar at the rear, with booths along the wall, most of them empty in the afternoon lull.

Mildred Fleming slipped into one of the booths and held up two fingers to the waitress behind the counter. The waitress came running with two heavy mugs, and fussed over my companion.

"Silly girl," she said when the waitress had bounced away. "She thinks I've got a pull. Nobody's got a pull any more." She leaned across the scarred table, sipping at her coffee. "Now tell me about poor Maude. Without coffee, I couldn't take it."

I had come to her for information, but first I told her what I thought was fit for her to know. What water had done to Olivia Slocum, what fire had done to Ryan, what strychnine had done to Maude. I left out Kilbourne and Mavis, and what they had done to each other.

She took it calmly, except that toward the end she needed her makeup more. She didn't say a word, till I mentioned Knudson and the fact that he had run me out of town.

"You shouldn't pay too much attention to what he said. I can imagine how he feels. I don't know whether I should tell you this—"

"You don't have to tell me. Knudson loved her, it was pretty obvious."

I was probing for a gap in her defenses. Most good secretaries had an occupational weakness: they gathered inside information and after they had gathered it they had to tell it to somebody.

She was piqued. "If you know the whole story already, why come to me?"

"I know damn little. I don't know who drowned Olivia Slocum or why Maude Slocum took strychnine. I came to you because you're her closest friend. I figured you had a right to know what happened and that you'd want to help me get to the bottom of it."

She was gratified. "I *do* want to help you. I've always been in Maude's confidence, and I can tell you she's had a tragic life." She called for more coffee, and turned back to me: "As far as her mother-in-law is concerned, didn't you say that this man Pat Ryan killed her?"

"That's Knudson's theory, and most of the evidence supports it. I've taken an option on it, but I haven't bought it yet."

"You don't think Maude—?" Her eyes shone blackly in the dim booth.

"I do not."

"I'm glad you don't. Anyone that knew her would tell you she couldn't hurt anyone. She was a gentle creature, in spite of everything."

"Everything?"

"Her whole damned messy life. Everything that made her want to suicide."

"You know why she did it then?"

"I guess I do, at that. She was crucified for fifteen years. She's the one woman I've ever known that wanted to do the right thing and couldn't make it. Everything about Maude was right except her life. She made a couple of mistakes that she couldn't wipe out. I'll tell you on one condition. Do you have a word of honor?"

"I have a word. I was an officer in the war, but the gentleman part didn't take."

The stern sharp glance raked me again. "I think I'd trust you as far as I would myself, no further. Give me your word that Cathy will never hear this, and that it won't affect Cathy in any way."

I guessed what she was going to tell me. "I can't do that if other people know it."

"Nobody but me," she said. "And Knudson, of course, and maybe Knudson's wife."

"So Knudson has a wife."

"He hasn't lived with her for fifteen or sixteen years, but they're still married, for keeps. She'll never divorce him, no matter what he does. She hates him. I guess she hates everyone in the world. She's going to be glad to hear that Maude killed herself."

"You know the woman, do you?"

"Do I know her! I lived in her house for nearly a year, and I know her better than I want to. Eleanor Knudson is one of these hard righteous women who wouldn't donate two pennies to close a dead man's eyes. Maude lived there too, we were room-mates: that's how the whole thing started. We were in our sophomore year at Berkeley."

"Mrs. Knudson ran a boarding house in Berkeley?"

"A rooming house for girls. Her husband was a sergeant with the Oakland police. She was older than he was; I never figured out how she managed to hook him. Probably the usual landlady-roomer business: propinquity and maternal care and more propinquity. She had brains and she wasn't bad-looking if you like the cold-steel type. Anyway, she and Ralph Knudson had been married for several years when we moved in."

"You and Maude, you mean?"

"Yes. We'd taken our freshman year in the Teachers' College in Santa Barbara, but we couldn't stay there. We both had to work our way through school, and there wasn't enough work in Santa Barbara. Maude's father was a rancher in Ventura—that's where we went to high school, in Ventura—but the depression had wiped him out. My father was dead and my mother couldn't help me. She was having a hard enough time supporting herself in 'thirty-two. So Maudie and I moved on to the big city. We both knew typing and shorthand and we made a go of it, doing public stenography and typing dissertations. Living was cheap in those days. We paid Mrs. Knudson ten dollars a month for our room, and did our own cooking. We even managed to get to some of our classes."

"I was around in those days," I said.

She supped the dregs of her coffee and lit a cigarette, regarding me somberly through the smoke. "They were wonderful sad days. There were lines a mile long at the mission soup-kitchens in San Francisco and Oakland, but we were going to be career girls and set the Bay on fire. I've realized since then that it was all my idea. Maudie just went along because I needed her. She had more brains than me, and more goodness. The pure female type, you know? All she really wanted was a husband and a home and a chance to raise some decent kids like herself. So she got herself tangled up with a man who could never marry her as long as he lived. As long as Eleanor Knudson lived, anyway. I watched it happen and couldn't do a thing to stop it. They were made for each other, Maudie and Ralph, like in the love stories. He was all man and she was all woman and his wife was a frigid bitch. They couldn't live in the same house without falling in love with each other."

"And making music together?"

"Damn your eyes!" she spat out suddenly. "You've

got a lousy attitude. It was the real thing, see. She was twenty and proud, she'd never gone with a man. He was the man for her and she was the woman for him. They were like Adam and Eve; it wasn't Maudie's fault he was married already. She went into it blind as a baby, and so did he. It just happened. And it was real," she insisted. "Look how it lasted."

"I have been looking."

She stirred uncomfortably, shredding her cigarette butt in her small hard fingers. "I don't know why I'm telling you these things. What do they mean to you? Is somebody paying you?"

"Maude gave me two hundred dollars; that's all gone by now. But once I'm in a case I sort of like to stay through to the end. It's more than curiosity. She must have died for a reason. I owe it to her or myself to find out the reason, to see the whole thing clear."

"Ralph Knudson knows the reasons. Eleanor Knudson knows: hell, it was her idea in a way. Maude had to spend her good years with a man she didn't love, and I guess she simply got sick of it."

"What do you mean, she had to marry Slocum?"

"You haven't given me your word," she said. "About Cathy."

"You don't have to worry about Cathy. I feel sorry for the girl. I wouldn't touch her."

"I suppose it doesn't matter a hell of a lot after all. James Slocum must have known she wasn't his child. They said she was a seven-months' baby, but Slocum must have known."

"Knudson is Cathy's father then."

"Who else? When he found out Maude was pregnant he begged his wife for a divorce. He offered her everything he had. No soap. So Knudson left his wife and his job and cleared out. He was crazy to take Maudie with him, but she wouldn't go. She was scared, and she was thinking about the baby she was carrying. James Slocum wanted to marry her, and she let him."

"How did he come into the picture?"

"Maude had been typing for him all winter. He was

doing graduate work in drama, and he seemed to be well-heeled. That wasn't really why she married him, though, at least not the only reason. He had a faggot tendency, you know? He claimed he needed her, that she could save him. I don't know whether she did or not. Chances are she didn't."

"She was still trying," I said. "You should be doing my work, Miss Fleming."

"You mean I notice things? Yes, I do. But where Maudie was concerned I didn't have to: we were like sisters. We talked the whole thing out before she gave Slocum her answer. I advised her to marry him. I made a mistake. I often make mistakes." A bitter smile squeezed her mouth and eyes. "I'm not really a Miss, incidentally. My name is Mrs. Mildred Fleming Kraus Peterson Daniels Woodbury. I've been married four times."

"Congratulations four times."

"Yeah," she answered dryly. "As I was saying, I make mistakes. For most of them I take the rap myself. Maude took the rap for this one. She and Slocum left school before the end of the spring semester and went to live with his mother in Nopal Valley. She was determined to be a good wife to him, and a good mother to the kid, and for twelve years she stuck it out. Twelve years.

"In 1946 she came across a picture of Knudson in the *Los Angeles Times*. He was a police lieutenant in Chicago, and he'd run down some ex-con or other. It suddenly hit Maude that she still loved him, and that she was losing her life. She came down here and told me about it and I told her to beat her way to Chicago if she had to hitchhike. She had some money saved, and she went. Knudson was still living by himself. He hasn't been since.

"That fall the Chief of Police in Nopal Valley was fired for bribery. Knudson applied for the job and got it. He wanted to be near Maude, and he wanted to see his daughter. So they finally got together, in a way." She sighed. "I guess Maude couldn't stand the strain of having a lover. She wasn't built for intrigue."

"No. It didn't work out well."

"Maude had enough maturity to see what had to be done, if she could do it. She'd have gone away with Knudson this time. But it was too late. She had Cathy to think about. The hell of it was that Cathy didn't like Knudson. And she was crazy about Slocum."

"Too crazy," I said.

"I know what you mean." The dark sharp eyes veiled themselves, and unveiled. "Of course, she believes Slocum is her father. I think she'd better go on believing that, don't you?"

"It's not my problem."

"Nor mine. I'm glad it isn't. Whatever happens to Cathy, I'm sorry for her. It's a shame, she's a wonderful kid. I think I'll go up and see her over the weekend.—I almost forgot, the funeral. When is the funeral?"

"I wouldn't know. You better call her house."

She stood up quickly, and offered me her hand. "I must be going now—some work to finish up. What time is it?"

I looked at my watch. "Four o'clock."

"Goodbye, Mr. Archer. Thanks for listening to me."

"I should be thanking you."

"No. I had to talk to somebody about it. I felt guilty. I still do."

"Guilty of what?"

"Being alive, I guess." She flashed me a difficult smile, and darted away.

I sat over a third cup of coffee and thought about Maude Slocum. Hers was one of those stories without villains or heroes. There was no one to admire, no one to blame. Everyone had done wrong for himself and others. Everyone had failed. Everyone had suffered.

Perhaps Cathy Slocum had suffered most of all. My sympathies were shifting from the dead woman to the living girl. Cathy had been born into it innocent. She had been weaned on hatred and schooled in a quiet hell where nothing was real but her love for her father. Who wasn't really her father.

CHAPTER 25

The ride to Quinto, on an old bus sardined with weekenders, was long and slow and hot. A girl who exhaled beer fumes and mauve-scented perfume regaled me with stories of her bowling triumphs in the twenty-alley Waikiki Bowl on Figueroa Boulevard. At the Quinto junction I bade her a quick farewell and walked out to the pier.

My car was where I had left it. A parking-ticket was tucked under the windshield wiper. I tore it into eight pieces and tossed them into the ocean one by one. I didn't intend to come back to Quinto if I could help it.

Over the pass again to Nopal Valley. The central street was choked with late afternoon traffic, and parked cars lined the curbs. One of them pulled out ahead of me and I backed into its place. I walked a block to Antonio's and took a seat at the end of the crowded bar. Antonio saw me and nodded in recognition.

Without a word spoken he went to his safe and opened it. When he came to take my order, the clumsy newspaper package was in his hands. I thanked him. He said I was welcome. I asked for a double bourbon, which he brought. I paid him for it.

He lit my cigarette. I drank the bourbon straight and walked out with the money in my pocket.

Gretchen Keck was standing in front of the butane stove just inside the door of her trailer. She was wearing a halter and slacks. Her yellow hair was pulled up into a top-knot, held in place by an elastic band. The egg that she was frying spluttered and popped like a tiny machine gun riddling my guts with hunger.

She didn't notice me until I rapped on the open door. Then she saw who it was. She picked up the frying-pan and brandished it clublike. The egg fell onto the floor and lay there drooling yellow. "Get away from me."

"In a minute."

"You're a dirty bull, ain't you, one of the ones that bumped Pat? I got nothing to say."

"I have."

"Not to me you haven't. I don't know nothing. You can amscray." With the frying-pan upraised, ready to throw, she should have looked ridiculous. There was nothing ridiculous about her.

I talked fast: "Pat gave me something for you before he died—"

"Before you killed him, you mean."

"Shut up and listen to me, girl. I haven't got all day."

"All right, finish your pitch. I know you're lying, copper. You're trying to hook me in, only I don't know nothing. How could I know he was going to murder somebody?"

"Put it down and listen to me. I'm coming in."

"In a pig's eye!"

I stepped across the threshold, wrenched the iron pan from her hand, pushed her down into the solitary chair: "Pat didn't murder anybody, can you understand that?"

"It said he did in the paper. Now I know you're lying." But her voice had lost its passionate conviction. Her soft mouth drooped uncertainly.

"You don't have to believe what you read in the papers. Mrs. Slocum died by accident."

"Why did they kill Pat then if he didn't murder her?"

"Because he claimed he did. Pat heard a policeman tell me she was dead. He went to the man he was working for and convinced him that he killed her."

"Pat wasn't that crazy."

"No. He was crazy like a fox. The big boss gave him ten grand lamster's money. Pat talked himself into getting paid for a murder he didn't do."

"Jesus!" Her eyes were wide with admiration. "I told you he had a brain on him."

"He had a heart, too." That lie left a bile taste on my tongue. "When he saw he wasn't going to make it, he gave me the ten grand to give to you. He told me you were his heir."

"No. He told you that?" The cornflower eyes spilled over. "What else did he say?"

My tongue wagged on: "He said he wanted you to have it on one condition: that you get out of Nopal Valley and go some place where you can live a decent life. He said it would all be worth it if you did that."

"I will!" she cried. "Did you say ten grand? Ten thousand dollars?"

"Right." I handed her the package. "Don't spend it in California or they might try to trace it. Don't tell anybody what I've told you. Go to another state and put it in a bank and buy a house or something. That's what Pat wanted you to do with it."

"Did he say that?" She had torn off the wrappings and crushed the bright bills to her breast.

"Yes. He said that." And I told her what she wanted to hear because there was no reason not to: "He also said that he loved you."

"Yes," she whispered. "I loved him, too."

"I have to go now, Gretchen."

"Wait a minute." She rose, her mouth working awkwardly, trying to frame a question. "Why did you—I mean I guess you really was his friend, like you said.

I'm sorry. I thought you was a copper. And here you just came to bring me the money from Pat."

"Put it away," I said. "Get out of town tonight if you can."

"Yeah. Sure. I'll do just what Pat wanted me to. He really was a swell guy after all."

I turned and went out the door, so that she wouldn't see my face. "Goodbye, Gretchen."

The money wouldn't do her any permanent good. She'd buy a mink coat or a fast car, and find a man to steal one or wreck the other. Another Reavis, probably. Still, it would give her something to remember different from the memories that she had. She had no souvenirs and I had too many. I wanted no mementos of Reavis or Kilbourne.

Mrs. Strang ushered me into James Slocum's bedroom. It was a very manly room, equipped with red leather chairs and solid dark furniture. Prints of old sailing vessels, like portholes opening on a motionless sea, adorned the paneled oak walls. Built-in bookcases, crammed with volumes, covered the length and height of one wall. The kind of room a hopeful mother might furnish for her son.

Olivia Slocum's son was sitting up at the end of the great four-poster bed. His face was bloodless and thin. In the late gray light from the windows he looked like a silver image of a man. Francis Marvell was sitting on his own feet in a chair beside him. Both of them were intent on a chessboard set with black and white ivory pieces that rested on the edge of the bed between them.

Slocum's hand emerged from his scarlet silk sleeve and moved a black knight. "There."

"Jolly good," Marvell said. "Oh, jolly good."

Slocum withdrew his dreaming gaze from the board and turned it on me. "Yes?"

"You said you would see Mr. Archer?" the housekeeper faltered.

"Mr. Archer? Oh. Yes. Come in, Mr. Archer." Slocum's voice was weak and vaguely peevish.

Mrs. Strang left the room. I stood where I was.

Slocum and Marvell projected an atmosphere, a circle of intimacy, which I didn't care to enter. Nor did they want me to enter it. Their heads were turned toward me at the same impatient angle, willing me to be gone. To leave them to the complex chess-play between them.

"I hope that you're recovering, Mr. Slocum." I had nothing better to say.

"I don't know, I have had a perfectly dreadful series of shocks." Self-pity squeaked behind the words like a rat behind the wall. "I have lost my mother, I have lost my wife, my own daughter has turned against me now."

"I'm standing by, dear fellow," Marvell said. "You can count on me, you know." Slocum smiled weakly. His hand moved toward Marvell's, which was resting slack by the chessboard, but paused short of it.

"If you've come about the play," Marvell said to me, "I'm afraid I have to confess we've given it up. After all that's happened, it may be months or years before I can regain the world of imagination. Poor dear James may never act again."

"No great loss to the theatre," Slocum said with quiet pathos. "But Mr. Archer isn't interested in the play, Francis. I'd supposed you knew by now that he's a detective. I imagine that he's looking for his pay."

"I have been paid."

"That's just as well. You'd never have a penny out of me. May I hazard a guess as to who paid you?"

"You needn't. It was your wife."

"Of course it was! And shall I tell you why?" He leaned forward, clutching the bedclothes. His eyes were bright with fever or passion. The silver face was peaked and hollowed like an old man's. "Because you helped her to murder my mother, didn't you? Didn't you?"

Marvell uncoiled his legs and stood up, his face averted in embarrassment.

"No, Francis, please don't go. I want you to hear

this. I want you to know the sort of woman I've had to spend my life with."

Marvell slumped back into the chair and began to bite his knuckles.

"Go on," I said. "This is interesting."

"It came to me the night before last. I lay here thinking the night through, and I saw the whole thing plainly. She'd always hated my mother, she wanted her money, she wanted to leave me. But she didn't dare to murder her without assistance. You were to lend the professional touch, were you not?"

"And what was my particular contribution?"

His voice was soft and sly: "You provided the scapegoat, Mr. Archer. No doubt Maude drowned mother herself; she wouldn't delegate that task, not she. You were there to make sure that Reavis took the blame. My suspicion was confirmed yesterday when Reavis's cap was found in the grove by the pool. I knew that Reavis didn't leave it there. He'd left it on the front seat of the car. I saw it in the car myself. I suggest that you saw it there too, and realized what could be done with it."

"I'm not very suggestible, Mr. Slocum. But let's assume that what you say is true. What are you going to do about it?"

"There is nothing I can do." With his eyes turned up toward the ceiling, his hands now gripping each other, he looked like a mad saint. "In order to have you punished, I should have to trumpet my shame, my wife's shame, to the world. You can rest easy, unless you have a conscience. Last night I did my duty to my dead mother. I told my wife what I have told you. She killed herself. It was fitting."

Hard words rose in me. I held them back with clenched teeth. Slocum had retreated from reality. If I told him that he had driven his wife to suicide for no good reason, it would only drive him further into the unreal world.

Maude Slocum hadn't killed herself because she murdered her mother-in-law. Her husband's story of the cap had simply told her that Reavis hadn't done it. Which meant that someone else had.

I said to Marvell: "If you care about this man, you'd better get him a damn good doctor."

He batted his eyes at me, and stuttered something incoherent against his knuckles. Slocum's face was still turned to the ceiling, wearing a sad holy smile. I went out. From the hallway I heard him say: "It's your move, Francis."

I went through the house alone, thinking of Maude Slocum and looking for her daughter. The rooms and corridors were empty and still. The tide of violence running in the house had permanently ebbed and drawn the life out with it. The veranda and the loggia and the terraces were empty of life, except for the flowers burning in the fading light. I avoided the pool, which glimmered through the trees like a wicked blade. At the end of the funereal alley of cypresses I came to the old lady's garden.

Cathy was sitting on a stone bench islanded among the lake of flowers. Her face was turned to the west, where a while before the sun had died in glory. Her young look traveled up beyond the fieldstone wall of the garden to the mountains. She was watching their purple masses as if they formed the walls of a great prison where she had been sentenced to live alone forever.

I called to her over the gate: "Cathy. May I come in?"

She turned slowly, the mountains huge and ancient in her eyes. Her voice was flat: "Hello, Mr. Archer. Do come in."

I released the redwood latch and stepped into the garden.

"Don't close it," she said. "You can leave it open."

"What are you doing?"

"Just thinking." She moved aside on the bench, to make room for me. The concrete surface still held the sun's heat.

"What about?"

"Me. I used to think this was all so beautiful, and

now it doesn't mean a thing. Coleridge was right about nature, I guess. You see the beauty there if you have it in your heart. If your heart is desolate, the world is a wilderness. Did you ever read his 'Ode to Dejection'?"

I said I never had.

"I understand it now. I'd kill myself if I had my mother's courage. As it is, I suppose I'll sit around and wait for something to happen to me. Something good or something bad, it doesn't really matter."

I didn't know what to say. I settled for something meaningless and soothing: "All the bad things have happened, haven't they?"

"Except the desolation in the heart." If she hadn't been completely earnest, the phrase would have sounded foolish.

I said: "Talk it out to me."

"What do you mean?"

She met my gaze. For a long moment we looked at each other. Her body narrowed and shrunk, drawing away from me. "I don't know what you mean."

"You killed your grandmother," I said. "You might as well tell me about it."

She bowed her head and shoulders and sat there, dry-eyed and quiet. "Does everybody know?"

"Nobody knows, Cathy. Just me and Ralph Knudson."

"Yes. He talked to me today. Mr. Knudson is my father. Why didn't they tell me sooner? I'd never have sent that letter."

"Why did you send it?" I said.

"I hated my mother. She was cheating on my father—Mr. Slocum. I saw her and Mr. Knudson together one day, and I wanted to make her suffer. And I thought if my father—if Mr. Slocum found out he'd make her leave and we could be together. Don't you see, they were always quarreling or giving each other the silent treatment. I wanted them separated so there would be some peace. But the letter didn't seem to make any difference at all."

For a while she had seemed a woman; more than

that, an ageless sybil speaking from ancient wisdom. She had become a child again, a harried child trying to explain the inexplicable: how one could do a murder with the best intentions in the world.

"So you did it the hard way," I said. "You thought your grandmother's money would blow them apart. Your mother would run off with her lover, and you could live happily ever after with your father."

"Mr. Slocum," she corrected me. "He isn't my father. Yes, I thought that. I am a hideous creature." And she wailed.

A mockingbird in the cypresses took it up. The sobbing howls of the girl and the bird demented the twilight. I laid one arm across Cathy's shuddering back. She said: "I am hideous. I should die."

"No, Cathy. Too many people have died."

"What are you going to do with me? I deserve to die. I really hated Grandma, I wanted to kill her. She twisted my father from the time he was a little boy, she made him what he is. You know what an Oedipus complex is, don't you?"

"Yes. I've also heard of an Electra complex."

She missed that. It was just as well, because I shouldn't have said it. She knew too much already, more than she could bear.

She had given over crying, but the bird still howled from the tree like a disembodied conscience.

I said: "Cathy. I'm not going to do anything to you. I haven't the right."

"Don't be nice to me. I don't deserve anything nice from anybody. From the moment I decided to do it, I've felt as if I was cut off from every human being. I know what they mean by the mark of Cain, I have it." She covered her high fair brow with her hand, as if it might actually be branded.

"I understand how you feel. I was responsible, in a way, for Pat Reavis's death. Once I killed another man with my hands. I did it to save my own life, but his blood is on my hands."

"You are being too good to me, and so was Mr. Knudson. My father." The word sounded remarkable from her lips, as if it stood for something great and mysterious and new. "He blamed himself for everything that happened. Now you're blaming yourself. I'm the one that did it, though. I even intended Pat to take the blame for me. I did see him here that night. I lied to you when I told you that I didn't. He wanted me to run away with him, and I tried to want to, but I couldn't. He was drunk; I sent him away. Then I saw the cap he'd left in the car, and that was when I decided I could do it. It was terrible. Once I saw what I could do, I felt as if I had to do it. You know?"

"I think I know."

"I felt as if I'd sold my soul to the devil, even before it happened—No, I mustn't say it *happened,* because I made it happen. Still I thought if I could get away from here, it wouldn't have to happen. I saw you coming out of the house, and I got into your car. But you wouldn't take me away."

"I'm sorry."

"Don't be sorry, you couldn't help it. What could you have done with me? Anyway, you left me there. I knew Grandma was sitting here in the garden. I couldn't go back into the house until it was done. I went down by the pool and hid Pat's cap in the hedge, then I called her. I told her there was a dead bird in the pool. She came to look and I pushed her in. I went into the house and went to bed. I didn't sleep all night, or last night either. Do you think I can sleep tonight, now that other people know?"

She turned her face to me. It was open and tormented, its flesh gray and almost translucent, like the last falling light in the garden.

"I hope so, Cathy."

Her cold lips moved: "Do you think I'm insane? I've been afraid for years that I was going insane."

"No," I said, though I hadn't any idea.

A man's voice called her name from somewhere out of sight. The bird flew out of the tree and circled to another, where it took up a new cry.

Cathy's head came up like a deer's. "I'm here." And

she added in the same clear voice: "father." The strange and ancient word.

Knudson appeared at the gate. He glowered when he saw me. "I told you to get out and stay out. Leave her alone."

"No," Cathy said. "He's been nice to me, father."

"Come here, Cathy."

"Yes, father." She went to him, her head bowed and watchful.

He spoke to her in a low voice, and she walked away in the direction of the house. She moved uncertainly, a traveler on new ground, and was lost in the cypress shadows.

I went to the gate and faced Knudson in the narrow opening between the fieldstone posts. "What are you going to do with her?"

"That's my business." He was taking off his coat. He was in civilian clothes, and his gunbelt was missing.

"I've made it my business, too."

"You've made a mistake. Several mistakes. You're going to suffer for them." He swung a fist at me.

I stepped out of reach. "Don't be childish, Knudson. Bloodletting won't help either of us. Or Cathy."

He said: "Take off your coat." He draped his over the swinging gate.

I threw mine on top of it. "If you insist."

He backed onto the grass, and I followed him. It was a long hard fight, and a useless one. Still it had to be fought through. He was bigger and heavier than I was, but I was faster. I hit him three times to his one. I knocked him down six times before he stayed, prone on his back with both hands over his face. Both of my thumbs were sprained and swelling tight. My right eye was almost closed by a mouse on the upper lid.

It was full dark when it ended. He sat up after a while and spoke between sobbing breaths. "I had to fight somebody. Slocum was no good to me. You fight well, Archer."

"I was trained by pros. What are you going to do with Cathy?"

Slowly he got to his feet. His face was striped with black blood which dropped from the end of his chin and splattered his torn shirt. He staggered and almost fell. I steadied him with my hand.

"Officially, you mean?" He mumbled, through puffed lips. "I turned in my resignation this afternoon. I didn't tell them why. You're not going to tell them, either."

"No," I said. "She's your baby."

"She knows that she's my baby. She's coming with me, back to Chicago. I'll put her in school there, and try to give her a home. Does that sound impossible to you? I've seen worse cases than Cathy straighten out and grow up into people. Not often, but it happens."

"Cathy will make it if anybody will. What does Slocum say?"

"Slocum can't stop me," he said. "He isn't going to try. Mrs. Strang is coming with me; she and Cathy are fond of each other."

"Good luck, then."

Around us and above us the darkness was immense. Our hands groped for each other and met. I left him there.

THE CHILL

To R.W. Lid

I

THE HEAVY red-figured drapes over the courtroom windows were incompletely closed against the sun. Yellow daylight leaked in and dimmed the electric bulbs in the high ceiling. It picked out random details in the room: the glass water cooler standing against the paneled wall opposite the jury box, the court reporter's carmine-tipped fingers playing over her stenotype machine. Mrs Perrine's experienced eyes watching me across the defense table.

It was nearly noon on the second and last day of her trial. I was the final witness for the defense. Her attorney had finished questioning me. The deputy D.A. waived cross-examination, and several of the jurors looked at him with puzzled frowns. The judge said I could go.

From my place on the witness stand I'd noticed the young man sitting in the front row of spectators. He wasn't one of the regular trial-watchers, housewives and pensioners filling an empty morning with other people's troubles. This one had troubles of his own. His brooding blue gaze stayed on my face, and I had the uncomfortable feeling that he might be willing to share his troubles with me.

He rose from his seat as I stepped down and intercepted me at the door. "Mr Archer, may I talk to you?"

"All right."

The bailiff opened the door and gestured urgently. "Outside, gentlemen. Court is still in session."

We moved out into the corridor. The young man scowled at the automatically closing door. "I don't like being pushed around."

"I'd hardly describe that as being pushed around. What's eating you, friend?"

I shouldn't have asked him. I should have walked briskly out to my car and driven back to Los Angeles. But he had that clean, crewcut All-American look, and that blur of pain in his eyes.

"I just got thrown out of the Sheriff's office. It came on top of a couple of other brushoffs from the local authorities, and I'm not used to that kind of treatment."

"They don't mean it personally."

"You've had a lot of detective experience, haven't you? I gathered that from what you said on the witness stand. Incidentally, you did a wonderful job for Mrs Perrine. I'm sure the jury will acquit her."

"We'll see. Never bet on a jury." I distrusted his compliment, which probably meant he wanted something more substantial from me. The trial in which I had just testified marked the end of a long uninteresting case, and I was planning a fishing trip to La Paz. "Is that all you wanted to say to me?"

"I have a lot to say, if you'll only listen. I mean, I've got this problem about my wife. She left me."

"I don't ordinarily do divorce work, if that's what you have in mind."

"Divorce?" Without making a sound, he went through the motions of laughing hollowly, once. "I was only married one day – less than one day. Everybody including my father keeps telling me I should get an annulment. But I don't want an annulment or a divorce. I want her back."

"Where is your wife now?"

"I don't know." He lit a cigarette with unsteady hands. "Dolly left in the middle of our honeymoon weekend, the day after we were married. She may have met with foul play."

"Or she may have decided she didn't want to be married, or not to you. It happens all the time."

"That's what the police keep saying: it happens all the time. As if that's any comfort! Anyway, I know that wasn't the case. Dolly loved me, and I loved – I love her."

He said this very intensely, with the entire force of his nature behind the words. I didn't know his nature but there was sensitivity and feeling there, more feeling than he could handle easily.

"You haven't told me your name."

"I'm sorry. My name is Kincaid, Alex Kincaid."

"What do you do for a living?"

"I haven't been doing much lately, since Dolly – since this thing happened. Theoretically I work for the Channel Oil Corporation. My father is in charge of their Long Beach office. You may have heard of him. Frederick Kincaid?"

I hadn't. The bailiff opened the door of the courtroom, and held it open. Court had adjourned for lunch, and the jurors filed out past him. Their movements were solemn, part of the ritual of the trial. Alex Kincaid watched them as if they were going out to sit in judgment on him.

"We can't talk here," he said. "Let me buy you lunch."

"I'll have lunch with you. Dutch." I didn't want to owe him anything, at least till I'd heard his story.

There was a restaurant across the street. Its main room was filled with smoke and the roar of conversation. The red-checkered tables were all occupied, mainly with the courthouse people, lawyers and sheriff's men and probation officers. Though Pacific Point was fifty miles south of my normal beat, I recognized ten or a dozen of them.

Alex and I went into the bar and found a couple of stools in a dim corner. He ordered a double scotch on the rocks. I went along with it. He drank his down like medicine and tried to order a second round immediately.

"You set quite a pace. Slow down."

"Are you telling me what to do?" he said distinctly and unpleasantly.

"I'm willing to listen to your story. I want you to be able to tell it."

"You think I'm an alcoholic or something?"

"I think you're a bundle of nerves. Pour alcohol on a bundle of nerves and it generally turns into a can of worms. While I'm making suggestions you might as well get rid of those chips you're wearing on both shoulders. Somebody's liable to knock them off and take a piece of you with them."

He sat for a while with his head down. His face had an almost fluorescent pallor, and a faint humming tremor went through him.

"I'm not my usual self, I admit that. I didn't know things like this could happen to people."

"It's about time you told me what did happen. Why not start at the beginning?"

"You mean when she left the hotel?"

"All right. Start with the hotel."

"We were staying at the Surf House," he said, "right here in

Pacific Point. I couldn't really afford it but Dolly wanted the experience of staying there – she never had. I figured a three-day weekend wouldn't break me. It was the Labour Day weekend. I'd already used my vacation time, and we got married that Saturday so that we could have at least a three-day honeymoon."

"Where were you married?"

"In Long Beach, by a judge."

"It sounds like one of these spur-of-the-moment weddings."

"I suppose it was, in a way. We hadn't known each other too long. Dolly was the one, really, who wanted to get married right now. Don't think I wasn't eager, I was. But my parents thought we should wait a bit, until we could find a house and have it furnished and so on. They would have liked a church wedding. But Dolly wanted to be married by a judge."

"What about her parents?"

"They're dead. She has no living relatives." He turned his head slowly and met my eyes. "Or so she claims."

"You seem to have your doubts about it."

"Not really. It's just that she got so upset when I asked her about her parents. I naturally wanted to meet them, but she treated my request as though I was prying. Finally she told me her entire family was dead, wiped out in an auto accident."

"Where?"

"I don't know where. When it comes right down to it, I don't know too much about my wife. Except that she's a wonderful girl," he added in a rush of loyal feeling slightly flavoured with whisky. "She's beautiful and intelligent and good and I know she loves me." He was almost chanting, as though by wishful thinking or sheer incantation he could bend reality back into shape around him.

"What was her maiden name?"

"Dolly McGee. Her name is really Dorothy. She was working in the university library and I was taking a summer course in Business Ad–"

"Just this summer?"

"That's correct." He swallowed, and his adam's apple throbbed like a grief in his throat. "We only knew each other for six weeks – six and a half weeks – before we were married. But we saw each other every day of those six and a half weeks."

"What did you do together?"

"I don't see that it matters."

"It could. I'm trying to get a line on her personal habits."

"She had no *bad* habits, if that's what you're looking for. She never let me drink when we were out together. She wasn't very keen on the coffee houses, either, or the movies. She was – she's a very serious girl. Most of our time we talked we talked and walked. We must have covered most of West Los Angeles."

"What did you talk about?"

"The meaning of life," he said, as if this went without saying. "We were trying to work out a plan to live by, a set of rules for our marriage and our children. The main thing for Dolly was the children. She wanted to bring them up to be real people. She thought it was more important to be an honest individual than to have security and worldly possessions and so on. I don't want to bore you with all this."

"You're not. I take it she was completely sincere?"

"Nobody was ever more sincere. I mean it. She actually wanted me to give up my job and go back and finish my MA. She didn't think I should take money from my family. She was willing to go on working to help me through. But we decided against that plan, when we made up our minds to get married."

"It wasn't a forced marriage?"

He looked at me stonily. "There was nothing like that between us. As a matter of fact we didn't even – I mean, I didn't touch her on our wedding night. The Surf House and Pacific Point seemed to get on her nerves, even though she was the one who wanted to come here. So we decided to postpone the physical bit. A lot of couples do that nowadays."

"How does Dolly feel about sex?"

"Fine. We talked about it very frankly. If you think she left me because she's afraid of it, you're way off the beam. She's a warm person."

"Why did she leave you, Alex?"

His eyes clouded with pain, which had scarcely left them. "I haven't been able to figure it out. It wasn't anything between me and Dolly, I'm sure of that. The man with the beard must have had something to do with it."

"How does he get into the picture?"

"He came to the hotel that afternoon – the day she left. I was down on the beach having a swim, and afterward I went to sleep in the sun. I must have been away from the room for a couple of hours. She was gone, bag and baggage, when I got back. The desk clerk told me she had this visitor before she left, a man with a short gray beard who stayed in the room about an hour."

"No name?"

"He didn't mention his name."

"Did he and your wife leave together?"

"The desk clerk said they didn't. The man left first. Then Dolly took a taxi to the bus station, but so far as I could find out she didn't buy a ticket. She didn't buy a railroad ticket or an airline ticket either. She had no car. So I've been going on the assumption that she's still here in Pacific Point. She couldn't walk down the freeway."

"She could hitchhike."

"Not Dolly."

"Where did she live before you were married?"

"In Westwood, in a furnished apartment. She gave it up and we moved her typewriter and things into my apartment on Saturday morning just before the ceremony. All the stuff is still there, and it's one of the things that worry me. I've been over it with a fine-toothed comb for clues, but she didn't leave any behind – nothing really personal at all."

"Do you think she planned to marry you and leave you?"

"No, I don't. What would be the point?"

"I can think of several possibilities. Do you carry much insurance, for example?"

"A fair amount. Dad insured me when I was born. But he's still the beneficiary."

"Does your family have money?"

"Not that much. Dad makes a good living, but he works for it. Anyway, what you're hinting at is out of the question. Dolly's completely honest, and she doesn't even care about money."

"What does she care about?"

"I thought she cared about me," he said with his head down. "I still believe she does. Something must have happened to her. She may have gone out of her mind."

"Is she mentally unstable?"

He considered the question, and his answer to it. "I don't

think so. She had her black spells. I guess most people do. I was talking loosely."

"Keep on talking loosely. You can't tell what may be important. You've been making a search for her, of course?"

"As much of a search as I could. But I can't do it all by myself, without any cooperation from the police. They write down what I say on little pieces of paper and put them away in a drawer and give me pitying looks. They seem to think Dolly found out something shameful about me on our wedding night."

"Could there be any truth in that?"

"No! We're crazy about each other. I tried to tell that to the Sheriff this morning. He gave me one of those knowing leers and said he couldn't act unless there was some indication of a breach of the peace. I asked him if a missing woman wasn't some indication, and he said no. She was free and twenty-one and she left under her own power and I had no legal right to force her to come back. He advised me to get an annulment. I told him what he could do with his advice, and he ordered two of his men to throw me out of his office, I found out where the deputy D.A. was, in court, and I was waiting to put in a complaint when I saw you on the stand."

"Nobody sent you to me, then?"

"No, but I can give you references. My father–"

"You told me about your father. He thinks you should get an annulment, too."

Alex nodded dolefully. "Dad thinks I'm wasting my time, on a girl who isn't worth it."

"He could be right."

"He couldn't be more wrong. Dolly is the only one I've ever loved and the only one I ever will love. If you won't help me, I'll find somebody who will!"

I liked his insistence. "My rates are high. A hundred a day and expenses."

"I've got enough to pay you for at least a week." He reached for his billfold and slammed it down on the bar, so hard that the bartender looked at him suspiciously. "Do you want a cash advance?"

"There's no hurry," I said. "Do you have a picture of Dolly?"

He removed a folded piece of newspaper from the billfold and handed it to me with a certain reluctance, as if it was more valuable than money. It was a reproduction of a photograph which had been unfolded and refolded many times.

"Among happy honeymooners at the Surf House," the caption said, "are Mr and Mrs Alex Kincaid of Long Beach." Alex and his bride smiled up at me through the murky light. Her face was oval and lovely in a way of its own, with a kind of hooded intelligence in the eyes and humour like a bittersweet taste in the mouth.

"When was this taken?"

"Three weeks ago Saturday, when we arrived at the Surf House. They do it for everybody. They printed it in the Sunday morning paper, and I clipped it. I'm glad I did. It's the only picture I have of her."

"You could get copies."

"Where?"

"From whoever took it."

"I never thought of that. I'll see the photographer at the hotel about it. How many pictures do you think I should ask him for?"

"Two or three dozen, anyway. It's better to have too many than too few."

"That will run into money."

"I know, and so will I."

"Are you trying to talk yourself out of a job?"

"I don't need the work, and I could use a rest."

"To hell with you then."

He snatched at the flimsy picture between my fingers. It tore across the middle. We faced each other like enemies, each of us holding a piece of the happy honeymooners.

Alex burst into tears.

II

I AGREED over lunch to help him find his wife. That and the chicken-pot pie calmed him down. He couldn't remember when he had eaten last, and he ate ravenously.

We drove out to the Surf House in separate cars. It was on the sea at the good end of town: a pueblo hotel whose Spanish gardens were dotted with hundred-dollar-a-day cottages. The terraces in front of the main building descended in wide green steps to its own marina. Yachts and launches were bobbing at the slips. Further out on the water, beyond the curving promontory that gave Pacific Point its name, white sails leaned against a low gray wall of fog.

The desk clerk in the Ivy League suit was very polite, but he wasn't the one who had been on duty on the Sunday I was interested in. That one had been a summer replacement, a college boy who had gone back to school in the East. He himself, he regretted to say, knew nothing about Mrs Kincaid's bearded visitor or her departure.

"I'd like to talk to the hotel photographer. Is he around today?"

"Yes, sir. I believe he's out by the swimming-pool."

We found him, a thin spry man wearing a heavy camera like an albatross around his neck. Among the colored beach clothes and bathing-costumes, his dark business suit made him look like an undertaker. He was taking some very candid pictures of a middle-aged woman in a bikini who didn't belong in one. Her umbilicus glared at the camera like an eyeless socket.

When he had done his dreadful work, the photographer turned to Alex with a smile. "Hi. How's the wife?"

"I haven't seen her recently," Alex said glumly.

"Weren't you on your honeymoon a couple of weeks ago? Didn't I take your picture?"

Alex didn't answer him. He was peering around at the poolside loungers like a ghost trying to remember how it felt to be human. I said:

"We'd like to get some copies made of that picture you took. Mrs Kincaid is on the missing list, and I'm a private detective. My name is Archer."

"Fargo. Simmy Fargo." He gave me a quick handshake and the kind of glance a camera gives you when it records you for posterity. "In what sense on the missing list?"

"We don't know, she left here in a taxi on the afternoon of September the second. Kincaid has been looking for her ever since."

"That's tough," Fargo said. "I suppose you want the prints for circularization. How many do you think you'll be needing?"

"Three dozen?"

He whistled, and slapped himself on his narrow wrinkled forehead. "I've got a busy weekend coming up, and it's already started. This is Friday. I could let you have them by Monday. But I suppose you want them yesterday?"

"Today will do."

"Sorry." He shrugged loosely, making his camera bob against his chest.

"It could be important, Fargo. What do you say we settle for a dozen in two hours?"

"I'd like to help you. But I've got a job." Slowly, almost against his will, he turned and looked at Alex. "Tell you what I'll do. I'll call the wife in, and you can have your pictures. Only don't stand me up, the way the other one did."

"What other one?" I said.

"Big guy with a beard. He ordered a print of the same picture and he never came back for it. I can let you have that print now if you like."

Alex came out of his dark trance. He took hold of Fargo's arm with both hands and shook it. "You saw him then. Who is he?"

"I thought maybe you knew him." Fargo disengaged himself and stepped back. "As a matter of fact, I thought I knew him, too. I could have sworn I took his picture once. But I couldn't quite place the face. I see too many faces."

"Did he give you his name?"

"He must have. I don't take orders without a name. I'll see if I can find it for you, eh?"

We followed him into the hotel and through a maze of corridors to his small cluttered windowless office. He phoned his wife, then burrowed into the pile of papers on his desk and came up with a photographer's envelope.

Inside, between two sheets of corrugated paper, was a glossy print of the newly-weds. On the front of the envelope Fargo had written in pencil: "Chuck Begley, Wine Cellar."

"I remember now," he said. "He told me he was working at the Wine Cellar. That's a liquor store not too far from here. When Begley didn't claim his picture I called them. They said Begley wasn't working for them any more." Fargo looked from me to Alex. "Does the name Begley mean anything to you?"

We both said that it didn't. "Can you describe him, Mr

Fargo?"

"I can describe the part of him that wasn't covered with seaweed, I mean the beard. His hair is gray, like the beard, and very thick and wavy. Gray eyebrows and gray eyes, an ordinary kind of straight nose. I noticed it was peeling from the sun. He's not bad-looking for an older man, apart from his teeth, which aren't good. And he looks as though he's taken a beating or two in his time. Personally I wouldn't want to go up against him. He's a big man, and he looks pretty rough."

"How big?"

"Three or four inches taller than I am. That would make him six feet one or two. He was wearing a short-sleeve sport shirt, and I noticed the muscles in his arms."

"How did he talk?"

"Nothing special. He didn't have a Harvard accent, and he didn't say ain't."

"Did he give you any reason for wanting the picture?"

"He said he had a sentimental interest. He saw it in the paper, and it reminded him of somebody. I remember thinking he must have dashed right over. The paper with the picture in it came out Sunday morning, and he came in around Sunday noon."

"He must have gone to see your wife immediately afterward," I said to Alex. And to Fargo: "How did this particular picture happen to be used by the newspaper?"

"They picked it out of a batch I sent over. The *Press* often uses my pictures, as a matter of fact I used to work for them. Why they used this one instead of some of the others I couldn't say." He held up the print in the fluorescent light, then handed it to me. "It did turn out well, and Mr Kincaid and his wife make an attractive couple"

"Thanks very much," Alex said sardonically.

"I was paying you a compliment, fellow."

"Sure you were."

I took the print from Fargo and shunted Alex out of the place before it got too small for him. Black grief kept flooding up in him, changing to anger when it reached the air. It wasn't just grief for a one-day wife, it was also grief for himself. He didn't seem to know if he was a man or not.

I couldn't blame him or his feelings, but they made him no

asset to the kind of work I was trying to do. When I found the Wine Cellar, on a motel strip a few blocks inland, I left him outside in his little red sports car.

The interior of the liquor store was pleasantly cool. I was the only potential customer, and the man behind the counter came out from behind it to greet me.

"What can I do for you, sir?"

He wore a plaid waistcoat, and he had the slightly muzzy voice and liquid eyes and dense complexion of a man who drank all day and into the night.

"I'd like to see Chuck Begley."

He looked vaguely pained, and his voice took on a note of mild complaint. "I had to fire Chuck. I'd send him out with a delivery, and sometimes it'd arrive when it was supposed to, and sometimes it wouldn't."

"How long ago did you fire him?"

"Couple of weeks. He only worked for me a couple of weeks. He isn't cut out for that kind of work. I told him more than once it was beneath his capacity. Chuck Begley is a fairly bright man if he'd straighten up, you know."

"I don't know."

"I thought perhaps you were an acquaintance of his."

I showed him my photostat.

He blew the smell of peppermint in my face. "Is Begley on the run?"

"He may be. Why?"

"I wondered when he first came in why a man like him would take a part-time delivery job. What's he wanted for?"

"I wouldn't know. Can you give me his home address?"

"I think I can at that." He stroked his veined nose, watching me over his fingers. "Don't tell Begley I gave you the word. I don't want him bouncing back on me."

"I won't."

"He spends a lot of time in the home of one of my customers. You might say he's a non-paying guest of hers. I certainly wouldn't want to make trouble for her. But then," he reasoned, "if Begley's on the run I'm doing her a favor in seeing that he's picked up. Isn't that right?"

"I'd say so. Where does she live?"

"On Shearwater Beach, cottage number seventeen. Her

name's Madge Gerhardi. Take the freeway south and you'll see the Shearwater turnoff about two miles down the line. Only just don't tell either of them that it was me sent you. Okay?"

"Okay." I left him with his bottles.

III

We parked our cars at the top of the access lane, and I persuaded Alex to stay in his, out of sight. Shearwater Beach turned out to be a kind of expensive slum where several dozen cottages stood in a row. The changing blue reflection of the sea glared through the narrow gaps between them. Beyond their peaked rooftops, out over the water, a tern circled on flashing wings, looking for fish.

Number seventeen needed paint, and leaned on its pilings like a man on crutches. I knocked on the scabbed gray door. Slowly, like bodies being dragged, footsteps approached the other side. The bearded man opened it.

He was a man of fifty or so wearing an open-necked black shirt from which his head jutted like weathered stone. The sunlight struck mica glints from his eyes. The fingers with which he was holding the edge of the door were bitten down to the quick. He saw me looking at them and curled them into a fist.

"I'm searching for a missing girl, Mr Begley." I had decided on the direct approach. "She may have met with foul play and if she did you may have been one of the last people who saw her alive."

He rubbed the side of his face with his clenched knuckles. His face bore marks of old trouble, some of them done by hand: faintly quilted patches around the eyes, a thin scar on his temple divided like a miniature ruler by stitch-marks. Old trouble and the promise of further trouble.

"You must be crazy. I don't even know any girls."

"You know *me*," a woman said behind him.

She appeared at his shoulder and leaned on him, waiting for somebody to second the self-administered flattery. She was about Begley's age, and may have been older. Her body was very assertive in shorts and a halter. Frizzled by repeated dyeings and bleachings, her hair stuck up on her head like a yellow fright wig. Between their deep blue artificial shadows, her eyes were the color of gin.

"I'm very much afraid that you must be mistaken," she said to me with a cultivated Eastern-seaboard accent which lapsed immediately. "I swear by all that's holy that Chuck had nothing to do with any girl. He's been too busy looking after little old me." She draped a plump white arm across the back of his neck. "Haven't you, darling?"

Begley was immobilized between the woman and me. I showed him Fargo's glossy print of the honeymooners.

"You know this girl, don't you? Her name, her married name, is Dolly Kincaid."

"I never heard of her in my life."

"Witnesses tell me different. They say you went to see her at the Surf House three weeks ago this coming Sunday. You saw this picture of her in the paper and ordered a copy of it from the photographer at the Surf House."

The woman tightened her arm around his neck, more like a wrestling partner than a lover. "Who is she, Chuck?"

"I have no idea." But he muttered to himself: "So it's started all over again."

"What has started all over again?"

She was stealing my lines. "Could I please talk to Mr Begley alone?"

"He has no secrets from me." She looked up at him proudly, with a wilted edge of anxiety on her pride. "Have you, darling?" We're going to be married, aren't we, darling?"

"Could you stop calling me darling? Just for five minutes? Please?"

She backed away from him, ready to cry, her downturned red mouth making a lugubrious clown face.

"Please go inside," he said. "Let me talk to the man."

"This is my place. I have a right to know what goes on in my own place."

"Sure you do, Madge. But I have squatter's privileges, at least. Go in and drink some coffee."

"Are you in trouble?"

"No. Of course I'm not." But there was resignation in his voice. "Beat it, eh, like a good girl?"

His last word seemed to mollify her. Dawdling and turning, she disappeared down the hallway. Begley closed the door and leaned on it.

"Now you can tell me the truth," I said.

"All right, so I went to see her at the hotel. It was a stupid impulse. It doesn't make me a murderer."

"Nobody suggested that, except you."

"I thought I'd save you the trouble." He spread out his arms as if for instant crucifixion. "You're the local law, I gather."

"I'm working with them," I said hopefully. "My name is Archer. You haven't explained why you went to see Mrs Kincaid. How well did you know her?"

"I didn't know her at all." He dropped his outspread arms in emphasis. The sensitive areas around his mouth were hidden by his beard, and I couldn't tell what he was doing with them. His gray eyes were unrevealing. "I thought I knew her, but I didn't."

"What do you mean?"

"I thought she might be my daughter. There was quite a resemblance to her in the newspaper picture, but not so much in the flesh. The mistake on my part was natural. I haven't seen my daughter for so long."

"What's your daughter's name?"

He hesitated. "Mary. Mary Begley. We haven't been in touch for over ten years. I've been out of the country, on the other side of the world." He made it sound as remote as the far side of the moon.

"Your daughter must have been quite young when you left."

"Yeah. Ten or eleven."

"And you must have been quite fond of her," I said, "to order a picture just because it reminded you of her."

"I was fond of her."

"Why didn't you go back for the picture then?"

He went into a long silence. I became aware of something impressive in the man, the untouchable still quality of an aging animal.

"I was afraid that Madge would be jealous," he said. "I happen to be living on Madge."

I suspected he was using the bald statement to tell a lie. But it may have come from a deeper source. Some men spend their lives looking for ways to punish themselves for having been born, and Begley had some of the stigmata of the trouble-prone. He said:

"What do you think happened to Mrs Kincaid?" His question was cold and formal, disclaiming all interest in the answer to it.

"I was hoping you'd have some ideas on the subject, She's been missing for nearly three weeks. I don't like it. It's true that girls are always disappearing, but not on their honeymoons – not when they love their husbands."

"She loves hers, does she?"

"He thinks so. How was she feeling when you saw her? Was she depressed?"

"I wouldn't say that. She was surprised to see me."

"Because she hadn't seen you for so long?"

He sneered at me hairily. "Don't bother trying to trap me. I told you she wasn't my daughter. She didn't know me from Adam."

"What did you find to talk about with her?"

"We didn't talk." He paused. "Maybe I asked her a few questions."

"Such as?"

"Who her father was. Who her mother was. Where she came from. She said she came from Los Angeles. Her maiden name was Dolly something – I forget the name. Her parents were both dead. That's about all."

"It took you quite a while to get that much out of her."

"I was only there five or ten minutes, maybe fifteen."

"The desk clerk said an hour."

"He made a mistake."

"Or maybe you did, Mr Begley. Time passes very rapidly sometimes."

He clutched at this dubious excuse. "Maybe I did stay longer than I realized. I remember now, she wanted me to stay and meet her husband." His eyes held steady, but they had taken on a faint lying sheen. "He didn't come and didn't come so I left."

"Did you suggest seeing her again?"

"No. She wasn't that interested in my story."

"You told her your story?"

"I told her about my daughter, naturally, just like I told you."

"I don't understand it. You say you were out of the country for ten years. Where?"

"In New Caledonia, mostly. I worked for a chrome mine there. They shut it down last spring and shipped us home."

"And now you're looking for your daughter?"

"I'd certainly like to put my hands on her."

"So she can be a bridesmaid at your wedding?" I wanted to see how sharp a needle he would take.

He took this one without a word.

"What happened to your wife?"

"She died." His eyes were no longer steady. "Look, do we have to go in to all this? It's bad enough losing your loved ones without having it raked up and pushed in your face." I couldn't tell if his self-pity was false: self-pity always is to some extent.

"It's too bad you lost your family," I said. "But what did you expect when you left the country for ten years?"

"It wasn't my choice. How would you like to get shanghaied and not be able to get back?"

"Is that your story? It isn't a likely one."

"My story is wilder than that, but we won't go into it. You wouldn't believe me, anyway. Nobody else has."

"You could always try me."

"It would take all day. You've got better things to do than talk to me."

"Name one."

"You said there's a young lady missing. Go and find her."

"I was hoping you could help me. I still am hoping, Mr Begley."

He looked down at his feet. He was wearing huaraches. "I've told you all I know about her, I should never have gone to that hotel in the first place. Okay, so I made a mistake. You can't hang a man for a little mistake in judgement.

"You've mentioned murder once, and hanging once, I wonder why."

"It was just a manner of speaking." But the confidence was seeping out of him through the holes my needle had made. He said with a rising inflection: "You think I murdered her?"

"No. I do think this. Something happened between you, or something was said, that might explain why she left so suddenly. Give it some thought, will you?"

Slowly, perhaps involuntarily, he raised his head and looked up at the sun. Under his tilted beard his neck was pale and scrawny. It gave the impression that he was wearing the kind of mask Greek actors wore, covering him completely from my eyes.

"No. Nothing was said like that."

"Was there any trouble between you?"

"No."

"Why did she let you come to her room?"

"I guess she was interested in my story. I talked to her on the house phone, said she resembled my daughter. It was just a foolish impulse. I knew as soon as I saw her that she wasn't."

"Did you make arrangements to see her again?"

"No. I'd certainly like to."

"Did you wait outside the hotel for her, or agree to meet her at the bus station?"

"I did not. What are you trying to nail me for? What do you want?"

"Just the truth. I'm not satisfied Ive been getting it from you."

He said in a sudden spurt of fury: "You've got as much as–" He began to regret the outburst before it was over, and swallowed the rest of the words.

But he turned his back on me and went inside, slamming the door. I waited for a little while, and gave up on him. I walked back along the sandy access lane to our cars.

The blonde woman, Madge Gerhardi, was sitting beside Alex in his red Porsche. He looked up with shining eyes.

"Mrs Gerhardi has seen her. She's seen Dolly."

"With Begley?"

"No, not with him." She opened the door and squeezed out of the little car. "It was at that garage that specializes in fixing foreign cars. I drive an MG myself, and I had it in for a lube job. The girl was there with an old woman. They went away together in an old brown Rolls. The girl was doing the driving."

"Are you certain of the identification?" I showed her the picture again.

She nodded over it emphatically. "I'm certain, unless she has a twin. I noticed her because she was so stunning."

"Do you know who the old woman was?"

"No, but the man at the garage ought to be able to tell you."

She gave us directions, and started to edge away. "I better get back to the house. I snuck out along the beach, and Chuck will be wondering where I am."

IV

A MECHANIC lying face up on a creeper rolled out from under the raised front end of a Jaguar sedan. I saw when he stood up that he was a plump Mediterranean type with "Mario" embroidered on his coverall. He nodded enthusiastically when I asked him about the old Rolls and the old lady.

"That's Mrs Bradshaw. I been looking after her Rolls for the last twelve years, ever since she bought it. It's running as good now as the day she bought it." He looked at his greasy hands with some satisfaction, like a surgeon recalling a series of difficult but successful operations. "Some of the girls she gets to drive her don't know how to treat a good car."

"Do you know the girl who's driving her at present?"

"I don't know her name. Mrs Bradshaw has quite a turnover with her drivers. She gets them from the college mostly. Her son is Dean at the college, and he won't let the old lady do her own driving. She's crippled with rheumatics, and I think she was in a smashup at one time."

I cut in on Mario's complicated explanations and showed him the print. "This girl?"

"Yeah. She was here with Mrs Bradshaw the other day. She's a new one. Like I said, Mrs Bradshaw has quite a turnover. She likes to have her own way, and these college girls don't take orders too well. Personally I always hit it off with Mrs Bradshaw–"

"Where does she live?"

Alex sounded anxious, and Mario was slightly infected by his anxiety. "What is it you want with her?"

"She's not the one I'm interested in. The girl is my wife."

"You and her are on the outs?"

"I don't know. I have to talk to her."

Mario looked up at the high corrugated-iron roof of the garage. "My wife divorced me a couple years ago. I been putting on weight ever since. A man don't have the same motivation."

"Where does Mrs Bradshaw live?" I said.

"Foothill Drive, not too far from here. Take the first cross street to the right, it runs into it. You can look up the house number in the phone book, on the desk there. It's in her son's name, Roy Bradshaw."

I thanked him. He lay down on the creeper and slid back under the Jaguar. The directory was under the telephone on top of the battered desk which stood in a corner. I found the listing: "Roy Bradshaw, 311 Foothill Drive."

"We could phone from here," Alex said.

"It's always better in person."

In spite of the housing tracts and the smokeless industries proliferating around it, Pacific Point had kept its identity. Foothill Drive was lined with trees, and had a dusty changeless quality. Settled old families still lived here behind mortised walls that had resisted earthquakes, or hedges that had outlived generations of gardeners.

The towering cypress hedge of 311 masked the house completely from the road. I turned in through the open iron gates with Alex following me. We passed a small white gatehouse with a green door and green shutters, rounded a bend in the driveway, and came in sight of the white Colonial house.

A woman with a wide straw hat tied under her chin was kneeling shoulder deep among the flowers in front of it. She had a pair of clippers in her gloved hands. They snicked in the silence when our engines died.

She rose cumbrously to her feet and came toward us, tucking wisps of gray hair under her hat. She was just an old lady in dirty tennis shoes but her body, indeterminate in a loose blue smock, carried itself with heavy authority, as if it recalled that it had once been powerful or handsome. The architecture of her face had collapsed under the weight of flesh and years. Still her black eyes were alert, like unexpected animal or bird life in the ruins of a building.

"Mrs Bradshaw?" Alex said eagerly.

"I am Mrs Bradshaw. What do you gentlemen want? I'm very busy, as you can see," She flourished the clippers. "I never trust anyone else to clip my roses. And still they die, poor things." Regret rustled in her voice.

"They look very beautiful to me," I said in an encouraging way. "Mr Kincaid and I hate to bother you. But he seems to have misplaced his wife, and we have reason to think she's working for you."

"For me? I employ no one but my Spanish couple. My son," she added with a trace of pride, "keeps me to a strict budget."

"Don't you have a girl driving for you?"

She smiled. "I completely forgot about her. She's just on a part-time basis. What's her name? Molly? Dolly? I never can remember the girls' names."

"Dolly," I said, and showed her the print. "Is this Dolly?"

She removed one gardening glove to take the picture. Her hand was gnarled by arthritis.

"I do believe it is. But she said nothing to me about being married. I'd never have hired her if I'd known, it makes for too much involvement. I like to take my little drives on schedule."

Alex interrupted her rather garrulous chatter. "Where is she now?"

"I couldn't say. She's done her day's stint for me. She may have walked over to the college, or she may be in the gatehouse. I let my girls use the gatehouse. Sometimes they abuse the privilege, but so far this one hasn't." She gave Alex a sharp black glance. "I hope she won't begin to, now that you've turned up."

"I don't expect she'll be going on–"

I cut him short. "Go and see if she's in the gatehouse." I turned back to Mrs Bradshaw: "How long has she been with you?"

"About two weeks. The semester started two weeks ago."

"Is she attending the college?"

"Yes. I get all my girls from there, except when I have to have a regular attendant, as I did when my son was abroad last summer. I hope I don't lose Dolly. She's brighter than most of them. But if she goes I suppose there are always others. You'll realize, when you've lived as long as I have, that the young ones leave the old ones. . ."

She turned to her roses, glowing red and yellow in the sunlight. She seemed to be looking for some way to finish the thought. None occurred to her. I said:

"What name is she using? What surname?"

"I'm afraid I don't remember. I call them by their first names. My son could tell you."

"Is he here?"

"Roy is at the college. He happens to be the Dean there."

"Is it far from here?"

"You can see it from where you stand."

Her arthritic hand curled on my elbow and turned me gently. Through a gap in the trees I could make out the metal cupola of a small observatory. The old lady spoke close to my ear, in a gossipy way:

"What happened between your young friend and his wife?"

"They came here on their honeymoon and she walked out on him. He's trying to find out why."

"What a strange thing to do," she said. I'd never have acted like that on my honeymoon. I had too much respect for my husband. But girls are different nowadays, aren't they? Loyalty and respect mean nothing to them. Are you married, young man?"

"I have been."

"I see. Are you the boy's father?"

"No. My name is Archer. I'm a private detective."

"Really? What do you make of all this?" She gestured vaguely with her clippers toward the gatehouse.

"Nothing so far. She may have left him on account of a girlish whim. Or she may have had deep dark reasons. All I can do is ask her. By the way, Mrs Bradshaw, have you ever heard her mention a man named Begley?"

"Begley?"

"He's a big man with a short gray beard. He visited her at the Surf House the day she left her husband. There's some possibility that he's her father."

She wet her seamed lips with the purple tip of her tongue. "She didn't mention him to me. I don't encourage the girls to unburden thenselves to me. Perhaps I should."

"What kind of a mood has Dolly been in lately?"

"It's hard to say. She's always the same. Quiet. She thinks her own thoughts."

Alex appeared, walking rapidly around the bend in the driveway. His face was bright.

"It's her definitely. I found her things in the closet."

"You weren't authorized to go in there," Mrs Bradshaw said.

"It's her house, isn't it?"

"It happens to be mine."

"But she has the use of it, hasn't she?"

"She does. You don't."

A quarrel with Dolly's employer was the last thing Alex needed. I stepped between them, turned him around, and walked him away from trouble for the second time.

"Get lost," I said when he was in his car. "You're in my way."

"But I have to see her."

"You'll see her. Go and check in at the Mariner's Rest Motel for both of us. It's on the strip between here and the Surf House–"

"I know where it is. But what about Dolly?"

"I'm going over to the college to talk to her. I'll bring her back with me, if she's willing."

"Why can't I go along to the college?" he said like a spoiled child.

"Because I don't want you to. Dolly has a separate life of her own. You may not like it, but you have no right to jump in and wreck it for her. I'll see you at the motel."

He drove away rapidly and angrily, spinning the wheels of his car. Mrs Bradshaw was back among her roses. I asked her very politely for permission to examine Dolly's things. She said that would have to be up to Dolly.

V

THE CAMPUS was an oasis of vivid green under the brown September foothills. Most of the buildings were new and very modern, ornamented with pierced concrete screens and semi-tropical plantings. A barefoot boy sitting under a roadside palm took time out from his Salinger to show me where the Administration Building was.

I parked in the lot behind it, among a scattering of transportation clunks with faculty stickers. A new black Thunderbird stood out among them. It was late Friday afternoon by now, and the long collegiate weekend was setting in. The glass information booth opposite the entrance of the building was empty. The corridors were practically deserted.

I found the Dean's office without much trouble. The paneled anteroom was furnished with convertible Danish pieces, and with a blonde secretary who sat at a typewriter guarding the closed inner door. She had a pale thin face, strained blue eyes that had worked too long under fluorescent light, and a suspicious voice:

"Can I help you, sir?"

"I'd like to see the Dean."

"Dean Bradshaw is very busy, I'm afraid. Perhaps I can assist you?"

"Perhaps. I'm trying to get in touch with one of your girl students. Her name is Dolly McGee, or Dolly Kincaid."

"Which? she said with a little gasp of irritation.

"Her maiden name is McGee, her married name is Kincaid, I don't know which she is using."

"Are you a parent?" she said delicately.

"No. I'm not her father. But I have good reason for wanting to see her."

She looked at me as if I was a self-confessed kingpin in the white slave traffic. "We have a policy of not giving out information about students, except to parents."

"What about husbands?"

"You're her husband?"

"I represent her husband. I think you'd better let me talk to the Dean about her,"

"I can't do that," she said in a final tone. "Dean Bradshaw is in conference with the department heads. About what do you wish to see Miss McGee?"

"It's a private matter."

"I see."

We had reached an impasse. I said in the hope of making her smile: "We have a policy of not giving out information."

She looked insulted, and went back to her typewriter. I stood and waited. Voices rose and fell behind the door of the inner office. "Budget" was the word I caught most frequently. After a while the secretary said:

"I suppose you could try Dean Sutherland if she's in. Dean Sutherland is Dean of Women. Her office is just across the hall."

Its door was standing open. The woman in it was the well-scrubbed ageless type who looks old in her twenties and young in her forties. She wore her brown hair rolled in a bun at the back of her neck. Her only concession to glamour was a thin pink line of lipstick accenting her straight mouth.

She was a good-looking woman in spite of this. Her face was finely chiseled. The front of her blouse curved out over her desk like a spinnaker going downwind.

"Come in," she said with a severity that I was getting used to. "What are you waiting for?"

Her fine eyes had me hypnotized. Looking into them was like looking into the beautiful core of an iceberg, all green ice and cold blazing light.

"Sit down," she said. "What is your problem."

I told her who I was and why I was there.

"But we have no Dolly McGee or Dolly Kincaid on campus."

"She must be using a third name, then. I know she's a student here. She has a job driving for Dean Bradshaw's mother." I showed her my photograph.

"But this is Dorothy Smith. Why would she register with us under a false name?"

"That's what her husband would like to know."

"Is this her husband in the picture with her?"

"Yes."

"He appears to be a nice enough boy."

"Apparently she didn't think so."

"I wonder why." Her eyes were looking past me, and I felt cheated. "As a matter of fact, I don't see how she *could* register under a false name, unless she came to us with forged credentials." She rose abruptly. "Excuse me for a minute, Mr Archer."

She went into the next room, where filing cabinets stood like upended metal coffins, and came back with a folder which she opened on her desk. There wasn't much in it.

"I see," she said more or less to herself. "She's been admitted provisionally. There's a note here to the effect that her transcript is on the way."

"How long is provisional admission good for?"

"Until the end of September." She consulted her desk calendar. "That gives her nine days to come up with a transcript. But she'll have to come up with an explanation rather sooner.

We don't look with favor on this sort of deception. And I had the impression that she was a straightforward girl." Her mouth turned down at the corners.

"You know her personally, Dean Sutherland?"

"I make a point of contacting all the new girls. I went out of my way to be useful to Miss or Mrs Smith-Kincaid. In fact I helped to get her a part-time job in the library."

"And the job with old Mrs Bradshaw?"

She nodded. "She heard that there was an opening there, and I recommended her." She looked at her watch. "She may be over there now."

"She isn't. I just came from Mrs Bradshaw's. Your Dean lives pretty high on the hog, by the way. I thought academic salaries were too low."

"They are, Dean Bradshaw comes from a wealthy old family. What was his mother's reaction to this?" She made an impatient gesture which somehow included me.

"She seemed to take it in stride. She's a smart old woman."

"I'm glad you found her so," she said, as if she had had other kinds of experience with Mrs Bradshaw. "Well, I suppose I'd better see if Mrs Smith-Kincaid is in the library."

"I could go over there and ask."

"I think not. I had better talk to her first, and try to find out what's going on in her little head."

"I didn't want to make trouble for her."

"Of course not, and you didn't. The trouble is and was there. You merely uncovered it. I'm grateful to you for that."

"Could your gratitude," I said carefully, "possibly take the form of letting me talk to her first?"

"I'm afraid not."

"I've had a lot of experience getting the facts out of people."

It was the wrong thing to say. Her mouth turned down at the corners again. Her bosom changed from a promise to a threat.

"I've had experience, too, a good many years of it, and I am a trained counselor. If you'll be good enough to wait outside, I'm going to try and phone her at the library." She flung a last shaft as I went out: "And please don't try to intercept her on the way here."

"I wouldn't dream of it, Miss Sutherland."

"Dean Sutherland, if you please."

I went and read the bulletin board beside the information booth. The jolly promises of student activities, dances and get-togethers and poetry clubs and breakfasts where French was spoken, only saddened me. It was partly because my own attempt at college hadn't worked out, partly because I'd just put the kibosh on Dolly's.

A girl wearing horn-rimmed glasses, and a big young fellow in a varsity sweater drifted in from outside and leaned against the wall. She was explaining something to him, something about Achilles and the tortoise. Achilles was chasing the tortoise, it seemed, but according to Zeno he would never catch it. The space between them was divisible into an infinite number of parts; therefore it would take Achilles an infinite period of time to traverse it. By that time the tortoise would be somewhere else.

The young man nodded. "I see that."

"But it isn't so," the girl cried. "The infinite divisibility of space is merely theoretical. It doesn't affect actual *movement* across space."

"I don't get it, Heidi."

"Of course you do. Imagine yourself on the football field. You're on the twenty-yard line and there's a tortoise crawling away from you toward the thirty-yard line."

I stopped listening. Dolly was coming up the outside steps towards the glass door, a dark-haired girl in a plaid skirt and a cardigan. She leaned on the door for a moment before she pushed it open. She seemed to have gone to pieces to some extent since Fargo had taken her picture. Her skin was sallow, her hair not recently brushed. Her dark uncertain glance slid over me without appearing to take me in.

She stopped short before she reached Dean Sutherland's office. Turning in a sudden movement, she started for the front door. She stopped again, between me and the two philosophers, and stood considering. I was struck by her faintly sullen beauty, her eyes dark and blind with thought. She turned around once more and trudged back along the hallway to meet her fate.

The office door closed behind her. I strolled past it after a while and heard the murmur of female voices inside, but nothing intelligible. From Dean Bradshaw's office across the hall the heads of departments emerged in a body. In spite of their glasses and their foreheads and their scholars' stoops, they looked a little like schoolboys let out for recess.

A woman with a short razorblade haircut came into the building and drew all their eyes. Her ash-blonde hair shone against the deep tan of her face. She attached herself to a man standing by himself in the doorway of the Dean's office.

He seemed less interested in her than she was in him. His good looks were rather gentle and melancholy, the kind that excite maternal passions in women. Though his brown wavy hair was graying at the temples, he looked rather like a college boy who twenty years after graduation glanced up from his books and found himself middle-aged.

Dean Sutherland opened the door of her office and made a sign to him. "Can you spare me a minute, Dr Bradshaw? Something serious has come up." She was pale and grim, lke a reluctant executioner.

He excused himself. The two deans shut themselves up with Dolly. The woman with the short and shining haircut frowned at the closed door. Then she gave me an appraising glance, as if she was looking for a substitute for Bradshaw. She had a promising mouth and good legs and a restless predatory air. Her clothes had style.

"Looking for someone?" she said.

"Just waiting."

"For Lefty or for Godot? It makes a difference."

"For Lefty Godot. The pitcher."

"The pitcher in the rye?"

"He prefers bourbon."

"So do I," she said. "You sound like an anti-intellectual to me, Mr –"

"Archer. Didn't I pass the test?"

"It depends on who does the grading."

"I've been thinking maybe I ought to go back to school. You make it seem attractive, and besides I feel so out of things when my intellectual friends are talking about Jack Kerouac and Eugene Burdick and other great writers, and I can't read. Seriously, if I were thinking of going back to college, would you recommend this place?"

She gave me another of her appraising looks. "Not for you, Mr Archer. I think you'd feel more at home in some larger urban university, like Berkeley or Chicago. I went to Chicago myself. This college presents quite a contrast."

"In what way?"

"Innumerable ways. The quotient of sophistication here is very low, for one thing. This used to be a denominational college, and the moral atmosphere is still in Victorian stays." As if to demonstrate that she was not, she shifted her pelvis. "They tell me when Dylan Thomas visited here – but perhaps we'd better not go into that. *De mortuis nil nisi bonum.*"

"Do you teach Latin?"

"No, I have small Latin and less Greek. I try to teach modern languages. My name is Helen Haggerty, by the way. As I was saying, I wouldn't really recommend Pacific Point to you. The standards are improving every year, but there's still a great deal of dead wood around. You can see some of it from here."

She cast a sardonic glance toward the entrance, where five or six of her fellow professors were conducting a post-mortem of their conference with the Dean.

"That was Dean Bradshaw you were talking to, wasn't it?"

"Yes. Is he the one you want to see?"

"Among others."

"Don't be put off by his rather forbidding exterior. He's a fine scholar – the only Harvard doctor on the faculty – and he can advise you better that I ever could. But tell me honestly, are you really serious about going back to college? Aren't you kidding me a little?"

"Maybe a little."

"You could kid me more effectively over a drink. And I could use a drink, preferably bourbon."

"It's a handsome offer." And a sudden one, I thought. "Give me a rain check, will you? Right now I have to wait for Lefty Godot."

She looked more disappointed than she had any right to be. We parted on fairly good, mutually suspicious terms.

The fatal door I was watching opened at last. Dolly backed out thanking the two Deans effusively, and practically curtsying. But I saw when she turned around and headed for the entrance that her face was white and set.

I went after her, feeling a little foolish. The situation reminded me of a girl I used to follow home from Junior High. I never did work up enough nerve to ask her for the privilege of carrying her books. But I began to identify Dolly with that unattainable girl whose name I couldn't even remember now.

She hurried along the mall that bisected the campus, and started up the steps of the library building. I caught up with her.

"Mrs Kincaid?"

She stopped as though I had shot her. I took her arm instinctively. She flung away my hand, and opened her mouth as if to call out for help. No sound came out. The other students around us, passing on the wide mall or chatting on the steps, paid no attention to her silent scream.

"I'd like very much to talk to you, Mrs Kincaid."

She pushed her hair back, so forcefully that one of her eyes slanted up and gave her a Eurasian look. "Who are you?"

"A friend of your husband's. You've given Alex a bad three weeks."

"I suppose I have," she said, as if she had only just thought of it.

"You must have had a bad three weeks yourself, if you're fond of him at all. Are you?"

"Am I what?" She seemed to be slightly dazed.

"Fond of Alex."

"I don't know. I haven't had time to think about it. I don't wish to discuss it, with you or anyone. Are you really a friend of Alex's?"

"I think I can claim to be. He doesn't understand what you're doing to him. He's a pretty sad young man."

"No doubt he caught it from me. Spreading ruin is my specialty."

"It doesn't have to be. Why don't you call it off, whatever you're doing, and give it another try with Alex? He's waiting for you here in town right now?"

"He can wait till doomsday. I'm not going back to him."

Her young voice was surprisingly firm, almost harsh. There was something about her eyes I didn't like. They were wide and dry and fixed, eyes which had forgotten how to cry.

"Did Alex hurt you in some way?"

"He wouldn't hurt a fly. You know that, if you're really a friend of his. He's a nice harmless boy, and *I* don't want to hurt *him*." She added with conscious drama: "Tell him to congratulate himself on his narrow escape."

"Is that the only message you have for your husband?"

"He isn't my husband, not really. Tell him to get an annulment. Tell him I'm not ready to settle down. Tell him I've decided to finish my education."

She made it sound like a solitary trip to the moon, one-way.

I went back to the Administration Building. The imitation flagstone pavement of the mall was flat and smooth, but I had the feeling that I was walking knee-deep in gopher holes. Dean Sutherland's door was closed and, when I knocked, her "Come in" was delayed and rather muffled.

Dean Bradshaw was still with her, looking more than ever like a college student on whom light frost had fallen during the night.

She was flushed, and her eyes were bright emerald green. "This is Mr Archer, Brad, the detective I told you about."

He gave my hand a fiercely competitive grip. "It's a pleasure to meet you, sir. Actually," he said with an attempt at a smile, "it's rather a mixed pleasure under the circumstances. I very much regret the necessity of your coming here to our campus."

"The kind of work I do has to be done," I said a little defensively. "Mrs Kincaid ran out on her husband, and some explanation is due him. Did she give any to you?"

Dean Sutherland put on her grim face. "She's not returning to him. She found out something on their wedding night so dreadful –"

Bradshaw raised his hand. "Wait a minute, Laura. The facts she divulged to you are in the nature of professional confidences. We certainly don't want this chap running back to her husband with them. The poor girl is frightened enough as it is."

"Frightened of her husband? I find that hard to believe," I said.

"She didn't pour out her heart to you," Laura Sutherland cried warmly. "Why do you suppose the poor child used a fake name? She was mortally afraid that he would track her down."

"You're being melodramatic, you know." Bradshaw's tone was indulgent. "The boy can't be as bad as all that."

"You didn't hear her, Brad. She told me things, as woman to woman, that I haven't even told you, and I don't intend to."

I said: "Perhaps she was lying."

"She most assuredly was not! I know the truth when I hear it. And my advice to you is to go back to that husband of hers, wherever he is, and tell him that you haven't been able to find her. She'll be safer and happier if you do."

"She seems to be safe enough. She certainly isn't happy. I talked to her outside for a minute."

Bradshaw tilted his head in my direction. "What did she say?"

"Nothing sensational. She made no accusations against Kincaid. In fact she blamed herself for the breakup. She says she wants to go on with her education."

"Good."

"Are you going to let her stay here?"

Bradshaw nodded. "We've decided to overlook her little deception. We believe in giving young people a certain amount of leeway, so long as it doesn't impinge on the rights of others. She can stay, at least for the present, and continue to use her pseudonym if she likes." He added with dry academic humor: "'A rose by any other name,' you know."

"She's going to have her transcripts sent to us right away," Dean Sutherland said. "Apparently she's had two years of junior college and a semester at the university."

"What's she planning to study here?"

"Dolly is majoring is psychology. According to Professor Haggerty, she has a flair for it."

"How would Profesor Haggerty know that?"

"She's Dolly's academic counselor. Apparently Dolly is deeply interested in criminal and abnormal psychology."

For some reason I thought of Chuck Begley's bearded head, with eyes opaque as a statue's. "When you were talking with Dolly, did she say anything about a man named Begley?"

"Begley?" They looked at each other and then at me. "Who," she asked, "is Begley?"

"It's possible he's her father. At any rate he had something to do with her leaving her husband. Incidentally I wouldn't put too much stock in her husband's Asiatic perversions or whatever it was she accused him of. He's a clean boy, and he respects her."

"Your entitled to your opinion," Laura Sutherland said, as though I wasn't. "But please don't act on it precipitately. Dolly is a sensitive young woman, and something has happened to shake her very deeply. You'll be doing them both a service by keeping them apart."

"I agree," Bradshaw said solemnly.

"The trouble is, I'm being paid to bring them together. But I'll think about it, and talk it over with Alex."

VI

In the parking lot behind the building Professor Helen Haggerty was sitting at the wheel of the new black Thunderbird convertible. She had put the top down and parked it beside my car, as if for contrast. The late afternoon sunlight slanting across the foothills glinted on her hair and eyes and teeth.

"Hello again."

"Hello again," I said. "Are you waiting for me?"

"Only if you're left-handed."

"I'm ambidextrous."

"You would be. You threw me a bit of a curve just now."

"I did?"

"I know who you are." She patted a folded newspaper on the leather seat beside her. The visible headline said: "MRS PERRINE ACQUITTED." Helen Haggerty said: "I think it's very exciting. The paper credits you with getting her off. But it's not quite clear how you did it."

"I simply told the truth, and evidently the jury believed me. At the time the alleged larceny was committed here in Pacific Point, I had Mrs Perrine under close surveillance in Oakland."

"What for? Another larceny?"

"It wouldn't be fair to say."

She made a mock-sorrowful mouth, which fitted the lines of her face too well. "All the interesting facts are confidential. But I happen to be checked out for security. In fact my father is a policeman. So get in and tell me all about Mrs Perrine."

"I can't do that."

"Or I have a better idea," she said with her bright unnatural smile. "Why don't you come over to my house for a drink?"

"I'm sorry, I have work to do."

"Detective work?"

"Call it that."

"Come *on*." With a subtle movement, her body joined in the invitation. "All work and no play makes Jack a dull boy. You don't want to be a dull boy and make me feel rejected. Besides, we have things to talk about."

"The Perrine case is over. Nothing could interest me less."

"It was the Dorothy Smith case I had in mind. Isn't that why you're on campus?"

"Who told you that?"

"The grapevine. Colleges have the most marvelously efficient grapevines, second only to penitentiaries."

"Are you familiar with penitentiaries?"

"Not intimately. But I wasn't lying when I told you my father was a policeman." A gray pinched expression touched her face. She covered it over with another smile. "We do have things in common. Why don't you come along?"

"All right. I'll follow you. It will save you driving me back."

"Wonderful."

She drove as rapidly as she operated, with a jerky nervousness and a total disregard for the rules of the road. Fortunately the campus was almost empty of cars and people. Diminished by the foothills and by their own long shadows, the buildings resembled a movie lot which had shut down for the night.

She lived back of Foothill Drive in a hillside house made out of aluminium and glass and black enameled steel. The nearest rooftop floated among the scrub oaks a quarter of a mile down the slope. You could stand in the living-room by the central fireplace and see the blue mountains rising up on one side, the gray ocean falling away on the other. The off-shore fog was pushing in to the land.

"Do you like my little eyrie?"

"Very much."

"It isn't really mine, alas. I'm only renting at present, though I have hopes. Sit down. What will you drink? I'm going to have a tonic."

"That will do nicely."

The polished tile floor was almost bare of furniture. I strolled around the large room, pausing by one of the glass walls to look out. A wild pigeon lay on the patio with its iridescent neck broken. Its faint spreadeagled image outlined in dust showed where it had flown against the glass.

I sat on a rope chair which probably belonged on the patio. Helen Haggerty brought our drinks and disposed herself on a canvas chaise, where the sunlight would catch her hair again, and shine on her polished brown legs.

"I'm really just camping for now," she said. "I haven't sent for my furniture, because I don't know if I want it around me any more. I may just leave it in storage and start all over, and to hell with the history. Do you think that's a good idea, Curveball Lefty Lew?"

"Call me anything, I don't mind. I'd have to know the history."

"Ha. You never will." She looked at me sternly for a minute, and sipped her drink. "You might as well call me Helen."

"All right, Helen.

"You make it sound so formal. I'm not a formal person, and neither are you. Why should we be formal with each other?"

"You live in a glass house, for one thing," I said smiling. "I take it you haven't been in it long."

"A month. Less than a month. It seems longer. You're the first really interesting man I've met since I arrived here."

I dodged the compliment. "Where did you live before?"

"Here and there. There and here. We academic people are such nomads. It doesn't suit me. I'd like to settle down permanently. I'm getting old."

"It doesn't show.

"You're being gallant. Old for a woman, I mean. Men never grow old."

Now that she had me where she apparently wanted me, she wasn't crowding so hard, but she was working. I wished that she would stop, because I liked her. I downed my drink. She brought me a second tonic with all the speed and efficiency of a cocktail waitress. I couldn't get rid of the dismal feeling that each of us was there to use the other.

With the second tonic she let me look down her dress. She was smooth and brown as far as I could see. She arranged herself on the chaise with one hip up, so that I could admire the curve. The sun, in its final yellow flareup before setting, took possession of the room.

"Shall I pull the drapes?" she said.

"Don't bother for me. It'll be down soon. You were going to tell me about Dolly Kincaid alias Dorothy Smith."

"Was I?"

"You brought the subject of her up. I understand you're her academic counselor."

"And that's why you're interested in me, *n'est-ce pas?*" Her tone was mocking.

"I was interested in you before I knew of your connection with Dolly."

"Really?"

"Really. Here I am to prove it."

"Here you are because I lured you with the magic words Dorothy Smith. What's she doing on this campus anyway?" She sounded almost jealous of the girl.

"I was sort of hoping you knew the answer to that."

"Don't you?"

"Dolly gives conflicting stories, probably derived from romantic fiction –"

"I don't think so," she said. "She's a romantic all right – one of these romantic idealists who are always a jump or two behind her unconscious mind. I ought to know, I used to be one myself. But I also think she has some real trouble – appalling trouble."

"What was her story to you?"

"It was no story. It was the lousy truth. We'll come to it later on, if you're a good boy." She stirred like an odalisque in the dying light, and recrossed her polished legs. "How brave are you, Mr Lew?"

"Men don't talk about how brave they are."

"You're full of copybook maxims," she said with some malice. "I want a serious answer."

"You could always try me."

"I may at that. I have a use – I mean, I need a man."

"Is that a proposal, or a business proposition, or are you thinking about some third party?"

"You're the man I have in mind. What would you say if I told you that I'm likely to be killed this weekend?"

"I'd advise you to go away for the weekend."

She leaned sideways toward me. Her breast hardly sagged. "Will you take me?"

"I have a prior commitment."

"If you mean little Mr Alex Kincaid, I can pay you better than he can. Not to mention fringe benefits," she added irrepressibly.

"That college grapevine is working overtime. Or is Dolly the source of your information?"

"She's one of them. I could tell you things about that girl that would curl your hair."

"Go ahead. I've always wanted curly hair."

"Why should I? You don't offer a *quid pro quo*. You don't even take me seriously. I'm not used to being turned down flat, by the way."

"It's nothing personal. I'm just the phlegmatic type. Anyway, you don't need me. There are roads going in three directions – Mexico, the desert, or Los Angeles – and you have a nice fast car."

"I'm too nervous to drive any distance."

"Scared?"

She nodded.

"You put up a good front."

"A good front is all I have."

Her face looked closed and dark, perhaps because the sunlight had faded from the room. Only her hair seemed to hold the light. Beyond the slopes of her body I could see the mountains darkening down.

"Who wants to kill you, Helen?"

"I don't know exactly. But I've been threatened."

"How?"

"Over the telephone. I didn't recognize the voice. I couldn't tell if it was a man or a woman, or something in between." She shuddered.

"Why would anybody threaten you?"

"I don't know," she said without meeting my eyes.

"Teachers do get threatened from time to time. It usually isn't serious. Have you had a run-in with any local crackpots?"

"I don't even know any local people. Except the ones at the college, of course."

"You may have a psychoneurotic in one of your classes."

She shook her head. "It's nothing like that. This is serious."

"How do you know?"

"I have my ways of knowing."

"Is it anything to do with Dolly Kincaid?"

"Perhaps. I can't say for sure. The situation is so complicated."

"Tell me about the complicated situation."

"It goes a long way back," she said, "all the way back to Bridgeton."

"Bridgeton?"

"The city where I was born and raised. The city where everything happened. I ran away, but you can't run away from the landscape of your dreams. My nightmares are still set in the streets of Bridgeton. The voice on the telephone threatening to kill me was Bridgeton catching up with me. It was the voice of Bridgeton talking out of the past."

She was unconscious of herself, caught in a waking nightmare, but her description of it sounded false. I still didn't know whether to take her seriously.

"Are you sure you're not talking nonsense out of the present?"

"I'm not making this up," she said. "Bridgeton will be the death of me. Actually I've always known it would."

"Towns don't kill people."

"You don't know the proud city of my birth. It has quite a record along those lines."

"Where is it?"

"In Illinois, south of Chicago."

"You say that everything happened there. What do you mean?"

"Everything important – it was all over before I knew it had started. But I don't want to go into the subject."

"I can't very well help you unless you do."

"I don't believe you have any intention of helping me. You're simply trying to pump me for information."

It was true. I didn't care for her as she wished to be cared for by someone. I didn't entirely trust her. Her handsome body seemed to contain two alternating persons, one sensitive and candid, one hard and evasive.

She rose and went to the glass wall that faced the mountains. They had turned lavender and plum, with dark nocturnal blue in their clefts and groins. The entire evening, mountains and sky and city, was inundated with blue.

"*Die blaue Stunde*," she said more or less to herself. "I used to love this hour. Now it gives me the mortal shivers."

I got up and stood behind her. "You're deliberately working on your own emotions."

"You know so much about me."

"I know you're an intelligent woman. Act like one. If the place is getting you down leave it, or stay here and take precautions. Ask for police protection."

"You're very free with brilliant suggestions not involving you. I asked for protection yesterday after I got the threatening telephone call. The Sheriff sent a man out. He said such calls were common, and usually involved teenagers."

"Could it have been a teenager?"

"I don't think so. But the deputy said they sometimes disguise their voices. He told me not to worry."

"So don't worry."

"I can't help it. I'm afraid, Lew. Stay with me?"

She turned and leaned on my chest, moving her body tentatively against me. The only real feeling I had for her was pity. She was trying to use me, and using herself in order to use me.

"I have to run along," I said. "I told you at the start I have a prior commitment. But I'll check back on you."

"Thanks so much!"

She pulled away from me, so violently that she thudded like a bird against the glass wall.

VII

I DROVE downhill through deepening twilight toward the Mariner's Rest Motel, telling myself in various tones of voice that I had done the right thing. The trouble was, in the scene I had just walked out of, there was no right thing to do – only sins of commission or omission.

A keyboy wearing a gold-braided yachting cap who looked as though he had never set foot on a dock told me that Alex Kincaid had registered and gone out again. I went to the Surf House for dinner. The spotlit front of the big hotel reminded me of Fargo and all the useless pictures I had ordered from him.

He was in the dark room adjoining his little office. When he came out he was wearing rectangular dark glasses against the light. I couldn't see his eyes, but his mouth was hostile. He picked up a bulky manila envelope from the desk and thrust it at me.

"I thought you were in a hurry for these prints."

"I was. Things came up. We found her."

"So now you don't want 'em? My wife worked in this sweatbox half the afternoon to get 'em ready."

"I'll take them. Kincaid will have a use for them if I don't. How much?"

"Twenty-five dollars including tax. It's actually $24.96."

I gave him two tens and a five, and his mouth went through three stages of softening. "Are they getting back together?"

"I don't know yet."

"Where did you find her?"

"Attending the local college. She has a job driving for an old lady named Bradshaw."

"The one with the Rolls?"

"Yes. You know her?"

"I wouldn't say that. She and her son generally eat Sunday buffet lunch in the dining-room. She's quite a character. I took a candid picture of them once, on the chance they'd order some copies, and she threatened to smash my camera with her cane. I felt like telling the old biddy her face was enough to smash it."

"But you didn't?"

"I can't afford such luxuries." He spread out his chemical-stained hands. "She's a local institution, and she could get me fired."

"I understand she's loaded."

"Not only that. Her son is a big wheel in educational circles. He seems like a nice enough joe, in spite of the Harvard lah-de-dah. As a matter of fact he calmed her down when she wanted to smash my Leica. But it's hard to figure a guy like that, a good-looking guy in his forties still tied to his old lady's apron-strings."

"It happens in the best of families."

"Yeah, especially in the best. I see a lot of these sad cookies waiting around for the money, and by the time they inherit it's too late. At least Bradshaw had the guts to go out and make a career for himself." Fargo looked at his watch. "Speaking of careers, I've already put in a twelve-hour day and I've got about two hours of developing to do. See you."

I started toward the hotel coffee-shop. Fargo came running after me along the corridor. The rectangular dark glasses lent his face a robotlike calm which went oddly with the movements of his legs and arms.

"I almost forgot to ask you. You get a line on this Begley?"

"I talked to him for quite a while. He didn't give too much. He's living with a woman on Shearwater Beach."

"Who's the lucky woman?" Fargo said.

"Madge Gerhardi is her name. Do you know her?"

"No, but I think I know who he is. If I could take another look at him –"

"Come over there now."

"I can't. I'll tell you who I *think* he is under all that sea-weed, if you promise not to quote me. There's such a thing as accidental resemblance, and a libel suit is the last thing I need."

"I promise not to quote you."

"See that you don't." He took a deep breath like a skin diver getting ready to go for the bottom. "I think he's a fellow named Thomas McGee who murdered his wife in Indian Springs about ten years ago. I took a picture of McGee when I was a cub reporter on the paper, but they never used the picture. They never play up those Valley cases."

"You're sure he murdered his wife?"

"Yeah, it was an open-and-shut case. I don't have time to go into details, in fact they're getting pretty hazy at this late date. But most of the people around the courthouse thought he should have been given first degree. Gil Stevens convinced the jury to go for second degree, which explains how he's out so quick."

Remembering Begley's story about his ten years on the other side of the world, the other side of the moon, I thought that ten years wasn't so very quick.

The fog was dense along Shearwater Beach. It must have been high tide: I could hear the surf roaring up under the cottages and sucking at their pilings. The smell of iodine hung in the chilly air.

Madge Gerhardi answered the door and looked at me rather

vaguely. The paint on her eyelids couldn't hide the fact that they were swollen.

"You're the detective, aren't you?"

"Yes. May I come in?"

"Come in if you want. It won't do you any good. He's gone."

I'd already guessed it from her orphaned air. I followed her along a musty hallway into the main room, which was high and raftered. Spiders had been busy in the angles of the rafters, which were webbed and blurred as if fog had seeped in at the corners. The rattan furniture was coming apart at the joints. The glasses and empty bottles and half-empty bottles standing around on the tables and the floor suggested that a party had been going on for some days and might erupt again if I wasn't careful.

The woman kicked over an empty bottle on the way to the settee, where she flung herself down.

"It's your fault he's gone," she complained. "He started to pack right after you were here this afternoon."

I sat on a rattan chair facing her. "Did Begley say where he was going?"

"Not to me he didn't. He did say I wasn't to expect him back, that it was all off. Why did you have to scare him, anyway? Chuck never did anybody any harm."

"He scares very easily."

"Chuck is sensitive. He's had a great deal of trouble. Many's the time he told me that all he wanted was a quiet nook where he could write about his experiences. He's writing an autobiographical novel about his experiences."

"His experiences in New Caledonia?"

She said with surprising candor: "I don't think Chuck ever set foot in New Caledonia. He got that business about the chrome mine out of an old *National Geographic* magazine. I don't believe he ever left this country."

"Where has he been?"

"In the pen," she said. "You know that, or you wouldn't be after him. I think it's a dirty crying shame, when a man has paid his debt to society and proved that he can rehabilitate himself–"

It was Begley she was quoting. Begley's anger she was expressing, but she couldn't sustain the anger or remember the end of the quotation. She looked around the wreckage of the room in dim alarm, as if she had begun to suspect that his rehabilitation was not complete.

"Did he tell you what he was in for, Mrs Gerhardi?"

"Not in so many words. He read me a piece from his book the other night. This character in the book was in the pen and he was thinking about the past and how they framed him for a murder he didn't commit. I asked him if the character stood for him. He wouldn't say. He went into one of his deep dark silences."

She went into one of her own. I could feel the floor trembling under my feet. The sea was surging among the pilings like the blithe mindless forces of dissolution. The woman said:

"Was Chuck in the pen for murder?"

"I was told tonight that he murdered his wife ten years ago. I haven't confirmed it. Can you?"

She shook her head. Her face had lengthened as if by its own weight, like unbaked dough. "It must be a mistake."

"I hope so. I was also told that his real name is Thomas McGee. Did he ever use that name?"

"No."

"It does tie in with another fact," I said, thinking aloud. "The girl he went to visit at the Surf House had the same name before she was married. He said the girl resembled his daughter. I think she is his daughter. Did he ever talk about her?"

"Never."

"Or bring her here?"

"No. If she's his daughter, he wouldn't bring her here." She reached for the empty bottle she had kicked over, set it on its base, and slumped back onto the settee, as if morally exhausted by the effort.

"How long did Begley, or McGee, live here with you?"

"A couple of weeks is all. We were going to be married. It's lonely living here without a man."

"I can imagine."

She drew a little life from the sympathy in my voice: "They just don't stay with me. I try to make things nice for them, but they don't stay. I should have stuck with my first husband." Her eyes were far away and long ago. "He treated me like a queen but I was young and foolish. I didn't know any better than to leave him."

We listened to the water under the house.

"Do you think Chuck went away with this girl you call his daughter?"

"I doubt it," I said. "How did he leave here, Mrs Gerhardi? By car?"

"He wouldn't let me drive him. He said he was going up to the corner and catch the L.A. bus. It stops at the corner if you signal it. He walked up the road with his suitcase and out of sight." She sounded both regretful and relieved.

"About what time?"

"Around three o'clock."

"Did he have any money?"

"He must have had some for the bus fare. He couldn't have had much. I've been giving him a little money, but he would only take what he needed from me, and then it always had to be a loan. Which he said he would pay back when he got his book of experiences on the market. But I don't care if he never pays me back. He was nice to have around."

"Really?"

"Really he was. Chuck is a smart man. I don't care what he's done in the course of his life. A man can change for the better. He never gave me a bad time once." She made a further breakthrough into candor: "I was the one who gave him the bad times. I have a drinking problem. He only drank with me to be sociable. He didn't want me to drink alone." She blinked her gin-colored eyes. "Would you like a drink?"

"No, thanks. I have to be on my way." I got up and stood over her. "You're sure he didn't tell you where he was going?"

"Los Angeles is all I know. He promised I'd hear from him but I don't expect it. It's over."

"If he should write or phone will you let me know?"

She nodded. I gave her my card, and told her where I was staying. When I went out, the fog had moved inland as far as the highway.

VIII

I STOPPED at the motel again on my way to the Bradshaw house. The keyboy told me that Alex was still out. I wasn't surprised when I found his red Porsche parked under the Bradshaw's hedge beside the road.

The moon was rising behind the trees. I let my thoughts rise with it, imagining that Alex had got together with his bride and they were snug in the gatehouse, talking out their troubles. The sound of the girl's crying wiped out the hopeful image. Her voice was loud and terrible, almost inhuman. Its compulsive rhythms rose and fell like the ululations of a hurt cat.

The door of the gatehouse was slightly ajar. Light spilled around its edges, as if extruded by the pressure of the noise inside. I pushed it open.

"Get out of here," Alex said.

They were on a studio bed in the tiny sitting-room. He had his arms around her, but the scene was not domestic. She seemed to be fighting him, trying to struggle out of his embrace. It was more like a scene in a closed ward where psychiatric nurses will hold their violent patients, sometimes for hours on end, rather than strap them in canvas jackets.

Her blouse was torn, so that one of her breasts was almost naked. She twisted her unkempt head around and let me see her face. It was gray and stunned, and it hardly changed expression when she screamed at me:

"Get out!"

"I think I better stick around," I said to the both of them.

I closed the door and crossed the room. The rhythm of her crying was running down. It wasn't really crying. Her eyes were dry and fixed in the gray flesh. She hid them against her husband's body.

His face was shining white.

"What happened, Alex?"

"I don't really know. I was waiting for her when she got home a few minutes ago. I couldn't get much sense out of her. She's awfully upset about something."

"She's in shock," I said, thinking that he was close to it himself. "Was she in an accident?"

"Something like that."

His voice trailed off in a mumble. His look was inward, as if he was groping for the strength to handle this new problem.

"Is she hurt, Alex?"

"I don't think so. She came running down the road, and then she tried to run away again. She put up quite a battle when I tried to stop her."

As if to demonstrate her prowess as a battler, she freed her hands and beat at his chest. There was blood on her hands. It left red dabs on his shirt-front.

"Let me go," she pleaded. "I want to die. I deserve to."

"She's bleeding, Alex."

He shook his head. "It's somebody else's blood. A friend of hers was killed."

"And it's all my fault," she said in a flat voice.

He caught her wrists and held her. I could see manhood biting into his face. "Be quiet Dolly. You're talking nonsense."

"Am I? She's lying in her blood, and I'm the one who put her there."

"Who is she talking about?" I said to Alex.

"Somebody called Helen. I've never heard of her."

I had.

The girl began to talk in her wispy monotone, so rapidly and imprecisely that I could hardly follow. She was a devil and so was her father before her and so was Helen's father and they had the bond of murder between them which made them blood sisters and she had betrayed her blood sister and done her in.

"What did you do to Helen?"

"I should have kept away from her. They die when I go near them."

"That's crazy talk," Alex said softly. "You never hurt anybody."

"What do you know about me?"

"All I need to. I'm in love with you."

"Don't say that. It only makes me want to kill myself." Sitting upright in the circle of his arms, she looked at her bloody hands and cried some more of her terrible dry tears. "I'm a criminal."

Alex looked up at me, his eyes blue-black. "Can you make

any sense of it?"

"Not much."

"You can't really think she killed this Helen person?" We were talking past Dolly as if she was deaf or out of her head, and she accepted this status.

"We don't even know that anybody's been killed," I said. "Your wife is loaded with some kind of guilt, but it may belong to somebody else. I found out a little tonight about her background, or I think I did." I sat on the shabby brown studio bed beside them and said to Dolly: "What's your father's name?"

She didn't seem to hear me.

"Thomas McGee?"

She nodded abruptly, as if she'd been struck from behind. "He's a lying monster. He made me into a monster."

"How did he do that?"

The question triggered another nonstop sentence. "He shot her," she said with her chin on her shoulder, "and left her lying in her blood but I told Aunt Alice and the policemen and the court took care of him but now he's done it again."

"To Helen?"

"Yes, and I'm responsible. I caused it to happen."

She seemed to take a weird pleasure in acknowledging her guilt. Her gray and jaded looks, her tearless crying, her breathless run-on talking and her silences, were signs of an explosive emotional crisis. Under the raw melodrama of her self-accusations, I had the sense of something valuable and fragile in danger of being permanently broken.

"We'd better not try to question her any more," I said. "I doubt right now she can tell the difference between true and false."

"Can't I?" she said malignly. "Everything I remember is true and I can remember everything from year one, the quarrels and the beatings, and then he finally shot her in her blood –"

I cut in: "Shut up, Dolly, or change the record. You need a doctor. Do you have one in town here?"

"No. I don't need a doctor. Call the police. I want to make a confession."

She was playing a game with us and her own mind, I thought, performing dangerous stunts on the cliff edge of reality, daring the long cloudy fall.

"You want to confess that you're a monster," I said.

It didn't work. She answered matter-of-factly: "I am a monster."

The worst of it was, it was happening physically before my eyes. The chaotic pressures in her were changing the shape of her mouth and jaw. She peered at me dully through a fringe of hair. I'd hardly have recognized her as the girl I had talked to on the library steps that day.

I turned to Alex. "Do you know any doctors in town?"

He shook his head. His short hair stood up straight as if live electricity was running through him from his contact with his wife. He never let go of her.

"I could call Dad in Long Beach."

"That might be a good idea, later."

"Couldn't we take her to the hospital?"

"Not without a private doctor to protect her."

"Protect her from what?"

"The police, or the psycho ward. I don't want her answering any official questions until I have a chance to check on Helen."

The girl whimpered. "I don't want to go to the psycho ward. I had a doctor in town here a long time ago." She was sane enough to be frightened, and frightened enough to cooperate.

"What's his name?"

"Dr Godwin. Dr James Godwin. He's a psychiatrist. I used to come in and see him when I was a little girl."

"Do you have a phone in the gatehouse?"

"Mrs Bradshaw lets me use her phone."

I left them and walked up the driveway to the main house. I could smell fog even at this level now. It was rolling down from the mountains, flooding out the moon, as well as rising from the sea.

The big white house was quiet, but there was light behind some of the windows. I pressed the bell push. Chimes tinkled faintly behind the heavy door. It was opened by a large dark woman in a cotton print dress. She was crudely handsome, in spite of the pitted acne scars on her cheekbones. Before I could say anything she volunteered that Dr Bradshaw was out and Mrs Bradshaw was on her way to bed.

"I just want to use the phone. I'm a friend of the young lady in the gatehouse."

She looked me over doubtfully. I wondered if Dolly's contagion had given me a wild irrational look.

"It's important," I said. "She needs a doctor."

"Is she sick?"

"Quite sick."

"You shouldn't ought to leave her alone."

"She isn't alone. Her husband's with her."

"But she is not married."

"We won't argue about it. Are you going to let me call a doctor?"

She stepped back reluctantly and ushered me past the foot of a curved staircase into a book-lined study where a lamp burned like a night light on the desk. She indicated the telephone beside it, and took up a watchful position by the door.

"Could I have a little privacy, please? You can search me on the way out."

She sniffed, and withdrew out of sight. I thought of calling Helen's house, but she wasn't in the telephone directory. Dr James Godwin fortunately was. I dialed his number. The voice that eventually answered was so quiet and neutral that I couldn't tell if it was male or female.

"May I speak to Dr Godwin?"

"This is Dr Godwin." He sounded weary of his identity.

"My name is Lew Archer. I've just been talking to a girl who says she used to be your patient. Her maiden name was Dolly or Dorothy McGee. She's not in a good way."

"Dolly? I haven't seen her for ten or eleven years. What's troubling her?"

"You're the doctor, and I think you'd better see her. She's hysterical, to put it mildly, talking incoherently about murder."

He groaned. With my other ear I could hear Mrs Bradshaw call hoarsely down the stairs:

"What's going on down there, Maria?"

"The girl Dolly is sick, he says."

"Who says?"

"I dunno. Some man."

"Why didn't you tell me she was sick?"

"I just did."

Dr Godwin was talking in a small dead voice that sounded

like the whispering ghost of the past: "I'm not surprised this material should come up. There was a violent death in her family when she was a child, and she was violently exposed to it. She was in the immediate pre-pubic period, and already in a vulnerable state."

I tried to cut through the medical jargon: "Her father killed her mother, is that right?"

"Yes." The word was like a sigh. "The poor child found the body. Then they made her testify in court. We permit such barbarous things–" He broke off, and said in a sharply different tone: "Where are you calling from?"

"Roy Bradshaw's house. Dolly is in the gatehouse with her husband. It's on Foothill Drive–"

"I know where it is. In fact I just got in from attending a dinner with Dean Bradshaw. I have another call to make, and then I'll be right with you."

I hung up and sat quite still for a moment in Bradshaw's leather-cushioned swivel chair. The walls of books around me, dense with the past, formed a kind of insulation against the present world and its disasters. I hated to get up.

Mrs Bradshaw was waiting in the hallway. Maria had disappeared. The old woman was breathing audibly, as if the excitement was a strain on her heart. She clutched the front of her pink wool bathrobe against her loosely heaving bosom.

"What's the trouble with the girl?"

"She's emotionally upset."

"Did she have a fight with her husband? He's a hothead, I could hardly blame her."

"The trouble goes a little deeper than that. I just called Dr Godwin the psychiatrist. She's been his patient before."

"You mean to tell me the girl is –?" She tapped her veined temple with a swollen knuckle.

A car had stopped in the driveway, and I didn't have to answer her question. Roy Bradshaw came in the front door. The fog had curled his hair tight, and his thin face was open. It closed up when he saw us standing together at the foot of the stairs.

"You're late," Mrs Bradshaw said in an accusing tone. "You go out wining and dining and leave me here to cope all by myself. Where were you, anyway?"

"The Alumni banquet. You can't have forgotten that. You know how those banquets drag on, and I'm afraid I made my own contribution to the general boredom." He hesitated, becoming aware of something in the scene more serious than an old woman's possessiveness. "What's up, Mother?"

"This man tells me the little girl in the gatehouse has gone out of her mind. Why did you have to send me a girl like that, a psychiatric patient?"

"I didn't send her."

"Who did?"

I tried to break in on their foolishness, but neither of them heard me. They were intent on their game of emotional ping-pong, which had probably been going on since Roy Bradshaw was a boy.

"It was either Laura Sutherland or Helen Haggerty," he was saying. "Professor Haggerty is her counselor, and it was probably she."

"Whichever one it was, I want you to instruct her to be more careful next time. If you don't care about my personal safety –"

"I *do* care about your safety. I care very much about your safety." His voice was strained thin between anger and submissiveness. "I had no idea there was anything the matter with the girl."

"There probably wasn't," I said. "She's had a shock. I just called a doctor for her. Dr Godwin."

Bradshaw turned slowly in my direction. His face was strangely soft and empty, like a sleeping boy's.

"I know Dr Godwin," he said. "What kind of a shock did she sustain?"

"It isn't clear. I'd like to talk to you in private."

Mrs Bradshaw announced in a trembling voice: "This is my house, young man."

She was telling me, but she was also reminding Bradshaw, flicking the economic whip at him. He felt it sting:

"I live here, too. I have my duties to you, and I try to perform them satisfactorily. I also have my duties to the students."

"You and your precious students." Her bright black eyes were scornful. "Very well. You can have your privacy. I'll go outside."

She actually started for the front door, drawing her bathrobe around her lumpy body, as if she was being cast out into a blizzard. Bradshaw went after her. There were pullings and haulings and cajolings and a final goodnight embrace, from which I averted my eyes, before she climbed heavily up the stairs, with his assistance.

"You mustn't judge Mother too harshly," he said when he came down. "She's getting old, and it makes it hard for her to adjust to crises. She's really a generous-hearted soul, as I have good reason to know."

I didn't argue with him. He knew her better than I did.

"Well, Mr Archer, shall we go into my study?"

"We can save time if we talk on the road."

"On the road?"

"I want you to take me to Helen Haggerty's place if you know where it is. I'm not sure I can find it in the dark."

"Why on earth? Surely you're not taking Mother seriously? She was simply talking to hear herself talk."

"I know. But Dolly's been doing some talking, too. She says that Helen Haggerty is dead. She has blood on her hands, by way of supporting evidence. I think we'd better go up there and see where the blood came from."

He gulped. "Yes. Of course. It isn't far from here. In fact it's only a few minutes by the bridle path. But at night we'll probably get there faster in my car."

We went out to his car. I asked him to stop at the gatehouse, and glanced in. Dolly was lying on the studio bed with her face turned to the wall. Alex had covered her with a blankert. He was standing by the bed with his hands loose.

"Dr Godwin is on his way," I said in a low voice. "Keep him here till I get back, will you?"

He nodded, but he hardly appeared to see me. His look was still inward, peering into depths he hadn't begun to imagine until tonight.

IX

BRADSHAW'S COMPACT car was equipped with seat-belts, and he made me fasten mine before we set out. Between his house and Helen's I told him as much as I thought he needed to know about Dolly's outpourings. His response was sympathetic. At my suggestion, he left his car by the mailbox at the foot of Helen's lane. When we got out I could hear a foghorn moaning from the low sea.

Another car, a dark convertible whose shape I could barely make out through the thickening air, was parked without lights down the road. I ought to have shaken it down. But I was pressed by my own private guilt, and eager to see if Helen was alive.

Her house was a faint blur of light high among the trees. We started up the hairpinning gravel driveway. An owl flew low over our heads, silent as a traveling piece of fog. It lit somewhere in the gray darkness, called to its mate, and was answered. The two invisible birds seemed to be mocking us with their sad distant foghorn voices.

I heard a repeated crunching up ahead. It resolved itself into footsteps approaching in the gravel. I touched Bradshaw's sleeve, and we stood still. A man loomed up above us. He had on a topcoat and a snap-brim hat. I couldn't quite see his face.

"Hello."

He didn't answer me. He must have been young and bold. He ran straight at us, shouldering me, spinning Bradshaw into the bushes. I tried to hold him but his downhill momentum carried him away.

I chased his running footfalls down to the road, and got there in time to see him climbing into the convertible. Its engine roared and its parking lights came on as I ran toward it. Before it leaped away, I caught a glimpse of a Nevada license and the first four figures of the license number. I went back to Bradshaw's car and wrote them down in my notebook: FT37.

I climbed up the driveway a second time. Bradshaw had reached the house. He was sitting on the doorstep with a sick look on his face. Light poured over him from the open door and cast his bowed shadow brokenly on the flagstones.

"She *is* dead, Mr Archer."

I looked in. Helen was lying on her side behind the door. Blood had run from a round bullet-hole in her forehead and formed a pool on the tiles. It was coagulating at the edges, like frost on a dark puddle. I touched her sad face. She was already turning cold. It was nine-seventeen by my watch.

Between the door and the pool of blood I found a faint brown hand-print still sticky to the touch. It was about the size of Dolly's hand. She could have fallen accidentally, but the thought twisted through my head that she was doing her best to be tried for murder. Which didn't necessarily mean that she was innocent.

Bradshaw leaned like a convalescent in the doorway. "Poor Helen. This is a heinous thing. Do you suppose the fellow who attacked us –?"

"I'd say she's been dead for at least two hours. Of course he may have come back to wipe out his traces or retrieve his gun. He acted guilty."

"He certainly did."

"Did Helen Haggerty ever mention Nevada?"

He looked surprised. "I don't believe so. Why?"

"The car our friend drove away in had a Nevada license."

"I see. Well, I suppose we must call the police."

"They'll resent it if we don't?"

"Will you? I'm afraid I'm feeling rather shaken."

"It's better if you do, Bradshaw. She worked for the college, and you can keep the scandal to a minimum."

"Scandal? I hadn't even thought of that."

He forced himself to walk past her to the telephone on the far side of the room. I went through the other rooms quickly. One bedroom was completely bare except for a kitchen chair and a plain table which she had been using as a working desk. A sheaf of test papers conjugating French irregular verbs lay on top of the table. Piles of books, French and German dictionaries and grammars and collections of poetry and prose, stood around it. I opened one at the flyleaf. It was rubber-stamped in purple ink: Professor Helen Haggerty, Maple Park College, Maple Park, Illinois.

The other bedroom was furnished in rather fussy elegance with new French Provincial pieces, lambswool rugs on the polished tile floor, soft heavy handwoven drapes at the enormous window. The wardrobe contained a row of dresses and skirts with Magnin and Bullocks labels, and under them a row of new shoes to match. The chest of drawers was stuffed with sweaters and more intimate garments, but nothing really intimate. No letters, no snapshots.

The bathroom had wall-to-wall carpeting and a triangular sunken tub. The medicine chest was well supplied with beauty cream and cosmetics and sleeping pills. The latter had been prescriped by a Dr Otto Schrenk and dispensed by Thompson's Drug Store in Bridgeton, Illinois, on June 17 of this year.

I turned out the bathroom wastebasket on the carpet. Under crumpled wads of used tissue I found a letter in an airmail envelope postmarked in Bridgeton, Illinois, a week ago and addressed to Mrs Helen Haggerty. The single sheet inside was signed simply "Mother", and gave no return address.

Dear Helen

It was thoughtful of you to send me a card from sunny Cal my favourite state of the union even though it is years since I was out there. Your father keeps promising to make the trip with me on his vacation but something always comes up to put it off. Anyway his blood pressure is some better and that is a blessing. I'm glad you're well. I wish you would reconsider about the divorce but I suppose that's all over and done with. It's a pity you and Bert couldn't stay together. He is a good man in his way. But I suppose distant pastures look greenest.

Your father is still furious of course. He won't let me mention your name. He hasn't really forgiven you for when you left home in the first place, or forgiven himself either I guess, it takes two to make a quarrel. Still you are his daughter and you shouldn't have talked to him the way you did. I don't mean to recriminate. I keep hoping for a reconcilement between you two before he dies. He is not getting any younger, you know, and I'm not either, Helen. You're a smart girl with a good education and if you wanted to you could write him a letter that would make him feel different about "things." You are his only daughter after all and you've never taken it back that he was a crooked stormtrooper. That is a hard word for a policeman to swallow from anybody and it still rankles him after more than twenty years. Please write.

I put the letter back in the wastebasket with the other discarded paper. Then I washed my hands and returned to the main room. Bradshaw was sitting in the rope chair, stiffly formal even when alone. I wondered if this was his first experience of death. It wasn't mine by a long shot, but this death had hit me especially hard. I could have prevented it.

The fog outside was getting denser. It moved against the glass wall of the house, and gave me the queer sensation that the world had dropped away, and Bradshaw and I were floating together in space, unlikely *gemini* encapsulated with the dead woman.

"What did you tell the police?"

"I talked to the Sheriff personally. He'll be here shortly. I gave him only the necessary minimum. I didn't know whether or not to say anything about Mrs Kincaid."

"We have to explain our discovery of the body. But you don't have to repeat anything she said. It's purely hearsay so far as you're concerned."

"Do you seriously regard her as a suspect in this?"

"I have no opinion yet. We'll see what Dr Godwin has to say about her mental condition. I hope Godwin is good at his job."

"He's the best we have in town. I saw him tonight, oddly enough. He sat at the speaker's table with me at the Alumni dinner, until he was called away."

"He mentioned seeing you at dinner."

"Yes. Jim Godwin and I are old friends." He seemed to lean on the thought.

I looked around for something to sit on, but there was only Helen's canvas chaise. I squatted on my heels. One of the things in the house that puzzled me was the combination of lavish spending and bare poverty, as if two different women had taken turns furnishing it. A princess and a pauper.

I pointed this out to Bradshaw, and he nodded: "It struck me when I was here the other evening. She seems to have spent her money on inessentials."

"Where did the money come from?"

"She gave me to understand she had a private income. Heaven knows she didn't dress as she did on an assistant professor's salary."

"Did you know Professor Haggerty well?"

"Hardly. I did escort her to one or two college functions, as well as the opening concert of the fall season. We discovered a common passion for Hindemith." He made a steeple of his fingers. "She's a – she was a very presentable woman. But I wasn't close to her, in any sense. She didn't encourage intimacy."

I raised my eyebrows. Bradshaw colored slightly.

"I don't mean sexual intimacy, for heaven's sake. She wasn't my type at all. I mean that she didn't talk about herself to any extent."

"Where did she come from?"

"Some small college in the Middle West, Maple Park I believe. She'd already left there and come out here when we appointed her. It was an emergency appointment, necessitated by Dr Farrand's coronary. Fortunately Helen was available. I don't know what our Department of Modern Languages will do now, with the semester already under way."

He sounded faintly resentful of the dead woman's absenteeism. While it was natural enough for him to be thinking of the college and its problems, I didn't like it. I said with deliberate intent to jolt him:

"You and the college are probably going to have worse problems than finding a teacher to take her place."

"What do you mean?"

"She wasn't an ordinary female professor. I spent some time with her this afternoon. She told me among other things that her life had been threatened."

"How dreadful," he said, as though the threat of murder were somehow worse than the fact. "Who on earth –?"

"She had no idea, and neither have I. I thought perhaps you might. Did she have enemies on the campus?"

"I certainly can't think of any. You understand, I didn't know Helen at all well."

"I got to know her pretty well, in a hurry. I gathered she'd had her share of experience, not all of it picked up in graduate seminars and faculty teas. Did you go into her background before you hired her?"

"Not too thoroughly. It was an emergency appointment, as I said, and in any case it wasn't my responsibility. The head of her department, Dr Geisman, was favorably impressed by her credentials and made the appointment."

Bradshaw seemed to be delicately letting himself off the hook. I wrote down Geisman's name in my notebook.

"Her background ought to be gone into," I said. "It seems she was married, and recently divorced. I also want to find out more about her relations with Dolly. Apparently they were close."

"You're not suggesting a Lesbian attachment? We have had –" He decided not to finish the sentence.

"I'm not suggesting anything. I'm looking for information. How did Professor Haggerty happen to become Dolly's counselor?"

"In the normal way, I suppose."

"What is the normal way of acquiring a counselor?"

"It varies. Mrs Kincaid was an upperclassman, and we usually permit upperclassmen to choose their own counselors, so long as the counselor in question has an opening in his or her schedule."

"Then Dolly probably chose Professor Haggerty, and initiated the friendship herself?"

"She had every chance to. Of course it may have been pure accident."

As if we had each received a signal on a common wavelength, we turned and looked at Helen Haggerty's body. It seemed small and lonely at the far end of the room. Our joint flight with it through cloudy space had been going on for a long time. I looked at my watch. It was only nine-thirty-one, fourteen minutes since our arrival. Time seemed to have slowed down, dividing itself into innumerable fractions, like Zeno's space or marijuana hours.

With a visible effort, Bradshaw detached his gaze from the body. His moment of communion with it had cost him the last of his boyish look. He leaned toward me with deep lines of puzzlement radiating from his eyes and mouth:

"I don't understand what Mrs Kincaid said to you. Do you

mean to say she actually confessed this – this murder?"

"A cop or a prosecutor might say so. Fortunately none was present. I've heard a lot of confessions, good ones and phoney ones. Hers was a phoney one, in my opinion."

"What about the blood?"

"She may have slipped and fallen in it."

"Then you don't think we should mention any of it to the Sheriff?"

"If you don't mind stretching a point."

His face showed that he minded, but after some hesitation he said: "We'll keep it to ourselves, at least for the present. After all she was a student of ours, however briefly."

Bradshaw didn't notice his use of the past tense, but I did, and it depressed me. I think we were both relieved by the sound of the Sheriff's car coming up the hill. It was accompanied by a mobile laboratory. Within a few minutes a fingerprint man and a deputy coroner and a photographer had taken over the room and changed its character. It became impersonal and drab like any room anywhere in which murder had been committed. In a curious way the men in uniform seemed to be doing the murder a second and final time, annulling Helen's rather garish aura, converting her into laboratory meat and courtroom exhibits. My raw nerves jumped when the bulbs flashed in her corner.

Sheriff Herman Crane was a thick-shouldered man in a tan gabardine suit. His only suggestion of uniform was a slightly broad-brimmed hat with a woven leather band. His voice had an administrative ring, and his manner had the heavy ease of a politician, poised between bullying and flattery. He treated Bradshaw with noisy deference, as if Bradshaw was a sensitive plant of undetermined value but some importance.

Me he treated the way cops always treated me, with occupational suspicion. They suspected me of the misdemeanor of doing my own thinking. I did succeed in getting Sheriff Crane to dispatch a patrol car in pursuit of the convertible with the Nevada license. He complained that his department was seriously understaffed, and he didn't think road blocks were indicated at this stage of the game. At this stage of the game I made up my mind not to cooperate fully with him.

The Sheriff and I sat in the chaise and the rope chair respectively and had a talk while a deputy who knew speedwriting took notes. I told him that Dolly Kincaid, the wife of a client of mine, had discovered the body of her college counselor Professor Haggerty and reported the discovery to me. She had been badly shocked, and was under a doctor's care.

Before the Sheriff could press me for further details, I gave him a verbatim account, or as close to verbatim as I could make it, of my conversation with Helen about the death threat. I mentioned that she had reported it to his office, and he seemed to take this as a criticism:

"We're understaffed, like I said. I can't keep experienced men. Los Angeles lures 'em away with salaries we can't pay and pie in the sky." I was from Los Angeles, as he knew, and the implication was that I was obscurely to blame. "If I put a man on guard duty in every house that got a crank telephone call, I wouldn't have anybody left to run the department."

"I understand that."

"I'm glad you do. Something I don't understand – how did this conversation you had with the decedent happen to take place?"

"Professor Haggerty approached me and asked me to come up here with her."

"What time was this?"

"I didn't check the time. It was shortly before sundown. I was here for about an hour."

"What did she have in mind?"

"She wanted me to stay with her, for protection. I'm sorry I didn't." Simply having the chance to say this made me feel better.

"You mean she wanted to hire you, as a bodyguard?"

"That was the idea." There was no use going into the complex interchange that had taken place between Helen and me, and failed.

"How did she know you were in the bodyguard business?"

"I'm not, exactly. She knew I was an investigator because she saw my name in the paper."

"Sure enough," he said. "You testified in the Perrine case this morning. Maybe I ought to congratulate you because Perrine got off."

"Don't bother."

"No. I don't think I will. The Perrine broad was guilty as hell and you know it and I know it."

"The jury didn't think so," I said mildly.

"Juries can be fooled and witnesses can be bought. Suddenly you're very active in our local crime circles, Mr Archer." The words had the weight of an implied threat. He flung out a heavy careless hand toward the body. "This woman, Professor Haggerty here, you're sure she wasn't a friend of yours?"

"We became friends to a certain extent."

"In an hour?"

"It can happen in an hour. Anyway, we had a previous conversation at the college today."

"What about before today? Did you have other previous conversations?"

"No. I met her today for the first time."

Bradshaw, who had been hanging around us in various anxious attitudes, spoke up: "I can vouch for the truth of that, Sheriff, if it will save you any time."

Sheriff Crane thanked him and turned back to me: "So it was a purely business proposition between her and you?"

"It would have been if I had been interested." I wasn't telling the precise truth, but there was no way to tell it to Crane without sounding foolish.

"You weren't interested. Why not?"

"I had other business."

"What other business?"

"Mrs Kincaid had left her husband. He employed me to locate her."

"I heard something about that this morning. Did you find out why she left him?"

"No. My job was to locate her. I did."

"Where?"

I glanced up at Bradshaw. He gave me a reluctant nod. I said: "She's a student at the college."

"And now you say she's under a doctor's care? What doctor?"

"Dr Godwin."

"The psychiatrist, eh?" The Sheriff uncrossed his heavy legs and leaned toward me confidentially. "What does she need a psychiatrist for? Is she out of her head?"

"She was hysterical. It seemed like a good idea to call one."

"Where is she now?"

I looked at Bradshaw again. He said: "At my house. My mother employed her as a driver."

The Sheriff got up with a rowing motion of his arms. "Let's get over there and talk to her."

"I'm afraid that won't be possible," Bradshaw said.

"Who says so?"

"I do, and I'm sure the doctor would concur."

"Naturally Godwin says what his patients pay him to say. I've had trouble with him before."

"I know that." Bradshaw had turned pale, but his voice was under rigid control. "You're not a professional man, Sheriff, and I rather doubt that you understand Dr Godwin's code of ethics."

Crane reddened under the insult. He couldn't think of anything to say. Bradshaw went on:

"I very seriously doubt that Mrs Kincaid can or should be questioned at the present time. What's the point of it? If she had anything to hide, she wouldn't have rushed to the nearest detective with her dreadful news. I'm sure we don't want to subject the girl to cruel and unusual punishment, simply for doing her duty as a citizen."

"What do you mean, cruel and unusual punishement? I'm not planning to third-degree her."

"I hope and trust you're not planning to go near the child tonight. That would be cruel and unusual punishment in my opinion, Sheriff, and I believe I speak for informed opinion in this county."

Crane opened his mouth to expostulate, perhaps realized the hopelessness of trying to outtalk Bradshaw, and shut it again. Bradshaw and I walked out unaccompanied. I said when we were out of hearing of the house:

"That was quite a job you did of facing down the Sheriff."

"I've always disliked that blustering bag of wind. Fortunately he's vulnerable. His majority slipped badly in the last election. A great many people in this county, including Dr Godwin and myself, would like to see more enlightened and efficient law enforcement. And we may get it yet."

Nothing had changed visibly in the gatehouse. Dolly was still lying on the studio bed with her face turned to the wall. Bradshaw and I hesitated at the door. Walking with his head down, Alex crossed the room to speak to us.

"Dr Godwin went up to the house to make a phone call. He thinks she ought to be in a nursing home, temporarily."

Dolly spoke in a monotone: "I know what you're saying. You might as well say it out loud. You want to put me away."

"Hush, darling." It was a brave word.

The girl relapsed into silence. She hadn't moved at all. Alex drew us outside, keeping the door open so that he could watch her. He said in a low voice:

"Dr Godwin doesn't want to run the risk of suicide,"

"It's that bad, eh?" I said.

"*I* don't think so. Neither does Dr Godwin, really. He says it's simply a matter of taking reasonable security precautions. I told him I could sit up with her, but he doesn't think I should try to do it myself."

"You shouldn't," Bradshaw said. "You'll need to have something left for tomorrow."

"Yeah. Tomorrow." Alex kicked at the rusty boot-scraper attached to the side of the doorstep. "I better call Dad. Tomorrow's a Saturday, he ought to be able to come."

Footsteps approached from the direction of the main house. A big man in an alligator coat emerged from the fog, his bald head gleaming in the light from the doorway. He greeted Bradshaw warmly:

"Hello, Roy. I enjoyed your speech, what I heard of it. You'll elevate us yet into the Athens of the West. Unfortunately a patient dragged me out in the middle of it. She wanted to know if it was safe for her to see a Tennessee Williams movie all by herself. She really wanted me to go along with her and protect her from bad thoughts." He turned to me. "Mr Archer? I'm Dr Godwin."

We shook hands. He gave me a look of lingering intensity, as if he was going to paint my portrait from memory. Godwin had a heavy, powerful face, with eyes that changed from bright to dark like lamps being turned down. He had authority, which he was being careful not to use.

"I'm glad you called me. Miss McGee – Mrs Kincaid needed somthing to calm her down." He glanced in through the doorway. "I hope she's feeling better now."

"She's much quieter," Alex said. "Don't you think it will be all right for her to stay here with me?"

Godwin made a commiserating face. His mouth was very flexible, like an actor's. "It wouldn't be wise, Mr Kincaid. I've made arrangements for a bed in a nursing home I use. We don't want to take any chances with her life."

"But why should she try to kill herself?"

"She has a lot on her mind, poor girl. I always pay attention to suicide threats, or even the slightest hint of them."

"Have you found out just what she does have on her mind?" Bradshaw said.

"She didn't want to talk much. She's very tired. It can wait till morning."

"I hope so," Bradshaw said. "The Sheriff wants to question her about the shooting. I did my best to hold him off."

Godwin's mobile face became grave. "There actually has been a murder then? Another murder?"

"One of our new professors, Helen Haggerty, was shot in her home tonight. Mrs Kincaid apparently stumbled on the body."

"She's had dreadful luck." Godwin looked up at the low sky. "I sometimes feel as though the gods have turned their backs on certain people."

I asked him to explain what he meant. He shook his head: "I'm much too tired to tell you the bloody saga of the McGees. A lot of it has faded out of my memory, mercifully. Why don't you ask the courthouse people for details?"

"That wouldn't be a good idea under the circumstances."

"It wouldn't, would it? You can see how tired I am. By the time I get my patient safely disposed of for the night I'll have just enough energy left to make it home and to bed."

"We still need to talk, Doctor."

"What about?"

I didn't like to say it in front of Alex but I said it, watching him: "The possibility that she committed this second murder, or let's say the possibility that she'll be accused of it. She seems to want to be."

Alex rose to her defence: "She was out of her head, temporarily and you can't use what she said –"

Godwin laid a hand on his shoulder. "Take it easy, Mr Kincaid. We can't settle anything now. What we all need is a night's sleep – especially your wife. I want you to come along with me to the nursing home in case I need help with her on the way. You," he said to me, "can follow along in your car and bring him back. You'll want to know where the nursing home is, anyway, because I'll meet you there tomorrow morning at eight, after I've had an opportunity to talk to Mrs Kincaid. Got that?"

"Tomorrow morning at eight."

He turned to Bradshaw. "Roy, if I were you I'd go and see how Mrs Bradshaw is feeling. I gave her a sedative, but she's alarmed. She thinks, or pretends to think, that she's surrounded by maniacal assassins. You can talk her out of it better than I could."

Godwin seemed to be a wise and careful man. At any rate, his authority imposed itself. All three of us did as he said.

So did Dolly. Propped between him and Alex, she came out to his car. She didn't struggle or make a sound, but she walked as though she was on her way to the execution chamber.

X

AN HOUR later I was sitting on one of the twin beds in my motel room. There was nothing more I could do right now, except possibly stir up trouble if I went for information to the local authorities. But my mind kept projecting on the plaster wall rapid movies of actions I could be performing. Run down Begley-McGee. Capture the man from Nevada.

I shut off the violent images with an effort of will and forced myself to think about Zeno, who said that Achilles could never traverse the space between him and the tortoise. It was a soothing thought, if you were a tortoise, or maybe even if you were Achilles.

I had a pint of whisky in my bag. I was getting it out of its sock when I thought of Arnie Walters, a Reno colleague of mine who had split more than one pint with me. I put in a long-distance call to his office, which happened to be the front room of his house, Arnie was at home.

"Walters Detective Agency," he said in a reluctant midnight voice.

"This is Lew Archer."

"Oh. Good. I didn't really want to go to bed. I was only modeling my pajamas."

"Irony isn't your forte, so drop it. All I'm asking for is a small sevice which I will repay in kind at the earliest opportunity. Are you recording?"

I heard the click of the machine, and told it and Arnie about Helen's death. "A couple of hours after the shooting, the man I'm interested in came out of the murder house and drove away in a black or dark blue convertible, I think a late-model Ford, with a Nevada license. I think I got the first four figures –"

"You think?"

"It's foggy here, and it was dark. First four figures are probably FT37. The subject is young and athletic, height about five-eleven, wearing a dark topcoat and dark snap-brim fedora, I couldn't make out his face."

"Have you seen your oculist lately?"

"You can do better than that, Arnie. Try."

"I hear senior citizens can get free glaucoma tests nowadays."

Arnie was older than I was, but he didn't like to have this pointed out. "What's bugging you? Trouble with the wife?"

"No trouble," he said cheerfully. "She's waiting for me in bed."

"Give Phyllis my love."

"I'll give her my own. In case I come up with anything, which seems unlikely in view of the fragmentary information, where do I contact you?"

"I'm staying at the Mariner's Rest motel in Pacific Point. But you better call my answering service in Hollywood."

He said he would. As I hung up, I heard a gentle tapping on my door. It turned out to be Alex. He had pulled on his trousers over his pajamas.

"I heard you talking in here."

"I was on the phone."

"I didn't mean to interrupt."

"I'm through phoning. Come in and have a drink."

He entered the room cautiously, as if it might be booby-trapped. In the last few hours his movements had become very tentative. His bare feet made no sound on the carpet.

The bathroom cupboard contained two glasses wrapped in

wax paper. I unwrapped and filled them. We sat on the twin beds, drinking to nothing in particular. We faced each other like mirror images separated by an invisible wall of glass.

I was conscious of the differences between us, particularly of Alex's youth and lack of experience. He was at the age when everything hurts.

"I was thinking of calling Dad," he said. "Now I don't know whether I should or not."

There was another silence.

"He won't say 'I told you so,' in so many words. But that will be the general idea. Fools rush in where angels fear to tread and all that jazz."

"I think it makes just as much sense if you reverse it. Angels rush in where fools are afraid to tread. Not that I know any angels."

He got the message. "You don't think I'm a fool?"

"You've handled yourself very well."

"Thank you," he said formally. "Even if it isn't actually true."

"It is, though. It must have taken some doing."

Whisky and the beginnings of human warmth had dissolved the glass wall between us. "The worst of it," he said, "was when I put her in the nursing home just now. I felt as if I was – you know, consigning her to oblivion. The place is like something out of Dante, with people crying and groaning. Dolly's a sensitive girl. I don't see how she'll be able to take it."

"She can take it better than some other things, such as wandering around loose in her condition."

"You think she's insane, don't you?"

"What I think doesn't matter. We'll get an expert opinion tomorrow. There's no doubt she's temporarily off base. I've seen people further off, and I've seen them come back."

"You think she'll be all right then?"

He grabbed at what I said like a flying trapeze and swung up into hopefulness. Which I didn't think ought to be encouraged:

"I'm more concerned about the legal situation than the psychiatric one."

"You can't really believe she killed this friend of hers – Helen? I know she said so, but it isn't possible. You see, I know Dolly. She isn't aggressive at all. She's one of the really pro-life people.

She doesn't even like to kill a spider."

"It is possible, Alex, and that was all I said. I wanted Godwin to be aware of the possibility from the start. He's in a position to do a lot for your wife."

Alex said, "My wife," with a kind of wonder.

"She is your wife, legally. But nobody would consider that you owe her much. You have an out, if you want to use it."

The whisky slopped in his glass. I think he barely restrained himself from throwing it in my face.

"I'm not going to ditch her," he said. "If you think I ought to, you can go to hell."

I hadn't liked him thoroughly until now. "Somebody had to mention the fact that you have an out. A lot of people would take it."

"I'm not a lot of people."

"So I gather."

"Dad would probably call me a fool, but I don't care if she's guilty of murder. I'm staying."

"It's going to cost money."

"You want more money, is that it?"

"I can wait. So can Godwin. I was thinking about the future, Also there's the strong possibility that you'll need a lawyer tomorrow."

"What for?" He was a good boy, but a little slow on the uptake.

"Judging by tonight, your main problem is going to be to prevent Dolly from talking herself into deep trouble. That means keeping her out of the hands of the authorities, in a place where she can be properly looked after. A good lawyer can be a help in that. Lawyers generally don't wait for their money in criminal cases."

"Do you really think she's in such danger – such legal jeopardy? Or are you just trying to put the iron in my soul?"

"I talked to the local sheriff tonight, and I didn't like the gleam in his eye when we got on the subject of Dolly. Sheriff Crane isn't stupid. He knew that I was holding back on him. He's going to bear down on her when he catches on to the family connection."

"The family connection?"

"The fact that her father murdered her mother." It was cruel to hit him with it again, on top of everything else. Still it was better for him to hear if from me than from the dreary voice that talks from under the twisted pillow at three o'clock in the morning. "Apparently he was tried and convicted in the local courts. Sheriff Crane probably gathered the evidence for the prosecution."

"It's almost as though history is repeating itself." There was something approaching awe in Alex's voice. "Did I hear you say that this Chuck Begley character, the man with the beard, is actually her father?"

"He seems to be."

"He was the one who started the whole thing off," he said, as much to himself as to me. "It was after he visited her that Sunday that she walked out on me. What do you think happened between them, to make her do that?"

"I don't know, Alex. Maybe he bawled her out for testifying against him. In any case he brought back the past. She couldn't handle the old mess and her new marriage together, so she left you."

"I still don't get it," he said. "How could Dolly have a father like that?"

"I'm not a geneticist. But I do know most non-professional killers aren't criminal types. I intend to find out more about Begley-McGee and his murder. I suppose it's no use asking if Dolly ever talked about it to you?"

"She never said a word about either of her parents, except that they were dead. Now I can understand why. I don't blame her for lying –" He cut the sentence short, and amended it: "I mean, for not telling me certain things."

"She made up for it tonight."

"Yeah. It's been quite a night." He nodded several times, as though he was still absorbing its repercussions. "Tell me the honest truth, Mr Archer. Do you believe the things she said about being responsible for this woman's death? And her mother?"

"I can't even remember half of them."

"That's not an answer."

"Maybe we'll get some better answers tomorrow. It's a complex world. The human mind is the most complex thing in it."

"You don't give me much comfort."

"It's not my job to."

Making a bitter face over this and the last of his whisky, he rose slowly. "Well, you need your sleep, and I have a phone call to make. Thanks for the drink." He turned with his hand on the doorknob. "And thanks for the conversation."

"Any time. Are you going to call your father?"

"No. I've decided not to."

I felt vaguely gratified. I was old enough to be his father, with no son of my own, and that may have had something to do with my feeling.

"Who are you going to call, or is that a private matter?"

"Dolly asked me to try and get in touch with her Aunt Alice. I guess I've been putting it off. I don't know what to say to her aunt. I didn't even know she had an Aunt Alice until tonight."

"I remember she mentioned her. When did Dolly ask you to make the call?"

"In the nursing home the last thing. She wants her aunt to come and see her. I didn't know if that was a good idea or not."

"It would depend on the aunt. Does she live here in town?"

"She lives in the Valley, in Indian Springs. Dolly said she's in the county directory. Miss Alice Jenks."

"Let's try her."

I found her name and number in the phone book, placed the toll call, and handed the receiver to Alex. He sat on the bed, looking at the instrument as if he had never seen one before.

"What am I going to say to her?"

"You'll know what to say. I want to talk to her when you're finished."

A voice rasped from the receiver: "Yes? Who is this?"

"I'm Alex Kincaid. Is that Miss Jenks? . . . We don't know each other, Miss Jenks, but I married your niece a few weeks ago. . . . Your niece Dolly McGee. We were married a few weeks ago, and she's come down with a rather serious illness. . . . No, it's more emotional. She's emotionally disturbed, and she wants to see you. She's in the Whitmore Nursing Home here in Pacific Point. Dr Godwin is looking after her."

He paused again. There was sweat on his forehead. The voice at the other end went on for some time.

"She says she can't come tomorrow," he said to me; and into the receiver: "Perhaps Sunday would be possible?. . . Yes, fine.

You can contact me at the Mariner's Rest Motel, or. . . Alex Kincaid. I'll look forward to meeting you."

"Let me talk to her," I said.

"Just a minute, Miss Jenks. The gentleman here with me, Mr Archer, has something to say to you." He handed over the receiver.

"Hello, Miss Jenks."

"Hello, Mr Archer. And who are you, may I ask, at one o'clock in the morning?" It wasn't a light question. The woman sounded anxious and irritated, but she had both feelings under reasonable control.

"I'm a private detective. I'm sorry to disrupt your sleep with this, but there's more to the situation than simple emotional illness. A woman has been murdered here."

She gasped, but made no other comment.

"Your niece is a material witness to the murder. She may be more deeply involved than that, and in any case, she's going to need support. So far as I know you're her only relative, apart from her father –"

"You can leave him out. He doesn't count. He never has, except in a negative way." Her voice was flat and harsh. "Who was killed?"

"A friend and counselor of your niece's, Professor Helen Haggerty."

"I never heard of the woman," she said with combined impatience and relief.

"You'll be hearing a great deal about her, if you're at all interested in your niece. Are you close to her?"

"I was, before she grew away from me. I brought her up after her mother's death." Her voice became flat again: "Does Tom McGee have anything to do with this new killing?"

"He may have. He's in town here, or he was."

"I knew it!" she cried in bleak triumph. "They had no business letting him out. They should have put him in the gas chamber for what he did to my little sister."

She was choked with sudden emotion. I waited for her to go on. When she didn't, I said:

"I'm anxious to go into the details of that case with you, but I don't think we should do it over the phone. It really would be helpful if you could come here tomorrow."

"I simply can't. There's no use badgering me. I have a terribly important meeting tomorrow afternoon. Several state officials will be here from Sacramento, and it will probably go on into the evening."

"What about the morning?"

"I have to prepare for them in the morning. We're shifting over to a new state-county welfare program." Latent hysteria buzzed in her voice, the hysteria of a middle-aged spinster who has to make a change. "If I walked out on this project, I could lose my position."

"We don't want that to happen, Miss Jenks. How far is it from there to Pacific Point?"

"Seventy miles, but I tell you I can't make it."

"I can. Will you give me an hour in the morning, say around eleven?"

She hesitated. "Yes, if it's important. I'll get up an hour earlier and do my paperwork. I'll be at home at eleven. You have my address? It's just off the main street of Indian Springs."

I thanked her and got rid of Alex and went to bed, setting my mental alarm for six-thirty.

XI

ALEX WAS was still sleeping when I was ready to leave in the morning. I let him sleep, partly for selfish reasons, and partly because sleep was kinder to him than waking was likely to be.

The fog was thick outside. Its watery mass overlay Pacific Point and transformed it into a kind of suburb of the sea. I drove out of the motel enclosure into a gray world without perspective, came abruptly to an access ramp, descended onto the freeway where headlights swam in pairs like deep-sea fish, and arrived at a truck stop on the east side without any real sense that I had driven across the city.

I'd been having a little too much talk with people whose business was talking. It was good to sit at the counter of a working-class restaurant where men spoke when they wanted something, or simply to kid the waitress. I kidded her a little myself. Her name was Stella, and she was so efficient that she threatened to take the place of automation. She said with a flashing smile that this was her aim in life.

My destination was near the highway, on a heavily used thoroughfare lined mainly with new apartment buildings. Their faddish pastel colors and scant transplanted palms seemed dingy and desolate in the fog.

The nursing home was a beige stucco one-storeyed building taking up most of a narrow deep lot. I rang the bell at eight o'clock precisely, Dr Godwin must have been waiting behind the door. He unlocked it and let me in himself.

"You're a punctual man, Mr Archer."

His changeable eyes had taken the stoney color of the morning. I noticed when he turned to shut the door behind us that his shoulders were permanently stooped. He was wearing a fresh white smock.

"Sit down, won't you? This is as good a place to talk as any."

We were in a small reception-room or lounge. I sat in one of several worn armchairs aimed at a silent television set in one corner. Through the inner door I could hear the rattle of dishes and the bright voices of nurses beginning the day.

"Is this your place, Doctor?"

"I have an interest in it. Most of the patients here are mine. I've just been giving some shock treatments." He smoothed the front of his smock. "I'd feel less like a witch-doctor if I knew why electric shocks make depressed people feel better. So much of our science, or art, is still in the empirical stage. But the people do get better," he said with a sudden grin, too sudden to touch his watching, waiting eyes.

"Is Dolly?"

"Yes, I think she's somewhat better. We don't have overnight cures of course. I want to keep an eye on her for at least a week. Here."

"Is she fit to be questioned?"

"I don't want you to question her, or anyone else remotely connected with the – the world of crime and punishment." As if to remove the curse from his refusal, he flung himself loosely into the armchair beside me, asked me for a cigarette and let me light it.

"Why not?"

"I do not love the law in its current primitive state, where sick people are trapped into betraying themselves in their sickness and then treated by the courts as if they were well. I've been fighting the situation for a long time." He rested his ponderous bald head on the back of the chair, and blew smoke toward the ceiling.

"What you say suggests that Dolly is in danger from the law."

"I was making a general statement."

"Which applied specifically to Dolly. We don't have to play games, Doctor. We're both on the same side. I don't assume the girl is guilty of anything. I do think she has information which may help me to clear up a murder."

"But what if she's guilty?" he said, watching for my reaction.

"Then I'd want to cooperate with you in getting charges reduced, finding mitigating circumstances, making a case for merciful treatment by the court. Remember I'm working for her husband. Is she guilty?"

"I don't know."

"You have talked to her this morning?"

"She did most of the talking. I don't ask many questions. I wait and I listen. In the end you learn more that way." He gave me a meaningful look, as if I should start applying this principle.

I waited and listened. Nothing happened. A plump woman with long black hair straggling down the back of her cotton robe appeared in the inside doorway. She stretched out her arms to the doctor.

He lifted his hand like a weary king. "Good morning, Nell."

She gave him a bright agonized smile and softly withdrew, like a woman walking backward in her sleep. Her outstretched arms were the last I saw of her.

"It would be helpful if you told me what Dolly had to say this morning."

"And possibly dangerous." Godwin crushed out his cigarette in a blue ceramic ashtray which looked homemade. "There is after all a difference between you and me. What a patient says to me is a professional confidence. You have no professional standing. If you refused to repeat information in court you could be jailed for contempt. I could, under the law, but I'm not likely to be."

"I've sweated out contempt before. And the police won't get anything out of me that I don't choose to tell them. That's a guarantee."

"Very well." Godwin nodded his head once, decisively. "I'm concerned about Dolly and I'll try to tell you why without any professional jargon. You may be able to put together the objective jigsaw puzzle while I'm reconstructing the subjective one."

"You said no professional jargon, Doctor."

"Sorry. First there's her history. Her mother Constance McGee brought her to me at the instigation of her sister Alice, a woman I know slightly, when Dolly was ten years old. She wasn't a happy child. In fact she was in some danger of becoming really withdrawn, for good reason. There's always good reason. Her father McGee was an irresponsible and violent man who couldn't handle the duties of fatherhood. He blew hot and cold on the child, spoiled her and punished her, constantly fought with his wife and eventually left her, or was left, it hardly matters. I would have preferred to treat him instead of Dolly, since he was the main source of the trouble in the family. But he was unreachable."

"Did you ever see him?"

"He wouldn't even come in for an interview." Godwin said with regret. "If I could have reached him, I might have been able to prevent a murder. Perhaps not. From what I've been told he was a severely maladjusted man who needed help but never got it. You can understand my bitterness about the gap between psychiatry and the law. People like McGee are allowed to run around loose, without preventive action of any kind, until they commit a crime. Then of course they're hauled into court, and sent away for ten or twenty years. But not to a hospital. To a prison."

"McGee's out now. He's been in town here. Did you know that?"

"Dolly told me this morning. It's one of the many severe pressures on her. You can understand how a sensitive child brought up in an atmosphere of violence and instability would be plagued by anxiety and guilt. The worst guilt often arises when a child is forced, by sheer instinctive self-preservation, to turn against her parents. A clinical psychologist I work with helped Dolly to express her feelings in clay and doll-play and so on. There wasn't too much I could do for her myself, since children don't have the mental equipment to be analyzed. But

I did try to assume the role of the calm and patient father, provide some of the stability that was missing in her young life. And she was doing pretty well, until the disaster occurred."

"You mean the murder?"

He swung his head in sorrow. "McGee worked himself into a self-pitying rage one night, came to the aunt's house in Indian Springs where they were staying, and shot Constance through the heart. Dolly was alone in the house with her mother. She heard the shot and saw McGee taking off. Then she discovered the body."

His head went on swinging slowly like a heavy silent bell. I said:

"What was her reaction at the time?"

"I don't know. One of the peculiar difficulties of my work is that I often have to perform a public function with private means . I can't go out and lasso patients. Dolly never came back to me. She no longer had her mother to bring her in from the Valley, and Miss Jenks, her aunt, is a busy woman."

"But didn't you say that Alice Jenks suggested treatment for Dolly in the first place?"

"She did. She also paid for it. Perhaps with all the trouble in the family she felt she couldn't afford it any longer. At any rate, I didn't see Dolly again until last night, with one exception. I went to court the day she testified against McGee. As a matter of fact I bearded the judge in his chambers and told him that it shouldn't be allowed. But she was a key witness, and they had her aunt's permission, and they put her through her sad little paces. She acted like a pale little automaton lost in a world of hostile adults."

His large body trembled with feeling. His hands burrowed under his smock, searching for a cigarette. I gave him one and lit it, and lit one for myself.

"What did she say in court?"

"It was very short and simple. I suspect that she was thoroughly rehearsed. She heard the shot and looked out her bedroom window and saw her father running away with the gun in his hand. One other question had to do with whether McGee had threatened Constance with bodily harm. He had. That was all."

"You're sure?"

"Yes. This isn't my unaided recollection, as they say. I took written notes at the time, and I scanned them this morning."

"Why?"

"They're part of her history, evidently a crucial part." He blew out smoke and looked at me through it, long and cautiously.

I said: "Does she tell a different story now?"

His face was working with complex passions. He was a man of feeling, and Dolly was his office daughter lost for many years.

"She tells an absurd story," he burst out. "I not only can't believe it, I can't believe that she believes it. She isn't that sick."

He paused, drawing deep on his cigarette, trying to get himself under full control. I waited and listened. This time he did go on:

"She claims now that she didn't see McGee that night, and that in fact he had nothing to do with the murder. She says she lied on the witness stand because the various adults wanted her to."

"Why would she say that now?"

"I don't pretend to understand her. After an interval of ten years we've naturally lost what rapport we had. And of course she hasn't forgiven me for what she considers my betrayal – my failure to look after her in the disaster. But what could I do? I couldn't go to Indian Springs and kidnap her out of her aunt's house."

"You care about your patients, Doctor."

"Yes. I care. It keeps me tired." He stubbed his cigarette in the ceramic ashtray. "Nell made this ashtray, by the way. It's rather good for a first attempt."

I murmured something in agreement. Above the subsiding clamor of dishes, a wild old complaining voice rose in the depths of the building.

"That story of hers," I said, "may not be so very absurd. It fits in with the fact that McGee visited her on the second day of her honeymoon and hit her so hard with something that it knocked her right off the tracks."

"You're acute, Mr Archer. That's precisely what happened. He treated her to a long tirade on the subject of his innocence. You mustn't forget that she loved her father, however ambivalently. He was able to convince her that her memory was at fault, that he was innocent and she was guilty. Childhood memories are powerfully influenced by emotion."

"That she was guilty of perjury, you mean?"

"Murder." He leaned toward me. "She told me this morning she killed her mother herself."

"With a gun?"

"With her tongue. That's the absurd part. She claims she killed her mother and her friend, Helen, and sent her father to prison into the bargain, all with her poisonous tongue."

"Does she explain what she means by that?"

"She hasn't yet. It's an expression of guilt which may be only superficially connected with these murders."

"You mean she's using the murders to unload guilt which she feels about something else?"

"More or less. It's a common enough mechanism. I know for a fact that she didn't kill her mother, or lie about her father, essentially. I'm certain McGee was guilty."

"Courts can make mistakes, even in a capital case."

He said with a kind of muted arrogance: "I know more about that case than ever came out in court."

"From Dolly?"

"From various sources."

"I'd be obliged if you'd let me in on it."

His eyes veiled themselves. "I can't do that. I have to respect the confidences of my patients. But you can take my word for it that McGee killed his wife."

"Then what's Dolly feeling so guilty about?"

"I'm sure that will come out, in time. It probably has to do with her resentment against her parents. It's natural she'd want to punish them for the ugly failure of their marriage. She may well have fantasied her mother's death, her father's imprisonment, before those things emerged into reality. When the poor child's vengeful dreams came true, how else could she feel but guilty? McGee's tirade the other weekend stirred up the old feelings, and then this dreadful accident last night –" He ran out of words and spread his hands, palms upward and fingers curling, on his heavy thighs.

"The Haggerty shooting was no accident, Doctor. The gun is missing, for one thing."

"I realise that. I was referring to Dolly's discovery of the body, which was certainly accidental."

"I wonder. She blames herself for that killing, too. I don't see how you can explain that in terms of childhood resentments."

"I wasn't attempting to." There was irritation in his voice, It made him pull a little professional rank on me: "Nor is there any need for you to understand the psychic situation. You stick to the objective facts, and I'll handle the subjective." He softened this with a bit of philosophy: "Objective and subjective, the outer world and the inner, do correspond of course. But sometimes you have to follow the parallel lines almost to infinity before they touch."

"Let's stick to the objective facts then. Dolly said she killed Helen Haggerty with her poisonous tongue. Is that all she said on the subject?"

"There was more, a good deal more, of a rather confused nature. Dolly seems to feel that her friendship with Miss Haggerty was somehow responsible for the latter's death."

"The two women were friends?"

"I'd say so, yes, though there was twenty years' difference in their ages. Dolly confided in her, poured out everything, and Miss Haggerty reciprocated. Apparently she'd had severe emotional problems involving her own father, and she couldn't resist the parallel with Dolly. They both let down their back hair. It wasn't a healthy situation," he said dryly.

"Does she have anything to say about Helen's father?"

"Dolly seems to think he was a crooked policeman involved in a murder, but that may be sheer fantasy – a kind of secondary image of her own father."

"It isn't. Helen's father is a policeman, and Helen at least regarded him as a crook."

"How in the world would you know that?"

"I read a letter from her mother on the subject. I'd like to have a chance to talk to her parents."

"Why don't you?"

"They live in Bridgeton, Illinois."

It was a long jump, but not so long as the jump my mind made into blank possibility. I had handled cases which opened up gradually like fissures in the firm ground of the present, cleaving far down through the strata of the past. Perhaps

Helen's murder was connected with an obscure murder in Illinois more than twenty years ago, before Dolly was born. It was a wishful thought, and I didn't mention it to Dr Godwin.

"I'm sorry I can't be more help to you," he was saying. "I have to go now, I'm already overdue for my hospital rounds."

The sound of a motor detached itself from the traffic in the street, and slowed down. A car door was opened and closed. Men's footsteps came up the walk. Moving quickly for a big man, Godwin opened the door before they rang.

I couldn't see who his visitors were, but they were unwelcome ones. Godwin went rigid with hostility.

"Good morning, Sheriff," he said.

Crane responded folksily: "It's a hell of a morning and you know it. September's supposed to be our best month, but the bloody fog's so thick the airport's socked in."

"You didn't come here to discuss the weather."

"That's right, I didn't. I heard you got a fugitive from justice holed up here."

"Where did you hear that?"

"I have my sources."

"You'd better fire them, Sheriff. They're giving you misleading information."

"Somebody is, Doctor. Are you denying that Mrs Dolly Kincaid née McGee is in this building?"

Godwin hesitated. His heavy jaw got heavier. "She is."

"You said a minute ago she wasn't. What are you trying to pull, Doc?"

"What are *you* trying to pull? Mrs Kincaid is not a fugitive. She's here because she's ill."

"I wonder what made her ill. Can't she stand the sight of blood?"

Godwin's lips curled outward. He looked ready to spit in the other man's face. I couldn't see the Sheriff from where I sat, and I made no attempt to. I thought it was best for me to stay out of sight.

"It isn't just the weather that makes it a lousy day, Doc. We had a lousy murder in town last night. I guess you know that, too. Probably Mrs Kincaid told you all about it."

"Are you accusing her?" Godwin said.

"I wouldn't say that. Not yet, anyway."

"Then beat it."

"You can't talk like that to me."

Godwin held himself motionless but his breath shook him as though he had a racing engine inside of him. "You accused me in the presence of witnesses of harbouring a fugitive from justice. I could sue you for slander and by God I will if you don't stop harassing me and my patients."

"I didn't mean it that way." Crane's voice was much less confident. "Anyway, I got a right to question a witness."

"At some later time perhaps you have. At the present time Mrs Kincaid is under heavy sedation. I can't permit her to be questioned for at least a week."

"A week?"

"It may be longer. I strongly advise you not to press the point. I'm prepared to go before a judge and certify that police questioning at the present time would endanger her health and perhaps her life."

"I don't believe it."

"I don't care what you believe."

Godwin slammed the door and leaned on it, breathing like a runner. A couple of white-uniformed nurses who had been peeking through the inner door tried to look as if they had business there. He waved them away.

I said with unfeigned admiration: "You really went to bat for her."

"They did enough damage to her when she was a child. They're not going to compound it if I can help it."

"How did they know she was here?"

"I have no idea. I can usually trust the staff to keep their mouths shut." He gave me a probing look. "Did you tell anyone?"

"Nobody connected with the law. Alex did mention to Alice Jenks that Dolly was here."

"Perhaps he shouldn't have. Miss Jenks has worked for the county a long time, and Crane and she were old acquaintances."

"She wouldn't tattle on her own niece, would she?"

"I don't know what she'd do." Godwin tore off his smock and threw it at the chair where I had been sitting. "Well, shall I let you out?"

He shook his keys like a jailer.

XII

About halfway up the pass road I came out into sunlight, The fog below was like a sea of white water surging into the inlets of the mountains. From the summit of the pass, where I paused for a moment, further mountains were visible on the inland horizon.

The wide valley between was full of light. Cattle grazed among the live oaks on the hillsides. A covey of quail marched across the road in front of my car like small plumed tipsy soldiers. I could smell newmown hay, and had the feeling that I had dropped down into a pastoral scene where nothing much had changed in a hundred years.

The town of Indian Springs didn't entirely dispel the feeling, though it had its service stations and its drive-ins offering hamburgers and tacos. It had a bit of old-time Western atmosphere, and more than a bit of the old-time sun-baked poverty of the West. Prematurely aging women watched over their brown children in the dooryards of crumbling adobes. Most of the loiterers in the main street had Indian faces under their broad-brimmed hats. Banners advertising Old Rodeo Days hung limply over their heads.

Alice Jenks lived in one of the best houses on what appeared to be the best street. It was a two-storyed white frame house, with deep porches upstairs and down, standing far back from the street behind a smooth green lawn. I stepped onto the grass and leaned on a pepper tree, fanning myself with my hat. I was five minutes early.

A rather imposing woman in a blue dress came out on the veranda. She looked me over as if I might possibly be a burglar cleverly creeping up on her house at eleven o'clock in the morning. She came down the steps and along the walk toward me. The sun flashed on her glasses and lent her searchlight eyes.

Close up, she wasn't so alarming. The brown eyes behind the glasses were strained and anxious. Her hair was streaked with gray. Her mouth was unexpectedly generous and even soft, but it was tweezered like a live thing between the harsh lines that thrust down from the base of her nose. The stiff blue dress that curved like armour plate over her monolithic bosom was old-fashioned in cut, and gave her a dowdy look. The valley sun had parched and roughened her skin.

"Are you Mr Archer?"

"Yes. How are you, Miss Jenks?"

"I'll survive." Her handshake was like a man's. "Come up on the porch, we can talk there."

Her movements, like her speech, were so abrupt that they suggested the jitters. The jitters under firm, perhaps lifelong, control. She motioned me into a canvas glider and sat in a reed chair facing me, her back to the street. Three Mexican boys on one battered bicycle rode by precariously like high-wire artists.

"I don't know just what you want from me, Mr Archer. My niece appears to be in very serious trouble. I talked to a friend in the courthouse this morning –"

"The Sheriff?"

"Yes. He seems to think that Dolly is hiding from him."

"Did you tell Sheriff Crane where she was?"

"Yes. Shouldn't I have?"

"He trotted right over to the nursing home to question her. Dr Godwin wouldn't let him."

"Dr Godwin is a great one for taking matters into his own hands. I don't believe myself that people in trouble should be coddled and swaddled in cotton wool, and what I believe for the rest of the world holds true for my own family. We've always been a law-abiding family, and if Dolly is holding something back, she ought to come out with it, I say let the truth be told, and the chips fall where they may."

It was quite a speech. She seemed to be renewing her old disagreement with Godwin about Dolly's testimony at the trial.

"Those chips can fall pretty hard, sometimes, when they fall on people you love."

She watched me, her sensitive mouth held tight, as if I had accused her of a weakness. "People I love?"

I had only an hour, and no sure intuition of how to reach her. "I'm assuming you love Dolly."

"I haven't seen her lately – she seems to have turned against me – but I'll always be fond of her. That doesn't mean" – and the deep lines reasserted themselves at the corners of her mouth

– "that I'll condone any wrongdoing on her part. I have a public position –"

"Just what is your position?"

"I'm senior county welfare worker for this area," she announced. Then she looked anxiously behind her at the empty street, as if a posse might be on its way to relieve her of her post.

"Welfare begins at home."

"Are you instructing me in the conduct of my private life?" She didn't wait for an answer. "Let me tell you, you don't have to. Who do you think took the child in when my sister's marriage broke up? I did, of course. I gave them both a home, and after my sister was killed I brought my niece up as if she was my own daughter. I gave her the best of food and clothes, the best of education. When she wanted her own independence, I gave her that, too. I gave her the money to go and study in Los Angeles. What more could I do for her?"

"You can give her the benefit of the doubt right now. I don't know what the Sheriff said to you, but I'm pretty sure he was talking through his little pointed hat."

Her face hardened. "Sheriff Crane does not make mistakes."

I had the sense of doubleness again, of talking on two levels. On the surface we were talking about Dolly's connection with the Haggerty killing but underneath this, though McGee had not been mentioned, we were arguing the question of McGee's guilt.

"All policemen make mistakes," I said. "All human beings make mistakes. It's even possible that you and Sheriff Crane and the judge and the twelve jurors and everybody else were mistaken about Thomas McGee, and convicted an innocent man."

She laughed in my face, not riotously. "That's ridiculous, you didn't know Tom McGee. He was capable of anything. Ask anybody in this town. He used to get drunk and come home and beat her. More than once I had to stand him off with a gun, with the child holding onto my legs. More than once, after Constance left him, he came to this house and battered on the door and said he would drag her out of here by the hair. But I wouldn't let him." She shook her head vehemently, and a strand of iron-gray hair fell like twisted wire across her cheek.

"What did he want from her?"

"He wanted domination. He wanted her under his thumb. But he had no right to her. We Jenks are the oldest family in town. The McGees across the river are the scum of the earth, most of them are on welfare to this day. He was one of the worst of them but my sister couldn't see it when he came courting her in his white sailor suit. He married her against Father's bitter objections. He gave her a dozen years of hell on earth and then he finally killed her. Don't tell me he was innocent. You don't know him."

A scrub jay in the pepper tree heard her harsh obsessive voice and raised his own voice in counter-complaint. I said under his noise:

"Why did he kill your sister?"

"Out of sheer diabolical devilment. What he couldn't have he chose to destroy. It was as simple as that. It wasn't true that there was another man. She was faithful to him to the day she died. Even though they were living in separate houses, my sister kept herself pure."

"Who said there was another man?"

She looked at me. The hot blood left her face. She seemed to lose the confidence that her righteous anger had given her.

"There were rumours," she said weakly. "Foul, dirty rumors. There always are when there's bad blood between a husband and wife. Tom McGee may have started them himself. I know his lawyer kept hammering away at the idea of another man. It was all I could do to sit there and listen to him, trying to destroy my sister's reputation after that murdering client of his had already destroyed her life. But Judge Gahagan made it clear in his instructions to the jury that it was just a story he invented, with no basis in fact."

"Who was McGee's lawyer?"

"An old fox named Gil Stevens. People don't go to him unless they're guilty, and he takes everything they have to get them off."

"But he didn't get McGee off."

"He practically did. Ten years is a small price to pay for first-degree murder. It should have been first-degree. He should have been executed."

The woman was implacable. With a firm hand she pressed her stray lock of hair back into place. Her graying head was marcelled in neat little waves, all alike, like the sea in old steel engravings. Such implacability as hers, I thought, could rise from either one of two sources: righteous certainty, or a guilty dubious fear that she was wrong. I hesitated to tell her what Dolly had said, that she had lied her father into prison. But I intended to tell her before I left.

"I'm interested in the details of the murder. Would it be too painful for you to go into them?"

"I can stand a lot of pain. What do you want to know?"

"Just how it happened."

"I wasn't here myself. I was at a meeting of the Native Daughters. I was president of the local group that year." The memory of this helped to restore her composure.

"Still I'm sure you know as much about it as anyone."

"No doubt I do. Except Tom McGee," she reminded me.

"And Dolly."

"Yes, and Dolly. The child was here in the house with Constance. They'd been living with me for some months. It was past nine o'clock, and she'd already gone to bed. Constance was downstairs sewing. My sister was a fine seamstress, and she made most of the child's clothes. She was making a dress for her that night. It got all spotted with blood. They made it an exhibit at the trial."

Miss Jenks couldn't seem to forget the trial. Her eyes went vague, as if she could see it like a ritual continually being repeated in the courtroom of her mind.

"What were the circumstances of the shooting?"

"It was simple enough. He came to the front door. He talked her into opening it."

"Its strange that he could do that, after her bad experiences with him."

She brushed my objection aside with a flat movement of her hand. "He could talk a bird out of a tree when he wanted to. At any rate, they had an argument. I suppose he wanted her to come back with him, as usual, and she refused. Dolly heard their voices raised in anger."

"Where was she?"

"Upstairs in the front bedroom, which she shared with her mother." Miss Jenks pointed upward at the boarded ceiling of the veranda. "The argument woke the child up, and then she heard the shot. She went to the window and saw him run out to the street with the smoking gun in his hand. She came downstairs and found her mother in her blood."

"Was she still alive?"

"She was dead. She died instantaneously, shot through the heart."

"With what kind of a gun?"

"A medium-caliber hand-gun, the Sheriff thought. It was never found. McGee probably threw it in the sea. He was in Pacific Point when they arrested him next day."

"On Dolly's word?"

"She was the only witness, poor child."

We seemed to have an unspoken agreement that Dolly existed only in the past. Perhaps because we were both avoiding the problem of Dolly's present situation, some of the tension between us had evaporated. I took advantage of this to ask Miss Jenks if I could look over the house.

"I don't see what for."

"You've given me a very clear account of the murder. I want to try and relate it to the physical layout."

She said doubtfully: "I don't have much more time, and frankly I don't know how much more of this I can stand. My sister was very dear to me."

"I know."

"What are you trying to prove?"

"Nothing. I just want to understand what happened. It's my job."

A job and its imperatives meant something to her. She got up, opened the front door, and pointed out the place just inside it where her sister's body had lain. There was of course no trace of the ten-year-old crime on the braided rag rug in the hall. No trace of it anywhere, except for the blind red smear it had left in Dolly's mind, and possibly in her aunt's.

I was struck by the fact that Dolly's mother and her friend Helen had both been shot at the front door of their homes by the same caliber gun, possibly held by the same person. I didn't mention this to Miss Jenks. It would only bring on another outburst against her brother-in-law McGee.

"Would you like a cup of tea?" she said unexpectedly.

"No thanks."

"Or coffee? I use instant. It won't take long."

"All right. You're very kind."

She left me in the living-room. It was divided by sliding doors from the dining-room, and furnished with stiff old dark pieces reminiscent of a nineteenth-century parlor. There were mottoes on the walls instead of pictures, and one of them brought back with a rush and a pang my grandmother's house in Martinez. It said: *"He is the Silent Listener at Every Conversation."* My grandmother had hand-embroidered the same motto and hung it in her bedroom. She always whispered.

An upright grand piano with a closed keyboard stood in one corner of the room. I tried to open it, but it was locked. A photograph of two women and a child stood in the place of honor on the piano top. One of the women was Miss Jenks, younger but just as stout and overbearing. The other woman was still younger and much prettier. She held herself with the naïve sophistication of a small-town belle. The child between them, with one hand in each of theirs, was Dolly aged about ten.

Miss Jenks had come through the sliding doors with a coffee tray. "That's the three of us." As if two women and a little girl made a complete family. "And that's my sister's piano. She played beautifully. I never could master the instrument myself."

She wiped her glasses. I didn't know whether they were clouded by emotion or by the steam from the coffee. Over it she related some of Constance's girlhood triumphs. She had won a prize for piano, another for voice. She did extremely well in high school, especially in French, and she was all set to go to college, as Alice had gone before her, when that smooth-talking devil of a Tom McGee –"

I left most of my coffee and went out into the hallway. It smelled of the mold that invades old houses. I caught a glimpse of myself in the clouded mirror beside the deer-horn hatrack. I looked like a ghost from the present haunting a bloody moment in the past. Even the woman behind me had an insubstantial quality, as if her large body was a husk or shell from which the essential being had departed. I found myself associating the smell of mold with her.

A rubber-treaded staircase rose at the rear of the hall. I was moving toward it as I said:

"Do you mind if I look at the room Dolly occupied?"

She allowed my momentum to carry her along and up the stairs. "It's my room now."

"I won't disturb anything."

The blinds were drawn and she turned on the overhead light for me. It had a pink shade which suffused the room with pinkness. The floor was thickly carpeted with a soft loose pink material. A pink decorator spread covered the queen-sized bed. The elaborate three-mirrored dressing-table was trimmed with pink silk flounces, and so was the upholstered chair in front of it.

A quilted pink long chair stood by the window with an open magazine across its foot. Miss Jenks picked up the magazine and rolled it in her hands so that its cover wasn't visible, but I knew a *True Romance* when I saw one.

I crossed the room, sinking to the ankles in the deep pink pile of her fantasy, and raised the blind over the front window. I could see the wide flat second-storey porch, and through its railings the pepper tree, and my car in the street. The three Mexican boys came by on their bicycle, one on the handle-bars, one on the seat, one on the carrier, trailed by a red mongrel which had joined the act.

"They have no right to be riding like that," Miss Jenks said at my shoulder. "I have a good mind to report them to the deputy. And that dog shouldn't be running around loose."

"He's doing no harm."

"Maybe not, but we had a case of hydrophobia two years ago."

"I'm more interested in ten years ago. How tall was your niece at that time?"

"She was a good big girl for her age. About four feet and a half. Why?"

I adjusted my height by getting down on my knees. From this position I could see the lacy branches of the pepper tree, and through them most of my car, but nothing nearer. A man leaving the house would scarcely be visible until he passed the pepper tree, at least forty feet away. A gun in his hand could not be seen until he reached the street. It was a hasty and haphazard experiment, but its result underlind the question in my mind.

I got up off my knees. "Was it dark that night?"

She knew which night I meant. "Yes. It was dark."

"I don't see any street lights."

"No. We have none. This is a poor town, Mr Archer."

"Was there a moon?"

"No. I don't believe so. But my niece has excellent eyesight. She can spot the markings on a bird –"

"At night?"

"There's always some light. Anyway, she'd know her own father." Miss Jenks corrected herself: "She *knew* her own father."

"Did she tell you this?"

"Yes. I was the first one she told."

"Did you question her about it in any detail?"

"I didn't, no. She was quite broken up, naturally. I didn't want to subject her to the strain."

"But you didn't mind subjecting her to the strain of testifying to these things in court."

"It was necessary, necessary to the prosecution's case. And it did her no harm."

"Dr Godwin thinks it did her a lot of harm, that the strain she went through then is partly responsible for her breakdown."

"Dr Godwin has his ideas and I have mine. If you want my opinion, he's a dangerous man, a troublemaker. He has no respect for authority and I have no respect for a man like that."

"You used to respect him. You sent your niece to him for treatment."

"I know more about him now than I did then."

"Do you mind telling me why she needed treatment?"

"No. I don't mind." She was still trying to preserve a friendly surface, though we were both conscious of the disagreement simmering under it. "Dolly wasn't doing well in school. She wasn't happy or popular. Which was natural enough with her parents – I mean, her father, making a shambles of their home together.

"This isn't the backwoods," she said as if she suspected maybe it was, "and I thought the least I could do was see that she got a little help. Even the people on welfare get family counseling when they need it. So I persuaded my sister to take her into Pacific Point to see Dr Godwin. He was the best we had at that time. Constance drove her in every Saturday morning for about a year. The child showed considerable improvement, I'll say that much for Godwin. So did Constance. She seemed brighter and happier and surer of herself."

"Was she getting treatment, too?"

"I guess she had a little, and of course it did her good to get into town every Saturday. She wanted to move into town but there was no money for it. She left McGee and moved in with me instead. That took some of the strain off her. He couldn't stand to see that. He couldn't stand to see her getting her dignity back. He killed her like a dog in the manger."

After ten years her mind was still buzzing like a fly around the bloody moment.

"Why didn't you continue Dolly's therapy? She probably needed it more than ever afterward."

"It wasn't possible. I work Saturday mornings. I have to get my paperwork done some time. She fell silent, confused and tongue-tied as honest people can be by their own deviousness.

"Also you had a disagreement with Godwin about your niece's testimony at the trial."

"I'm not ashamed of it, no matter what *he* says. It did her no harm to speak out about her father. It probably did her good. She had to get it out of her system somehow."

"It isn't out of her system, though. She's still hung up on it." Just as you are, Miss Jenks. "But now she's changed her story."

"Changed her story?"

"She says now that she didn't see her father the night of the murder. She denies that he had anything to do with it."

"Who told you that?"

"Godwin. He'd just been talking to her. She told him she lied in court to please the adults." I was tempted to say more, but remembered in time that it would almost certainly be relayed to her friend the Sheriff.

She was looking at me as if I had questioned a basic faith of her life. "He's twisting what she said, I'm sure. He's using her to prove that he was right when he was wrong."

"I doubt that, Miss Jenks. Godwin doesn't believe her new story himself."

"You see! She's either crazy or she's lying! Don't forget she's got McGee blood in her!" She was appalled by her own outburst. She turned her eyes away, glancing around the pink room as though it might somehow vouch for the girlish innocence of her intentions. "I didn't really mean that," she said. "I love my niece. It's just – it's harder than I thought to rake over the past like this."

"I'm sorry, and I'm sure you love your niece. Feeling about her the way you do, and did, you couldn't have fed her a false story to tell in court."

"Who says I did?"

"No one. I'm saying you couldn't have. You're not the sort of woman who could bring herself to corrupt the mind of a twelve-year-old child."

"No," she said. "I had nothing to do with Dolly's accusation against her father. She came to me with it, the night it happened, within half an hour of the *time* it happened. I never questioned it for a minute. It had all the accents of truth."

But she had not. I didn't think she was lying, exactly. More likely she was suppressing something. She spoke carefully and in a low voice, so that the motto in the living-room wouldn't hear her. She still wasn't meeting my eyes. A slow dull flush rose from her heavy neck to her face. I said:

"I doubt that it was physically possible for her to identify anyone, even her own father, at this distance on a dark night – let alone pick out a smoking gun in his hand."

"But the police accepted it. Sheriff Crane and the D.A. both believed her."

"Policemen and prosecutors are usually glad to accept the facts, or the pseudo-facts, that fit their case."

"But Tom McGee was guilty. He was guilty."

"He may have been."

"Then why are you trying to convince me that he wasn't?"

The flush of shame in her face was going through the usual conversion into a flush of anger. "I won't listen."

"You might as well listen. What can you lose? I'm trying to open up that old case because it's connected, through Dolly, with the Haggerty case."

"Do you believe she killed Miss Haggerty?" she said

"No. Do you?"

"Sheriff Crane seems to regard her as the main suspect."

"Did he say so to you, Miss Jenks?"

"He as much as said so. He was feeling me out on what my reaction would be if he took her in for questioning."

"And what was your reaction?"

"I hardly know, I was so upset. I haven't seen Dolly for some time. She went and married behind my back. She was always a good girl, but she may have changed."

I had the feeling that Miss Jenks was talking out of her deepest sense of herself: She had always been a good girl, but she might have changed.

"Why don't you call Crane up and tell him to lay off? Your niece needs delicate handling."

"You don't believe she's guilty of this murder?"

"I said I didn't. Tell him to lay off or he'll lose the next election."

"I couldn't do that. He's my senior in county work." But she was thinking about it. She shook the thought off. "Speaking of which, I've given you all the time I possibly can. It must be past twelve."

I was ready to leave. It had been a long hour. She followed me downstairs and out onto the veranda. I had the impression as we said goodbye that she wanted to say something more. Her face was expectant. But nothing came.

XIII

THE FOG had thinned out a little along the coastline, but you still couldn't see the sun, only a sourceless white glare that hurt the eyes. The keyboy at the Mariner's Rest told me that Alex had driven away with an older man in a new Chrysler. His own red sports car was still in the parking enclosure, and he hadn't checked out.

I bought a sandwich at a drive-in down the street and ate it in my room. Then I made a couple of frustrating phone calls. The switchboard operator at the courthouse said there wasn't a chance of getting hold of a trial transcript this afternoon: everything was locked up tight for the weekend. I called the office of Gil Stevens, the lawyer who had unsuccessfully defended Tom McGee. His answering service said he was in Balboa. No, I couldn't reach him there. Mr Stevens was racing his yacht today and tomorrow.

I decided to drop in on Jerry Marks, the young lawyer who

had acted as Mrs Perrine's defense counsel. His office was in a new shopping center not too far from the motel strip. Jerry was unmarried and ambitious, and he might be in it, even on a Saturday afternoon.

The front door was open and I walked into the waiting room, which was furnished with maple and chintz. The secretary's cubicle behind the glass half-wall on the left was deserted for the weekend, but Jerry Marks was in the inner office.

"How are you, Jerry?"

"I'm all right."

He looked at me guardedly over the book he was reading, an enormous tome entitled *Rules of Evidence*. He wasn't very experienced in criminal practice, but he was competent and honest. His homely Middle-European face was warmed and lit by intelligent brown eyes.

"How's Mrs Perrine?" I said.

"I haven't seen her since she was released, and I don't expect to. I seldom see much of my ex-clients. I smell of the courtroom to them."

"I have the same experience. Are you free?"

"Yeah, and I'm going to stay that way. I promised myself a clear weekend of study, murder or no murder."

"You know about the Haggerty murder then."

"Naturally, it's all over town."

"What have you heard?"

"Really not very much. Somebody at the courthouse told my secretary that this lady professor was shot by a girl student at the college. I forget her name."

"Dolly Kincaid. Her husband is my client. She's in a nursing home, under a doctor's care."

"Psycho?"

"It depends on your definition of psycho. It's a complex situation, Jerry. I doubt that she's legally insane under the McNaghten rule. On the other hand I very much doubt that she did the shooting at all."

"You're trying to get me interested in the case," he said suspiciously.

"I'm not trying to do anything to you. Actually I came to you for information. What's your opinion of Gil Stevens?"

"He's the local old master. Get him."

"He's out of town. Seriously, is he a good lawyer?"

"Stevens is the most successful criminal lawyer in the county. He has to be good. He knows law, and he knows juries. He does pull some old-fashioned courtroom shenanigans that I wouldn't use myself. He's quite an actor, heavy with the emotion. It works, though. I can't remember when he's lost an important case."

"I can. About ten years ago he defended a man named Tom McGee who was convicted of shooting his wife."

"That was before my time."

"Dolly Kincaid is McGee's daughter. Also, she was the key witness for the prosecution at her father's trial."

Jerry whistled. "I see what you mean by complex." After a pause, he said: "Who's her doctor?"

"Godwin."

He pushed out his heavy lips. "I'd go easy with him."

"What do you mean?"

"I'm sure he's a good psychiatrist, but maybe not so much in the forensic department. He's a very bright man and he doesn't hide his light under a bushel, in fact he sometimes acts like a mastermind. Which puts people's backs up, especially if their name is Gahagan and they're sitting on the Superior Court bench. So I'd use him sparingly."

"I can't control the use that's made of him."

"No, but you can warn her attorney –"

"It would be a lot simpler if you were her attorney. I haven't had a chance to talk to her husband today, but I think he'll go along with my recommendation. His family isn't poverty-stricken, by the way."

"It wasn't the money I was thinking about," Jerry said coldly. "I promised myself that I'd spend this weekend with my books."

"Helen Haggerty should have picked another weekend to get herself shot."

It came out harsher than I intended. My own failure to do anything for Helen was eating me.

Jerry regarded me quizzically. "This case is a personal matter with you?"

"It seems to be."

"Okay, okay," he said. "What do you want me to do?"

"Just hold youself in readiness for the present."

"I'll be here all afternoon. After that my answering service will be able to contact me."

I thanked him and went back to the motel. Alex's room next to mine was still empty. I checked with my own answering service in Hollywood. Arnie Walters had left his number for me and I called Reno.

Arnie was out of the office, but his wife and partner Phyllis took the call. Her exuberant femininity bounced along the wires:

"I never *see* you, Lew. All I hear is your voice on the telephone. For all I know you don't exist any more, but simply made some tapes a number of years ago and somebody plays them to me from time to time."

"How do you explain the fact that I'm responsive? Like now."

"Electronics, I explain everything I don't understand electronically. It saves me no end of trouble. But when am I going to *see* you?"

"This weekend, if Arnie's tabbed the driver of the convertible."

"He hasn't quite done that, but he does have a line on the owner. She's a Mrs Sally Burke and she lives right here in Reno. She claims her car was stolen a couple of days ago. But Arnie doesn't believe her."

"Why not?"

"He's very intuitive. Also she didn't report the alleged theft. Also she has boyfriends of various types. Arnie's out doing legwork on them now."

"Good."

"I gather this is important," Phyllis said.

"It's a double murder case, maybe a triple. My client's a young girl with emotional problems. She's probably going to be arrested today or tomorrow, for something she almost certainly didn't do."

"You sound very intense."

"This case has gotten under my skin. Also I don't know where I'm at."

"I never heard you admit that before, Lew. Anyway, I was thinking before you called, maybe I could strike up an acquaintance with Mrs Sally Burke. Does that sound like a good idea to you?"

"An excellent idea." Phyllis was an ex-Pinkerton operative

who looked like an ex-chorus girl. "Remember Mrs Burke and her playmates may be highly dangerous. They may have killed a woman last night."

"Not this woman. I've got too much to live for." She meant Arnie.

We exchanged some further pleasantries in the course of which I heard people coming into Alex's room next door. After I said goodbye to Phyllis I stood by the wall and listened. Alex's voice and the voice of another man were raised in argument, and I didn't need a contact mike to tell what the argument was about. The other man wanted Alex to clear out of this unfortunate mess and come home.

I knocked on his door.

"Let me handle them," the other man said, as if he was expecting the police.

He stepped outside, a man of about my age, good-looking in a grayish way, with a thin face, narrow light eyes, a pugnacious chin. The mark of organization was on him, like an invisible harness worn under his conservative gray suit.

There was some kind of desperation in him, too. He didn't even ask who I was before he said: "I'm Frederick Kincaid and you have no right to chivvy my son around. He has nothing to do with that girl and her crimes. She married him under false pretences. The marriage didn't last twenty-four hours. My son is a respectable boy –"

Alex stepped out and pulled at the older man's arm. His face was miserable with embarrassment. "You'd better come inside, Dad. This is Mr Archer."

"Archer, eh? I understand you've involved my son in this thing –"

"On the contrary, he hired me."

"I'm firing you." His voice sounded as if it had often performed this function.

"We'll talk it over," I said.

The three of us jostled each other in the doorway. Kincaid senior didn't want me to come in. It was very close to turning into a brawl. Each of us was ready to hit at least one of the others.

I bulled my way into the room and sat down in a chair with my back to the wall. "What's happened, Alex?"

"Dad heard about me on the radio. He phoned the Sheriff

and found out where I was. The Sheriff called us over there just now. They found the murder gun."

"Where?"

Alex was slow in answering, as though the words in his mouth would make the whole thing realer when he let them out. His father answered for him:

"Where she hid it, under the mattress of the bed in that little hut she's been living in –"

"It isn't a hut," Alex said. "Its a gatehouse."

"Don't contradict me, Alex."

"Did you see the gun?" I said.

"We did. The Sheriff wanted Alex to identify it, which naturally he couldn't do. He didn't even know she had a gun."

"What kind of gun is it?"

"It's a Smith and Wesson revolver, .38 caliber, with walnut grips. Old, but in pretty fair condition. She probably bought it at a pawn shop."

"Is this the police theory?"

"The Sheriff mentioned the possibility."

"How does he know it's hers?"

"They found it under her mattress, didn't they?" Kincaid talked like a prosecutor making a case, using it to bring his son into line. "Who else could have hidden it there?"

"Practically anybody else. The gatehouse was standing open last night, wasn't it, Alex?"

"It was when I got there."

"Let me do the talking," his father said. "I've had more experience in these matters."

"It hasn't done you a hell of a lot of good. Your son is a witness, and I'm trying to get at the facts."

He stood over me with his hands on his hips, vibrating. "My son has nothing whatever to do with this case."

"Don't kid youself. He's married to the girl."

"The marriage is meaningless – a boyish impulse that didn't last one full day. I'm having it annulled. It wasn't even consummated, he tells me."

"You can't annul it."

"Don't tell me what I can do."

"I think I will, though. All you can do is annul yourself and your son. There's more to a marriage than sexual consummation or legal technicalities. The marriage is real because it's real for Alex."

"He wants out of it now."

"I don't believe you."

"It's true, isn't it, Alex, you want to come home with me and Mother? She's terribly worried about you. Her heart is kicking up again." Kincaid was throwing everything but the kitchen sink.

Alex looked from him to me. "I don't know. I just want to do what's right."

Kincaid started to say something, probably having to do with the kitchen sink, but I talked over him:

"Then answer another question or two, Alex. Was Dolly carrying a gun when she came running back to the gatehouse last night?"

"I didn't see one."

Kincaid said: "She probably had it concealed under her clothes."

"Shut up, Kincaid," I said calmly from my sitting position. "I don't object to the fact that you're a bloodless bastard. You obviously can't help it. I do object to your trying to make Alex into one. Leave him a choice, at least."

Kincaid sputtered a couple of times, and walked away from me. Alex said without looking at either of us: "Don't talk to my father that way, Mr Archer."

"All right. She was wearing a cardigan and a blouse and skirt. Anything else?"

"No."

"Carrying a bag?"

"I don't think so."

"Think."

"She wasn't."

"Then she couldn't have been carrying a concealed .38 revolver. You didn't see her hide it under the mattress?"

"No."

"And were you with her all the time, between the time she got back and the time she left for the nursing home?"

"Yes. I was with her all the time."

"Then it's pretty clear it isn't Dolly's gun, or at least it wasn't Dolly who hid it under the mattress. Do you have any idea who it could have been?"

"No."

"You said it was the murder gun. How did they establish that? They haven't had time for ballistics tests."

Kincaid spoke up from the far corner where he had been sulking: "It's the right caliber to fit the wound, and one shell had been fired, recently. It stands to reason it's the gun she used."

"Do you believe that, Alex?"

"I don't know."

"Have they questioned her?"

"They intend to. The Sheriff said something about waiting until they nailed it down with ballistic evidence. Monday."

That gave me a little time, if I could believe Alex. The pressures of the night and morning, on top of the uncertainties of the last three weeks, had left him punchy. He looked almost out on his feet.

"I think we all should wait," I said, "before we make up our minds about your wife. Even if she's guilty, which I very strongly doubt, you owe her all the help and support you can give her."

"He owes her nothing," Kincaid said. "Not a thing. She married him fraudulently. She lied to him again and again."

I kept my voice and temper down, for contrast. "She still needs medical care, and she needs a lawyer. I have a good local lawyer waiting to step in, but I can't retain him myself."

"You're taking quite a lot into your hands, aren't you?"

"Somebody has to assume responsibility. There's a lot of it floating around loose at the moment. You can't avoid it by crawling into a hole and pulling the hole in after you. The girl's in trouble, and whether you like it or not she's a member of your family."

Alex appeared to be listening. I didn't know if he was hearing me. His father shook his narrow gray head:

"She's no member of my family, and I'll tell you one thing for certain. She's not going to drag my son down into the underworld. And neither are you." He turned to Alex. "How much have you already paid this man?

"A couple of hundred."

Kincaid said to me: "You've been amply paid, exorbitantly paid. You heard me fire you. This is a private room and if you persist in intruding I'll call the management. If they can't handle you I'll call the police."

Alex looked at me and lifted his hands, not very far, in a helpless movement. His father put an arm around his shoulders: "I'm only doing what's best for you, son. You don't belong with these people. We'll go home and cheer up Mother. After all you don't want to drive her into her grave."

It came out smooth and pat, and it was the clincher. Alex didn't look at me again. I went back to my own room and phoned Jerry Marks and told him I had lost a client and so had he. Jerry seemed disappointed.

XIV

ALEX AND his father vacated their room and drove away. I didn't go out to see them off but I could hear the sound of their engines, quickly muffled by the fog. I sat and let my stomach unknot, telling myself I should have handled them better. Kincaid was a frightened man who valued his status the way some previous generations valued their souls.

I drove up Foothill to the Bradshaw house. The Dean was probably another breakable reed, but he had money, and he had shown some sympathy for Dolly, over and above his official interest in the case. I had no desire to continue it on my own. I needed a principal, preferably one who swung some weight locally. Alice Jenks met this requirement, more or less, but I didn't want her for a client.

A deputy was standing guard at the gatehouse. He wouldn't let me in to look around but he didn't object to my going up to the main house. The Spanish woman Maria answered the door.

"Is Dr Bradshaw home?"

"No, sir."

"Where can I find him?"

She shrugged. "I dunno. I think Mrs Bradshaw said he's gone for the weekend."

"That's queer. I'd like to talk to Mrs Bradshaw."

"I'll see if she's busy."

I stepped inside uninvited and sat down on a gilt chair in

the entrance hall while Maria went upstairs. She came down and told me that Mrs Bradshaw would be with me shortly.

It was a least half an hour before she came limping down. She had primped her gray head and rouged her cheeks and put on a dress with lace at her slack throat held in place by a diamond brooch. I wondered, as she made me the dubious gift of her hand, if all this had been done for my benefit.

The old lady seemed glad to see me. "How are you, Mr – it's Mr Archer, isn't it? I've been hoping somebody would call. This fog makes one feel so isolated, and with my driver gone –" She seemed to hear the note of complaint rising in her voice, and cut it off. "How is the girl?" she said briskly.

"She's being taken care of. Dr Godwin thinks she's better than she was last night."

"Good. You'll be glad to know," she said with a bright ironic stare, "that I'm somewhat better myself than I was last night. My son informed me this morning that I staged one of my exhibitions, as he calls them. Frankly, I was upset. Nights aren't my best season."

"It was a rough night for everybody."

"And I'm a selfish old woman. Isn't that what you're thinking?"

"People don't seem to change much as they get older."

"That has all the earmarks of an insult." But she was smiling, almost flirtatiously. "You imply that I've always been this way."

"You'd know better than I would."

She laughed outright. It wasn't a joyous sound, but there was humor in it. "You're a bold young man, and a bright one. I like bright young men. Come into the study and I'll see that you get a drink."

"Thank you, but I can't stay –"

"Then I'll sit here." She lowered herself carefully onto the gilt chair. "My moral qualities may not have altered for the worse. My physical capabilities certainly have. This fog is very bad for my arthritis." She added, with a gingerly shake of her head: "But I mustn't complain. I promised my son, in penance for last night, that I would go through an entire day without uttering a word of complaint."

"How are you doing."

"Not so well," she said with her wry and wrinkled smile. "It's like solitaire, you always cheat a little. Or don't you?"

"I don't play the game."

"You're not missing a great deal, but it helps to pass the days for me. Well, I won't keep you if you have business."

"I have business with Dr Bradshaw. Do you know where I can contact him?"

"Roy flew to Reno this morning."

"Reno?"

"Not to gamble, I assure you. He hasn't an iota of gambling instinct. In fact I sometimes think he's excessively cautious. Roy is a bit of a mother's boy, wouldn't you say?" She looked up at me with complex irony, unembarrassed by his condition or her complicity in it.

"I'm a little surprised that he'd go away in the middle of this murder case."

"So was I, but there was no stopping him. He isn't exactly running away from it. They're holding a conference of small-college deans at the University of Nevada. It's been planned for months, and Roy is slated as one of the principal speakers. He felt it was his duty to be there. But I could see very well that he was eager to go. He loves the public eye, you know – he's always been a bit of an actor – but he isn't so terribly fond of the responsibilities that go with it."

I was amused and intrigued and a little appalled by her realism. She seemed to be enjoying it herself. Conversation was better than solitaire.

Mrs Bradshaw rose creakingly and leaned on my arm. "You might as well come into the study. It's drafty here. I've taken a fancy to you, young man."

I didn't know if this was a blessing or a curse. She grinned up into my face as if she could read my doubts there. "Don't worry, I won't eat you." She placed the emphasis on the final word, as though she had already eaten her son for breakfast.

We went into the study together and sat in facing high-backed leather chairs. She rang for Maria and ordered me a highball. Then she leaned back and scanned the bookshelves. The phalanxes of books seemed to remind her of Bradshaw's importance.

"Don't misunderstand me. I love my son profoundly and I'm proud of him. I'm proud of his good looks and I'm proud of his brains. He graduated *summa cum laude* from Harvard and went on to take a most distinguished doctorate. One of these days he's going to be the president of a major university or a great foundation."

"Is he ambitious, or are you?"

"I used to be, for him. As Roy became more ambitious, I became less so. There are better things in life than climbing an endless ladder. I haven't entirely given up hope that he'll marry." She cocked a bright old eye at me. "He *likes* women, you know."

"I'm sure he does."

"In fact I was beginning to persuade myself that he was interested in Miss Haggerty. I've never known him to pay so much attention to any other woman." She dropped the statement so that it became a question.

"He mentioned to me that he took her out several times. But he also said that they were never close in any way. His reaction to her death confirmed that."

"What was his reaction to her death?"

I'd done a lot of pumping in my time, and I knew when it was being done to me. "I mean his general reaction. He wouldn't have flown to Reno this morning, deans' conference or no deans' conference, if he had been really fond of Helen Haggerty. He'd be here in Pacific Point trying to find out who did her in."

"You seem quite let down about it."

"I was looking for his help. He seemed genuinely concerned about Dolly Kincaid."

"He is. We both are. In fact Roy asked me at breakfast to do what I could for the girl. But what can I do?" She displayed her crumpled hands, making a show of her helplessness.

Maria came in with my clinking highball, handed it to me unceremoniously, and asked her employer if there was anything else. There wasn't. I sipped my drink, wondering if Mrs Bradshaw was a client I could possibly handle, if she became my client. She had the money, all right. The diamonds winking at her throat would have bought my services for several years.

"You can hire me," I said.

"Hire you?"

"If you really want to do something for Dolly, and not just sit there paying lip-service to the idea. Do you think we could get along?"

"I was getting along with men when you were in the cradle, Mr Archer. Are you implying I can't get along with people?"

"I seem to be the one who can't. Alex Kincaid just fired me, with a strong assist from his father. They want no part of Dolly and her problems, now that the chips are down."

Her black eyes flashed. "I saw through that boy immediately. He's a mollycoddle."

"I don't have the resources to go on by myself. It isn't good practice, anyway. I need somebody to back me, preferably somebody with local standing and – I'll be frank – a substantial bank balance."

"How much would it cost me?"

"It depends on how long the case goes on and how many ramifications develop. I get a hundred a day and expenses. Also I have a team of detectives in Reno working on a lead that may be a hot one."

"A lead in Reno?"

"It originated here, last night."

I told her about the man in the convertible which belonged to Mrs Sally Burke, a woman with many boy friends. She leaned forward in her chair in mounting interest:

"Why aren't the police working on that lead?"

"They may be. If they are, I don't know about it. They seem to have settled for the idea that Dolly's guilty and everything else is irrelevant. It's simpler that way."

"You don't accept that idea?"

"No."

"In spite of the gun they found in her bed?"

"You know about that, then."

"Sheriff Crane showed it to me this morning. He wanted to know if I recognized it. Of course I didn't. I abhor the very sight of guns myself. I've never permitted Roy to own a gun."

"And you have no idea who owned that one?"

"No, but the Sheriff appeared to take it for granted that it was Dolly's, and that it tied her to the murder."

"We have no reason to think it was hers. If it was, the last place she'd put it would be under her own mattress. Her husband denies she did, and he was with her continuously once she got back to the gatehouse. There's the further point that there's no definite proof it's the murder weapon."

"Really?"

"Really. It will take ballistics tests and they're not scheduled until Monday. If my luck holds, I think I can throw more light on the situation by then."

"Do you have a definite theory of your own, Mr Archer?"

"I have an idea that the ramifications of this thing go far back beyond Dolly. It wasn't Dolly who threatened Miss Haggerty's life. She would have recognized her voice, they were close friends. I think Dolly walked up to her house simply to ask her advice about whether to go back to her husband. She stumbled over the body and panicked. She's still in panic."

"Why?"

"I'm not prepared to explain it. I want to go into her background further. I also want to go into Miss Haggerty's background."

"That might be interesting," she said, as if she was considering attending a double-feature movie. "How much is all this going to cost me?"

"I'll keep it as low as I can. But it could mount up in the thousands, two or three or even four."

"That's rather an expensive penance."

"Penance"

"For all my selfishness, past and present and future. I'll think about it, Mr Archer."

"How long do you need to think about it?"

"Call me tonight. Roy will be telephoning me around dinner-time – he telephones me every night when he's away – and I couldn't possibly give you an answer before I discuss it with him. We live on a tighter budget than you might think," she said earnestly, fingering the diamonds at her throat.

XV

I DROVE up under the dripping trees to Helen Haggerty's place. Two deputies messing around outside the front door wouldn't let me in or answer any questions. It was turning out to be a bad day.

I drifted over to the campus and into the Administration Building. I had some idea of talking to Laura Sutherland, the Dean of Women, but her office was locked. All the offices were locked. The building was deserted except for a white-headed man in blue jeans who was sweeping the corridor with a long-handled push-broom. He looked like Father Time, and I had a nightmare moment of thinking that he was sweeping Helen's last vestiges away.

In a kind of defensive reflex I got out my notebook and looked up the name of the chairman of the modern languages department. Dr Geisman. The old man with the push-broom knew where his office was:

"It's in the new Humanity Building, down the line." He pointed. "But he won't be there on a Saturday afternoon."

The old man was mistaken. I found Geisman in the department office on the first floor of the Humanities Building, sitting with a telephone receiver in one hand and a pencil in the other. I had seen him coming out of Bradshaw's conference the day before, a heavy middle-aged man with thick spectacles imperfectly masking anxious little eyes.

"One moment," he said to me; and into the telephone: "I'm sorry you can't help us, Mrs Bass. I realize you have your family responsibilities and of course the remuneration is not great for a special lecturer."

He sounded foreign, though he had no accent. His voice was denatured, as if English was just another language he had learned.

"I am Dr Geisman," he said as he hung up and stroked out a name on the list in front of him. "Are you Dr de Falla?"

"No. My name is Archer."

"What are your qualifications? Do you have an advanced degree?"

"In the university of hard knocks."

He didn't respond to my smile. "A member of our faculty is defunct, as you must know, and I've had to give up my Saturday to an attempt to find a replacement for her. If you expect me to take your application seriously –"

"I'm not applying for anything, Doctor, except possibly a little information. I'm a private detective investigating Professor Haggarty's death, and I'm interested in how she happened to land here."

"I have no time to go into all that again. There are classes which must be met on Monday. If this Dr de Falla doesn't arrive, or proves impossible, I don't know what to do." He peered at his wristwatch. "I'm due at the Los Angeles airport at six-thirty."

"You can spare five minutes, anybody can."

"Very well. Five minutes." He tapped the crystal of his watch. "You wish to know how Miss Haggerty came here? I can't say, except that she appeared in my office one day and asked for a position. She had heard about Professor Farrand's heart attack. This is our second emergency in a month."

"Who told her about the heart attack?"

"I don't know. Perhaps Dean Sutherland. She gave Dean Sutherland as a local reference. But it was common knowledge, it was in the paper."

"Was she living here before she applied for a job with you?"

"I believe so. Yes, she was. She told me she already had a house. She liked the place, and wished to remain. She was very eager for the post. Frankly, I had some doubts about her. She had a master's degree from Chicago but she wasn't fully qualified. The school where she had been teaching, Maple Park, is not credentialed on our level. But Dean Sutherland told me she needed the position and I let her have it, unfortunately."

"I understood she had a private income."

He pursed his lips and shook his head. "Ladies with a private income don't take on four sections of French and German, plus counseling duties, at a salary of less than five thousand dollars. Perhaps she meant her alimony. She told me she was having difficulty collecting her alimony." His spectacles glinted as he looked up. "You knew that she had been recently divorced?"

"I heard that. Do you know where her ex-husband is?"

"No. I had very few words with her at any time. Do you suspect him?"

"I have no reason to. But when a woman is killed you normally look for a man who had a motive to kill her. The local police have other ideas."

"You don't agree with them?"

"I'm keeping my mind open, Doctor."

"I see. They tell me one of our students is under suspicion."

"So I hear. Do you know the girl?"

"No. She was registered for none of our departmental courses, fortunately."

"Why fortunately?"

"She is psychoneurotic, they tell me." His myopic eyes looked as vulnerable as open oysters under the thick lenses of his glasses. "If the administration employed proper screening procedures we would not have students of that sort on the campus, endangering our lives. But we are very backward here in some respects." He tapped the crystal of his watch again. "You've had your five minutes."

"One more question, Doctor. Have you been in touch with Helen Haggerty's family?"

"Yes, I phoned her mother early this morning. Dean Bradshaw asked me to perform that duty, though properly I should think it was his duty. The mother, Mrs Hoffman, is flying out here and I have to meet her at the Los Angeles airport."

"At six-thirty?"

He nodded dismally. "There seems to be no one else available. Both of our deans are out of town –"

"Dean Sutherland, too?"

"Dean Sutherland, too. They've gone off and left the whole business on my shoulders." His glasses blurred with self-pity, and he took them off to wipe them. "It's foggy, and I can't see to drive properly. My eyesight is so poor that without my glasses I can't tell the difference between you and the Good Lord himself."

"There isn't much difference."

He put on his glasses, saw that this was a joke, and emitted a short barking laugh.

"What plane is Mrs Hoffman coming in on, Doctor?"

"United, from Chicago. I promised to meet her at the United baggage counter."

"Let me."

"Are you serious?"

"It will give me a chance to talk to her. Where do you want me to bring her?"

"I reserved her a room at the Pacific Hotel. I could meet you there at eight, say."

"Fine."

He got up and came around the desk and shook my hand vigorously. As I was leaving the building, a small, old man in a black hat and a greenish black cloak came sidling out of the fog. He had a dyed-looking black mustache, hectic black eyes, a wine flush on his hollow cheeks.

"Dr de Falla?"

He nodded. I held the door for him. He swept off his hat and bowed.

"Merci beaucoup."

His rubber-soled shoes made no more sound than a spider. I had another one of my little nightmare moments. This one was Doctor Death.

XVI

IT WAS a slow drive up the coast but the fog lifted before I reached the airport, leaving a thickish twilight in the air. I parked my car at the United building. It was exactly six-twenty-five, according to the ticket the girl in the parking lot handed me. I crossed the road to the bright enormous building and found the baggage carrousel, besieged by travelers.

A woman who looked like a dried-up older Helen was standing on the edge of the crowd beside her suitcase. She had on a black dress under a black coat with a ratty fur collar, black hat, and black gloves.

Only her garish red hair was out of keeping with the occasion. Her eyes were swollen, and she seemed dazed, as if a part of her mind was still back in Illinois.

"Mrs Hoffman?"

"Yes. I'm Mrs Earl Hoffman."

"My name is Archer. Your daughter's department head, Dr Geisman, asked me to pick you up."

"That was nice of him," she said with a poor vague smile. "And nice of you."

I picked up her suitcase, which was small and light. "Would you like something to eat, or drink? There's a pretty good restaurant here."

"Oh, no, thanks. I had dinner on the plane. Swiss steak. It

was a very interesting flight. I never flew in a jet before. But I wasn't the least bit frightened."

She didn't know what she was. She stared around at the bright lights and the people. The muscles of her face were tensing up as if she might be getting ready to cry some more. I got hold of her thin upper arm and hustled her out of there and across the road to my car. We circled the parking lot and got onto the freeway.

"They didn't have this when I was here before. I'm glad you decided to meet me. I'd get lost," she said in a lost voice.

"How long is it since you were here before?"

"Nearly twenty years. It was when Hoffman was in the Navy, he was a warrant officer in the Shore Patrol. They assigned him to San Diego and Helen had already run – left home, and I thought I might as well get the benefit of the travel. We lived in San Diego for over a year, and it was very nice." I could hear her breathing as if she was struggling up to the rim of the present. She said carefully: "Pacific Point is quite near San Diego, isn't it?"

"About fifty miles."

"Is that right?" After another pause, she said: "Are you with the college?"

"I happen to be a detective."

"Isn't that interesting? My husband is a detective. He's been on the Bridgeton force for thirty-four years. He's due to retire next year. We've talked about retiring in California but this will probably turn him against it. He pretends not to care, but he cares. I think he cares just as much as I do." Her voice floated along above the highway noises like a disembodied spirit talking to itself.

"It's too bad he couldn't fly out with you today."

"He could have, if he'd wanted to. He could have taken time off. I think he was afraid he couldnt face it. And he has his blood pressure to consider." She hesitated again. "Are you investigating my daughter's murder?"

"Yes."

"Dr Geisman said on the phone that you have a suspect, a young girl. What would make a student shoot one of her teachers? I never heard of such a thing."

"I don't think she did, Mrs Hoffman."

"But Dr Geisman said it was practically open and shut." The sorrow in her voice had changed into a kind of vengeful justice.

"That may be." I had no desire to argue with a potentially valuable witness. "I'm investigating other angles, and you may be able to help me."

"How is that?"

"Your daughter's life was threatened. She talked to me about it before she was shot. Somebody called her on the telephone. It was a voice she didn't recognize, but she said a strange thing about it. She said it sounded like the voice of Bridgeton."

"Bridgeton? That's where we live."

"I know that, Mrs Hoffman. Helen said it was Bridgeton catching up with her. Do you have any idea what she meant?"

"She always hated Bridgeton. From the time that she was in high school she blamed it for everything that went wrong with her life. She couldn't wait to get out of Bridgeton."

"I understand she ran away from home."

"I wouldn't put it that way," although she almost had. "She only dropped out of sight for the one summer, and she was working all the time. She had a job, with a newspaper in Chicago. Then she started in at the university, and she let me know where she was. It was just her father –" She cut this sentence off short. "I used to help her out of my housekeeping money until we went into the Navy."

"What was the trouble between her and her father?"

"It had to do with his professional work. At least that was what the final big battle was about."

"When Helen called him a crooked stormtrooper?"

She turned in the seat to look at me. "Helen told you that, eh? Are you – were you her boy friend or something like that?"

"We were friends." I found that I could say it with some conviction. We had spent a single angry hour together but her death had turned a light on it which hurt my eyes.

She leaned closer to study my face. "What else did she tell you?"

"There was a murder involved in her quarrel with her father."

"That's a lie. I don't mean Helen was lying, but she was mistaken. The Deloney shooting was an accident pure and simple. If Helen thought she knew more about it than her father, she was dead wrong."

"Dead" and "wrong" were heavy words to lay on the dead. Her black-gloved hand flew up to her mouth. She rode for a while in hunched and fearful silence, a thin dry cricket of a woman who had lost her chirp.

"Tell me about the Deloney shooting, Mrs Hoffman."

"I don't see the point of doing that. I never talk about my husband's cases. He doesn't like me to."

"But he isn't here."

"In a way he is. We've been together so long. Anyway it's all past history."

"History is always connected with the present. That case may have something to do with Helen's death."

"How could that be? It was twenty years ago, longer than that, and it didn't amount to anything at the time. The only reason it made an impression on Helen was that it happened in our apartment building. Mr Deloney was cleaning a gun, and it went off and shot him, and that was the whole story."

"Are you sure?"

"Hoffman said so, and Hoffman doesn't lie." It sounded like an incantation which she had used before."

"What made Helen think he was lying?"

"Imagination pure and simple. She said she talked to a witness who saw somebody shoot Mr Deloney, but I say she dreamed it. No witness ever turned up, and Hoffman said there couldn't have been a witness. Mr Deloney was alone in the apartment when it happened. He tried to clean a loaded gun and shot himself in the face. Helen must have dreamed the other. She had a bit of a crush on Mr Deloney. He was a good-looking man, and you know how young girls are."

"How old was she?"

"Nineteen. That was the summer she left home."

It was full dark now. Away off to the right the lights of Long Beach, where I had spent my own uneasy youth, were reflected like a dying red fire from the overcast.

"Who was Mr Deloney?"

"Luke Deloney," she said. "He was a very successful contractor in Bridgeton and throughout the state. He owned our apartment building and other buildings in town. Mrs Deloney still owns them. They're worth a lot more than they were then, and even then he was close to a millionaire."

"Deloney has a surviving widow?"

"Yes, but don't go jumping to conclusions. She was miles away, in the main house, when it happened. Sure there was a lot of talk in town, but she was as innocent as a newborn babe. She came from a very good family. She was one of the famous Osborne sisters in Bridgeton."

"What were they famous for?"

"Their father was the US Senator. I remember when I was in grade school, back before the World War One, they used to ride to hounds in red coats. But they were always very democratic."

"Good for them." I brought her back to the Deloney case. "You say Deloney was shot in the building where you had your own apartment?"

"Yes. We were in an apartment on the ground floor. We got it dirt cheap because we used to collect the rent for Mr Deloney. He kept the roof apartment for himself. He used it for a kind of private office, and a place to throw parties for visiting firemen and so on. A lot of big men from the state house were friends of his. We used to see them coming and going," she said in a privileged way.

"And he shot himself in this penthouse apartment?"

"The gun shot him," she corrected me. "It was an accident."

"What sort of man was Deloney?"

"He was a self-made man, I guess you'd say. He came from the same section of town Hoffman and I did, which is how we got the job collecting rent for him, and that *helped,* in the depression. The depression didn't faze Luke Deloney. He borrowed the money to start his own contracting business and came up fast on his own initiative, and married Senator Osborne's oldest daughter. There's no telling where he might have got to. He was only a young man of forty when he died."

"Helen was interested in him, you say?"

"Not seriously, I don't mean that. I doubt if they ever said two words to each other. But you know how young girls are, dreaming about older men. He was the most successful man around, and Helen was always very ambitious. It's funny, she blamed her father for being a failure, which he isn't. But when she finally got around to marrying she had to pick Bert Haggerty, and he's a failure if there ever was one."

She was talking much more freely, but her loquacity tended to fly off in all directions. It was natural enough. Her daughter's murder had dropped a depth charge into her life.

"Assume there is a connection," I said, "between Helen's death and the Deloney shooting – do you have any notion what it could be?"

"No, she must have been imagining things. She was always a great one for that."

"But she said she knew a witness who saw Deloney shot by someone else?"

"She was talking foolishness."

"Why?"

"You mean why would she say such things to her father? To get under his skin. There was always bad blood between them, from the time that Hoffman first raised his hand to her. Once they got arguing, there wasn't anything she wouldn't say."

"Did she name the witness?"

"How could she? There was no such person. Her father challenged her to mention a name. She admitted that she couldn't, that she was just talking."

"She admitted it?"

"She had to. Hoffman made her. But she never took back the hard words she spoke to him."

"Is it possible that Helen herself was the witness?"

"That's crazy and you know it. How could she be a witness to something that never happened?" But there was a shrill edge on her certitude.

"Deloney's dead, remember. So is she. It tends to confirm the things she told her friends before she died."

"About Bridgeton, you mean?"

"Yes."

She lapsed into silence again. Below the harbor cities we entered the fog zone. I was afraid of running into a pileup and I slowed down. Mrs Hoffman kept looking back as if she could feel Bridgeton catching up.

"I hope Hoffman isn't drinking," she said after a while. "It isn't good for his blood pressure. I'll blame myself if anything happens to him."

"One of you had to come out here."

"I suppose so. Anyway Bert is with him and whatever else

he may be Bert is no drunk."

"Helen's ex-husband is staying with her father?"

"Yes. He came over from Maple Park this morning and drove me to the airport. Bert's a good boy. I shouldn't call him a boy, he's a grown man in his forties, but he always seems younger than he is."

"Does he teach at Maple Park?"

"That's right, only he hasn't got his degree. He's been working on it for years. He teaches journalism and English, and he helps put out the school paper. He used to be a newspaperman, that was how Helen met him."

"When she was nineteen?"

"You have a good memory. You and Hoffman would get along. Hoffman's middle name is memory. There was a time before we got our wartime expansion when he knew every building in Bridgeton. Every factory, every warehouse, every residence. Pick any house on any street and he could tell you who built it and who owned it. He could tell you who lived there and who used to live there and how many children they had and how much income and anything else you wanted to know about them. I'm not exaggerating, ask any of his fellow officers. They used to predict great things for him, but he never made it higher than Lieutenant."

I wondered why the great things hadn't materialized. She gave me a kind of answer, which I suspected was more of a legend than a fact:

"Helen got her memory from him. They were more alike than either of them admitted. And they were crazy about each other, under all the trouble there was between them. It broke his heart when Helen left home and never wrote. He never asked about her, either, but he did a lot of brooding. He was never the same man again."

"Did she marry Bert Haggerty right away?"

"No, she kept him dangling for five or six years. He was away in the army part of that time. Bert did well in the war – a lot of men did well in the war that never did so well before or since – and he was full of confidence for a while. He was going to write a book, start his own newspaper, take her to Europe on their honeymoon. They did get to Europe, on the GI Bill – I gave them part of the money to make the trip – but that was all that ever came of his plans. He never could settle down to any one thing, and when he finally did it was too late. Last spring they came to the parting of the ways. I didn't like it, but I can hardly blame her. She always did better than he did, from the time that they were married. And one thing I'll say for Helen, she always had class."

"I agree."

"But maybe she should have stuck with Bert. Who knows? Maybe this wouldn't have happened. I sometimes think that any man is better than no man at all."

Later, as we were entering Pacific Point, she said: "Why couldn't Helen marry an upstanding husband? It's funny. She had brains and looks *and* class, but she never could attract an upstanding man."

I could feel her eyes on my profile, trying to chart the lost continent of her daughter's life.

XVII

THE PACIFIC Hotel stood on a corner just above the economic equator that divided the main street into a prosperous section and a not so prosperous one. The lobby was almost empty on this Saturday night. Four old men were playing bridge in the light of a standing lamp. The only other human being in sight was Dr Geisman, if he qualified.

He got up out of a shabby green plastic armchair and shook hands formally with Mrs Hoffman.

"I see that you've arrived safely. How are you?"

"I'm all right, thanks."

"Your daughter's unexpected demise came as quite a blow to us."

"To me, too."

"In fact I've been endeavouring all day to find a replacement for her. I still haven't succeeded. This is the worst possible time of year to try to recruit teaching personnel."

"That's too bad."

I left them trying to breathe life into their stillborn conversation and went into the bar for a drink. A single customer sat trading sorrows with the fat lugubrious bartender. Her hair was dyed black, with a greenish sheen on it like certain ducks.

I recognized the woman – I could have spotted Mrs Perrine at a thousand yards – and I started to back out of the room. She turned and saw me.

"Fancy meeting you here." She made a large gesture which almost upset the empty glass in front of her, and said to the bartender: "This is my friend Mr Archer. Pour my friend a drink."

"What'll you have?"

"Bourbon. I'm paying. What is the lady drinking?"

"Planter's punch," she said, "and thanks for the 'lady'. Thanks for everything in fact. I'm celebrating, been celebrating all day."

I wished she hadn't been. The granite front she had kept up at her trial had eroded, and the inner ruin of her life showed through. While I didn't know all of Mrs Perrine's secrets, I knew the record she had left on the police blotters of twenty cities. She had been innocent of this one particular crime, but she was a hustler who had worked the coasts from Acapulco to Seattle and from Montreal to Key West.

The bartender limped away to make our drinks. I sat on the stool beside her. "You should pick another town to celebrate in."

"I know. This town is a graveyard. I felt like the last living inhabitant, until you sashayed in."

"That isn't what I mean, Mrs Perrine."

"Hell, call me Bridget, you're my pal, you've earned the right."

"Okay, Bridget. The police didn't like your acquittal, you couldn't expect them to. They'll pick you up for any little thing."

"I haven't stepped out of line. I have my own money."

"I'm thinking about what you might do if you go on celebrating. You can't afford to jaywalk in this town."

She considered this problem, and her twisting face mimicked the efforts of her mind. "You may be right at that. I been thinking of going to Vegas in the morning. I have a friend in Vegas."

The bartender brought our drinks. Mrs Perrine sipped at hers, making a sour face, as if she'd suddenly lost her taste for it. Her gaze strayed to the mirror behind the bar.

"My gosh," she said. "Is that me? I look like the wrath of God."

"Take a bath and get some sleep."

"It isn't so easy to sleep. I get lonely at night." She ogled me, more or less automatically.

She wasn't my baby. I finished my drink and put two dollar bills on the bar.

"Good night, Bridget. Take it easy. I have to make a phone call."

"Sure you do. See you at the Epworth League."

The bartender limped toward her as I walked out. Mrs Hoffman and Dr Geisman were no longer in the lobby. I found the telephone booths in a cul-de-sac behind the main desk and called the Bradshaw house.

Before the phone had rung more than once, the old lady's voice came quavering over the line. "Roy? Is that you, Roy?"

"This is Archer."

"I was so hoping it would be Roy. He always telephones by this time. You don't suppose something has happened to him?"

"No. I don't."

"Have you seen the paper?"

"No."

"There's an item to the effect that Laura Sutherland went to the Reno conference with him. Roy didn't tell me that. Do you suppose he's interested in Laura?"

"I wouldn't know."

"She's a lovely young woman, don't you think?"

I wondered if she'd had some wine at dinner that made her silly. "I have no opinion on the subject, Mrs Bradshaw. I called to see if you're willing to follow through on our conversation this afternoon."

"I'm afraid I couldn't possibly, not without Roy's consent. He handles the money in the family, you know. Now I'm going to ask you to cut this short, Mr Archer. I'm expecting to hear from Roy at any moment."

She hung up on me. I seemed to be losing my touch with little old ladies. I went into the washroom and looked at my face in the mirror above the row of basins. Someone had written in pencil on the wall: *Support Mental Health or I'll kill you.*

A small brown newsboy came into the washroom and caught me grinning at my reflection. I pretended to be examining my teeth. He looked about ten years old, and conducted himself like a miniature adult.

"Read all about the murder," he suggested.

I bought a local paper from him. The lead story was headlined: "PPC Teacher Shot," with the subhead: "Mystery Student to be Questioned." In effect, it tried and convicted Dolly. She had "registered fraudulently, using an alias". Her friendship with Helen was described as "a strange relationship". The S and W thirty-eight found in her bed was "the murder weapon". She had "a dark secret in her past" – the McGee killing – and was "avoiding questioning by the police".

No other possible suspect was mentioned. The man from Reno didn't appear in the story.

In lieu of doing something constructive I tore the paper to pieces and dropped the pieces in the trash basket. Then I went back to the telephone booths. Dr Godwin's answering service wanted to know if it was an emergency.

"Yes. It has to do with a patient of Dr Godwin's."

"Are you the patient, sir?"

"Yes," I lied, wondering if this meant I needed help.

The switchboard girl said in a gentler voice: "The last time the doctor called in he was at home."

She recited his number but I didn't use it. I wanted to talk to Godwin face to face. I got his address out of the directory and drove across town to his house.

It was one of a number of large houses set on the edge of the mesa which normally overlooked the harbor and the city. Tonight it was islanded by the fog.

Behind the Arizona fieldstone front of the house a tenor and a soprano were singing a heartbreaking duet from *La Bohème*.

The door was answered by a handsome woman wearing a red silk brocade coat and the semi-professional smile that doctors' wives acquire. She seemed to recognize my name.

"I'm sorry, Mr Archer. My husband was here until just a few minutes ago. We were actually listening to music for a change. Then a young man called – the husband of one of his patients – and he agreed to meet him at the nursing home."

"It wasn't Alex Kincaid who called?"

"I believe it was, Mr Archer?" She stepped outside, a brilliant and very feminine figure in her red coat. "My husband has spoken of you. I understand you're working on this criminal case he's involved with."

"Yes."

Her hand touched my arm. "I'm worried about him. He's taking this thing so seriously. He seems to think that he let the girl down when she was his patient before, and that it makes him responsible for everything that's happened." Her fine long eyes looked up at me, asking for reassurance.

"He isn't," I said.

"Will you tell him so? He won't listen to me. There are very few people he will listen to. But he seems to have some respect for you, Mr Archer."

"It's mutual. I doubt that he'd want my opinion on the subject of his responsibility, though. He's a very powerful and temperamental man, easy to cross."

"You're telling me," she said. "I suppose I had no right to ask you to speak to him. But the way he pours his life away into those patients of his –" Her hand moved from her breast in an outward gesture.

"He seems to thrive on it."

"I don't." She made a wry face. "Physician's wife, heal thyself, eh?"

"You're thriving by all appearances," I said. "That's a nice coat, by the way."

"Thank you. Jim bought it for me in Paris last summer."

I left her smiling less professionally, and went to the nursing home. Alex's red Porsche was standing at the curb in front of the big plain stucco building. I felt my heartbeat pounding in my ears. Something good could still happen.

A Spanish American nurse's aide in a blue and white uniform unlocked the door and let me into the front room to wait for Dr Godwin. Nell and several other bathrobed patients were watching a television drama about a pair of lawyers, father and son. They paid no attention to me. I was only a real-life detective, unemployed at the moment. But not, I hoped, for long.

I sat in an empty chair to one side. The drama was well directed and well played but I couldn't keep my mind on it. I began to watch the four people who were watching it. Nell the somnambulist, her black hair hanging like tangled sorrows down her back, held cupped in her hands the blue ceramic ashtray she had made. A young man with an untrimmed beard and rebellious eyes looked like a conscientious objector to everything. A thin-haired man, who was trembling with excitement, went on trembling right through the commerical. An old woman had a translucent face through which her life burned like a guttering candle. Step back a little and you could almost imagine that they were three generations of one family, grandmother, parents, and son, at home on a Saturday night.

Dr Godwin appeared in the inner doorway and crooked his finger at me. I followed him down the hallway through a thickening hospital odor, into a small cramped office. He switched on a lamp over the desk and sat behind it. I took the only other chair.

"Is Alex Kincaid with his wife?"

"Yes. He called me at home and seemed very eager to see her, though he hasn't been around all day. He also wanted to talk to me."

"Did he say anything about running out on her?"

"No."

"I hope he's changed his mind." I told Godwin about my meeting with Kincaid senior, and Alex's departure with his father.

"You can't entirely blame him for falling by the wayside momentarily. He's young, and under great strain." Godwin's changeable eyes lit up. "The important thing, for him as well as Dolly, is that he decided to come back."

"How is she?"

"Calmer, I think. She didn't want to talk tonight, at least not to me."

"Will you let me have a try at her?"

"No."

"I almost regret bringing you into this case, Doctor."

"I've been told that before, and less politely," he said with a stubborn smile. "But once I'm in I'm in, and I'll continue to do as I think best."

"I'm sure you will. Did you see the evening paper?"

"I saw it."

"Does Dolly know what's going on outside? About the gun, for instance?"

"No."

"Don't you think she should be told?"

He spread out his hands on the scarred desk-top. "I'm trying to simplify her problems, not add to them. She had so many pressures on her last night, from both the past and the present, that she was on the verge of a psychotic breakthrough. We don't want that to happen."

"Will you be able to protect her from police questioning?"

"Not indefinitely. The best possible protection would be a solution to this case absolving her."

"I'm working on it. I talked to her Aunt Alice this morning, and looked over the scene of the McGee killing. I became pretty well convinced that even if McGee did kill his wife, which I doubt, Dolly couldn't have identified him as he left the house. In other words her testimony at his trial was cooked."

"Alice Jenks convinced you of this?"

"The physical layout did. Miss Jenks did her best to convince me of the opposite, that McGee was guilty. I wouldn't be surprised if she was the main motive power behind the case against him."

"He *was* guilty."

"So you've said. I wish you'd go into your reasons for believing that."

"I'm afraid I can't. It has to do with the confidences of a patient."

"Constance McGee?"

"Mrs McGee wasn't formally a patient. But you can't treat a child without treating the parents."

"And she confided in you?"

"Naturally, to some extent. For the most part we talked about her family problems." Godwin was feeling his way carefully. His face was bland. Under the lamp his bald head gleamed like a metal dome in moonlight.

"Her sister Alice made an interesting slip. She said there was no other man in Constance's life. I didn't ask her. Alice volunteered the information."

"Interesting."

"I thought so. Was Constance in love with another man at the time she was shot?"

Godwin nodded almost imperceptibly.

"Who was he?"

"I have no intention of telling you. He's suffered enough."

A shadow of the suffering passed across his own face. "I've told you this much because I want you to understand that McGee had a motive, and was certainly guilty."

"I think he was framed, just as Dolly is being framed."

"We agree on the latter point. Why can't we settle for that?"

"Because there have been three killings, and they're connected. They're connected subjectively, as you would say, in Dolly's mind, I believe they're objectively connected, too. They may all have been done by the same person."

Godwin didn't ask me who. It was just as well. I was talking over my head, and I had no suspect.

"What third killing are you referring to?"

"The death of Luke Deloney, a man I never heard of until tonight. I met Helen Haggerty's mother at the L.A. airport and had a talk with her on the way down here. According to her, Deloney shot himself by accident while cleaning a gun. But Helen claimed he was murdered and said she knew a witness. The witness may have been herself. At any rate she quarreled with her father on the issue – he seems to have been the detective in charge of the case – and ran away from home. All this was over twenty years ago."

"You seriously think it's connected with the present case?"

"Helen thought so. Her death makes her an authority on the subject."

"What do you propose to do about it?"

"I'd like to fly to Illinois tonight and talk to Helen's father. But I can't afford to do it on my own hook."

"You could phone him."

"I could. My sense of the situation is that it would do more harm than good. He may be a tough nut to crack."

Godwin said after a minute's thought: "I might consider backing you."

"You're a generous man."

"A curious one," he said. "Remember I've been living with this case for over ten years. I'd give a good deal to see it ended."

"Let me talk to Alex first, and ask him how he feels about laying out more money."

Godwin inclined his head and remained bowing as he stood up. He wasn't bowing to me. It was more of a general and habitual bow, as if he could feel the weight of the stars and was asking their permission to take part of the weight on human shoulders.

"I'll get him out of there. He's stayed long enough."

Godwin disappeared down the hallway. A few minutes later Alex came back alone. He walked like a man in a tunnel underground, but his face was more serene than I'd ever seen it.

He paused in the doorway. "Dr Godwin said you were here."

"I'm surprised to see you."

Hurt and embarrassment flickered across the upper part of his face. He brushed at it impatiently with his fingers. Then he stepped into the office, shutting the door behind him and leaning on it.

"I made a fool of myself today. I tried to chicken out."

"It takes guts to admit it."

"Don't gloss it over," he said sharply. "I was really lousy. It's funny, when Dad gets upset it has a peculiar effect on me. It's like sympathetic vibrations: he goes to pieces, I go to pieces. Not that I'm blaming *him*."

"I'm blaming him."

"Please don't. You have no right to." His eyebrows knitted. "The company's talking about bringing in computers to handle most of the work in the office. Dad's afraid he can't adjust, and I guess it makes him afraid of things in general."

"You've been doing some thinking."

"I had to. You started me off with what you said about annulling myself. I felt that way when I went home with Dad – as though I wasn't a man any more." He pushed himself clear of the door and balanced himself on his feet, his arms swinging slightly at his sides. "It's really amazing, you know? You really can make a decision inside yourself. You can decide to be one thing or the other."

The only trouble was that you had to make the decision every hour on the hour. But he would have to find that out for himself.

"How is your wife?" I said

"She actually seemed glad to see me. Have you talked to her?"

"Dr Godwin wouldn't let me."

"He wouldn't let me, either, till I promised not to ask her any questions. I didn't, but the subject of the revolver came up. She'd heard two of the aides talking about some newspaper story –"

"It's in the local paper. What did she have to say about the gun?"

"It isn't hers. Somebody must have hidden it under her mattress. She asked me to describe it, and she said it sounded like her Aunt Alice's revolver. Her aunt used to keep it on her bedside table at night. Dolly was sort of fascinated by it when she was a little girl." He breathed deeply. "Apparently she saw her aunt threaten her father with it. I didn't want her to go into all that stuff but I couldn't prevent her. She calmed down again after a while."

"At least she's stopped blaming herself for Helen Haggerty's death."

"She hasn't though. She still says it was her fault. Everything's her fault."

"In what way?"

"She didn't go into it. I didn't want her to."

"You mean Dr Godwin didn't want you to."

"That's right. He's calling the shots. I guess he knows more about her than I ever will."

"I take it you're going on with your marriage?" I said.

"We have to. I realized that today. People can't walk out on each other when they're in this kind of trouble. I think maybe Dolly realizes it, too. She didn't turn her back on me or anything."

"What else did you talk about?"

"Nothing important. The other patients, mostly. There's one old lady with a broken hip who doesn't want to stay in bed. Dolly's been sort of looking after her." It seemed important to him. "She can't be so very sick herself." It was an implied question.

"You'll have to take that up with the doctor."

"He isn't saying much. He wants to give her some psychological tests tomorrow. I told him to go ahead."

"Do I have your go-ahead, too?"

"Naturally. I was hoping you'd take that for granted. I want you to do everything you can to settle this thing. I'll give you a written contract –"

"That won't be necessary. But it's going to cost you money."

"How much money?"

"A couple of thousand, maybe a good deal more."

I told him about the Reno end of the case, which Arnie and Phyllis Walters were handling, and about the Bridgeton situation which I wanted to explore. I also advised him to talk to Jerry Marks first thing in the morning.

"Will Mr Marks be availabe on a Sunday?"

"Yes. I've already set him up for you. Of course you're going to have to give him a retainer."

"I have some savings bonds," he said thoughtfully, "and I can borrow on my insurance policy. Meantime I can sell the car. It's paid for, and I've been offered two five for it. I was getting pretty tired of sport car rallies and all that jazz. It's kid stuff."

XVIII

THE FRONT doorbell rang. Someone trotted past the office to answer it. It was getting late for visitors, and I went out and followed the aide along the hallway. The four patients were still watching the television screen as if it was a window on the outside world.

Whoever had rung the bell was knocking now, rather violently.

"Just a minute," the aide said through the door. She got her key into the lock and opened it partly. "Who is it? Who do you want to see?"

It was Alice Jenks. She tried to push her way in, but the aide had her white shoe against the door.

"I wish to see my niece, Dolly McGee."

"We have no such patient."

"She calls herself Dolly Kincaid now."

"I can't let you in to see anyone without Doctor's permission."

"Is Godwin here?"

"I think so."

"Get him," Miss Jenks said peremptorily.

The girl's Latin temper flared. "I don't take orders from you," she said in a hissing whisper. "And keep your voice down. We have people trying to rest."

"Get Dr Godwin."

"Don't worry, I intend to. But you'll have to wait outside."

"It will be a pleasure."

I stepped between them before the nurse closed the door and said to Miss Jenks: "May I speak to you for a minute?"

She peered at me through fogged glasses. "So you're here, too."

"I'm here, too."

I stepped out under the outside light and heard the door shut behind me. The air was chilly after the hot-house atmosphere of the nursing home.

Miss Jenks had on a thick fur-collared coat which made her figure massive in the gloom. Droplets of water glistened in the fur, and in her graying hair.

"What do you want with Dolly?"

"It's none of your business. She's my flesh and blood, not yours."

"Dolly has a husband. I represent him."

"You can go and represent him in some other constituency. I'm not interested in you *or* her husband."

"But suddenly you're interested in Dolly. Does it have anything to do with the story in the paper?"

"Maybe it has and maybe it hasn't." In her language, that meant yes. She added defensively: "I've been interested in Dolly since she was born. I know better than a lot of strangers what's good for her."

"Dr Godwin isn't a stranger."

"No. I wish he was."

"I hope you're not thinking of taking her out of here."

"Maybe I am and maybe I'm not." She dug some Kleenex out of her purse and used it to clean her glasses. I could see a newspaper folded small in the purse.

"Miss Jenks, did you read the description of the revolver that was found in Dolly's bed?"

She replaced her glasses quickly, as though to cover the startled look in her eyes. " Naturally I read it."

"Did it ring any bell with you?"

"Yes. It sounded like the revolver I used to have, so I came into town to the courthouse to have a look at it. It looks like mine all right."

"You admit that?"

"Why shouldn't I? I haven't seen it for over ten years."

"Can you prove it?"

"Of course I can prove it. It was stolen from my house before Constance was shot. Sheriff Crane theorized at the time that it might have been the gun McGee used on her. He still thinks so. McGee could easily have taken it. He knew where it was, in my bedroom."

"You didn't tell me all this this morning."

"I didn't think of it. It was only theory, anyway. You were interested in facts."

"I'm interested in both, Miss Jenks. What's the police theory now. That McGee killed Miss Haggerty and tried to frame his daughter?"

"I wouldn't put it past him. A man who would do what he did to his wife –" Her voice sank out of hearing in her throat.

"And they want to use his daughter to nail McGee again?"

She didn't answer me. Lights went on inside, and there were sounds of movement culminating in Godwin's opening the door. He shook his keys at us, grinning fiercely.

"Come inside, Miss Jenks."

She stamped up the concrete steps. Godwin had cleared the front room of everyone but Alex, who was sitting on a chair against the wall. I stood unobtrusively in the corner beside the silent television set.

She faced him, almost as tall in heels as he was, almost as wide in her coat, almost as stubborn in her pride. "I don't approve of what you're doing, Dr Godwin."

"What am I doing?" He sat on the arm of a chair and crossed his legs.

"You know what I'm referring to. My niece. Keeping her cooped up here in defiance of the constituted authorities."

"There's no defiance involved. I try to do my duty, the Sheriff tries to do his. Sometimes we come into conflict. It doesn't necessarily mean that Sheriff Crane is right and I'm wrong."

"It does to me."

"I'm not surprised. We've disagreed before, on a similar issue. You and your friend the Sheriff had your way on that occasion, unfortunately for your niece."

"It did her no harm to testify. Truth is truth."

"And trauma is trauma. It did her incalculable harm, which

she's still suffering under."

"I'd like to see that for myself."

"So you can make a full report to the Sheriff?"

"Good citizens cooperate with the law," she said sententiously. "But I'm not here on the Sheriff's behalf. I came here to help my niece."

"How do you propose to help her?"

"I'm going to take her home with me."

Godwin stood up shaking his head.

"You can't stop me. I've been her guardian since her mother died. The law will back me up."

"I think not," Godwin said coldly. "Dolly's of age, and she's here of her own free will."

"I'd like to ask her that question for myself."

"You're not going to ask her any questions."

The woman took a step toward him and thrust her head forward on her neck. "You think you're a little tin god, don't you, masterminding my family's affairs? I say you've got no right to keep her here under duress, making us all look bad. I've got a position to keep up in this county. I spent the day with some very high-level people from Sacramento."

"I'm afraid I don't follow your logic. But keep your voice down, please." Godwin himself was using the slow weary monotone that I had first heard on the telephone twenty-four hours before. "And let me assure you again, your niece is here of her own free will."

"That's right." Alex came forward into the verbal line of fire. "I don't believe we've met. I'm Alex Kincaid, Dolly's husband."

She disregarded his hand.

"I think it's important for her to stay here," he said. "I have confidence in the doctor, and so has my wife."

"I'm sorry for you then. He had me bamboozled, too, until I found out what went on in his office."

Alex looked inquiringly at Godwin. The doctor turned his hands out as if he was feeling for rain. He said to Miss Jenks:

"You graduated in sociology, I believe."

"What if I did?"

"From a woman of your training and background, I'd expect a more professional attitude toward the practice of psychiatry."

"I'm not talking about the practice of psychiatry. I'm talking about the practice of other things."

"What other things?"

"I wouldn't soil my tongue on them. But please don't think I didn't know my sister and what went on in her life. I've been remembering things – the way she used to primp and preen Saturday mornings before she came in to town. And then she wanted to move here, to be closer."

"Closer to me?"

"So she told me."

Godwin's face was white, as if all its color had been drawn into the darkness of his eyes. "You're a silly woman, Miss Jenks, and I've had enough of you. I'll ask you to leave now."

"I'm staying here till I see my niece. I want to know what you're practicing on her."

"It would do her no good. In your present mood you'd do no good to anyone." He moved around her to the door and held it open. "Good night."

She didn't move or look at him. She stood with her head down, a little dazed by the anger that had gone through her like a storm.

"Do you wish to be forcibly removed?"

"Try it. You'll end up in court."

But a kind of shame had begun to invade her face. Her mouth was twitching like a small injured thing. It had said more than she intended.

When I took her by the arm and said, "Come on, Miss Jenks," she let me lead her to the door. Godwin closed it on her.

"I have no patience with fools," he said.

"Have a little patience with me, though, will you Doctor?"

"I'll give it a try, Archer." He took a deep breath and let it out as a sigh. "You want to know if there's any truth in her innuendo."

"You make it easy for me."

"Why not? I love the truth. My entire life is a search for it."

"Okay, was Constance McGee in love with you?"

"I suppose she was, in a way. Women patients traditionally fall in love with their doctors, particularly in my field. It didn't persist in her case."

"This may strike you as a foolish question, but did you love her?"

"I'll give you a foolish answer, Mr Archer. Of course I loved her. I loved her the way a doctor loves his patients, if he's any good. It's a love that's more maternal than erotic." He spread his large hands on his chest, and spoke from there: "I wanted to serve her. I didn't succeed too well."

I was silenced.

"And now, gentlemen, if you'll excuse me, I have hospital rounds in the morning." He swung his keys.

Alex said to me in the street: "Do you believe him?"

"Unless or until I have proof that he's lying. He's not telling all he knows but people seldom do, let alone doctors. I'd take his word ahead of Alice Jenks's."

He started to climb into his car, then turned back toward me, gesturing in the direction of the nursing home. Its plain rectangular façade loomed in the fog like a blockhouse, the visible part of an underground fortress.

"You think she's safe there, Mr Archer?"

"Safer than she'd be on the streets, or in jail, or in a psycho ward with a police psychiatrist quizzing her."

"Or at her aunt's?"

"Or at her aunt's. Miss Jenks is one of these righteous women who doesn't let her left lobe know what her right lobe is doing. She's quite a tiger."

His eyes were still on the front of the nursing home.

Deep inside the building, the wild old voice I had heard that morning rose again. It faded like the cry of a seabird flying away, intermitted by wind.

"I wish I could stay with Dolly, and protect her," Alex said.

He was a good boy.

I broached the subject of money. He gave me most of the money in his wallet. I used it to buy an airline ticket to Chicago and return, and caught the late flight from International Airport.

XIX

I LEFT the toll road, which bypassed Bridgeton, and drove my rented car through the blocks of housing tracts on the outskirts of the city. I could see the clumps of sawed-off skyscrapers in the business district ahead, and off to the left, across the whole south side, the factories. It was Sunday morning, and only one of their stacks was pouring smoke into the deep-blue sky.

I stopped for gas at a service station and looked up Earl Hoffman's address in the telephone directory. When I asked the attendant how to get to Cherry Street, where Hoffman lived, he pointed in the general direction of the factories.

It was a middle-class street of substantial two-storey houses which had been touched but not destroyed by the blight that creeps outward from the centers of cities. Hoffman's house was of grimy white brick like the others, but the front porch had been painted within living memory. An old Chevrolet coupé stood at the curb in front of it.

The doorbell didn't work. I knocked on the screen door. An old young man with more nose than chin opened the inner door and looked at me through the screen in a sad way.

"Mr Haggerty?"

"Yes."

I told him my name and trade and where I was from. "I was with your wife – your ex-wife – shortly before she was killed."

"It's a dreadful thing."

He stood absently in the doorway, forgetting to ask me in. He had a frowzy sleepless look as if he'd been up most of the night. Though there was no gray on his head, white hairs glistened in his day-old beard. His small eyes had the kind of incandescence that goes with conscious suffering.

"May I come in, Mr Haggerty?"

"I don't know if it's such a good idea. Earl's pretty broken up."

"I thought he and his daughter had been on the outs for a long time."

"They were. It only makes it harder for him, I think. When

you're angry with someone you love, you always expect at the back of your mind there'll be a reconciliation some day. But now there will never be anything."

He was speaking for his father-in-law but also for himself. His empty hands moved aimlessly at his sides. The fingers of his right hand were stained dark yellow by nicotine.

"I'm sorry," I said, "that Mr Hoffman isn't feeling well. I'm afraid I'll have to talk to him anyway. I didn't come from California for the ride."

"No. Obviously not. What is it you have to discuss with him?"

"His daughter's murder. He may be able to help me understand it."

"I thought it was already solved."

"It isn't."

"Has the girl student been cleared?"

"She's in process of being cleared," I said with deliberate vagueness. "You and I can go into all that later. Right now I'm very eager to talk to Hoffman."

"If you insist. I only hope you can get some sense out of him."

I saw what he meant when he took me through the house to "Earl's den," as Haggerty called it. It was furnished with a closed roll-top desk, an armchair, a studio couch. Through a haze compounded of whisky fumes and smoke I could see a big old man sprawled in orange pajamas on the couch, his head propped up by bolsters. A strong reading light shone on his stunned face. His eyes seemed out of focus, but he was holding a magazine with an orange cover that almost matched his pajamas. The wall above him was decorated with rifles and shotguns and hand guns.

"When I recall the loss of all my perished years," he said huskily.

Old cops didn't talk like that, and Earl Hoffman looked like no exception to the rule. His body was massive, and could have belonged to a professional football player or a wrestler gone to pot. His nose had once been broken. He had a clipped gray head and a mouth like bent iron.

"That's beautiful poetry, Bert," the iron mouth said.

"I suppose it is."

"Who's your friend, Bert?"

"Mr Archer, from California."

"California, eh? That's where my poor little Helen got knocked off."

He sobbed, or hiccuped, once. Then he swung himself onto the edge of the couch, letting his bare feet fall heavily to the floor. "Do you know – did you know my little daughter Helen?"

"I knew her."

"Isn't that remarkable." He rose swaying and clasped my hands in both of his, using me to support him. "Helen was a remarkable girl. I've just been reading over one of her poems. Wrote it when she was just a teen-age girl at City College. Here, I'll show you."

He made a fairly elaborate search for the orange-covered magazine, which was lying in plain sight on the floor where he had dropped it. The name of it was the *Bridgeton Blazer*, and it looked like a school production.

Haggerty picked it up and handed it to him: "Please don't bother with it, Earl. Helen didn't write it anyway."

"Didn't write it? 'Course she wrote it. It's got her initials on it." Hoffman flipped through the pages. "See?"

"But she was only translating from Verlaine."

"Never heard of him." Hoffman turned to me, thrusting the magazine into my hands. "Here, read this. See what a remarkable gift poor little Helen had."

I read:

When the violins
Of the autumn winds
Begin to sigh
My heart is torn
With their forlorn
Monotony.

And when the hour
Sounds from the tower
I weep tears
For I recall
The loss of all
My perished years.

And then I go
With the winds that blow
And carry me
There and here
Like a withered and sere
Leaf from a tree. – H.H.

Hoffman looked at me with one of his unfocused eyes. "Isn't that beautiful poetry, Mr Arthur?"

"Beautiful."

"I only wisht I understood it. Do you understand it?"

"I think so."

"Then keep it. Keep it in memory of poor little Helen."

"I couldn't do that."

"Sure you can. Keep it." He snatched it out of my hands, rolled it up, and thrust it into my jacket pocket, breathing whisky in my face.

"Keep it," Haggerty whispered at my shoulder. "You don't want to cross him."

"You heard him. You don't want to cross me."

Hoffman grinned loosely at me. He clenched his left fist, examined it for defects, then used it to strike himself on the chest. He walked on spraddled legs to the roll-top desk and opened it. There were bottles and a single smeared tumbler inside. He half-filled the tumbler from a fifth of bourbon and drank most of it down. His son-in-law said something under his breath, but made no move to stop him.

The heavy jolt squeezed sweat out on Hoffman's face. It seemed to sober him a little. His eyes focused on me.

"Have a drink?"

"All right. I'll take water and ice in mine, please." I didn't normally drink in the morning but this was an abnormal occasion.

"Get some ice and a glass, Bert. Mr Arthur wants a drink. If you're too mucky-muck to drink with me, Mr Arthur isn't."

"The name is Archer."

"Get *two* glasses," he said with a foolish grin. "Mr Archer wants a drink, too. Sit down," he said to me. "Take the load off your feet. Tell me about poor little Helen."

We sat on the couch. I filled him in quickly on the circumstances of the murder, including the threat that preceded it, and Helen's feeling that Bridgeton was catching up with her.

"What did she mean by that?" The lines of the grin were still in his face like clown marks but the grin had become a rictus.

"I've come a long way to see if you can help me answer that question."

"Me? Why come to me? I never knew what went on in her mind, she never *let* me know. She was too bright for me." His mood swayed into heavy drunken self-pity. "I sweated and slaved to buy her an education like I never had, but she wouldn't give her poor old father the time of day."

"I understand you had a bad quarrel and she left home."

"She told you, eh?"

I nodded. I had decided to keep Mrs Hoffman out of it. He was the kind of man who wouldn't want his wife ahead of him in anything.

"She tell you the names she called me, crook and Nazi, when all I was doing was my bounden duty? You're a cop, you know how a man feels when your own family undermines you." He peered at me sideways. "You are a cop, aren't you?"

"I have been."

"What do you do for a living now?"

"Private investigation."

"Who for?"

"A man named Kincaid, nobody you know. I knew your daughter slightly, and I have a personal interest in finding out who killed her. I think the answer may be here in Bridgeton."

"I don't see how. She never set foot in this town for twenty years, until last spring. She only came home then to tell her mother she was getting a divorce. From *him*." He gestured toward the back of the house, where I could hear ice being chipped.

"Did she do any talking to you?"

"I only saw her the once. She said hello-how-are-you and that was about it. She told her mother that she'd had it with Bert and her mother couldn't talk her out of it. Bert even followed her out to Reno to try and convince her to come back, but it was no go. He isn't enough of a man to hold a woman."

Hoffman finished his drink and set his tumbler down on the floor. He remained slumped forward for about a minute, and

I was afraid he was going to get sick or pass out on me. But he came back up to a sitting position and muttered something about wanting to help me.

"Fine. Who was Luke Deloney?"

"Friend of mine. Big man in town back before the war. She told you about him, too, eh?"

"You could tell me more, Lieutenant. I hear you have a memory like an elephant."

"Did Helen say that?"

"Yes." The lie didn't cost me anything, not even a pang of conscience.

"At least she had some respect for her old man, eh?"

"A good deal."

He breathed with enormous relief. It would pass, as everything passes when a man is drinking seriously to kill awareness. But for the moment he was feeling good. He believed his daughter had conceded a point in their bitter life-long struggle.

"Luke was born in nineteen-oh-three on Spring Street," he said with great care, "in the twenty-one-hundred block, way out on the south side – two blocks over from where I lived when I was a kid. I knew him in grade school. He was the kind of a kid who saved up his paper-route money to buy a Valentine for everybody in his class. He actually did that. The principal used to take him around to the various rooms to show off his mental arithmetic. He did have a good head on his shoulders. I'll give him that. He skipped two grades. He was a comer.

"Old man Deloney was a cement finisher, and cement started to come in strong for construction after the World War. Luke bought himself a mixer with money he'd saved and went into business for himself. He did real well in the twenties. At his peak he had over five hundred men working for him all over the state. Even the depression didn't cramp his style. He was a wheeler and a dealer as well as a builder. The only things going up in those days were public works, so he went out in a big way for the federal and state contracts. He married Senator Osborne's daughter, and that didn't do him any harm, either."

"I hear Mrs Deloney's still alive."

"Sure she is. She lives in the house the Senator built in nineteen-oh-one on Glenview Avenue on the north side. Number one-oh-three, I think." He was straining to live up to his encyclopedic reputation.

I made a mental note of the address. Preceded by clinking, Bert Haggerty came into the room with ice and water and glasses on a tin tray. I cleared a space on the desk and he set the tray down. It had originally belonged to the Bridgeton Inn.

"You took long enough," Hoffman said offhandedly.

Haggerty stiffened. His eyes seemed to regroup themselves more closely at the sides of his nose.

"Don't talk to me like that, Earl. I'm not a servant."

"If you don't like it you know what you can do."

"I realize you're tight, but there's a limit –"

"Who's tight? I'm not tight."

"You've been drinking for twenty-four hours."

"So what? A man has a right to drown his sorrows. But my brain is as clear as a bell. Ask Mr Arthur here. Mr Archer."

Haggerty laughed, mirthlessly, falsetto. It was a very queer sound, and I tried to cover it over with a broad flourish:

"The Lieutenant's been filling me in one some ancient history. He has a memory like an elephant."

But Hoffman wasn't feeling good any more. He rose cumbrously and advanced on Haggerty and me. One of his eyes looked at each of us. I felt like a man in a cage with a sick bear and his keeper.

"What's funny, Bert? You think my sorrow is funny, is that it? She wouldn't be dead if you were man enough to keep her at home. Why didn't you bring her home from Reno with you?"

"You can't blame me for everything," Haggerty said a little wildly. "I got along with her better than you did. If she hadn't had a father-fixation –"

"Don't give me that, you lousy intellectual. Ineffectual. Ineffectual intellectual. You're not the only one that can use four-bit words. And stop calling me Earl. We're not related. We never would have been if I had any say in the matter. We're not even related and you come into my house spying on my personal habits. What are you, an old woman?"

Haggerty was speechless. He looked at me helplessly.

"I'll break your neck," his father-in-law said.

I stepped between them. "Let's have no violence, Lieutenant. It wouldn't look good on the blotter."

"The little pipsqueak accused me. He said I'm drunk. You

tell him he's mistaken. Make him apologize."

I turned to Haggerty, closing one eye. "Lieutenant Hoffman is sober, Bert. He can carry his liquor. Now you better get out of here before something happens."

He was glad to. I followed him out into the hall.

"This is the third or fourth time," he said in a low voice. "I didn't mean to set him off again."

"Let him cool for a bit. I'll sit with him. I'd like to talk to you afterward."

"I'll wait outside in my car."

I went back into the bear cage. Hoffman was sitting on the edge of the couch with his head supported by his hands.

"Everything's gone to hell in a hand-car," he said. "That pussy willow of a Bert Haggerty gets under my skin. I dunno what he thinks he's sucking around for." His mood changed. "You haven't deserted me, anyway. Go ahead, make yourself a drink."

I manufactured a light highball and brought it back to the couch. I didn't offer Hoffman any. In wine was truth, perhaps, but in whisky, the way Hoffman sluiced it down, was an army of imaginary rats climbing your legs.

"You were telling me about Luke Deloney and how he grew."

He squinted at me. "I don't know why you're so interested in Deloney. He's been dead for twenty-two years. Twenty-two years and three months. He shot himself, but I guess you know that, eh?" A hard intelligence glinted momentarily in his eyes and drew them into focus on my face.

I spoke to the hard intelligence: "Was there anything between Helen and Deloney?"

"No, she wasn't interested in *him*. She had a crush on the elevator boy, George. I ought to know, she made me get him the job. I was sort of managing the Deloney Apartments at the time. Luke Deloney and me, we were like that."

He tried to cross his second finger over his forefinger. It kept slipping. He finally completed the maneuver with the help of his other hand. His fingers were thick and mottled like uncooked breakfast sausages.

"Luke Deloney was a bit of a womanizer," he said indulgently, "but he didn't mess around with the daughters of his friends. He never cared for the young stuff, anyway. His wife must of been ten years older than he was. Anyway, he wouldn't touch my daughter. He knew I'd kill him."

"Did you?"

"That's a lousy question, mister. If I didn't happen to like you I'd knock your block off."

"No offense."

"I had nothing against Luke Deloney. He treated me fair and square. Anyway, I told you he shot himself."

"Suicide?"

"Naw. Why would he commit suicide? He had everything, money and women and a hunting lodge in Wisconsin. He took me up there personally more than once. The shooting was an accident. That's the way it went into the books and that's the way it stays."

"How did it happen, Lieutenant?"

"He was cleaning his .32 automatic. He had a permit to tote it on his person – I helped him get it myself – because he used to carry large sums of money. He took the clip out all right but he must of forgot the shell that was in the chamber. It went off and shot him in the face."

Where?"

"Through the right eye."

"I mean where did the accident occur?"

"In one of the bedrooms in his apartment. He kept the roof apartment in the Deloney building for his private use. More than once I drank with him up there. Prewar Green River, boy." He slapped my knee, and noticed the full glass in my hand. "Drink up your drink."

I knocked back about half of it. It wasn't prewar Green River. "Was Deloney drinking at the time of the shooting?"

"Yeah. I think so. He knew guns. He wouldn't of made that mistake if he was sober."

"Was anybody with him in the apartment?"

"No."

"Can you be sure?"

"I can be sure. I was in charge of the investigation,"

"Did anybody share the apartment with him?"

"Not on a permanent basis, you might say. Luke Deloney had various women on the string. I checked them out, but none of them was within a mile of the place at the time it happened."

"What kind of women?"

"All the way from floozies to one respectable married woman here in town. Their names didn't go into the record then and they're not going to now."

There was a growl in his voice. I didn't pursue the subject. Not that I was afraid of Hoffman exactly. I had a least fifteen years on him, and a low alcohol content. But if he went for me I might have to hurt him badly.

"What about Mrs Deloney?" I said.

"What about her?"

"Where was she when all this was going on?"

"At home, out on Glenview. They were sort of separated. She didn't believe in divorce."

"People who don't believe in divorce sometimes believe in murder."

Hoffman moved his shoulders belligerently. "You trying to say that I hushed up a murder?"

"I'm not accusing you of anything, Lieutenant."

"You better not. I'm a cop, remember, first last and always." He raised his fist and rotated it before his eyes like a hypnotic device. "I been a good cop all my life. In my prime I was the best damn cop this burg ever saw. I'll have a drink on that." He picked up his tumbler. "Join me?"

I said I would. We were moving obscurely on a collision course. Alcohol might soften the collision, or sink him. I finished my drink and handed him my glass. He filled it to the brim with neat whisky. Then he filled his own. He sat down and stared into the brown liquid as if it was a well where his life had drowned.

"Bottoms up," he said.

"Take it easy, Lieutenant. You don't want to kill youself." It occurred to me as I said it that maybe he did.

"What are you, another pussy willow? Bottoms up."

He drained his glass and shuddered. I held mine in my hand. After a while he noticed this.

"You didn't drink your drink. What are you trying to do, pull a fast one on me? Insult my hosh – my hoshpit –?" His lips were too numb to frame the word.

"No insult intended. I didn't come here for a drinking party, Lieutenant. I'm seriously interested in who killed your daughter. Assuming Deloney was murdered –"

"He wasn't."

"Assuming he was, the same person may have killed Helen. In view of everything I've heard, from her and other people, I think it's likely. Don't you?

I was trying to get his mind under my control; the sloppy drunken sentimental part, and the drunken violent part, and the hard intelligent part hidden at the core.

"Deloney was an accident," he said clearly and stubbornly.

"Helen didn't think so. She claimed it was murder, and that she knew a witness to the murder."

"She was lying, trying to make me look bad. All she ever wanted to do was make her old man look bad."

His voice had risen. We sat and listened to its echoes. He dropped his empty glass, which bounced on the rug, and clenched the fist which seemed to be his main instrument of expression. I got ready to block it, but he didn't throw it at me.

Heavily and repeatedly, he struck himself in the face, on the eyes and cheeks, on the mouth, under the jaw. The blows left dull red welts in his clay-colored flesh. His lower lip split.

Hoffman said through the blood: "I clobbered my poor little daughter. I chased her out of the house. She never came back."

Large tears the color of pure distilled alcohol or grief rolled from his puffing eyes and down his damaged face. He fell sideways on the couch. He wasn't dead. His heart was beating strongly. I straightened him out – his legs were as heavy as sandbags – and put a bolster under his head. With blind eyes staring straight up into the light, he began to snore.

I closed the roll-top desk. The key was in it, and I turned it on the liquor and switched off the light and took the key outside with me.

XX

BERT HAGGERTY was sitting in the Chevrolet coupé, wearing a stalled expression. I got in beside him and handed him the key.

"What's this?"

"The key to the liquor. You better keep it. Hoffman's had as much as he can take."

"Did he throw you out?"

"No. He passed out, while hitting himself in the face. Hard."

Haggerty thrust his long sensitive nose toward me. "Why would Earl do a thing like that?"

"He seemed to be punishing himself for hitting his daughter a long time ago."

"Helen told me about that. Earl treated her brutally before she left home. It's one thing I can't forgive him for."

"He can't forgive himself. Did Helen tell you what they quarreled about?"

"Vaguely. It was something to do with a murder here in Bridgeton. Helen believed, or pretended to believe, that her father deliberately let the murderer go free."

"Why do you say she pretended to believe it?"

"My dear dead wife," he said, wincing at the phrase, "had quite a flair for the dramatic, especially in her younger days."

"Did you know her before she left Bridgeton?"

"For a few months. I met her in Chicago at a party in Hyde Park. After she left home I helped her to get a job as a cub reporter. I was working for the City News Bureau then. But as I was saying, Helen always had this dramatic flair and when nothing happened in her life for it to feed on she'd *make* something happen or pretend that it had happened. Her favorite character was Mata Hari," he said with a chuckle that was half a sob.

"So you think she invented this murder?"

"I suppose I thought so at the time, because I certainly didn't take it seriously. I have no opinion now. Does it matter?"

"It could matter very much. Did Helen ever talk to you about Luke Deloney?"

"Who?"

"Luke Deloney, the man who was killed. He owned the apartment building they lived in, and occupied the penthouse himself."

Haggerty lit a cigarette before he answered. His first few words came out as visible puffs of smoke: "I don't recall the name. If she talked about him, it couldn't have made much of an impression on me."

"Her mother seems to think Helen had a crush on Deloney."

"Mrs Hoffman's a pretty good woman, and I love her like a mother, but she gets some wild ideas."

"How do you know that this one is so wild. Was Helen in love with *you* then?"

He took a deep drag on his cigarette, like an unweaned child sucking on a dry bottle. It burned down to his yellow fingers. He tossed it into the street with a sudden angry gesture.

"She never was in love with me. I was useful to her, for a while. Later, in some sense, I was the last chance. The faithful follower. The last chance for gas before the desert."

"The desert?"

"The desert of love. The desert of *un*love. But I don't think I'll go into the long and dreary chronicle of my marriage. It wasn't a lucky one, for either of us. I loved her, as far as I'm able to love, but she didn't love me. Proust says it's always that way. I'm teaching Proust to my sophomore class this fall, if I can summon up the *élan* to go on teaching."

"Who did Helen love?"

"It depends on which year you're talking about. Which month of which year." He didn't move, but he was hurting himself, hitting himself in the face with bitter words.

"Right at the beginning, before she left Bridgeton."

"I don't know if you'd call it love, but she was deeply involved with a fellow-student at the City College. It was a Platonic affair, the kind bright young people have, or used to have. It consisted largely of reading aloud to each other from their own works and others'. According to Helen, she never went to bed with him. I'm pretty sure she was a virgin when I met her."

"What was his name?"

"I'm afraid I don't remember. It's a clear case of Freudian repression."

"Can you describe him?"

"I never met him. He's a purely legendary figure in my life. But obviously he isn't the elusive murderer you're searching for. Helen would have been happy to see *him* go free." He had withdrawn from the pain of memory and was using an almost flippant tone, as if he was talking about people in a play, or watching ceiling movies at the dentist's. "Speaking of murder, as we seem to be doing, you were going to tell me about my ex-wife's death. She's completely ex now, isn't she, exed out?"

I cut in on his sad nonsense and gave him the story in some detail, including the man from Reno who ran away in the fog, and my attempts to get him identified. "Earl tells me you went to Reno last summer to see your wife. Did you run into any of her acquaintances there?"

"Did I not. Helen played a trick on me involving a couple of them. Her purpose was to stall off any chance for an intimate talk with me. Anyway, the one evening we spent together she insisted on making it a foursome with this woman named Sally something and her alleged brother."

"Sally Burke?"

"I believe that *was* her name. The hell of it was, Helen arranged it so that I was the Burke woman's escort. She wasn't a bad-looking woman, but we had nothing in common, and in any case it was Helen I wanted to talk to. But she spent the entire evening dancing with the brother. I'm always suspicious of men who dance too well."

"Tell me more about this brother, he may be our man."

"Well, he struck me as a rather sleazy customer. That may be projected envy. He was younger than I am, and healthier, and better looking. Also, Helen seemed to be fascinated by his line of chatter, which I thought was pointless – all about cars and horses and gambling odds. How a highly educated woman like Helen could be interested in such a man –" He tired of the sentence, and dropped it.

"Were they lovers?"

"How would I know? She wasn't confiding in me."

"But you know your own wife, surely."

He lit another cigarette and smoked half of it. "I'd say they weren't lovers. They were simply playmates. Of course she was using him to hit at me."

"For what?"

"For being her husband. For having been her husband. Helen and I parted on bad terms. I tried to put the marriage together again in Reno, but she wasn't even remotely interested."

"What broke up your marriage?"

"It had a major fracture in it from the beginning." He looked past me at the house where Earl Hoffman was lying senseless under the past. "And it got worse. It was both our faults. I couldn't stop nagging her and she couldn't stop – doing what she was doing."

I waited and listened The church-bells were ringing, in different parts of the city.

"She was a tramp," Haggerty said "A campus tramp. I started her on it when she was a nineteen-year-old babe in the woods in Hyde Park. Then she went on without me. Toward the end she was even taking money."

"Who from?"

"Men with money, naturally. My wife was a corrupt woman, Mr Archer. I played a part in making her what she was, so I have no right to judge her." His eyes were brilliant with the pain that came and went like truth in him.

I felt sorry for the man. It didn't prevent me from saying: "Where were you Friday night?"

"At home in Maple Park in our – in my apartment, grading themes."

"Can you prove it?"

"I have the marked papers to prove it. They were turned in to me Friday, and I marked them Friday night. I hope you're not imagining I did something fantastic like flying to California and back?"

"When a woman is murdered, you ask her estranged husband where he was at the time. It's the corollary of *cherchez la femme*."

"Well, you have my answer. Check it out if you like. But you'll save yourself time and trouble simply by believing me. I've been completely frank with you – inordinately frank."

"I appreciate that."

"But then you turn around and accuse me –"

"A question isn't an accusation, Mr Haggerty."

"It carried that implication," he said in an aggrieved and slightly nagging tone. "I thought the man in Reno was your suspect."

"He's one of them."

"And I'm another?"

"Let's drop it, shall we?"

"You brought it up."

"Now I'm dropping it. Getting back to the man in Reno, can you remember his name?"

"I was introduced to him, of course, but I don't recall his surname. The women called him Jud. I'm not sure whether it was a given name or a nickname."

"Why did you refer to him as Mrs Burke's alleged brother?"

"They didn't strike me as brother and sister. They acted toward each other more like – oh – intimate friends who were simply going along with Helen's gag. I intercepted a couple of knowing glances, for example."

"Will you describe the man in detail for me?"

"I'll try. My visual memory isn't too good. I'm strictly the verbal type."

But under repeated questions, he built up an image of the man: age about thirty-two or -three, height just under six feet, weight about 175; muscular and active, good-looking in an undistinguished way; thinning black hair, brown eyes, no scars. He had worn a light gray silk or imitation silk suit and pointed low black shoes in the Italian style. Haggerty had gathered that the man Jud worked in some undetermined capacity for one of the gambling clubs in the Reno-Tahoe area.

It was time I went to Reno. I looked at my watch: nearly eleven: and remembered that I would gain time on the flight west. I could still have a talk with Luke Deloney's widow, if she was available, and get to Reno at a reasonable hour.

I went into the house with Haggerty, called O'Hare Airport, and made a reservation on a late afternoon flight. Then I called Mrs Deloney. She was at home, and would see me.

Bert Haggerty offered to drive me out to her house. I told him he'd better stay with his father-in-law. Hoffman's snores were sounding through the house like muffled lamentations, but he could wake up at any time and go on the rampage.

XXI

GLENVIEW AVENUE wound through the north side of the north side, in a region of estates so large that it almost qualified as country. Trees lined the road and sometimes met above it. The light that filtered through their turning leaves onto the great lawns was the color of sublimated money.

I turned in between the brick gate-posts of 103 and shortly came in sight of an imposing old red-brick mansion. The driveway led to a brick-columned *porte-cochère* on the right. I was hardly out of my car when a Negro maid in uniform opened the door.

"Mr Archer?"

"Yes."

"Mrs Deloney is expecting you, in the downstairs sitting-room."

She was sitting by a window looking out on a countryside where red sumac blazed among less brilliant colors. Her hair was white, and bobbed short. Her blue silk suit looked like Lily Daché. Her face was a mass of wrinkles but its fine bones remained in all their delicacy. She was handsome in the way an antique object can be handsome without regard to the condition of the materials. Her mind must have been very deep in the past, because she didn't notice us until the maid spoke.

"Mr Archer is here, Mrs Deloney."

She rose with the ease of a younger woman, putting down a book she was holding. She gave me her hand and a long look. Her eyes were the same color as her blue silk suit, unfaded and intelligent.

"So you've come all the way from California to see me. You must be disappointed."

"On the contrary."

"You don't need to flatter me. When I was twenty I looked like everybody else. Now I'm past seventy, I look like myself. It's a liberating fact. But do sit down. This chair is the most comfortable. My father Senator Osborne preferred it to any other."

She indicated a red leather armchair polished and dark with use. The chair she sat in opposite me was a ladder-backed rocker with worn cushions attached to it. The rest of the furnishings in the room were equally old and unpretentious, and I wondered if she used it as a place to keep the past.

"You've had a journey," she reminded herself. "Can I give you something to eat or drink?"

"No, thanks."

She dismissed the maid. "I'm afraid you're going to be doubly disappointed. I can add very little to the official account of my husband's suicide. Luke and I hadn't been in close touch for some time before it occurred."

"You already have added something," I said. "According to the official account it was an accident."

"So it was. I'd almost forgotten. It was thought best to omit the fact of suicide from the public reports."

"Who thought it best."

"I did, among others. Given my late husband's position in the state, his suicide was bound to have business and political repercussions. Not to mention the personal ugliness."

"Some people might think it was uglier to alter the facts of a man's death."

"Some people might think it," she said with a *grande dame* expression. "Not many of them would say it in my presence. In any case the fact was not altered, only the report of it. I've had to live with the fact of my husband's suicide."

"Are you perfectly certain that it is a fact?"

"Perfectly."

"I've just been talking to the man who handled the case, Lieutenant Hoffman. He says your husband shot himself by accident while he was cleaning an automatic pistol."

"That was the story we agreed upon. Lieutenant Hoffman naturally sticks to it. I see no point in your trying to change it at this late date."

"Unless Mr Deloney was murdered. Then there would be some point."

"No doubt, but he was *not* murdered." Her eyes came up to mine, and they hadn't changed, except that they may have become a little harder.

"I've heard rumors that he was, as far away as California."

"Who's been spreading such nonsense?"

"Lieutenant Hoffman's daughter Helen. She claimed she knew a witness to the killing. The witness may have been herself."

The insecurity that had touched her face changed into cold anger. "She has no right to tell such lies. I'll have her stopped!"

"She's been stopped," I said. "Somebody stopped her Friday night, with a gun. Which is why I'm here."

"I see. Where in California was she killed?"

"Pacific Point. It's on the coast south of Los Angeles."

Her eyes flinched, ever so slightly. "I'm afraid I never heard of it. I'm naturally sorry that the girl is dead, though I never knew her. But I can assure you that her death had nothing to do with Luke. You're barking up the wrong tree, Mr Archer."

"I wonder."

"There's no need to. My husband wrote me a note before he shot himself which made the whole thing very clear. Detective Hoffman brought it to me himself. No one knew it existed except him and his superiors. I hadn't intended to tell you."

"Why?"

"Because it was ugly. In effect he blamed me and my family for what he intended to do. He was in financial hot water, he'd been gambling in stocks and other things, his business was overextended. We refused to help him, for reasons both personal and practical. His suicide was an attempt to strike back at us. It succeeded, even though we altered the facts, as you put it." She touched her flat chest. "I was hurt, as I was meant to be."

"Was Senator Osborne alive at the time?"

"I'm afraid you don't know your history," she chided me. "My father died on December 14, 1936, three and a half years before my husband killed himself. At least my father was spared that humiliation."

"You referred to family."

"I meant my sister Tish and my late Uncle Scott, the guardian of our trust. He and I were responsible for refusing further assistance to Luke. The decision was essentially mine. Our marriage had ended."

"Why?"

"The usual reason, I believe. I don't care to discuss it." She rose and went to the window and stood there straight as a soldier looking out. "A number of things ended for me in 1940. My marriage, and then my husband's life, and then my sister's. Tish died in the summer of that same year, and I cried for her all that fall. And now it's fall again," she said with a sigh. "We used to ride together in the fall. I taught her to ride when she was five years old and I was ten. That was before the turn of the century."

Her mind was wandering off into remoter and less painful times. I said:

"Forgive me for laboring the point, Mrs Deloney, but I have to ask you if that suicide note still exists."

She turned, trying to smooth the marks of grief from her face.

They persisted. "Of course not. I burned it. You can take my word as to its contents."

"It isn't your word that concerns me so much. Are you absolutely certain your husband wrote it?"

"Yes. I can't be mistaken about his handwriting."

"A clever forgery can fool almost anybody."

"That's absurd. You're talking the language of melodrama."

"We live it every day, Mrs Deloney."

"But who would forge a suicide note?"

"It's been done, by other murderers."

She flung back her white head and looked at me down her delicate curved nose. She resembled a bird, even in the sound of her voice:

"My husband was not murdered."

"It seems to me you're resting a great deal of weight on a single handwritten note which might have been forged."

"It was not forged. I know that by internal evidence. It referred to matters that only Luke and I were privy to."

"Such as?"

"I have no intention of telling you, or anyone. Besides, Luke had been talking for months about killing himself, especially when he was in his cups."

"You said you hadn't been close to him for months."

"No, but I got reports, from mutual friends."

"Was Hoffman one of them?"

"Hardly. I didn't consider him a friend."

"Yet he hushed up your husband's suicide for you. Your husband's alleged suicide."

"He was ordered to. He had no choice."

"Who gave the order?"

"Presumably the Commissioner of Police. He *was* a friend of mine, and a friend of Luke's."

"And that made it all right for him to order the falsification of records?"

"It's done every day," she said, "in every city in the land. Spare me your moralizing, Mr Archer. Commissioner Robertson is long since dead. The case itself is a dead issue."

"Maybe it is to you. It's very much on Hoffman's mind. His daughter's murder revived it."

"I'm sorry for both of them. But I can't very well alter the past to accommodate some theory you may have. What are you trying to prove, Mr Archer?"

"Nothing specific. I'm trying to find out what the dead woman meant when she said that Bridgeton had caught up with her."

"No doubt she meant something quite private and personal. Women usually do. But as I said, I never knew Helen Hoffman."

"Was she involved with your husband?"

"No. She was not. And please don't ask me how I can be sure. We've scratched enough at Luke's grave, don't you think? There's nothing hidden there but a poor suicide. I helped to put him there, in a way."

"By cutting off his funds?"

"Precisely. You didn't think I was confessing to shooting him?"

"No," I said. "Would you like to?"

Her face crinkled up in a rather savage smile. "Very well. I shot him. What do you propose to do about it?"

"Nothing. I don't believe you."

"Why would I say it if it wasn't true?" She was playing the kind of fantastic girlish game old women sometimes revert to.

"Maybe you wanted to shoot you husband. I have no doubt you did want to. But if you actually had, you wouldn't be talking about it."

"Why not? There's nothing you could possibly do. I have too many good friends in this city, official and otherwise. Who incidentally would be greatly disturbed if you persisted in stirring up that old mess."

"Am I to take that as a threat?"

"No, Mr Archer," she said with her tight smile, "I have nothing against you except that you're a zealot in your trade, or do you call it a profession? Does it really matter so much how people died? They're dead, as we all shall be, sooner or later. Some of us sooner. And I feel I've given you enough of my remaining time on earth."

She rang for the maid.

XXII

I STILL had time for another try at Earl Hoffman. I drove back toward his house, through downtown streets depopulated by the Sabbath. The questions Mrs Deloney had raised, or failed to answer, stuck in my mind like fishhooks which trailed their broken lines into the past.

I was almost certain Deloney hadn't killed himself, by accident or intent. I was almost certain somebody else had, and that Mrs Deloney knew it. As for the suicide note, it could have been forged, it could have been invented, it could have been misread or misremembered. Hoffman would probaby know which.

As I turned into Cherry Street, I saw a man in the next block walking away from me. He had on a blue suit and he moved with the heavy forcefulness of an old cop, except that every now and then he staggered and caught himself. I saw when I got closer that it was Hoffman. The orange cuffs of his pajama legs hung below his blue trousers.

I let him stay ahead of me, through slums that became more blighted as we went south. We entered a Negro district. The adult men and women on the sidewalk gave Hoffman a wide berth. He was walking trouble.

He wasn't walking too well. He stumbled and fell on his hands and knees by a gap-toothed picket fence. Some children came out from behind the fence and followed him, prancing and hooting, until he turned on them with upraised arms. He turned again and went on.

We left the Negro district and came to a district of very old three-storeyed frame houses converted into rooming houses and business buildings. A few newer apartment buildings stood among them, and Hoffman's destination was one of these.

It was a six-storey concrete structure with a slightly run-down aspect: cracked and yellowing blinds in the rows of windows, brown watermarks below them. Hoffman went in the front entrance. I could see the inscription in the concrete arch above it: Deloney Apartments, 1928. I parked my car and followed

Hoffman into the building.

He had evidently taken the elevator up. The tarnished brass arrow above the elevator door slowly turned clockwise to seven and stuck there. I gave up pushing the button after a while – Hoffman had probably left the door ajar – and found the fire stairs. I was breathing hard by the time I reached the metal door that let out onto the roof.

I opened the door a crack. Except for some pigeons coo-hooing on a neighboring rooftop, everything outside seemed very quiet. A few potted shrubs and a green plexiglas windscreen jutting out at right angles from the wall of the penthouse had converted a corner of the roof into a terrace.

A man and a woman were sunning themselves there. She was lying face down on an air mattress with the brassière of her Bikini unfastened. She was blonde and nicely made. He sat in a deck chair, with a half-empty cola bottle on the table beside him. He was broad and dark, with coarse black hair matting his chest and shoulders. He wore a diamond ring on the little finger of his left hand, and had a faint Greek accent.

"So you think the restaurant business is low class? When you say that you're biting the hand that feeds you. The restaurant business put mink on your back."

"I didn't say it. What I said, the insurance business is a nice clean business for a man."

"And restaurants are dirty? Not my restaurants. I even got violet rays in the toilets –"

"Don't talk filthy," she said.

"Toilet is not a filthy word."

"It is in my family."

"I'm sick of hearing about your family. I'm sick of hearing about your good-for-nothing brother Theo."

"Good-for-nothing?" She sat up, exposing a pearly flash of breast before she fastened its moorings. "Theo made the Million Dollar Magic Circle last year."

"Who bought the policy that put him over the top? I did. Who set him up in the insurance agency in the first place? I did."

"Mr God." Her face was a beautiful blank mask. It didn't change when she said: "Who's that moving around in the house? I sent Rosie home after breakfast."

"She came back maybe."

"It doesn't sound like Rosie. It sounds like a man."

"Could be Theo coming to sell me this year's Magic Circle policy."

"That isn't funny."

"I think it's very funny."

He laughed to prove it. He stopped laughing when Earl Hoffman came out from behind the plexiglas windscreen. Every mark on his face was distinct in the sunlight. His orange pajamas were down over his shoes.

The dark man got out of his deck chair and pushed air toward Hoffman with his hands. "Beat it. This is a private roof."

"I can't do that," Hoffman said reasonably. "We got a report of a dead body. Where is it?"

"Down in the basement. You'll find it there." The man winked at the woman.

"The basement? They said the penthouse." Hoffman's damaged mouth opened and shut mechanically, like a dummy's, as if the past was ventriloquizing through him. "You moved it, eh? It's against the law to move it."

"*You* move yourself out of here." The man turned to the woman, who had covered herself with a yellow terrycloth robe: "Go in and phone the you-know-who."

"I am the you-know-who," Hoffman said. "And the woman stays. I have some questions to ask her. What's your name?"

"None of your business," she said.

"Everything's my business." Hoffman flung one arm out and almost lost his balance. "I'm detective inves'gating murder."

"Let's see your badge, detective."

The man held out his hand, but he didn't move toward Hoffman. Neither of them had moved. The woman was on her knees, with her beautiful scared face slanting up at Hoffman.

He fumbled in his clothes, produced a fifty-cent piece, looked at it in a frustrated way, and flung it spinning over the parapet. Faintly, I heard it ring on the pavement six stories down.

"Must of left it home," he said mildly.

The woman gathered herself together and made a dash for the penthouse. Moving clumsily and swiftly, Hoffman caught her around the waist. She didn't struggle, but stood stiff and white-faced in the circle of his arm.

"Not so fast now, baby. Got some questions to ask you. You

the broad that's been sleeping with Deloney?"

She said to the man: "Are you going to let him talk to me this way? Tell him to take his hands off me."

"Take your hands off my wife," the man said without force.

"Then tell her to sit down and cooperate."

"Sit down and cooperate," the man said

"Are you crazy? He smells like a still. He's crazy drunk."

"I know that."

"Then *do* something."

"I am doing something. You got to humor them."

Hoffman smiled at him like a public servant who was used to weathering unjust criticism. His hurt mouth and mind made the smile grotesque. The woman tried to pull away from him. He only held her closer, his belly nudging her flank.

"You look a little bit like my dau'er Helen. You know my dau'er Helen?"

The woman shook her head frantically. Her hair fluffed out.

"She says there was a witness to the killing. Were you there when it happened, baby?"

"I don't even know what you're talking about."

"Sure you do. Luke Deloney. Somebody drilled him in the eye and tried to make it look like suicide."

"I remember Deloney," the man said. "I waited on him in my father's hamburg joint once or twice. He died before the war."

"Before the war?"

"That's what I said. Where you been the last twenty years, detective?"

Hoffman didn't know. He looked around at the rooftops of his city as if it was a strange place. The woman cried out:

"Let me go, fatso."

He seemed to hear her from a long way off. "You speak with some respect to your old man."

"If you were my old man I'd kill myself."

"Don't give me no more of your lip. I've had as much of your lip as I'm going to take. You hear me?"

"Yes, I hear you. You're a crazy old man and take your filthy paws off me."

Her hooked fingers raked at his face, leaving three bright parallel tracks. He slapped her. She sat down on the gravel roof. The man picked up the half-empty cola bottle. Its brown contents gushed down his arm as he raised it, advancing on Hoffman.

Hoffman reached under the back of his coat and took a revolver out of his belt. He fired it over the man's head. The pigeons flew up from the neighboring rooftop, whirling in great spirals. The man dropped the bottle and stood still with his hands raised. The woman, who had been whimpering, fell silent.

Hoffman glared at the glaring sky. The pigeons diminished into it. He looked at the revolver in his hand. With my eyes focused on the same object, I stepped out into the sunlight.

"You need any help with these witnesses, Earl?"

"Naw, I can handle 'em. Everythin's under control." He squinted at me. "What was the name again? Arthur?"

"Archer." I walked toward him, pushing my squat shadow ahead of me across the uneven surface of the gravel. "You'll get some nice publicity out of this, Earl. Solving the Deloney killing singlehanded."

"Yeah. Sure." His eyes were deeply puzzled. He knew I was talking nonsense, as he knew he had been acting nonsense out, but he couldn't admit it, even to himself. "They hid the body in the basement."

"That means we'll probably have to dig."

"Is everybody crazy?" the man said between his upraised arms.

"Keep quiet, you," I said. "You better call for reinforcements, Earl. I'll hold the gun on these characters."

He hesitated for a stretching moment. Then he handed me the revolver and went into the penthouse, bumping the door-frame heavily with his shoulder.

"Who are you?" the man said.

"I'm his keeper. Relax."

"Did he escape from the insane asylum?"

"Not yet."

The man's eyes were like raisins thumbed deep into dough. He helped his wife to her feet, awkwardly brushing off the seat of her robe. Suddenly she was crying in his arms and he was patting her back with his diamonded hand and saying something emotional in Greek.

Through the open door I could hear Hoffman talking on the phone: "Six men with shovels an' a drill for concrete. Her body's under the basement floor. Want 'em here in ten minutes or somebody gets reamed!"

The receiver crashed down, but he went on talking. His voice rose and fell like a wind, taking up scattered fragments of the past and blowing them together in a whirl. "He never touched her. Wouldn't do that to the daughter of a friend. She was a good girl, too, a clean little daddy's girl. 'Member when she was a little baby, I used to give her her bath. She was soft as a rabbit. I held her in my arms, she called me Da." His voice broke. "What happened?"

He was silent. Then he screamed. I heard him fall to the floor with a thud that shook the penthouse. I went inside. He was sitting with his back against the kitchen stove, trying to remove his trousers. He waved me back.

"Keep away from me. There's spiders on me."

"I don't see any spiders."

"They're under my clothes. Black widows. The killer's trying to poison me with spiders."

"Who is the killer, Earl?"

His face worked. "Never found out who put the chill on Deloney. Word came down from the top, close off the case. What can a man –?" Another scream issued from his throat. "My God, there's hundreds of 'em crawling on me."

He tore at his clothes. They were in blue and orange rags when the police arrived, and his old wrestler's body was naked and writhing on the linoleum.

The two patrolmen knew Earl Hoffman. I didn't even have to explain.

XXIII

THE RED sun sank abruptly when the plane came down into the shadow of the mountains. I had wired my ETA to the Walters agency, and Phyllis was waiting for me at the airport.

She took my hand and offered me her cheek. She had a peaches-and-cream complexion, a little the worse for sun, and opaque smiling eyes the color of Indian enamel.

"You look tired, Lew. But you do exist."

"Don't tell me. It makes me feel tireder. You look wonderful."

"It gets more difficult as I get older. But then some other things get easier." She didn't say what things. We walked toward her car in the sudden evening. "What were you doing in Illinois, anyway? I thought you were working on a case in Pacific Point."

"It's in both places. I found an old pre-war murder in Illinois which seems to be closely tied in with the current ones. Don't ask me how. It would take all night to explain, and we have more important things to do."

"You do, anyway. You have a dinner date at eight-thirty with Mrs Sally Burke. You're an old friend of mine from Los Angeles, business unspecified. You take it from there."

"How did you fix it?"

"It wasn't hard. Sally dotes on free dinners and unattached men. She wants to get married again."

"But how did you get to know her?"

"I sort of happened into her at the bar where she hangs out and we got drunk together last night. One of us got drunk, anyway. She did some talking about her brother Judson, who may be the man you want."

"He is. Where does he live?"

"Somewhere on the South Shore. It's a hard place to find people, as you know. Arnie's out there looking for him now."

"Lead me to the sister."

"You sound like a lamb asking to be led to the slaughter. Actually she's a pretty nice gal," she said with female solidarity. "Not bright, but she has her heart in the right place. She's very fond of her brother."

"So was Lucrezia Borgia."

Phyllis slammed the car door. We drove toward Reno, a city where nothing good had ever happened to me, but I kept hoping.

Mrs Sally Burke lived close in on Riley Street in the upper flat of an old two-storey house. Phyllis dropped me off in front of it at eight-twenty-nine, having extracted my promise to come back and spend the night with Arnie and her. Mrs Burke was waiting in full panoply on the upper landing: tight black sheath with foxes, pearls and earrings, four-inch heels. Her hair was mingled brown and blonde, as if to express the complexity of her personality. Her brown eyes appraised me, as I came up to her level, the way an antebellum plantation owner might look over an able-bodied slave on the auction block.

She smelled nice, anyway, and she had a pleasant friendly anxious smile. We exchanged greetings and names. I was to call her Sally right away.

"I'm afraid I can't ask you in, the place is a mess. I never seem to get anything done on Sunday. You know the old song, 'Gloomy Sunday'? That is, since my divorce. Phyllis says you're divorced."

"Phyllis is right."

"It's different for a man," she said with some faint resentment. "But I can see you could use a woman to look after you."

She was one of the fastest and least efficient workers I'd ever met. My heart went down toward my boots. She was looking at my boots, and at the clothes I had slept in on the plane. On the other hand I was able-bodied. I had climbed the stairs unaided.

"Where shall we eat?" she said. "The Riverside is nice."

It was nice and expensive. After a couple of drinks I ceased to care about spending Alex's money. I began to be fascinated, in a way, by Sally Burke's conversation. Her ex-husband, if I could believe her, was a combination of Dracula, Hitler, and Uriah Heep. He made at least twenty-five thousand a year as a salesman in the Northwest, but more than once she had to attach his salary to collect her measley six-hundred-a-month alimony. She was having a rough time making ends meet, especially now that her little brother had lost his job at the club.

I ordered her another drink and indicated mild sympathy. "Jud's a good boy," she said, as if somebody had just denied it. "He played football at Washington State and led the team in rushing. A lot of people in Spokane thought he would have made All-American if he'd played for a better-known school. But he never got due recognition, he never has. He lost his coaching job out of sheer politics pure and simple. The charges they made were a lot of poppycock, he told me so himself."

"What charges?"

"Nothing. They were a lot of poppycock. I mean it." She finished her fourth martini and regarded me with simple cunning over the empty glass. "I don't believe you told me what kind of business that you're in, Lew?"

"I don't believe I did. I run a small agency in Hollywood."

"Isn't that interesting? Jud has always been interested in acting. He hasn't done any, actually, but he's said to be a very handsome boy. Jud was down in Hollywood last week."

"Looking for an acting job?"

"Anything,"she said. "He's a willing worker, but the trouble is he isn't trained for anything, I mean after he lost his teaching credentials, and then the dance studio folded. Do you think you could get him something to do in Hollywood?"

"I'd certainly like to talk to him," I said truthfully.

She was tipsy and hopeful, and she wasn't surprised by my interest in her brother.

"*That* can be arranged," she said. "As a matter of fact he's at my apartment right now. I could call him and tell him to come over here."

"Let's have dinner first."

"*I* don't mind paying for Jud's dinner." She realized she had made a tactical error, and quickly back-tracked: "But I guess three's company, eh? I mean two."

She talked so much about her brother at dinner that it was almost like having him there. She recited his old football statistics. She told me, with a kind of vicarious enthusiasm, all about his prowess with the ladies. She explained about the brilliant ideas Jud was always hatching. The one I liked best was a plan for a condensed version of the Bible, with all the offensive passages removed, for family reading.

Sally couldn't drink. She was coming apart by the time we finished eating. She wanted to pick up her brother and go and hell around in the clubs, but my heart wasn't in it. I took her home. In the cab she went to sleep on my shoulder. This I didn't mind.

I woke her up on Riley Street and got her into the house and up the stairs. She seemed very large and loosely put together, and the foxes kept slipping. I felt as if I'd been nursing drunks all weekend.

A man in shirtsleeves and form-fitting trousers opened the door of her flat. With Sally leaning on me, I got a quick impression of him: a man of half-qualities who lived in a half-world:

he was half-handsome, half-lost, half-spoiled, half-smart, half-dangerous. His pointed Italian shoes were scuffed at the toes.

"Need any help?" he said to me.

"Don't be ridic," Sally said. "I'm in perfect control. Mr Archer, meet brother Jud, Judson Foley."

"Hello," he said. "You shouldn't have let her drink. She's got a weak head for liquor. Here, I'll take her."

With weary skill he looped her arm over his shoulders, clasped her around the waist, walked her through the front room into a lighted bedroom, laid her out on the Hollywood bed, and turned off the light.

He seemed unpleasantly surprised to find me still in the front room. "Good night, Mr Archer, or whatever your name is. We're closing up for the night now."

"You're not very hospitable."

"No. My sister is the hospitable one." He cast a sour glance around the little room, at overflowing ashtrays, clouded glasses, scattered newspapers. "I never saw you before, I'll never see you again. Why should I be hospitable?"

"You're sure you never saw me before? Think hard."

His brown eyes studied my face, and then my body. He scratched nervously at the front of his thinning hair. He shook his head.

"If I ever saw you before I must have been drunk at the time. Did Sally bring you here when I was drunk?"

"No. Were you drinking last Friday night?"

"Let's see, what night was that? I think I was out of town. Yeah. I didn't get back here until Saturday morning." He was trying to sound casual and look unconcerned. "It must have been two other guys."

"I don't think so, Jud. I ran into you, or you ran into me, about nine last Friday night in Pacific Point."

Panic brightened his face like a flash of lightning. "Who are you?"

"I chased you down Helen Haggerty's driveway, remember? You were too fast for me. It took me two days to catch up."

He was breathing as if he'd just finished the run. "Are you from the police?"

"I'm a private detective."

He sat down in a Danish chair, gripping the fragile arms so

hard I thought they might break. He snickered. It was very close to a sob.

"This is Bradshaw's idea, isn't it?"

I didn't answer him. I cleared a chair and sat in it.

"Bradshaw said he was satisfied with my story. Now he sends you up against me." His eyes narrowed. "I suppose you were pumping my sister about me."

"She doesn't need much priming."

Twisting in the chair, he threw a wicked look in the direction of her bedroom. "I wish she'd keep her mouth shut about my business."

"Don't blame her for what you did yourself."

"But the hell of it is I didn't *do* anything, I *told* Bradshaw that, and he believed me, at least he said he did."

"Are you talking about Roy Bradshaw?"

"Who else?" He recognized me the other night, or thought he did. I didn't know who it was I bumped in the dark. I just wanted out of there."

"Why?"

He lifted his heavy shoulders and sat with them lifted, head down between them. "I didn't want trouble with the law."

"What were you doing at Helen's?"

"She *asked* me to come. Hell, I went there as a good Samaritan. She called me at the motel in Santa Monica and practically begged me to come and spend the night. It wasn't my beautiful blue eyes. She was frightened, she wanted company."

"What time did she call you?"

"Around seven or seven-thirty. I was just coming in from getting something to eat." He dropped his shoulders. "Listen, you know all this, you got it from Bradshaw, didn't you? What are you trying to do, trap me into a mistake?"

"It's an idea. What sort of a mistake did you have in mind?"

He shook his head, and went on shaking it as he spoke. "I didn't have anything particular in mind. I mean, I can't afford to make any mistakes."

"You already made the big one, when you ran."

"I know. I panicked." He shook his head some more. "There she was with a bullet hole in her skull and there I was a natural setup for a patsy. I heard you fellows coming, and I panicked. You've got to believe me."

They always said that. "Why do I have to believe you?"

"Because I'm telling the truth. I'm innocent as a little child."

"That's pretty innocent."

"I didn't mean in general. I meant in this particular situation. I went a long way out of my way to give Helen a helping hand. It doesn't make sense I'd go there to knock her off. I *liked* the girl. She and I had a lot in common."

I didn't know if this was a compliment to either of them. Bert Haggerty had described his ex-wife as corrupt. The man in front of me was a dubious character. Behind the mask of his good looks he seemed dilapidated, as if he'd painfully bumped down several steps in the social scale. In spite of this, I half-believed his story, I would never more than half-believe anything he said.

"What did you and Helen have in common?"

He gave me a quick sharp up-from-under look. This wasn't the usual line of questioning. He thought about his answer. "Sports. Dancing. Fun and games. We had some real fun times, I mean it. I almost died when I found her the other night."

"How did you happen to meet her?"

"You *know* all this," he said impatiently. "You're working for Bradshaw, aren't you?"

"Put it this way: Bradshaw and I are on the same side." I wanted to know why Roy Bradshaw loomed so large in Foley's mind, but other questions had priority. "Now why don't you humor me and tell me how you knew Helen?"

"It's simple enough." He jabbed his thumb downward like a decadent emperor decreeing death. "She rented the downstairs apartment when she was putting in her six weeks this summer. She and my sister hit it off, and eventually I got into the act. The three of us used to go places together."

"In Sally's car?"

"I had my own car then – sixty-two Galaxie five hundred," he said earnestly. "This was back in August before I lost my job and couldn't keep up with the payments."

"How did you happen to lose your job?"

"That wouldn't interest you. It had nothing to do with Helen Haggerty, nothing whatever."

His over insistence on the point made me suspicious. "What were you working at?"

"I said you wouldn't be interested."

"I can easily find out where you were working. You might as well tell me."

He said with his eyes down: "I was in the cashier's cage at the Solitaire in Stateline. I guess I made one mistake too many." He looked at his strong square fumbling hands.

"So you were looking for work in Los Angeles?"

"Correcto." He seemed relieved to get away from the subject of his job and why he lost it. "I didn't make a connection, but I've got to get out of this place."

"Why?"

He scratched his hair. "I can't go on living on my sister. It *cuts* me, being on the ding. I'm going down to L.A. again and have another look around."

"Let's go back to the first time. You say Helen called you at your motel Friday night. How did she know you were there?"

"I already called her earlier in the week."

"What for?"

"The usual. I mean, I thought we could get together, have some fun." He kept talking about having fun but he looked as if he hadn't had any for years. "Helen already had a date that night, Wednesday night. As a matter of fact she had a date with Bradshaw. They were going to some concert. She said she'd call me back another time. Which she did, Friday night."

"What did she say on the telephone?"

"That somebody threatened to kill her, and she was scared. I never heard her talk like that before. She said that she had nobody to turn to but me. And I got there too late." There seemed to be grief in him, but even this was ambiguous, as if he felt defrauded by Helen's death.

"Were Helen and Bradshaw close?"

He answered cautiously: "I wouldn't say that. I guess they lucked into each other last summer the same way Helen and I did. Anyway, he was busy Friday night. He had to give a speech at some big dinner. At least that's what he told me this morning."

"He wasn't lying. Did Bradshaw and Helen meet here in Reno?"

"Where else?"

"I thought Bradshaw spent the summer in Europe?"

"You thought wrong. He was here all through August, anyway."

"What was he doing here?"

"He told me once he was doing some kind of research at the University of Nevada. He didn't say what kind. I hardly knew him, actually. I ran into him a couple of times with Helen, and that was it. I didn't see him again until today."

"And you say he recognized you Friday night and came here to question you?"

"That's the truth. He came here this morning, gave me quite a grilling. *He* believed I didn't do that murder. I don't see why you can't believe me."

"I'll want to talk to Bradshaw before I make up my mind. Where is he now, do you know?"

"He said he was staying at the Lakeview Inn, on the North Shore. I don't know if he's still there or not."

I stood up and opened the door. "I think I'll go and see."

I suggested to Jud that he stay where he was, because a second runout would make him look very bad. He nodded. He was still nodding when a counter-impulse took hold of him and he rushed me. His heavy shoulder caught me under the ribs and slammed me back against the doorframe wheezing for air.

He threw a punch at my face. I shifted my head. His fist crunched into the plaster wall. He yipped with pain. He hit me low in the belly with his other hand. I slid down the door-frame. He kneed me, a glancing blow on the side of the jaw.

This impelled me to get up. He rushed me again, head down. I stepped to one side and chopped the back of his neck as he went by. He staggered rapidly through the door and across the landing, and plunged down. At the foot of the stairs he lay still.

But he was conscious when the police arrived. I rode along to the station to make sure they nailed him down. We hadn't been there five minutes when Arnie came in. He had an understanding with the officers. They booked Foley for assault and related charges, and promised to hold him.

XXIV

ARNIE DROVE me out to the Lakeview Inn, a rambling California Gothic pile which must have dated from the early years of the century. Generations of summer visitors had marched through the lobby and trampled out any old-world charm it might once have had. It seemed an unlikely place for Roy Bradshaw to be staying.

But Bradshaw was there, the elderly night clerk said. He took a railroad watch out of his vest pocket and consulted it. "It's getting pretty late, though. They may be asleep."

"They?"

"Him and his wife. I can go up and call him, if you want me to. We never did put telephones in the rooms."

"I'll go up. I'm a friend of Dr Bradshaw's."

"I didn't know he was a doctor."

"A doctor of philosophy," I said. "What's his room number?"

"Thirty-one, on the top floor." The old man seemed relieved at not having to make the climb.

I left Arnie with him and went up to the third floor. Light shone through the transom of 31, and I could hear the indistinct murmur of voices. I knocked. There was a silence, followed by the noise of slippered feet.

Roy Bradshaw spoke through the door. "Who is it?"

"Archer."

He hesitated. A sleeper in the room across the hall, perhaps disturbed by our voices, began to snore. Bradshaw said:

"What are you doing here?"

"I have to see you."

"Can't it wait till morning?" His voice was impatient, and he had temporarily mislaid his Harvard accent.

"No. It can't. I need your advice on what to do about Judson Foley."

"Very well, I'll get dressed."

I waited in the narrow ill-lit hallway. It had the faintly acrid smell which old buildings seem to absorb from the people who pass through them night by night, the smell of transient life.

The snoring man was uttering terrible moans between his snores. A woman told him to turn over, and he subsided.

I could hear a quick interchange of voices in Bradshaw's room. The woman's voice seemed to want something, which Bradshaw's voice denied. I thought I recognized the woman's voice, but I couldn't be sure.

I was sure when Bradshaw finally opened the door. He tried to slip out without letting me see in, but I caught a glimpse of Laura Sutherland. She was sitting upright on the edge of the unmade bed in a severely cut Paisley robe. Her hair was down around her shoulders, and she was rosy and beautiful.

Bradshaw jerked the door shut. "So now you know."

He had pulled on slacks and a black turtleneck sweater which made him look more undergraduate than ever. In spite of the tension in him, he seemed quite happy.

"I don't know what I know," I said.

"This is not an illicit liaison, believe me. Laura and I were married some time ago. We're keeping our marriage secret, for the present. I'm going to ask you to go along with that."

I didn't say whether I would or not. "Why all the secrecy?"

"We have our reasons. For one thing, under the college regulations, Laura would have to give up her post. She intends to, of course, but not immediately. And then there's Mother. I don't know how I'm going to break it to her."

"You could just tell her. She'll survive."

"It's easy enough to say. It isn't possible."

The thing that made it impossible, I thought, was Mother's money. Having money and looking forward to inheriting more were difficult habits for a man to break in early middle age. But I felt a sneaking admiration for Bradshaw. He had more life in him than I'd suspected.

We went downstairs and through the lobby, where Arnie was playing gin rummy with the night clerk. The bar was a gloomy cavern with antlers on the walls instead of stalactites and customers instead of stalagmites. One of the customers, a local man wearing a cap and windbreaker and carrying a load, wanted to buy Bradshaw and me a drink. The bartender told him it was time to go home. Surprisingly, he went, and most of the others drifted out after him.

We sat at the bar. Bradshaw ordered a double bourbon and

insisted on one for me, though I didn't need it. There was some aggression in his insistence. He hadn't forgiven me for stumbling on his secret, or for dragging him away from his wife's bed.

"Well," he said, "what about Judson Foley"

"He tells me you recognized him Friday night."

"I had an intuition that it was he." Bradshaw had recovered his accent, and was using it as a kind of vocal mask.

"Why didn't you say so? You could have saved a lot of legwork and expense."

He looked at me solemnly over his drink. "I had to be certain and I was very far from being that. I couldn't accuse a man, and set the police on his trail, unless I were certain."

"So you came here to make certain?"

"It happened to work out that way. There are times in a man's life when everything seems to fall together into place, have you noticed?" A momentary flash of glee broke through his earnestness. "Laura and I had been planning to steal a weekend here for some time, and the conference gave us the opportunity. Foley was a side issue, but of course a very important one. I looked him up this morning and questioned him thoroughly. He seems completely innocent to me."

"Innocent of what?"

"Of Helen's murder. Foley went to her house to give her what protection he could, but she was already beyond protection when he got there. He lost his nerve and ran."

"What was he afraid of?"

"A false accusation, what he calls a frameup. He's had some trouble with the law in the past. It had to do with shaving points, as they call it, in football games."

"How do you know?"

"He told me. I have," he said with a chuckle of vanity, "a certain capacity to inspire confidence in these – ah – disaffiliates. The man was utterly forthright with me, and in my considered opinion he had nothing to do with Helen's murder."

"You're probably right. I'd still like to find out more about him."

"I know very little about him. He was a friend of Helen's. I saw him once or twice in her company."

"In Reno."

"Yes. I spent a part of the summer in Nevada. It's another

fact about myself that I'm not publicizing." He added rather vaguely: "A man has a right to some private life, surely."

"You mean you were here with Laura?"

He dropped his eyes. "She was with me part of the time. We hadn't quite made up our minds to get married. It was quite a decision. It meant the end of her career and the end of my – life with Mother," he concluded lamely.

"I can understand your reason for keeping it quiet. Still I wish you'd told me that you met Foley and Helen last month in Reno."

"I should have. I apologize. One acquires the habit of secrecy." He added in a different, passionate voice: "I'm deeply in love with Laura. I'm jealous of anything that threatens to disturb our idyl." His words were formal and old-fashioned, but the feeling behind them seemed real.

"What was the relationship between Foley and Helen?"

"They were friends, nothing more, I'd say. Frankly I was a little surprised at her choice of companion. But he was younger than she, and I suppose that was the attraction. Presentable escorts are at a premium in Reno, you know. I had quite a time myself fending off the onslaught of various predatory females."

"Does that include Helen?"

"I suppose it does." Through the gloom I thought I could discern a faint blush on his cheek. "Of course she didn't know about my – my *thing* with Laura. I've kept it a secret from everyone."

"Is that why you don't want Foley taken back for questioning?"

"I didn't say that."

"I'm asking you."

"I suppose that's partly it." There was a long silence. "But if you think it's necessary, I won't argue. Laura and I have nothing really to hide."

The bartender said: "Drink up, gentlemen. It's closing time."

We drank up. In the lobby Bradshaw gave me a quick nervous handshake, muttering something about getting back to his wife. He went up the stairs two at a time, on his toes.

I waited for Arnie to finish his game of gin. One of the things that made him a first-rate detective was his ability to merge with almost any group, nest into almost any situation, and start a conversation rolling. He and the night man shook hands when we left the hotel.

"The woman your friend registered with," he said in the car, "is a good-looking brownette type, well stacked, who talks like a book."

"She's his wife."

"You didn't tell me Bradshaw was married," he said rather irritably.

"I just found out. The marriage is *sub rosa.* The poor beggar has a dominating mother in the background. In the foreground. The old lady has money, and I think he's afraid of being disinherited."

"He better come clean with her, and take his chances."

"That's what I told him."

Arnie put the car in gear and as we drove west and south along the lakeshore, recounted a long story about a client he had handled for Pinkerton in San Francisco before the war. She was a well-heeled widow of sixty or so who lived in Hillsborough with her son, a man in his thirties. The son was always home by midnight, but seldom before, and the mother wanted to know what he was doing with his evenings. It turned out he had been married for five years to an ex-waitress whom he maintained, with their three small children, in a row house in South San Francisco.

Arnie seemed to think that this was the end of the story.

"What happened to the people?" I asked him.

"The old lady fell in love with her grandchildren and put up with the daughter-in-law for their sake. They all lived happily ever after, on her money."

"Too bad Bradshaw hasn't been married long enough to have any children."

We drove in silence for a while. The road left the shore and tunneled among trees which enclosed it like sweet green coagulated night. I kept thinking about Bradshaw and his unsuspected masculinity.

"I'd like to do some checking on Bradshaw, Arnie."

"Has this marriage business escalated him into a suspect?"

"Not in my book. Not yet, anyway. But he did suppress the fact that he met Helen Haggerty in Reno last summer. I want to know exactly what he was doing here in the month of August.

He told Judson Foley he was doing research at the University of Nevada, but that doesn't seem likely."

"Why not?"

"He's got a doctorate from Harvard, and he'd normally do his research there or at Berkeley or Stanford. I want you to do some checking on Foley, too. Find out if you can why Foley was fired by the Solitaire Club."

"That shouldn't be too hard. Their top security man is an old friend of mine." He looked at his watch in the light from the dash. "We could go by there now but he probably won't be on duty this late on a Sunday night."

"Tomorrow will do."

Phyllis was waiting for us with food and drink. We sat up in her kitchen foolishly late, getting mildly drunk on beer and shared memories and exhaustion. Eventually the conversation came full circle, back to Helen Haggerty and her death. At three o'clock in the morning I was reading aloud her translated poem in the *Bridgeton Blazer* about the violins of the autumn winds.

"It's terribly sad," Phyllis said. "She must have been a remarkable young girl, even it if is only a translation."

"That was her father's word for her. Remarkable. He's remarkable, too, in his own way."

I tried to tell them about the tough old drunken heart-broken cop who had sired Helen. Suddenly it was half-past three and Phyllis was asleep with her head resting like a tousled dahlia among the bottles on the kitchen table. Arnie began gathering up the bottles, carefully, so as not to wake her unnecessarily soon.

Alone in their guest room I had one of those intuitions that come sometimes when you're very tired and emotionally stirred up. I became convinced that Hoffman had given me the *Blazer* for a reason. There was something in it he wanted me to see.

I sat there in my underwear on the edge of the open fresh-smelling bed and read the little magazine until my eyes crossed. I learned a good deal about student activities at Bridgeton City College twenty-two years ago, but nothing of any apparent consequence to my case.

I found another poem I liked, though. It was signed with the initials G.R.B., and it went:

If light were dark
and dark were light,
Moon a black hole
In the blaze of night,

A raven's wing
As bright as tin,
Then you, my love,
Would be darker than sin.

I read it aloud at breakfast. Phyllis said she envied the woman it had been written to. Arnie complained that his scrambled eggs weren't moist. He was older than Phyllis, and it made him touchy.

We decided after breakfast to leave Judson Foley sitting for the present. If Dolly Kincaid were arrested and arraigned, Foley would make a fairly good surprise witness for the defense. Arnie drove me to the airport, where I caught a Pacific flight to Los Angeles.

I picked up an L.A. paper at International Airport, and found a brief account of the Haggerty killing in the Southland News on an inside page. It informed me that the wife-slayer Thomas McGee, released from San Quentin earlier in the year, was being sought for questioning. Dolly Kincaid wasn't mentioned.

XXV

AROUND NOON I walked into Jerry Marks's store-front office. His secretary told me that Monday was the day for the weekly criminal docket and Jerry had spent the morning in court. He was probably having lunch somewhere near the courthouse. Yes, Mr Kincaid had got in touch with Mr Marks on Sunday, and retained him.

I found them together in the restaurant where Alex and I had lunched the day it began. Alex made room for me on his side of the booth, facing the front. Business was roaring, and there was a short lineup inside the front door.

"I'm glad the two of you got together," I said.

Alex produced one of his rare smiles. "So am I. Mr Marks has been wonderful."

Jerry flapped his hand in a depreciating way. "Actually I haven't been able to do anything yet. I had another case to dispose of this morning. I did make an attempt to pick Gil Steven's brain, but he told me I'd better go to the transcript of the trial, which I plan to do this afternoon. Mrs Kincaid," he said, with a sidelong glance at Alex, "was just as uncommunicative as Stevens."

"You've talked to Dolly then?"

He lowered his voice. "I tried, yesterday. We've got to know where we stand before the police get to her."

"Is that going to happen?"

Jerry glanced around him at the courthouse crowd, and lowered his voice still further. "According to the grapevine, they were planning to make their move today, when they completed their ballistics tests. But something's holding them up. The Sheriff and the experts he brought in are still down in the shooting gallery under the courthouse."

"The bullet may be fragmented. It often is in head wounds. Or they may have shifted their main attention to another suspect. I see in the paper they've put out an APB for Thomas McGee."

"Yes, it was done yesterday. He's probably over the Mexican border by now."

"Do you consider him a major suspect, Jerry?"

"I'll want to read the transcript before I form an opinion. Do you?"

It was a hard question. I was spared having to answer it by a diversion. Two elderly ladies, one in serviceable black and one in fashionable green, looked in through the glass front door. They saw the waiting queue and turned away. The one in black was Mrs Hoffman, Helen's mother. The other was Luke Deloney's widow.

I excused myself and went out after them. They had crossed the street in the middle of the block and were headed downtown, moving through light and shadow under the giant yuccas that hedged the courthouse grounds. Though they seemed to keep up an incessant conversation, they walked together like strangers, out of step and out of sympathy. Mrs Deloney was much the older, but she had a horsewoman's stride. Mrs Hoffman stubbed along on tired feet.

I stayed on the other side of the street and followed them at a distance. My heart was thudding. Mrs Deloney's arrival in California confirmed my belief that her husband's murder and Helen's were connected, and that she knew it.

They walked two blocks to the main street and went into the first restaurant they came to, a tourist trap with empty tables visible though its plate glass windows. There was an open-fronted cigar store diagonally across the street, I looked over its display of paperbacks, bought a pack of cigarettes, and smoked three or four which I lit at the old-fashioned gas flame, and eventually bought a book about ancient Greek philosophy. It had a chapter on Zeno which I read standing. The old ladies were a long time over lunch.

"Archer will never catch the old ladies," I said.

The man benind the counter cupped his ear. "What was that?"

"I was thinking aloud."

"It's a free country. I like to talk to myself when I'm off work. In the store here it wouldn't be appropriate." He smiled over the word, and his gold teeth flashed like jewelry.

The old ladies came out of the restaurant and separated. Mrs Hoffman limped south, toward her hotel. Mrs Deloney strode in the opposite direction, moving rapidly now that she was unencumbered by her companion. From the distance you could have taken her for a young woman who had unaccountably bleached her hair white.

She turned off the main street in the direction of the courthouse, and halfway down the block disappeared into a modern concrete and glass building. "Law Offices of Stevens and Ogilvy," said the brass sign beside the entrance. I walked on to the next corner, sat on a bench at a bus stop, and read in my new book about Heraclitus. All things flow like a river, he said; nothing abides. Parmenides, on the other hand, believed that nothing ever changed, it only seemed to. Both views appealed to me.

A cab pulled up in front of the Stevens and Ogilvy office. Mrs Deloney came out, and the cab took her away. I made a note of its license number before I went into the building.

It was a large office, and a working one. Typewriters were clacking in a row of cubicles behind the waiting-room. A very junior attorney in a flannel suit was telling the middle-aged woman at the front desk how he wanted a brief got up on her typewriter.

He went away. Her steel-gray glance met mine, and we happened to smile at each other. She said:

"I was typing briefs when he was just a gleam in his daddy's eye. Can I help you?"

"I'm very eager to see Mr Gil Stevens. My name is Archer."

She looked in her appointment book, and then at her watch. "Mr Stevens is due for lunch in ten minutes. He won't be coming back to the office today. I'm sorry."

"It has to do with a murder case."

"I see. I may be able to slip you in for five minutes if that will do any good."

"It might."

She talked to Stevens on the phone and waved me past the cubicles to an office at the end of the hall. It was large and sumptuous. Stevens sat on leather behind mahogany, flanked by a glass-faced cabinet of yachting trophies. He was lion-faced, with a big soft masterful mouth, a high brow overhung by broken wings of yellowish white hair, pale blue eyes that had seen everything at least once and were watching the second time around. He wore tweeds and a florid bow tie.

"Close the door behind you, Mr Archer, and sit down."

I parked myself on a leather settee and started to tell him what I was doing there. His heavy voice interrupted me:

"I have only a very few minutes. I know who you are, sir, and I believe I know what you have in mind. You want to discuss the McGee case with me."

I threw him a curve: "And the Deloney case."

His eyebrows went up, forcing the flesh above them into multiple corrugations. Sometimes you have to give away information on the chance of gaining other information. I told him what had happened to Luke Deloney.

He leaned forward in his chair. "You say this is connected in some way with the Haggerty murder?"

"It has to be. Helen Haggerty lived in Deloney's appartment

building. She said she knew a witness to Deloney's murder."

"Strange she didn't mention it." He wasn't talking to me. He was talking to himself about Mrs Deloney. Then he remembered that I was there. "Why do you come to me with this?"

"I thought you'd be interested, since Mrs Deloney is your client."

"Is she?"

"I assumed she was."

"You're welcome to your assumptions. I suppose you followed her here"

"I happened to see her come in. But I've wanted to get in touch with you for a couple of days."

"Why?"

"You defended Tom McGee. His wife's death was the second in a series of three related murders which started with Deloney and ended with Helen Haggerty. Now they're trying to pin the Haggetty death on McGee or his daughter, or both of them. I believe McGee is innocent, and has been all along."

"Twelve of his peers thought otherwise."

"Why did they, Mr Stevens?"

"I get no pleasure from discussing past mistakes."

"This could be very relevant to the present. McGee's daughter admits she lied on the witness stand. She says she lied her father into prison."

"Does she now? The admission comes a little belatedly. I should have borne down on her in cross, but McGee didn't want me to. I made the mistake of respecting his wishes."

"What was the motive behind them?"

"Who can say? Paternal love, perhaps, or his feeling that the child had been made to suffer enough. Ten years in prison is a big price to pay for such delicacies of feeling."

"You're convinced that McGee was innocent?"

"Oh, yes. The daughter's admission that she was lying removes any possible doubt." Stevens took a blotched green cigar out of a glass tube, clipped it and lit it. "I take it that is highly confidential advice."

"On the contrary, I'd like to see it publicized. It might help to bring McGee in. He's on the run, as you probably know."

Stevens neither affirmed nor denied this. He sat like a

mountain behind a blue haze of smoke.

"I'd like to ask him some questions," I said.

"What about?"

"The other man, for one thing – the man Constance McGee was in love with. I understand he played some part in your case."

"He was my hypothetical alternative." Steven's face crumpled in a rueful smile. "But the judge wouldn't let him in, except in my summing-up, unless I put McGee on the stand. Which didn't seem advisable. That other man was a two-edged weapon. He was a motive for McGee as well as an alternative suspect. I made the mistake of going for an outright acquittal."

"I don't quite follow."

"It doesn't matter. It's only history." He waved his hand and the smoke shifted around him like strata of time in an old man's memory.

"Who was the other man?"

"Come now, Mr Archer, you can't expect to walk in off the street and pump me dry. I've been practicing law for forty years."

"Why did you take McGee's case?"

"Tom used to do some work on my boats. I rather liked him."

"Aren't you interested in clearing him?"

"Not at the expense of another innocent man."

"You know who the other man is?"

"I know who he is, if Tom can be believed." While he still sat solidly in his chair, he was withdrawing from me like a magician through dissolving mirrors. "I don't divulge the secrets that come to me. I bury 'em, sir. That's why they come to me."

"It would be a hell of a thing if they put Tom back in San Quentin for the rest of his life, or gassed him."

"It certainly would. But I suspect you're trying to enlist me in your cause, rather than Tom's."

"We could certainly use you."

"Who are 'we'?"

McGee's daughter Dolly and her husband Alex Kincaid, Jerry Marks and me."

"And what *is* your cause?"

"The solution of those three murders."

"You make it sound very simple and neat," he said. "Life never is. Life always has loose ends, and it's sometimes best to let them ravel out."

"Is that what Mrs Deloney wants?"

"I wasn't speaking on behalf of Mrs Deloney. I don't expect to." He worked a speck of tobacco on to the tip of his tongue, and spat it out.

"Did she come to you for information about the McGee case?"

"No comment."

"That probably means yes. It's a further indication that the McGee case and the Deloney killing are connected."

"We won't discuss it," he said shortly. "As for your suggestion that I join forces with you, Jerry Marks had the same idea this morning. As I told him, I'll think about it. In the meantime I want you and Jerry to think about something. Tom McGee and his daughter may be on opposite sides of this issue. They certainly were ten years ago."

"She was a child then, manipulated by adults."

"I know that." He rose, bulking huge in his light tweed suit. "It's been interesting talking to you but I'm overdue for a luncheon meeting." He moved past me to the door, gesturing with his cigar. "Come along."

XXVI

I WALKED down the main street to the Pacific Hotel and asked for Mrs Hoffman. She had just checked out, leaving no forwarding address. The bellhop who handled her bag said she had ridden away in a taxi with another old lady wearing a green coat. I gave him five dollars and my motel address and told him it would be worth another five to find out where they'd gone.

It was past two o'clock, and my instinct told me this was the crucial day. I felt cut off from what was happening in the private offices of the court house, in the shooting gallery and laboratory where the ballistics tests were being conducted, behind the locked door of the nursing home. Time was slipping away, flowing past me like Heraclitus' river, while I was checking up on the vagaries of old ladies.

I went back to the telephone booths behind the hotel lobby and called Godwin's office. The doctor was with a patient, and wouldn't be available until ten minutes to three. I tried Jerry Marks. His secretary told me he was still out.

I made a collect call to the Walters agency in Reno. Arnie answered the phone:

"Nice timing, Lew. I just got the word on your boy."

"Which one? Bradshaw or Foley?"

"Both of them in a way. You wanted to know why Foley lost his job at the Solitaire Club. The answer is he used his position in the cashier's cage to find out how much Bradshaw was worth."

"How did he do that?"

"You know how the clubs check up on their customers when they open an account. They put in a query to the customer's bank, get an approximate figure on his bank balance, and set a limit to his credit accordingly. 'Low three' means a three-figure bank balance on the low side, and maybe a limit of a couple of hundred. A 'high four' might be seven or eight thousand, and a 'low five' maybe twenty or thirty thousand. Which incidentally is Bradshaw's bracket."

"Is he a gambler?"

"He isn't. That's the point. He never opened an account at the Solitaire, or anywhere else that I know of, but Foley put in a query on him anyway. The club caught it, did a double check on Foley, and got him out of there fast."

"It smells like possible blackmail, Arnie."

"More than possible," he said. "Foley admits to a bit of a record in that line."

"What else does he admit?"

"Nothing else yet. He claims he got the information for a friend."

"Helen Haggerty?"

"Foley isn't saying. He's holding back in the hope of making a deal."

"Go ahead and deal with him. He got hurt worse than I did. I'm willing to drop charges."

"It may not be necessary, Lew."

"Deal with him. Assuming blackmail, which I do, the question is what makes Bradshaw blackmailable."

"Could be his divorce," Arnie said smoothly. "You were interested in what Bradshaw was doing in Reno between the middle of July and the end of August. The answer is on the court record. He was establishing residence for a divorce from a woman named Letitia O. Macready."

"Letitia who?"

"Macready." He spelled it out. "I haven't been able to get any further information on the woman. According to the lawyer who handled the divorce, Bradshaw didn't know where she lived. Her last known address was in Boston. The official notice of the proceedings came back from there with a 'Gone – No Order' stamp."

"Is Bradshaw still at Tahoe?"

"He and his new wife checked out this morning. They were on their way back to Pacific Point. That makes him your baby."

"Baby isn't quite the word for Bradshaw. I wonder if his mother knows about the first marriage."

"You could always ask her."

I decided to try and talk to Bradshaw first. I got my car out of the courthouse lot and drove out to the college. The students on the mall and in the corridors, particularly the girls, wore subdued expressions. The threat of death and judgement had invaded the campus. I felt a little like its representative.

The blonde secretary in the Dean's outer office looked tense, as if only her will was holding her, and the whole institution, together.

"Dean Bradshaw isn't in."

"Not back from the weekend yet?"

"Of couse he's back." She added in a defensive tone: "Dean Bradshaw was here this morning for over an hour."

"Where is he now?"

"I don't know. I guess he went home."

"You sound kind of worried about him."

She answered me with a machine-gun burst from her typewriter. I retreated, across the hall to Laura Sutherland's office. Her secretary told me she hadn't come in today. She'd phoned in the middle of the morning that she was afraid she was coming down with something. I hoped it wasn't something serious, like death and judgement.

I drove back to Foothill and along it to the Bradshaw house.

Wind rustled in the trees. The fog had been completely dissipated, and the afternoon sky was a brilliant aching blue. The mountains rising into it were distinct in every scarred and wrinkled detail.

I was more aware than usual of these things, but I felt cut off from them. I must have had some empathy for Roy Bradshaw and his new wife and was afraid of being hurt in my empathy. I drove past his gate without seeing it and had to turn in the next driveway and come back to the Bradshaw house. I was somewhat relieved to be told by the Spanish woman, Maria, that Bradshaw wasn't there and hadn't been all day.

Mrs Bradshaw called from the stairs in a cracked penetrating voice: "Is that you, Mr Archer? I want to talk to you."

She came down the steps in a quilted dressing-robe and cloth slippers. The weekend had aged her. She looked very old and haggard.

"My son hasn't been home for three days," she complained, "and he hasn't telephoned once. What do you suppose has happened to him?"

"I'd like to discuss that question with you in private."

Maria who had been listening with her entire body, went off in a hip-swinging dudgeon. Mrs Bradshaw took me to a room I hadn't been in before, a small sitting-room opening on a patio at the side of the house. Its furnishings were informal and old-fashioned, and they reminded me slightly of the room where I had interviewed Mrs Deloney.

This room was dominated by an oil painting over the fireplace. It was a full-length portrait, almost life-size, of a handsome gentleman wearing sweeping white mustaches and a cutaway. His black eyes followed me across the room to the armchair which Mrs Bradshaw indicated. She sat in an upholstered platform rocker with her slippered feet on a small petit-point hassock.

"I've been a selfish old woman," she said unexpectedly. "I've been thinking it over and I've decided to pay your expenses after all. I don't like what they're doing to that girl."

"You probably know more about it than I do."

"Probably. I have some good friends in this city." She didn't elaborate.

"I appreciate the offer," I said, "but my expenses are being taken care of. Dolly's husband came back."

"Really? I'm so glad," She tried to warm herself at the thought, and failed. "I'm deeply concerned about Roy."

"So am I, Mrs Bradshaw." I decided to tell her what I knew, or part of it. She was bound to find out soon about his marriage, his marriages. "You don't have to worry about his physical safety. I saw him last night in Reno, and he was in good shape. He checked in at the college today."

"His secretary lied to me then. I don't know what they're trying to do to me out there, or what my son is up to. What was he really doing in Reno?"

"Attending a conference, as he said. He also went there to look into a suspect in Helen Haggerty's murder."

"He must have been very fond of her, after all, to go to such lengths."

"He was involved with Miss Haggerty. I don't think the involvement was romantic."

"What was it then?"

"Financial. I think he was paying her money, and incidentally he got her a job at the college, through Laura Sutherland. To put it bluntly, the Haggerty women was blackmailing your son. She may have called it something different herself. But she used a crooked friend in Reno to check on his bank balance before she ever came here. This was the same man Roy went to Reno to talk to."

Mrs Bradshaw didn't throw a fit, as I was afraid she might. She said in a grave tone: "Are these facts, Mr Archer, or are you exercising your imagination?"

"I wish I were. I'm not."

"But how could Roy be blackmailed? He's led a blameless life, a dedicated life. I'm his mother. I ought to know."

"That may be. But the standard varies for different people. A rising college administrator has to be lily-white. An unfortunate marriage, for instance, would queer his chances for that university presidency you were telling me about."

"An unfortunate marriage? But Roy has never been married."

"I'm afraid he has," I said. "does the name Letitia Macready mean anything to you?"

"It does not."

She was lying. The name drew a net of lines across her face, reduced her eyes to bright black points and her mouth to a purse with a drawstring. She knew the name and hated it, I thought; perhaps she was even afraid of Letitia Macready.

"The name ought to mean something to you, Mrs Bradshaw. The Macready woman was your daughter-in-law."

"You must be insane. My son has never married."

She spoke with such force and assurance that I had a moment of doubt. It wasn't likely that Arnie had made a mistake – he seldom did – but it was possible that there were two Roy Bradshaws. No, Arnie had talked to Bradshaw's lawyer in Reno, and must have made a positive identification.

"You have to get married," I said, "before you can get a divorce. Roy got a Reno divorce a few weeks ago. He was in Nevada establishing residence for it from the middle of July till the end of August."

"Now I know you're insane. He was in Europe all that time, and I can prove it." She got up, on creaking reluctant limbs, and went to the eighteenth-century secretary against one wall. She came back toward me with a sheaf of letters and postcards in her shaking hands. "He sent me these. You can see for yourself that he was in Europe."

I looked over the postcards. There were about fifteen of them, arranged in order: the Tower of London (postmarked London, July 18), the Bodleian Library (Oxford, July 21), York Cathedral (York, July 25), Edinburgh Castle (Edinburgh, July 29), The Giant's Causeway (Londonderry, August 3), The Abbey Theatre (Dublin, August 6), Land's End (St. Ives, August 8), The Arc de Triomphe (Paris, August 12), and so on through Switzerland and Italy and Germany. I read the card from Munich (a view of the English Gardens, postmarked August 25):

> Dear Moms:
>
> Yesterday I visited Hitler's eyrie at Berchtesgaden – a beautiful setting made grim by its associations – and today, by way of contrast, I took a bus to Oberammergau, where the Passion Play is performed. I was struck by the almost Biblical simplicity of the villagers. This whole Bavarian countryside is studded with the most stunning little churches. How I wish you could enjoy them with me! I'm sorry to hear

that your summer companion is presenting certain prickly aspects. Well, the summer will soon be over and I for one will be happy to turn my back on the splendors of Europe and come home. All my love.

Roy

I turned to Mrs Bradshaw. "Is this your son's handwriting?"

"Yes. It's unmistakable. I know he wrote those cards, and those letters, too."

She brandished several letters under my nose. I looked at the postmarks: London, July 19; Dublin, August 7; Geneva, August 15; Rome, August 20; Berlin, August 27; Amsterdam, August 30. I started to read the last one ("Dear Moms: Just a hasty note, which may arrrive after I do, to tell you how I loved your letter about the blackbirds. . .") but Mrs Bradshaw snatched it out of my hand.

"Please don't *read* the letters. My son and I are very close, and he wouldn't like me to show our correspondence to a stranger." She gathered all the letters and cards and locked them up in the secretary. "I believe I've proved my point, that Roy couldn't have been in Nevada when you say he was."

For all her assurance, her voice was questioning. I said:

"Did you write letters to him while he was away?"

"I did. That is to say, I dictated them to Miss What's-her-name, except for once or twice when my arthritis allowed me to write. I had a nurse-companion during the summer. Miss Wadley her name was. She was one of these completely self-centred young women –"

I cut in: "Did you write a letter about the blackbirds?"

"Yes. We had an invasion of them last month. It was more of a fanciful little tale than a letter, having to do with blackbirds baked in a pie."

"Where did you send the blackbird letter?"

"Where? I think to Rome, to American Express in Rome. Roy gave me an itinerary before he left here."

He was supposed to be in Rome on August 20. The blackbird letter was answered from Amsterdam on August 30."

"You have an impressive memory, Mr Archer, but I fail to see what you're getting at."

"Just this. There was a lapse of at least ten days between the receiving and the answering of that letter – time enough for an accomplice to pick it up in Rome, airmal it to Roy in Reno, get his airmail reply in Amsterdam, and remail it to you here."

"I don't believe it." But she half-believed it. "Why would he go to such lengths to deceive his mother?"

"Because he was ashamed of what he was actually doing – divorcing the Macready woman in Reno – and he didn't want you, or anyone else, to know about it. Has he been to Europe before?"

"Of course. I took him there soon after the war, when he was in graduate school at Harvard."

"And did you visit many of these same places?"

"Yes. We did. Not Germany, but most of the others "

"Then it wouldn't have been hard for him to fake the letters. As for the postcards, his accomplice must have bought them in Europe and mailed them to him."

"I dislike your use of the word 'accomplice' in connection with my son. There is, after all, nothing criminal about this – this deception. It's a purely personal matter."

"I hope so, Mrs Bradshaw."

She must have known what I meant. Her face went through the motions of swallowing pain. She turned her back on me and went to the window. Several white-eyed blackbirds were walking around on the tiles of the patio. I don't suppose she saw them. One of her hands combed roughly at her hair, over and over, until it stuck up like molting thistles. When she turned around at last, her eyes were half-closed, and her face seemed tormented by the light.

"I'm going to ask you to keep all this in confidence, Mr Archer."

Roy Bradshaw had used very similar language last night, about his marriage to Laura.

"I can try," I said.

"Please do. It would be tragic if Roy's career were to be ruined by a youthful indiscretion. That's all it was, you know – a youthful indiscretion. It would never have happened if his father had lived to give him a father's guidance." She gestured toward the portrait over the fireplace.

"By 'it' you mean the Macready woman?"

"Yes."

"You know her then?"

"I know her."

As if the admission had exhausted her, she collapsed in the platform rocker, leaning her head on the high cushioned back. Her loose throat seemed very vulnerable.

"Miss Macready came to see me once," she said. "It was before we left Boston, during the war. She wanted money."

"Blackmail money?"

"That's what it amounted to. She asked me to finance a Nevada divorce for her. She'd picked Roy up on Scollay Square and tricked the boy into marrying her. She was in a position to wreck his future. I gave her two thousand dollars. Apparently she spent it on herself and never bothered getting a divorce." She sighed. "Poor Roy."

"Did he know that you knew about her?"

"I never told him. I thought I had ended the threat by paying her money. I wanted it over with and forgotten, with no recriminations between my son and me. But apparently she's been haunting him all these years."

"Haunting him in the flesh?"

"Who knows? I thought I understood my son, and all the details of his life. It turns out that I don't."

"What sort of woman is she?"

"I saw her only once, when she came to my house in Belmont. I formed a most unfavorable impression. She claimed to be an actress, unemployed, but she dressed and talked like a member of an older profession than that." Her voice rasped with irony. "I suppose I have to admit that the redheaded hussy was handsome, in a crude way. But she was utterly unsuitable for Roy, and of course she knew it. He was an innocent lad, hardly out of his teens. She was obviously an experienced woman."

"How old was she?"

"Much older than Roy, thirty at least."

"So she'd be pushing fifty now."

"At least," she said.

"Have you ever seen her in California?"

She shook her head so hard that her face went loose and wobbly.

"Has Roy?"

"He's never mentioned her to me. We've lived together on

the assumption that the Macready woman never existed. And I beg you not to tell him what I've told you. It would destroy all confidence between us."

"There may be more important considerations, Mrs Bradshaw."

"What could be more important?"

"His neck."

She sat with her thick ankles crossed, more stunned than impassive. Her broad sexless body made her resemble a dilapidated Buddha. She said in a hushed voice:

"Surely you can't suspect my son of murder?"

I said something vague and soothing. The eyes of the man in the portrait followed me out. I was glad the father wasn't alive, in view of what I might have to do to Roy.

XXVII

I HADN'T eaten since breakfast, and on my way into town I stopped at a drive-in. While I was waiting for my sandwich, I made another call to Arnie Walters from an outside booth.

Arnie had made his deal with Judson Foley. It was Helen Haggerty who had wanted the word on Bradshaw's financial status. Foley couldn't or wouldn't swear that she had blackmail in mind. But shortly after he sold her the information she came into sudden wealth, by Foley's standards.

"How much did she pay Foley?"

"Fifty dollars, he says. Now he feels cheated."

"He always will," I said. "Did she tell Foley what she had on Bradshaw?"

"No. She was very careful not to, apparently. But there's a piece of negative evidence: She didn't mention to Foley that Bradshaw had been married, or was getting a divorce. Which probably means that that information was worth money to her."

"It probably does."

"One other fact came out, Lew. The Haggerty woman knew Bradshaw long before they met in Reno."

"Where and how?"

"Foley says he doesn't know, and I believe him. I offered to pay him for any information that checked out. It broke his heart when he couldn't do business with me."

I found Jerry Marks in the law library on the second floor of the courthouse. Several bound volumes of typescript were piled on the table in front of him. There was dust on his hands, and a smudge on the side of his nose.

"Have you turned up anything, Jerry?"

"I've come to one conclusion. The case against McGee was weak. It consisted of two things, mainly: prior abuse of his wife, and the little girl's testimony, which some judges would have thrown out of court. I've been concentrating on her testimony, because I'm going to have a chance to question her under pentothal."

"When?"

"Tonight at eight, at the nursing home. Dr Godwin isn't free till then."

"I want to be there."

"That suits me, if Godwin can be persuaded. It was all I could do to get myself invited, and I'm her lawyer."

"I think Godwin is sitting on something. There's a job that needs doing between now and eight. It's properly my job but this is your town and you can do it faster. Find out if Roy Bradshaw's alibi for Helen Haggerty's murder is waterproof and dustproof and antimagnetic."

Jerry sat up straight and used his forefinger to smudge his nose some more. "How should I go about it?"

"Bradshaw addressed an alumni banquet Friday evening. I want to know if he could have slipped out during one of the other speeches, or left in time to kill her. You have a right to any facts the sheriff's men and the pathologist can provide about time of death."

"I'll do my best," he said, pushing his chair back.

"One other thing, Jerry. Is there any word on the ballistics tests?"

"The rumor says they're still going on. The rumor doesn't say why. Do you suppose they're trying to fake something?"

"No, I don't. Ballistics experts don't go in for fakery."

I left him gathering up his transcripts and walked downtown to the Pacific Hotel. My bellhop had contacted Mrs Deloney's cab-driver, and told me in return for a second five that the two elderly ladies had checked in at the Surf House. I bought a drip-dry shirt and some underwear and socks and went back to my motel to shower and change. I needed that before I tackled Mrs Deloney again.

Someone was knocking as I stepped out of the shower, tapping ever so gently as if the door was fragile.

"Who's there?"

"Madge Gerhardi. Let me in."

"As soon as I'm dressed."

It took a little time. I had to pick the pins out of my new shirt, and my hands were jerking.

"*Please* let me in," the woman said at the door. "I don't want to be seen."

I pulled on my trousers and went to the door in my bare feet." She pressed in past me as if there was a storm at her back. Her garish blonde hair was windblown. She took hold of my hands with both of her clammy ones.

"The police are watching my house. I don't know if they followed me here or not. I came along the beach."

"Sit down," I said, and placed a chair for her. "I'm sure the police aren't after you. They're looking for your friend Begley-McGee."

"Don't call him that. It sounds as though you're making fun of him." It was an avowal of love.

"What do you want me to call him?"

"I still call him Chuck. A man has a right to change his name, after what they did to him, and what they're doing. Anyway, he's a writer, and writers use pen names."

"Okay, I'll call him Chuck. But you didn't come here to argue about a name."

She fingered her mouth, pushing her full lower lip from side to side. She wasn't wearing lipstick or any other make-up. Without it she looked younger and more innocent.

"Have you heard from Chuck?" I said.

She nodded almost imperceptibly, as if too great a movement would endanger him.

"Where is he, Madge?"

"In a safe place. I'm not to tell you where unless you promise not to tell the police."

"I promise."

Her pale eyes brightened. "He wants to talk to you."

"Did he say what about?"

"I didn't talk to him personally. A friend of his down at the harbor telephoned the message."

"I take it he's somewhere around the harbor then."

She gave me another of her barely visible nods.

"You've told me this much," I said. "You might as well tell me the rest. I'd give a lot for an interview with Chuck."

"And you won't lead the police to him?"

"Not if I can help it. Where is he, Madge?"

She screwed up her face and made the plunge: "He's on Mr Stevens's yacht, the *Revenant*."

"How did he get aboard her?"

"I'm not sure. He knew that Mr Stevens was racing her at Balboa over the weekend. I think he went there and surrendered to Mr Stevens."

I left Madge in my room. She didn't want to go out again by herself, or ride along with me. I took the waterfront boulevard to the harbour. While a few tugboats and tuna-fishers used its outer reaches, most of the boats moored at the slips or anchored within the long arm of the jetty were the private yachts and cruisers of weekend sailors.

On a Monday, not many of them were at sea, but I noticed a few white sails on the horizon. They were headed shoreward, like homing dreams.

A man in the harbormaster's glass-enclosed lookout pointed out Stevens's yacht to me. Though she rode at the far end of the outer slip, she was easy to spot because of her towering mast. I walked out along the floating dock to her.

Revenant was long and sleek, with a low streamlined cabin and a racing cockpit. Her varnish was smooth and clear, her brass was bright. She rocked ever so slightly on the enclosed water, like an animal trembling to run.

I stepped aboard and knocked on the hatch. No answer, but it opened when I pushed. I climbed down the short ladder and made my way past some short-wave radio equipment and a tiny galley smelling of burned coffee, into the sleeping quarters. An oval of sunlight from one of the ports, moving reciprocally with the motion of the yacht, fluttered against the bulkhead like a bright and living soul. I said to it:

"McGee?"

Something stirred in an upper bunk. A face appeared at eye level. It was a suitable face for the crew of a boat named *Revenant.* McGee had shaved off his beard, and the lower part of his face had a beard-shaped pallor. He looked older and thinner and much less sure of himself.

"Did you come here by yourself?" he whispered.

"Naturally I did."

"That means you don't think I'm guilty, either," he was reduced to such small momentary hopefulnesses.

"Who else doesn't think you're guilty?"

"Mr Stevens."

"Was this his idea?" I said, with a gesture that included McGee and myself.

"He didn't say I *shouldn't* talk to you."

"Okay, McGee, what's on your mind?"

He lay still watching me. His mouth was twitching, and his eyes held a kind of beseeching brightness. "I don't know where to start. I've been living in my thoughts for ten years – so long it hardly seems real. I know what happened to me but I don't know why. Ten years in the pen, with no chance of parole because I wouldn't admit that I was guilty. How could I? I was bum-rapped. And now they're getting ready to do it again."

He gripped the polished mahogany edge of the bunk. "I can't go back to 'Q', brother. I did ten years and it was *hard* time. There's no time as hard as the time you do for somebody else's mistake. God, but the days crawled. There weren't enough jobs to go round and half the time I had nothing to do but sit and think.

"I'll kill myself," he said, "before I let them send me back again."

He meant it, and I meant what I said in reply: "It won't happen, McGee. That's a promise."

"I only wish I could believe you. You get out of the habit of believing people. They don't believe you, you don't believe them."

"Who killed your wife?"

"I don't know."

"Who do you think killed her?"

"I'm not saying."

"You've gone to a lot of trouble, and taken quite a risk, to get me out here and tell me you're not saying. Let's go back to where it started, McGee. Why did your wife leave you?"

"I left her. We had been separated for months when she was killed. I wasn't even in Indian Springs that night, I was here in the Point."

"Why did you leave her?"

"Because she asked me to. We weren't getting along. We never did get along after I came back from the service. Constance and the kid spent the war years living with her sister, and she couldn't adjust to me after that. I admit I was a wild man for a while then. But her sister Alice promoted the trouble between us."

"Why?"

"She thought the marriage was a mistake. I guess she wanted Constance all to herself. I just got in the way."

"Did anybody else get in the way?"

"Not if Alice could help it."

I phrased my question more explicitly: "Was there another man in Constance's life?"

"Yeah. There was." He seemed ashamed, as if the infidelity had been his. "I've given it a lot of thought over the years, and I don't see much point in opening it up now. The guy had nothing to do with her death. I'm sure of that. He was crazy about her. He wouldn't hurt her."

"How do you know?"

"I talked to him about her, not long before she was killed. The kid told me what was going on between him and her."

"You mean your daughter Dolly?"

"That's right. Constance used to meet the guy every Saturday, when she brought Dolly in to see the doctor. On one of my visiting days with the kid – the last one we ever had together, in fact – she told me about those meetings. She was only eleven or twelve and she didn't grasp the full significance, but she knew something fishy was going on.

"Every Saturday afternoon Constance and the guy used to park her in a double-feature movie and go off by themselves someplace, probably some motel. Constance asked the kid to cover for her, and she did. The guy even gave her money to tell Alice that Constance went to those movies with her. I thought that was a lousy trick." McGee tried to warm over his old anger but he had suffered too much, and thought too much, to be able to. His face hung like a cold moon over the edge of the bunk.

"We might as well use his name," I said. "Was it Godwin?"

"Hell, no. It was Roy Bradshaw. He used to be a professor at the college." He added with a kind of mournful pride: "Now he's the Dean out there."

He wouldn't be for long, I thought; his sky was black with chickens coming home to roost.

"Bradshaw was one of Dr Godwin's patients," McGee was saying. "That's where he and Connie met, in Godwin's waiting-room. I think the doctor kind of encouraged the thing between them."

"What makes you think that?"

"Bradshaw told me himself the doctor said it was good for them, for their emotional health. It's a funny thing, I went to Bradshaw's house to get him to lay off Connie, even if I had to beat him up. But by the time he was finished talking he had me half-convinced that he and Connie were right, and I was wrong. I still don't know who was right and who was wrong. I know I never gave her any real happiness, after the first year. Maybe Bradshaw did."

"Is that why you didn't inject him into your trial?"

"That was one reason. Anyway, what was the use of fouling it up? It would only make me look worse." He paused. A deeper tone rose from a deeper level of his nature: "Besides, I loved her. I loved Connie. It was the one way I had to prove I loved her."

"Did you know that Bradshaw was married to another woman?"

"When?"

"For the last twenty years. He divorced her a few weeks ago."

McGee looked shocked. He'd been living on illusions for a long time, and I was threatening his sustenance. He pulled himself back into the bunk, almost out of sight.

"Her name was Letitia Macready – Letitia Macready Bradshaw. Have you ever heard of her?"

"No. How could he be married? He was living at home with his mother?"

"There are all kinds of marriages," I said. "He may not have seen his wife in years, and then again he may have. He may have had her living here in town, unknown to his mother or any of his friends. I suspect that was the case, judging from the lengths he went to cover up his divorce."

McGee said in a confused and shaken voice: "I don't see what it has to do with me."

"It may have a very great deal. If the Macready woman was in town ten years ago, she had a motive for killing your wife – a motive as strong as your own."

He didn't want to think about the woman. He was too used to thinking about himself. "I *had* no motive. I wouldn't hurt a hair of her head."

"You did, though, once or twice."

He was silent. All I could see of him was his wavy gray hair, like a dusty wig, and his large dishonest eyes trying to be honest:

"I hit her a couple of times, I admit it. I suffered the tortures of the damned afterward. You've got to understand, I used to get mean when I got plastered. That's why Connie sent me away, I don't blame her. I don't blame her for anything. I blame myself." He drew in a long breath and let it out slowly.

I offered him a cigarette, which he refused. I lit one for myself. The bright trembling patch of sunlight was climbing the bulkhead. It would soon be evening.

"So Bradshaw had a wife," McGee said. He had had time to absorb the information. "And he told me he intended to marry Connie."

"Maybe he did intend to. It would strengthen the woman's motive."

"You honestly think she did it?"

"She's a prime suspect. Bradshaw is another. He must have been a suspect to your daughter, too. She enrolled in his college and took a job in his household to check on him. Was that your idea, McGee?"

He shook his head.

"I don't understand her part in all this. She hasn't been much help in explaining it, either."

"I know," he said. "Dolly's done a lot of lying, starting away back when. But when a little kid lies you don't put the same construction on it as you would an adult."

"You're a forgiving man."

"Oh, no, I'm not. I went to her with anger in my heart that Sunday I saw her picture in the paper, with her husband. What right did she have to a happy marriage after what she did to me? That's what was on my mind."

"Did you tell her what was on your mind?"

"Yessir, I did. But my anger didn't last. She reminded me so of her mother in appearance. It was like going back twenty years to happier times, when we were first married. We had a real good year when I was in the Navy and Connie was pregnant, with her."

His mind kept veering away from his current troubles. I could hardly blame him, but I urged him back to them:

"You gave your daughter a hard time the other Sunday, didn't you?"

"I did at first. I admit that. I asked her why she lied about me in court. That was a legitimate question, wasn't it?"

"I should say so. What was her reaction?"

"She went into hysterics and said she wasn't lying, that she saw me with the gun and everything and heard me arguing with her mother. Which was false, and I told her so. I wasn't even in Indian Springs that night. That stopped her cold."

"Then what?"

"I asked her why she had lied about me." He licked his lips and said in a hushed voice: "I asked her if she shot her mother herself, maybe by accident, the way Alice kept that revolver lying around loose. It was a terrible question, but it had to come out. It's been on my mind for a long time."

"As long ago as your trial?"

"Yeah. Before that."

"And that's why you wouldn't let Stevens cross-examine her?"

"Yeah. I should have let him go ahead. I ended up cross-questioning her myself ten years later."

"What was the result?"

"More hysterics. She was laughing and crying at the same time. I never felt so sorry for anybody. She was as white as a sheet and the tears popped out of her eyes and ran down her face. Her tears looked so *pure*."

"What did she say?"

"She said she didn't do it, naturally."

"Could she have? Did she know how to handle a gun?"

"A little. I gave her a little training, and so did Alice. It doesn't take much gun-handling to pull a trigger, especially by accident."

"You still think it could have happened that way?"

"I don't know. It's mainly what I wanted to talk to you about."

These words seemed to release him from an obscure bondage. He climbed down out of the upper bunk and stood facing me in the narrow aisle. He had on a seaman's black turtleneck, levis, and rubber-soled deck shoes.

"You're in a position to go and talk to her," he said. "I'm not. Mr Stevens won't. But you can go and ask her what really happened."

"She may not know."

"I realize that. She got pretty mixed up the other Sunday. God knows I wasn't trying to mix her up. I only asked her some questions. But she didn't seem to know the difference between what happened and what she said in court.

"That story she told in court – did she definitely admit she made it up?"

"She made it up with a lot of help from Alice. I can imagine how it went. 'This is the way it happened, isn't it?' Alice would say. 'You saw your old man with the gun, didn't you?' And after a while the kid had her story laid out for her."

"Would Alice deliberately try to frame you?"

"She wouldn't put it that way to herself. She'd know for a fact I was guilty. All she was doing was making sure I got punished for my crime. She probably fed the kid her lines without knowing she was faking evidence. My dear sister-in-law was always out to get me, anyway."

"Was she out to get Connie, too?"

"Connie? She doted on Connie. Alice was more like her mother than her sister. There was fourteen-fifteen years' difference in their ages."

"You said she wanted Connie to herself. Her feelings for Connie could have changed if she found out about Bradshaw."

"Not *that* much. Anyway, who would tell her?"

"Your daughter might have. If she told you, she'd tell Alice."

McGee shook his head. "You're really reaching."

"I have to. This is a deep case, and I can't see the bottom of it yet. Did Alice ever live in Boston, do you know?"

"I think she always lived here. She's a Native Daughter. I'm a native son, but nobody ever gave me a medal for it."

"Even Native Daughters have been known to go to Boston. Did Alice ever go on the stage, or marry a man named Macready, or dye her hair red?"

"None of those things sound like Alice."

I thought of her pink fantastic bedroom, and wondered.

"They sound more," McGee was saying, and then he stopped. He was silent for a watching moment. "I'll take that cigarette you offered me."

I gave him a cigarette and lighted it. "What were you going to say?"

"Nothing. I must have been thinking aloud."

"Who were you thinking about?"

Nobody you know. Forget it, eh?"

"Come on, McGee. You're supposed to be leveling with me."

"I still have a right to my private thoughts. It kept me alive in prison."

"You're out of prison now. Don't you want to stay out?"

"Not if somebody else has to go in."

"Sucker," I said. "Who are you covering for now?"

"Nobody."

"Madge Gerhardi?"

"You must be off your rocker."

I couldn't get anything more out of him. The long slow weight of prison forces men into unusual shapes. McGee had become a sort of twisted saint.

XXVIII

He was about to be given another turn of the screw. When I climbed out into the cockpit I saw three men approaching along the floating dock. Their bodies, their hatted heads, were dark as iron against the exploding sunset.

One of them showed me a deputy's badge and a gun, which he held on me while the others went below. I heard McGee cry out once. He scrambled up through the hatch with blue handcuffs on his wrists and a blue gun at his back. The single look he gave me was full of fear and loathing.

They didn't handcuff me, but they made me ride to the courthouse with McGee in the screened rear compartment of the Sheriff's car. I tried to talk to him. He wouldn't speak to me or look in my direction. He believed I had turned him in, and perhaps I had without intending to.

I sat under guard outside the interrogation room while they questioned him in tones that rose and fell and growled and palavered and yelled and threatened and promised and refused and wheedled. Sheriff Crane arrived, looking tired but important. He stood over me smiling, with his belly thrust out.

"Your friend's in real trouble now."

"He's been in real trouble for the last ten years. You ought to know, you helped to cook it for him."

The veins in his cheeks lit up like intricate little networks of infra-red tubing. He leaned toward me spewing martini-scented words:

"I could put you in jail for loose talk like that. You know where your friend is going? He's going all the way to the green room this time.

"He wouldn't be the first innocent man who was gassed."

"Innocent? McGee's a mass murderer, and we've got the evidence to prove it. It took my experts all day to nail it down: The bullet in the Haggerty corpse came from the same gun as the bullet we found in McGee's wife – the same gun he stole from Alice Jenks in Indian Springs."

I'd succeeded in provoking the Sheriff into an indiscretion. I tried for another. "You have no proof he stole it. You have no proof he fired it either time. Where's he been keeping the gun for the last ten years?"

"He cached it someplace, maybe on Stevens's boat. Or maybe an accomplice kept it for him."

"Then he hid it in his daughter's bed to frame her?"

"That's the kind of man he is."

"Nuts!"

"Don't talk to me like that!" He menaced me with the cannonball of his belly.

"Don't talk like that to the Sheriff," the guard said.

"I don't know of any law against the use of the word 'nuts'. And incidentally I wasn't violating anything in the California Code when I went out to the yacht to talk to McGee. I'm cooperating with a local attorney in this investigation and I have a right to get my information where I can and keep it confidential."

"How did you know he was there?"

"I got a tip."

"From Stevens?"

"Not from Stevens. You and I could trade information, Sheriff. How did *you* know he was there?"

"I don't make deals with suspects."

"What do you suspect me of? Illegal use of the word 'nuts'?"

"It isn't so funny. You were taken with McGee. I have a right to hold you."

"I have a right to call an attorney. Try kicking my rights around and see where it gets you. I have friends in Sacramento."

They didn't include the Attorney General or anybody close to him, but I liked the sound of the phrase. Sheriff Crane did not. He was half a politician, and like most of his kind he was an insecure man. He said after a moment's thought:

"You can make your call."

The Sheriff went into the interrogation room – I caught a glimpse of McGee hunched gray-faced under a light – and added his voice to the difficult harmony there. My guard took me into a small adjoining room and left me by myself with a telephone. I used it to call Jerry Marks. He was about to leave for his appointment with Dr Godwin and Dolly, but he said he'd come right over to the courthouse and bring Gil Stevens with him if Stevens was available.

They arrived together in less than fifteen minites. Stevens shot me a glance from under the broken white wings of his hair. It was a covert and complex glance which seemed to mean that for the record we were strangers. I suspected the old lawyer had advised McGee to talk to me, and probably set up the interview. I was in a position to use McGee's facts in ways that he couldn't.

With soft threats of *habeas corpus* proceedings, Jerry Marks sprung me out. Stevens remained behind with the Sheriff and a Deputy D.A. It was going to take longer to spring his client.

A moon like a fallen fruit reversing gravity was hoisting itself above the rooftops. It was huge and slightly squashed.

"Pretty," Jerry said in the parking-lot.

"It looks like a rotten orange to me."

"Ugliness is in the eye of the beholder. I learned that at my mother's knee and other low joints, as a well-known statesman said." Jerry always felt good when he tried something he learned in law school, and it worked. He walked to his car swiftly, on the balls of his feet, and made the engine roar. "We're late for our appointment with Godwin."

"Did you have time to check on Bradshaw's alibi?"

"I did. It seems to be impregnable." He gave me the details as we drove across town. "Judging by temperature loss, rate of blood coagulation, and so on, the Deputy Coroner places the time of Miss Haggerty's death as no later than eight-thirty. From about seven until about nine-thirty Dean Bradshaw was sitting, or standing up talking, in front of over a hundred witnesses. I talked to three of them, three alumni picked more or less at random, and they all agreed he didn't leave the speaker's table during that period. Which lets him out."

"Apparently it does."

"You sound disappointed, Lew."

"I'm partly that, and partly relieved. I rather like Bradshaw. But I was pretty certain he was our man."

In the remaining minutes before we reached the nursing home, I told him briefly what I'd learned from McGee, and from the Sheriff. Jerry whistled, but made no other comment.

Dr Godwin opened the door for us. He wore a clean white smock and an aggrieved expression.

"You're late, Mr Marks. I was just about ready to call the whole thing off."

"We had a little emergency. Thomas McGee was arrested about seven o'clock tonight. Mr Archer happened to be with him, and he was arrested, also."

Godwin turned to me. "*You* were with McGee?"

"He sent for me, and he talked. I'm looking forward to comparing his story with his daughter's."

"I'm afraid you aren't – ah – co-opted to this session." Godwin said with some embarrassment. "As I pointed out to you before, you don't have professional immunity."

"I do if I'm acting on Mr Marks's instructions. Which I am."

"Mr Archer is correct, on both counts," Jerry said.

Godwin let us in reluctantly. We were outsiders, interlopers in his shadowy kingdom. I had lost some of my confidence in his benevolent despotism, but I kept to to myself for the present.

He took us to the examination room where Dolly was waiting. She was sitting on the end of a padded table, wearing a sleeveless white hospital gown. Alex stood in front of her, holding both her hands. His eyes stayed on her face, hungry and worshipping, as if she was the priestess or the goddess of a strange one-member cult.

Her hair was shining and smooth. Her face was composed. Only her eyes had a sullen restlessness and inwardness. They moved across me and failed to give any sign of recognition.

Godwin touched her shoulder. "Are you ready, Dolly?"

"I suppose I am."

She lay back on the padded table. Alex held on to one of her hands.

"You can stay if you like, Mr Kincaid. It might be easier if you didn't."

"Not for me," the girl said. "I feel safer when he's with me. I want Alex to know all about – everything."

"Yes, I want to stay."

Godwin filled a hypodermic needle, inserted it in her arm, and taped it to the white skin. He told her to count backward from one hundred. At ninety-six the tension left her body and an inner light left her face. It flowed back in a diffused form when the doctor spoke to her:

"Do you hear me, Dolly?"

"I hear you," she murmured.

"Speak louder. I can't hear you."

"I hear you," she repeated, her voice was faintly slurred.

"Who am I?"

"Dr Godwin."

"Do you remember when you were a little girl you used to come and visit me in my office?"

"I remember."

"Who used to bring you to see me?"

"Mommy did. She used to bring me in in Aunt Alice's car."

"Where were you living then?"

"In Indian Springs, in Aunt Alice's house."

"And Mommy was living there, too?"

"Mommy was living there, too. She lived there, too."

She was flushed, and talking like a drunken child. The doctor turned to Jerry Marks with a handing-over gesture. Jerry's dark eyes were mournful.

"Do you remember a certain night," he said, "when your Mommy was killed?"

"I remember. Who are you?"

"I'm Jerry Marks, your lawyer. It's all right to talk to me."

"It's all right," Alex said.

The girl looked up at Jerry sleepily. "What do you want me to tell you?"

"Just the truth. It doesn't matter what I want, or anybody else. Just tell me what you remember."

"I'll try.

"Did you hear the gun go off?"

"I heard it." She screwed up her face as if she was hearing it now. "I am – it frightened me."

"Did you see anyone?"

"I didn't go downstairs right away. I was scared."

"Did you see anyone out the window?"

"No. I heard a car drive away. Before that I heard her running."

"You heard *who* running?" Jerry said.

"I thought it was Aunt Alice at first, when she was talking to Mommy at the door. But it couldn't have been Aunt Alice. She wouldn't shoot Mommy. Besides, her gun was missing."

"How do you know?"

"She said I took it from her room. She spanked me with a hairbrush for stealing it."

"When did she spank you?"

"Sunday night, when she came home from church. Mommy said she had no right to spank me. Aunt Alice asked Mommy if *she* took the gun."

"Did she?"

"She didn't say – not while I was there. They sent me to bed."

"*Did* you take the gun?"

"No. I never touched it. I was afraid of it."

"Why?"

"I was afraid of Aunt Alice."

She was rosy and sweating. She tried to struggle up onto her elbows. The doctor eased her back into her supine position, and made an adjustment to the needle. The girl relaxed again, and Jerry said:

"Was it Aunt Alice talking to your Mommy at the door?"

"I thought it was at first. It sounded like her. She had a big scary voice. But it couldn't have been Aunt Alice."

"Why couldn't it?"

"It just couldn't."

She turned her head in a listening attitude. A lock of hair fell over her half-closed eyes. Alex pushed it back with a gentle hand. She said:

"The lady at the door said it had to be true, about Mommy and Mr Bradshaw. She said she got it from Daddy's own lips, and Daddy got it from me. And then she shot my Mommy and ran away."

There was silence in the room, except for the girl's heavy breathing. A tear as slow as honey was exuded from the corner of one eye. It fell down her temple. Alex wiped the blue-veined hollow with his handkerchief. Jerry leaned across her from the other side of the table:

"Why did you say your Daddy shot your Mommy?"

"Aunt Alice wanted me to. She didn't say so, but I could tell. And I was afraid she'd think that I did it. She spanked me for taking the gun, and I *didn't* take it. I said it was Daddy. She made me say it over and over and over."

There were more tears than one now. Tears for the child she had been, frightened and lying, and tears for the woman she was painfully becoming. Alex wiped her eyes. He looked close to tears himself.

"Why," I said, "did you try to tell us that you killed your mother?"

"Who are you?"

"I'm Alex's friend Lew Archer."

"That's right," Alex said.

She lifted her head and let if fall back. "I forgot what you asked me."

"Why did you say you killed your mother?"

"Because it was all my fault. I told my Daddy about her and

Mr Bradshaw, and that's what started everything.

"How do you know?"

"The lady at the door said so. She came to shoot Mommy because of what Daddy told her."

"Do you know who she was?"

"No."

"Was it your Aunt Alice?"

"No."

"Was it anyone you knew?"

"No."

"Did your mother know her?"

"I don't know. Maybe she did."

"Did she talk as if she knew her?"

"She called her by name."

"What name?"

"Tish. She called her Tish. I could tell Mommy didn't like her though. She was afraid of her, too."

"Why haven't you ever told anyone this before?"

"Because it was all my fault."

"It wasn't," Alex said. "You were only a child. You weren't responsible for what the adults did."

Godwin shushed him with his finger to his lips. Dolly rolled her head from side to side:

"It was all my fault."

"This has gone on long enough," Godwin whispered to Jerry. "She's made some gains. I want to have a chance to consolidate them."

"But we haven't even got to the Haggerty case."

"Make it short then." Godwin said to the girl: "Dolly, are you willing to talk about last Friday night?"

"Not about finding her." She screwed up her face until her eyes were hidden.

"You needn't go into the details of finding the body," Jerry said. "But what were you doing there?"

"I wanted to talk to Helen. I often walked up the hill to talk to her. We were friends."

"How did that happen to be?"

"I ingratiated myself with Helen," she said with queer blank candor. "I thought at first she might be the lady – the woman who shot my mother. The rumor was going round the campus that she was close to Dean Bradshaw."

"And you were on the campus to find that woman?"

"Yes. But it wasn't Helen. I found out she was new in town, and she told me herself there was nothing between her and Bradshaw. I had no right to drag her into this."

"How did you drag her in?"

"I told her everything, about my mother and Bradshaw and the murder and the woman at the door. Helen was killed because she knew too much."

"That may be," I said, "but she didn't learn it from you."

"She did! I told her everything."

Godwin pulled at my sleeve. "Don't argue with her. She's coming out of it fast, but her mind is still operating below the conscious level."

"Did Helen ask you questions?" I said to the girl.

"Yes. She asked me questions."

"Then you didn't force the information on her."

"No. She wanted to know."

"What did she want to know?"

"All about Dean Bradshaw and my mother."

"Did she say why?"

"She wanted to help me in my crusade. I went on a sort of crusade after I talked to Daddy in the hotel. A children's crusade." Her giggle turned into a sob before it left her throat. "The only thing it accomplished was the death of my good friend Helen. And when I found her body –"

Her eyes opened wide. Then her mouth opened wide. Her body went rigid, as if it was imitating the rigor of the dead. She stayed like that for fifteen or twenty seconds.

"It was like finding Mommy again," she said in a small voice, and came fully awake. "Is it all right?"

"It's all right," Alex said.

He helped her up to a sitting position. She leaned on him, her hair mantling his shoulder. A few minutes later, still leaning on him, she walked across the hallway to her room. They walked like husband and wife.

Godwin closed the door of the examination room. "I hope you gentlemen got what you wanted," he said with some distaste.

"She talked very freely," Jerry said. The experience had left him drained.

"It was no accident. I've been preparing her for the last three days. Pentothal, as I've told you before, is no guarantee of truth. If a patient is determined to lie, the drug can't stop him."

"Are you implying she wasn't telling the truth?"

"No. I believe she was, so far as she knows the truth. My problem now is to enlarge her awareness and make it fully conscious. If you gentlemen will excuse me?"

"Wait a minute," I said. "You can spare me a minute, Doctor. I've spent three days and a lot of Kincaid's money developing facts that you already had in your possession."

"Have you indeed?" he said coldly.

"I have indeed. You could have saved me a good deal of work by filling me in on Bradshaw's affair with Constance McGee."

"I'm afraid I don't exist for the purpose of saving detectives work. There's a question of ethics involved here which you probably wouldn't understand. Mr Marks probably would."

"I don't understand the issue," Jerry said, but he edged between us as if he expected trouble. He touched my shoulder. "Let's get out of here, Lew, and let the doctor get about his business. He's cooperated beautifully and you know it."

"Who with? Bradshaw?"

Godwin's face turned pale. "My first duty is to my patients."

"Even when they murder people?"

"Even then. But I know Roy Bradshaw intimately and I can assure you he's incapable of killing anyone. Certainly he didn't kill Constance McGee. He was passionately in love with her."

"Passion can cut two ways."

"He didn't kill her."

"A couple of days ago you were telling me McGee did. You can be mistaken, doctor."

"I know that, but not about Roy Bradshaw. The man has lived a tragic life."

"Tell me about it."

"He'll have to tell you himself. I'm not a junior G-man, Mr Archer. I'm a doctor."

"What about the woman he recently divorced, Tish or Letitia? Do you know her?"

He looked at me without speaking. There was sad knowledge in his eyes. "You'll have to ask Roy about her," he said finally.

XXIX

On his way to the courthouse to question McGee, Jerry dropped me at the harbor, where my car had been left sitting. The moon was higher now, and had regained its proper shape and color. Its light converted the yachts in the slips into a ghostly fleet of Flying Dutchmen.

I went back to my motel to talk to Madge Gerhardi. She had evaporated, along with the rest of the whisky in my pint bottle. I sat on the edge of the bed and tried her number and got no answer.

I called the Bradshaw house. Old Mrs Bradshaw seemed to have taken up a permanent position beside the telephone. She picked up the receiver on the first ring and quavered into it:

"Who is that, please?"

"It's only Archer. Roy hasn't come home, has he?"

"No, and I'm worried about him, deeply worried. I haven't seen him or heard from him since early Saturday morning. I've been calling his friends –"

"I wouldn't do that, Mrs Bradshaw."

"I have to do something."

"There are times when it's better to do nothing. Keep still and wait."

"I can't. You're telling me there's something terribly wrong, aren't you?"

"I think you know it."

"Does it have to do with that dreadful woman – that Macready woman?"

"Yes. We have to find out where she is. I'm pretty sure your son could tell me, but he's made himself unavailable. Are you sure you haven't seen the woman since Boston?"

"I'm quite certain. I saw her only once, when she came to me for money."

"Can you describe her for me?"

"I thought I had."

"In more detail, please. It's very important."

She paused to think. I could hear her breathing over the line, a faint rhythmic huskiness. "Well, she was quite a large woman, taller than I, red-haired. She wore her hair bobbed. She had quite a good figure, rather lush, and quite good features, too – a kind of brassy good looks. And she had green eyes, murky green eyes which I didn't like at all. She wore very heavy makeup, more appropriate for the stage than the street, and she was hideously overdressed."

"What was she wearing?"

"It hardly seems relevant, after twenty years. But she had on a leopardskin – an imitation leopardskin coat, as I recall, and under it something striped. Sheer hose, with runs in them. Ridiculously high heels. A good deal of costume jewelry."

"How did she talk?"

"Like a woman of the streets. A greedy, pushing, lustful woman." The moral indignation in her voice hardly surprised me. She had almost lost Roy to the woman, and might yet.

"Would you know her if you saw her again, in different clothes, with her hair perhaps a different color?"

"I think so, if I had a chance to study her."

"You'll have that chance when we find her."

I was thinking that the color of a woman's eyes was harder to change than her hair. The only green-eyed woman connected with the case was Laura Sutherland. She had a conspicuously good figure and good features, but nothing else that seemed to jibe with the description of the Macready woman. Still, she might have changed. I'd seen other women change unrecognizably in half the time.

"You know Laura Sutherland, Mrs Bradshaw?"

"I know her slightly."

"Does she resemble the Macready woman?"

"Why do you ask that?" she said on a rising note. "Do you suspect Laura?"

"I wouldn't go that far. But you haven't answered my question."

"She couldn't possibly be the same woman. She's a wholly different type."

"What about her basic physical characteristics?"

"I suppose there is some resemblance," she said dubiously. "Roy has always been attracted to women who are obviously mammals."

And obviously mother figures, I thought. "I have to ask you one other question, a more personal question."

"Yes?" She seemed to be bracing herself for a blow.

"I suppose you're aware that Roy was Dr Godwin's patient."

"Dr Godwin's patient? I don't believe it. He wouldn't go behind my back." For all her half-cynical insight into his nature she seemed to know very little about him.

"Dr Godwin says he did, apparently for some years."

"There must be a mistake. Roy has nothing the matter with his mind." There was a vibrating silence. "Has he?"

"I was going to ask you, but I'm sorry I brought it up. Take it easy, Mrs Bradshaw."

"How can I, with my boy in jeopardy?"

She wanted to hold me on the line. Siphoning comfort into her frightened old ears, but I said good night and hung up. One suspect had been eliminated: Madge Gerhardi: the description didn't fit her and never could have. Laura was still in the running.

It wouldn't make sense, of course, for Bradshaw to divorce her and remarry her immediately. But I had only Bradshaw's word for his recent marriage to Laura. I was gradually realizing that his word stretched like an elastic band, and was as easily broken. I looked up Laura's address – she lived in College Heights – and was copying it into my notebook when the phone rang.

It was Jerry Marks. McGee denied having told the woman Tish or anyone else about the affair between Bradshaw and his wife. The only one he had discussed the subject with was Bradshaw.

"Bradshaw may have told the woman himself," I said. "Or possibly the woman overheard McGee."

"Possibly, but hardly likely. McGee says his conversation with Bradshaw took place in Bradshaw's house."

"He could have had the woman there while his mother was away."

"You think she lives around here?"

"Somewhere in Southern California, anyway. I believe Bradshaw's been leading a split-level life with her, and that she's responsible for both the McGee and the Haggarty killings. I just got an improved description of her from Bradshaw's mother. Better pass it along to the police. Do you have something to write on?"

"Yes. I'm sitting at the Sheriff's desk."

I recited Letitia Macready's description, but I didn't say anything about Laura Sutherland. I wanted to talk to her myself.

College Heights was a detached suburb on the far side of the campus from the city. It was a hodgepodge of tract houses and fraternity houses, duplexes and apartment buildings, interspersed with vacant lots sprouting for-sale signs. A boy with a guitar in one of the lighted fraternity houses was singing that this land belongs to you and me.

Laura lived in one of the better apartments, a garden apartment built around an open court with a swimming-pool. A shirt-sleeved man slapping mosquitoes in a deck chair by the pool pointed out her door to me and mentioned with some complacency that he owned the place.

"Is anybody with her?"

"I don't think so. She did have a visitor, but he went home."

"Who was he?"

The man peered up at my face. "That's her private business, mister."

"I expect it was Dean Bradshaw, from the college."

"If you know, why ask?"

I walked to the back of the court and knocked on her door. She opened it on a chain. Her face had lost a good deal of its rosy beauty. She had on a dark suit, as if she was in mourning.

"What do you want? It's late."

"Too late for us to have a talk, Mrs Bradshaw?"

"I'm not Mrs Bradshaw," she said without much conviction. "I'm not married."

"Roy said you were last night. Which one of you is lying?"

"Please, my landlord's out there." She unchained the door and stepped back out of the widening light. "Come inside if you must."

She closed the door and chained it behind me. I was looking at her instead of the room, but I had the impression of a tastefully decorated place where shaded lights gleamed peacefully on wooden and ceramic surfaces. I was searching her face for traces of a past wholly different from her present. There were no visible traces, no cruel lines or pouches of dissipation. But she hadn't much peace in her. She was watching me as though I was a burglar.

"What are you afraid of?"

"I'm not afraid," she said in a frightened voice. She tried to control it with her hand at her throat. "I resent your barging into my home and making personal remarks."

"You invited me in, more of less."

"Only because you were talking indiscreetly."

"I called you by your married name. What's your objection to it?"

"I *have* no objection," she said with a wan smile. "I'm very proud of it. But my husband and I are keeping it a secret."

"A secret from Letitia Macready?"

She showed no particular reaction to the name. I'd already given up on the idea that it could be hers. No matter how well preserved her body or her skin might be, she was clearly too young. When Bradshaw married Letitia, Laura couldn't have been more than a girl in her teens.

"Letitia who?" she said.

"Letitia Macready. She's also known as Tish."

"I have no idea who you're talking about."

"I'll tell you if you really want to know. May I sit down?"

"Please do," she said without much warmth. I was the messenger who brought bad tidings, the kind they used to kill in the old days.

I sat on a soft leather hassock with my back against the wall. She remained standing.

"You're in love with Roy Bradshaw, aren't you?"

"I wouldn't have married him if I weren't."

"Just when did you marry him?"

"Two weeks ago last Saturday, September the tenth." A little color returned to her cheeks with the memory of the day. "He'd just got back from his European tour. We decided to go to Reno on the spur of the moment."

"Had you spent some time with him there earlier in the summer?"

She frowned in a puzzled way, and shook her head.

"Whose idea was it to go to Reno?"

"Roy's of course, but I was willing. I've been willing for some time," she added in a spurt of candor.

"What held up the marriage?"

"It wasn't held *up*, exactly. We postponed it, for various reasons. Mrs Bradshaw is a very possessive mother, and Roy has nothing of his own except his salary. It may sound mercenary –" She paused in some embarrassment, and tried to think of a better way to phrase it.

"How old is his mother?"

"Somewhere in her sixties. Why?"

"She's a vigorous woman, in spite of her infirmities. She may be around for a long time yet."

Her eyes flashed with some of their fine old iceberg fire. "We're not waiting for her to die, if that's what you think. We're simply waiting for the psychological moment. Roy hopes to persuade her to take a more personal view of – of me. In the meantime –" She broke off, and looked at me distrustfully. "But none of this is any concern of yours. You promised to tell me about the Macready person, whoever she is. Tish Macready? The name sounds fictitious."

"I assure you the woman isn't. Your husband divorced her in Reno shortly before he married you."

She moved to a chair and sat down very suddenly, as if her legs had lost their strength. "I don't believe it. Roy has never been married before."

"He has, though. Even his mother admitted it, after a struggle. It was an unfortunate marriage, contracted when he was a student at Harvard. But he waited until this summer to end it. He spent part of July and all of August establishing residence in Nevada."

"Now I know you're mistaken, Roy was in Europe all that time."

"I suppose you have letters and postcards to prove it?"

"Yes I do," she said with a relieved smile.

She went into another room and came back with a handful of mail tied with a red ribbon. I riffled through the postcards and put them in chronological order: Tower of London (postmarked London, July 18), Bodleian Library (Oxford, July 21), and so on down to the view of the English Gardens (Munich, August 25). Bradshaw had written on the back of this last card:

Dear Laura:

Yesterday I visited Hitler's eyrie at Berchtesgaden – a beautiful setting made grim by its associations – and today, by way of contrast, I took a bus to Oberammergau, where the Passion Play is performed. I was struck by the almost Biblical simplicity of the villagers. This whole Bavarian countryside is studded with the most stunning little churches. How I wish you could enjoy them with me! I'm sorry to hear that your summer has turned out to be a lonely one. Well, the summer will soon be over and I for one will be happy to turn my back on the splendors of Europe and come home. All my love.

Roy

I sat and reread the incredible message. It was almost word by word the same as the one Mrs Bradshaw had shown me. I tried to put myself in Bradshaw's place, to understand his motive. But I couldn't imagine what helpless division in a man's nature, what weary self-mockery or self-use, would make him send identical lying postcards to his mother and his fiancée.

"What's the matter?" Laura said.

"Merely everything."

I gave her back her documents. She handled them lovingly. "Don't try to tell me Roy didn't write these. They're in his writing and his style."

"He wrote them in Reno," I said, "and shipped them for remailing to a friend or accomplice who was traveling in Europe."

"Do you *know* this?"

"I'm afraid I do. Can you think of any friend of his who might have helped him?"

She bit her lower lip. "Dr Godwin spent the late summer traveling in Europe. He and Roy are very close. In fact Roy was his patient for a long time."

"What was Godwin treating him for?"

"We haven't discussed it, really, but I expect it had something to do with his excessive – his excessive dependence on his mother." A slow angry flush mounted from her neck to her cheekbones. She turned away from the subject. "But why would two grown men collaborate in such a silly letter-writing game?"

"It isn't clear. Your husband's professional ambitions probably enter into it. He obviously didn't want anyone to know about his previous, bad marriage, or his divorce, and he went to great lengths to keep everything quiet. He got off a similar set of European post-cards and letters to his mother. He may have sent a third set to Letitia."

"Who is she? *Where* is she?"

"I think she's here in town, or was as recently as last Friday night. She's very likely been here for the last ten years. I'm surprised your husband never gave it away, even to someone as close as you."

She was still standing over me, and I looked up into her face. Her eyes were heavy. She shook her head.

"Or maybe is isn't so surprising. He's very good at deceiving people, living on several levels, maybe deceiving himself to a certain extent. Mother's boys get that way sometimes. They need their little escape hatches from the hot-house."

Her bosom rose. "He isn't a mother's boy. He may have had a problem when he was younger, but now he's a virile man, and I *know* he loves me. There must be a reason for all this." She looked down at the cards and letters in her hand.

"I'm sure there is. I suspect the reason has to do with our two murders. Tish Macready is the leading suspect for both of them."

"*Two* murders?"

"Actually there have been three, spaced over a period of twenty-two years: Helen Haggerty on Friday night, Constance McGee ten years ago, Luke Deloney in Illinois before the war."

"Deloney?"

"Luke Deloney. You wouldn't know about him, but I think Tish Macready does."

"Is he connected with the Mrs Deloney at the Surf House?"

"She's his widow. You know her?"

"Not personally. But Roy was talking to her on the telepohone shortly before he left here."

"What did he say?"

"Simply that he was coming over to see her. I asked him who she was, but he was in too great a hurry to explain."

I got up. "If you'll excuse me, I'll see if I can catch him at the hotel. I've been trying to catch him all day."

"He was here, with me." She smiled slightly, involuntarily, but her eyes were confused. "Please don't tell him I told you. Don't tell him I told you anything."

"I'll try, but it may come out."

I moved to the door and tried to open it. The chain delayed my exit.

"Wait," she said behind me. "I've remembered something – something he wrote in a book of poems he lent me."

"What did he write?"

"Her name."

She started into the other room. Her hip bumped the door-frame, and Bradshaw's cards and letters fell from her hands. She didn't pause to pick them up.

She returned with an open book and thrust it at me a little blindly. It was a well-worn copy of Yeats's *Collected Poems*, open to the poem "Among School Children". The first four lines of the fourth stanza were underlined in pencil, and Bradshaw had written in the margin beside them the single word, "Tish".

I read the four lines to myself:

> Her present image floats into the mind –
> Did Quattrocento finger fashion it
> Hollow of cheek as though it drank the wind
> And took a mess of shadows for its meat?

I wasn't certain what they meant, and said so.

Laura answered bitterly: "It means that Roy still loves her. Yeats was writing about Maud Gonne – the woman he loved all his life. Roy may even have lent me the Yeats to let me know about Tish. He's very subtle."

"He probably wrote her name there long ago, and forgot about it. If he still loved her, he wouldn't have divorced her and married you. I have to warn you, though, that your marriage may not be legal."

"Not legal?" She was a conventional woman, and the possibility jarred her. "But we were married in Reno by a judge."

"His divorce from Tish," I said, "is probably voidable. I gather she wasn't properly informed of Bradshaw's action. Which means that under California law he's still married to her. If she wants it that way."

Shaking her head, she took the book of poems from my hands and tossed it with some violence into a chair. A piece of paper fluttered from between the leaves. I picked it up from the floor.

It was another poem, in Bradshaw's handwriting:

TO LAURA

If light were dark
And dark were light,
Moon a black hole
In the blaze of night,

A raven's wing
As bright as tin,
then you, my love,
Would be darker than sin.

At breakfast I had read the same poem aloud to Arnie and Phyllis, It had been printed twenty-odd years ago in the *Bridgeton Blazer,* over the initials G.R.B. I had a gestalt, and Bridgeton and Pacific Point came together in a roaring traffic of time. G.R.B. George Roy Bradshaw.

"When did he write this peom to you, Laura?"

"Last spring, when he lent me the Yeats."

I left her reading it over to herself, trying to recapture the spring.

XXX

PASSING THROUGH the lobby of the Surf House, I noticed Helen's mother sitting by herself in a far corner. She was deep in thought and she didn't look up until I spoke:

"You're sitting up late, Mrs Hoffman."

"I don't have much choice," she said resentfully. "I'm supposed to be sharing a cottage with Mrs Deloney, and it was entirely her idea. But she put me out so she can entertain her friend in private."

"You mean Roy Bradshaw?"

"That's what he calls himself now. I knew George Bradshaw

when he was glad to be given a good hot meal, and I served him more than one in my own kitchen."

I pulled up a chair beside hers. "All this adds up to an interesting coincidence."

"I think it does, too. But I'm not supposed to talk about it."

"Who says so?"

"Mrs Deloney."

"Does she tell you what to do?"

"No, but it was nice of her to take me out of that crummy room in the Pacific Hotel and –" She paused, considering.

"And stash you in the lobby here?"

"It's only temporary."

"So is life. Are you and your husband going to take orders from people like the Deloneys until the day you die? You get nothing out of it, you know, except the privilege of being pushed around."

"Nobody pushes Earl around," she said defensively. "You leave Earl out of this."

"Have you heard from him?"

"I haven't, and I'm worried about Earl. I tried to phone home two nights in a row, and nobody answered. I'm afraid he's drinking."

"He's in the hospital," I said.

"Is he sick?"

"He made himself sick with too much whisky."

"How do you know that?"

"I helped to get him to the hospital. I was in Bridgeton yesterday morning. Your husband talked to me, quite freely toward the end. He admitted Luke Deloney had been murdered but he had orders from the top to let it go as an accident."

Her eyes darted around the lobby, shyly and shamefully. There was no one in sight but the night clerk and a couple who didn't look married renting a room from him. But Mrs Hoffman was as nervous as a cricket on a crowded floor.

"You might as well tell me what you know," I said. "Let me buy you a cup of coffee."

"I'd be up all night."

"A cup of cocoa then.

"Cocoa sounds good."

We went into the coffee shop. Several orchestra members in

mauve jackets were drinking coffee at the counter and complaining in the language of their tribe about the pay. I sat in a booth facing Mrs Hoffman and the plate glass door, so that I could see Bradshaw if he came out through the lobby.

"How did you come to know Bradshaw, Mrs Hoffman?"

"Helen brought him home from City College. I think she was stuck on him for a while, but I could see that he wasn't stuck on her. They were more friends. They had interests in common."

"Like poetry?"

"Like poetry and play-acting. Helen said he was very talented for a boy his age, but he was having a hard time staying in college. We wangled him a part-time job running the elevator in the apartments. All it paid was five a week, but he was glad to have it. He was as thin as a rake and as poor as Job's turkey when we knew him. He claimed he came from a wealthy family in Boston, that he ran away from his freshman year at Harvard to be on his own. I never really believed him at the time – I thought he was maybe ashamed of his folks and putting on the dog – but I guess it was true after all. They tell me his mother is loaded." She gave me a questioning look.

"Yes. I know her."

"Why would a young fellow run away from all that money? I spent most of my own life trying to get a little to stick to my fingers."

"Money usually has strings atached to it."

I didn't go into a fuller explanation. The waitress brought Mrs Hoffman's cocoa and my coffee. I said when she had retreated behind the counter:

"Have you ever known a woman named Macready? Letitia O. Macready?"

Mrs Hoffman's hand fumbled with her cup and spilled some brown liquid in the saucer. I was fleetingly conscious that her hair was dyed an unlikely shade of red and that she might once have been a handsome woman with a good figure and a gaudy taste in clothes. But she couldn't be Tish Macready. She'd been married to Earl Hoffman for over forty years.

She put a folded paper napkin under her cup to absorb the spillage. "I knew her to say hello to."

"In Bridgeton?"

"I'm not supposed to talk about Letitia. Mrs Deloney –"

"Your daughter's in a refrigerated drawer and all you give me is Mrs Deloney."

She bowed her head over the shiny formica table. "I'm afraid of her," she said, "of what she can do to Earl."

"Be afraid of what she's already done to him. She and her political pals made him seal up the Deloney case, and it's been festering inside of him ever since."

"I know. It's the first time Earl ever laid down on the job deliberately."

"You admit that?"

"I guess I have to. Earl never said it out in so many words, but I knew, and Helen knew. It's why she left us."

And why, perhaps, in the long run Helen couldn't stay honest.

"Earl had a great respect for Luke Deloney," the woman was saying, "even if Luke did have his human failings. He was the one who made good for all of us in a manner of speaking. His death hit Earl real hard, and he started drinking right after, seriously I mean. I'm worried about Earl." She reached across the table and touched the back of my hand with her dry fingertips. "Do you think he'll be all right?"

"Not if he keeps on drinking. He ought to survive this bout. I'm sure he's being well taken care of. But Helen isn't."

"Helen? What can anybody do for Helen?"

"You can do something for her by telling the truth. Her death deserves an explanation at least."

"But I don't know who killed her. If I did I'd shout it from the housetops. I thought the police were after that man McGee who killed his wife."

"McGee has been cleared. Tish Macready killed his wife, and probably your daughter as well."

She shook her head solemnly. "You're mistaken, mister. What you say isn't possible. Tish Macready – Tish Osborne that was – she died long ago before either of those tragedies happened. I admit there were rumors about her at the time of Luke Deloney's death, but then she had her own tragedy, poor thing."

"You said 'Tish Osborne that was'."

"That's right. She was one of Senator Osborne's girls – Mrs Deloney's sister. I told you about them the other night when we were driving down here from the airport, how they used to ride to hounds." She smiled faintly, nostalgically, as if she had caught a flash of red coats from her childhood.

"What were the rumors about her, Mrs Hoffman?"

"That she was carrying on with Luke Deloney before his death. Some people said she shot him herself, but I never believed that."

"Was she having an affair with Luke Deloney?"

"She used to spend some time in his apartment, that was no secret. She was kind of his unofficial hostess when Luke and Mrs Deloney were separated. I didn't think too much about it. She was already divorced from Val Macready. And she was Luke's sister-in-law after all, I guess she had a right to be in his penthouse."

"Did she have red hair?"

"More auburn I'd say. She had beautiful auburn hair." Mrs Hoffman absently stroked her own dyed curls. "Tish Osborne had a lot of life in her. I was sorry to hear when she died."

"What happened to her?"

"I don't know exactly. She died in Europe when the Nazis ran over France. Mrs Deloney still hasn't got over it. She was talking about her sister's death today."

Something that felt like a spider with wet feet climbed up the back of my neck into the short hairs and made them bristle. The ghost of Tish or a woman (or a man?) using her name had come to the door of the house in Indian Springs ten years ago, more than ten years after the Germans overran France.

"Are you certain she's dead, Mrs Hoffman?"

She nodded. "There was quite a writeup in the papers, even the Chicago papers. Tish Osborne was the belle of Bridgeton in her time. I can remember back in the early twenties her parties were famous. The man she married, Val Macready, had meat-packing money on his mother's side."

"Is he still alive?"

"The last I heard of him. He married an Englishwoman during the war and was living in England. He wasn't a Bridgeton boy and I never really knew him. I just read the society pages and the obituaries."

She sipped her cocoa. Her look, her self-enclosed posture, seemed to be telling me that she had survived. Her daughter Helen had been brighter, Tish Osborne had been wealthier, but she was the one who had survived. She would survive Earl, too, and probably make a shrine of the study where he kept his liquor in the roll-top desk.

Well, I had caught one of the old ladies. The other one would be tougher.

"Why did Mrs Deloney fly out here?"

"I guess it was just a rich woman's whim. She said she wanted to help me out in my time of trouble."

"Were you ever close to her?"

"I hardly knew her. Earl knows her better."

"Was Helen close to her?"

"No. If they ever met each other, it's news to me."

"Mrs Deloney came a long way to help out a comparative stranger. Has she given you any particular help, apart from changing hotels?"

"She bought me lunch and dinner. I didn't want her to pay, but she insisted."

"What were you to do in return for the free room and board?"

"Nothing."

"Didn't she ask you not to talk about her sister Tish?"

"That's true, she did. I wasn't to say anything about her carrying on with Luke Deloney, or the rumors that went around about his death. She's very sensitive about her sister's reputation."

"Abnormally sensitive, if Tish has really been dead for over twenty years. Who weren't you supposed to mention these things to?"

"Anybody, especially you."

She drowned her nervous little giggle in the remains of her cocoa.

XXXI

I WENT out into the grounds of the hotel. The high moon floated steadily in the sky and in the ornamental pools of the Spanish garden. There was yellower light behind the shutters of Mrs Deloney's cottage, and the sound of voices too low to be eaves-dropped on.

I knocked on the door.

"What is it?" she said.

"Service." Detective service.

"I didn't order anything."

But she opened the door. I slipped in past her and stood against the wall. Bradshaw was sitting on an English sofa beside the fireplace in the opposite wall. A low fire burned in the grate, and gleamed on the brass fittings.

"Hello," he said.

"Hello, George."

He jumped visibly.

Mrs Deloney said: "Get out of here." She seemed to have perfectly round blue eyes in a perfectly square white face, all bone and will. "I'll call the house detective."

"Go ahead, if you want to spread the dirt around."

She shut the door.

"We might as well tell him," Bradshaw said. "We have to tell someone."

The negative jerk of her head was so violent it threw her off balance. She took a couple of backward steps and regrouped her forces, looking from me to Bradshaw as if we were both her enemies.

"I absolutely forbid it," she said to him. "Nothing is to be said."

"It's going to come out anyway. It will be better if we bring it out ourselves."

"It is *not* going to come out. Why should it?"

"Partly," I said, "because you made the mistake of coming here. This isn't your town, Mrs Deloney. You can't put a lid on events the way you could in Bridgeton."

She turned her straight back on me. "Pay no attention to him, George."

"My name is Roy."

"Roy," she corrected herself. "This man tried to bluff me yesterday in Bridgeton, but he doesn't know a thing. All we have to do is remain quiet."

"What will that get us?"

"Peace."

"I've had my fill of that sort of peace," he said. "I've been living close up to it all these years. You've been out of contact.

You have no conception of what I've been through." He rested his head on the back of the sofa and lifted his eyes to the ceiling.

"You'll go through worse," she said roughly, "if you let down your back hair now."

"At least it will be different."

"You're a spineless fool. But I'm not going to let you ruin what remains of my life. If you do, you'll get no financial help from me."

"Even that I can do without."

But he was being careful to say nothing I wanted to know. He'd been wearing a mask so long that it stuck to his face and controlled his speech and perhaps his habits of thought. Even the old woman with her back turned was playing to me as if I was an audience.

"This argument is academic, in more than one sense," I said. "The body isn't buried any longer. I know your sister Letitia shot your husband, Mrs Deloney. I know she later married Bradshaw in Boston. I have his mother's word for it –"

"His mother?"

Bradshaw sat up straight. "I do have a mother after all." He added in his earnest cultivated voice, with his eyes intent on the woman's: "I'm still living with her, and she has to be considered in this matter, too."

"You lead a very complicated life," she said.

"I have a very complicated nature."

"Very well, young Mr Complexity, the ball is yours. Carry it." She went to a love-seat in a neutral corner of the room and sat down there.

"I thought the ball was mine," I said, "but you're welcome to it, Bradshaw. You can start where everything started, with the Deloney killing. You were Helen's witness, weren't you?"

He nodded once. "I shouldn't have gone to Helen with that heavy knowledge. But I was deeply upset and she was the only friend I had in the world."

"Except Letitia."

"Yes. Except Letitia."

"What was your part in the murder."

"I was simply there. And it wasn't a murder, properly speaking. Deloney was killed in self-defense, virtually by accident."

"This is where I came in."

"It's true. He caught us in bed together in his penthouse."

"Did you and Letitia make a habit of going to bed together?"

"It was the first time. I'd written a poem about her, which the college magazine printed, and I showed it to her in the elevator. I'd been watching her, admiring her, all through the spring. She was much older than I was, but she was fascinating. She was the first woman I ever had." He spoke of her with a kind of awe still.

"What happened in the penthouse bedroom, Bradshaw?"

"He caught us, as I said. He got a gun out of the chest of drawers and hit me with the butt of it. Tish tried to stop him. He beat her face in with the gun. She got her hands on it somehow, and it went off and killed him."

He touched the lid of his right eye, and nodded toward the old woman. She was watching us from the corner, from the distance of her years.

"Mrs Deloney hushed the matter up, or had it hushed up. You can hardly blame her, under the circumstances. Or blame us. We went to Boston, where Tish spent months in and out of the hospital having her face rebuilt. Then we were married. I was in love with her, in spite of the discrepancy in our ages. I suppose my feeling for my own mother prepared me to love Tish."

His hooded intelligence flared up in his eyes so bright it was half-insane. His mouth was wry.

"We went to Europe on our honeymoon. My mother put French detectives on our trail. I had to leave Tish in Paris and come home to make my peace with Mother and start my sophomore year at Harvard. The war broke out in Europe that same month. I never saw Tish again. She fell sick and died before I knew it."

"I don't believe you. There wasn't time for all that."

"It happened very rapidly, as tragedy does."

"Not yours, it's been dragging on for twenty-two years."

"No," Mrs Deloney said. "He's telling the truth, and I can prove it to you."

She went into another room of the cottage and came back with a heavily creased document which she handed me. It was an *acte de décès* issued in Bordeaux and dated July 16, 1940. It stated in French that Letitia Osborne Macready, aged 45, had died of pneumonia.

I gave it back to Mrs Deloney. "You carry this with you wherever you go?"

"I happened to bring it with me."

"Why?"

She couldn't think of an answer.

"I'll tell you why. Because your sister is very much alive and you're afraid she'll be punished for her crimes."

"My sister committed no crime. The death of my husband was either justifiable homicide or accident. The police commissioner realized that or he'd never have quashed the case."

"That may be. But Constance McGee and Helen Haggerty weren't shot by accident."

"My sister died long before either of those women."

"Your own actions deny it, and they mean more than this phony death certificate. For instance, you visited Gil Stevens today and tried to pump him about the McGee case."

"He broke my confidence, did he?"

"There was nothing there to be broken. You're not Stevens's client. He's still representing McGee."

"He didn't tell me."

"Why should he? This isn't your town."

She turned in confusion to Bradshaw. He shook his head. I crossed the room and stood over him.

"If Tish is safely buried in France, why did you go to such elaborate trouble to divorce her?"

"So you know about the divorce. You're quite a digger for facts, aren't you, quite a Digger Indian? I begin to wonder if there's anything you don't know about my private life."

He sat there, looking up at me brightly and warily. I was a little carried away by the collapse of his defenses, and I said:

"Your private life, or your private lives, are something for the book. Have you been keeping up two establishments, dividing your time between your mother and your wife?"

"I suppose it's obvious that I have," he said tonelessly.

"Does Tish live here in town?"

"She lived in the Los Angeles area. I have no intention of telling you where, and I can assure you you'll never find the place. There'd be no point in it, anyway, since she's no longer there."

"Where and how did she die this time?"

"She isn't dead. That French death certificate is a fake, as you guessed. But she is beyond your reach. I put her on a plane to Rio de Janeiro on Saturday, and she'll be there by now."

Mrs Deloney said: "You didn't tell me that!"

"I hadn't intended to tell anyone. However, I have to make Mr Archer see that there's no point in pressing this thing any further. My wife – my ex-wife – is an old woman, and a sick one, and she's beyond extradition. I've arranged for her to have medical care, psychiatric care in a South American city which I won't name."

"You're admitting that she killed Helen Haggerty?"

"Yes. She confessed to me when I went to see her in Los Angeles early Saturday morning. She shot Helen and hid the gun in my gatehouse. I contacted Foley in Reno primarily to find out if he had witnessed anything. I didn't want him blackmailing me –"

"I thought he already was."

"Helen was," he said. "She learned about my pending divorce in Reno, and she jumped to a number of conclusions, including the fact that Tish was still alive. I gave her a good deal of money, and got her a job here, in order to protect Tish."

"And yourself."

"And myself. I do have a reputation to protect, though I've done nothing illegal."

"No. You're very good at arranging for other people to do your dirty work. You brought Helen here as a kind of decoy, didn't you."

"I'm afraid I don't understand you." But he shifted uneasily.

"You took Helen out a few times and passed the word that she was your intended. She wasn't, of course. You were already married to Laura and you hated Helen, with good reason."

"That's not true. We were on quite a friendly basis, in spite of her demands. She was a very old friend, after all, and I couldn't help sympathizing with her feeling that she deserved something from the world."

"I know what she got – a bullet in her head. The same thing Constance McGee got. The same thing Laura would have got if you hadn't set Helen up as a substitute victim for Tish."

"I'm afraid you're getting much too complicated."

"For a complicated nature like yours?"

He looked around the room as if he felt imprisoned in it, or in the maze of his own nature. "You'll never prove any complicity on my part in Helen's death. It came as a fearful shock to me. Letitia's confession was another shock."

"Why? You must have known she killed Constance McGee."

"I didn't know it till Saturday. I admit I had my suspicions. Tish was always savagely jealous. I've lived with the dreadful possibility for ten years, hoping and praying that my suspicions were unfounded –"

"Why didn't you ask her?"

"I suppose I couldn't face it. Things were already so difficult between us. It would have meant admitting my love for Connie." He heard his own words, and sat quiet for a moment, his eyes downcast, as if he was peering down into a chasm in himself. "I really did love her, you know. Her death almost finished me."

"But you survived to love again."

"Men do," he said. "I'm not the sort of man who can live without love. I loved even Tish as long and as well as I could. But she got *old,* and sick."

Mrs Deloney made a spitting sound. He said to her:

"I wanted a wife, one who could give me children."

"God help any children of yours, you'd probably abandon them. You broke all your promises to my sister."

"Everyone breaks promises. I didn't intend to fall in love with Connie. It simply happened. I met her in a doctor's waiting room quite by accident. But I didn't turn my back on your sister. I never have. I've done more for her than she ever did for me."

She sneered at him with the arrogance of a second-generation aristocrat. "My sister lifted you out of the gutter. What were you – an elevator boy?"

"I was a college student, and an elevator boy by my own choice."

"Very likely."

He leaned toward her, fixing her with his bright eyes. "I had family resources to draw on if I had wished."

"Ah yes, your precious mother."

"Be careful what you say about my mother."

There was an edge on his words, the quality of a cold threat, and it silenced her. This was one of several moments when I sensed that the two of them were playing a game as complex as chess, a game of power on a hidden board. I should have tried to force it into the open. But I was clearing up my case, and as long as Bradshaw was willing to talk I didn't care about apparent side-issues.

"I don't understand the business of the gun," I said. "The police have established that Connie McGee and Helen were shot with the same gun – a revolver that belonged originally to Connie's sister Alice. How did Tish get hold of it?"

"I don't really know."

"You must have some idea. Did Alice Jenks give it to her?"

"She very well may have."

"That's nonsense, Bradshaw, and you know it. The revolver was stolen from Alice's house. Who stole it?"

He made a steeple of his fingers and admired its symmetry. "I'm willing to tell you if Mrs Deloney will leave the room."

"Why should I?" she said from her corner. "Anything my sister could endure to live through I can endure to hear."

"I'm not trying to spare your sensibilities," Bradshaw said. "I'm trying to spare myself."

She hesitated. It became a test of wills. Bradshaw got up and opened the inner door. Through it I could see across a hall into a bedroom furnished in dull luxury. The bedside table held an ivory telephone and a leather-framed photograph of a white-mustached gentleman who looked vaguely familiar."

Mrs Deloney marched into the bedroom like a recalcitrant soldier under orders. Bradshaw closed the door sharply behind her.

"I'm beginning to hate old women," he said.

"You were going to tell me about the gun."

"I was, wasn't I?" He returned to the sofa. "It's not a pretty story. None of it is. I'm telling you the whole thing in the hope that you'll be completely satisfied."

"And not bring in the authorities?"

"Don't you see there's nothing to be gained by bringing them in? The sole effect would be to turn the town on its ear, wreck the standing of the college which I've worked so hard to build up, and ruin more than one life."

"Especially yours and Laura's?"

"Especially mine and Laura's. She's waited for me, God knows. And even I deserve something more than I've had. I've lived my entire adult life with the consequences of a neurotic involvement that I got into when I was just a boy."

"Is that what Godwin is treating you for?"

"I needed *some* support. Tish hasn't been easy to deal with. She drove me half out of my mind sometimes with her animal violence and her demands. But now it's over." His eyes changed the statement into a question and a plea.

"I can't make any promises," I said. "Let's have the entire story, then we'll think about the next step. How did Tish get hold of Alice's revolver?"

"Connie took it from her sister's room and gave it to me. We had some wild idea of using it to cut the Gordian knot."

"Do you mean kill Tish with it?"

"It was sheer fantasy," he said, "*folie à deux*. Connie and I would never have carried it out, desperate as we were. You'll never know the agony I went through dividing myself between two wives, two lovers – one old and rapacious, the other young and passionate. Jim Godwin warned me that I was in danger of spiritual death."

"For which murder is known to be a sure cure."

"I'd never have done it. I couldn't. Actually Jim made me see that. I'm not a violent man."

But there was violence in him now, pressing against the conventional fears that corseted his nature and held him still, almost formal, under my eyes. I sensed his murderous hatred for me. I was forcing all his secrets into the open, as I thought.

"What happened to the gun Connie stole for you?"

"I put it away in what I thought was a safe place, but Tish must have found it."

"In your house?"

"In my mother's house. I sometimes took her there when Mother was away."

"Was she there the day McGee called on you?"

"Yes." He met my eyes. "I'm amazed that you should know about that day. You're very thorough. It was the day when everything came to a head. Tish must have found the gun in the lockbox in my study where I'd hidden it. Before that she must have heard McGee complaining to me about my interest in his wife. She took the gun and turned it against Constance. I suppose there was a certain poetic justice in that."

Bradshaw might have been talking about an event in someone else's past, the death of a character in history or fiction. He no longer cared for the meaning of his own life. Perhaps that was what Godwin meant by spiritual death.

"Do you still maintain you didn't know Tish killed her until she confessed it last Saturday?"

"I suppose I didn't let myself realize. So far as I knew the gun had simply disappeared. McGee might very well have taken it from my study when he was in the house. The offical case against him seemed very strong."

"It was put together with old pieces of string, and you know it. McGee and his daughter are my main concern. I won't be satisfied until they're completely cleared."

"But surely that can be accomplished without draging Letitia back from Brazil."

"I have only your word that she's in Brazil," I said. "Even Mrs Deloney was surprised to hear it."

"Good heavens, don't you believe me? I've literally exposed my entrails to you."

"You wouldn't do that unless you had a reason. I think you're a liar, Bradshaw, one of those virtuosos who use real facts and feelings to make their stories plausible. But there's a basic implausibility in this one. If Tish was safe in Brazil, it's the last thing you'd ever tell me. I think she's hiding out here in California."

"You're quite mistaken."

His eyes came up to mine, candid and earnest as only an actor's can be. A telephone chirring behind the bedroom door interrupted our staring contest. Bradshaw moved toward the sound. I was on my feet and I moved more rapidly, shouldering him against the doorframe, picking up the bedside phone before it rang a third time.

"Hello."

"Is that you, darling?" It was Laura's voice. "Roy, I'm frightened. She *knows* about us. She called here just a minute ago and said she was coming over."

"Keep the door locked and chained. And you better call the

police."

"That isn't Roy. Is it?"

Roy was behind me. I turned in time to see the flash of brass as the poker in his fist came down on my head.

XXXII

MRS DELONEY was slapping my face with a wet towel. I told her to quit it. The first thing I saw when I got up was the leather-framed photograph beside her telephone. It seemed to my blurred vision to be a photograph of the handsome old black-eyed gentleman whose portrait hung over the fireplace in Mrs Bradshaw's sitting room.

"What are you doing with a picture of Bradshaw's father?"

"It happens to be my own father, Senator Osborne."

I said: "So Mrs Bradshaw's a virtuoso, too."

Mrs Deloney looked at me as if my brains had been addled by the poker. But the blow had been a glancing one, and I couldn't have been out for more than a few seconds. Bradshaw was leaving the hotel parking lot when I got there.

His light car turned uphill away from the ocean. I followed him to Foothill Drive and caught him long before he reached his house. He made it easy for me by braking suddenly. His car slewed sideways and came to a shuddering halt broadside across the road.

It wasn't me he was trying to stop. Another car was coming downhill toward us. I could see its headlights approaching under the trees like large calm insane eyes, and Bradshaw silhouetted in their beam. He seemed to be fumbling with his seat-belt. I recognized Mrs Bradshaw's Rolls in the moment before, with screeching brakes, it crashed into the smaller car.

I pulled off the road, set out a red blinker, and ran uphill toward the point of impact. My footsteps were loud in the silence after the crash. The crumpled nose of the Rolls was nuzzled deep in the caved-in side of Bradshaw's car. He lolled in the driver's seat. Blood ran down his face from his forehead and nose and the corners of his mouth.

I went in through the undamaged door and got his seat-belf

unbuckled. He toppled limply into my arms. I laid him down in the road. The jagged lines of blood across his face resembled cracks in a mask through which live tissue showed. But he was dead. He lay pulseless and breathless under the iron shadows of the tree branches.

Old Mrs Bradshaw had climbed down out of her high protected seat. She seemed unhurt. I remember thinking at the moment that she was an elemental power which nothing could ever kill.

"It's Roy, isn't it? Is he all right?"

"In a sense he is. He wanted out. He's out."

"What do you mean?"

"I'm afraid you've killed him, too."

"But I didn't mean to hurt him. I couldn't hurt my own son, the child of my womb."

Her voice cracked with maternal grief. I think she half believed she was his mother, she had lived the rôle so long. Reality had grown dim as the moonlit countryside around her.

She flung herself on the dead man, holding him close, as if her old body could somehow warm him back to life and rekindle his love for her. She wheedled and cooed in his ear, calling him a naughty malingering boy for trying to scare her.

She shook him. "Wake up! It's Moms."

As she had told me, night wasn't her best season. But she had a doubleness in her matching Roy's, and there was an element of play-acting in her frenzy.

"Leave him alone," I said. "And let's drop the mother bit. The situation is ugly enough without that."

She turned in queer slow furtiveness and looked up at me. "The mother bit?"

"Roy Bradshaw wasn't your son. The two of you put on a pretty good act – Godwin would probably say it fitted both your neurotic needs – but it's over."

She got up in a surge of anger which brought her close to me. I could smell her lavender, and feel her force.

"I *am* his mother. I have his birth certificate to prove it."

"I bet you do. Your sister showed me a death certificate which proved that you died in France in 1940. With your kind of money you can document anything. But you can't change the facts by changing them on paper. Roy married you in Boston after you killed Deloney. Eventually he fell in love with Constance McGee. You killed her. Roy lived with you for another ten years, if you can call it living, terrified that you'd kill again if he ever dared to love anyone again. But finally he dared, with Laura Sutherland. He managed to convince you that it was Helen Haggarty he was interested in. So you went up the bridle path on Friday night and shot her. Those are all facts you can't change."

Silence set in between us, thin and bleak like a quality of the moonlight. The woman said:

"I was only protecting my rights. Roy owed me faithfulness at least. I gave him money and background, I sent him to Harvard, I made all his dreams come true."

We both looked down at the dreamless man lying in the road.

"Are you ready to come downtown with me and make a formal statement about how you protected your rights over the years? Poor Tom McGee is back in jail, still sweating out your rap."

She pulled herself erect. "I won't permit you to use such language to me. I'm not a criminal."

"You were on your way to Laura Sutherland's, weren't you? What were you planning to do to her, old woman?"

She covered the lower part of her face with her hand. I thought she was ill, or overcome with shame. But she said:

"You mustn't call me that. I'm not old. Don't look at my face, look into my eyes. You can see how young I am."

It was true in a way. I couldn't see her eyes clearly, but I knew they were bright and black and vital. She was still greedy for life, like the imaginary Letitia, the weird projection of herself in imitation leopardskin she had used to hide behind.

She shifted her hand to her heavy chin and said: "I'll give you money."

"Roy took your money. Look what happened to him."

She turned abruptly and started for her car. I guessed what was in her mind: another death, another shadow to feed on: and got to the open door of the Rolls before her. Her black leather bag was on the floor where it had fallen in the collision. Inside the bag I found the new revolver which she had intended to use on Roy's new wife.

"Give me that."

She spoke with the authority of a Senator's daughter and the more terrible authority of a woman who had killed two other women and two men.

"No more guns for you," I said.

No more anything, Letitia.

THE GOODBYE LOOK

To Henri Coulette

I

THE LAWYER, WHOSE name was John Truttwell, kept me waiting in the outer room of his offices. It gave the room a chance to work me over gently. The armchair I was sitting in was covered in soft green leather. Oil paintings of the region, landscapes and seascapes, hung on the walls around me like subtle advertisements.

The young pink-haired receptionist turned from the switchboard. The heavy dark lines accenting her eyes made her look like a prisoner peering out through bars.

'I'm sorry Mr Truttwell's running so late. It's that daughter of his,' the girl said rather obscurely. 'He should let her go ahead and make her own mistakes. The way I have.'

'Oh?'

'I'm really a model. I'm just filling in at this job because my second husband ran out on me. Are you really a detective?'

I said I was.

'My husband is a photographer. I'd give a good deal to know who—where he's living.'

'Forget it. It wouldn't be worth it.'

'You could be right. He's a lousy photographer. Some very good judges told me that his pictures never did me justice.'

It was mercy she needed, I thought.

A tall man in his late fifties appeared in the open doorway. High-shouldered and elegantly dressed, he was handsome and seemed to know it. His thick white hair was carefully arranged on his head, as carefully arranged as his expression.

'Mr Archer? I'm John Truttwell.' He shook my hand with restrained enthusiasm and moved me along the corridor to his office. 'I have to thank you for coming down from Los Angeles so promptly, and I apologize for keeping you waiting. Here I'm supposed to be semi-retired but I've never had so many things on my mind.'

Truttwell wasn't as disorganized as he sounded. Through the flow of language his rather sad cold eyes were looking me over carefully. He ushered me into his office and placed me in a brown-leather chair facing him across his desk.

A little sunlight filtered through the heavily draped windows, but the room was lit by artificial light. In its diffused whiteness Truttwell himself looked rather artificial, like a carefully made wax image wired for sound. On a wall shelf above his right shoulder was a framed picture of a clear-eyed blonde girl who I supposed was his daughter.

'On the phone you mentioned a Mr and Mrs Lawrence Chalmers.'

'So I did.'

'What's their problem?'

'I'll get to that in a minute or two,' Truttwell said. 'I want to make it clear at the beginning that Larry and Irene Chalmers are friends of mine. We live across from each other on Pacific Street. I've known Larry all my life, and so did our parents before us. I learned a good deal of my law from Larry's father, the judge. And my late wife was very close to Larry's mother.'

Truttwell seemed proud of the connection in a slightly unreal way. His left hand drifted softly over his side hair, as if he was fingering an heirloom. His eyes and voice were faintly drowsy with the past.

'The point I'm making,' he said, 'is that the Chalmerses are valuable people—personally valuable to me. I want you to handle them with great care.'

The atmosphere of the office was teeming with social pressures. I tried to dispel one or two of them. 'Like antiques?'

'Somewhat, but they're not old. I think of the two of them as objects of art, the point of which is that they don't have to be useful.' Truttwell paused, and then went on as if struck by a new thought. 'The fact is Larry hasn't accomplished much since the war. Of course he's made a great deal of money, but even that was handed to him on a silver platter. His mother left him a substantial nest egg, and the bull market blew it up into millions.'

There was an undertone of envy in Truttwell's voice, suggesting that his feelings about the Chalmers couple were complicated and not entirely worshipful. I let myself react to the nagging undertone:

'Am I supposed to be impressed?'

Truttwell gave me a startled look, as if I'd made an obscene noise, or allowed myself to hear one. 'I can see I haven't succeeded in making my point. Larry Chalmers's grandfather fought in the Civil War, then came to California and married a Spanish land-grant heiress. Larry was a war hero himself, but he doesn't talk about it. In our instant society that makes him the closest thing we have to an aristocrat.' He listened to the sound of the sentence as though he had used it before.

'What about Mrs Chalmers?'

'Nobody would describe Irene as an aristocrat. But,' he added with unexpected zest, 'she's a hell of a good-looking woman. Which is all a woman really has to be.'

'You still haven't mentioned what their problem is.'

'That's partly because it's not entirely clear to me.' Truttwell picked up a sheet of yellow foolscap from his desk and frowned over the scrawling on it. 'I'm hoping they'll speak more freely to a stranger. As Irene laid out the situation to me, they had a burglary at their house while they were away on a long weekend in Palm Springs. It was a rather peculiar burglary. According to her, only one thing of value was taken—an old gold box that was kept in the study safe. I've seen that safe—Judge Chalmers had it put in back in the twenties—and it would be hard to crack.'

'Have Mr and Mrs Chalmers notified the police?'

'No, and they don't plan to.'

'Do they have servants?'

'They have a Spanish houseman who lives out. But they've

had the same man for over twenty years. Besides, he drove them to Palm Springs.' He paused, and shook his white head. 'Still it does have the feel of an inside job, doesn't it?'

'Do you suspect the servant, Mr Truttwell?'

'I'd rather not tell you whom or what I suspect. You'll work better without too many preconceptions. Well as I know Irene and Larry, they're very private people, and I don't pretend to understand their lives.'

'Have they any children?'

'One son, Nicholas,' he said in a neutral tone.

'How old is he?'

'Twenty-three or -four. He's due to graduate from the university this month.'

'In January?'

'That's right. Nick missed a semester in his freshman year. He left school without telling anyone, and dropped out of sight completely for several months.'

'Are his parents having trouble with him now?'

'I wouldn't put it that strongly.'

'Could he have done this burglary?'

Truttwell was slow in replying. Judging by the changes in his eyes, he was trying out various answers mentally: they ranged from prosecution to defense.

'Nick could have done it,' he said finally. 'But he'd have no reason to steal a gold box from his mother.'

'I can think of several possible reasons. Is he interested in women?'

Truttwell said rather stiffly: 'Yes, he is. He happens to be engaged to my daughter Betty.'

'Sorry.'

'Not at all. You could hardly be expected to know that. But do be careful what you say to the Chalmerses. They're accustomed to leading a very quiet life, and I'm afraid this business has really upset them. The way they feel about their precious house, it's as if a temple had been violated.'

He crumpled the yellow foolscap in his hands and threw it into a wastebasket. The impatient gesture gave the impression that he would be glad to be rid of Mr and Mrs Chalmers and their problems, including their son

II

PACIFIC STREET ROSE like a slope in purgatory from the poor lower town to a hilltop section of fine old homes. The Chalmerses' California Spanish mansion must have been fifty or sixty years old, but its white walls were immaculate in the late-morning sun.

I crossed the walled courtyard and knocked on the iron-bound front door. A dark-suited servant with a face that belonged in a Spanish monastery opened the door and took my name and left me standing in the reception hall. It was an enormous two-storied room that made me feel small and then, in reaction, large and self-assertive.

I could see into the great white cave of the living room. Its walls were brilliant with modern paintings. Its doorway was equipped with black wrought-iron gates, shoulder high, which gave the place a museum atmosphere.

This was partly dispelled by the dark-haired woman who came in from the garden to greet me. She was carrying a pair of clippers and a clear red Olé rose. She laid the clippers down on a hall table but kept the rose, which exactly matched the color of her mouth.

Her smile was bright and anxious. 'Somehow I expected you to be older.'

'I'm older than I look.'

'But I asked John Truttwell to get me the head of the agency.'

'I'm a one-man agency. I co-opt other detectives when I need them.'

She frowned. 'It sounds like a shoestring operation to me. Not like the Pinkertons.'

'I'm not big business, if that's what you want.'

'It isn't. But I want somebody good, really good. Are you experienced in dealing with—well—' Her free hand indicated first herself and then her surroundings—'people like me?'

'I don't know you well enough to answer that.'

'But *you're* the one we're talking about.'

'I assume Mr Truttwell recommended me, and told you I was experienced.'

'I have a right to ask my own questions, don't I?'

Her tone was both assertive and lacking in self-assurance. It was the tone of a handsome woman who had married money and social standing and never could forget that she might just as easily lose these things.

'Go ahead and ask questions, Mrs Chalmers.'

She caught my gaze and held it, as if she were trying to read my mind. Her eyes were black and intense and impervious.

'All I really want to know is this. If you find the Florentine box—I assume John Truttwell told you about the gold box?'

'He said that one was missing.'

She nodded. 'Assuming you find it, and find out who took it, is that as far as it goes? I mean, you won't march off to the authorities and tell them all about it?'

'No. Unless they're already involved?'

'They aren't, and they're not going to be,' she said. 'I want this whole thing kept quiet. I wasn't even going to tell John Truttwell about the box, but he wormed it out of me. However, him I trust. I think.'

'And me you think you don't?'

I smiled, and she decided to respond. She tapped me on the cheek with her red rose, then dropped it on the tile floor as if it had served its purpose. 'Come into the study. We can talk privately there.'

She led me up a short flight of steps to a richly carved oak door.

Before she closed it behind us I could see the servant in the reception hall picking up after her, first the clippers, then the rose.

The study was an austere room with dark beams supporting the slanting white ceiling. The single small window, barred on the outside, made it resemble a prison cell. As if the prisoner had been looking for a way out, there were shelves of old law books against one wall.

On the facing wall hung a large picture which appeared to be an oil painting of Pacific Point in the old days, done in primitive perspective. A seventeenth-century sailing vessel lay in the harbor inside the curve of the point; beside it naked brown Indians lounged on the beach; over their heads Spanish soldiers marched like an army in the sky.

Mrs Chalmers seated me in an old calf-covered swivel chair in front of a closed roll-top desk.

'These pieces don't go with the rest of the furniture,' she said as if it mattered. 'But this was my father-in-law's desk, and that chair you're sitting in was the one he used in court. He was a judge.'

'So Mr Truttwell told me.'

'Yes, John Truttwell knew him. I never did. He died a long time ago, when Lawrence was just a small boy. But my husband still worships the ground his father walked on.'

'I'm looking forward to meeting your husband. Is he at home?'

'I'm afraid not. He went to see the doctor. This burglary business has him all upset.' She added: 'I wouldn't want you to talk to him, anyway.'

'Does he know I'm here?'

She moved away from me, leaning over a black oak refectory table. She fumbled a cigarette from a silver box and lit it with a matching table lighter. The cigarette, which she puffed on furiously, laid down a blue smokescreen between us.

'Lawrence didn't think it was a good idea to use a private detective. I decided to go ahead with you anyway.'

'Why did he object?'

'My husband likes his privacy. And this box that was stolen—well, it was a gift to his mother from an admirer of hers. I'm not supposed to know that, but I do.' Her smile was crooked. 'In addition to which, his mother used it to keep his letters in.'

'The admirer's letters?'

'My husband's letters. Larry wrote her a lot of letters during the war, and she kept them in the box. The letters are missing, too—not that they're of any great value, except maybe to Larry.'

'Is the box valuable?'

'I think it is. It's covered with gold, and very carefully made. It was made in Florence during the Renaissance.' She stumbled on the word, but got it out. 'It has a picture on the lid, of two lovers.'

'Insured?'

She shook her head, and crossed her legs. 'It hardly seemed necessary. We never took it out of the safe. It never occurred to us that the safe could be broken into.'

I asked to be allowed to see the safe. Mrs Chalmers took down the primitive painting of the Indians and the Spanish soldiers. Where it had hung a large cylindrical safe was set deep in the wall. She turned the dial several times and opened it. Looking over her shoulder, I could see that the safe was about the diameter of a sixteen-inch gun and just as empty.

'Where's your jewelry, Mrs Chalmers?'

'I don't have much, it never has interested me. What I do have, I keep in a case in my room. I took the case along with me to Palm Springs. We were there when the gold box was taken.'

'How long has it been missing?'

'Let me see now, this is Tuesday. I put it in the safe Thursday night. Next morning we went to the desert. It must have been stolen after we left, so that makes four days, or less. I looked in the safe last night when we got home, and it was gone.'

'What made you look in the safe last night?'

'I don't know. I really don't,' she added, making it sound like a lie.

'Did you have some idea that it might be stolen?'

'No. Certainly not.'

'What about the servant?'

'Emilio didn't take it. I can vouch for him, absolutely.'

'Was anything taken besides the box?'

She considered the question. 'I don't think so. Except the letters, of course, the famous letters.'

'Were they important?'

'They were important to my husband, as I said. And of course to his mother. But she's been dead a long time, since the end of the war. I never met her myself.' She sounded a little worried, as if she'd been denied a maternal blessing, and still felt defrauded.

'Why would a burglar take them?'

'Don't ask me. Probably because they were in the box.' She made a face. 'If you do find them, don't bother to bring them back. I've already heard them, or most of them.'

'Heard them?'

'My husband used to read them aloud to Nick.'

'Where is your son?'

'Why?'

'I'd like to talk to him.'

'You can't.' She was frowning again. Behind her beautiful mask there was a spoiled girl, I thought, like a faker huddled in the statue of a god. 'I wish John Truttwell had sent me someone else. Anyone else.'

'What did I do wrong?'

'You ask too many questions. You're prying into our family affairs, and I've already told you more than I should.'

'You can trust me.' Immediately I regretted saying it.

'Can I really?'

'Other people have.' I could hear an unfortunate selling note in my voice. I wanted to stay with the woman and her peculiar little case: she had the kind of beauty that made you want to explore its history. 'And I'm sure Mr Truttwell would advise you not to hold back with me. When a lawyer hires me I have the same privilege of silence as he does.'

'Exactly what does that mean?'

'It means I can't be forced to talk about what I find out. Not even a Grand Jury with contempt powers can make me.'

'I see.' She had caught me off base, trying to sell myself, and now in a certain sense she could buy me; not with money, necessarily. 'If you promise to be absolutely close-mouthed, even with John Truttwell, I'll tell you something. This may not be an ordinary burglary.'

'Do you suspect it was an inside job? There's no sign that the safe was forced.'

'Lawrence pointed that out. It's why he didn't want you brought into the case. He didn't even want me to tell John Truttwell.'

'Who does he think stole the box?'

'He hasn't said. I'm afraid he suspects Nick, though.'

'Has Nick been in trouble before?'

'Not this kind of trouble.' The woman's voice had dropped almost out of hearing. Her whole body had slumped, as if the thought of her son was a palpable weight inside of her.

'What kind of trouble has he had?'

'Emotional problems so called. He turned against Lawrence and me for no good reason. He ran away when he was nineteen. It took the Pinkertons months to find him. It cost us thousands of dollars.'

'Where was he?'

'Working his way around the country. Actually, his psychiatrist said it did him some good. He's settled down to his studies since. He's even got himself a girl.' She spoke with some pride, or hope, but her eyes were somber.

'And you don't think he stole your box?'

'No, I don't.' She tilted up her chin. 'You wouldn't be here if I thought so.'

'Can he open the safe?'

'I doubt it. We've never given him the combination.'

'I noticed you've got it memorized. Do you have it written down anywhere?'

'Yes.'

She opened the bottom right-hand drawer of the desk, pulled it all the way out and turned it over, dumping the yellow bank statements it contained. Taped to the bottom of the drawer was a slip of paper bearing a series of typewritten numbers. The tape was yellow and cracked with age, and the paper was so worn that the figures on it were barely decipherable.

'That's easy enough to find,' I said. 'Is your son in need of money?'

'I can't imagine what for. We give him six or seven hundred a month, more if he needs it.'

'You mentioned a girl.'

'He's engaged to Betty Truttwell, who is not exactly a gold digger.'

'No other girls or women in his life?'

'No.' But her answer was slow and dubious.

'How does he feel about the box?'

'Nick?' Her clear forehead wrinkled, as if my question had taken her by surprise. 'As a matter of fact, he used to be interested in it when he was little. I used to let him and Betty play with it. We used—they used to pretend that it was Pandora's box. Magic, you know?'

She laughed a little. Her whole body was dreaming of the past. Then her eyes changed again. Her mind came up to their surface, hard and scared. She said in a thinner voice:

'Maybe I shouldn't have built it up so much. But I still can't believe he took it. Nick has usually been honest with us.'

'Have you asked him if he took it?'

'No. We haven't seen him since we got back from the desert. He has his own apartment near the university, and he's taking his final exams.'

'I'd like to talk to him, at least get a yes or no. Since he is under suspicion—'

'Just don't tell him his father suspects him. They've been getting along so well these last couple of years, I'd hate to see it spoiled.'

I promised her to be tactful. Without any further persuasion she gave me Nick Chalmers's phone number and his address in the university community. She wrote them on a slip of paper in a childish unformed hand. Then she glanced at her watch.

'This has taken longer than I thought. My husband will be coming home for lunch.'

She was flushed and brilliant-eyed, as if she was terminating an assignation. She hurried me out to the reception hall, where the dark-suited servant was standing with a blank respectful face. He opened the front door, and Mrs Chalmers practically pushed me out.

A middle-aged man in a fine tweed suit got out of a black Rolls Royce in front of the house. He crossed the courtyard with a kind of military precision, as if each step he took, each movement of his arms, was separately controlled by orders sent down from on high. The eyes in his lean brown face had a kind of bright blue innocence. The lower part of his face was conventionalized by a square-cut, clipped brown mustache.

His pale gaze drifted past me. 'What's going on here, Irene?'

'Nothing. I mean—' She drew in her breath. 'This is the insurance man. He came about the burglary.'

'You sent for him?'

'Yes.' She gave me a shame-faced look. She was lying openly and asking me to go along with it.

'That was rather a silly thing to do,' her husband said. 'The Florentine box wasn't insured, at least not to my knowledge.' He looked at me in polite inquiry.

'No,' I said in a wooden voice.

I was angry with the woman. She had wrecked my rapport with her, and any possible rapport with her husband.

'Then we won't keep you further,' he said to me. 'I apologize for Mrs Chalmers's blunder. I'm sorry your time has been wasted.'

Chalmers moved toward me smiling patiently under his mustache. I stepped to one side. He edged past me in the deep doorway, taking care not to brush against me. I was a commoner, and it might be catching.

III

I STOPPED AT a gas station on the way to the university, and called Nick's apartment from an outdoor pay phone. A girl's voice answered:

'Nicholas Chalmers's residence.'

'Is Mr Chalmers there?'

'No he is not.' She spoke with a professional lilt. 'This is his answering service.'

'How can I get in touch with him? It's important.'

'I don't know *where* he is.' An unprofessional note of anxiety had entered her voice. 'Is this connected with his missing his exams?'

'It may very well be,' I said in an open-ended way. 'Are you a friend of Nick's?'

'Yes I am. Actually I'm not his answering service. I'm his fiancée.'

'Miss Truttwell?'

'Do I know you?'

'Not yet. Are you in Nick's apartment?'

'Yes. Are you a counselor?'

'Roughly speaking, yes. My name is Archer. Will you wait there in the apartment for me, Miss Truttwell? And if Nick turns up, will you ask him to wait for me, too?'

She said she would. 'I'll do anything that will help Nick.' The implication seemed to be that he needed all the help he could get.

The university stood on a mesa a few miles out of town, beyond the airport. From a distance its incomplete oval of new buildings looked ancient and mysterious as Stonehenge. It was the third week in January, and I gathered that the midyear exams were in progress. The students I saw as I circled the campus had a driven preoccupied air.

I'd been there before, but not for several years. The student body had multiplied in the meantime, and the community attached to the campus had turned into a city of apartment buildings. It was strange, after Los Angeles, to drive through a city where everyone was young.

Nick lived in a five-storied building which called itself the Cambridge Arms. I rode the self-service elevator to the fifth floor and found the door of his apartment, which was number 51.

The girl opened the door before I knocked. Her eyes flickered when she saw it was only me. She had clean straight yellow hair that brushed the shoulders of her dark slacks suit. She looked about twenty.

'No Nick?' I said.

'I'm afraid not. You're Mr Archer?'

'Yes.'

She gave me a quick probing look, and I realized she was older than I'd thought. 'Are you really a counselor, Mr Archer?'

'I said roughly speaking. I've done a lot of counseling in an amateur sort of way.'

'What do you do in a professional sort of way?'

Her voice wasn't unfriendly. But her eyes were honest and sensitive, ready to be affronted. I didn't want that to happen. She was the nicest thing I'd come across in some time.

'I'm afraid if I tell you, Miss Truttwell, you won't talk to me.'

'You're a policeman, aren't you?'

'I used to be. I'm a private investigator.'

'Then you're perfectly right. I don't want to talk to you.'

She was showing signs of alarm. Her eyes and nostrils were dilated. Her face had a kind of sheen or glare on it. She said:

'Did Nick's parents send you here to talk to me?'

'How could they have? You're not supposed to be here. Since we are talking, by the way, we might as well do it inside.'

After some hesitation, she stepped back and let me in. The living room was furnished in expensive but dull good taste. It looked like the kind of furniture the Chalmerses might have bought for their son without consulting him.

The whole room gave the impression that Nick had kept himself hidden from it. There were no pictures on the walls. The only personal things of any kind were the books in the modular bookcase, and most of these were textbooks, in politics, law, psychology, and psychiatry.

I turned to the girl. 'Nick doesn't leave much evidence of himself lying around.'

'No. He's a very secret boy—man.'

'Boy or man?'

'He may be trying to make up his mind about that.'

'Just how old is he, Miss Truttwell?'

'He just turned twenty-three last month—December 14. He's graduating half a year late because he missed a semester a few years ago. That is, he'll graduate if they let him make up his exams. He's missed three out of four now.'

'Why?'

'It's not a school problem. Nick's quite brilliant,' she said as though I'd denied it. 'He's a whizz in poli sci, which is his major, and he's planning to study law next year.' Her voice was a little unreal, like that of a girl reciting a dream or trying to recall a hope.

'What kind of a problem is it, Miss Truttwell?'

'A life problem, as they call it.' She took a step toward me and stood with her hands hanging loose, palms facing me. 'All of a sudden he quit caring.'

'About you?'

'If that was all, I could stand it. But he cut loose from everything. His whole life has changed in the last few days.'

'Drugs?'

'No. I don't think so. Nick knows how dangerous they are.'

'Sometimes that's an attraction.'

'I know, I know what you mean.'

'Has he discussed it with you?'

She seemed confused for a second. 'Discussed what?'

'The change in his life in the last few days.'

'Not really. You see, there's another woman involved. An older woman.' The girl was wan with jealousy.

'He must be out of his mind,' I said by way of complimenting her.

She took it literally. 'I know. He's been doing things he couldn't do if he were completely sane.'

'Tell me about the things he's been doing.'

She gave me a look, the longest one so far. 'I *can't* tell you. I don't even know you.'

'Your father does.'

'Really?'

'Call him up if you don't believe me.'

Her gaze wandered to the telephone, which stood on an end table by the chesterfield, then came back to my face. 'That means you are working for the Chalmerses. They're Dad's clients.'

I didn't answer her.

'What did Nick's parents hire you to do?'

'No comment. We're wasting time. You and I both want to see Nick get back inside his skin. We need each other's help.'

'How can I help?'

I felt I was reaching her. 'You obviously want to talk to someone. Tell me what Nick's been up to.'

I was still standing like an unwanted guest. I sat down on the chesterfield. The girl approached it carefully, perching on one arm beyond my reach.

'If I do, you won't repeat it to his parents?'

'No. What have you got against his parents?'

'Nothing, really. They're nice people, I've known them all my life as friends and neighbors. But Mr Chalmers is pretty hard on Nick; they're such different types, you know. Nick is very critical of the war, for example, and Mr Chalmers considers that unpatriotic. He served with distinction in the last war, and it's made him kind of rigid in his thinking.'

'What did he do in the war?'

'He was a naval pilot when he was younger than Nick is now. He thinks Nick is a terrible rebel.' She paused. 'He isn't really. I admit he was pretty wild-eyed at one time. That was several years ago, before Nick settled down to study. He was doing so well until last week. Then everything went smash.'

I waited. Tentative as a bird, she slid off the arm of the chesterfield and plopped down beside me. She made a sour face and shut her eyes tight, holding back tears. In a minute she went on:

'I think that woman is at the bottom of it. I know what that makes me. But how can I help being jealous? He dropped me like a hotcake and took up with a woman old enough to be his mother. She's even married.'

'How do you know that?'

'He introduced her to me as Mrs Trask. I'm pretty sure she's from out of town—there are no Trasks in the phone book.'

'He introduced you?'

'I forced him to. I saw them together in the Lido Restaurant. I went to their table and stayed there until Nick introduced me to her and the other man. His name was Sidney Harrow. He's a bill collector from San Diego.'

'Did he tell you that?'

'Not exactly. I found out.'

'You're quite a finder-outer.'

'Yes,' she said, 'I am. Ordinarily I don't believe in snooping.' She gave me a half-smile. 'But there are times when snooping is called for. So when Mr Harrow wasn't looking I picked up his parking ticket, which was lying on the table beside his plate. I took it out to the Lido parking lot and got the attendant to show me which was his car. It was a junky old convertible, with the back window torn out. The rest was easy. I got his name and address from the car registration in the front and put in a call to his place in San Diego, which turned out to be a collection agency. They said he was on his vacation. Some vacation.'

'How do you know he isn't?'

'I haven't finished.' For the first time she was impatient, carried along by her story. 'It was Thursday noon when I met them in the restaurant. I saw the old convertible again on Friday night. It was parked in front of the Chalmerses' house. We live diagonally across the street and I can see their house from the window of my workroom. Just to make sure that it was Mr Harrow's car, I went over there to check on the registration. This was about nine o'clock Friday night.

'It was his, all right. He must have heard me close the car door. He came rushing out of the Chalmerses' house and asked me what I was doing there. I asked him what he was doing. Then he slapped my face and started to twist my arm. I must have let out some kind of a noise, because Nick came out of the house and knocked Mr Harrow down. Mr Harrow got a revolver out of his car and I thought for a minute he was going to shoot Nick. They had a funny look on both their faces, as if they were both going to die. As if they really *wanted* to kill each other and be killed.'

I knew that goodbye look. I had seen it in the war, and too many times since the war.

'But the woman,' the girl said, 'came out of the house and stopped them. She told Mr Harrow to get into his car. Then she got in and they drove away. Nick said that he was sorry, but couldn't talk to me right then. He went into the house and closed the door and locked it.'

'How do you know he locked it?'

'I tried to get in. His parents were away, in Palm Springs, and he was terribly upset. Don't ask me why. I don't understand it at all, except that that woman is after him.'

'Do you know that?'

'She's that kind of woman. She's phony blonde with a big red sloppy mouth and poisonous eyes. I can't understand why he would flip over her.'

'What makes you think he has?'

'The way she talked to him, as if she owned him.' She spoke with her face and the front of her body averted.

'Have you told your father about this woman?'

She shook her head. 'He knows I'm having trouble with Nick. But I can't tell him what it is. It makes Nick look so bad.'

'And you want to marry Nick.'

'I've waited for a long time.' She turned and faced me. I could feel the pressure of her cool insistence, like water against a dam. 'I intend to marry him, whether my father wants me to or not. I'd naturally prefer to have his approval.'

'But he's opposed to Nick?'

Her face thinned. 'He'd be opposed to any man whom I wanted to marry. My mother was killed in 1945. She was younger then than I am now,' she added in faint surprise. 'Father never remarried, for my sake. I wish for my sake he had.'

She spoke with the measured emphasis of a young woman who had suffered.

'How old are you, Betty?'

'Twenty-five.'

'How long is it since you've seen Nick?'

'Not since Friday night, at his house.'

'And you've been waiting for him here since then?'

'Part of the time. Dad would worry himself sick if I didn't come home at night. Incidentally, Nick hasn't slept in his own bed since I started waiting for him here.'

'When was that?'

'Saturday afternoon.' She added with a seasick look: 'If he wants to sleep with her, let him.'

At this point the telephone rang. She rose quickly and

answered it. After listening for a moment she spoke rather grimly into the receiver:

'This is Mr Chalmers's answering service. . . . No, I don't know where he is . . . Mr Chalmers does not provide me with that information.'

She listened again. From where I sat I could hear a woman's emotional voice on the line, but I couldn't make out her words. Betty repeated them: ' "Mr Chalmers is to stay away from the Montevista Inn." I see. Your husband has followed you there. Shall I tell him that? . . . All right.'

She put the receiver down, very gently, as if it was packed with high explosives. The blood mounted from her neck and suffused her face in a flush of pure emotion.

'That was Mrs Trask.'

'I was wondering. I gather she's at the Montevista Inn.'

'Yes. So is her husband.'

'I may pay them a visit.'

She rose abruptly. 'I'm going home. I'm not going to wait here any longer. It's humiliating.'

We went down together in the elevator. In its automatic intimacy she said:

'I've spilled all my secrets. How do you make people do it?'

'I don't. People like to talk about what's hurting them. It takes the edge off the pain sometimes.'

'Yes, I believe it does.'

'May I ask you one more painful question?'

'This seems to be the day for them.'

'How was your mother killed?'

'By a car, right in front of our house on Pacific Street.'

'Who was driving?'

'Nobody knows, least of all me. I was just a small baby.'

'Hit-run?'

She nodded. The doors slid open at the ground floor, terminating our intimacy. We went out together to the parking lot. I watched her drive off in a red two-seater, burning rubber as she turned into the street.

IV

MONTEVISTA LAY ON the sea just south of Pacific Point. It was a rustic residential community for woodland types who could afford to live anywhere.

I left the freeway and drove up an oak-grown hill to the Montevista Inn. From its parking lot the rooftops below seemed to be floating in a flood of greenery. I asked the young man in the office for Mrs Trask. He directed me to Cottage Seven, on the far side of the pool.

A bronze dolphin spouted water at one end of the big old-fashioned pool. Beyond it a flagstone path meandered through live oaks toward a white stucco cottage. A red-shafted flicker took off from one of the trees and crossed a span of sky, wings opening and closing like a fan lined with vivid red.

It was a nice place to be, except for the sound of the voices from the cottage. The woman's voice was mocking. The man's was sad and monotonous. He was saying:

'It isn't so funny, Jean. You can wreck your life just so many times. And my life, it's my life, too. Finally you reach a point where you can't put it back together. You should learn a lesson from what happened to your father.'

'Leave my father out of this.'

'How can I? I called your mother in Pasadena last night, and she says you're still looking for him. It's a wild-goose chase, Jean. He's probably been dead for years.'

'No! Daddy's alive. And this time I'm going to find him.'

'So he can ditch you again?'

'He never ditched me.'

'That's the way I heard it from your mother. He ditched you

both and took off with a piece of skirt.'

'He did not.' Her voice was rising. 'You mustn't say such things about my father.'

'I can say them if they're true.'

'I won't listen!' she cried. 'Get out of here. Leave me alone.'

'I will not. You're coming home to San Diego with me and put up a decent front. You owe me that much after twenty years.'

The woman was silent for a moment. The sounds of the place lapped in like gentle waves: a towhee foraging in the underbrush, a kinglet rattling. Her voice, when she spoke again, was calmer and more serious:

'I'm sorry, George, I truly am, but you might as well give up. I've heard everything you're saying so often, it just goes by like wind.'

'You always came back before,' he said with a note of hopefulness in his voice.

'This time I'm not.'

'You have to, Jean.'

His voice had thinned. Its hopefulness had twisted into a kind of threat. I began to move around the side of the cottage.

'Don't you dare touch me,' she said.

'I have a legal right to. You're my wife.'

He was saying and doing all the wrong things. I knew, because I'd said and done them in my time. The woman let out a small scream, which sounded as if she was tuning up for a bigger one.

I looked around the corner of the cottage, where the flatstone path ran into a patio. The man had pinned the woman in his arms and was kissing the side of her blond head. She had turned her face away, in my direction. Her eyes were chilly, as if her husband's kisses were freezing cold.

'Let go of me, George. We have company.'

He released her and backed away, red-faced and wet-eyed. He was a large middle-aged man who moved awkwardly, as if he was the intruder instead of me.

'This is my wife,' he said, more in self-excuse than introduction.

'What was she yelling about?'

'It's all right,' the woman said. 'He wasn't hurting me. But you better leave now, George, before something does happen.'

'I have to talk to you some more.' He reached out a thick red hand toward her. The gesture was both menacing and touching, like something done by Frankenstein's innocent monster.

'You'd only get stirred up again.'

'But I've got a right to plead my case. You can't cut me off without a hearing. I'm not a criminal like your father was. But even a criminal gets his day in court. You've got to give me a hearing.'

He was getting very excited, and it was the kind of spinning excitement that could change to violence if it came up tails.

'You better go, Mr Trask.'

His wild wet gaze roved to me. I showed him an old Special Deputy badge I carried. He examined it closely, as if it was a curio.

'Very well, I'll go.' He turned and walked away, pausing at the corner of the building to call back: 'I'm not going very far.'

The woman turned to me, sighing. Her hair had been disarranged, and she was fixing it with nervous fingers. It was done in a fluffy doll-like fashion that didn't go with her forty years or so. But in spite of Betty's description of her, she wasn't a bad-looking woman. She had a good figure under her blouse, and a handsome, heavy face.

She also had a quality that bothered me, a certain doubt and dimness about the eyes, as if she had lost her way a long time ago.

'That was good timing,' she said to me. 'You never know what George is going to do.'

'Or anybody else.'

'Are you the security man around here?'

'I'm filling in.'

She looked me up and down, like a woman practicing to be a divorcee. 'I owe you a drink. Do you like Scotch?'

'On the rocks, please.'

'I have some ice. My name is Jean Trask, by the way.'

I told her my name. She took me into the living room of the cottage and left me there while she went into the kitchen. Around the walls of the room a series of English hunting prints followed some red-coated hunters and their hounds over hills and through valleys to the death of the fox.

Ostensibly studying the prints, I circled the room to the open door of the bedroom and looked in. On the nearest of the two beds a woman's blue weekend case lay open, and the gold box was in it. On its painted lid a man and a woman in skimpy antique clothes disported themselves.

I was tempted to walk in and take the box, but John Truttwell wouldn't have liked that. Even without him, I'd probably have let the thing lie. I was beginning to sense that the theft of the box was just a physical accident of the case. Any magic it possessed, black or white or gold, was soaked up from the people who handled it.

But I took two steps into the bedroom and lifted the heavy lid of the box. It was empty. I heard Mrs Trask crossing the living room, and I retreated in her direction. She slammed the bedroom door.

'We won't be using that room.'

'What a pity.'

She gave me a startled look, as if she was unaware of her own rough candor. Then she shoved a lowball glass at me. 'Here.'

She went into the kitchen and returned with a dark-brown drink for herself. As soon as she had taken a swallow or two, her eyes turned moist and bright and her color rose. She was a drinker, I thought, and I was there essentially because she didn't want to drink alone.

She knocked her drink back in a hurry and made herself another, while I nursed mine. She sat down in an armchair facing me across a coffee table. I was almost enjoying myself. The room was large and tranquil, and through the open front door I could hear quail muttering and puttering.

I had to spoil it. 'I was admiring your gold box. Is it Florentine?'

'I suppose it is,' she said, offhandedly.

'Don't you know? It looks quite valuable.'

'Really? Are you an expert?'

'No. I was thinking in terms of security. I wouldn't leave it lying around like that.'

'Thanks for your advice,' she said unthankfully. She was quiet for a minute, sipping her drink. 'I didn't mean to be rude just now; I have things on my mind.' She leaned toward me in a show of interest. 'Have you been in the security business long?'

'Over twenty years, counting my time with the police.'

'You used to be a policeman?'

'That's right.'

'Perhaps you can help me. I'm involved in a kind of nasty situation. I don't feel up to explaining it all right now, but I hired a man named Sidney Harrow to come here with me. He claimed to be a private detective but it turned out his main experience is repossessing cars. He's a fast man with a tow bar. Also he's dangerous.' She finished her drink, and shivered.

'How do you know he's dangerous?'

'He almost killed my boyfriend. He's a fast man with a gun, too.'

'You also have a boyfriend?'

'I call him my boyfriend,' she said with a half-smile. 'Actually we're more like brother and sister, or father and daughter—I mean mother and son.' Her smile turned to a simper.

'What's his name?'

'That has no bearing on what I'm telling you. The point is that Sidney Harrow nearly shot him the other night.'

'Where did this happen?'

'Right out in front of my boyfriend's house. I realized then that Sidney was a wild man, and he's been no use to me since. He has the picture and stuff but he's not doing anything with them. I'm afraid to go and ask for it back.'

'And you want me to?'

'Maybe. I'm not committing myself yet.' She spoke with the foolish wisdom of a woman who had no feeling for men and would always make the wrong decisions about them.

'What would Sidney be doing with the picture and stuff?'

'Finding out facts,' she said carefully. 'That's what I hired him to do. But I made the mistake of giving him some money and all he does is sit in his motel room and drink. I haven't even heard from him in two days.'

'Which motel?'

'The Sunset, on the beach.'

'How did you get involved with Sidney Harrow?'

'I'm not *involved* with him. A man I know brought him to the house last week and he seemed so lively and alert, just the man I was looking for.' As if to renew the promise of that occasion, she raised her glass and drained the last few drops, coaxing them with her tongue. 'He reminded me of my father when he was a young man.'

For a moment she seemed at ease in the double memory. But her feelings were very shifty, and she couldn't hold this one long. I could see her quick-remembered happiness dying in her eyes.

She rose and started for the kitchen, then stopped abruptly, as if she'd come up against invisible glass. 'I'm drinking too much,' she said. 'And I'm talking too much.'

She left her glass in the kitchen and came back and stood over me. Her unhappy eyes regarded me suspiciously, as if I was the source of the unhappiness.

'Please get out of here, will you? Forget what I said to you, eh?'

I thanked her for the drink and drove downhill to the Ocean Boulevard and along it to the Sunset Motor Hotel.

V

IT WAS ONE of the older buildings on the Pacific Point waterfront, two-storied and solidly constructed of red brick. In the harbour across the boulevard, sailboats lay in their slips like birds with their wings folded. A few Capris and Seashells were scudding down the channel before the January wind.

I parked in front of the motor hotel and went into the office. The gray-haired woman behind the desk gave me a bland experienced glance that took in my age and weight, my probable income and credit rating, and whether I was married.

She said she was Mrs Delong. When I asked for Sidney Harrow, I could see my credit rating slip in the ledger of her eyes.

'Mr Harrow has left us.'

'When?'

'Last night. In the course of the night.'

'Without paying his bill?'

Her look sharpened. 'You know Mr Harrow, do you?'

'Just by reputation.'

'Do you know where I can get in touch with him? He gave us a San Diego business address. But he only worked part-time for them, they said, and they wouldn't assume any responsibility or give me his home address—if he has a home.' She paused for breath. 'If I knew where he lived I could get the police after him.'

'I may be able to help you.'

'How is that?' she said with some suspicion.

'I'm a private detective, and I'm looking for Harrow, too. Has his room been cleaned?'

'Not yet. He left his Do Not Disturb card out, which he did most of the time anyway. It was just a little while ago I noticed his car was gone and used my master key. You want to look over the room?'

'It might be a good idea. While we think of it, Mrs Delong, what's his car license number?'

She looked it up in her file. 'KIT 994. It's an old convertible, tan-colored with the back window torn out. What's Harrow wanted for?'

'I don't know yet.'

'Are you sure you're a detective?'

I showed her my photostat, and it satisfied her. She made a careful note of my name and address, and handed me the key to Harrow's room. 'It's number twenty-one on the second floor at the back.'

I climbed the outside stairs and went along the alley toward the rear. The windows of number twenty-one were closely draped. I unlocked the door and opened it. The room was dim, and sour with old smoke. I opened the drapes and let the light sluice in.

The bed had apparently not been slept in. The spread was rumpled, though, and several pillows were squashed against the headboard. A half-empty fifth of rye stood on the bedside table on top of a girlie magazine. I was a little surprised that Harrow had left behind a bottle with whisky in it.

He had also left, in the bathroom cabinet, a toothbrush and a tube of toothpaste, a three-dollar razor, a jar of hair grease, and a spray can of a spicy scent called Swingeroo. It looked as if Harrow had planned to come back, or had left in a great hurry.

The second possibility seemed more likely when I found an unmatched shoe in the darkest corner of the closet. It was a new pointed black Italian shoe for the left foot. Along with the shoe for the right foot it would have been worth at least twenty-five dollars. But I couldn't find the right shoe anywhere in the room.

In the course of looking for it I did find, on the high self of the closet under spare blankets, a brown envelope containing a small-size graduation picture. The smiling young man in the picture resembled Irene Chalmers and was probably, I decided, her son Nick.

My guess was pretty well confirmed when I found the Chalmerses' address, 2124 Pacific Street, penciled on the back of the envelope. I slid the picture back into the envelope and put it in my inside pocket and took it away with me.

After reporting the general situation to Mrs Delong, I crossed the street to the harbor. The boats caught in the maze of floating docks rocked and smacked the water. I felt like getting into one of them and sailing out to sea.

My brief dip into Sidney Harrow's life had left a stain on my nerves. Perhaps it reminded me too strongly of my own life. Depression threatened me like a sour smoke drifting in behind my eyes.

The ocean wind blew it away, as it nearly always could. I walked the length of the harbor and crossed the asphalt desert of the parking lots toward the beach. The waves were collapsing like walls there, and I felt like a man escaping from his life.

You can't, of course. An old tan Ford convertible with a torn-out rear window was waiting for me at the end of my short walk. It was parked by itself in a drift of sand at the far edge of the asphalt. I looked in through the rear window and saw the dead man huddled on the back seat with dark blood masking his face.

I could smell whisky and the spicy odor of Swingeroo. The doors of the convertible weren't locked, and I could see the keys in the ignition. I was tempted to use them to open the trunk.

Instead I did the right thing, for prudential reasons. I was outside of Los Angeles County, and the local police had a very strong sense of territory. I found the nearest telephone, in a bait and tackle shop at the foot of the breakwater, and called the police. Then I went back to the convertible to wait for them.

The wind spat sand in my face and the sea had a shaggy green theatening look. High above it, gulls and terns were wheeling like a complex mobile suspended from the sky. A city police car crossed the parking lot and skidded to a stop beside me.

Two uniformed officers got out. They looked at me, at the dead man in the car, at me again. They were young men, with few discernible differences except that one was dark, one fair. Both had heavy shoulders and jaws, unmoved eyes, conspicuous guns in their holsters, and hands ready.

'Who is he?' said the blue-eyed one.

'I don't know.'

'Who are you?'

I told them my name, and handed over my identification.

'You're a private detective?'

'That's right.'

'But you don't know who this is in the car?'

I hesitated. If I told them it was Sidney Harrow, as I guessed, I'd have to explain how I found that out and would probably end up telling them everything I knew.

'No,' I said.

'How did you happen to find him?'

'I was passing by.'

'Passing by to where?'

'The beach. I was going to take a walk on the beach.'

'That's a funny place to take a walk on a day like this,' said the fair one.

I was ready to agree. The place had changed. The dead man had bled it of life and color. The men in uniform had changed its meaning. It was a dreary official kind of place with a cold draft blowing.

'Where you from?' the dark one asked me.

'Los Angeles. My address is on my photostat. I want it back, by the way.'

'You'll get it back when we're finished with you. You got a car, or you come to town by public carrier?'

'Car.'

'Where is your car?'

It hit me then, in a reaction that had been delayed by the shock of finding Harrow, if that's who he was. My car was parked in front of the Sunset Motor Hotel. Whether I told them about it or not, the police would find it there. They'd talk to Mrs Delong and learn that I'd been on Harrow's trail.

That was what happened. I told them where my car was, and before long I was in an interrogation room in police headquarters being questioned by two sergeants. I asked several times for a lawyer, specifically the lawyer who had brought me to town.

They got up and left me alone in the room. It was an airless cubicle whose dirty gray plaster walls had been scribbled with names. I passed the time reading the inscriptions. Duke the Dude from Dallas had been there on a bum rap. Joe Hespeler had been there, and Handy Andy Oliphant, and Fast Phil Larrabee.

The sergeants came back and regretted to say that they hadn't been able to get in touch with Truttwell. But they wouldn't let me try to phone him myself. In a way this breach of my rights encouraged me: it meant that I wasn't a serious suspect.

They were on a fishing expedition, hoping I'd done their work for them. I sat and let them do some of mine. The dead man was Sidney Harrow, without much question: his thumbprint matched the thumbprint on his driver's license. He'd been shot in the head, once, and been dead for at least twelve hours. That placed the time of death no later than last midnight, when I had been at home in my apartment in West Los Angeles.

I explained this to the sergeants. They weren't interested. They wanted to know what I was doing in their county, and what my interest in Harrow was. They wheedled and begged and coaxed and pleaded and threatened me and made jokes. It gave me a queer feeling, which I didn't mention to them, that I had indeed inherited Sidney Harrow's life.

VI

A MAN IN plain dark clothes came quietly into the room. Both the sergeants stood up, and he dismissed them. He had clipped gray hair, eyes that were hard and sober on either side of a scarred and broken nose. His mouth was chewed and ravaged by lifelong doubt and suspicion, and it kept working now. He sat down facing me across the table.

'I'm Lackland, Captain of Detectives. I hear you been giving our boys a bad time.'

'I thought it was the other way around.'

His eyes searched my face. 'I don't see any marks on you.'

'I have a right to a lawyer.'

'We have a right to your cooperation. Try bucking us and you could end up flat on your rear end without a license.'

'That reminds me, I want my photostat back.'

Instead, he took a manila envelope out of his inside pocket and opened it. Among other things it contained a snapshot, or a piece of snapshot, which Lackland pushed across the table to me.

It was a picture of a man in his forties. He had fair thinning hair, bold eyes, a wry mouth. He looked like a poet who had missed his calling and had had to settle for grosser satisfactions.

His picture had been cut from a larger picture which had included other people. I could see girls' dresses on either side of him, but not the girls. The thing looked like a blown-up snapshot at least twenty years old.

'Know him?' Captain Lackland said.

'No.'

He thrust his scarred face toward me like a warning of what my face might become. 'You're sure about that, are you?'

'I'm sure.' There was no use mentioning my unsupported guess that this was a picture Jean Trask had given Harrow, and that it was a picture of her father.

He leaned toward me again. 'Come on now, Mr Archer, help us out. Why was Sidney Harrow carrying this?' His forefinger jabbed at the blown-up snapshot.

'I don't know.'

'You must have some idea. Why were *you* interested in Harrow?'

'I have to talk to John Truttwell. After that I may be able to say something.'

Lackland got up and left the room. In about ten minutes he came back accompanied by Truttwell. The lawyer looked at me with concern.

'I understand you've been here for some time, Archer. You should have got in touch with me before.' He turned to Lackland. 'I'll talk to Mr Archer in private. He's employed by me in a confidential capacity.'

Lackland retreated slowly. Truttwell sat down across from me. 'Why are they holding you, anyway?'

'A part-time bill collector named Sidney Harrow was shot last night. Lackland knows I was following Harrow. He doesn't know that Harrow was one of several people involved in the theft of the gold box.'

Truttwell was startled. 'You've found that out already?'

'It wasn't hard. This is the sloppiest burglary in history. The woman who has the box now keeps it lying around in plain view.'

'Who is she?'

'Her married name is Jean Trask. Who she really is is another question. Apparently Nick stole the box and gave it to her. Which is why I can't talk freely, to Lackland or anyone else.'

'I should certainly say you can't. Are you sure about all this?'

'Unless I've been having delusions.' I stood up. 'Can't we finish this outside?'

'Of course. Wait here for a minute.'

Truttwell went out, closing the door behind him. He came back smiling and handed me the photostat of my license. 'You're sprung. Oliver Lackland's a fairly reasonable man.'

In the narrow corridor that led to the parking lot, I ran the gauntlet of Lackland and his sergeants. They nodded at me, too many times for comfort.

I told Truttwell what had happened as we drove across town in his Cadillac. He turned up Pacific Street.

'Where are we going?'

'To my house. You made quite an impression on Betty. She wants to ask your advice.'

'What about?'

'It's probably something to do with Nick. He's all she thinks about.' Truttwell added after a long pause: 'Betty seems to believe I'm prejudiced against him. That's really not the case. But I don't want her to make any unnecessary mistakes. She's the only daughter I have.'

'She told me she's twenty-five.'

'Betty's very young for her age, though. Very young and vulnerable.'

'Superficially, maybe. She struck me as a resourceful woman.'

Truttwell gave me a look of pleased surprise. 'I'm glad you think so. I brought her up by myself, and it's been quite a responsibility.' After another pause he added: 'My wife died when Betty was only a few months old.'

'She told me her mother was killed by a hit-run driver.'

'Yes, that's true.' Truttwell's voice was almost inaudible.

'Was the driver ever caught?'

'I'm afraid not. The Highway Patrol found the car, near San Diego, but it was a stolen car. Strangely enough, whoever it was had made an attempt to burglarize the Chalmerses' house. My wife apparently saw them enter the house and scared them out of there. They ran her down when they made their getaway.'

He gave me a bleak look which resisted further questions. We drove in silence the rest of the way to his house, which was diagonally across the street from the Chalmerses' Spanish mansion. He dropped me at the curb, said he had a client waiting, and drove away.

The architecture on upper Pacific Street was traditional but eclectic. Truttwell's house was a white colonial one, with green shutters upstairs and down.

I knocked on the green front door. It was answered by a gray little woman in a housekeeper's dim quasi-uniform. The formal lines which bracketed her mouth softened when I told her who I was.

'Yes. Miss Truttwell is expecting you.' She led me up a curving stair to the door of a front room. 'Mr Archer is here to see you.'

'Thanks, Mrs Glover.'

'Can I get you anything, dear?'

'No thanks.'

Betty delayed her appearance till Mrs Glover had gone. I could see why. Her eyes were swollen and her color was bad. She held her body tensely, like a kicked animal expecting to be kicked again.

She stood back to let me enter the room, and closed the door behind me. It was a young woman's study, bright with chintz and Chagall, its shelves loaded with books. She faced me standing up, with her back to the windows overlooking the street.

'I've heard from Nicholas.' She indicated the orange telephone on the worktable. 'You won't tell Father, will you?'

'He already suspects it, Betty.'

'But you won't tell him anything more?'

'Don't you trust your father?'

'About anything else, yes. But you mustn't tell him what I'm going to tell you.'

'I'll do my best, that's all I can promise. Is Nick in trouble?'

'Yes.' She hung her head, and her bright hair curtained her face. 'I think he intends to kill himself. I don't want to live, either, if he does.'

'Did he say why?'

'He's done something terrible, he says.'

'Like kill a man?'

She flung her hair back and looked at me with blazing dislike. 'How can you say such a thing?'

'Sidney Harrow was shot on the waterfront last night. Did Nick mention him?'

'Of course not.'

'What *did* he say?'

She was quiet for a minute, remembering. Then she recited slowly: 'That he didn't deserve to live. That he'd let me down, and let his parents down, and he couldn't face any of us again. Then he said goodbye to me—a final goodbye.' A hiccup of grief shook her.

'How long ago did he make the call?'

She looked at the orange phone, and then at her watch. 'About an hour. It seems like forever, though.'

She moved vaguely past me to the other side of the room and took a framed photograph down from a wall bracket. I moved up behind her and looked at it over her shoulder. It was a larger copy of the photograph in my pocket, which I had found in the closet of Harrow's motel room. I noticed now that in spite of his smiling mouth, the young man in the picture had somber eyes.

'I take it that's Nick,' I said.

'Yes. It's his graduation picture.'

She replaced it on its bracket, with a faintly ritual air, and went to the front windows. I followed her. She was looking out across the street toward the closed white front of the Chalmers house.

'I don't know what to do.'

'We've got to find him,' I said. 'Did he say where he was calling from?'

'No, he didn't.'

'Or anything else at all?'

'I don't remember anything else.'

'Did he say what suicide method he had in mind?'

She hid her face behind her hair again and answered in a hushed voice: 'He didn't say, this time.'

'You mean he's gone through this routine before?'

'Not really. And you mustn't speak of it in that way. He's terribly serious.'

'So am I.' But I was angry at the boy for what he had done

and was doing to the girl. 'What did he do or say the other times?'

'He often talked about suicide when he got depressed. I don't mean that he threatened to do it. But he talked about ways and means. He never held anything back from me.'

'Maybe it's time he started.'

'You sound like Father. You're both prejudiced against him.'

'Suicide is a cruel business, Betty.'

'Not if you love the person. A depressed person can't help the way he feels.'

I didn't argue any further. 'You were going to tell me how he planned to do it.'

'It wasn't a *plan*. He was simply talking. He said a gun was too messy, and pills were uncertain. The cleanest way would be to swim out to sea. But the thing that really haunted him, he said, was the thought of the rope.'

'Hanging?'

'He told me he'd thought of hanging himself ever since he was a child.'

'Where did he get that idea?'

'I don't know. But his grandfather was a Superior Court judge, and some people in town considered him a hanging judge—one who liked to sentence people to death. It may have influenced Nick, in a negative way. I've read of stranger things in history.'

'Did Nick ever mention the hanging judge in the family?'

She nodded.

'And suicide?'

'Many times.'

'That's quite a courtship he's been treating you to.'

'I'm not complaining. I love Nick, and I want to be of some use to him.'

I was beginning to understand the girl, and the more I understood the better I liked her. She had a serviceability that I had noticed before in widowers' daughters.

'Think back to his telephone call,' I said. 'Did he give any indication of where he was?'

'I don't remember any.'

'Give it some time. Go and sit by the telephone.'

She sat in a chair beside the table, with one hand on the instrument as if to keep it quiet.

'I could hear noises in the background.'

'What kind of noises?'

'Wait a minute.' She raised her hand for silence, and sat listening. 'Children's voices, and splashing. Pool noises. I think he must have called me from the public booth at the Tennis Club.'

VII

THOUGH I'D VISITED the Tennis Club before, the woman at the front desk was strange to me. But she knew Betty Truttwell, and greeted her warmly.

'We never see you any more, Miss Truttwell.'

'I've been terribly busy. Has Nick been here today?'

The woman answered with some reluctance: 'As a matter of fact, he has been. He came in an hour or so ago, and went into the bar for a while. He wasn't looking too well when he came out.'

'Do you mean that he was drunk?'

'I'm afraid he was, Miss Truttwell, since you asked me. The woman with him, the blonde, was under the weather, too. After they left I gave Marco a piece of my mind. But he said he only served them two drinks each. He said the woman was tight when they arrived, and Mr Chalmers can't handle liquor.'

'He never could,' Betty agreed. 'Who was the woman?'

'I forget her name—he's brought her in once before.' She consulted the guest register which lay on the desk in front of her. ' "Jean Swain." '

'Not Jean Trask?' I said.

'It looks like "Swain" to me.'

She pushed the register toward me, indicating with her red fingertips where Nick had signed the woman's name and his own. It looked like 'Swain' to me, too. Her home address was given as San Diego. 'Is she a fairly large blonde with a good figure, fortyish?'

'That's her. A good figure,' she added, 'if you like the fleshy type.' She herself was very thin.

Betty and I walked toward the bar along the gallery that overlooked the pool. The children were still making pool noises. A few adults were stretched out on long chairs in corners, catching the thin warmth of the January sun.

The bar was empty except for a couple of men prolonging their lunch. The bartender and I exchanged nods of recognition. Marco was a short, quick, dark man in a red waistcoat. He admitted gloomily that Nick had been there.

'Matter of fact, I asked him to leave.'

'Did he have a lot to drink?'

'Not here he didn't. I served him two single shots of bourbon, and you can't make a federal case out of that. What happened, did he wreck his car?'

'I hope not. I'm trying to catch up with him before he wrecks anything. Do you know where he went?'

'No, but I'll tell you one thing, he was in a hell of a mood. When I wouldn't give him a third drink, he wanted to put up a fight. I had to show him my pool cue.' Marco reached under the bar and showed it to us: the sawed-off butt of a heavy cue about two feet long. 'I hated to pull it on a member, you know, but he was carrying a gun and I wanted him out of here, fast. Anyone else, I would have called the sheriff.'

'He had a gun?' Betty said in a small, high voice.

'Yeah, it was in the pocket of his jacket. He kept it out of sight but you can't hide a big heavy gun like that.' He leaned across the bar and peered into Betty's eyes. 'What's the matter with him, anyway, Miss Truttwell? He never acted like this before.'

'He's in trouble,' she said.

'Does the dame have anything to do with his trouble? The blonde dame? She drinks like she's got a hollow leg. She shouldn't be making him drink.'

'Do you know who she is, Marco?'

'No. But she looks like trouble to me. I don't know what he thinks he's doing with *her*.'

Betty started for the door, then turned back to Marco again. 'Why didn't you take the gun away from him?'

'I don't fool around with guns, Miss. That isn't my department.'

We went out to Betty's two-seater in the parking lot. The club was on a cove of the Pacific, and I caught a whiff of the sea. It was a raw and rueful smell, conjuring up the place where I had found Sidney Harrow.

Betty and I were both silent and thoughtful as she drove up the long hill to the Montevista Inn. The young man in the office remembered me.

'You're just in time if you want to see Mrs Trask. She's getting ready to leave.'

'Did she say why?'

'I think she's had bad news. It must be serious, because she didn't even put up an argument when I had to charge her for an extra day. They usually put up an argument.'

I made my way through the oak grove and tapped on the screen door of the stucco cottage.

The inner door was open, and Jean Trask answered from the bedroom: 'My bags are ready, if you want to carry them out.'

I crossed the living room and entered the bedroom. The woman was sitting at the dressing table, shakily applying lipstick.

Our eyes met in the mirror. Her hand wandered, describing a red clown mouth around her real one. She turned and got up clumsily, upsetting her stool.

'They sent you for my bags?'

'No. But I'll be glad to carry them.' I picked up her matched blue bags. They were light enough.

'Put them down,' she said. 'Who are you anyway?'

She was ready to be afraid of anyone for any reason—so full of fear that some of it slopped over into me. Her huge red mouth alarmed me. Chilly laughter convulsed my stomach.

'I asked about you at the office,' she said. 'They told me they don't have a security guard. So what are you doing here?'

'At the moment I'm looking for Nick Chalmers. We don't have to beat around the bush. You must know he's in serious emotional trouble.'

She answered as if she was glad to have someone to talk to: 'He certainly is. He's talking about suicide. I thought a couple of drinks would do him good. They only made him worse.'

'Where is he now?'

'I made him promise to go home and sleep it off. He said he would.'

'Home to his apartment?'

'I guess so.'

'You're pretty vague, Mrs Trask.'

'I try to keep myself that way. It's less painful,' she added wryly.

'How did you get so interested in Nick?'

'It's none of your business. And I'm not taking any static from you.'

Her voice rose as she gained confidence in her own anger. But a steady trill of fear ran through it.

'What are you so afraid of, Mrs Trask?'

'Sidney Harrow got himself zapped last night.' Her voice was rough with self-concern. 'You must know that.'

'How do *you* happen to know it?'

'Nick told me. I'm sorry I ever opened this can of worms.'

'Did he kill Sidney?'

'I don't think he knows—that's how far off base he is. And I'm not waiting around to find out.'

'Where are you going?'

She refused to tell me.

I went back to Betty and told her what I had learned, or part of it. We decided to go out to the university community in separate cars. My car was where it was supposed to be, in front of the Sunset Motor Motel. There was a parking ticket under the windshield wiper.

I tried to follow Betty's red two-seater, but she drove too fast for me, close to ninety on the straightaway. She was waiting for me when I reached the parking lot of the Cambridge Arms.

She ran toward me. 'He's here. At least that's his car.'

She pointed at a blue sports car standing beside her red one. I went and touched the hood. The engine was hot. The key was in the ignition.

'You stay down here,' I said.

'No. If he makes trouble—I mean he won't if I'm there.'

'That's a thought.'

We went up together in the elevator. Betty knocked on Nick's door and called his name. 'This is Betty.'

There was a long waiting silence. Betty knocked again. Abruptly the door was pulled open. She took an involuntary step into the room, and ended up with her face against Nick's chest. He held her with one hand and with the other he pointed a heavy revolver at my stomach.

I couldn't see his eyes, which were hidden by dark wrap-around glasses. In contrast, his face was very pale. His hair was uncombed and hung down over his forehead. His white shirt was dirty. My mind recorded these things as if they might add up to my last sight of the world. I felt resentment more than fear. I hated the idea of dying for no good reason at the hands of a mixed-up overgrown boy I didn't even know.

'Drop it,' I said routinely.

'I don't take orders from you.'

'Come on now, Nick,' Betty said.

She moved closer to him, trying to use her body to distract him. Her right arm slid around his waist, and she pressed one thigh forward between his legs. She raised her left arm as if she was going to loop it around his neck. Instead she brought it sharply down on his gun arm.

The revolver was pointing at the floor now. I dove for it and wrenched it out of his hand.

'Damn you!' he said. 'Damn you both!'

A boy with a high voice or a girl with a low one came out of the apartment across the hall. 'What's going on?'

'Initiation,' I said.

Nick tore himself loose from Betty and swung at my face. I shifted and let his fist go by. I lowered my head and bulled him backward into his living room. Betty shut the door and leaned on it. Her color was high. She was breathing through her mouth.

Nick came at me again. I went under his fists and hit him solidly in the solar plexus. He lay down gasping for breath.

I spun the cylinder of his revolver. One shell had been fired. It was a Colt ·45. I got out my black notebook and made a record of its number.

Betty moved between us. 'You didn't have to hurt him.'

'Yes I did. But he'll get over it.'

She kneeled beside him and touched his face with her hand. He rolled away from her. The sounds he made fighting for breath gradually subsided. He sat up with his back against the chesterfield.

I sat on my heels facing him, and showed him his revolver. 'Where did you get this, Nick?'

'I don't have to answer that. You can't make me incriminate myself.'

His voice had a queer inhuman tone, as if it was being played back on tape. I couldn't tell what the tone meant. His eyes were effectively masked by the wrap-around glasses.

'I'm not a policeman, Nick, if that's what you think.'

'I don't care what you are.'

I tried again. 'I'm a private detective working on your side. But I'm not quite clear what your side is. Do you want to talk about it?'

He shook his head like a child in a tantrum, whipping it rapidly from side to side until his hair blurred out. Betty said in a pained voice:

'Please don't do that, Nicholas. You'll hurt your neck.'

She smoothed his hair with her fingers. He sat perfectly still.

'Let me look at you,' she said.

She took off his dark glasses. He grabbed for them, but she held them out of his reach. His eyes were black and glistening like asphalt squeezed from a crevice. They seemed to be leading a strange life of their own, with an inward look and an outward look alternating anxiety and aggression. I could understand why he wore the glasses to hide his sad changing eyes.

He covered his eyes with his hands and peered between his fingers.

'Please don't do that, Nick.' The girl was kneeling beside him again. 'What happened? Please tell me what happened.'

'No. You wouldn't love me any more.'

'Nothing could stop me loving you.'

'Even if I killed somebody?' he said between his hands.

'Did you kill somebody?' I said.

He nodded slowly, once, keeping his head down and his face hidden.

'With this revolver?'

His head jerked downward in the affirmative.

Betty said: 'He's in no condition to talk. You mustn't force him.'

'I think he wants to get it off his chest. Why do you suppose he phoned you from the club?'

'To say goodbye.'

'This is better than saying goodbye. Isn't it?'

She answered soberly: 'I don't know. I don't know how much I can stand.'

I turned to Nick again. 'Where did you get the revolver?'

'It was in his car.'

'Sidney Harrow's car?'

He dropped his hands from his face. His eyes were puzzled and fearful. 'Yes. It was in his car.'

'Did you shoot him in his car?'

His whole face clenched like a frightened baby's getting ready to cry. 'I don't remember.' He struck himself on the forehead with his fist. Then he struck himself in the mouth, hard.

'You're tormenting him,' the girl said. 'Can't you see he's sick?'

'Stop mothering him. He already has a mother.'

His head came up in a startled movement. 'You mustn't tell my mother. Or my father. Dad will kill me.'

I made no promises. His parents would have to be told. 'You were going to tell me where the shooting occurred, Nick.'

'Yes. I remember now. We went to the hobo jungle back of Ocean Boulevard. Someone had left a fire burning and we sat by the coals. He wanted me to do a bad thing.' His voice was naïve, like a child's. 'I took his gun and shot him.'

He made another scowling baby-face, so tight that it hid his eyes. He began to sob and moan, but no tears came. It was hard to watch his dry crying.

Betty put her arms around him. I said across the rhythms of his noise:

'He's had breakdowns before, hasn't he?'

'Not like this.'

'Did he stay at home, or was he hospitalized?'

'Home.' She spoke to Nick. 'Will you come home with me?'

He said something that might have been yes. I called the Chalmerses' number and got the servant, Emilio. He brought Irene Chalmers to the phone.

'This is Archer. I'm with your son in his apartment. He's not in a good way, and I'm bringing him home.'

'Is he hurt?'

'He's mentally hurt, and talking about suicide.'

'I'll get in touch with his psychiatrist,' she said. 'Dr Smitheram.'

'Is your husband there?'

'He's in the garden. Do you want to talk to him?'

'It isn't necessary. But you'd better prepare him for this.'

'Can you handle Nick?'

'I think so. I have Betty Truttwell with me.'

Before we left the apartment I called the Bureau of Criminal Investigation in Sacramento. I gave the number of the revolver to a man I knew named Roy Snyder. He said he'd try to check the name of the original owner. When we went down to my car I put the revolver in the trunk, locked in an evidence case.

VIII

WE RODE IN my car, with Betty driving and Nick on the front seat between us. He didn't speak or move until we stopped in front of his parents' house. Then he begged me not to make him go in.

I had to use a little force to get him out of the car. With one hand on his arm, and Betty walking on his far side, I marched him across the courtyard. He moved with deep reluctance, as if we planned to stand him up against the white wall and execute him.

His mother came out before we reached the front door. 'Nick? Are you all right?'

'I'm okay,' he said in his tape-recorder tone.

As we moved into the reception hall she said to me: 'Do you *have* to talk to my husband?'

'Yes I do. I asked you to prepare him.'

'I just couldn't do it,' she said. 'You'll have to tell him yourself. He's in the garden.'

'What about the psychiatrist?'

'Dr Smitheram had a patient with him, but he'll be here in a little while.'

'You'd better call John Truttwell, too,' I said. 'This thing has legal angles.'

I left Nick with the two women in the living room. Betty was solemn and quiet, as if Irene Chalmers's dark beauty cast a shadow over her.

Chalmers was in the walled garden, working among the plants. In clean, sun-faded Levis he looked thin, almost fragile. He was digging vigorously with a spade around some bushes which had been cut back for the winter and looked like dead thorny stumps.

He glanced up sharply at me, then slowly straightened, striking his spade upright in the earth. Greek and Roman statues stood around like nudists pitted by years of inclement weather.

Chalmers said rather severely: 'I thought it was understood that the Florentine box was not insured.'

'I wouldn't know about that, Mr Chalmers. I'm not in the insurance business.'

He got a little pale and tense. 'I understood you to say you were.'

'It was your wife's idea. I'm a private detective. John Truttwell called me in on your wife's behalf.'

'Then he can damn well call you off again.' Chalmers did a mental double take. 'You mean my wife went to Truttwell behind my back?'

'It wasn't such a bad idea. I know you're concerned about your son, and I just brought him home. He's been running around with a gun, talking very loosely about suicide and murder.'

I filled Chalmers in on what had been said and done. He was appalled. 'Nick must be out of his mind.'

'He is to a certain extent,' I said. 'But I don't think he was lying.'

'You believe he committed a murder?'

'A man named Sidney Harrow is dead. There was bad blood between him and Nick. And Nick has admitted shooting him.'

Chalmers swayed slightly and leaned on his spade, head down. There was a bald spot on the crown of his head, with a little hair brushed over it as if to mask his vulnerability. The moral beatings that people took from their children, I was thinking, were the hardest to endure and the hardest to escape.

But Chalmers wasn't thinking of himself. 'Poor Nick. He was doing so well. What's happened to him?'

'Maybe Dr Smitheram can tell you. It seems to have started with the gold box. Apparently Nick took it from your safe and gave it to a woman named Jean Trask.'

'I never heard of her. What would she want with my mother's gold box?'

'I don't know. It seems important to her.'

'Have you talked to this Trask woman?'

'Yes I have.'

'What did she do with my letters to my mother?'

'I don't know. I looked in the box, but it was empty.'

'Why didn't you ask her?'

'She's a difficult woman to deal with. And more important things kept coming up.'

Chalmers bit his mustache in chagrin. 'Such as?'

'I learned that she hired Sidney Harrow to come to Pacific Point. Apparently they were searching for her father.'

Chalmers gave me a puzzled look which wandered across the garden and over the wall to the sky. 'What has all this got to do with us?'

'It isn't clear, I'm afraid. I have a suggestion, subject to John Truttwell's approval. And yours, of course. It might be a good idea to turn the gun over to the police and let them make ballistics tests.'

'You mean give up without a fight?'

'Let's take this a step at a time, Mr Chalmers. If it turns out that Nick's gun didn't kill Harrow, his confession is probably fantasy. If it did kill Harrow, we can decide then what to do next.'

'We'll take it up with John Truttwell. I don't seem to be thinking too clearly.' Chalmers put his fingers to his forehead.

'It still wouldn't be hopeless,' I said, 'even if Nick did kill him. I believe there may have been mitigating circumstances.'

'How so?'

'Harrow had been throwing his weight around. He threatened Nick with a gun, possibly the same gun. This happened in front of your house the other night, when the box was stolen.'

Chalmers gave me a doubtful look. 'I don't see how you can possibly know that.'

'I have an eyewitness.' But I didn't name her.

'Do you have the gun with you?'

'It's in the trunk of my car. I'll show it to you.'

We went through a screened lanai into the house and down a corridor to the reception hall. Nick and his mother and Betty were sitting in a stiff little group on a sofa in the living room, like people at a party that had died some time ago. Nick had put on his dark glasses again, like a black bandage over his eyes.

Chalmers went into the living room and stood in front of him looking down as if from a great height. 'Is it true that you shot a man?'

Nick nodded dully. 'I'm sorry. I didn't want to come home. I meant to kill myself.'

'That's cowardly talk,' Chalmers said. 'You've got to act like a man.'

'Yes, Dad,' he said without hope.

'We'll do everything we can for you. Don't despair. Promise me that, Nick.'

'I promise, Dad. I'm sorry.'

Chalmers turned with a kind of military abruptness and came

back to me. His face was stoical. Both he and Nick must have been aware that no real communication had taken place.

We went out the front door. On the sidewalk Chalmers looked down at his gardening clothes self-consciously.

'I hate to appear like this in public,' he said, as if the neighbors might be watching him.

I opened the trunk of my car and showed him the revolver without removing it from the evidence case. 'Have you ever seen it before?'

'No. As a matter of fact Nick never owned a gun. He's always detested the whole business of guns.'

'Why?'

'I suppose he got it by osmosis from me. My father taught me to hunt when I was a boy. But the war destroyed my pleasure in hunting.'

'I hear you had quite a lot of war experience.'

'Who told you that?'

'John Truttwell.'

'I wish John would keep his own counsel. And mine. I prefer not to talk about my part in the war.' He looked down at the revolver with a kind of sad contempt, as if it symbolized all the forms of violence. 'Do you really think we should entrust this gun to John?'

'What do you suggest?'

'I know what I'd *like* to do. Bury it ten feet deep and forget about it.'

'We'd only have to dig it up again.'

'I suppose you're right,' he said.

Truttwell's Cadillac came into view, far down Pacific Street. He parked it in front of his own house and came across the street at a half-trot. He absorbed the bad news about Nick as if his mind had been tuned in to receive it.

'And this is the gun. It's loaded.' I handed him the case with the key in the lock. 'You better take charge of it until we decide what to do. I have a query in on its original ownership.'

'Good.' He turned to Chalmers. 'Where's Nick?'

'In the house. We're expecting Dr Smitheram.'

Truttwell laid his hand on Chalmers's bony shoulder. 'Too bad you and Irene have to go through it again.'

'Please. We won't discuss it.' Chalmers pulled away from Truttwell's hand. He turned abruptly and marched in his stoical way toward the front door.

I followed Truttwell across the street to his house. In his study, he locked the evidence case in a fireproof steel cabinet. I said:

'I'm glad to get that off my hands. I didn't want Lackland to catch me with it.'

'Do you think I should turn it over to him today?'

'Let's see what Sacramento says about ownership. What did you mean, by the way, about Chalmers going through it all again? Has Nick been in this kind of trouble before?'

Truttwell took his time about answering. 'It depends on what you mean by this kind of trouble. He's never been mixed up in a homicide before, at least not to my knowledge. But he's had one or two episodes—isn't that what the psychiatrists call them? A few years ago he ran away, and it took a nationwide search to bring him home.'

'Was he on the hippie kick?'

'Not really. Actually he was trying to support himself. When the Pinkertons finally tracked him down on the east coast, he was working as a busboy in a restaurant. We managed to persuade him that he should come home and finish his education.'

'How does he feel about his parents?'

'He's very close to his mother,' Truttwell said dryly, 'if that's desirable. I think he idolizes his father, but feels he can't measure up. Which is exactly how Larry Chalmers felt about his own father, the Judge. I suppose these patterns have to go on repeating themselves.'

'You mentioned more than one episode,' I prompted him.

'So I did.' He said down facing me. 'It goes much further back, fourteen or fifteen years, and it may be the root of Nick's trouble.

Dr Smitheram seems to think so. But beyond a certain point he won't discuss it with me.'

'What happened?'

'That's what Smitheram won't discuss. I think Nick was picked up by some sort of sexual psychopath. His family got him back in a hurry, but not before Nick was frightened out of his wits. He was only eight years old at the time. You can understand why nobody likes to talk about it.'

I wanted to ask Truttwell some more questions, but the housekeeper tapped on the study door and opened it. 'I heard you come in, Mr Truttwell. Is there anything I can get you?'

'No thanks, Mrs Glover. I'm going right out again. Where's Betty, by the way?'

'I don't know, sir.' But the woman looked at me, rather accusingly.

'She's at the Chalmers house,' I said.

Truttwell got to his feet, his entire body making an angry gesture. 'I don't like that at all.'

'It couldn't be helped. She was with me when I took Nick. She handled herself very well. And handled him.'

Truttwell struck his thigh with his fist. 'I didn't bring her up to be nurse to a psycho.'

The housekeeper had a terrified expression. She withdrew and closed the door without any sound.

'I'm going over there and bring her home,' Truttwell said. 'She's wasted her entire girlhood on that weakling.'

'She doesn't seem to think it was all waste.'

'So you're on *his* side?' He sounded like a rival.

'No. I'm on Betty's side, and probably yours. This is a hell of a time to force a decision on her.'

Truttwell got the message after a moments thought. 'You're right, of course.'

IX

BEFORE HE LEFT the house, Truttwell filled a pipe and lit it with a kitchen match. I stayed behind in his study to make a phone call to Roy Snyder in Sacramento. It was five minutes to five by my watch, and I was just in time to catch Snyder before he quit for the night.

'Archer again. Do you have any information on the ownership of the Colt?'

'Yes, I do. It was bought new by a Pasadena man named Rawlinson. Samuel Rawlinson.' Snyder spelled out the surname. 'He made the purchase in September of 1941, and at the same time he got a permit to carry it from the Pasadena police. The permit was allowed to lapse in 1945. That's all I have.'

'What reason did Rawlinson give for carrying a gun?'

'Business protection. He was the president of a bank,' Snyder added dryly. 'The Pasadena Occidental Bank.'

I thanked him and dialed Pasadena Information. The Pasadena Occidental Bank was not listed, but Samuel Rawlinson was.

I put in a person-to-person call to Rawlinson. A woman answered. Her voice was rough and warm.

'I'm sorry,' she explained to the operator. 'It's hard for Mr Rawlinson to come to the phone. Arthritis.'

'I'll talk to her,' I said.

'Go ahead, sir,' the operator said.

'This is Lew Archer. Who am I talking to?'

'Mrs Shepherd. I look after Mr Rawlinson.'

'Is he ill?'

'He's old,' she said. 'We all get old.'

'You're so right, Mrs Shepherd. I'm trying to trace possession of a gun which Mr Rawlinson bought in 1941. A ·45 Colt revolver. Will you ask him what he did with it?'

'I'll ask him.'

She left the phone for a minute or two. It was a noisy line, and I could hear distant babblings, scraps of conversation fading just before I could grasp their meaning.

'He wants to know who you are,' Mrs Shepherd said. 'And what right you have to ask him about any gun.' She added apologetically: 'I'm only quoting what Mr Rawlinson said. He's a stickler.'

'So am I. Tell him I'm a detective. The gun may or may not have been used last night to commit a crime.'

'Where?'

'In Pacific Point.'

'He used to spend his summers there,' she said. 'I'll ask him again.' She went away and came back. 'I'm sorry, Mr Archer, he won't talk. But he says if you want to come here and explain what it's all about, he'll discuss it with you.'

'When?'

'This evening if you want. He never goes out evenings. The number is 245 on Locust Street.'

I said I'd be there as soon as I could make it.

I was in my car, ready to go, when I realized I couldn't leave just yet. A black Cadillac convertible with a medical caduceus was parked just ahead of me. I wanted to have a word with Dr Smitheram.

The front door of the Chalmers house was standing open, as if its security had been breached. I walked into the reception hall. Truttwell stood with his back to me, arguing with a large balding man who had to be the psychiatrist. Lawrence and Irene Chalmers were on the fringes of the argument.

'The hospital is contraindicated,' Truttwell was saying. 'We can't be sure what the boy will say, and hospitals are always full of leaks.'

'My clinic isn't,' the large man said.

'Possibly, just possibly, it isn't. Even so, if you or one of your employees were asked a question in court, you'd have to answer it. Unlike the legal profession—'

The doctor interrupted Truttwell: 'Has Nick committed a crime of some sort?'

'I'm not going to answer that question.'

'How can I look after a patient without information?'

'You have plenty of information, more than I have.' Truttwell's voice seemed to buzz with an old resentment. 'You've sat on that information for fifteen years.'

'At least you recognize,' Smitheram said, 'that I haven't gone running to the police with it.'

'Would the police be interested, doctor?'

'I'm not going to answer that question.'

The two men faced each other in a quiet fury. Lawrence Chalmers tried to say something to them but they paid no attention.

His wife moved toward me, and drew me to one side. Her eyes were dull and unsurprised, as if she'd been hit by something that she'd seen coming from a long way off.

'Dr Smitheram wants to take Nick to his clinic. What do you think we should do?'

'I agree with Mr Truttwell. Your son needs legal security as well as medical.'

'Why?' she said bluntly.

'He killed a man last night, he says, and he's been talking about it quite freely.'

I paused to let the fact sink in. She handled it almost as if she'd been expecting it. 'Who is the man?'

'Sidney Harrow is his name. He was involved in the theft of your Florentine box. So was Nick, apparently.'

'Nick was?'

'I'm afraid so. With all these things on his mind, I don't think you should put him in any kind of clinic or hospital. Hospitals are always full of leaks, as Truttwell says. Couldn't you keep him at home?'

'Who would watch him?'

'You and your husband.'

She glanced at her husband, appraisingly. 'Maybe. I don't know if Larry is up to it. It doesn't show but he's terribly emotional, especially where Nick is concerned.' She moved closer, letting me feel the influence of her body. 'Would you, Mr Archer?'

'Would I what?'

'Stand watch over Nick tonight?'

'No.' The word came out hard and definite.

'We're paying your salary, you know.'

'And I've been earning it. But I'm not a psychiatric nurse.'

'I'm sorry I asked you.'

There was a sting in her words. She turned her back on me and moved away. I decided I'd better get out of town before she had me fired. I went and told John Truttwell where I was going and why.

Truttwell's argument with the doctor had cooled down. He introduced me to Smitheram, who gave me a soft handclasp and a hard look. There was a troubled intelligence in his eyes.

I said: 'I'd like to ask you some questions about Nick.'

'This isn't the time or the place.'

'I realize that, doctor. I'll see you at your office tomorrow.'

'If you insist. Now if you'll excuse me, I have a patient to attend to.'

I followed him as far as the living-room gates, and glanced in. Betty and Nick were sitting on a rug, not together but near each other. Her body was turned toward him, supported by one straight arm. Nick's face was pressed against his own raised knees.

Neither of them seemed to move, even to breathe. They looked like people lost in space, frozen forever in their separate poses, his of despair, hers of caring.

Dr Smitheram went and sat down near them on the floor.

X

I DROVE INLAND by way of Anaheim. It was a bad time of day, and in places the traffic crawled like a wounded snake. It took me ninety minutes to get from Chalmers's house to Rawlinson's house in Pasadena.

I parked in front of the place and sat for a minute, letting the freeway tensions drip off my nerve ends. It was one of a block of three-storied frame houses. They were ancient, as time went in California, ornamented with turn-of-the-century gables and cupolas.

Half a block further on, Locust Street came to an end at a black-and-white-striped barricade. Beyond it a deep wooded ravine opened. Twilight was overflowing the ravine, flooding the yards, soaking up into the thick yellow sky.

A light showed in Rawlinson's house as the front door opened and closed. A woman crossed the veranda and came down the steps skipping a broken one.

I saw as she approached my car that she must have been close to sixty. She moved with the confidence of a much younger woman. Her eyes were bright black behind her glasses. Her skin was dark, perhaps with a tincture of Indian or Negro blood. She wore a staid gray dress and a multi-colored Mexican apron.

'Are you the gentleman who wants to see Mr Rawlinson?'

'Yes. I'm Archer.'

'I'm Mrs Shepherd. He's just sitting down to dinner and he won't mind if you join him. He likes to have some company with his food. I only prepared enough for the two of us, but I'll be glad to pour you a cup of tea.'

'I could use a cup of tea, Mrs Shepherd.'

I followed her into the house. The entrance hall was impressive if you didn't look too closely. But the parquetry floor was buckling and loose underfoot, and the walls were dark with mold.

The dining room was more cheerful. Under a yellowing crystal chandelier with one live bulb, a table had been set for one person, with polished silver on a clean white cloth. An old white-headed man in a rusty dinner coat was finishing off what looked like a bowl of beef stew.

The woman introduced me to him. He put his spoon down and struggled to his feet, offering me a gnarled hand. 'Take it easy with my arthritis, please. Sit down. Mrs Shepherd will get you a cup of coffee.'

'Tea,' she corrected him. 'We're out of coffee.' But she lingered in the room, waiting to hear what was said.

Rawlinson's eyes had a mica glint. He spoke with impatient directness. 'This revolver you telephoned about—I gather it's been used for some illegal purpose?'

'Possibly. I don't know that it has.'

'But if it hasn't you've come a long way for nothing.'

'In my job everything has to be checked out.'

'I understand you're a private detective,' he said.

'That's correct.'

'Employed by whom?'

'A lawyer named Truttwell in Pacific Point.'

'John Truttwell?'

'Yes. Do you know him?'

'I met John two or three times through one of his clients. That was a long time ago, when he was young and I was middle-aged. It must be close to thirty years—Estelle's been dead for nearly twenty-four.'

'Estelle?'

'Estelle Chalmers—Judge Chalmers's widow. She was a hell of a woman.' The old man smacked his lips like a wine-taster.

The woman still lingering by the door was showing signs of distress. 'All that is ancient history, Mr Rawlinson. The gentleman isn't interested in ancient history.'

Rawlinson laughed. 'It's the only kind of history I know. Where's that tea you were so freely offering, Mrs Shepherd?' She went out, closing the door with emphasis. He turned to me. 'She thinks she owns me. She doesn't, though. If I don't have a right to my memories, there isn't a great deal left at my time of life.'

'I'm interested in your memories,' I said, 'specifically in the Colt revolver you bought in September 1941. It was probably used to shoot a man last night.'

'What man?'

'Sidney Harrow was his name.'

'I never heard of him,' Rawlinson said, as if this cast some doubt on Harrow's reality. 'Is he dead?'

'Yes.'

'And you're trying to connect my gun with his death?'

'Not exactly. It either is connected or it isn't. I want to know which.'

'Wouldn't ballistics show?'

'Possibly. The tests haven't been made yet.'

'Then I think I should wait, don't you?'

'You certainly should if you're guilty, Mr Rawlinson.'

He laughed so hard his upper teeth slipped. He pushed them back into place with thumb and forefinger. Mrs Shepherd appeared in the doorway with a tea tray.

'What's so funny?' she asked him.

'You wouldn't consider it funny, Mrs Shepherd. Your sense of humor is deficient.'

'Your sense of fittingness is. For an eighty-year-old man who used to be the president of a bank—' She set the tea tray down with a slight clash that completed her thought. 'Milk or lemon, Mr Archer?'

'I'll take it black.'

She poured our tea in two bone china cups that didn't match. The rundown elegance of the household made me wonder if Rawlinson was a poor man or a miser; and what in hell had happened to his bank.

'Mr Archer suspects me of committing a murder,' he said to the woman in a slightly bragging tone.

She didn't think it was funny at all. Her dark face got darker, grim around the mouth and in the eyes. She turned on Rawlinson fiercely.

'Why don't you tell him the truth then? You know you gave that revolver to your daughter, and you know the exact date.'

'Be quiet.'

'I will not. You're playing tricks with yourself and I won't let you. You're a smart man but you don't have enough to occupy your mind.'

Rawlinson showed no anger. He seemed to be pleased by her almost wifely concern. And his holding back about the gun had been just a game, apparently.

Mrs Shepherd was the worried one. 'Who got shot?'

'A part-time detective named Sidney Harrow.'

She shook her head. 'I don't know who that would be. Drink up your tea while it's hot. Can I get you a piece of fruitcake, Mr Archer? There's some left over from Christmas.'

'No thanks.'

'I'll have some,' Rawlinson said. 'With a scoop of ice cream.'

'We're out of ice cream.'

'We seem to be out of everything.'

'No, there's enough to eat. But money only stretches so far.'

She left the room again. With her warmth and energy subtracted, the room changed. Rawlinson looked around it a little uneasily, as if he was feeling the cold weight of his bones.

'I'm sorry she saw fit to sic you onto my daughter. And I hope you won't go dashing off in her direction now. There'd be no point in it.'

'Why?'

'It's true I gave Louise the gun in 1945. But it was stolen from her house some years later, in 1954, to be exact.' He recited the dates as if he was proud of his memory. 'This is not an *ad hoc* story.'

'Who stole the gun?'

'How should we know? My daughter's house was burglarized.'

'Why did you give her the gun in the first place?'

'It's an old story and a sad one,' he said. 'My daughter's husband abandoned her and left her stranded with Jean.'

'Jean?'

'My granddaughter Jean. The two helpless females were left alone in the house. Louise wanted the gun for protection.' He grinned suddenly. 'I think Louise may have been hoping that he would come back.'

'That who would come back.'

'Her husband. My egregious son-in-law Eldon Swain. If Eldon had come back, I have no doubt she'd have shot him. With my blessing.'

'What did you have against your son-in-law?'

He laughed abruptly. 'That's an excellent question. But with your permission I don't think I'll answer it.'

Mrs Shepherd brought us two narrow wedges of cake. She noticed that I wolfed mine.

'You're hungry. I'll make you a sandwich.'

'Don't bother. I'm on my way to dinner.'

'It wouldn't be any bother.'

Her divided attention made Rawlinson uncomfortable. He said with the air of a comedian: 'Mr Archer wants to know what Eldon Swain did to me. Shall I tell him?'

'No. You're talking too much, Mr Rawlinson.'

'Eldon's defalcations are common knowledge.'

'Not any more they're not. I say let it lie. We could all be a lot worse off than we are. I told Shepherd the same thing. When you talk about old trouble sometimes you can talk it back to life.'

He reacted with jealous irritation. 'I thought your husband was living in San Diego.'

'Randy Shepherd isn't my husband. He's my ex.'

'Have you been seeing him?'

She shrugged. 'I can't help it when he comes back for a visit. I do my best to discourage him.'

'So that's where the ice cream and coffee have been going!'

'It isn't so. I never give Shepherd a morsel of your food or a cent of your money.'

'You're a liar.'

'Don't call me that, Mr Rawlinson. There are things I won't put up with, even from you.'

Rawlinson looked quite happy again. He had the woman's attention, and all her heat, focused on him.

I stood up. 'I've got to be going.'

Neither of them offered any argument. Mrs Shepherd accompanied me to the front door.

'I hope you got what you came for.'

'Part of it, anyway. Do you know where his daughter lives?'

'Yessir.' She gave me another address in Pasadena. 'Just don't tell her I told you. Mrs Eldon Swain doesn't approve of me.'

'You seem to be bearing up under it,' I said. 'Is Jean Trask Mrs Swain's daughter?'

'Yes. Don't tell me Jean's mixed up in all this.'

'I'm afraid so.'

'That's too bad. I can remember when Jean was an innocent little angel. Jean and my own little girl were best friends for years. Then everything went sour.' She heard herself, and sucked her lips inward. 'I'm talking too much myself, bringing the past back to life.'

XI

LOUISE SWAIN LIVED on a poor street off Fair Oaks, between Old Town and the ghetto. A few children of various shades were playing under the light at the corner, islanded in the surrounding darkness.

There was a smaller light on the front porch of Mrs Swain's stucco cottage, and a Ford sedan standing at the curb in front of it. The Ford was locked. I shone my flashlight into it. It was registered to George Trask, 4545 Bayview Avenue, San Diego.

I made a note of the address, got out my contact mike, and went around to the side of the stucco cottage, following two strips of concrete which made an exigent driveway. An old black Volkswagen with a crumpled fender stood under a rusty carport. I moved into its shadow and leaned on the wall beside a blinded window.

I didn't need my microphone. Inside the house, Jean's voice was raised in anger: 'I'm not going back to George—'

An older woman spoke in a more controlled voice: 'You better take my advice and go back to him. George still cares about you and he was asking for you early this morning—but it won't last forever.'

'Who cares?'

'You ought to care. If you lose him you won't have anybody, and you don't know how that feels until you've tried it. Don't think you're coming back to live with me.'

'I wouldn't stay if you begged me on your knees.'

'That won't happen,' the older woman said dryly. 'I've got just enough room and enough money and enough energy left for myself.'

'You're a cold woman, Mother.'

'Am I? I wasn't always. You and your father made me that way.'

'You're jealous!' Jean's voice had changed. A hiss of pleasure underlay her anger and distress. 'Jealous of your own daughter and your own husband. It all comes clear. No wonder you gave him Rita Shepherd.'

'I didn't give him Rita. She threw herself at his head.'

'With a good strong assist from you, Mother. You probably planned the whole thing.'

The older woman said: 'I suggest you leave here before you say any more. You're nearly forty years old and you're not my responsibility. You're lucky to have a husband willing and able to look after you.'

'I can't stand him,' Jean said. 'Let me stay here with you. I'm scared.'

'So am I,' her mother said. 'I'm afraid for you. You've been drinking again, haven't you?'

'I did a little celebrating.'

'What have *you* got to celebrate?'

'Wouldn't you like to know, Mother?' Jean paused. 'I'll tell you if you ask me pretty please.'

'If you have something to tell me, then tell me. Don't fool around.'

'Now I'm not going to tell you.' Jean sounded like a child playing a teasing game. 'You can find out for yourself.'

'There's nothing to find out,' her mother said.

'Is that a fact? What would you say if I told you that Daddy's alive?'

'Really alive?'

'You bet he is,' Jean said.

'Have you seen him?'

'I soon will. I've picked up his trail.'

'Where?'

'That's my little secret, Mother.'

'Augh, you've been imagining things again. I'd be crazy to believe you.'

Jean made no answer that I could hear. I suspected the two women had exhausted the conversation and each other. I moved from the shadow of the carport into the dim street.

Jean came out onto the lighted porch. The door was slammed behind her. The light went out. I waited for her beside her car.

She backed away from me, stumbling on the broken sidewalk. 'What do you want?'

'Give me the gold box, Jean. It isn't yours.'

'Yes it is. It's an old family heirloom.'

'Come off it.'

'It's true,' she said. 'The box belonged to my Grandmother Rawlinson. She said it would come down to me. And now it has.'

I half believed her. 'Could we talk a little in your car?'

'That never does any good. The more you talk the more it hurts.'

Her face was mournful and her body dragged. She gave off a peculiar feeling, that she was a ghost or cloudy emanation of the actual Jean Trask; her sense of herself was a vacuum, a cold emptiness.

'What's hurting, Jean?'

'My whole life.' She spread both hands on her breasts as if the pain was overflowing her fingers. 'Daddy ran off to Mexico with Rita. He didn't even send me a birthday card.'

'How old were you?'

'Sixteen. I never had any fun after that.'

'Is your father alive?'

'I think he is. Nick Chalmers said he saw him in Pacific Point.'

'Where in Pacific Point?'

'Down by the railroad yards. That was a long time ago, when Nick was just a child. But he identified Daddy by his picture.'

'How did Nick get into this?'

'He's my witness that Daddy is alive.' Her voice rose in pitch and amplitude, as if she was speaking to the woman in the house instead of me: 'Why shouldn't he be alive? He'd only be—let's see, I'm thirty-nine and Daddy was twenty-four when I was born. That makes him sixty-three, doesn't it?'

'Thirty-nine and twenty-four makes sixty-three.'

'And sixty-three isn't old, especially not nowadays. He was always very youthful for his age. He could dive and dance and spin like a top,' she said. 'He bounced me on his knee.'

It sounded like something repeated from her childhood. Her mind was being carried down the stream of memory, swept willy-nilly through subterranean passages toward roaring falls.

'I'm going to find my Daddy,' she said. 'I'll find him dead or alive. If he's alive I'll cook and keep house for him. And I'll be happier than I ever was in my born days. If he's dead I'll find his grave and do you know what I'll do then? I'll crawl in with him and go to sleep.'

She unlocked her car and drove away, turning south onto the boulevard. Perhaps I should have followed her, but I didn't.

XII

I KNOCKED ON the front door of the stucco cottage. After an interval, the porch light came on over my head. Then the door was opened about four inches on a chain.

A woman with fading blond hair peered at me through the opening. Her face was set grimly, as if she'd expected to see her daughter again. The atmosphere around her was still charged.

'What is it?'

'I've just been talking to your father,' I said. 'About a Colt revolver he bought in 1941.'

'I don't know anything about a revolver.'

'Aren't you Mrs Eldon Swain?'

'Louise Rawlinson Swain,' she corrected me. But then she asked: 'Has something come up about my husband?'

'Possibly. Could we talk inside? I'm a private detective.'

I handed her my photostat through the crack. She looked it over carefully, and did everything but bite it. Finally she handed it back.

'Who are you working for, Mr Archer?'

'A lawyer in Pacific Point named John Truttwell. I'm looking into a couple of related crimes—a theft and a murder.' I didn't bother adding that her daughter was connected with one of the crimes, possibly both.

She let me in. Her front room was poor and small. As in Rawlinson's house, there were relics of better days. On the mantel over the gas fire a Dresden shepherd and shepherdess exchanged adoring glances.

A small Oriental rug lay not on the floor, which was covered with worn matting, but over the back of the chesterfield. Facing the chesterfield was a television set with an electric clock on top of it, and beside it a telephone table with a drawer. Everything was clean and well-dusted, but the room had a musty taint, as if neither it nor the woman in it had been fully used.

Mrs Swain didn't invite me to sit down. She stood facing me, a large woman like her daughter, with the same kind of heavy good looks.

'Who was murdered?'

'I'll come to that, Mrs Swain. I wanted to ask you first about a box that was stolen. It's a Florentine gold box with classical figures on the lid, a man and a woman.'

'My mother had a box like that,' she said. 'She used it as a jewel case. I never did know where it disappeared to after Mother died.' But her eyes were alive with roving speculation. 'What is this all about? Has Eldon been heard from?'

'I don't know.'

'You said "possibly." '

'I didn't want to rule anything out. I really came here to talk about the revolver your father gave you. But we'll talk about anything you like.'

'There's nothing I want to discuss.' But after a moment she asked me: 'What did Father say?'

'Simply that he gave you the Colt for protection, after your husband left you. The year he mentioned was 1945.'

'All that is perfectly true,' she said carefully. 'Did he mention the circumstances in which Eldon left?'

I threw her a slow curve. 'Mrs Shepherd wouldn't let him.'

It jarred her. 'Was Mrs Shepherd present at the conversation?'

'She was in and out of the dining room.'

'She would be. What else did my father say in front of her?'

'I don't remember if this was said in front of Mrs Shepherd.

But he told me that your house was burglarized in 1954 and the Colt was taken.'

'I see.' She looked around the room as if to see how the story fitted into it.

'Did it happen in this house?' I asked her.

She nodded.

'Was the burglar ever caught?'

'I don't know. I don't believe so.'

'Did you report the burglary to the police?'

'I don't remember.' She wasn't a good liar, and she screwed up her mouth in a kind of self-disgust. 'Why is it important?'

'I'm trying to trace possession of the revolver. If you have any idea who the burglar was, Mrs Swain—' I left the sentence unfinished, and glanced at the electric clock. It was half past eight. 'About twenty hours ago, that revolver may have been used to kill a man. A man named Sidney Harrow.'

She knew the name. Her whole face caught and held it. The delicate skin around her eyes puckered in distress. After a moment she spoke.

'Jean didn't tell me. No wonder she was frightened.' Mrs Swain wrung her hands and walked away from me as far as the room would let her. 'Do you suspect Eldon of killing Sidney Harrow?'

'Possibly. Was it your husband who took the gun in 1954?'

'Yes, it was.' She spoke with her head down and her face averted, like a woman in a storm. 'I didn't want to tell Father that Eldon had come back, or that I had seen him. So I made up a lie about a burglary.'

'Why did you have to tell your father anything?'

'Because he asked me for the gun the very next morning. I believe he'd heard that Eldon had been in town, and he intended to shoot him with the gun. But Eldon already had it. That's quite an irony, isn't it?'

It wasn't the kind I could live on, but I agreed. 'How did Eldon get hold of the revolver? You didn't give it to him?'

'No. I wouldn't do that. I kept it at the back of the telephone drawer.' Her eyes moved past me to the telephone table. 'I got it out when Eldon tapped on the door. I suspected it was Eldon, his knock was so distinctive. Shave and a haircut, two-bits, you know? That was Eldon's speed. He was capable of coming back after spending nine years in Mexico with another girl. And all the other dreadful things he did to me and my family. And expect to smile it all away and charm us as he used to in the old days.'

She looked at the door. 'I didn't have the chain on the door at that time—I had it put on the following day. The door wasn't locked, and Eldon came in smiling, calling my name. I wanted to shoot him, but I couldn't pull the trigger of the gun. He walked right up and took it away from me.'

Mrs Swain sat down as if her strength had been taken away. She leaned back against the Oriental rug. I sat down beside her tentatively.

'What happened then?'

'Just what you'd expect of Eldon. He denied everything. He hadn't taken the money. He hadn't gone to Mexico with the girl. He ran away because he'd been falsely accused, and had been living in strictest celibacy. He even argued that my family owed him something, because Father publicly called him an embezzler and blackened his reputation.'

'What was your husband supposed to have done?'

'There's no supposition about it. He was the cashier of my father's bank, and he embezzled over half a million dollars. You mean Father didn't tell you?'

'No, he didn't. When did all this happen?'

'July the first, 1945—the blackest day of my life. He ruined my father's bank and sold me into slavery.'

'I don't quite follow, Mrs Swain.'

'Don't you?' She tapped her knee with her fist like a judge gaveling for order. 'In the spring of 1945 I lived in a big house in San Marino. Before the summer was over, I had to move in here.

Jean and I could have gone to live with Father on Locust Street, but I wouldn't live in the same house with Mrs Shepherd. That meant I had to get out and find a job. The only thing I ever learned to do well is sew. For over twenty years now I've been demonstrating sewing machines. That's what I mean by slavery.' Her fist clenched on her knee. 'Eldon robbed me of all the good things of life, and then tried to deny it to my face.'

'I'm sorry.'

'So am I. I'm sorry I didn't shoot him. If I had another chance—' She took a deep breath and let it out in a sigh.

'It wouldn't do any good, Mrs Swain. And there are worse places than this. One of them is the women's prison at Corona.'

'I know that. I was just talking.' But she leaned toward me intently. 'Tell me, has Eldon been seen in Pacific Point?'

'I don't know.'

'The reason I ask, Jean claims she found some trace of him. It's why she employed that Harrow person.'

'Did you know Harrow?'

'Jean brought him here last week. I didn't think much of him. But Jean was always impulsive about men. Now you tell me that he's dead.'

'Yes.'

'Shot with the revolver that Eldon took from me,' she said dramatically. 'Eldon would kill if he had to, you know. He'd kill anyone who tried to drag him back here and put him in jail.

'That wasn't what Jean planned to do, though.'

'I know that. She idolized his memory, foolishly. But Sidney Harrow may have had other ideas. Harrow looked like a bum to me. And don't forget Eldon has stacks of money—over half-a-million.'

'Provided he hung on to it.'

She smiled fiercely. 'You don't know Eldon. He wouldn't throw money away. Money was all he ever wanted in life. He went about getting it coldly and methodically. The bank examiners said that he'd been preparing his theft for well over a year. And when he got to Mexico he probably invested the whole thing at ten per cent.'

I listened to her, without entirely believing her. According to her own story, she hadn't seen her husband since 1954. Her account of him had the swooping certainty of a mind tracking on fantasy. A woman could do a lot of dreaming in twenty years of demonstrating sewing machines.

'Are you still married to him, Mrs Swain?'

'Yes, I am. He may have gotten a Mexican divorce but if he did I never heard of it. He's still living in sin with that Shepherd girl. Which is the way I want it.'

'You're talking about Mrs Shepherd's daughter?'

'That's right. Like mother like daughter. I allowed Rita Shepherd into my home and treated her like my own daughter. So she stole my husband.'

'Which theft came first?'

She was puzzled for a moment. Then her brow cleared. 'I see what you mean. Yes, Eldon was carrying on with Rita before he stole the money. I caught on to them very early in the game. It was during a swimming party at our house—we had a forty-foot pool where we lived in San Marino.' Her voice sank almost out of hearing. 'I can't bear to think about it.'

The woman had been punished severely in the past hour, and I was weary of my part in it. I rose to go, and thanked her. But she wouldn't let me leave.

She got up heavily. 'Do detectives ever do things on a contingency basis?'

'What do you have in mind?'

'I don't have the money to pay you. But if I could get back some of the money Eldon took—' Her sentence dangled in the air, hopefully, hopelessly. 'We'd all be rich again,' she said in a hushed and prayerful voice. 'And of course I'd pay you very generously.'

'I'm sure you would.' I edged toward the door. 'I'll keep my eyes open for your husband.'

'Do you know what he looks like?'

'No.'

'Wait. I'll get a picture of him, if my daughter left me any.'

She went into a back room where I could hear her lifting and shoving things around. When she came back she had a dusty photograph in her hand and a smear of grime on her cheek, like a miner. 'Jean took all my good family pictures, all my San Marino albums,' she complained. 'She used to sit and study them the way other young women read movie magazines. George tells me—George is her husband—that she's still watching the home movies we took in San Marino.'

I took the photograph from her: a man of thirty-five or so, fair-haired, bold-eyed. He looked like the man whose picture Captain Lackland had found on Sidney Harrow. But the photograph wasn't clear enough to be absolutely certain.

XIII

I HAD DINNER in Pasadena and drove home to West Los Angeles. The air in my second-floor apartment was warm and stale. I opened a window and a bottle of beer, and sat down with the bottle in the near-darkness of my front room.

I lived in a quiet section, away from the main freeways. Still I could hear them humming, remote yet intimate, like the humming of my own blood in my veins.

Cars went by in the street from time to time, flinging brief lights across the ceiling. The case I was on seemed as hard to hold in the mind as the vanishing lights and the humming city were.

The shape and feeling of the case were changing. They always changed as you moved around in them. Eldon Swain had come into the center, pulling his whole family with him. If he was alive, he could give me some answers I needed. If he was dead, the people who knew his history would have to provide the answers.

I turned on the light and got out my black notebook and put down some notes about the people:

'The Colt ·45 I took off Nick Chalmers was bought in September 1941 by Samuel Rawlinson, president of the Pasadena Occidental Bank. Around July 1, 1945, he gave it to his daughter Louise Swain. Her husband, Eldon, cashier of the bank, had just embezzled over a half a million and ruined the bank. He ran off, reportedly to Mexico, with Rita Shepherd, daughter of Rawlinson's housekeeper (and onetime 'best friend' of his own daughter, Jean).

'Eldon Swain turned up at his wife's house in 1954 and took the Colt from her. How did it get from Swain to Nick Chalmers? Via Sidney Harrow, or through other people?

'N.B. San Diego: Harrow lived there, ditto Swain's daughter Jean and her husband, George Trask, ditto Mrs Shepherd's ex-husband.'

When I finished writing it was nearly midnight. I called John Truttwell's house in Pacific Point and at his request I read my notes to him, twice. I said it might be a good idea after all to turn the Colt revolver over to Lackland for testing. Truttwell said he already had. I went to bed.

At seven by my radio clock the phone jarred me awake. I picked up the receiver and pronounced my own name with a dry mouth.

'Captain Lackland here. I know it's early to call. But I've been up all night myself, supervising tests on the revolver you turned in to your lawyer.'

'Mr Truttwell isn't my lawyer.'

'He's been doing your talking for you. But under present circumstances that isn't good enough.'

'What are the circumstances?'

'I don't believe in discussing evidence over the phone. Can you be here in the station in an hour?'

'I can try.'

I skipped breakfast and walked into Lackland's office at two minutes to eight by the electric clock on his wall. He nodded curtly. His eyes had sunk deeper into his head. Glinting gray beard had sprouted on his face, like wire growing out from a central steel core.

His desk was cluttered with photographs. The top one was a blown-up microphotograph of a pair of bullets. Lackland waved me into a hard chair opposite him.

'It's time you and I had a meeting of minds.'

'You make it sound more like a clash of personalities, Captain.'

Lackland didn't smile. 'I'm in no mood for wisecracks. I want to know where you got hold of this gun.' He pulled the revolver on me suddenly, producing a plywood board to which it had been attached with wire.

'I can't tell you that. The law says I don't have to.'

'What do you know about the law?'

'I'm working under a good lawyer. I accept his interpretation.'

'I don't.'

'You make that clear, Captain. I'm willing to cooperate in any way I can. The fact that you have the gun is proof of that.'

'The real proof would be for you to tell me where you got it.'

'I can't do that.'

'Would it change your mind if I told you we know?'

'I doubt it. Try me.'

'Nick Chalmers was known to be carrying a gun yesterday. I have a witness. Another witness places him in the vicinity of the Sunset Motor Hotel at the approximate time of the Harrow killing.'

Lackland's voice was dry and official, as if he was already testifying at Nick's trial. He was watching my eyes as he spoke. I tried to keep them unresponsive, as cold as his were.

'No comment,' I said.

'You'll have to answer in court.'

'That's doubtful. Also, we're not in court.'

'We may be sooner than you think. Right now I probably have

enough for a Grand Jury indictment.' He slapped the pile of photographs on his desk. 'I have positive proof that this revolver killed Harrow. The bullets we test-fired from it match up with the slug recovered from his brain. You want to take a look?'

I studied the microphotographs. I was no ballistics expert, but I could see that the slugs matched. The evidence against Nick was piling up.

There was almost too much evidence. Beside it, Nick's confession that he had murdered Harrow in the hobo jungle seemed less and less real.

'You don't waste any time, Captain.'

The compliment depressed Lackland. 'I wish that that was true. I've been working on this case for fifteen years—nearly all of it wasted.' He gave me a long appraising look. 'I really could use your help, you know. I like to cooperate as well as the next man.'

'So do I. I don't understand what you mean about fifteen years.'

'I wish I understood it myself.' He lifted his microphotographs out of the way and produced some other pictures from the manila envelope he'd shown me yesterday. 'Look here.'

The first picture was the cropped one I'd already seen. It was Eldon Swain, all right, flanked by girls' dresses, with the girls cut away.

'Know him?'

'I may.'

'You do or you don't,' Lackland said.

There was no reason not to tell him. Lackland would trace the Colt revolver to Samuel Rawlinson, if he hadn't already done so. From there it was only a step to Rawlinson's son-in-law. I said:

'His name is Eldon Swain. He used to live in Pasadena.'

Lackland smiled and nodded, like a teacher whose backward pupil is making progress. He brought out another picture from his manila envelope. It was a flash picture which showed the weary face of a sleeping man. I blinked, and saw that the sleeping man was dead.

'How about *him*?' Lackland said.

The man's hair had faded almost white. There were smudges of dirt or ashes on his face, and it had been burned by harsh suns. His mouth showed broken teeth and around it the marks of broken hopes.

'It could be the same man, Captain.'

'That's my opinion, too. It's why I dug him out of the files.'

'Is he dead?'

'For a long time. Fifteen years.' Lackland's voice had a certain rough tenderness, which he seemed to reserve for the dead. 'He got himself knocked off down in the hobo jungle. That was in 1954—I was a sergeant at the time.'

'Was he murdered?'

'Shot through the heart. With this gun.' He lifted the revolver on the board. 'The same gun that killed Harrow.'

'How do you know that?'

'Ballistics again.' From a drawer in his desk he got out a labelled box which was lined with cotton, and took out a slug. 'This bullet matches the ones we test-fired last night, and it's the one that killed the man in the jungle. I thought of it,' he said with careful pride, 'because Harrow was carrying this other picture.' He tapped the cropped photograph of Eldon Swain. 'And I was struck by the resemblance to the dead man in the jungle.'

'I think the dead man is Swain,' I said. 'The timing is right.' I told Lackland what I had learned about the passage of the revolver from Rawlinson's hands, into his daughter's, and from her hands into her wandering husband's.

Lackland was deeply interested. 'You say Swain had been in Mexico?'

'For eight or nine years, apparently.'

'That tends to confirm the identification. The dead man was dressed like a wetback, in Mexican clothes. It's one reason we didn't follow it up like maybe we should have. I used to be a border guard during the war, and I know how hard it is to trace a Mex.'

'No fingerprints?'

'That's right, no fingerprints. The body was left with its hands in a fire—the coals of a bonfire.' He showed me a hideous picture of the charred hands. 'I don't know if it was accidental or not. Some wild things happen in the hobo jungle.'

'Did you have any suspects at the time?'

'We rounded up the transients, of course. One of them looked promising at first—an ex-con named Randy Shepherd. He was carrying too much money for a tramp, and he'd been seen with the decedent. But he claimed they'd just met casually on the road and shared a bottle. We couldn't prove otherwise.'

He shifted to further questions about Eldon Swain and the revolver, which I answered. Finally he said: 'We've covered everything except the essential point. How did you get hold of the gun yesterday?'

'Sorry, Captain. At least you're not trying to pin this old hobo-jungle killing on Nick Chalmers. He was hardly big enough for a cap pistol at the time.'

Lackland was as implacable as a chess player: 'Children have been known to fire a gun.'

'You can't be serious.'

Lackland gave me a chilly smile which seemed to say that he knew more than I did, and always would.

XIV

I STOPPED BY Truttwell's office to report to him. His pink-haired receptionist seemed relieved to see me.

'I've been trying to get you. Mr Truttwell says it's urgent.'

'Is he here?'

'No. He's at Mr Chalmers's house.'

The Chalmerses' servant, Emilio, let me in. Truttwell was sitting with Chalmers and his wife in the living room. The scene looked like a wake with the corpse missing.

'Has something happened to Nick?'

'He ran away,' Chalmers said. 'I didn't get any sleep last night, and I'm afraid he caught me with my wits down. He locked himself in an upstairs bathroom. It never occurred to me that he could squeeze himself out the window. But he did.'

'How long ago?'

'Hardly more than half an hour,' Truttwell said.

'That's too damn bad.'

'I know it is.' Chalmers was taut and anxious. The slow grinding passage of the night had worn flesh from his face. 'We were hoping you could help us get him back.'

'We can't use the police, you see,' his wife said.

'I understand that. How was he dressed, Mr Chalmers?'

'In the same clothes as he was wearing yesterday—he wouldn't undress last night. He had on a gray suit, a white shirt, and a blue tie. Black shoes.'

'Did he take anything else with him?'

Truttwell answered for them: 'I'm afraid he did. He took all the sleeping pills in the medicine cabinet.'

'At least they're missing,' Chalmers said.

'Exactly what is missing?' I asked him.

'Some chloral hydrate capsules, and quite a few ¾-grain Nembutal.'

'And a good deal of Nembu-Serpin,' his wife added.

'Did he have money?'

'I presume he did,' Chalmers said. 'I didn't take his money away. I was trying to avoid anything that would upset him.'

'Which way did he go?'

'I don't know. It took me a few minutes to realize he was gone. I'm not a very good jailer, I'm afraid.'

Irene Chalmers made a clucking noise with her tongue. It was hardly audible, and she made it only once, but it conveyed the idea that she could think of other things he wasn't very good at.

I asked Chalmers to show me Nick's escape route. He took me up a short tile staircase and along a windowless corridor to the bathroom. The rifled medicine cabinet was standing open. The window, set deep in the far wall, was about two feet wide by three feet high. I opened it and leaned out.

In a flower bed about twelve feet below the window I could see deep footprints, toes pointed inward to the house. Nick must have climbed out feet first, I thought, hung from the sill and dropped. There was no other trace of them.

We went downstairs to the living room where Irene Chalmers was waiting with Truttwell. 'You're wise,' I said, 'not to think in terms of the police. I wouldn't tell them, or anyone, that he's gone.'

'We haven't, and we don't intend to,' Chalmers said.

'What kind of emotional state was he in when he left?'

'Pretty fair, I thought. He didn't sleep much, but we did some quiet talking in the course of the night.'

'Do you mind telling me what about?'

'I don't mind. I talked about our need to stick together, our willingness to support him.'

'How did he react?'

'Hardly at all, I'm afraid. But at least he didn't get angry.'

'Did he mention the shooting of Harrow?'

'No. Nor did I ask him.'

'Or the shooting of another man fifteen years ago?'

Chalmers's face lengthened in surprise. 'What on earth do you mean?'

'Skip it for now. You've got enough on your mind.'

'I prefer not to skip it.' Irene Chalmers rose and moved toward me. She had dark circles under her eyes; her skin was yellowish; her lips moved uncertainly. 'You can't be accusing my son of another shooting?'

'I simply asked a question.'

'It was a terrible question.'

'I agree.' John Truttwell got to his feet and came over to me. 'I think it's time we got out of here. These people have put in a hellish night.'

I gave them a semiapologetic salute and followed Truttwell toward the front door. Emilio came running to let us out. But Irene Chalmers intercepted him and us.

'Where did this alleged shooting take place, Mr Archer?'

'In the local hobo jungle. Apparently it was done with the same gun that killed Harrow.'

Chalmers came up behind his wife. 'How can you know that?' he said to me.

'The police have ballistic evidence.'

'And they suspect Nick? Fifteen years ago he was only eight.'

'I pointed that out to Captain Lackland.'

Truttwell turned on me in surprise. 'You've already discussed this with him?'

'Not in the sense that I answered his questions. He's the source for most of my information about that earlier killing.'

'How did it come up between you?' Truttwell said.

'Lackland brought it up. I mentioned it just now because I thought I should.'

'I see.' Truttwell's manner to me was smooth and neutral. 'If you don't mind, I'd like to discuss this in private with Mr and Mrs Chalmers.'

I waited outside in my car. It was a bright January day, with enough wind to put an edge on its sparkle. But the weight of what had happened in the house, and what had been said, lay heavily on my mind. I was afraid the Chalmerses were going to fire me off the case. It wasn't an easy case, but after a day and a night with the people involved in it, I wanted to finish it.

Truttwell came out eventually and got into the front seat of my car. 'They asked me to dismiss you. I talked them out of it.'

'I don't know if I should thank you.'

'Neither do I. They're not easy people to deal with. They had to be convinced you weren't playing footsie with Lackland.'

He meant it as a question, which I answered: 'I wasn't. I do have to cooperate with him, though. He's been on this case for fifteen years. I've been on it less than one day.'

'Did he specifically accuse Nick of anything?'

'Not quite. He mentioned that a child could fire a gun.'

Truttwell's eyes grew small and bright, like little pellets of ice. 'Do you think that really happened?'

'Lackland seems to be playing with the idea. Unfortunately, he has a dead man to back him up.'

'Do you know who the dead man was?'

'It isn't definitely established. It may have been a wanted man named Eldon Swain.'

'Wanted for what?'

'Embezzlement. There's one other thing which I hate to mention but I have to.' I paused. I really did hate to mention it. 'Before I brought Nick in yesterday he made a sort of confession to a shooting. His confession fits the old shooting, the Swain shooting, better than the shooting of Harrow. Actually he may have been confessing both at once.'

Truttwell rapped his fists together several times. 'We have to get him back before he talks his life away.'

'Is Betty at home?'

Her father glanced sharply at me. 'You're not going to use her as a decoy, or a bird dog.'

'Or a woman? She is one.'

'Before everything else she's my daughter.' It was one of Truttwell's more self-revealing statements. 'She's not getting mixed up in a murder case.'

I didn't bother reminding him that she already was. 'Does Nick have any other friends I could talk to?'

'I doubt it. He's always been pretty much of a loner. Which was one of my objections—' Truttwell cut himself short. 'Dr Smitheram may be your best bet, if you can get him to talk. I've been trying to for fifteen years.' He added dryly: 'He and I suffer from professional incompatibility, I'm afraid.'

'When you say fifteen years—?'

Truttwell answered my half-finished question: 'I remember that something did happen involving Nick when he was in second or third grade. One day he didn't come home from school. His mother phoned me and asked me what to do. I gave her some standard advice. Whether or not she followed it I still don't know. But the boy was home the following day. And Smitheram's been treating him off and on ever since. Not too successfully, I might add.'

'Did Mrs Chalmers give you any idea of what happened?'

'Nick either ran away or was abducted. I think the latter. And I think—' Truttwell wrinkled his nose as if at a bad smell—'sex was involved.'

'So you said yesterday. What kind of sex?'

'Abnormal,' he said shortly.

'Did Mrs Chalmers say so?'

'Not explicitly. It was everyone's deep silence on the subject.' His voice trailed off.

'Murder makes for even deeper silence.'

Truttwell sniffed. 'An eight-year-old boy is incapable of murder, in any real sense.'

'I know that. But eight-year-old boys don't know it, especially if the whole thing is hushed up around them.'

Truttwell moved uncomfortably in the seat, as if he was being crowded by ugly images. 'I'm afraid you're jumping to conclusions, Archer.'

'These aren't conclusions. They're hypotheses.'

'Aren't we getting rather far afield from your initial assignment?'

'We always expected to, didn't we? Incidentally, I wish you'd reconsider about Betty. She may know where Nick is.'

'She doesn't,' Truttwell said shortly. 'I asked her myself.'

XV

I DROPPED TRUTTWELL off downtown. He told me how to get to Dr Smitheram's clinic, which turned out to be a large new building on the fashionable borders of Montevista. 'Smitheram Clinic, 1967' was cut in the stone facing over the main door.

A handsome woman with dark-brown hair came out into the windowless waiting room and asked me if I had an appointment.

I said I hadn't. 'There's an emergency involving one of Dr Smitheram's patients.'

'Which one?'

Her blue eyes were concerned. There was a slash of grey in her brown hair, as if time had thrust a loving hand through it.

'I'd rather tell the doctor,' I said.

'You can discuss it with me. I'm Mrs Smitheram, and I work professionally with my husband.' She gave me a smile which may have been professional but felt real. 'Are you a relative?'

'No. My name is Archer—'

'Of course,' she said. 'The detective. Dr Smitheram has been expecting you to call.' She scanned my face, and frowned a little. 'Has something else happened?'

'All hell has been breaking loose. I wish you'd let me talk to the doctor.'

She looked at her watch. 'I simply can't. He has a patient with him, with half an hour to go. I can't interrupt them except in a serious emergency.'

'This is one. Nick's run away again. And I think the police are getting ready to make a move.'

She reacted as if she was Nick's co-conspirator: 'To arrest him?'

'Yes.'

'That's foolish and unfair. He was just a small boy—' She cut the sentence in half, as if a censor had come awake in her head.

'Just a small boy when he did what, Mrs Smitheram?'

She drew a deep angry breath and let it out in a faint droning sound of resignation. She went through an inner door and closed it behind her.

Eventually Smitheram came out, enormous in a white smock. He looked slightly remote, like a man coming out of a waking dream, and he shook hands with me impatiently.

'Where has Nick gone to, anyway?'

'I have no idea. He just took off.'

'Who was looking after him?'

'His father.'

'That's preposterous. I warned them that the boy needed security, but Truttwell vetoed that.' His anger was running on, finding new objects, as if it was really anger with himself. 'If they refuse to take my advice I'll wash my hands of the business.'

'You can't do that and you know it,' his wife said from the doorway. 'The police are after Nick.'

'Or soon will be,' I said.

'What have they got on him?'

'Suspicion of two killings. You probably know more about the details than I do.'

Dr Smitheram's eyes met mine in a kind of confrontation. I could feel that I was up against a strong devious will.

'You're assuming a good deal.'

'Look, doctor. Couldn't we put down the foils and talk like human beings? We both want to bring Nick home safe, keep him out of jail, get his sickness cured—whatever it is.'

'That's a large order,' he said with a cheerless smile. 'And we don't seem to be making much progress, do we?'

'All right. Where would he go?'

'That's hard to say. Three years ago he was gone for several months. He wandered all over the country as far as the east coast.'

'We don't have three months, or three days. He took along

several batches of sleeping pills and tranquilizers—chloral hydrate, Nembutal, Nembu-Serpin.'

Smitheram's eyes wavered and darkened. 'That's bad. He's sometimes suicidal, as you undoubtedly know.'

'Why is he suicidal?'

'He's had an unfortunate life. He blames himself, as if he was criminally responsible for his misfortunes.'

'You mean he isn't?'

'I mean that no one is.' He said if as if he believed it. 'But you and I shouldn't be standing here talking. In any case, I'm not going to divulge my patient's secrets.' He made a move toward the inner door.

'Wait a minute, doctor. Just one minute. Your patient's life may be in danger, you know that.'

'Please,' Mrs Smitheram said. 'Talk to the man, Ralph.'

Dr Smitheram turned back to me, bowing his head in a slightly exaggerated attitude of service. I didn't ask him the question I wanted to, about the dead man in the hobo jungle; it would only produce widening circles of silence.

'Did Nick talk to you at all last night?' I said.

'He did to some extent. His parents and his fiancée were present most of the time. They were an inhibiting influence, naturally.'

'Did he mention any names of people or places? I'm trying to get a line on where he might have gone.'

The doctor nodded. 'I'll get my notes.'

He left the room and brought back a couple of sheets of paper, illegibly scrawled over. He put on reading glasses and scanned them rapidly.

'He mentioned a woman named Jean Trask whom he's been seeing.'

'How did he feel about her?'

'Ambivalent. He seemed to blame her for his troubles—it wasn't clear why. At the same time he seemed rather interested in her.'

'Sexually interested?'

'I wouldn't put it that way. His feeling was more fraternal. He also referred to a man named Randy Shepherd. In fact he wanted my help in finding Shepherd.'

'Did he say why?'

'Apparently Shepherd was or may have been a witness to something that happened long ago.'

Smitheram left me before I could ask any further questions. His wife and I exchanged the numbers of our respective telephone-answering services. But she wouldn't let me go just yet. Her eyes were slightly wilted, as if she'd disappointed herself in some way.

'I know it's exasperating,' she said, 'not to be given the facts. We operate this way because we have to. My husband's patients hold nothing back, you see. It's essential to treatment.'

'I understand that.'

'And please believe me when I say that we're very much in Nick's corner. Both Dr Smitheram and I are very fond of him—of his whole family. They've had more than their share of misfortune, as he said.'

Both the Smitherams were masters of the art of talking quite a lot without saying much. But Mrs Smitheram seemed to be a lively woman who would have liked to talk freely. She followed me to the door, still dissatisfied with what she'd said or left unsaid.

'Believe me, Mr Archer, there are things in my files you wouldn't want to know.'

'And in mine. Someday we'll exchange histories.'

'That will be a day,' she said with a smile.

There was a public phone in the lobby of the Smitheram building. I called San Diego Information, got George Trask's number, and put in a call to his home. The phone rang many times before the receiver was lifted.

'Hello?' It was Jean Trask's voice, and it sounded scared and dim. 'Is that you, George?'

'This is Archer. If Nick Chalmers shows up there—'

'He better not. I don't want anything more to do with him.'

'If he does, though, keep him with you. He's carrying a pocketful of barbiturates, and I think he plans to take them.'

'I suspected he was psycho,' the woman said. 'Did he kill Sidney Harrow?'

'I doubt it.'

'He did, though, didn't he? Is he after me? Is that why you called?' The quick forced rhythms of fear had entered her voice.

'I have no reason to think so.' I changed the subject: 'Do you know a Randy Shepherd, Mrs Trask?'

'It's funny you should ask me that. I was just—' Her voice stopped dead.

'You were just what?'

'Nothing. I was thinking of something else. I don't know anybody by that name.'

She was lying. But you can't unravel lies on the telephone. San Diego was an easy trip, and I decided to go there, unannounced.

'Too bad,' I said, and hung up.

I tried Information again. Randy Shepherd had no phone listed in the San Diego area. I called Rawlinson's house in Pasadena, and Mrs Shepherd answered.

'Archer speaking. Remember me?'

'Naturally, I remember you. If it's Mr Rawlinson you want, he's still in bed.'

'It's you I want, Mrs Shepherd. How can I get in touch with your former husband?'

'You can't through me. Has he done wrong again?'

'Not to my knowledge. A boy I know is carrying a lot of sleeping pills and planning suicide. Shepherd may be able to lead me to him.'

'What boy are you talking about?' she said in a guarded tone.

'Nick Chalmers. You wouldn't know him.'

'No, I wouldn't. And I can't give you Shepherd's address, I doubt he has one. He lives someplace in the Tijuana River Valley, down by the Mexican border.'

XVI

I GOT TO San Diego shortly before noon. The Trask house on Bayview Avènue stood near the base of Point Loma, overlooking North Island and the bay. It was a solid hillside ranchhouse with a nicely tended lawn and flowerbeds.

I knocked on the front door with an iron knocker shaped like a seahorse. No answer. I knocked and waited, and tried the knob. The door didn't open.

I walked around the outside of the house, peering into the windows, trying to act like a prospective purchaser. The windows were heavily draped. Apart from a glimpse of birch cupboard and a stainless-steel sink pagodaed with dirty dishes, I couldn't see anything. The attached garage was latched on the inside.

I went back to my car, which I'd parked diagonally across the street, and settled down to wait. The house was ordinary enough, but somehow it gripped my attention. The traffic of the harbor and the sky, ferries and fishing boats, planes and gulls, all seemed to move in relation to it.

The waiting minutes were long-drawn-out. Delivery vans went by, and a few carsful of children chauffeured by mothers. The street wasn't much used by the people who lived on it, except for transportation. The people kept to their houses, as if to express a sense of property, and a sense of isolation.

An old car that didn't belong on the street came up the hill trailing oil smoke and preceded by the clatter of a fan belt that needed lubrication. A big rawboned man wearing a dirty gray windbreaker and a dirty gray beard got out and crossed the street, silent in worn sneakers. He was carrying a round Mexican basket under one arm. He knocked, as I had, on the Trask's front door. He tried the knob, as I had.

He looked up and down the street and at me, the movements of his head as quick and instinctive as an old animal's. I was reading a San Diego County road map. When I looked at the man again, he had opened the door and was closing it behind him.

I got out of my car and noted the registration of his: Randolph Shepherd, Conchita's Cabins, Imperial Beach. His keys were in the ignition. I put them in the same pocket as my keys.

A folded copy of the Los Angeles *Times* lay on the right side of the front seat, open at the third page. Under a two-column head there was an account of Sidney Harrow's death and a picture of his young swinger's face, which I had never really seen.

I was named as the discoverer of the body, nothing more. Nick Chalmers wasn't named. But Captain Lackland was quoted as saying that he expected to make an arrest within the next twenty-four hours.

My head was still in Shepherd's car when he opened the door of the Trask house. He came out furtively but rapidly, almost with abandon, as if he'd been pushed out by an explosion in the house. For a moment his eyes were perfectly round, like clouded marbles, and his mouth a round red hole in his beard.

He stopped short when he saw me. He looked up and down the open sunlit street as if he was in a cul-de-sac surrounded by high walls.

'Hello, Randy.'

He showed his brown teeth in a grin of puzzlement. With enormous unwillingness, like a man wading into a cold deepening sea, he came across the road toward me. He let his grin become loose and foolish.

'I was just bringing Miss Jean some tomatoes. I used to tend the garden for Miss Jean's daddy. I got a real green thumb, see.'

He raised his thumb. It was big and spatulate, grained with dirt, and armed with a jagged dirty nail.

'Do you always pick the lock when you make a delivery, Randy?'

'How come you know my name? Are you a cop?'

'Not exactly.'

'How come you know my name?'

'You're famous. I've been wanting to meet you.'

'Who are you? A cop?'

'A private cop.'

He made a quick bad decision. He had been making them all his life: his scarred face bore the record of them. He jabbed at my eyes with his thumbnail. At the same time he tried to knee me.

I caught his jabbing hand and twisted it. For a moment we were perfectly poised and still. Shepherd's eyes were bright with rage. He couldn't sustain it, though. His face went through a series of transformations, like stop-time pictures of a man growing tired and old. His hand went limp, and I let go of it.

'Listen, boss, is it all right if I go now? I got a lot of other deliveries to make.'

'What are you delivering? Trouble?'

'No sir. Not me.' He glanced at the Trask house as if its presence on the street had caught him by surprise. 'I got a quick temper but I wouldn't hurt nobody. I didn't hurt *you*. You were the one hurt me. I'm the one that's always getting hurt.'

'But not the only one.'

He winced as if I had made a cruel remark. 'What are you getting at, mister?'

'There've been a couple of killings. That isn't news to you.' I reached for the newspaper on the seat of his car and showed him Harrow's picture.

'I never saw him in my life,' he said.

'You had the paper open at this story.'

'Not me. I picked it up that way at the station. I always pick up my papers at the station.' He leaned toward me, sweaty and jumpy. 'Listen, I got to go now, okay? I got a serious call of nature.'

'This is more important.'

'Not to me it isn't.'

'To you, too. You know a young man named Nick Chalmers?'

'He isn't—' He caught himself, and started over: 'What did you say?'

'You heard me. I'm looking for Nick Chalmers. He may be looking for you.'

'What for? I never touched him. When I found out that Swain was planning a snatch—' He caught himself again and covered his mouth with his hand, as if he could force the words back in or hide them like birds in his beard.

'Did Swain snatch the Chalmers boy?'

'Why ask me? I'm as clean as a whistle.' But he peered up at the sky with narrowed eyes as if he could see a sky hook or a noose descending toward him. 'I gotta get out of this sun. It gives me skin cancer.'

'It's a nice slow death. Swain died a quicker one.'

'You'll never pin it on me, 'bo. Even the cops at the Point turned me loose.'

'They wouldn't have if they'd known what I do.'

He moved closer to me, cringing on bent knees, making himself look smaller. 'I'm clean, honest to God. *Please* let me go now, mister.'

'We've barely started.'

'But we can't just stand here.'

'Why not?'

His head turned on his neck like an automatic mechanism, and he looked at the Trask house once again. My gaze followed his. I noticed that the front door was a few inches ajar.

'You left the front door open. We better go over and shut it.'

'You shut it,' he said. 'I got a bad charley horse in my leg. I gotta sit down or I'll fall down.'

He climbed in behind the wheel of his jalopy. He wouldn't get far without an ignition key, I thought, and I crossed the street. Looking through the crack between the door and the lintel, I could see red tomatoes scattered on the floor of the hallway. I went in, stepping carefully to avoid them.

There was a smell of burning from the kitchen. I found that a glass coffeemaker on an electric plate had boiled dry and cracked. Jean Trask was lying near it on the green vinyl floor.

I pulled the plug of the electric plate, and knelt down beside Jean. She had stab wounds in her breast and one great gash in her throat. Her body was clothed in pajamas and a pink nylon robe, and it was still warm.

Even though Jean was dead, I could hear breathing somewhere. It sounded as if the house itself was breathing. An open door led through the back kitchen, past the washer and dryer, into the attached garage.

George Trask's Ford Sedan was standing in the garage. Nick Chalmers was lying face up beside it on the concrete floor. I loosened his shirt collar. Then I looked at his eyes: they were turned up. I slapped him hard, once on each side of his face. No response. I heard myself groan.

Three empty drugstore tubes of varying sizes lay near him on the floor. I picked them up and put them in my pocket. There was no time for any further search. I had to get Nick to a stomach pump.

I raised the garage door, crossed the street for my car, and backed it into the driveway. I lifted Nick in my arms—he was a big man and it wasn't easy—and laid him on the back seat. I closed the garage. I pulled the front door of the house shut.

I noticed then that Randy Shepherd and his jalopy had gone. No doubt he was just as good at starting keyless cars as he was at opening locked doors. Under the circumstances, I could hardly blame him for leaving.

XVII

I DROVE DOWN Rosecrans to Highway 80 and delivered Nick at the ambulance entrance of the hospital. There had been a recent auto accident, and everybody on the emergency ward was busy. Looking for a stretcher, I opened the door and saw a dead man and closed the door again.

I found a wheeled stretcher in another room, took it outside and heaved Nick onto it. I pushed him up to the emergency desk.

'This boy needs a stomach pump. He's full of barbiturates.'

'Another one?' the nurse said.

She produced a paper form to be filled out. Then she glanced at Nick's face and I think she was touched by his inert good looks. She dispensed with red tape for the present. She helped me to wheel Nick into a treatment room and called in a young doctor with an Armenian name.

The doctor checked Nick's pulses and respiration, and looked at the pupils of his eyes, which were contracted. He turned to me.

'What did he take, do you know?'

I showed him the drug containers I had picked up in the Trasks' garage. They had Lawrence Chalmers's name on them, and the names and amounts of the three drugs they had contained: chloral hydrate, Nembutal and Nembu-Serpin.

He looked at me inquiringly. 'He hasn't taken all of these?'

'I don't know if the prescriptions were full. I don't think they were.'

'Let's hope the chloral hydrate wasn't, anyway. Twenty of those capsules are enough to kill two men.'

As he spoke, the doctor began to thread a flexible plastic tube into Nick's nostril. He told the nurse to cover him with a blanket, and prepare a glucose injection. Then he turned to me again.

'How long ago did he swallow the stuff?'

'I don't know exactly. Maybe two hours. What's Nembu-Serpin, by the way?'

'A combination of Nembutal and reserpine. It's a tranquilizer used in treating hypertension, also in psychiatric treatment.' His eyes met mine. 'Is the boy emotionally disturbed?'

'Somewhat.'

'I see. Are you a relative?'

'A friend,' I said.

'The reason I ask, he'll have to be admitted. In suicide attempts like this the hospital requires round-the-clock nurses. That costs money.'

'It shouldn't be any problem. His father's a millionaire.'

'No kidding.' He was unimpressed. 'Also, his regular doctor should see him before he's admitted. Okay?'

'I'll do my best, doctor.'

I found a telephone booth and called the Chalmerses' house in Pacific Point. Irene Chalmers answered.

'This is Archer. May I speak to your husband?'

'Lawrence isn't here. He's out looking for Nick.'

'He can stop looking. I found him.'

'Is he all right?'

'No. He took the drugs, and he's having his stomach pumped out. I'm calling from the San Diego Hospital. Have you got that?'

'The San Diego Hospital, yes. I know the place, I'll be there as soon as I can.'

'Bring Dr Smitheram with you, and John Truttwell.'

'I'm not sure I can do that.'

'Tell them it's a major emergency. It really is, Mrs Chalmers.'

'Is he dying?'

'He could die. Let's hope he doesn't. Incidentally you'd better bring a checkbook. He's going to need special nurses.'

'Yes, of course. Thank you.' Her voice was blank, and I couldn't tell if she had really heard me.

'You'll bring a checkbook, then, or some cash.'

'Yes. Certainly. I was just thinking, life is so strange, it seems to go in circles. Nick was born in that same hospital, and now you say he may die there.'

'I don't think he will, Mrs Chalmers.'

But she had begun to cry. I listened to her for a little while, until she hung up on me.

Because it wasn't good policy to leave a murder unreported, I called the San Diego Police Department and gave the sergeant on duty George Trask's address on Bayview Avenue. 'There's been an accident.'

'What kind of an accident?'

'A woman got cut.'

The sergeant's voice became louder and more interested: 'What is your name, please?'

I hung up and leaned on the wall. My head was empty. I think I almost fainted. Remembering that I'd missed my breakfast, I wandered through the hospital and found the cafeteria. I drank a couple of glasses of milk and had some toast with a soft-boiled egg, like an invalid. The morning's events had hit me in the stomach.

I went back to the emergency ward where Nick was still being worked on.

'How is he?'

'It's hard to tell,' he doctor said. 'If you'll fill out his form we'll admit him provisionally and put him in a private room. Okay?'

'That's fine. His mother and his psychiatrist should be here within an hour or so.'

The doctor raised his eyebrows. 'How sick is he?'

'You mean in the head? Sick enough.'

'I was wondering.' He reached under his white coat and produced a torn scrap of paper. 'This fell out of his breast pocket.'

He handed it to me. It was a penciled note:

'I am a murderer and deserve to die. Forgive me, Mother and Dad. I love you Betty.'

'He isn't a murderer, is he?' the doctor said.

'No.'

My denial sounded unconvincing to me, but the doctor accepted it. 'Ordinarily the police would want to see that suicide note. But there's no use making further trouble for the guy.'

I folded the note and put it in my wallet and got out of there before he changed his mind.

XVIII

I DROVE SOUTH to Imperial Beach. The cashier of a drive-in restaurant told me how to find Conchita's Cabins. 'You wouldn't want to stay in them, though,' she advised me.

I saw what she meant when I got there. It was a ruined place, as ancient-looking as an archeological digging. A sign on the office said: 'One dollar per person. Children free.' The cabins were small stucco cubes that had taken a beating from the weather. The largest building, with 'Beer and Dancing' inscribed across its front, had long since been boarded up.

The place was redeemed by a soft green cottonwood tree and its soft gray shade. I stood under it for a minute, waiting for somebody to discover me.

A heavy-bodied woman came out of one of the cabins. She wore a sleeveless dress which showed her large brown arms, and a red cloth on her head.

'Conchita?'

'I'm Mrs Florence Williams. Conchita's been dead for thirty years. Williams and I kept on with her name when we bought the cabins.' She looked around her as if she hadn't really seen the place for a long time. 'You wouldn't think it, but these cabins were a real moneymaker during the war.'

'There's a lot more competition now.'

'You're telling me.' She joined me in the shadow of the tree.

'What can I do for you? If you're selling don't even bother to open your mouth. I just lost my second-to-last roomer.' She made a farewell gesture toward the open door of the cabin.

'Randy Shepherd?'

She stepped away from me and looked me up and down. 'You're after him, eh? I figured somebody was, the way he took off and left his things. The only trouble is, they're not worth much. They're not worth ten per cent of the money he owes me.'

She was looking at me appraisingly, and I returned the look. 'How much would that be, Mrs Williams?'

'It adds up to hundreds of dollars, over the years. After my husband died, he talked me into investing money in his big treasure hunt. That was back around 1950, when he got out of the clink.'

'Treasure hunt?'

'For buried money,' she said. 'Randy rented heavy equipment and dug up most of my place and half the county besides. This place has never been the same since, and neither have I. It was like a hurricane went through.'

'I'd like to buy a piece of that treasure hunt.'

She countered rapidly: 'You can have my share for a hundred dollars, even.'

'With Randy Shepherd thrown in?'

'I don't know about *that.*' The talk of money had brightened her dusty eyes. 'This wouldn't be blood money that we're talking about?'

'I'm not planning to kill him.'

'Then what's he so a-scared of? I never saw him scared like this before. How do I know you won't kill him?'

I told her who I was and showed her my photostat. 'Where has he gone, Mrs Williams?'

'Let's see the hundred dollars.'

I got two fifties out of my wallet and gave her one of them. 'I'll give you the other after I talk to Shepherd. Where can I find him?'

She pointed south along the road. 'He's on his way to the border. He's on foot, and you can't miss him. He only left here about twenty minutes ago.'

'What happened to his car?'

'He sold it to a parts dealer up the hike. That's what makes me think he's crossing over to Mexico. I know he's done it before, he's got friends to hide him.'

I started for my car. She followed me, moving with surprising speed.

'Don't tell him I told you, will you? He'll come back some dark night and take it out of my hide.'

'I won't tell him, Mrs Williams.'

With my road map on the seat beside me, I drove due south through farmland. I passed a field where Holstein cattle were grazing. Then the tomato fields began, spreading in every direction. The tomatoes had been harvested, but I could see a few hanging red and wrinkled on the withering vines.

When I had travelled about a mile and a half, the road took a jog and ran through low chaparral. I caught sight of Shepherd. He was tramping along quickly, almost loping, with a bedroll bouncing across his shoulders and a Mexican hat on his head. Not far ahead of him Tijuana sloped against the sky like a gorgeous junk heap.

Shepherd turned and saw my car. He began to run. He plunged off the road into the brush and reappeared in the dry channel of a river. He had lost his floppy Mexican hat but still had his bedroll.

I left my car and went after him. A rattlesnake buzzed at me from under an ocotillo, and focused my attention. When I looked for Shepherd again, he had disappeared.

Making as little noise as possible, and keeping my head down, I moved through the chaparral to the road which ran parallel with the border fence. The road map called it Monument Road. If Shepherd planned to cross the border, he would have to cross Monument Road first. I settled down in the ditch beside it, keeping an alternating watch in both directions.

I waited for nearly an hour. The birds in the brush got used to me, and the insects became familiar. The sun moved very slowly down the sky. I kept looking one way and then the other, like a spectator at a languid tennis match.

When Shepherd made his move, it was far from languid. He came out of the brush about two hundred yards west of me, scuttled across the road with his bedroll bouncing, and headed up the slope toward the high wire fence that marked the border.

The ground between the road and the fence had been cleared. I cut across it and caught Shepherd before he went over. He turned with his back to the fence and said between hard breaths:

'You stay away from me. I'll cut your gizzard.'

A knife blade stuck out of his fist. On the hillside beyond the fence a group of small boys and girls appeared as if they had sprouted from the earth.

'Drop the knife,' I said a little wearily. 'We're attracting a lot of attention.'

I pointed up the hill toward the children. Some of them pointed back at me. Some waved. Shepherd was tempted to look, and turned his head a little to one side.

I moved hard on his knife arm and put an armlock on it which forced him to drop the knife. I picked it up and closed it and tossed it over the fence into Mexico. One of the little boys came scrambling down the hill for it.

Further up the hill, where the houses began, an invisible musician began to play bullfight music on a trumpet. I felt as if Mexico was laughing at me. It wasn't a bad feeling.

Shepherd was almost crying. 'I'm not going back to a bum murder rap. You put me behind the walls again, it'll kill me.'

'I don't think you killed Jean Trask.'

He gave me an astonished look, which quickly faded. 'You're just saying that.'

'No. Let's get out of here, Randy. You don't want the border patrol to pick you up. We'll go some place where we can talk.'

'Talk about what?'

'I'm ready to make a deal with you.'

'Not me. I allus get the short end of the deals.'

He had the cynicism of a small-time thief. I was getting impatient with him.

'Move, con.'

I took him by the arm and walked him down the slope toward the road. A child's voice nearly as high as a whistle called to us from Mexico above the sound of the trumpet:

'Adios.'

XIX

SHEPHERD AND I walked east along Monument Road to its intersection with the road that ran north and south. He hung back when he saw my car. It could take him so fast and so far, all the way back to the penitentiary.

'Get it through your head, Randy, I don't want you. I want your information.'

'And what do *I* get out of it?'

'What do you want?'

He answered quickly and ardently, like a man who has been defrauded of his rights: 'I want a fair shake for once in my life. And enough money to live on. How can a man help breaking the law if he don't have money to live on?'

It was a good question.

'If I had my rights,' he went on, 'I'd be a rich man. I wouldn't be living on tortillas and chili.'

'Are we talking about Eldon Swain's money?'

'It ain't Swain's money. It belongs to anybody who finds it. The statute of limitations ran out years ago,' he said in the legalese of a cell-block lawyer, 'and the money's up for grabs.'

'Where is it?'

'Someplace in this very area.' He made a sweeping gesture which took in the dry riverbed and the empty fields beyond. 'I been making a study of this place for twenty years, I know it like the back of my hand.' He sounded like a prospector who had worn out his wits in the desert looking for gold. 'All I need is to get real lucky and find me the coordinates. I'm Eldon Swain's legal heir.'

'How so?'

'We made a deal. He was interested in a relative of mine.' He probably meant his daughter. 'And so we made a deal.'

The thought of it lifted his spirits. He got into my car without argument, hoisting his bedroll into the back seat.

'Where do we go from here?' he said.

'We might as well stay where we are for the present.'

'And then?'

'We go our separate ways.'

He glanced quickly at my face, as if to catch me in a false expression. 'You're conning me.'

'Wait and see. Let's get one thing out of the way first. Why did you go to Jean Trask's house today?'

'Take her some tomatoes.'

'Why did you pick the lock?'

'I thought maybe she was sleeping. Sometimes she sleeps real heavy, when she's been drinking. I didn't know she was dead, man. I wanted to talk to her.'

'About Sidney Harrow?'

'That was part of it. I knew the cops would be asking her questions about him. The fact is, I was the one introduced her to Sidney, and I wanted Miss Jean not to mention my name to the cops.'

'Because you were a suspect in Swain's death?'

'That was part of it. I knew they'd be opening up that old case. If my name came up and they traced my connection with Swain, I'd be right back on the hooks. Hell, my connection with Swain went back thirty years.'

'Which is why you didn't identify his body.'

'That's right.'

'And you let Jean go on thinking her father was alive, and go on looking for him.'

'It made her feel better,' he said. 'She never found out how he died.'

'Who shot him?'

'I don't know. Honest to God. I only know I didn't.'

'You mentioned a snatch.'

'That's right. It's where him and I parted company. I admit I been a thief in my time, but strong-arm stuff was never for me. When he started to plan this snatch, I backed out on him.' Shepherd added meditatively: 'When Swain came back from Mexico in 1954, he wasn't the man he used to was. I think he went a little crazy down there.'

'Did Swain kidnap Nick Chalmers?'

'That's the one he was talking about. I never saw the boy myself. I was long gone when it happened. And it never came out in the papers. I guess the parents hushed it up.'

'Why would a man with half a million dollars attempt a kidnapping?'

'Ask me another. Swain kept changing his story. Sometimes he claimed he had the half million, sometimes he said he didn't. Sometimes he claimed he had it and lost it. He said once he was highjacked by a border guard. His wildest story was the one about Mr Rawlinson. Mr Rawlinson was the president of the bank that Eldon Swain worked for, and he claimed Mr Rawlinson took the money and framed him for it.'

'Could that have happened?'

'I don't see how. Mr Rawlinson wouldn't ruin his own bank. And he's been on his uppers ever since. I know that for certain because I got a relative works for him.'

'Your ex-wife.'

'You get around,' he said in some surprise. 'Did you talk to her?'

'A little.'

He leaned toward me, keenly interested. 'What did she say about me?'

'We didn't discuss you.'

Shepherd seemed disappointed, as if he had been robbed of a dimension. 'I see her from time to time. I bear no grudges, even if she did divorce me when I was in the pen. I was kind of glad to make the break,' he said dolefully. 'She's got mixed blood, you probably noticed that. It kind of hurt my pride to be married to her.'

'We were talking about the money,' I reminded him. 'You're pretty certain that Swain took it and kept it.'

'I know he did. He had it with him at Conchita's place. This was right after he lifted it.'

'You saw it?'

'I know somebody who did.'

'Your daughter?'

'No.' He added with a touch of belligerence: 'Leave my daughter out of this. She's going straight.'

'Where?'

'Mexico. She went to Mexico with him and never came back from there.' His answer sounded a little glib, and I wondered if it was true.

'Why did Swain come back?'

'He always planned to, that's my theory. He left the money buried on this side of the border, he told me so himself more than once. He offered me a share of it if I would go partners with him and drive him around and grubstake him. Like I said, he wasn't in very good shape when he came back. Fact is, he needed a keeper.'

'And you were his keeper?'

'That's right. I owed him something. He was a pretty good man at one time, Eldon Swain was. When I hit the pavement the first time, on parole, he took me on as a gardener at his place in San Marino. It was a real showplace. I used to grow him roses as big as dahlias. It's a terrible thing when a man like that ends up dead of lead poisoning in a railroad yard.'

'Did you drive Swain to Pacific Point in 1954?'

'I admit that much. But that was before he started to talk about snatching the boy. I wouldn't drive him on that caper. I got out of town in a hurry. I wanted no part—'

'You didn't shoot him before you left, by any chance?'

He gave me a shocked look. 'No *sir*. You don't know much about me, mister. I'm not a man of violence. I specialize in staying out of trouble, out of jail. And I'm still working at it.'

'What were you sent up for?'

'Car theft. Break and enter. But I never carried a gun.'

'Maybe somebody else shot Swain and you burned off his fingerprints.'

'That's crazy. Why would I do that?'

'So that you wouldn't be traced through him. Let's say you took the ransom money from Swain.'

'What ransom money? I never saw any ransom money. I was back here on the border by the time he took the boy.'

'Was Eldon Swain a child molester?'

Shepherd squinted at the sky. 'Could be. He always liked 'em young, and the older he got the younger he liked 'em. Sex was always his downfall.'

I didn't believe Shepherd. I didn't disbelieve him. The mind that looked at me through his eyes was like muddy water continually stirred by fears and fantasies and greeds. He was growing old in the desperate hope of money, and by now he was willing to become whatever the hope suggested.

'Where are you going now, Randy? To Mexico?'

He was quiet for a moment, peering out across the flatland toward the sun, which was halfway down the west. A Navy jet flew over like a swallow towing the noise of a freight train. Shepherd watched it out of sight, as if it represented his last disappearing luck.

'I better not tell you where I'm going, mister. If we need to get in touch again I'll get in touch with you. Just don't try to pull a fast one on me. So you saw me at Miss Jean's house. That puts you on the same spot.'

'Not quite. But I won't turn you in unless I find some reason.'

'You won't. I'm clean as soap. And you're a white man,' he added, sharing with me his one dubious distinction. 'How about a little travelling money?'

I gave him fifty dollars and my name, and he seemed satisfied. He got out of the car with his bedroll and stood waiting by the roadside until I lost sight of him in my rear-view mirror.

I drove back to the cabins and found Mrs Williams still working in the one that Shepherd had vacated. When I appeared in the doorway, she looked up from her sweeping with pleased surprise.

'I never thought you'd come back,' she said. 'I guess you didn't find him, eh?'

'I found him. We had a talk.'

'Randy's a great talker.'

She was stalling, unwilling to ask me outright for the second installment of her money. I gave her the other fifty. She held it daintly in her fingers, as if she had captured some rare specimen of moth or butterfly, then tucked it away in her bosom.

'I thank you kindly. I can use this money. I guess you know how it is.'

'I guess I do. Are you willing to help me with more information, Mrs Williams?'

She smiled. 'I'll tell you anything but my age.'

She sat down on the stripped mattress of the bed, which creaked and sank under her weight. I took the only chair in the room. A shaft of sunlight fell through the window, swarming with brilliant dust. It laid down a swatch of brightness between us on the worn linoleum floor.

'What do you want to know?'

'How long has Shepherd been staying here?'

'Off and on since the war. He comes and he goes. When he got really hungry he used to travel with the fruit pickers sometimes. Or he'd pick up a dollar or two weeding somebody's garden. He was a gardener at one time.'

'He told me that. He worked for a Mr Swain in San Marino. Did he ever mention Eldon Swain to you?'

The question made her unhappy. She looked down at her knee and began pleating her skirt. 'You want me to tell it like it is, like the kids say?'

'Please do.'

'It don't make me look good. The trouble is in this business you get so you'll do things for money that you wouldn't start out doing when you're young and fresh. There's nothing people won't do for money.'

'I know that. What are you leading up to, Florence?'

She said in a hurried monotone, as if to reduce the size and duration of her guilt: 'Eldon Swain stayed here with his girl friend. She was Randy Shepherd's daughter. That's what brought Randy here in the first place.'

'When was this?'

'Let's see. It was just before the trouble with the money, when Mr Swain took off for Mexico. I don't have a good head for dates, but it was sometime along toward the end of the war.' She added after a thinking pause: 'I remember the Battle of Okinawa was going on. Williams and I used to follow the battles, so many of our roomers were sailor boys, you know.'

I brought her back to the subject: 'What happened when Shepherd came here?'

'Nothing much. A lot of loud talk mainly. I couldn't help but overhear some of it. Randy wanted to be paid for the loan of his daughter. That was the way his mind worked.'

'What kind of a girl was the daughter?'

'She was a beautiful child.' Mrs Williams's eyes grew misty with the quasi-maternal feelings of a procuress. 'Dark and tender-looking. It's hard to understand a girl like that, going with a man more than twice her age.' She readjusted her position on the bed, and its springs squeaked in tired rhythms. 'I don't doubt she was after her share of the money.'

'This was before the money, you said.'

'Sure, but Swain was already planning to take it.'

'How do you know that, Mrs Williams?'

'The officers said so. This place was swarming with officers the week after he took off. They said that he'd been planning it for at least a year. He picked this place for his final jumping-off place to Mexico.'

'How did he cross the border?'

'They never did find out. He may have gone over the border fence, or crossed in the regular way under another name. Some of the officers thought he left the money behind. That's probably where Randy got the idea.'

'What happened to the girl?'

'Nobody knows.'

'Not even her father?'

'That's right. Randy Shepherd isn't the kind of father a girl would keep in touch with if she had a choice. Randy's wife felt the same way about him. She divorced him while he was in the pen the last time, and when he got out he came back here. He's been here off and on ever since.'

We sat in silence for a little while. The rectangle of sunlight on the linoleum was lengthening perceptibly, measuring out the afternoon and the movement of the earth. Finally she asked me:

'Will Randy be coming back here, do you think?'

'I don't know, Mrs Williams.'

'I sort of hope he does. He's got a lot against him. But over the years a woman gets used to seeing a man around. It doesn't even matter what kind of man he is.'

'Besides,' I said, 'he was your second-to-last roomer.'

'How do you know that?'

'You told me.'

'So I did. I'd sell this place if I could find a buyer.'

I got up and moved toward the door. 'Who's your last roomer?'

'Nobody you would know.'

'Try me.'

'A young fellow named Sidney Harrow. And I haven't seen *him* for a week. He's off on one of Randy Shepherd's wild-goose chases.'

I produced the copy of Nick's graduation picture. 'Did Shepherd give this to Harrow, Mrs Williams?'

'He may have. I remember Randy showed me that picture. He wanted to know if it reminded me of anybody.'

'Did it?'

'Nope. I'm not much good at faces.'

XX

I WENT BACK to San Diego and drove out Bayview Avenue to George Trask's house. The sun had just set and everything was reddish, as if the blood in the kitchen of the house had formed a weak solution with the light.

A car I had seen before but couldn't remember where—a black Volkswagen with a crumpled fender—stood in the driveway of the Trask house. A San Diego police car was at the curb. I drove on by, and made my way back to the hospital.

Nick was in Room 211 on the second floor, the woman at the information desk told me. 'But he's not allowed to have visitors unless you're immediate family.'

I went up anyway. In the visitors' lounge across from the elevator Mrs Smitheram, the psychiatrist's wife, was reading a magazine. A coat folded with the lining turned out was draped across the back of her chair. For some reason I was very glad to see her. I crossed to the lounge and sat down near her.

She wasn't reading after all, just holding the magazine. She was looking right at me, but she didn't see me. Her blue eyes were turned inward on her thoughts, which lent her face a grave beauty. I watched the changes in her eyes as she gradually became aware of me, and finally recognized me.

'Mr Archer!'

'I wasn't expecting to see you, either.'

'I just came along for the ride,' she said. 'I lived in San Diego County for several years during the war. I haven't been back here since.'

'That's a long time.'

She inclined her head. 'I was just thinking about that long time and how it grew. But you're not interested in my autobiography.'

'I am, though. Were you married when you lived here before?'

'In a sense. My husband was overseas most of the time. He was a flight surgeon on an escort carrier.' Her voice had a rueful pride which seemed to belong entirely to the past.

'You're older than you look.'

'I married young. Too young.'

I liked the woman, and it was a pleasure to talk for once about something that had no bearing on my case. But she brought the conversation back to it:

'The latest on Nick is that he's coming out of it. The only question is in what condition.'

'What does your husband think?'

'It's too early for Ralph to commit himself. Right now he's in consultation with a neurologist and a brain surgeon.'

'They don't do brain surgery for barbiturate poisoning, do they?'

'Unfortunately, that's not the only thing the matter with Nick. He has a concussion. He must have fallen and hit the back of his head.'

'Or been hit?'

'That's possible, too. How did he get to San Diego, anyway?'

'I don't know.'

'My husband said you brought him here to the hospital.'

'That's true. But I didn't bring him to San Diego.'

'Where did you find him?'

I didn't answer her.

'Don't you want to tell me?'

'That's right.' I changed the subject, not very smoothly. 'Are Nick's parents here?'

'His mother's sitting with him. His father is on his way. There's nothing either you or I can do.'

I stood up. 'We could have dinner.'

'Where?'

'The hospital cafeteria if you like. The food is fair.'

She made a face. 'I've eaten too many hospital-cafeteria dinners.'

'I thought you mightn't want to go too far.' The phrase had a double meaning that we both heard.

She said: 'Why not? Ralph will be tied up for hours. Why don't we go out to La Jolla?'

'Is that where you used to live during the war?'

'You're a good guesser.'

I helped her on with her coat. It was silver-blue mink complementing the slash of gray in her hair. In the elevator, she said:

'This is on one condition. You mustn't ask me questions about Nick and his family constellation. I can't answer certain questions, just as you can't, so why spoil things.'

'I won't spoil things, Mrs Smitheram.'

'My name is Moira.'

She was born in Chicago, she told me at dinner, and trained as a psychiatric social worker in the University of Michigan Hospital. There she met and married Ralph Smitheram, who was completing his residency in psychiatry. When he joined the Navy and was assigned to the San Diego Naval Hospital, she came along to California.

'We lived in a little old hotel here in La Jolla. It was sort of rundown but I loved it. After we finish dinner I want to go and see if it's still there.'

'We can do that.'

'I'm taking a chance, coming back here. I mean, you can't imagine how beautiful it was. It was my first experience of the ocean. When we went down to the cove in the early morning, I felt like Eve in the garden. Everything was fresh and new and spare. Not like this at all.'

With a movement of her hand she dismissed her present surroundings: the thick pseudo-Hawaiian decor, the uniformed black waiters, the piped-in music, all the things that went with the fifteen-dollar Chateaubriand for two.

'This part of the town has changed,' I agreed.

'Do you remember La Jolla in the forties?'

'Also the thirties. I lived in Long Beach then. We used to come down for the surf here and at San Onofre.'

'Does "we" refer to you and your wife?'

'Me and my buddies,' I said. 'My wife wasn't interested in surf.'

'Past tense?'

'Historical. She divorced me back in those same forties. I don't blame her. She wanted a settled life, and a husband she could count on to be there.'

Moira received my ancient news in silence. After a while she spoke half to herself: 'I wish I'd gotten a divorce then.' Her eyes came up to mine. 'What did *you* want, Archer?'

'This.'

'Do you mean being here with me?' I thought she was overeager for a compliment, then realized she was kidding me a little. 'I hardly justify a lifetime of effort.'

'The life is its own reward,' I countered. 'I like to move into people's lives and then move out again. Living with one set of people in one place used to bore me.'

'That isn't your real motivation. I know your type. You have a secret passion for justice. Why don't you admit it?'

'I have a secret passion for mercy,' I said. 'But justice is what keeps happening to people.'

She leaned toward me with that female malice which carries some sexual heat. 'You know what's going to happen to you? You'll grow old and run out of yourself. Will that be justice?'

'I'll die first. That will be mercy.'

'You're terribly immature, do you know that?'

'Terribly.'

'Don't I make you angry?'

'Real hostility does. But you're not being hostile. On the contrary. You're off on the usual nurse kick, telling me I better marry again before I get too old, or I won't have anybody to nurse me in my old age.'

'You!' She spoke with angry force, which changed into laughter.

After dinner we left my car where it was in the restaurant parking lot, and walked down the main street toward the water. The surf was high and I could hear it roaring and retreating like a sea lion frightened by the sound of his own voice.

We turned right at the top of the last slope and walked past a brand-new multistoried office building, toward a motel which stood on the next corner. Moira stood still and looked it over.

'I thought this was the corner, but it isn't. I don't remember that motel at all.' Then she realized what had happened. 'This *is* the corner, isn't it? They tore down the old hotel and put up the motel in its place.' Her voice was full of emotion, as if a part of her past had been demolished with the old building.

'Wasn't it called the Magnolia Hotel?'

'That's right. The Magnolia. Did you ever stay there?'

'No,' I said. 'But it seems to have meant quite a lot to you.'

'It did and does. I lived on there for two years after Ralph shipped out. I think now it was the realest part of my life. I've never told anyone about it.'

'Not even your husband?'

'Certainly not Ralph.' Her voice was sharp. 'When you try to tell Ralph something, he doesn't hear it. He hears your motive for saying it, or what he thinks is your motive. He hears some of the implications. But he doesn't really hear the obvious meaning. It's an occupational hazard of psychiatrists.'

'You're angry with your husband.'

'Now you're doing it!' But she went on: 'I'm deeply angry with him, and with myself. It's been growing on me for quite a while.'

She had begun to walk, drawing me across the lighted corner and away from it downhill toward the sea. Spray hung in luminous clouds around the scattered lights. The green common and the waterfront path were virtually deserted. She began to talk again as we walked along the path.

'At first I was angry with myself for doing what I did. I was only nineteen when it started, and full of normal adolescent guilt. Later I was angry with myself for not following through.'

'You're not making yourself entirely clear.'

She had raised the collar of her coat against the spray. Now she looked at me over it like a desperado wearing a partial face mask: 'I don't intend to, either.'

'I think you want to, though.'

'What's the use? It's all gone—completely past and gone.'

Her voice was desolate. She walked quietly away from me, and I followed her. She was in an uncertain mood, a middle-aging woman groping for a line of continuity in her life. The path was dark and narrow, and it would be easy by accident or design to fall among the rocks in the boiling surf.

I caught up with her at the cove, the physical center of the past she had been talking about. The broken white water streamed up the slope of the beach. She took her shoes off and led me down the steps. We stood just above the reach of the water.

'Come and get me,' she said to it or me or someone else.

'Were you in love with a man who died in the war?'

'He wasn't a man. He was just a boy who worked in the post office.'

'Was he the one who came down here with you, when you felt like Eve in the garden?'

'He was the one. I still feel guilty about it. I lived here on the beach with another boy while Ralph was overseas defending his country.' Her voice flattened sardonically whenever she spoke of her husband. 'Ralph used to write me long dutiful letters, but somehow they made no difference. I actually wanted to undercut him, he was so superconfident and know-it-all. Do you think I'm slightly crazy?'

'No.'

'Sonny was, you know. More than slightly.'

'Sonny?'

'The boy I lived with in the Magnolia. Actually he'd been one of Ralph's patients, which is how I got to know him in the first place. Ralph suggested that I keep an eye on him. There's an irony for you.'

'Stop it, Moira. I think you're reaching for trouble.'

'Some reach for it,' she said. 'Others have it thrust upon them. If I could just go back to that time and change a few things—'

'What would you change?'

'I'm not quite sure.' She sounded rather dreary. 'Let's not talk about it any more now.'

She walked away from me. Her naked feet left wasp-waisted impressions in the sand. I admired the grace of her departing movements, but she came back toward me clumsily. She was walking backward, trying to fit her feet again into the prints she had made and not succeeding.

She walked into me and turned, her furred breast against my arm. I put my arm around her and held her. There were tears on her face, or spray. Anyway, it tasted salt.

XXI

THE MAIN STREET was quiet and bright when we walked back to the car. The stars were all in order, and quite near. I don't remember seeing any other people until I went into the restaurant to phone George Trask.

He answered right away, in a moist, overused voice: 'This is the Trask residence.'

I said I was a detective and would like to talk to him about his wife.

'My wife is dead.'

'I'm sorry. May I come over and ask you a few questions?'

'I guess so.' He sounded like a man who had no use for time.

Moira was waiting for me in the car, like a silver-blue cat in a cave.

'Do you want to be dropped at the hospital? I have an errand to do.'

'Take me along.'

'It's a fairly unpleasant errand.'

'I don't care.'

'You would if you lost your marriage and ended up with me. I spend a lot of my nights doing this kind of thing.'

Her hand pressed my knee. 'I know that I could be hurt. I've already made myself vulnerable. But I'm sick of always doing the professional thing for prudential reasons.'

I took her along to Bayview Avenue. The police car was gone. The black Volkswagen with the crumpled fender was still in George Trask's driveway. I remembered now where I had seen it before; under Mrs Swain's rusty carport in Pasadena.

I knocked on the front door and George Trask let us in. His gangling body was carefully dressed in a dark suit and black tie. He had an air of having made himself the servant of the situation, like a mortician. His grief showed only in his reddened eyes, and in the fact that he didn't remember me.

'This is Mrs Smitheram, Mr Trask. She's a psychiatric social worker.'

'It's nice of you to come,' he said to her. 'But I don't need that kind of help. Everything's under control. Come into the living room and sit down, won't you? I'd offer to make you some coffee but I'm not allowed to go into the kitchen. And anyway,' he went on, as if his voice was being piped in from someplace beyond his control, 'the coffeemaker got broken this morning when my wife was murdered.'

'I'm sorry,' Moira said.

We followed George Trask into the living room and sat down beside each other, facing him. The window drapes were partly open, and I could see the lights of the city wavering on the water. The beauty of the scene and the woman beside me made me more aware of the pain George Trask was suffering, like solitary confinement in the world.

'The company is being very understanding,' he said conversationally. 'They're giving me a leave of absence, open-ended, with full pay. That will give me a chance to get everything squared away, eh?'

'Do you know who murdered your wife?'

'We have a pretty good suspect—man with a criminal record as long as your arm—he's known Jean all her life. The police asked me not to mention his name.'

It had to be Randy Shepherd. 'Has he been picked up?'

'They expect to get him tonight. I hope they do, and *when* they do, put him in the gas chamber. You know and I know why crime and murder are rampant. The courts won't convict and when they do convict they won't mete out the death penalty. And even when they do the law is flouted right and left. Convicted murderers walk free, they don't gas anybody any more, no wonder we have a breakdown of law and order.' His eyes were wide and staring, as if they were seeing a vision of chaos.

Moira rose and touched his head. 'Don't talk so much, Mr Trask. It makes you upset.'

'I know. I've been talking all day.'

He put his large hands on his glaring face. I could see his eyes bright as coins between his fingers. His voice went on unmuffled, as if it were independent of his will:

'The dirty old son deserves to be gassed, even if he didn't kill her he's directly responsible for her death. He got her started on this latest mania of looking for her father. He came here to the house last week with his schemes and stories, told her he knew where her father was and she could be with him again. And that's what happened,' he added brokenly. 'Her father's dead in his grave and Jean is with him.'

Trask began to cry. Moira quieted him with small noises more than words.

I noticed after a while that Louise Swain was standing in the hall doorway looking like her daughter's ruined ghost. I got up and went to her:

'How are you, Mrs Swain?'

'Not very well.' She drew a hand across her forehead. 'Poor Jean and I could never get along—she was her father's daughter—but we cared about each other. Now I have no one left.' She shook her head slowly from side to side. 'Jean should have listened to me. I knew she was getting into deep water again, and I tried to stop her.'

'What kind of deep water do you mean?'

'All kinds. It wasn't good for her to go wandering off into the past, imagining that her father was alive. And it wasn't safe. Eldon was a criminal and he consorted with criminals. One of them killed her because she found out too much.'

'Do you know this, Mrs Swain?'

'I know it in my bones. There are hundreds of thousands of dollars at stake, remember. For that kind of money anyone would murder anyone else.' Her eyes seemed to be squinting against a bright light. 'A man would even murder his own daughter.'

I maneuvered her into the hallway, out of hearing of the living room. 'Could your husband still be alive, in your opinion?'

'He could be. Jean thought so. There has to be a reason for everything that's happened. I've heard of men changing their faces with plastic surgery so they could come and go.' Her narrowed gaze swung to my face and stayed on it, as if she was looking for surgical scars that would mark me as Eldon Swain.

And other men, I was thinking, had disappeared and left in their places dead men who resembled them. I said to the woman:

'About fifteen years ago, at the time your husband came back from Mexico, a man was shot dead in Pacific Point. He's been identified as your husband. But the identification has to be tentative: it's based on pictures which aren't the best in the world. One of them is the photograph you gave me last night.'

She looked at me in bewilderment. 'Was that only last night?'

'Yes. I know how you feel. You mentioned last night that your daughter had all your best family pictures. You also mentioned some home movies. They could be useful in this investigation.'

'I see.'

'Are they here in this house?'

'Some of them are, anyway. I've just been going through them.' She spread her fingers. 'It's how I got the dust on my fingers.'

'May I have a look at the pictures, Mrs Swain?'

'That depends.'

'On what?'

'Money. Why should I give you anything free?'

'It may be evidence in your daughter's murder.'

'I don't *care*,' she cried. 'Those pictures are the only things I have left—all I have to show for my life. Whoever gets them has to pay for them, the way I've had to pay for things. And you can go and tell Mr Truttwell that.'

'How did he get into this?'

'You're working for Truttwell, aren't you? I asked my father about him, and he says Truttwell can well afford to pay me!'

'How much are you asking?'

'Let him make a bid,' she said. 'Incidentally, I found the gold box you were inquiring about—my mother's Florentine box.'

'Where was it?'

'That's none of your business. The point is that I have it and it's for sale as well.'

'Was it really your mother's?'

'It certainly was. I've found out what happened to it after her death. My father gave it to another woman. He didn't want to admit it when I asked him about it last night. But I forced it out of him.'

'Was the other woman Estelle Chalmers?'

'You know about his liaison with her, eh? I guess everyone knows. He had his gall giving her Mother's jewel box. It was supposed to go to Jean, you know.'

'What makes it so important, Mrs Swain?'

She thought for a moment. 'I guess it stands for everything that has happened to my family. Our whole life went to pieces. Other people ended up with our money and our furniture and even our little objects of art.' She added after another thinking moment: 'I remember when Jean was just a small child, my mother used to let her play with the box. She told her the story of Pandora's box—you know?—and Jean and her friends pretended that was what it was. When you lifted the lid you released all the troubles of the world.' The image seemed to frighten her into silence.

'May I see the box and the pictures?'

'No you don't! This is my last chance to get a little capital together. Without capital you're nobody, you don't exist. You're not going to cheat me out of my last chance.'

She seemed to be full of anger, but it was probably sorrow she was feeling. She'd stepped on a rotten place and fallen through the floor and knew she was trapped in poverty forever. The dream she was defending wasn't a dream for the future. It was a dreaming memory of the past, when she had lived in San Marino with a successful husband and a forty-foot pool.

I told her I would discuss the matter with Truttwell, and advised her to take good care of the box and the pictures. Then Moira and I said good night to George Trask, and went out to my car.

'Poor people.'

'You were a help.'

'I wish I could have been.' Moira paused. 'I know that certain questions are out of bounds. But I'm going to ask one anyway. You don't have to answer.'

'Go ahead.'

'When you found Nick today, was he in this neighborhood?'

I hesitated, but not for long. She was married to another man, and in a profession with different rules from mine. I gave her a flat no.

'Why?'

'Mr Trask told me his wife was involved with Nick. He didn't know Nick's name, but his description was accurate. Apparently he saw them together in Pacific Point.'

'They spent some time together,' I said shortly.

'Were they lovers?'

'I have no reason to think so. The Trasks and Nick make a very unlikely triangle.'

'I've seen unlikelier,' she said.

'Are you trying to tell me Nick may have killed the woman?'

'No, I'm not. If I thought so I wouldn't be talking about it. Nick has been our patient for fifteen years.'

'Since 1954?'

'Yes.'

'What happened in 1954?'

'Nick became ill,' she said levelly. 'I can't discuss the nature of his illness. I've already said too much.'

We were almost back where we started. Not quite. Driving back to the hospital I could feel her leaning close to me, tentatively, lightly.

XXII

MOIRA LEFT ME at the hospital entrance to fix her face, as she said. I took the elevator to the second floor and found Nick's parents in the visitors' room. Chalmers was snoring in an armchair with his head thrown back. His wife sat near him, dressed in elegant black.

'Mrs Chalmers?'

She rose with her finger to her lips, moving toward the door. 'This is the first rest Larry's had.' She followed me into the corridor. 'We're both deeply grateful to you, for finding Nick.'

'I hope it wasn't too late.'

'It wasn't.' She managed a pale smile. 'Dr Smitheram and the other doctors are most encouraging. Apparently Nick regurg—' She stumbled over the word. 'He vomited some of the pills before they could take effect.'

'What about his concussion?'

'I don't think it's too serious. Do you have any idea how he got it?'

'He fell or was hit,' I said.

'Who hit him?'

'I don't know.'

'Where did you find him, Mr Archer?'

'Here in San Diego.'

'But where?'

'I'd rather report the details through Mr Truttwell.'

'But he's not here. He refused to come. He said he had other clients to attend to.' Her feelings had risen close to the surface, and anger broke through. 'If he thinks he can give us the brush-off, he'll be sorry.'

'I'm sure he didn't mean that.' I changed the subject. 'Since Truttwell isn't available. I should probably tell you I've been talking to a Mrs Swain. She's Jean Trask's mother and she has some family pictures that I'd like to have a look at. But Mrs Swain wants money for them.'

'How much money?'

'Quite a lot. I may be able to get them for a thousand or so.'

'That's ridiculous! The woman must be crazy.'

I didn't press the point. Nurses were coming and going in the corridor. They already knew Mrs Chalmers, and they smiled and nodded and looked inquiringly at her hot black eyes. Breathing deeply, she got herself under some control.

'I insist that you tell me where you found Nick. If he was the victim of foul play—'

I cut her short: 'I wouldn't get off on that kick, Mrs Chalmers.'

'What do you mean?'

'Let's take a little walk.'

We turned a corner and loitered along a hallway past offices that had been closed for the night. I told her in detail where I had found her son, in the garage next to the kitchen where Jean Trask had been murdered. She leaned on the white wall, her head hanging sideways as if I had struck her violently in the face. Without her coloring, her foreshortened shadow looked like that of a hunched old woman.

'You think he killed her, don't you?'

'There are other possibilities. But I haven't reported any of this to the police, for obvious reasons.'

'Am I the only one you've told?'

'So far.'

She straightened up, using her hands to push herself away from the wall. 'Let's keep it that way. Don't tell John Truttwell—he's turned against Nick on account of that girl of his. Don't even tell my husband. His nerves are exhausted as it is, and he can't take it.'

'But you can?'

'I have to.' She was quiet for a moment, getting her thoughts in order. 'You said there were other possibilities.'

'One is that your son was framed. Say the murderer found him drugged and put him in the Trask garage as a patsy. It would be hard to convince the police of that one.'

'Do they have to be brought in?'

'They're in. The question is how much we have to tell them. We'll need legal advice on that. My neck is out a mile as it is.'

She wasn't much interested in the state of my neck. 'What are the other possibilities?'

'I can think of one other. We'll get to that in a minute.' I took out my wallet and produced the suicide note which had fallen from Nick's pocket. 'Is this Nick's writing?'

She held it up to the light. 'Yes, it is. It means he's guilty, doesn't it?'

I took it back. 'It means he feels guilty of something. He may have stumbled across Mrs Trask's body and had an overwhelming guilt reaction. That's the other possibility that occurred to me. I'm no psychiatrist, and I'd like your permission to talk this over with Dr Smitheram.'

'No! Not even Dr Smitheram.'

'Don't you trust him?'

'He knows too much about my son already.' She leaned toward me urgently. 'You can't trust anybody, don't you know that?'

'No,' I said, 'I don't know that. I was hoping we'd reached a point where the people responsible for Nick could do some candid talking with each other. The hush-hush policy hasn't been working too well.'

She looked at me with a kind of wary surprise. 'Do you like Nick?'

'I've had no chance to like him, or get to know him. I feel responsible for him. I hope you do, too.'

'I love him dearly.'

'You may love him too damn dearly. I think you and your husband have been giving him a bad break in trying to overprotect him. If he actually killed anyone the facts are going to have to be brought out.'

She shook her head resignedly. 'You don't know the circumstances.'

'Then tell me.'

'I can't.'

'You might save yourself a lot of time and money, Mrs Chalmers. You might save your son's sanity, or his life.'

'Dr Smitheram says his life is not in danger.'

'Dr Smitheram hasn't been talking to the people I've been talking to. There have been three killings over a period of fifteen years—'

'Be quiet.'

Her voice was low and frantic. She looked up and down the corridor, her gesture mocked and cartooned by her shadow on the wall. In spite of her sex and her elegance I was reminded of Randy Shepherd's furtive sidelong peerings.

'I won't be quiet,' I said. 'You've lived in fear so long you need a taste of reality. There have been three killings, as I said, and they all seem to be connected. I didn't say that Nick was guilty of all three. He may not have done any of them.'

She shook her head despairingly.

I went on: 'Even if he killed the man in the railroad yards, it was a far cry from murder. He was protecting himself against a kidnapper, a wanted man named Eldon Swain who was carrying a gun. As I reconstruct the shooting, he made a rough pass at your little boy. The boy got hold of his gun and shot him in the chest.'

She looked up in surprise. 'How do you know all this?'

'I don't know all of it. It's partly reconstruction from what Nick told me himself. And I had a chance to talk today with an old con named Randy Shepherd. If I can believe him at all, he went to Pacific Point with Eldon Swain but got cold feet when Swain started planning the kidnapping.'

'Why did they pick on us?' she said intently.

'That didn't come out. I suspect Randy Shepherd was more deeply involved than he admits. Shepherd seems to be connected with all three killings, at least as a catalyst. Sidney Harrow was a friend of Shepherd's, and Shepherd was the one who got Jean Trask interested in looking for her father.'

'Her father?'

'Eldon Swain was her father.'

'And you say that this Swain person was carrying a gun?'

'Yes. We know it was the same gun that killed him, and the same gun that killed Sidney Harrow. All of which makes me doubt that Nick killed Harrow. He couldn't very well have kept that gun hidden for the last fifteen years.'

'No.' Her eyes were wide and bright yet somehow abstract, like a hawk's, looking over the entire span of those years. 'I'm sure he didn't,' she said finally.

'Did he ever mention the gun to you?'

She nodded. 'When he came home—he found his own way home. He said a man picked him up on our street and took him to the railroad yards. He said he grabbed a gun and shot the man. Larry and I didn't believe him—we thought it was little-boy talk—till we saw it in the paper next day, about the body being found in the yards.'

'Why didn't you go to the police?'

'By that time it was too late.'

'It's not too late even now.'

'It is for me—for all of us.'

'Why?'

'The police wouldn't understand.'

'They'd understand very well if he killed in self-defense. Did he ever tell you why he shot the man?'

'He never did.' She paused, and her eyes were suffused with feeling.

'And what happened to the gun?'

'He left it lying there, I guess. The police said in the paper the weapon couldn't be found, and Nicky certainly didn't bring it home with him. Some hobo must have picked it up.'

My mind went back to Randy Shepherd. He had been on or near the spot, and he had been very eager to disconnect himself from the kidnapping. I shouldn't have let him go, I thought: a half million dollars was a critical mass of money, enough to convert any thief into a murderer.

XXIII

MRS CHALMERS AND I walked back to the visitors' room, where Dr Smitheram and his wife were talking to Larry Chalmers.

The doctor greeted me with a smile that failed to touch his dubious, probing eyes. 'Moira tells me you took her to dinner. Thanks very much.'

'It was a pleasure. What are my chances of talking to your patient?'

'Minimal. Nonexistent, in fact.'

'Even for a minute?'

'It wouldn't be a good idea, for both physical and psychiatric reasons.'

'How is he?'

'He has a giant hangover, of course, and he's depressed both physically and emotionally. That's partly the overdose of reserpine. Also he has a bit of a concussion.'

'What caused it?'

'I'd say he was hit on the back of the head with a blunt object. But forensic medicine is not my line. Anyway, he's doing surprisingly well. I owe you a vote of thanks for getting him here in time.'

'We all do,' Chalmers said, and shook hands with me formally. 'You saved my son's life.'

'We were lucky, both of us. It would be nice if the luck continued.'

'What do you mean, exactly?'

'I think Nick's room should be guarded.'

'You think he might get away again?' Chalmers said.

'That's a thought. It hadn't occurred to me. What I had in mind was protection for him.'

'He has round-the-clock nurses,' Dr Smitheram said.

'He needs an armed guard. There have been several killings; we don't want another.' I turned to Chalmers: 'I can get you three shifts for about a hundred dollars a day.'

'By all means,' Chalmers said.

I went downstairs and made a couple of phone calls. The first was to a Los Angeles guard service with a San Diego branch. They said they would have a man named Maclennan on duty in half an hour. Then I called Conchita's Cabins in Imperial Beach. Mrs Williams answered in a hushed and worried voice.

'This is Archer. Has Randy Shepherd been back?'

'No, and he probably won't be.' She lowered her voice even further. 'You're not the only one looking for him. They have the place staked out.'

I was glad to hear it, because it meant I wouldn't have to stake it out myself.

'Thanks, Mrs Williams. Take it easy.'

'That's easier said than done. Why didn't you tell me Sidney Harrow was dead?'

'It wouldn't have done you any good to know.'

'You can say that again. I'm putting this place up for sale as soon as I get *them* out of my hair.'

I wished her good luck, and went out the front door for some air. After a while Moira Smitheram came out and joined me.

She lit a cigarette from a fresh pack and smoked it as if she was being timed by a stop watch. 'You don't smoke, do you?'

'I gave it up.'

'So did I. But I still smoke when I'm angry.'

'What are you angry about now?'

'Ralph again. He's going to sleep in the hospital tonight so he can be on call. I might as well be married to a Trappist.'

Her anger sounded superficial, as if it was masking some deeper feeling. I waited for that feeling to show itself. She threw her cigarette away and said: 'I hate motels. You wouldn't be driving back to the Point tonight?'

'West Los Angeles. I can drop you off on the way.'

'You're very kind.' Under the formal language I could sense an excitement echoing mine. 'Why are you going to West Los Angeles?'

'I live there. I like to sleep in my own apartment. It's just about the only continuity in my life.'

'I thought you abhorred continuity. You said at dinner you liked to move in and out of people's lives.'

'That's true. Particularly the people I meet in my work.'

'People like me?'

'I wasn't thinking of you.'

'Oh? I thought you were stating a general policy,' she said with some irony, 'to which everyone was expected to conform.'

A tall, wide young man with a crew cut and wearing a dark suit emerged from the shadows of the parking lot and headed for the hospital entrance. I called to him:

'Maclennan?'

'Yessir.'

I told Moira I'd be right back, and took Maclennan up in the elevator. 'Don't let anyone in,' I told him, 'except hospital personnel—doctors and nurses—and the immediate family.'

'How do I know who *they* are?'

'I'll get you started with them. The main thing I want you to look for is men, wearing white coats or not. Don't let any man in unless he's vouched for by a nurse or a doctor you know.'

'You expecting a murder attempt?'

'It could happen. You're armed?'

Maclennan pulled back his jacket and showed me the butt of the automatic in his armpit. 'Who do I look out for?'

'I don't know, unfortunately. You have one other duty. Don't let the boy run away. But don't use a gun on him, or anything else. He's what it's all about.'

'Sure, I understand that.' He had a large man's calmness.

I took him to the door of Nick's room and asked the private nurses for Smitheram. The doctor opened the door wide as he came out. I caught a glimpse of Nick lying still with his eyes closed, his nose pointed at the ceiling, his parents sitting on either side of him. The three of them looked like something in a frieze, a ritual in which the raised hospital bed served as a kind of sacrificial altar.

The door closed on them silently. I introduced Maclennan to Dr Smitheram, who gave us both a bored and weary look:

'Are all these alarms and excursions really necessary?'

'I think so.'

'I don't. I'm certainly not going to let you plant this man in the room.'

'He'd be more effective there.'

'Effective against what?'

'A possible murder attempt.'

'That's ridiculous. The boy's perfectly safe here. Who would want to murder him?'

'Ask him.'

'I will not.'

'Will you let me ask him?'

'No. He's in no condition—'

'When will he be?'

'Never, if you plan to bullyrag him.'

' "Bullyrag" is a loaded word. Are you trying to make me sore?'

Smitheram let out a clever little laugh. 'If I were, I appear to have succeeded.'

'What are you sitting on, doctor?'

His eyes narrowed and his mouth talked very rapidly: 'I'm standing—standing on my right and duty to protect my patient.

And no Junior G-men are going to talk to him now or ever, if I can help it. Is that clear?'

'What about me?' Maclennan said. 'Am I hired or fired?'

I turned to him, swallowing my anger. 'You're hired. Dr Smitheram wants you to stay outside in the corridor. If anyone questions your right to be here, tell them you're employed by Nick Chalmers's parents to protect him. Dr Smitheram or one of the nurses will introduce you to the parents when it's convenient.'

'I can hardly wait,' Maclennan said under his breath.

XXIV

MOIRA WASN'T WAITING downstairs or in my car. I found her eventually in a parking lot reserved for doctors' cars. She was sitting behind the wheel of her husband's Cadillac convertible.

'I got tired of waiting,' she said lightly. 'I thought I'd test your investigative skills.'

'This is a hell of a time to be playing hide-and-seek.'

My voice must have been rough. She closed her eyes in reaction. Then she climbed out of the convertible. 'I was only kidding. But not really. I wanted to see if you would look for me.'

'I looked. Okay?'

She took my arm and shook it gently. 'You're still angry.'

'I'm not angry at you. It's your goddam husband.'

'What did Ralph do now?'

'He pulled rank on me and called me a junior G-man. That's the personal part. The other part is more serious. He refused to let me talk to Nick, now or ever. If I could have just five minutes with Nick, I could clear up a lot of points.'

'I hope you're not asking me to take it up with Ralph?'

'No.'

'I don't want to be caught in the middle between you.'

'If you don't want that,' I said, 'you better go and find a better place to hide.'

She looked up at me slantwise. I caught a glint of her naked self, shy and mercurial and afraid of being hurt. 'Did you mean that? You want me to get lost?'

I took hold of her and answered her without words. After a minute, she broke away.

'I'm ready to go home now. Are you?'

I said I was, but I wasn't quite. My feeling about Smitheram, anger deepened now by suspicion, got in the way of my feeling for his wife. And it started me thinking along less pleasant lines: the possibility that I might use her to get back at him, or get at him. I pushed these thoughts away but they crouched like unwanted children in the shadows, waiting for the lights to be turned out.

We headed north on the highway. Moira noticed my preoccupation. 'If you're tired I can drive.'

'It's not that kind of tired.' I tapped my skull. 'I have a few problems to work through, and my computer is a fairly early pre-binary model. It doesn't say yes and no. It says mainly maybe.'

'About me?'

'About everything.'

We rode in silence past San Onofre. The great sphere of the atomic reactor loomed in the darkness like a dead and fallen moon. The actual moon hung in the sky above it.

'Is this computer of yours programmed for questions?'

'Some questions. Others put it completely out of whack.'

'Okay.' Moira's voice became soft and serious. 'I think I know what's on your mind, Lew. You gave it away when you said five minutes with Nick could clear up everything.'

'Not everything. A lot.'

'You think he killed all three of them, don't you? Harrow and poor Mrs Trask and the man in the railroad yards?'

'Maybe.'

'Tell me what you really think.'

'What I really think is maybe. I'm reasonably sure he killed the man in the railroad yards. I'm not sure about the others, and I'm getting less sure all the time. Right now I'm going on the assumption that Nick was framed for the others and may know who framed him. Which means he may be next.'

'Is that why you didn't want to come with me?'

'I didn't say that.'

'I felt it, though. Look, if you feel you have to turn around and go back there, I'll understand.' She added: 'I can always leave my body to medical science. Or put in an application for equal time.'

I laughed.

'It's not funny,' Moira said. 'Things keep happening, and the world keeps moving so fast, it's hard for a woman to compete.'

'Anyway,' I said, 'there's no point in going back. Nick is well guarded. He can't get out, and nobody can get in.'

'Which takes care of both your maybes, doesn't it?'

We were silent for a long time. I would have liked to question her at length, about both Nick and her husband. But if I started to use the woman and the occasion, I'd be using a part of myself and my life that I tried to keep unused: the part that made the difference between me and a computer, or a spy.

The unasked question simmered down after a while, and my mind hung loose in silence. The sense of living inside the case, which I sometimes used as a drug to keep me going, slowly left me.

The woman beside me had a sensitive antennae. As if I'd withdrawn a protective shield, she moved in close to me. I drove with her warmth all down my right side and spreading through my body.

She lived on the Montevista shore in a rectilinear cliff-top house made of steel and glass and money.

'Put your car in the carport if you like. You will come in for a drink?'

'A short one.'

She couldn't unlock the front door.

'You're using your car key,' I told her.

She paused to consider. 'I wonder what that means?'

'That you probably need glasses.'

'I do use glasses for reading.'

She let me in and turned on a light in the hall. We went down some steps into an octagonal room which was mostly window. I could see the moon almost close enough to touch, and, far below, the scrawled white lines of the breakers.

'It's a nice place.'

'Do you think so?' She seemed surprised. 'God knows the place was beautiful before we built on it, and when we were planning it with the architect. But the house never seemed to capture it.' She went on after a moment: 'Building a house is like putting a bird in a cage. The bird being yourself, I guess.'

'Is that what they tell you at the clinic?'

She turned to me with a quick smile. 'Am I being terribly talky?'

'You did mention a drink.'

She leaned toward me, silver-faced, dark-eyed, and dark-mouthed in the thin light from outside. 'What will you have?'

'Scotch.' Then her eyes moved and I caught that naked glint of her again, like a light hidden deep in a building. I said: 'May I change my mind?'

She was willing to be taken. We shed our clothes, more or less, and lay down like wrestlers going to the mat under special rules, where pinning and being pinned were equally lucky and meritorious.

She said at one point, between falls, that I was a gentle lover.

'There are some advantages in getting older.'

'It isn't that. You remind me of Sonny, and he was only twenty. You make me feel like Eve in the garden again.'

'That's pretty fancy talk.'

'I don't care.' She rose on one elbow, and her silver breast lay heavy on me. 'Does it upset you when I mention Sonny?'

'Oddly enough, it doesn't.'

'It shouldn't, either. He was a poor little nothing boy. But we were happy together. We lived like silly angels doing things for each other. He'd never been with a girl before, and I'd only been with Ralph.'

Her voice changed on her husband's name, and my feeling also changed. 'Ralph was always so terribly technical and self-assured. He came on in bed like an army pacifying an undeveloped country. But with Sonny it was different. He was so gentle and nutty. Love was like a game, a fantasy that we lived in, playing house together. Sometimes he pretended to be Ralph. Sometimes I pretended to be his mother. Does that sound sick?' she said with a nervous little laugh.

'Ask Ralph.'

'I'm boring you, aren't I?'

'On the contrary. How long did this affair go on?'

'Nearly two years.'

'Then Ralph came home?'

'Eventually he did. But I'd already broken with Sonny. The fantasy was running out of control and so was he. Besides, I couldn't just leap from his bed into Ralph's. As it was the guilt nearly killed me.'

I looked down along her body. 'You don't strike me as the guilt-ridden type.'

She answered after a moment. 'You're right. It wasn't guilt. It was simple pain. I'd given up my one true love. For what? A hundred-thousand-dollar house and four-hundred-thousand-dollar clinic. In neither of which I'd be caught dead if I could help it. I'd rather be back in one room at the Magnolia.'

'It isn't there any more,' I said. 'Aren't you building up the past a little large?'

She answered thoughtfully. 'Maybe I am exaggerating, especially the good parts. Women do tend to make up stories featuring ourselves.'

'I'm glad men never do.'

She laughed. 'I bet Eve made up the story of the apple.'

'And Adam made up the story of the garden.'

She crawled close against me. 'You're a nut. That's a diagnosis. I'm glad I told you all this. Are you?'

'I can stand it. Why did you?'

'Various reasons. Also you have the advantage of not being my husband.'

'That's the finest thing any woman ever said to me.'

'I mean it seriously. If I told Ralph what I've told you, it would be the end of me as a person. I'd become just another of his famous psychiatric trophies. He'd probably have me stuffed and hang me up on the office wall with his diplomas.' She added: 'In a way that's what he has done.'

There were questions I wanted to ask her about her husband but the time and place were wrong, and I was still determined not to use them. 'Forget about Ralph. Whatever happened to Sonny?'

'He found another girl and married her.'

'And you're jealous?'

'No. I'm lonely. I have no one.'

We merged our lonelinesses once again, in something less than love but sweeter than self. I didn't get home to West Los Angeles after all.

XXV

IN THE MORNING I left early without waking Moira. Fog had moved in from the sea, blanketing the cliff-top house and the whole Montevista shore. I drove up the road very slowly between lines of phantom trees.

I came to the end of the fog suddenly. The sky was cloudless except for a couple of smeared jet contrails. I drove downtown and checked in at the police station.

Lackland was in his office. The electric clock on the wall above his head said that it was exactly eight o'clock. It bothered me for a minute. It made me feel as if Lackland had brought me in again at this particular time by the exertion of some occult force.

'Glad you dropped by,' he said. 'Sit down. I was wondering where everybody was.'

'I went to San Diego on a lead.'

'And you took your clients with you?'

'Their son had an accident. They went to San Diego to look after him.'

'I see.' He waited for a while, twisting and biting his lips as if to punish his mouth for asking questions. 'What kind of an accident did he have, or is it a family secret?'

'Barbiturate, mainly. He also has a head injury.'

'Was it a suicide attempt?'

'Could be.'

Lackland leaned forward abruptly, pushing his face toward mine. 'After he knocked off Mrs Trask?'

I wasn't ready for the question, and I avoided answering it directly. 'The prime suspect in the Trask killing is Randy Shepherd.'

'I know that,' Lackland said, making it clear that I hadn't given him anything. 'We have an APB on Shepherd from San Diego.'

'Does it mention that Shepherd knew Eldon Swain from 'way back?'

Lackland gnawed at his upper lip. 'Do you know that for a fact?'

'Yes. I talked to Shepherd yesterday, before he was regarded as a suspect. He told me that Swain ran off with his daughter Rita and half a million dollars. Apparently Shepherd has spent his life trying to latch onto a piece of that money. It's fairly clear, by the way, that Shepherd talked Mrs Trask into hiring Sidney Harrow and coming here to the Point. He was using them as cat's-paws to find out what he could without the risk of coming here himself.'

'So Shepherd had a motive to kill Swain after all.' Lackland's voice was low, as if his fifteen years on the case had used up all his energy at last. 'And he had a motive to burn off Swain's fingerprints. Where did you talk to him?'

'On the Mexican border near Imperial Beach. He wouldn't be there any more.'

'No. As a matter of fact, Shepherd was seen in Hemet last night. He stopped for gas, heading north in a stolen car, a late-model Merc convertible, black.'

'Better check Pasadena. Shepherd came from there, and so did Eldon Swain.'

I filled Lackland in on the Pasadena end of the case, on Swain and Mrs Swain and their murdered daughter, and Swain's embezzlement from Rawlinson's bank. 'Once you know these facts,' I concluded, 'you can't seriously go on blaming Nick Chalmers for everything. He wasn't even born when Eldon Swain took the money from the bank. But that was the real beginning of the case.'

Lackland was silent for a while. His face in repose was like an eroded landscape in a dry season. 'I know some history, too. Rawlinson, the man who owned the bank, used to spend his summers here back in the twenties and thirties. I could tell you more.'

'Please do.'

Lackland produced one of his rare smiles. It wasn't very different from his mouth-gnawings, except that a shy light flickered in his eyes. 'I hate to disappoint you, Archer. But no matter how far back you go, Nick Chalmers is in the picture. Sam Rawlinson had a girl friend here in town, and after her husband died they spent their summers together. You want to know who his girl friend was?'

'Nick's grandmother,' I said. 'Judge Chalmers's widow.'

Lackland was disappointed. He lifted a typed sheet from his

in-basket, read it carefully, crushed in up in a ball, and threw it at a trash can in the corner of his office. It missed. I scooped it up and dropped it in.

'How did you find that out?' he asked me finally.

'I've been doing some digging in Pasadena, as I told you. But I still don't see how Nick comes into this. He's not responsible for his grandmother.'

For once Lackland failed to offer an argument. But I thought as I left the police station that perhaps the reverse was true, and Nick's dead grandmother was responsible for him. Certainly there had to be a meaning in the old connection between the Rawlinson family and the Chalmers family.

I passed the courthouse on my way downtown. In a cast stone bas-relief above the entrance, a big old Justice with bandaged eyes fumbled at her scales. She needed a seeing-eye man, I told her silently. I was feeling dangerously good.

After a breakfast of steak and eggs I went into a barber-shop and had a shave. By this time it was close to ten o'clock, and Truttwell should be in his office.

He wasn't, though. The receptionist told me that he had just left and hadn't said when he'd be back. She was wearing a black wig this morning, and took my troubled stare as a compliment.

'I like to change my personality. I get sick of having the same old personality.'

'Me, too.' I made a face at her. 'Did Mr Truttwell go home?'

'I don't know. He received a couple of long-distance calls and then he just took off. If he goes on this way, he'll end up losing his practice.' The girl smiled intensely up at me, as if she was already looking for a new opening. 'Do you think black hair goes with my complexion? Actually I'm a natural brownette. But I like to keep experimenting with myself.'

'You look fine.'

'I thought so, too,' she said, overconfidently.

'Where did the distance calls come from?'

'The one call came from San Diego—that was Mrs Chalmers.

I don't know who the other one was, she wouldn't give her name. It sounded like an older woman.'

'Calling from where?'

'She didn't say, and it was dialed direct.'

I asked her to call Truttwell's house for me. He was there, but he wouldn't or couldn't come to the phone. I talked to Betty instead.

'Is your father all right?'

'I guess he is. I hope so.' The young woman's voice was serious and subdued.

'Are you?'

'Yes.' But she sounded doubtful.

'If I come right over, will he be willing to talk to me?'

'I don't know. You'd better hurry. He's going out of town.'

'Where out of town?'

'I don't know,' she repeated glumly. 'If you do miss him, Mr Archer, I'd still like to talk to you myself.'

Truttwell's Cadillac was standing in front of his house when I got there. Betty opened the front door for me. Her eyes were rather dull and unresponsive. Even her bright hair looked a little tarnished.

'Have you seen Nick?' she said.

'I've seen him. The doctor gave him a fairly good report.'

'But what did Nick say?'

'He wasn't talkable.'

'He'd talk to me. I wanted so badly to go to San Diego.' She raised her fists and pressed them against her breast. 'Father wouldn't let me.'

'Why not?'

'He's jealous of Nick. I know that's a disloyal thing to say. But Father made it very clear. He said when Mrs Chalmers dismissed him this morning that I would have to choose between him and Nick.'

'Why did Mrs Chalmers dismiss him?'

'You'll have to ask Father. He and I are not communicating.'

Truttwell appeared in the hallway behind her. Though he must have heard what she'd just said, he made no reference to it. But he gave her a hard impatient look that I saw and she didn't.

'What's this, Betty? We don't keep visitors standing in the doorway.'

She turned away without speaking, moving into another room and shutting the door behind her. Truttwell spoke in a complaining way, with a thin note of malice running through his complaint:

'She's losing her mind over that sad sack. She wouldn't listen to me. Maybe she will now. But come in, Archer. I have news for you.'

Truttwell took me into his study. He was even more carefully dressed and groomed than usual. He wore a fresh sharkskin suit, a button-down shirt with matching silk tie and handkerchief, and the odors of bay rum and masculine scent.

'Betty tells me you're parting company with the Chalmerses. You look as if you're celebrating.'

'Betty shouldn't have told you. She's losing all sense of discretion.'

His handsome pink face was fretful. He pressed and patted his white hair. Betty had hurt him in his vanity, I thought, and apparently he didn't have much else to fall back on.

I was more disturbed by the change in Truttwell than by the change in his daughter. She was young, and would change again before she settled on a final self.

'She's a good girl,' I said.

Truttwell closed the study door and stood against it. 'Don't sell her to me. I know what she is. She let that creep get to her and poison her mind against me.'

'I don't think so.'

'You're not her father,' he said, as if paternity conferred the gift of second sight. 'She's put herself down on his level. She's even using the same crude Freudian jargon.' His face was red now and his voice was choked. 'She actually accused me of taking an unhealthy interest in her.'

I said to myself: This is a healthy interest?

Truttwell went on: 'I know where she picked up those ideas—from Dr Smitheram via Nick. I also know,' he said, 'why Irene Chalmers terminated their association with me. She made it quite clear on the telephone that the great and good Dr Smitheram insisted on it. He was probably standing at her elbow telling her what to say.'

'What reason did she give?'

'I'm afraid you were one reason, Archer. I don't mean to be critical,' though he did. 'I gathered that you asked too many questions to suit Dr Smitheram. He seems determined to mastermind the entire show, and that could be disastrous. No lawyer can defend Nick without knowing what he's done.'

Truttwell gave me a careful look. As our talk moved back onto more familiar ground, he had regained some of his lawyer's poise. 'You're better acquainted with the facts than I could possibly be.'

It was a question. I didn't answer it right away. My attitude to Truttwell was undergoing an adjustment. It wasn't a radical one, since I had to admit to myself that from the beginning of the case I hadn't wholly understood or trusted his motivations.

It was becoming fairly evident now that Truttwell had been using me and intended to go on using me. In the same way as Harrow had served as Randy Shepherd's cat's-paw, I was Truttwell's. He was waiting now, handsome and quick-eyed and well-groomed as a cat, for me to spill the dirt on his daughter's friend. I said:

'Facts are hard to come by in this case. I don't even know who I'm working for. Or if I'm working.'

'Of course you are,' he said benevolently. 'You'll be paid in full for everything you've done, and I'll guarantee payment through today at least.'

'Who will be doing the paying?'

'The Chalmerses, naturally.'

'But you don't represent them any more.'

'Don't let that worry you. Just submit your bill through me, and they'll pay it. You're not exactly a migratory worker, and I won't let them treat you as one.'

His good will was self-serving, I thought, and would probably last only as long as he could use me. I was embarrassed by it, and by the conflict that had risen. In cases like this, I was usually the expendable one.

'Shouldn't I report to the Chalmerses?'

'No. They've already dismissed you. They don't want the truth about Nick.'

'How is he?'

Truttwell shrugged. 'His mother didn't say.'

'Who do I report to now?'

'Report to me. I've represented the Chalmers family for nearly thirty years, and they're going to find that I'm not so very readily dispensable.' He made the prediction with a smile, but there was the hint of a threat in it.

'What if they don't?'

'They will, I guarantee it. But if you're concerned about your money, I'll undertake to pay you personally as of today.'

'Thanks. I'll give it some thought.'

'You'd better think in a hurry,' he said smiling. 'I'm on my way to Pasadena to meet Mrs Swain. She phoned me this morning about investing in her family pictures—after Mrs Chalmers dismissed me. I'd like to have you come along, Archer.'

In my trade you don't often have your own way. If I refused to deal with John Truttwell, he could push me off the case and probably close the county to me. I said:

'I'll take my own car and meet you at Mrs Swain's house. That's where you're going, isn't it?—Pasadena?'

'Yes, I can count on you to follow me then?'

I said he could, but I didn't follow him right away. There was something more to be said between me and his daughter.

XXVI

BETTY CAME TO the front door, as if by prearrangement, and asked me in again. 'I have the letters,' she said quietly, 'the letters that Nick took from his father's safe.'

She led me upstairs to her workroom and brought a manila envelope out of a drawer. It was stuffed with airmail letters arranged for the most part in serial order. There must have been a couple of hundred of them.

'How do you know Nick took them from the safe?'

'He told me so himself the night before last. Dr Smitheram left us alone for awhile. Nick told me where he'd hidden them in his apartment. I went and got them yesterday.'

'Did Nick say why he took them?'

'No.'

'Do you know why?'

She perched on a large multicolored hassock. 'I've had a lot of different thoughts,' she said. 'It has to do with the whole father-son business, I suppose. In spite of all the trouble, Nick has always had a lot of respect for his father.'

'Does that go for you and your father?'

'We aren't talking about me,' she said in a stiff-mouthed way. 'Anyway, girls are different—we're much more ambiguous. A boy either wants to be like his father or he doesn't. I think Nick does.'

'It still doesn't explain why Nick stole the letters.'

'I didn't say I could explain it. But maybe he was trying, you know, to steal his father's bravery and so on. The letters were important to him.'

'Why?'

'Mr Chalmers made them important. He used to read them aloud to Nick—parts of them, anyway.'

'Recently?'

'No. When Nick was a little boy.'

'Eight?'

'It started about that age. I think Mr Chalmers was trying to indoctrinate him, make a man of him and all like that.' Her tone was a little contemptuous, not so much of Nick or his father as of the indoctrination.

'When Nick was eight,' I said, 'he had a serious accident. Do you know about it, Betty?'

She nodded deeply. Her hair slid forward, covering most of her face. 'He shot a man, he told me the other night. But I don't want to talk about it, okay?'

'Just one question. What was Nick's attitude toward that shooting?'

She hugged herself as if she was chilly. Encircled by her arms and masked by her hair, she huddled on the hassock like a gnome. 'I don't want to talk about it.'

She pulled up her knees and rested her face against them, almost as if she was imitating Nick in his posture of despair.

I carried the letters to a table by a front window. From where I sat I could see the façade of the Chalmerses' house glistening white under its red tile roof. It looked like a building with a history, and I read the first of the letters in the hope of filling in my knowledge of it.

Mrs Harold Chalmers
2124 Pacific Street
Pacific Point, Calif.

Pearl Harbor
October 9, 1943

Dear Mother:

All I have time for is a short letter. But I wanted you to know as soon as possible that I have got my exact wish. This letter will be censored for military details, I am told, so I will simply mention the sea and the air, and you will understand what kind of duty I have been assigned to. I feel as if I had just been knighted, Mother. Please tell Mr Rawlinson my good news.

The trip from the mainland was dull but rather pleasant. A number of my fellow pilots spent their time on the fantail shooting at flying fish. I finally told some of them that they were wasting their time and spoiling the beauty of the day. I thought for a while that I might have to fight four or five of them at once. But they recognized the moral superiority of my view, and retreated from the fantail.

I hope you are well and happy, dear Mother. I have never been happier in my life. Your affectionate son,

Larry

I suppose I had been expecting some further light on the case, and the letter was a disappointment to me. It had evidently been written by an idealistic and rather conceited boy who was unnaturally eager to get into the war. The only remarkable thing about it was the fact that the boy had since become a dry stick of a man like Chalmers.

The second letter from the top had been written about eighteen months after the first. It was longer and more interesting, the work of a more mature personality sobered by the war.

Lt (j.g.) L Chalmers
SS Sorel Bay (CVE 185)
March 15, 1945

Mrs Harold Chalmers
2124 Pacific Street

Pacific Point, Calif.

Dearest Mother:

Here I am in the forward area again so my letter won't go off for a while. I find it hard to write a letter that I have to hold on to. It's like keeping a diary, which I detest, or carrying on a conversation with a dictaphone. But writing to you, my dearest, is another matter.

Apart from the things that wouldn't get past the censor, the news about me is very much the same. I fly, sleep, read, eat, dream of home. We all do. For a nation that has built up not only the most powerful but the most expert Navy in the world, we Americans are a bunch of awful landlubbers. All we want is to get back to Mother Earth.

This applies to regular Navy men, who constantly look forward to shore duty and retirement, all but the brass hats, who are having a career. It's even true of the British Navy, some of whose officers I met not long ago in a certain port. A rumour of Germany's collapse reached us that night, and it was touching to see the hopeful wishing of those Britishers. The rumor turned out to be premature, as you must know, but Germany may be finished by the time you get this letter. Give Japan one year after that.

I met a couple of fellow pilots who had been over Tokyo and they told me how it felt: pretty good, they said, because none of the planes in their group got hit. (My squadron has not been so lucky.) They were on their way back to the U.S. after completing their missions and they were happy about that. But they were tensed up, their faces were stiff and reacted quite violently to their emotions. There's something about pilots that reminds you of racehorses—developed almost to an unhealthy point. I hope I'm not that way to other eyes.

Our squadron leader Commander Wilson is, though. (He's no longer censoring mail so I can say this.) He's been in for over four years now, but he seems to be exactly the same gentlemanly Yale man he was when he came in. He has, however, a certain air of arrested development. He has given his best to the war, and will never become the man he was meant to be. (He plans to go into the consular service afterwards.)

Apart from one or two rain squalls the weather has been good: bright sun and shining blue sea, which helps with the flying. But there's a fairly strong swell, which doesn't. The old tub lurches and strains along, and every now and then she wiggles like a hula girl and things slide off onto the floor. The cradle of the deep, to coin a phrase. Well, I'm off to bed.

Affectionately,

Larry

It was a fairly impressive letter, with a certain sadness running gray through its perceptions. One sentence stayed in my mind—'He has given his best to the war, and will never become the man he was meant to be'—because it seemed to apply to Chalmers himself as well as his squadron commander. The third letter was dated 4 July 1945:

Dearest Mother:

We're fairly near the equator and the heat is pretty bad, though I don't mean to complain. If we're still anchored at this atoll tomorrow I'm going to try to get off the ship for a swim, which I haven't had since we left Pearl months ago. One of my big daily pleasures, though, is the shower I take every night before going to bed. The water isn't cold, because the sea at temperatures around 90 can't cool it, and you're not supposed to use much, because all the water we use on board has to be condensed from seawater. Still, I like my shower.

Other things I would like: fresh eggs for breakfast, a glass of cold milk, a sail off the Point, a chance to sit and chat with you, Mother, in our garden between the mountains and the sea. I'm terribly sorry to hear that you are ill and your sight has failed. Please thank Mrs Truttwell on my behalf (hi, Mrs Truttwell!) for reading aloud to you.

You have no cause to worry about me, Mother. After a not-unexciting period (in which our squadron lost Commander Wilson, and too many others) we are fighting a safe war. So safe I feel guilty, but not so guilty that I'm going to jump overboard and swim rapidly in the direction of Japan. Good news from there, eh?—I mean re the destruction of their cities. It's no secret by now that we're going to do to Japan what we've already done to that certain island (which shall be nameless) where I flew so many missions.

Affectionately,
Larry

I put the letters back in the envelope. They seemed to mark points on a curve. The boy or man who had written them had passed from the eager idealism of the first letter into the rather impressive quick maturity of the second, and declined in the third into a kind of tiredness. I wondered what Chalmers himself could see in his letters that made him want to read them aloud to his son.

I turned to the girl, who hadn't moved from her hassock: 'Have you read these letters, Betty?'

She raised her head. The look in her eyes was very dark and far. 'I beg your pardon? I was thinking.'

'Have you read these letters?'

'Some of them. I wanted to see what all the shouting was about. *I* think they're boring. I *hated* the one about bombing Okinawa.'

'May I keep the three I've read?'

'Keep them all, why don't you? If Father finds them here, I'll have to explain where I got them. And it will be just another nail in Nick's coffin.'

'He isn't in his coffin. It doesn't help matters to talk as if he is.'

'Don't fatherize, please, Mr Archer.'

'Why not? I don't believe people know everything at birth and forget it as they get older.'

She reacted positively to my sharp tone. 'That's the doctrine of Platonic reminiscence. I don't believe it, either.' She slid off the hassock and out of her lethargy and came toward me. 'Why don't you give the letters to Mr Chalmers? You wouldn't have to tell him where you got them.'

'Is he at home?'

'I'm afraid I have no idea. I don't really spend all my time at this window watching the Chalmers house.' She added with a quick wan smile: 'Not more than six or eight hours a day, anyway.'

'Don't you think it's time you broke the habit?'

She gave me a disappointed look. 'Are you against Nick, too?'

'Obviously I'm not. But I hardly know him. You're the one I know. And I hate to see you caught here, between two fairly dismal alternatives.'

'You mean Nick and my father, don't you? I'm not caught.'

'You are, though, like a maiden in a tower. This low-grade war of attrition with your father may feel like a battle for freedom, but it isn't. You just get more and more deeply engaged with him. Even if you do succeed in breaking away, it won't be into freedom. You've got it arranged so another demanding male will take you over. And I do mean Nick.'

'You've got no right to attack him—'

'I'm attacking you,' I said. 'Or rather the situation you've put yourself in. Why don't you move out of the middle?'

'Where could I go?'

'You shouldn't have to ask me. You're twenty-five.'

'But I'm afraid.'

'What of?'

'I don't know. I'm just afraid.' After a silence she said in a hushed voice: 'You know what happened to my mother. I told you, didn't I? She looked out this very window— this used to be her sewing room—and she saw a light in the Chalmers house when there wasn't supposed to be one. She went over there and the burglars chased her out and ran over her and killed her.'

'Why did they kill her?'

'I don't know. It may have been just an accident.'

'What did the burglars want from the Chalmers house?'

'I don't know.'

'When did it happen, Betty?'

'In the summer of 1945.'

'You were too young to remember, weren't you?'

'Yes, but my father told me about it. I've been afraid ever since.'

'I don't believe you. You didn't act afraid the other night, when Mrs Trask and Harrow came to Chalmers house.'

'I was afraid, though, terribly. And I should never have gone there. They're both dead.'

I was beginning to understand the fear that held her. She believed or suspected that Nick had killed both Harrow and Mrs

Trask, and that she herself had acted as a catalyst. Perhaps in some dark place of her mind, back beyond memory and below the level of speech, was the false but guilty knowledge that her infant self had somehow killed her mother in the street.

XXVII

THE MOVEMENT OF a car below the window drew my thoughts out of the past. It was Chalmers's black Rolls. He got out and moved rather uncertainly across the courtyard to his house. He unlocked the front door and went in.

'Now you've got me doing it,' I said to Betty.

'Doing what?'

'Watching the Chalmers house. They're not all that interesting.'

'Maybe not. But they're special people, the kind other people watch.'

'Why don't they watch us?'

She entered into my mood. 'Because they're more interested in themselves. They couldn't care less about us.' She smiled not very cheerfully. 'Okay, I get the message. I have to become more interested in myself.'

'Or something. What *are* you interested in?'

'History. I've been offered a traveling fellowship. But I felt I was needed here.'

'To pursue a career of house-watching.'

'You've made your point, Mr Archer. Don't spoil it now.'

I left her and, after putting the letters in the trunk of my car, crossed the street to the Chalmers house. I was having a delayed reaction to the death of Betty's mother, which seemed now to be an integral part of the case. If Chalmers was willing, he might be able to help me understand it.

He came to the door himself. A worried look had lengthened

his bony brown face. His tan looked rather sallow, and his eyes were reddish and tired.

'I wasn't expecting to see *you*, Mr Archer.' His tone was polite and neutral. 'I understood my wife had severed diplomatic relations.'

'We're still talking to each other, I hope. How is Nick doing?'

'Quite well.' He went on in a careful voice: 'My wife and I have reason to be grateful for your help. I want you to know that. Unfortunately, you were caught in the middle, between Truttwell and Dr Smitheram. They can't cooperate, and under the circumstances we have to stay with Smitheram.'

'The doctor's assuming a great deal of responsibility.'

'I suppose he is. But that's not your affair.' Chalmers was getting a little edgy. 'And I hope you didn't come here to make an attack on Dr Smitheram. In a situation like this, a man has to lean on someone. We're not islands, you know,' he said surprisingly. 'We can't bear the weight of these problems all alone.'

His angry sorrow bothered me. 'I agree with you, Mr Chalmers. I'd still like to help if I can.'

He looked at me suspiciously. 'In what way?'

'I'm getting the feeling of the case. I think it started before Nick was born, and that his part in it is fairly innocent. I can't promise to get him off the hook entirely. But I hope to prove that he's a victim, a patsy.'

'I'm not sure I understand you,' Chalmers said. 'But come inside.'

He took me into the study where the case had begun. I felt slightly cramped and smothered, as if everything that had happened in the room was still going on, using up space and air. I was struck by the thought that Chalmers, with family history breathing down his neck, may have felt smothered and cramped most of the time.

'Will you have some sherry, old man?'

'No thanks.'

'Then neither will I.' He turned the swivel chair in front of the desk and sat facing me across the refectory table. 'You were going to give me an overview of the situation, I think.'

'I'll try, with your help, Mr Chalmers.'

'How can I help? Events have gone quite beyond me.' He made a helpless gesture with his hands.

'With your forbearance, then. I've just been talking to Betty Truttwell about her mother's death.'

'That was a tragic accident.'

'I think it may have been more than an accident. I understood Mrs Truttwell was your mother's closest friend.'

'She was indeed. Mrs Truttwell was wonderfully kind to my mother in her last days. If I have any criticism at all, it has to do with her failure to tell me how bad things were with Mother. I was still overseas that summer, and I had no idea that Mother was close to death. You can imagine my feelings when my ship came back to the West Coast in mid-July, and I found that both of them were dead.' His troubled blue gaze came up to mine. 'Now you tell me Mrs Truttwell's death may not have been an accident.'

'I'm raising the question, anyway. The question of accident versus murder isn't crucial, really. When someone is killed in the course of a felony, it's murder under the law, in any case. But I'm beginning to suspect Mrs Truttwell was intentionally killed. She was your mother's closest friend, she must have known all her secrets.'

'My mother had no secrets. The whole community looked up to her.'

Chalmers rose angrily, spinning the creaky swivel chair. He took up a stance with his back to me, which reminded me oddly of a stubborn boy. Facing him was the primitive picture that concealed the door of the safe: the sailing ship, the naked Indians, the Spanish soldiers marching in the sky.

'If the Truttwells have been maligning my mother,' he said, 'I'll sue them for slander.'

'Nothing like that happened, Mr Chalmers. Nothing's been said against your mother by anyone. I'm trying to get at who the people were that broke into the house in 1945.'

He turned. 'They certainly wouldn't have been known to my mother. Her friends were the best people in California.'

'I don't doubt it. But your mother was probably known to the burglars, and they probably knew what was in the house that made it worth breaking into.'

'I can answer that,' Chalmers said. 'My mother kept her money in the house. It was a habit she inherited from my father, along with the money itself. I repeatedly urged her to put it in the bank, but she wouldn't.'

'Did the burglars get it?'

'No. The money was intact when I got home from overseas. But Mother was dead. And Mrs Truttwell, too.'

'Was there very much money involved?'

'Quite a sum, yes. Several hundred thousand.'

'Where did it come from?'

'I told you: Mother inherited it from my father.' He gave me a pale suspicious look, as if I was planning to insult her again. 'Are you suggesting the money wasn't hers?'

'Certainly not. Couldn't we forget her for a bit?'

'I can't.' He added in a kind of gloomy pride: 'I live with the thought of my mother constantly.'

I waited, and tried again: 'What I'm trying to get at is this. Two burglaries or at least two thefts occurred in this house, in this very room, over twenty-three years apart. I think they were connected.'

'In what way?'

'Through the people involved.'

Chalmers's eyes were puzzled. He sat down opposite me again. 'I'm afraid you've lost me.'

'I'm simply trying to say that some of the same people, with the same motives, may have been involved in both these burglaries. We know who did the recent one. It was your son

Nick, acting under pressure from a couple of other people, Jean Trask and Sidney Harrow.'

Chalmers leaned forward, resting his forehead on his hand. His bald spot gleamed, defenseless as a tonsure.

'Did he kill those people?'

'I doubt it, as you know, but I can't prove he didn't. Yet. Let's stick to the burglaries for now. Nick took a gold box which had your letters in it.' I was being careful not to name his mother. 'The letters were probably incidental. The gold box was the main thing: Mrs Trask wanted it. Do you know why?'

'Presumably because she was a thief.'

'She didn't think so, though. She was quite open about the box. Apparently, it had belonged to Mrs Trask's grandmother, and after her grandmother's death it was given to your mother by her grandfather.'

Chalmers's head sank lower. The fingers supporting it raked up through his hair. 'You're talking about Mr Rawlinson, aren't you?'

'I'm afraid I am.'

'This is infinitely depressing to me,' he said. 'You're twisting a harmless relationship between an elderly man and a mature woman—'

'Let's forget about the relationship.'

'I can't,' he said. 'I can't forget about it.' His head had sunk closer to the table, guarded by his hands and arms.

'I'm not judging anyone, Mr Chalmers, certainly not your mother. The point is simply that there was a connection between her and Samuel Rawlinson. Rawlinson ran a bank, the Pasadena Occidental, and it was ruined by embezzlement around the time of the burglary. His son-in-law, Eldon Swain, was blamed for the embezzlement, perhaps correctly. But it's been suggested to me that Mr Rawlinson may have looted his own bank.'

Chalmers sat up rigidly. 'Who suggested that, for heaven's sake?'

'Another figure in the case—a convicted burglar named Randy Shepherd.'

'And you'd take the word of a man like that, and let him blacken my mother's name?'

'Who said anything about your mother?'

'Aren't you about to offer me the precious theory that my mother took stolen money from that whoremaster? Isn't that what you have on your rotten mind?'

Hot wet rage had flooded his eyes. He stood up blinking and swung an open hand at my face. It was a feeble attempt. I caught his arm by the wrist and handed it back to him.

'I'm afraid we can't talk, Mr Chalmers. I'm sorry.'

I went out to my car and turned downhill toward the freeway. Fog still lay in a grey drift across the foot of the town.

XXVIII

INLAND IN PASADENA the sun was hot. Children were playing in the road in front of Mrs Swain's house. Truttwell's Cadillac, which stood at the curb, acted like a magnet on the children.

Truttwell was sitting in the front seat, engrossed in business papers. He glanced up impatiently at me.

'You took your time about getting here.'

'Something came up. Also, I can't afford a Cadillac.'

'*I* can't afford to waste hours waiting for people. The woman said she'd be here at twelve.'

It was twelve thirty by my wristwatch. 'Is Mrs Swain driving from San Diego?'

'I presume so. I'll give her until one o'clock to get here.'

'Maybe her car broke down, it's pretty old. I hope nothing's happened to her.'

'I'm sure nothing has.'

'I wish I could be sure. The leading suspect in her daughter's death was seen in Hemet last night. Apparently, he was heading this way in a stolen car.'

'Who are you talking about?'

'Randy Shepherd. He's the ex-con who used to work for Mrs Swain and her husband.'

Truttwell didn't seem much interested. He turned to his papers, and rattled them at me. From what I could see of them, they were Xeroxed copies of the articles of incorporation of something called the Smitheram Foundation.

I asked Truttwell what it was. He didn't answer me, or even look up. Irritated by his bad manners, I went and got the envelope of letters out of the trunk of my car.

'Have I mentioned,' I said in a casual voice, 'that I recovered the letters?'

'Chalmers's letters? You know very well you haven't. Where did you get hold of them?'

'They were in Nick's apartment.'

'I'm not surprised,' he said. 'Let's have a look at them.'

I slid into the front seat beside him and handed him the envelope. He opened it and peered at its contents:

'God, but this brings back the past. Estelle Chalmers lived for these letters, you know. The early ones were nothing much, as I recall. But Larry's epistolary style improved with practice.'

'You've read them?'

'Some of them. Estelle gave me no choice. She was so proud of her young hero.' His tone was just faintly ironic. 'Toward the end, when her sight failed completely, she asked us—my wife and me—to read them aloud to her as they came. We tried to persuade her to hire a nurse-companion, but she refused. Estelle had a very strong sense of privacy, and it got stronger as she got older. The main burden of looking after her fell on my wife.' He added in quiet regret: 'I shouldn't have let it happen to my young wife.'

He fell into a silence, which I finally broke: 'What was the matter with Mrs Chalmers?'

'I believe she had glaucoma.'

'She didn't die of glaucoma.'

'No. I think she died of grief—grief for my wife. She gave up eating, she gave up everything. I took the liberty of calling a doctor, very much against her wishes. She lay in bed with her face to the wall and wouldn't let the doctor examine her, or even look at her. And she wouldn't let me try to get Larry home from overseas.'

'Why not?'

'She claimed to be perfectly well, though obviously she wasn't. She wanted to die alone and unseen, I think. Estelle had been a real beauty, and some of it lasted almost to the end. Also, as she grew older, she became a bit of a miser. You'd be surprised how many older women do. The idea of having a doctor come to the house, or hiring a nurse, seemed like a horrible extravagance to Estelle. Her poor-mouthing actually had me convinced. But of course she'd been quite wealthy all along.

'I'll never forget the day following her funeral. Larry was finally en route home after the usual snafu, and in fact he arrived a couple of days later. But the County Administrator didn't want to wait to check the house and its contents. As a member of the courthouse crowd he'd known Estelle all his life. I think he knew or suspected that she kept her money in the house, as Judge Chalmers had before her. And of course there had been the attempted burglary. If I had been in full possession of my faculties, I'd have checked the safe the morning after the break-in. But I had troubles of my own.'

'You mean your wife's death?'

'The loss of my wife was the main disaster, of course. It left me with full responsibility for an infant girl.' He looked at me with painful candor. 'A responsibility I haven't handled too well.'

'The point is that it's over. Betty's grown up. She has to make her own choices.'

'But I can't let her marry Nick Chalmers.'

'She will if you keep saying that.'

Truttwell went into another of his silences. He seemed to be catching up at last with great snatches of lost time. When his eyes changed back to present time, I said:

'Do you have any idea who killed your wife?'

He shook his white head. 'The police failed to come up with a single suspect.'

'What was the date of her death?'

'July 3, 1945,'

'Exactly how did it happen?'

'I'm afraid I don't really know. Estelle Chalmers was the only surviving witness, and she was blind and saw nothing. Apparently my wife noticed something wrong at the Chalmers house and went over there to investigate. The thieves chased her out into the road and ran her down with their car. Actually it wasn't their car—it had been stolen. The police recovered it in the tules below San Diego. There were—physical evidences on the bumper that proved it had been used to murder my wife. The murderers probably escaped over the border.'

Truttwell's forehead was shining with sweat. He wiped it with a silk handkerchief.

'I'm afraid I can't tell you anything more about the events of that night. I was in Los Angeles on business. I got home in the small hours and found my wife in the morgue and my little girl being cared for by a policewoman.'

His voice broke, and for once I saw through Truttwell's surface into his hidden self. He lived with a grief so central and consuming that it drained the energy from his external life and made him seen a smaller man than he was, or had once been.

'I'm sorry, Mr Truttwell. I had to ask you these questions.'

'I don't quite see their relevance.'

'Neither do I, yet. When I interrupted you, you were telling me about the County Administrator checking the house.'

'So I was. As the representative of the Chalmers family I opened the house for him. I also turned over the combination of the safe, which Estelle had given me some time before. It turned out to be stuffed with money, of course.'

'How much?'

'I don't recall the exact figure. Certainly it was up in the hundreds of thousands. It took the Administrator most of the day to count it, even though some of the notes were in large denominations, up to ten thousand.'

'Where did it come from, do you know?'

'Her husband probably left her some of it. But Estelle was widowed when she was still quite young, and it's not exactly a secret that there were other men in her life. One or two of them were very successful men. I suppose they gave her money, or told her how to make it.'

'And how to avoid taxes on it?'

Truttwell shifted uneasily in the car seat. 'It hardly seems necessary to raise that question. All this is far away and long ago.'

'It seems here and now to me.'

'If you must know,' he said impatiently, 'the tax issue is dead. I persuaded the government to settle for inheritance taxes on the full amount. They had no way of proving the source of the money.'

'The source is what interests me. I understand the Pasadena banker Rawlinson was one of the men in Mrs Chalmers's life.'

'He was, for many years. But that was a long time before her death.'

'Not so very,' I said. 'In one of these letters, written in the fall of 1943, Larry asked to be remembered to him. Which means that his mother was still seeing Rawlinson.'

'Really? How did Larry feel about Rawlinson?'

'The letter was noncommittal.'

I could have given Truttwell a fuller answer, but I had decided to suppress my interview with Chalmers, at least for the present. I knew that Truttwell wouldn't approve of it.

'What are you getting at, Archer? You're not suggesting that Rawlinson was the source of Mrs Chalmers's money?'

As if he had pushed a significant button which closed a circuit, the phone began to ring in Mrs Swain's front room. It rang ten times, and stopped.

'It was your idea,' I said.

'But I was speaking generally about the men in Estelle's life. I didn't single out Samuel Rawlinson. As you perfectly well know, he was ruined by the embezzlement.'

'His bank was.'

Truttwell's face twisted in surprise. 'You can't mean he embezzled the money himself.'

'The idea has come up.'

'Seriously?'

'I hardly know. I got it from Randy Shepherd. It originated with Eldon Swain. Which doesn't help to make it true.'

'I should think not. We *know* that Swain ran off with the money.'

'We know that he ran off. But the truth isn't always so obvious; in fact, it's usually just as complex as the people who make it. Consider the possibility that Swain took some of the bank's money and Rawlinson caught him at it and took a great deal more. He used Mrs Chalmers's safe to cache the money, but she died before he could recover it.'

Truttwell gave me a look of appalled interest. 'You have a tortuous imagination, Archer.' But he added: 'What was the date of the embezzlement?'

I consulted my black notebook. 'July 1, 1945.'

'That was just a couple of weeks before Estelle Chalmers died. It rules out the possibility you suggest.'

'Does it? Rawlinson didn't know she was going to die. They may have been planning to use the money, go someplace and live together.'

'An old man and a blind woman? It's ridiculous!'

'That still doesn't rule it out. People are always doing ridiculous things. Anyway, Rawlinson wasn't so very old in 1945. He was about the age that you are now.'

Truttwell flushed. He was self-conscious about his age. 'You'd better not mention this wild idea of yours to anyone else. He'd slap a libel suit on you.' He turned and gave me another curious look. 'You don't think much of bankers, do you?'

'They're no different from anyone else. But you can't help noticing that a high proportion of embezzlers are bankers.'

'That's a simple matter of opportunity.'

'Exactly.'

The phone in Mrs Swain's house began to ring again. I counted fourteen rings before it stopped. At the moment my sensibility was pretty highly keyed, and I felt as if the house had been trying to say something to me.

It was one o'clock. Truttwell climbed out of the car and began to pace the broken sidewalk. A clownish youngster walked behind him, aping his movements, until Truttwell shooed him away. I got the envelope of letters out of the front seat and locked them in a metal evidence case in the trunk of my car.

When I looked up, Mrs Swain's old black Volkswagen had entered the little street. It turned onto the strips of concrete that formed her driveway. Some of the children lifted their hands to her and said: 'Hi.'

Mrs Swain got out and walked towards us across the brown January grass. She moved awkwardly in her high heels and tight black dress. I introduced her to Truttwell and they shook hands stiffly.

'I'm awfully sorry to keep you waiting,' she said. 'A policeman came to my son-in-law's house just as I was about to leave. He asked me questions for over an hour.'

'What about?' I asked her.

'Several matters. He wanted a full history of Randy Shepherd from the time he was our gardener in San Marino. He seemed to think that Randy might come after me next. But I'm not afraid of Randy, and I don't believe he killed Jean.'

'Who do you suspect?' I said.

'My husband is capable of it, if he's alive.'

'It's pretty definite that he's dead, Mrs Swain.'

'What happened to the money, if he's dead?' She leaned toward me, both hands out, like a starving beggar.

'Nobody knows.'

She shook my arm. 'We've got to find the money. I'll give you half if you find it for me.'

There was a high shrieking in my head. I thought I was having a bad reaction to poor old Mrs Swain. Then I realized that the shrieking wasn't in me.

It came from a siren whirling its whip of sound over the city. The sound grew louder but it was still far away and irrelevant.

On the boulevard there was another, nearer, sound of tires shuddering and squealing. An open black Mercury convertible turned into the little street. It skidded wide on the turn and scattered the children like confetti, nearly running some of them down.

The man at the wheel had a beardless face and bright red synthetic-looking hair. In spite of it I recognized Randy Shepherd. And he recognized me. He kept on going past us to the end of the block, and turned north out of sight. At the other end of the block a police car appeared for an instant. Without turning or pausing, it fled on up the boulevard.

I followed Shepherd, but it was a hopeless chase. He was on home territory, and his stolen convertible had more speed than my almost-paid-for car. Once I caught a glimpse of it crossing a bridge far ahead, with Shepherd's bright red hair like artificial fire in the front seat.

XXIX

I FOUND MYSELF in a blind street ending in a barricade. Beyond it a deep ravine opened. I turned off my engine and sat getting my bearings.

At just about my level, a red-tailed hawk was circling over the treetops in the ravine. There were scrub oak and sycamores along the hidden watercourse. I realized after a while that this was the same ravine that cut across Locust Street, where Rawlinson lived. But I was on the other side of it, facing west.

I drove the long way around to Locust Street. The first thing I saw when I entered it was an open black Mercury convertible standing at the curb half a block from Rawlinson's house. The keys were in the ignition. I put them in my pocket.

I left my own car in front of Rawlinson's house and mounted the veranda uneasily, tripping on the broken step. Mrs Shepherd opened the door with her finger to her lips. Her eyes were deeply troubled.

'Be quiet,' she whispered. 'Mr Rawlinson is taking his nap.'

'Can I talk to you for a minute?'

'Not right now. I'm busy.'

'I've come all the way from Pacific Point.'

This information seemed to fascinate her. Without removing her gaze from my face, she closed the front door quietly behind her and stepped out onto the veranda.

'What's going on in Pacific Point?'

It sounded like a routine question, but it probably stood for questions she was afraid to ask in detail. She gave the impression that in her age she had stumbled back into all the desperate uncertainties of youth.

'More of the same,' I said. 'Trouble for everybody. I think it all started with this.'

I showed her the copy of Nick's graduation picture that I'd taken from Sidney Harrow. She shook her head over it:

'I don't know who it would be.'

'Are you sure?'

'I'm sure.' She added solemnly: 'I never saw that young man in my life.'

I almost believed her. But she had neglected to ask me who he was.

'His name is Nick Chalmers. This was supposed to be his graduation picture. But Nick won't be graduating.'

She didn't say, 'Why not?' But her eyes said it.

'Nick's in the hospital recovering from a suicide attempt. The trouble started, as I said, when a man named Sidney Harrow came to town and began hounding Nick. He brought this picture with him.'

'Where did he get it?'

'From Randy Shepherd,' I said.

Her face had taken on an underlying pallor which made it almost gray. 'Why are you telling me these things?'

'You're obviously interested.' I went on in the same quiet tone: 'Is Randy in the house now?'

Her uncontrolled upward glance probably meant that Shepherd was upstairs. She didn't speak.

'I'm pretty sure he's in there, Mrs Shepherd. If I were you I wouldn't try to hide him. The police are after him, and they'll be arriving any time now.'

'What do they want him for this time?'

'Murder. The murder of Jean Trask.'

She moaned. 'He didn't tell me.'

'Is he armed?'

'He has a knife.'

'No gun?'

'I didn't see one.' She reached out and touched my chest. 'Are you certain Randy gave that picture to the other man—the man who went to the Point?'

'I'm sure now, Mrs Shepherd.'

'Then he can burn in hell.' She started down the steps.

'Where are you going?'

'The neighbors' to phone the police.'

'I wouldn't do that, Mrs Shepherd.'

'Maybe you wouldn't. But I've suffered enough in my life on his account. I'm not going to jail for him.'

'Let me go in and talk to him.'

'No. It's *my* neck. And I'm calling the police.' She turned away again.

'Don't be in such a hurry. We have to get Mr Rawlinson out of there first. Where *is* Randy?'

'In the attic. Mr Rawlinson's in the front parlor.'

She went in and helped the old man to walk out. He was limping and yawning, and blinking against the sun. I put him in the front seat of my car and drove him to the barricade at the end of the street. The police used a lot of firepower nowadays.

The old man turned to me impatiently. 'I'm afraid I don't understand what we're doing here.'

'It would take a long time to explain. Briefly, we're wrapping up the case that started in July 1945.'

'When Eldon Swain robbed me blind?'

'If it was Eldon.'

Rawlinson turned his head to look at me, the flesh of his neck twisting in stringy folds. 'Is there some doubt that Eldon was responsible?'

'The question has been raised.'

'Nonsense. He was the cashier. Who else could have embezzled all that money?'

'You could have, Mr Rawlinson.'

His eyes grew small and bright in their nests of wrinkles. 'You must be joking.'

'No. I admit the question is partly hypothetical.'

'And pretty damn insulting,' he said without much real heat. 'Do I look like the kind of man who would ruin his own bank?'

'Not unless you had a powerful reason.'

'What possible reason could I have?'

'A woman.'

'What woman?'

'Estelle Chalmers. She died rich.'

He manufactured a quick small rage. 'You're throwing dirt on the memory of a fine woman.'

'I don't think so.'

'I do. If you persist in following this line, I refuse to talk with you.' He made a move to get out of my car.

'You better stay here, Mr Rawlinson. Your house isn't safe. Randy Shepherd's in the attic, and the police will be here soon.'

'Is this Mrs Shepherd's doing? Did she let him in?'

'He probably didn't give her any choice.' I brought out my picture of Nick again, and showed it to Rawlinson. 'Do you know who this is?'

He took the picture in his swollen arthritic fingers. 'I'm afraid I don't know his name. I could guess who the boy is, but you don't want that.'

'Go ahead and guess.'

'It's someone near and dear to Mrs Shepherd. I saw this in her room early last week. Then it disappeared, and she blamed me for it.'

'She should have blamed Randy Shepherd. He was the one who took it.' I lifted the picture out of his hands and replaced it in the inside pocket of my jacket.

'That's what she gets for letting him into my house!' His eyes were moist, leaking away his old-man's anger. 'The police are coming, you say. What's Randy been up to now?'

'He's wanted for murder, Mr Rawlinson. The murder of your granddaughter Jean.'

He made no response, except that he sank a little lower in the seat. I felt sorry for the man. He had had everything and bit by bit lost nearly all of it. Now he had outlived his own granddaughter.

I looked out over the ravine, hoping to lose my borrowed pain in its deep green spaces. The red-tailed hawk I had seen from the other side was visible from this side, too. He turned, and his ruddy wedge of tail flashed in the sun.

'You knew about Jean, Mr Rawlinson?'

'Yes. My daughter Louise phoned me yesterday. But she didn't say that Shepherd was responsible.'

'I don't think he is.'

'Then what is this all about?'

'The police think he is.'

Almost as if he could hear us talking about him, Randy Shepherd appeared at the side of Rawlinson's house and looked in our direction. He was wearing a wide-brimmed Panama hat with a striped band, and a moth-eaten tan polo coat.

'Hold on there, that's my hat!' Rawlinson cried. 'By God, that's my coat, too!'

He started to get out of the car. I told him to stay where he was, in a tone which he obeyed.

Shepherd sauntered up the street like a gentleman out for a stroll. Then he scampered across to the black convertible, holding the loose hat on his head with one hand. He sat in the car for a frantic minute, looking for the keys, then got out and headed for the parkway.

By this time the sirens were rising in the distance, curdling the daylight at the edges. Shepherd stopped dead and stood perfectly still in a listening attitude. He turned and started back in our direction, pausing for an instant at the Rawlinson house as if he was thinking of going back in.

Mrs Shepherd came out on the front porch. By this time two patrol cars were in the street and rolling toward Shepherd. He looked at them over his shoulder, and all around at the long Victorian faces of the houses. Then he ran in my direction. His Panama hat flew off. His coat billowed out behind.

I got out of the car to head him off. It was an unconsidered reflex. The patrol cars stopped abruptly, ejecting four policemen who began to fire their revolvers at Shepherd.

He went down flat on his face and slid a little. Then splashes on the back of his neck and down the back of his light coat were darker and realer than his slipping red wig.

A bullet ripped into my shoulder. I fell sideways against the open door of my car. Then I lay down and pretended to be as dead as Shepherd was.

XXX

I ENDED UP high on pentothal in a Pasadena hospital room. A surgeon had had to dig for the slug, and my arm and shoulder would be immobilized for some time.

Fortunately, it was the left shoulder. This was pointed out more than once by the police and DA's men who came to visit me late that afternoon. The police apologized for the incident, while managing to suggest at the same time that I had collided with the bullet, not it with me. They offered to do what they could for me, and agreed at my suggestion to have my car brought to the hospital parking lot.

Still, their visit made me angry and concerned. I felt as if my case had run away and left me lying. I had a bedside phone, and I used it to make a call to Truttwell's house. The housekeeper said he wasn't at home, and neither was Betty. I put in a call to Truttwell's office and left my name and number with his answering service.

Later, as night was coming on, I got out of bed and opened the door of the closet. I was feeling a little lightheaded but I was worried about my black notebook. My jacket was hanging in the closet with my other clothes and in spite of the blood and the bullet hole the notebook was in the pocket where I'd put it. So was Nick's picture.

As I was on my way back to bed the floor tilted up and smacked me on the right side of the face. I blacked out for a while. Then I sat up with my back against a leg of the bed.

The night nurse looked in. She was pretty and dedicated and wore a Los Angeles General cap. Her name was Miss Cowan.

'What in the world are you doing?'

'Sitting on the floor.'

'You can't do *that*.' She helped me to get to my feet and into bed. 'I hope you weren't trying to get out of here.'

'No, but it's a good idea. When do you think I'll be sprung?'

'It's up to the doctor. He may be able to tell you in the morning. Now do you feel up to a visitor?'

'It depends on who it is.'

'She's an elderly woman. Her name is Shepherd. Is that the same Shepherd—?' Delicately, she left the question unfinished.

'Same Shepherd.' My pentothal high had changed to a pentothal low, but I told the nurse to send the woman in.

'You're not afraid she'll try to pull something on you?'

'No. She's not the type.'

Miss Cowan went away. Shortly afterwards, Mrs Shepherd came in. Gray pallor seemed to have become her permanent color. Her dark eyes were very large, as if they had been distended by the events they'd witnessed.

'I'm sorry you were injured, Mr Archer.'

'I'll survive. It's too bad about Randy.'

'Shepherd was no loss to anybody,' she said. 'I just finished telling that to the police and now I'm telling you. He was a bad husband and a bad father, and he came to a bad end.'

'That's a lot of badness.'

'I know whereof I speak.' Her voice was solemn. 'Whether he killed Miss Jean or not, I know what Shepherd did to his own daughter. He ruined her life and drove her to her death.'

'Is Rita dead?'

My use of the name stopped her. 'How do you know my daughter's name?'

'Somebody mentioned it. Mrs Swain, I think.'

'Mrs Swain was no friend of Rita's. She blamed my daughter for everything that happened. It wasn't fair. Rita was beneath the age of consent when Mr Swain got interested in her. And her own father pandered to Mr Swain and took money from him for her.'

The words came pouring out of her under pressure, as if Shepherd's death had opened a deep volcanic fissure in her life.

'Did Rita go to Mexico with Swain?'

'Yes.'

'And died there?'

'Yes. She died there.'

'How do you know that, Mrs Shepherd?'

'Mr Swain told me himself. Shepherd brought him to see me when he came back from Mexico. He said she died and was buried in Guadalajara.'

'Did she leave any children?'

Her dark eyes wavered and then held firm, meeting mine. 'No. I have no grandchildren of any kind.'

'Who's the boy in the picture?'

'The picture?' she said with a show of puzzlement.

'If you want to refresh your memory, it's in my jacket in the closet.'

She glanced at the closet door. I said:

'I mean the one Randy Shepherd stole from your room.'

Her puzzlement became real. 'How do you know that? How come you're digging so deep in my family affairs?'

'You know why, Mrs Shepherd. I'm trying to wrap up a case that started nearly a quarter of a century ago. On July 1, 1945.'

She blinked. Apart from this tiny movement of her eyelids, her face had recovered its immobility. 'That was the date that Mr Swain robbed Mr Rawlinson's bank.'

'Is that what really happened?'

'What other story did you hear?'

'I've found a few bits and pieces of evidence pointing another way. And I'm beginning to wonder if Eldon Swain ever got the money.'

'Who else could have taken it?'

'Your daughter Rita, for one.'

She reacted angrily, but not as angrily as she should have. 'Rita was sixteen years old in 1945. Children don't plan bank robberies. You *know* it had to be somebody in the bank.'

'Like Mr Rawlinson?'

'That's just plain silly, and you know it.'

'I thought I'd try it on you.'

'You'll have to try harder than that. I don't know why you're straining so hard to make Mr Swain into a whited sepulchre. I know he took that money, and I know Mr Rawlinson didn't. Why, the poor man lost everything. He's lived from hand to mouth ever since.'

'On what?'

She answered quietly: 'He has a little pension, and I have my savings. For a long time I worked as a nurse's aide. That helped to keep him going.'

What she said sounded like the truth. Anyway, I couldn't help believing her.

Mrs Shepherd was looking at me more kindly, as if she sensed a change in our relations. Very gently, she touched my bandaged shoulder with her fingers. 'Poor man, you need a rest. You oughtn't to be troubling your head with all these questions. Aren't you tired?'

I admitted that I was.

'Then why don't you get some sleep?' Her voice was soporific. She laid her palm on my forehead. 'I'll stay in the room and watch for a while if you don't mind. I like the smell of hospitals. I used to work in this very hospital.'

She sat down in the armchair between the closet and the window. The imitation-leather cushions creaked under her weight.

I closed my eyes and slowed down my breathing. But I was very far from going to sleep. I lay and listened to Mrs Shepherd. She was completely still. Sounds drifted in through the window: the sounds of cars, a mockingbird tuning up for a night song. He kept postponing his song until the sense of something about to happen had screwed my nerves up tight.

The imitation-leather cushions of the chair emitted a tiny noise. There was the faintest possible sibilance from Mrs Shepherd's feet sliding across the composition floor, the rattle of a doorknob, the paired whispers of a door opening and closing.

I opened my eyes. Mrs Shepherd wasn't visible. Apparently she had shut herself up in the closet. Then its door began to open slowly again. She came out sideways, and held the picture of Nick up to the light. Her face was full of love and longing.

She glanced at me, and saw that my eyes were open. But she thrust the picture under her coat and left the room quietly, without a word.

I didn't say anything to her, or do anything. After all, it was her picture.

I turned out the light and lay listening to the mockingbird. He was singing all-out now, and still singing when I went to sleep. I dreamed that I was Nick and that Mrs Shepherd was my grandmother who used to live with birds in the garden in Contra Costa County.

XXXI

IN THE MORNING, as I was eating a poached egg on a damp piece of toast, the resident surgeon came in.

'How are you feeling?'

'Fine,' I lied. 'But I'll never build up my strength on this kind of rations. When can I get out of here?'

'Don't be in such a hurry. I'm going to have to ask you to take it easy for at least a week.'

'I can't stay here for a week.'

'I didn't say you had to. You're going to have to look after yourself, though. Regular hours, mild exercise followed by rest, no rough stuff.'

'Sure,' I said.

I rested very carefully all morning. Truttwell failed to return my call, and the waiting began to get in the way of the resting and finally displaced it.

Shortly before noon I called his office again. The switchboard girl informed me that he wasn't there.

'*Really* not there?'

'Really. I don't know where he is.'

I did some more resting and waiting. A Pasadena motorcycle officer brought me the keys to my car and told me where to find it in the hospital parking lot. I took this as an omen.

After an early lunch I got out of bed and to a certain extent put on my clothes. By the time I had on underwear, trousers, and shoes I was wet and shaking. I sort of draped my bloody shirt over my chest and shoulders and covered it with my jacket.

In the corridor, the nurses and nurses' aides were still busy with lunch. I crossed the corridor to a gray metal door that opened on the fire stairs and walked down three stories to the ground floor.

A side exit let me out into the parking lot. I found my car and got in and sat for a while. Mild exercise followed by rest.

The freeway was crowded and slow. Even with all the concentration I was giving it, my driving wasn't too good. My attention kept slipping away from the traffic. I was moving in. Once I had to burn rubber to avoid running into the rear end of another car.

I'd originally intended to drive to Pacific Point. I barely made it to West Los Angeles. In the last block of the trip, on my home street, I caught a glimpse in the rear-view mirror of a bearded man carrying a bedroll. But when I turned to look at him directly he wasn't there.

I left my car at the curb and climbed the outside stairs to my apartment. The phone started to ring, like an aural booby-trap, just as I opened the door. I picked it up and carried it to my armchair.

'Mr Archer? This is Helen at the answering service. You've had a couple of urgent calls, from a Mr Truttwell and a Miss Truttwell. I've been ringing your office.'

I looked at the electric clock. It was just two o'clock. Helen gave me the number of Truttwell's office, and the less familiar number his daughter had left.

'Anything else?'

'Yes, but there must be some mistake about this call, Mr Archer. A hospital in Pasadena claims that you owe them a hundred and seventy dollars. That includes the cost of the operating room, they said.'

'It's no mistake. If they call again, tell them I'm putting a check in the mail.'

'Yessir.'

I got out my checkbook and looked at the balance and decided to call Truttwell first. Before I did, I went out to the kitchen and put a frozen steak in the gas broiler. I tasted the milk in the refrigerator, found that it was still sweet, and drank half of the remaining quart. I wanted a shot of whisky as a chaser, but it was exactly what I didn't need.

My call to Truttwell's office was taken by a junior member of the firm named Eddie Sutherland. Truttwell wasn't in at the moment, he said, but he had set up an appointment for me at four thirty. It was very important that I should be there, though Sutherland didn't seem to know why.

I remembered as I was dialing the number Betty had left that it belonged to the phone in Nick's apartment.

Betty answered. 'Hello?'

'This is Archer speaking.'

She drew in her breath. 'I've been trying to get you all day.'

'Is Nick with you?'

'No. I only wish he were. I'm very concerned about him. I went to San Diego yesterday afternoon to try and see him. They wouldn't let me into his room.'

'Who wouldn't?'

'The guard on the door, backed up by Dr Smitheram. They seemed to think I was spying for my father. I did manage to get a glimpse of Nick, and let him see me. He asked me to get him out. He said they were holding him against his will.'

' "They?" '

'I think he meant Dr Smitheram. Anyway, it was Dr Smitheram who ordered him to be moved last night.'

'Moved where?'

'I don't know for certain, Mr Archer. I think they're holding him prisoner in the Smitheram Clinic. That's where the ambulance took him.'

'And you seriously believe that he's a prisoner?'

'I don't know what I believe. But I'm afraid. Will you help me?'

I said that she would have to help me first, since I wasn't up to driving. She agreed to pick me up in an hour.

I went out to the kitchen and turned my steak. It was hot and sizzling on one side, frozen solid on the other, like schizophrenic people I had known. I wondered just how crazy Nick Chalmers was.

The immediate problem was clothes. My not very extensive wardrobe included a stretchable nylon shirt that I managed to get into without putting the left arm in the armhole. I completed my costume with a soft cardigan jacket.

By this time my schizoid steak was brown on both sides and red in the center. It bled on the plate when I stabbed it. I let it cool and ate it with my fingers.

I finished the quart of milk. Then I went back to the armchair in the front room and rested. For just about the first time in my life I knew how it must feel to get old. My body was demanding special privileges and offering not much in return.

The yelp of Betty's horn brought me out of a half-sleep. She gave me a hard look as I climbed rather awkwardly into her car.

'Are you sick, Mr Archer?'

'Not exactly. I took a slug in the shoulder.'

'Why didn't you tell me?'

'You mightn't have come. I want to be in at the end of this thing.'

'Even if it kills you?'

'It won't.'

If I was looking worse, she was looking better. She had decided after all not to be a gnome who lived in the gray underground.

'Who on earth shot you?'

'A Pasadena cop. He was aiming at another man. I got in the way. Didn't your father tell you any of this?'

'I haven't seen my father since yesterday.' She spoke these words rather formally, as if they constituted an announcement.

'Are you leaving home?'

'Yes, I am. Father said I had to choose between him and Nick.'

'I'm sure he didn't mean it.'

'Yes, he did.'

She made her engine roar. At the last moment I remembered that Chalmers's war letters were still in the trunk of my car. I went back to get them, and looked over the top ones again as Betty drove me to the freeway.

The heading of the second letter stopped me:

Lt. (j.g.) L Chalmers
USS Sorrel Bay (CVE 185)
March 15, 1945

I turned to Betty. 'You mentioned Nick's birthday the other day. Didn't you say it was in December?'

'December 14,' she said.

'And what year was he born?'

'Nineteen forty-five. He was twenty-three last month. Is it important?'

'It could be. Did Nick rearrange these letters, with certain ones up front and out of chronological order?'

'He may have. I think he had been reading them. Why?'

'Mr Chalmers wrote a letter at sea in the forward area, dated March 15, 1945.'

'I'm not too good at arithmetic, especially when I'm driving. Is it nine months from March 15 to December 14?'

'Exactly.'

'Isn't that strange? Nick always suspected that his fa—that Mr Chalmers wasn't his real father. He used to think he was adopted.'

'Maybe he was.'

I put the three top letters in my wallet. The girl turned up on the on-ramp to the freeway. She drove with angry speed under a brown firmament of smog.

XXXII

SOUTHWARD ALONG THE coast it was a bright, windy day. From the mesa above Pacific Point I could see occasional whitecaps on the water, and a few sails leaning far over.

Betty took me directly to the Smitheram Clinic. The well-groomed, rather formal young woman who presided over the reception desk said that Dr Smitheram was with a patient and couldn't possibly see us. He would be with patients all the rest of the day, including the evening.

'What about a week from Tuesday at midnight?'

The young woman looked me over disapprovingly. 'Are you sure you don't want the emergency ward at the hospital?'

'I'm sure. Is Nicholas Chalmers a patient here?'

'I'm not authorized to answer questions like that.'

'Can I see Mrs Smitheram?'

The young woman didn't answer for a while. She pretended to be busy with her papers. Finally she said:

'I'll see. What did you say your name was, again?'

I told her. She opened an inner door. Before she closed it behind her, I heard a flash of noise that made the back of my neck bristle. It was a high yell; someone crying out wordlessly in pain and desolation.

Betty and I looked at each other. 'That may be Nick,' she said. 'What are they doing to him?'

'Nothing. You shouldn't be here.'

'Where should I be?'

'At home reading a book.'

'Dostoevsky?' she said sharply.

'Something lighter than that.'

'Like *Little Women*? I'm afraid you don't understand me, Mr Archer. You're fatherizing again.'

'You're daughterizing.'

Moira and the receptionist opened the inner door and came out unaccompanied by any sound. Moira gave me a look of surprise and Betty a more complex look which seemed to combine both envy and contempt. Betty was younger, Moira's look seemed to say, but she herself had survived longer.

She moved toward me. 'What on earth's been happening, Mr Archer?'

'I was accidentally shot, if you mean this.' I touched my left arm. 'Is Nick Chalmers here?'

'Yes. He is.'

'Was that him yelling?'

'Yelling? I don't believe so.' She was flustered. 'We have several patients in the closed wing. Nick isn't one of the more disturbed ones.'

'Then you won't object if we see him. Miss Truttwell is his fiancée—'

'I know that.'

'—and she's quite concerned about him.'

'There's no need to feel that way.' But she herself seemed deeply concerned. 'I'm sorry I can't let you see him. Dr Smitheram makes these decisions. He evidently thinks that Nick needs seclusion.'

Her mouth twisted sideways. The strain of keeping up her public face and voice was telling on Moira.

'Could we discuss this in private, Mrs Smitheram?'

'Yes. Come into my office, please.'

The invitation excluded Betty. I followed Moira into an office which was partly sitting room and partly file room. The room was windowless but hung with abstract paintings, like inward windows replacing the outward ones. Moira closed the door and locked it and stood against it.

'Am I your prisoner?' I said.

She answered without trying to be light: 'I'm the prisoner. I wish I could get out of this.' A slight upward movement of her hands and shoulders suggested the almost insupportable weight of the building. 'But I can't.'

'Won't your husband let you?'

'It's a little more complicated than that. I'm the prisoner of all my past mistakes—I'm feeling sententious today—and Ralph is one of them. You're a more recent one.'

'What did I do wrong?'

'Nothing. I thought you liked me, is all.' She had dropped her public face and voice entirely. 'I acted on that assumption the other night.'

'So did I. It was a true assumption.'

'Then why are you giving me a bad time?'

'I didn't mean to. But we seem to be ending up on different sides.'

She shook her head. 'I don't believe it. All I want is a decent life, a possible life, for the people concerned.' She added: 'Including me.'

'What does your husband want?'

'The same thing, according to his lights. We don't agree about everything, of course. And I made the mistake of going along with all his large ideas.' Once again the movement of her arms referred to the entire building. 'As if we could save our marriage by giving birth to a clinic.' She added wryly: 'We should have rented one.'

She was a complex woman, spinning off ambiguities, talking too much. I moved solidly against her, held her not very masterfully with one arm, and silenced her mouth.

The wound in my shoulder was beating like an auxiliary heart.

As if she could sense the pain directly, Moira said:

'I'm sorry you're hurt.'

'I'm sorry *you're* hurt, Moira.'

'Don't waste your sympathy on me.' Her tone reminded me that she was or had been a kind of nurse. 'I'll survive. But it isn't going to be much fun, I'm afraid.'

'You're losing me again. What are we talking about?'

'Disaster. I can feel it in my bones. I'm partly Irish, you know.'

'Disaster for Nick Chalmers?'

'For all of us. He's part of it, of course.'

'Why don't you let me take him out of here?'

'I can't.'

'Is his life in danger?'

'Not as long as he stays here.'

'Will you let me see him?'

'I can't. My husband won't allow it.'

'Are you afraid of him?'

'No. But he's a doctor and I'm just a technician. I simply can't second-guess him.'

'How long is he proposing to keep Nick here?'

'Until the danger is over.'

'Who's the source of the danger?'

'I can't tell you that. Please don't ask any more questions, Lew. The questions spoil everything.'

We stood and held each other for a while, leaning against the locked door. The warmth of her body and her mouth revived me, even though our minds were at odds and part of my mind was keeping track of the time.

She said in a low voice, 'I wish we could walk out of here this minute, you and I, and never come back.'

'You have a marriage.'

'It isn't going to last.'

'On account of me?'

'Of course not. Will you promise me one thing, though?'

'After I know what it is.'

'Don't tell anyone about Sonny. You know, my little La Jolla postal clerk. I made a mistake in talking about him to you.'

'Has Sonny cropped up again?'

She nodded. Her eyes were somber. 'You won't tell anyone, will you?'

'I have no reason to.'

I was hedging a little, and she sensed this. 'Lew? I know you're a powerful man, and a very one-way man. Promise me you won't do anything to us. Give Ralph and me a chance to work this thing out.'

I stepped away from her. 'I can't make a blind commitment. And you're not being clear, as you bloody well know.'

She made an anguished monkey-face which wiped out her good looks. 'I can't be clear. This is a problem that won't be solved by talking. There are too many people involved, and too many years of life.'

'Who are the people involved?'

'Ralph and I and the Chalmerses and the Truttwells—'

'And Sonny?'

'Yes. He's in it.' The focus of her eyes shifted to something beyond my knowledge. 'That's why you mustn't tell anyone what I told you.'

'Why did you tell me?'

'I thought you might be able to advise me, that we might become better friends than we have.'

'Give it more time.'

'That's what I'm asking you for.'

XXXIII

BETTY WAS WAITING impatiently in the parking lot. Her gaze narrowed on the lower part of my face.

'There's lipstick on you. Wait.' She got a piece of tissue out of her bag and dabbed at me quite hard. 'There. That looks better.'

In her car, she spoke to me in a neutral voice: 'Are you having an affair with Mrs Smitheram?'

'We're friends.'

She said in the same neutral tone: 'No wonder I can't trust anybody, or do anything for Nick.' She turned to me: 'If you're such a good friend of Mrs Smitheram's, why won't she let me see Nick?'

'Her husband is the doctor. She's only a technician, she says.'

'Why won't her husband let him go?'

'They're holding Nick for his protection. Against what or who isn't clear, but I agree he needs protection. It shouldn't be handled entirely by his doctor, though. He needs legal counsel.'

'If you're trying to bring my father into this—' Her knuckles struck the wheel of her car in a sharp blow that must have hurt her.

'He is in it, Betty. There's not much use arguing about it. And you're not really helping Nick by turning against your father.'

'He's the one who turned against *us*—against Nick and me.'

'Maybe so. But we need his help.'

'*I* don't,' she said loudly and indecisively.

'Anyway, I need yours. Will you drive me to his office?'

'All right. But I'm not going in.'

She took me to the parking lot behind her father's building. A polished black Rolls was standing in one of the Reserved slots.

'That's the Chalmerses' car,' Betty said. 'I thought they'd had a falling-out with Father.'

'Maybe they're falling back in. What time is it?'

She looked at her wristwatch. 'Four thirty-five. I'll wait out here for you.'

I was interested in the Rolls. I went and looked it over, admiring its deep leather upholstery and walnut trim. The whole car was immaculate, except for a yellow spillage on a plaid traveling rug in the back seat. It looked like a dried froth of vomit.

I scraped some of it up with the edge of a plastic credit card. When I looked up a thin man in a dark suit and a chauffeur's cap was coming toward me across the parking lot. It was the Chalmerses' houseman, Emilio.

'Get away from that car,' he said.

'All right.'

I slammed the rear door of the Rolls and stepped away from it. Emilio's black eyes focused on the card in my hand. He made a grab for it. I pulled it out of his reach.

'Give me that.'

'The hell I will. Who's been sick in the car, Emilio?'

The question worried him. I asked it again. His anger evaporated suddenly. He turned away from me and climbed in behind the wheel of the Rolls, raising the automatic window on my side.

'What was all that about?' Betty said as we walked away.

'I'm not sure. What kind of a character is he?'

'Emilio? He's pretty dour.'

'Is he honest?'

'He must be. He's been with the Chalmerses for over twenty years.'

'What sort of life does he lead?'

'A very quiet bachelor life, I believe. But I'm no great authority on Emilio. What's that yellow stuff on the card?'

'That's a good question. Do you have an envelope?'

'No. But I'll get one.'

She entered the building through the back door and came out

right away with one of her father's business envelopes. I put my findings in it, with her help, sealed and initialed it.

'What laboratory does your father use?'

'Barnard's. It's between here and the courthouse.'

I handed her the envelope. 'I want this tested for chloral hydrate and Nembutal. They're fairly simple tests, I believe, and they can be done right now if you tell them your father says it's urgent. And tell them to take good care of the sample, will you?'

'Yes sir.'

'Will you bring me the results? I'll probably still be in your father's office. You can wear a disguise or something.'

She refused to smile. But she trotted dutifully away on the errand. I could feel new adrenalin in my own veins, making me feel stronger and more aggressive. If my hunch was good, the froth of vomit in the envelope could break the case.

I went into Truttwell's building and started along the corridor to the waiting room at the front. I was stopped at an open door by Truttwell's voice:

'Archer? I'd just about given up on you.'

He drew me into his law library, which was completely lined with shelves of reference books. A young man in an Ivy League suit was working over a film projector. A screen had already been set up at the far end of the room.

Truttwell surveyed me with not very sympathetic eyes. 'Where have you been?'

I told him, and dropped the subject. 'I gather you bought Mrs Swain's home movies.'

'No money changed hands,' he said with satisfaction. 'I persuaded Mrs Swain it was her duty to serve the truth. Also I let her keep the Florentine box, which was her mother's. In return she gave me some film. Unfortunately, the reel I'm about to show you is nearly twenty-six years old and in rather poor condition. It broke as I was running it through just now.' He turned to the young man at the projector. 'How are you doing, Eddie?'

'I'm splicing it. It should be ready in a minute.'

Truttwell said to me: 'Do me a favor, Archer. Irene Chalmers is in the waiting room.'

'Is she back in the fold?'

'She will be,' he said with a glint of teeth. 'At the moment she's here rather against her will. Just go and make sure she doesn't run away.'

'What are you planning to spring on her?'

'You'll see.'

'That her maiden name was really Rita Shepherd?'

Truttwell's satisfied look fell apart. A kind of rivalry had been growing between us, perhaps rising from the fact that Betty had trusted me.

'How long have you known that?' he said in a prosecutor's voice.

'About five seconds. I've suspected it since last night.' It wouldn't have been a good idea to tell him that the idea had come to me in a dream about my grandmother.

As I moved along the corridor, the dream came back into my mind and blunted my aggression. Mrs Shepherd merged with the memories of my grandmother long since buried in Martinez. The passion with which Mrs Shepherd had guarded her daughter's secret gave it some value.

Irene Chalmers lifted her face to me as I entered the waiting room. She didn't seem to know me right away. The switchboard girl spoke to me in a whisper, like someone speaking in the presence of illness or mental retardation:

'I didn't think you were going to make it. Mr Truttwell is in the library. He said to send you right in.'

'I've just been talking to him.'

'I see.'

I sat next to Irene Chalmers. She turned and looked at me with slow recognition, almost like a woman coming awake from a dream. As if the dream had been frightening, her mood was apologetic and subdued:

'I'm sorry, my mind's been wandering. You're Mr Archer.

But I thought you weren't with us any more.'

'I'm still on the case, Mrs Chalmers. By the way, I've recovered your husband's letters.'

She said without much interest: 'Do you have them with you?'

'Just a few of them. I'll return them through Mr Truttwell.'

'But he isn't our lawyer any longer.'

'I'm sure you can trust him to give you the letters, anyway.'

'I don't know.' She looked around the little room with a kind of primitive suspicion. 'We all used to be the best of friends. But we aren't any more.'

'On account of Nick and Betty?'

'I guess that was the last straw,' she said. 'But we had our real trouble some time ago, over money. It always seems to be over money, doesn't it? Sometimes I almost wish I was poor again.'

'You say you had trouble over money?'

'Yes, when Larry and I set up the Smitheram Foundation. John Truttwell refused to draw the papers for us. He said we were being taken by Dr Smitheram, setting him up in a free clinic. But Larry wanted to do it, and I thought it was a nice idea myself. I don't know where we'd be without Dr Smitheram.'

'He's done a lot for you, has he?'

'You know he has. He saved Nick from—you know what. I think John Truttwell is jealous of Dr Smitheram. Anyway, he isn't our friend any more. I only came here this afternoon because he threatened me.'

I wanted to ask her what she meant, but the girl at the switchboard was listening openly. I said to the girl:

'Go and ask Mr Truttwell if he's ready for us, please.'

Unwillingly, she went. I turned back to Mrs Chalmers.

'What did he threaten you with?'

She didn't respond defensively. She was acting as if a numbing blow had knocked all discretion out of her:

'It was Nick again. Truttwell went to San Diego today and dug up some new dirt. I don't think I should tell you what it was.'

'Did it have to do with Nick's birth?'

'He told you, then.'

'No, but I read some of your husband's letters. Apparently he was overseas when Nick was conceived. Is that true, Mrs Chalmers?'

She looked at me in confusion and then with hard disdain. 'You have no right to ask me that. You're trying to strip me naked, aren't you?'

Even in her anger there was an ambiguous erotic underplay, which seemed to ask for my complicity. I offered her a smile which felt strange from inside.

The switchboard girl came back and said that Mr Truttwell was waiting for us. We found him alone in the library, standing behind the projector.

Irene Chalmers reacted to the machine as if it was a complex weapon pointed at her. Her fearful gaze moved from Truttwell to me, standing between her and the door. I closed the door. Her face and body froze.

'You didn't say anything about movies,' she complained to Truttwell. 'You said you wanted to review the case with me.'

He answered smoothly, very much in command of the situation. 'This film is a part of the case. It was taken at a swimming party in San Marino in the summer of 1943. Eldon Swain, who gave the party, shot most of it himself. The bit at the end, where he appears, was taken by Mrs Swain.'

'Have you talked to Mrs Swain?'

'Somewhat. Frankly, I'm much more interested in your reaction.' He tapped the back of an armchair near the projector. 'Come and sit down and be comfortable, Irene.'

She remained stubbornly unmoving. Truttwell approached her smiling and took her arm. She moved slowly and heavily like a statue thawing reluctantly into flesh.

He settled her in the armchair, leaning over her from behind, withdrawing his hands lingeringly from her upper arms.

'Turn off the lights, will you, Archer?'

I flicked the switch and sat down beside Irene Chalmers. The projector whirred. Its quiet shotgun blast of light filled the screen with images. A large rectangular pool with a diving board and a slide reflected a blue old-fashioned sky.

A young blonde girl with a mature figure and an immature face climbed onto the diving board. She waved at the camera, bounced excessively, and did a comic dive with her legs apart and kicking like a frog's. She came up with a mouthful of water and spurted it at the camera. Jean Trask, young.

Irene Chalmers, née Rita Shepherd, was next on the diving board. She walked to the end of it gravely, as if the eye of the camera was judging her. The black rubber helmet in which her hair was hidden made her look oddly archaic.

She stood for quite a while with the camera on her, not once returning its stare. Then she bounced and did a swan dive, cutting the water without much splash. It wasn't until she disappeared from sight that I realized how beautiful she had been.

The camera caught her coming up, and she smiled and turned onto her back directly under it. Jean came up behind and ducked her, shouting or laughing, splashing water at the camera with her hands.

A third young person, a boy of eighteen or so whom I didn't immediately recognize, climbed up onto the board. Slowly, he walked to the forward end, with many backward looks, as if there were pirates behind him. There was one. Jean rushed him and shoved him into the water, laughing or shouting. He came up floundering, his eyes closed. A woman wearing a wide-brimmed hat held out a padded hook to him at the end of a long pole. She used it to tow him to the shallow end. He stood there, in water up to his waist, with his narrow back turned to the camera. His rescuer took off her floppy hat and bowed toward unseen spectators.

The woman was Mrs Swain, but Swain's camera failed to linger on her. It shifted to the spectators, a handsome older couple who were sitting together on a shaded swing. In spite of the shadow falling across him, I recognized Samuel Rawlinson and guessed that the woman beside him was Estelle Chalmers. The camera moved again before I had a chance to study her thin, passionate face.

Rita and Jean went down the slide, singly and together. They raced the length of the pool, with Jean coming out ahead. She splashed the hydrophobic boy still standing as if rooted in waist-deep water. Then she splashed Rita.

I caught a fuzzy background glimpse of Randy Shepherd, red-headed and red-bearded in gardener's dungarees, looking over a hedge at his daughter taking her place in the sun. I glanced sideways at Irene Chalmers's face, which was fitfully lit by the flickering inexact colors reflected from the screen. She looked as if she were dying under the soft bombardment of the past.

When my eyes returned to the screen, Eldon Swain was on the diving board. He was a man of middle size with a large handsome head. He bounced and did a swan dive. The camera met him coming up and followed him back onto the diving board. He performed flips, front and back.

Next came a double dive with Jean on his shoulders, and finally a double dive with Rita. As if controlled by a documentary interest, the camera followed the pair as Rita stood spraddled on the diving board, and Eldon Swain inserted his head between her legs and lifted her. Tottering slightly, he carried her out to the end of the board and stood for a long moment with his head projecting from between her thighs like the head of a giant smiling baby being born again.

The two fell off the board together and stayed underwater for what seemed a long time. The eye of the camera looked for them but caught only sparkling surfaces netted with light and underlaid by colored shadows dissolving in the water.

XXXIV

AFTER THE REEL ended, none of us spoke for a while. I turned on the lights. Irene Chalmers stirred and roused herself. I could sense her fear, so powerful it seemed to make her drowsy.

She said in an effort to throw it off: 'I was pretty in those days, wasn't I?'

'More than pretty,' Truttwell said. 'The word is beautiful.'

'A lot of good it ever did me.' Her voice and language were changing, as if she was falling back on her earlier self. 'Where did you get this movie—from Mrs Swain?'

'Yes. She gave me others.'

'She would. She's always hated me.'

'Because you took up with her husband?' I said.

'She hated me long before that. It was almost as if she knew it was going to happen. Or maybe she *made* it happen, I don't know. She sat around and watched Eldon, waiting for him to jump. If you do that to a man, sooner or later he's going to jump.'

'What made you jump?' I said.

'We won't talk about me.' She looked at me and then at Truttwell and then at nothing. 'I'm taking the fifth.'

Truttwell moved closer to her, gentle and suave as a lover. 'Don't be foolish, Irene. You're among friends here.'

'I bet.'

'It's true,' he said. 'I went to enormous trouble, and so did Mr Archer, to get hold of this evidence, get it out of the hands of potential enemies. In my hands it can't be used against you. I think I can guarantee it never will be.'

She sat up straight, meeting him eye to eye. 'What is this? Blackmail?'

Truttwell smiled. 'You're getting me confused with Dr Smitheram, I'm afraid. I don't want anything from you at all,

Irene. I do think we should have a free and frank discussion.'

She looked in my direction. 'What about him?'

'Mr Archer knows this case better than I do. I rely completely on his discretion.'

Truttwell's praise made me uneasy: I wasn't prepared to say the same things about him.

'I don't trust his discretion,' the woman said. 'Why should I? I hardly know him.'

'You know me, Irene. As your attorney—'

'So you're our lawyer again?'

'I never ceased to be, really. It must be clear to you by now that you need my help, and Mr Archer's help. Everything we've learned about the past is strictly in confidence among the three of us.'

'That is,' she said, 'if I go along. What if I don't?'

'I'm ethically bound to keep your secrets.'

'But they'd slip out anyway, is that the idea?'

'Not through me or Archer. Perhaps through Dr Smitheram. Obviously I can't protect your interests unless you let me.'

She considered Truttwell's proposition. 'I didn't want to break with you myself. Especially not at this time. But I can't speak for my husband.'

'Where is he?'

'I left him at home. These last few days have been awfully hard on Larry. He doesn't look it, but he's the nervous type.'

Her words touched a closed place in my mind. 'Was that your husband in the film? The boy who got pushed into the water?'

'Yes it was. It was the first day I met Larry. And his last free weekend before he went into the Navy. I could tell that he was interested in me, but I didn't get to know him that day, not really. I wish I had.'

'When did you get to know him?'

'A couple of years later. He grew up in the meantime.'

'What happened to you in the meantime?'

She turned away from me abruptly, her white neck ridged

with strain. 'I'm not going to answer that,' she said to Truttwell. 'I didn't hire a lawyer and a detective to dig up all the dirt in my own life. What kind of sense would that make?'

He answered her in a quiet careful voice: 'It makes more sense than trying to keep it secret. It's time the dirt, as you call it, was laid out on the table, among the three of us. I needn't remind you there have been several murders.'

'*I* didn't kill anybody.'

'Your son did,' I reminded her. 'We've already discussed that death in the hobo jungle.'

She turned back to me. 'It was a kidnapping. He killed in self-defense. You said yourself the police would understand.'

'I may have to take that back, now that I know more about it. You held back part of the story—all the really important parts. For example, when I told you that Randy Shepherd was involved in the kidnapping you didn't mention that Randy was your father.'

'A woman doesn't have to tell on her husband,' she said. 'Isn't it the same for a girl and her father?'

'No, but it doesn't matter now. Your father was shot dead in Pasadena yesterday afternoon.'

Her head came up. 'Who shot him?'

'The police. Your mother called them.'

'My mother did?' She was silent for a while. 'That doesn't really surprise me. The first thing I remember in my life is the two of them fighting like animals. I had to get away from that kind of life, even if it meant—' Our eyes met, and the sentence died under the impact.

I continued it for her: 'Even if it meant running off to Mexico with an embezzler.'

She shook her head. Her black hair fluffed out a little, and made her look both younger and cheaper.

'I never did.'

'You never ran off with Eldon Swain?'

She was silent.

'What did happen, Mrs Chalmers?'

'I can't tell you—not even at this late date. There are other people involved.'

'Eldon Swain?'

'He's the most important one.'

'You don't have to worry about protecting him, as you very well know. He's as safe as your father, and for the same reason.'

She gave me a lost look, as if her game with time had failed for a moment and she was caught in the limbo between her two lives. 'Is Eldon really dead?'

'You know he is, Mrs Chalmers. He was the dead man in the railroad yards. You must have known or suspected it at the time.'

Her eyes darkened. 'I swear to God I didn't.'

'You had to know. The body was left with its hands in the fire so that the fingerprints would be erased. No eight-year-old boy did that.'

'That doesn't mean it was me.'

'You were the one with the motivation,' I said. 'If the dead man was identified as Swain, your whole life would collapse. You'd lose your house and your husband and your social standing. You'd be Rita Shepherd again, back on your uppers.'

She was silent, her face working with thought. 'You said my father was involved with Eldon. It must have been my father who burned the body—did you say he burned the body?'

'The fingers.'

She nodded. 'It must have been my father. He was always talking about getting rid of his own fingerprints. He was a nut on the subject.'

Her voice was unreflective, almost casual. It stopped suddenly. Perhaps she had heard herself as Rita Shepherd, daughter of an ex-con, trapped again in that identity without any possible escape.

The knowledge of her predicament seemed to be striking down into her body and penetrating her mind through layers of indifference, years of forgetfulness. It struck a vital place and crumpled her in the chair, her face in her hands. Her hair fell forward from her nape and sifted over her fingers like black water.

Truttwell stood over her looking down with an intensity that didn't seem to include any kind of love. Perhaps it was pity he felt, laced with possession. She had passed through several hands and been slightly scorched by felony, but she was still very beautiful.

Forgetful of me, and of himself, Truttwell put his hands on her. He stroked her head very gently, and then her long tapering back. His caresses weren't sexual in any ordinary sense. Perhaps, I thought, his main feeling was an abstract legal passion which satisfied itself by having her as a client. Or a widower's underground desire held in check by the undead past.

Mrs Chalmers recovered after a while, and asked for water. Truttwell went to another room to fetch it. She spoke to me in an urgent whisper:

'Why did my mother call the police on Randy? She must have had a reason.'

'She had. He stole her picture of Nick.'

'The graduation picture I sent her?'

'Yes.'

'I shouldn't have sent it. But I thought for once in my life I could act like a normal human being.'

'You couldn't, though. Your father took it to Jean Trask and talked her into hiring Sidney Harrow. That's how the whole thing started.'

'What did the old man want?'

'Your husband's money, just like everyone else.'

'But not you, eh?' Her voice was sardonic.

'Not me,' I said. 'Money costs too much.'

Truttwell brought her a paper cup of water and watched her drink it. 'Are you feeling up to a little drive?'

Her body jerked in alarm. 'Where to?'

'The Smitheram Clinic. It's time we had a chat with Nick.'

She looked profoundly unwilling. 'Dr Smitheram won't let you in.'

'I think he will. You're Nick's mother. I'm his attorney. If Dr Smitheram won't cooperate, I'll slap a writ of *habeas corpus* on him.'

Truttwell wasn't entirely serious, but her mood of alarm persisted. 'No. Please, don't do anything like that. I'll talk to Dr Smitheram.'

On the way out I asked the switchboard girl if Betty had come back with the lab report. She hadn't. I left word for her that I'd be at the clinic.

XXXV

IRENE CHALMERS DISMISSED Emilio. She rode between Truttwell and me in the front seat of his Cadillac. When she got out of the car in the parking lot of the clinic she moved like a drugged woman. Truttwell gave her his arm and guided her into the reception room.

Moira Smitheram was behind the desk, as she had been the day I met her. It seemed like a long time ago. Her face had aged and deepened, or maybe I could see more deeply into her. She looked from Truttwell to me.

'You didn't give me much time.'

'We're running out of time.'

Truttwell said: 'It's very important that we talk to Nick Chalmers. Mrs Chalmers agrees.'

'You'll have to take that up with Dr Smitheram.'

Moira went and got her husband. He came through the inner door, striding angrily in his white smock.

'You don't give up easily, do you?' he said to Truttwell.

'I don't give up at all, old man. We're here to see Nick, and I'm very much afraid that you can't stop us.'

Smitheram turned his back on Truttwell and said to Mrs Chalmers: 'How do you feel about this?'

'You better let us in, doctor,' she said without raising her eyes.

'Have you re-engaged Mr Truttwell as your attorney?'

'Yes I have.'

'And has Mr Chalmers concurred?'

'He will.'

Dr Smitheram gave her a probing look. 'What sort of pressure are you under, anyway?'

Truttwell said: 'You're wasting time, doctor. We're here to talk to your patient, not to you.'

Smitheram swallowed his anger. 'Very well.'

He and his wife conducted us through the inner door, along a corridor to a second door which had to be unlocked and relocked. The wing beyond it contained eight or ten rooms beginning with a suicide room in which a woman sat on the padded floor looking out at us through thick glass.

Nick had a bed-sitting room with an open door. He sat in an armchair holding an open textbook. In his light wool robe he looked almost like any other young man interrupted at his studies. He stood up when he saw his mother, his black eyes large and bright in his pale face. His dark glasses were on the desk beside him.

'Hello, Mother, Mr Truttwell.' His glance traveled across our faces without pausing. 'Where's Dad? Where's Betty?'

'This isn't a social occasion,' Truttwell said, 'though it's good to see you. We have some questions to ask you.'

'Keep them as brief as possible,' Smitheram said. 'Sit down, Nick.'

Moira took his book and put a marker in it; then stood beside her husband in the doorway. Irene Chambers sat in the other chair, Truttwell and I on the single bed facing Nick.

'I'm not going to beat around the bush,' Truttwell said. 'About fifteen years ago, when you were a small boy, you shot a man in the railroad yards.'

Nick raised his eyes to Smitheram's and said in a flat disappointed tone: 'You told him.'

'No, I did not,' Smitheram said.

Truttwell said to the doctor: 'You took on quite a responsibility when you kept that shooting quiet.'

'I know that. I acted in the best interests of an eight-year-old who was threatened with autism. The law isn't the only guide to the conduct of human affairs. Even if it were, the homicide was justifiable or accidental.'

Truttwell said wearily: 'I didn't come here to argue law or ethics with you, doctor.'

'Then don't attack my motives.'

'Which are, of course, as pure as the driven snow.'

The doctor's large body made a small threatening move in Truttwell's direction. It was inhibited by Moira's hand on his elbow.

Truttwell turned back to Nick. 'Tell me about that shooting down by the tracks. Was it an accident?'

'I don't know.'

'Then just tell me how it happened. How did you get to the railroad yards in the first place?'

Nick answered haltingly as if his memory operated by fits and starts like a teletype ticker. 'I was on my way home from school when the man picked me up in his car. I know I shouldn't have got in. But he seemed terribly serious. And I felt sorry for him. He was sick and old.

'He asked me a lot of questions about who my mother was, and who my father was, and when and where I was born. Then he said that he was my father. I didn't exactly believe him, but I was interested enough to go along to the hobo jungle with him.

'He took me to a place behind the old roundhouse. Someone had left a fire burning and we added some wood and sat beside it. He got out a pint of whisky and took a pull and gave me a taste of it. It burned my mouth. But he drank it down like water, and finished the bottle.

'It made him foolish. He sang some old songs, and then he got sentimental. He said I was his darling boy and when he came into his rights he'd assume his true position and look after me. He started to paw me and kiss me, and that was when I shot him. He had a gun in the waistband of his trousers. I pulled it out and shot him, and he died.'

Nick's pale face was still composed. But I could hear his rapid breathing.

'What did you do with the gun?' I said.

'I didn't do anything with it. I left it lying there and walked home. Later I told my parents what I'd done. They didn't believe me at first. Then it came out in the paper, about the dead man, and they believed me. They brought me to Dr Smitheram. And,' he added with wry bitterness, 'I've been with him ever since. I wish I'd gone to the police in the first place.' His eyes were on his mother's half-averted face.

'It wasn't your decision,' I said. 'Now let's get on to the Sidney Harrow killing.'

'Good Lord, do you think I killed him, too?'

'You thought so, remember?'

His gaze turned inward. 'I was pretty confused, wasn't I? The trouble was I really felt like killing Harrow. I went to his motel room that night to have a showdown with him. Jean told me where he was staying. He wasn't there, but I found him in his car on the beach.'

'Alive or dead?'

'He was dead. The gun that killed him was lying beside his car. I picked it up to look at it and something clicked in my head. And the ground literally shifted under my feet. I thought at first it was an earthquake. Then I realized it was in me. I was confused for a long time, and suicidal.' He added: 'The gun seemed to want me to do something with it.'

'You already had done something with it,' I said. 'It was the same gun that you left in the railroad yards.'

'How could that be?'

'I don't know how it could be. But it was the same gun. The police have ballistic records that prove it. Are you sure you left the gun beside the body?'

Nick was confused again. His eyes looked at our faces in naked helplessness. He reached for his dark glasses and put them on. 'Harrow's body?'

'Eldon Swain's body. The man in the railroad yards who said he was your father. Did you leave the gun there beside him, Nick?'

'Yes. I know I didn't take it home with me.'

'Then someone else picked it up and kept it for fifteen years and used it on Harrow. Who would that be?'

'I don't know.' The young man shook his head slowly from side to side.

Smitheram stepped forward. 'He's had enough. And you're not learning anything.' His eyes were full of anxiety, but whether it was for Nick I couldn't tell.

'I'm learning a good deal, doctor. So is Nick.'

'Yes.' The young man looked up. 'Was the man in the railroad yards really my father as he said?'

'You'll have to ask your mother.'

'Was he, Mother?'

Irene Chalmers looked around the room as if another trap had closed on her. The pressure of our silence forced words out of her:

'I don't have to answer that and I'm not going to.'

'That means he was my father.'

She didn't answer Nick or look at him. She sat with her head bowed. Truttwell stood up and put a hand on her shoulder. She inclined her head sideways so that her cheek rested against his knuckles. In contrast with her flawless skin, his hand was spotted with age.

Nick said insistently: 'I knew that Lawrence Chalmers couldn't be my father.'

'How did you know that?' I asked him.

'The letters he wrote from overseas—I don't remember the dates exactly, but the timing wasn't right.'

'Is that why you took the letters out of the safe?'

'Not really. I stumbled onto that aspect of it. Sidney Harrow and Jean Trask came to me with a wild story that my father—that Lawrence Chalmers had committed a crime. I took the letters to prove to them that they were mistaken. He was overseas at the time the theft occurred.'

'What theft?'

'Jean said he stole some money from her family—from her father—actually an enormous amount of money, half a million or so. But his letters proved that Jean and Harrow were wrong. On the day of the alleged theft—I think it was July 1, 1945—my fa—Mr Chalmers was at sea aboard his carrier.' He added with a look of sad irony: 'In proving that I also proved that he couldn't be my father. I was born on December 14, 1945, and nine months before, when I must have been—' He looked at his mother, and couldn't find the word.

'Conceived?' I said.

'When I must have been conceived, he was aboard his ship in the forward area. Do you hear that, Mother?'

'I hear you.'

'Haven't you any other comment?'

'You don't have to turn against me,' she said in a low tone. 'I'm your mother. What does it matter who your father was?'

'It matters to me.'

'Forget it. Why don't you forget it?'

'I have some of the letters here.' I brought out my wallet and showed Nick the three letters. 'I think these are the ones you were particularly interested in.'

'Yes. Where did you get them?'

'From your apartment,' I said.

'May I have them for a minute?'

I handed him the letters. He went through them quickly.

'This is the one he wrote on March 15, 1945: "Dearest

Mother: Here I am in the forward area again, so my letter won't go off for a while." That would seem to prove conclusively that whoever my father was, he wasn't and isn't Lieutenant (j.g.) L. Chalmers.' He looked at his mother again in murky speculation: 'Was it the man in the railroad yards, Mother? The man I killed?'

'You don't want an answer,' she said.

'That means the answer is yes,' he said in bleak satisfaction. 'At least I know that much for certain. What did you say his name was? My father's name?'

She didn't answer.

'Eldon Swain,' I said. 'He was Jean Trask's father.'

'She *said* we were brother and sister. You mean it's really true?'

'I don't have the answers. You're the one who seems to have them.' I paused, and went on: 'There's one very important answer I have to ask you for, Nick. What took you to Jean Trask's house in San Diego?'

He shook his head. 'I don't recall. The whole thing is a blank. I don't even remember *going* to San Diego.'

Dr Smitheram came forward again. 'I have to call a halt now. I'm not going to let you undo what we've done for Nick in the last couple of days.'

'Let's finish it off,' Truttwell said. 'After all, it's been dragging on now for most of Nick's young life.'

'I want to finish it, too,' Nick said, 'if I can.'

'And so do I.' It was Moira coming out of a long silence.

The doctor turned on her coldly. 'I don't remember asking for your opinion.'

'You have it, anyway. Let's get it over with.'

Moira's voice had overtones of weary guilt. The two of them confronted each other for a moment as if they were the only ones in the room.

I said to Nick: 'When did you start remembering in San Diego?'

'When I woke up in the hospital that night. I was missing the whole day.'

'And what was the last you remembered before that?'

'When I got up that morning. I'd been awake all night, with one thing and another, and I was feeling awfully depressed. That horrible scene in the railroad yards kept coming back. I could smell the fire and the whisky.

'I decided to turn off my mind with a sleeping pill or two, and I got up and went into the bathroom where they kept them. When I saw the red and yellow capsules in the bottles I changed my mind. I decided to take a lot of them and turn off my mind for good.'

'Was that when you wrote your suicide note?'

He considered my question. 'I wrote it just before I took the pills. Yes.'

'How many did you take?'

'I didn't count them. A couple of handfuls, I guess, enough to kill me. But I couldn't just sit in the bathroom and wait. I was afraid they'd find me and not let me die. I climbed out the bathroom window and dropped to the ground. I must have fallen and hit my head on something.' He balanced the letters on his knee and touched the side of his head tenderly. 'Next thing I knew I was in the San Diego hospital. I've already told Dr Smitheram all this.'

I glanced at Smitheram. He wasn't listening. He was talking in intense, low tones to his wife.

'Dr Smitheram?'

He turned abruptly, but not in response to me. He reached for the letters in Nick's lap. 'Let's have a look at these, eh?'

Smitheram riffled through the flimsy pages and began to read aloud to his wife: ' "There's something about pilots that reminds you of racehorses—developed almost to an unhealthy point. I hope I'm not that way to other eyes.

' "Commander Wilson is, though. (He's no longer censoring mail so I can say this.) He's been in for over four years now, but he seems to be exactly the same gentlemanly Yale man he was when he came in. He has, however, a certain air of arrested development. He has given his best to the war—" '

Truttwell said dryly: 'You read beautifully, doctor, but this is hardly the occasion.'

Smitheram acted as if he hadn't heard Truttwell. He said to his wife: 'What was the name of my squadron leader on the Sorrel Bay?'

'Wilson,' she said in a small voice.

'Do you remember I made this comment about him in a letter I wrote you in March 1945?'

'Vaguely. I'll take your word for it.'

Smitheram wasn't satisfied. He went through the pages again, his furious fingers almost tearing them. 'Listen to this, Moira: "We're very near the equator and the heat is pretty bad, though I don't mean to complain. If we're still anchored at this atoll tomorrow I'm going to try to get off the ship for a swim, which I haven't had since we left Pearl months ago. One of my big daily pleasures, though, is the shower I take every night before going to bed." And so on. Later, the letter mentions that Wilson was shot down over Okinawa. Now I distinctly remember writing this to you in the summer of 1945. How do you account for that, Moira?'

'I don't,' she said with her eyes down. 'I won't attempt to account for it.'

Truttwell stood up and looked past Smitheram's shoulder at the letter. 'I take it this isn't your writing. No, I see it's not.' He added after a pause: 'It's Lawrence Chalmers' writing, isn't it?' And after a further pause: 'Does this mean his war letters to his mother were all a fake?'

'They certainly were.' Smitheram shook the documents in his fist. His eyes were on his wife's downcast face. 'I still don't understand how these letters got written.'

'Was Chalmers ever a Navy pilot?' Truttwell said.

'No. He did make an attempt to get into the pilot training

program. But he was hopelessly unqualified. In fact, he was given a general discharge by the Navy a few months after he enlisted.'

'Why was he discharged?' I said.

'For reasons of mental health. He broke down in boot camp. It happened to quite a few schizoid boys when they tried to assume a military role. Particularly those whose mothers were the dominant parent, as in Larry's case.'

'How do you know so much about his case, doctor?'

'I was assigned to it, in the Navy Hospital in San Diego. Before we turned him loose on the world, we gave him a few weeks of treatment. He's been my patient ever since—except for my two years' sea duty.'

'Was he the reason you settled here in the Point?'

'One of the reasons. He was grateful to me and he offered to help set me up in practice. His mother had died and left him a good deal of money.'

'One thing I don't understand,' Truttwell said, 'is how he could fool us with these phony letters. He must have had to fake Fleet Post Office envelopes and markings. And how could he receive answers if he wasn't in the Navy?'

'He had a job in the Post Office,' Smitheram said. 'I got him that job myself before I shipped out. I suppose he set up a special box for his own mail.' As if his head was being wrenched around by an external force, Smitheram looked at his wife again. 'What *I* don't understand, Moira, is how he got a chance—repeated chances—to copy my letters to you.'

'He must have taken them,' she said.

'Did you know he was taking them?'

She nodded glumly. 'Actually, he borrowed them to read, or so he said. But I can understand why he copied them. He hero-worshipped you. He wanted to be like you.'

'How did he feel about you?'

'He was fond of me. He made no secret of it, even before you left.'

'After I left, did you see him regularly?'

'I could hardly help it. He lived next door.'

'Next door in the Magnolia Hotel? You mean you lived in adjoining rooms?'

'You asked me to keep an eye on him,' she said.

'I didn't tell you to live with him. Did you live with him?' He was speaking in the hectoring voice of a man who was hurting himself and knew it but kept on doing it.

'I lived with him,' his wife said. 'I'm not ashamed of it. He needed someone. I may have had just as much to do with saving his mind as you had.'

'So it was therapy, was it? That's why you wanted to come here after the war. That's why he's—'

She cut him short: 'You're off the track, Ralph. You usually are where I'm concerned. I quit with him before you ever came home.'

Irene Chalmers lifted her head. 'That's true. He married me in July—'

Truttwell leaned toward her and touched her mouth with his finger. 'Don't volunteer any information, Irene.'

She lapsed into silence, and I could hear Moira's intense low voice.

'You knew about my relationship with him,' she was saying to her husband. 'You can't treat a patient for twenty-five years without knowing that much about him. But you chose to act as if you hadn't known.'

'If I did,' he said—'I'm not admitting anything but if I did, I was acting in my patient's interest, not my own.'

'You really believe that, don't you, Ralph?'

'It's true.'

'You're fooling yourself. But you're not fooling anyone else. You knew Larry Chalmers was a fake, just as I did. We conspired with his fantasy and went on taking his money.'

'I'm afraid you're fantasying, Moira.'

'You know I'm not.'

He looked around at our faces to see if we were judging him. His wife brushed past him and left the room. I followed her down the corridor.

XXXVI

I CAUGHT MOIRA at the locked door beside the suicide room. For the second time in our acquaintance she was having trouble unlocking a door. I mentioned this.

She turned on me with hard bright eyes. 'We won't talk about the other night. It's all in the past—so long ago I hardly remember your name.'

'I thought we were friends.'

'So did I. But you broke that.'

She flung one arm out toward Nick's room. The woman in the suicide room began to moan and cry.

Moira unlocked the door which let us out of the wing and took me to her office. The first thing she did there was to take her handbag out of a drawer and set it on top of the desk, ready to go.

'I'm leaving Ralph. And don't say anything, please, about me going with you. You don't like me well enough.'

'Do you always think people's thoughts for them?'

'All right—I don't like *myself* well enough.' She paused and looked around her office. The glowing paintings on the walls seemed to reflect her anger with herself, like subtle mirrors. 'I don't like making money from other people's suffering. Do you know what I mean?'

'I ought to. It's how I live.'

'But you don't do it for the money, do you?'

'I try not to,' I said. 'When your income passes a certain point you lose touch. All of a sudden the other people look like geeks or gooks, expendables.'

'That happened to Ralph. I won't let it happen to me.' She

sounded like a woman in flight, but more hopeful than afraid. 'I'm going back to social work. It's what I really love. I was never happier than when I lived in La Jolla in one room.'

'Next door to Sonny.'

'Yes.'

'Sonny was Lawrence Chalmers, of course.'

She nodded.

'And the other girl he took up with was Irene Chalmers?'

'Yes. She called herself Rita Shepherd in those days.'

'How do you know?'

'Sonny told me about her. He'd met her at a swimming party in San Marino a couple of years before. Then one day she walked into the post office where he worked. He was terribly upset by the meeting at first, and now I can understand why. He was afraid his secret would leak out, and his mother would learn he was just a postal clerk instead of a Navy pilot.'

'Did you know about the deception?'

'Naturally I knew he was living a fantasy life. He used to dress up in officers' clothes and walk the streets at night. But I didn't know about his mother—there were some things he didn't talk about, even to me.'

'How much did he tell you about Rita Shepherd?'

'Enough. She was living with an older man who kept her stashed in Imperial Beach.'

'Eldon Swain.'

'Was that his name?' She added after a thinking pause: 'It all comes together, doesn't it? I didn't realize how much life, and death, I was involved with. I guess we never do until afterwards. Anyway, Rita shifted to Sonny and I moved to the sidelines. By then I didn't much care. It was pretty wearing, looking after Sonny, and I was willing to pass him on to the next girl.'

'What I don't understand is how you could stay interested in him for over two years. Or why a woman like his wife would fall for him.'

'Women don't always go for the solid virtues,' she said. 'Sonny had a wild psychotic streak. He would try almost anything once.'

'I'll have to cultivate my wild psychotic streak. But I must say Chalmers keeps his pretty well hidden.'

'He's older now, and under tranquilizers all the time.'

'Tranquilizers like Nembu-Serpin?'

'I see you've been boning up.'

'Just how sick is he?'

'Without supportive therapy, and drugs, he'd probably have to be hospitalized. But with these things he manages to lead a fairly well-adjusted life.' She sounded like a salesman who didn't quite believe in her product.

'Is he dangerous, Moira?'

'He *could* be dangerous, under certain circumstances.'

'If somebody found out that he was a fake, for example?'

'Perhaps.'

'You're very perhapsy all of a sudden. He's been your husband's patient for twenty-five years, as you pointed out. You must know something about him.'

'We know a good deal. But the doctor-patient relationship involves a right to privacy.'

'Don't lean too heavily on that. It doesn't apply to a patient's crimes, or potential crimes. I want to know if you and Dr Smitheram considered him a threat to Nick.'

She sidestepped the question. 'What kind of a threat?'

'A mortal threat,' I said. 'You and your husband knew that he was dangerous to Nick, didn't you?'

Moira didn't answer me in words. She moved around her office and began to take the pictures down from the walls and pile them on the desk. In a token way she seemed to be trying to dismantle the clinic and her place in it.

A knock on the door interrupted her work. It was the young receptionist. 'Miss Truttwell wants to speak to Mr Archer. Shall I send her in?'

'I'll go out,' I said.

The receptionist looked around in dismay at the empty walls.

'What happened to all your pictures?'

'I'm moving out. You could help me.'

'I'll be glad to, Mrs Smitheram,' the young woman said brightly.

Betty was standing in the middle of the outer room. She looked windblown and excited.

'The lab said there was quite a lot of Nembutal in the sample. Also some chloral hydrate, but they couldn't tell how much without further testing.'

'I'm not surprised.'

'What does it mean, Mr Archer?'

'It means that Nick was in the back of the family Rolls some time after he took his overdose of pills. He vomited some of them up, and that may have saved his life.'

'How is he?'

'Doing quite well. I had a talk with him just now.'

'Can I see him?'

'That isn't up to me. His mother, and your father, are with him right now.'

'I'll wait.'

I waited with her, each of us thinking his own thoughts. I needed quiet. The case was coming together in my mind, constructing itself in inner space like a movie of a falling building reversed.

The inner door opened, and Irene Chalmers came through on Truttwell's arm, leaning on him heavily, like a survivor. She had shifted her weight from Chalmers to Truttwell, I thought, as she had once shifted it from Eldon Swain to Chalmers.

Truttwell became aware of his daughter. His eyes moved nervously, but he didn't try to disengage himself from Irene Chalmers. Betty gave them a so-that's-how-it-is look.

'Hello, Dad. Hello, Mrs Chalmers. I hear Nick is much better.'

'Yes, he is,' her father said.

'Can I talk with him for a minute?'

He hesitated for a thoughtful moment. His gaze flicked across my face, and back to his daughter's. He answered her in a careful, gentle voice: 'We'll take it up with Dr Smitheram.'

He led Betty through the inner door and closed it carefully behind them.

I was alone in the reception room with Irene Chalmers. As she knew. She looked at me with a kind of dull formality, in the hope that nothing real would be said between us.

'I'd like to ask you a few questions, Mrs Chalmers.'

'That doesn't mean I have to answer them.'

'Once and for all, now, was Eldon Swain Nick's father?'

She faced me in passive subbornness. 'Probably. Anyway he thought he was. But you can't expect me to tell Nick he killed his own natural father—'

'He knows it now,' I said. 'And you can't go on using Nick to hide behind.'

'I don't understand what you meant.'

'You suppressed the facts about Eldon Swain and his death for your own sake, not for Nick's. You let him carry the burden of the guilt, and take the rap for you.'

'There isn't any rap. We kept everything quiet.'

'And let Nick live in mental torment for fifteen years. It was a lousy trick to pull on your own son, or anybody's son.'

She bowed her head as if in shame. But what she said was: 'I'm not admitting anything.'

'You don't have to. I've got enough physical evidence, and enough witnesses, to make a case against you. I've talked to your father and your mother, and Mr Rawlinson, and Mrs Swain. I've talked to Florence Williams.'

'Who in hell is she?'

'She owns Conchita's Cabins, in Imperial Beach.'

Mrs Chalmers raised her head and swept her fingers across her face, as if there was dust or cobwebs in her eyes. 'I'm sorry I ever set foot in that dump, I can tell you. But you can't make anything out of it, not at this late date. I was just a juvenile at the time. And anything I did away back then—the statute of limitations ran out on it long ago.'

'What did you do away back then?'

'I'm not going to testify against myself. I said before that I was taking the fifth.' She added in a stronger voice: 'John Truttwell will be back in a minute, and this is his department. If you want to get rough, he can get rougher.'

I knew I was on uncertain ground. But this might be the only chance I would have to reach Mrs Chalmers. And both her responses to my accusations, and her failures to respond, had tended to confirm my picture of her. I said:

'If John Truttwell knew what I know about you, he wouldn't touch you with a sterilized stick.'

She had no answer this time. She moved to a chair near the inner door and sat down inexactly and abruptly. I followed and stood over her.

'What happened to the money?'

She twisted sideways away from me. 'Which money do you mean?'

'The money Eldon Swain embezzled from the bank.'

'He took it across the Mexican border with him. I stayed behind in Dago. He said he'd send for me but he never did. So I married Larry Chalmers. That's the whole story.'

'What did Eldon do with the money in Mexico?'

'I heard he lost it. He ran into a couple of bandits in Baja and they took it off him and that was that.'

'What were the bandits' names, Rita?'

'How should I know? It was just a rumor I heard.'

'I'll tell you a better rumor. The bandits' names were Larry and Rita, and they didn't steal the money in Mexico. Eldon Swain never got it across the border. You set him up for a highjacking, and fingered him for Larry. And the two bandits lived happily ever after. Until now.'

'You'll never prove that! You can't!'

She was almost shouting, as if she hoped to drown out the

sound of my voice and the rumors of the past. Truttwell opened the inner door.

'What's going on?' He gave me a stern look. 'What are you trying to prove?'

'We were discussing what happened to Swain's half million. Mrs Chalmers claims that Mexican bandits got it. But I'm fairly certain she and Chalmers highjacked it from Swain. It must have happened a day or two after Swain embezzled the money and brought it to San Diego, where she was waiting for him.'

Mrs Chalmers glanced up, as if my freewheeling reconstruction had touched on a factual detail. Truttwell noticed the giveaway movement of her eyes. His whole face opened and closed like a grasping hand.

'They stole a car,' I went on, 'and brought the money here to Pacific Point, to his mother's house. This was July 3, 1945. Larry and Rita staged a burglary in reverse. It wasn't hard, since Larry's mother was blind and Larry must have had keys to the house, as well as the combination of the safe. They put the money in the safe and left it.'

Mrs Chalmers got to her feet and went to Truttwell and took hold of his arm. 'Don't believe him. I wasn't within fifty miles of here that night.'

'Was Larry?' Truttwell said.

'Yes! It was all Larry's doing. His mother never used the safe after she lost her sight and he figured it was a perfect place to stash—I mean—'

Truttwell took her by the shoulders with both hands and held her at arm's length.

'You were here with Larry that night. Weren't you?'

'He forced me to come along. He held a gun on me.'

'That means you were driving.' Truttwell said. 'You killed my wife.'

The woman hung her head. 'It was Larry's fault. She recognized him, see. He twisted the wheel and stomped on my foot and speeded up the car. I couldn't stop it. I went right over her. He wouldn't let me stop till we got back to Dago.'

Truttwell shook her. 'I don't want to hear that. Where is your husband now?'

'At home. I already told you he isn't feeling well. He's just sitting around in a daze.'

'He's still dangerous,' I said to Truttwell. 'Don't you think we better call Lackland?'

'Not until I've had a chance to talk to Chalmers. You come along with me, eh? You too, Mrs Chalmers.'

Once again she sat between us in the front seat of Truttwell's car. She peered far ahead along the freeway like an accident-prone subject living in dread of still further disasters.

'The other morning,' I said, 'when Nick took all those sleeping pills and tranquilizers, where were you?'

'In bed asleep. I took a couple of chloral hydrates myself the night before.'

'Was your husband in bed asleep?'

'I wouldn't know. We have separate rooms.'

'When did he take off to look for Nick?'

'Right after you left that morning.'

'Driving the Rolls?'

'That's right.'

'Where did he go?'

'All over the place, I guess. When he gets excited he runs around like a maniac. Then he sits around like a dummy for a week.'

'He went to San Diego, Mrs Chalmers. And there's evidence that Nick rode along with him, lying unconscious under a rug in the back seat.'

'That doesn't make sense.'

'I'm afraid it did to your husband. When Nick climbed out the bathroom window, your husband intercepted him in the garden. He knocked him out with a spade or some other tool and hid him in the Rolls until he was ready to leave for San Diego.'

'Why would he do a thing like that to his own son?'

'Nick wasn't his son. He was Eldon Swain's son, and your husband knew it. You're forgetting your own life history, Mrs Chalmers.'

She gave me a quick sideways look. 'Yeah, I wish I could.'

'Nick knew or suspected whose son he was,' I said. 'In any case, he was trying to get at the truth about Eldon Swain's death. And he was getting closer all the time.'

'Nick shot Eldon himself.'

'We all know that now. But Nick didn't drag the dead man into the fire to burn off his fingerprints. That took adult strength, and adult motives. Nick didn't keep Swain's gun, to use it on Sidney Harrow fifteen years later. Nick didn't kill Jean Trask, though your husband did his best to frame him for it. That was why he took Nick to San Diego.'

The woman said in a kind of awe: 'Did Larry kill all those people?'

'I'm afraid he did.'

'But why?'

'They knew too much about him. He was a sick man protecting his fantasy.'

'Fantasy?'

'The pretend world he lived in.'

'Yeah, I see what you mean.'

We left the freeway at Pacific Street and drove up the long slope. Behind us at the foot of the town the low red sun was glaring on the water. In the queer, late night the Chalmers mansion looked insubstantial and dreamlike, a castle in Spain referring to a past that had never existed.

The front door was unlocked, and we went in. Mrs Chalmers called her husband—'Larry!'—and got no answer.

Emilio appeared laggingly in the corridor that led to the back of the house. Mrs Chalmers rushed toward him.

'Where is he?'

'I don't know, ma'am. He ordered me to stay in the kitchen.'

'Did you tell him I searched the Rolls?' I said.

Emilio's black eyes slid away from mine. He didn't answer me.

The woman had climbed the short flight of stairs to the study. She pounded with her fist on the carved oak door, sucked her bleeding knuckles, and pounded again.

'He's in there!' she cried. 'You've got to get him out. He'll do away with himself.'

I pushed her to one side and tried the door. It was locked. The room beyond it was terribly still.

Emilio went back to the kitchen for a screwdriver and a hammer. He used them to unhinge the door of the study.

Chalmers was sitting in the judge's swivel chair, his head inclined rather oddly to one side. He had on a blue naval uniform with a full commander's three gold stripes. Blood from his cut throat had run down over his row of battle ribbons, making them all one color. An old straight razor lay open beside his dangling hand.

His wife stood back from his body as if it gave off mortal laser rays.

'I knew he was going to do it. He wanted to do it the day they came to the front door.'

'Who came to the front door?' I said.

'Jean Trask and that muscle boy she traveled with. Sidney Harrow. I slammed the door in their faces, but I knew they'd be coming back. So did Larry. He got out Eldon's gun that he'd kept in the safe all those years. What he had in mind was a suicide pact. He wanted to shoot me and then himself. Dr Smitheram and I talked him into a trip to Palm Springs instead.'

'You should have let him shoot himself,' Truttwell said.

'And me too? Not on your life. I wasn't ready to die. I'm still not ready.'

She still had passion, if only for herself. Truttwell and I were silent. She said to him:

'Look, are you still my lawyer? You said you were.'

He shook his head. His eyes seemed to be looking through and beyond her, into a sad past or a cold future.

'You can't go back on me now,' she said. 'You think I haven't suffered enough? I'm *sorry* about your wife. I still wake up in the middle of the night and see her in the road, poor woman, laying there like a bundle of old clothes.'

Truttwell struck her face with the back of his hand. A little blood spilled from her mouth, drawing a line across her chin like a crack in marble.

I stepped between them so that he couldn't hit her again. It wasn't the sort of thing that Truttwell should be doing.

She took some courage from my gesture. 'You don't have to hurt me, John. I feel bad enough without that. My whole time here, it's been like living in a haunted house. I mean it. The very first night we came, when we were here in the study, putting the packages of money in the safe—Larry's blind old mother came down in the dark. She said: "Is that you, Sonny?" I don't know how she knew who it was. It was creepy.'

'What happened then?' I said.

'He took her back to her room and talked to her. He wouldn't tell me what he said to her, but she didn't bother us after that.'

'Estelle never mentioned it,' Truttwell said to me. 'She died without mentioning it to anyone.'

'Now we know what she died of,' I said. 'She found out what had become of her son.'

As though he had overheard me, the dead man seemed to have cocked his head in an attitude of stiff embarrassment. His widow moved toward him like a sleepwalker and stood beside him. She touched his hair.

I stayed with her while Truttwell phoned the police.

A & B CRIME

DENISE DANKS
Frame Grabber

JOHN DUNNING
Booked to Die

CHESTER HIMES
All Shot Up
The Big Gold Dream
Cotton Comes to Harlem
The Heat's On
Blind Man With a Pistol
The Crazy Kill
The Real Cool Killers
A Rage in Harlem

H. R. F. KEATING
A Remarkable Case of Burglary

JON LEWIS
Red Handed

TED LEWIS
Get Carter

ROSS MACDONALD
The Barbarous Coast
The Blue Hammer
The Far Side of the Dollar
The Galton Case
The Ivory Grin
Meet Me At The Morgue
The Way Some People Die
The Wycherly Woman
The Zebra-Striped Hearse
The Three Roads
The Chill
The Drowning Pool
The Moving Target
Black Money
The Goodbye Look

MARGARET MILLAR
Ask For Me Tomorrow
Mermaid
Rose's Last Summer

RICHARD STARK
Deadly Edge
The Handle
The Man With the Getaway Face
The Mourner
Point Blank
The Rare Coin Score
The Green Eagle Score
The Sour Lemon Score
Slayground

MARILYN WALLACE (ed.)
Sisters in Crime

DONALD WESTLAKE
Sacred Monster
The Mercenaries